Rapid Dreams

Tim '03

Rapid Dreams

A Novel

Inspired by True Events

By

Debbie Kling & Jim Quinn

ISBN: 979-8-9899263-0-5
Ebook ISBN: 979-8-9899263-1-2

Manufactured in the United States of America.

Frontispiece image by Jim Quinn.
Produced by Dean Burrell
Design by Maureen Forys, Happenstance Type-O-Rama

Website: www.rapiddreamsthenovel.com

10 9 8 7 6 5 4 3 2 1

For Emily,
the best big sister Rapid
Dreams could ever have.
And the best daughter
we could ever ask for.

Rapid Dreams

LIST OF DREAMERS

CUBA →

Guy Stockman

RAPID CITY

The Morans

James

Jennie

John

Billy

The Rosens

Bernie

Lana

Dinah

The Williams

Clarence Sr.

Cherry Mae

Clarence Jr.

Violet

Other Dreamers

Martha Muffling

Glen Merritt

← NYC

Joel Meznik

Rivkah Slotnick

THE BALL PLAYERS (RAPID CITY CHIEFS)

Guy Stockman (Manager, catcher)

Joel Meznik (pitcher)

Clarence Williams (catcher, outfield)

Dick Quarles (pitcher, 1st base)

Darren Hoades (2nd base, catcher)

Frank Hacker (outfield)

Clyde Kibbee (outfield)

Len Hunt (outfield)

Andy Richkas (1st base)

Lee Casey (shortstop)

Hank Paskiewicz (3rd base)

Tony Schunot (shortstop)

Harlan Dalluge (pitcher)

Dave Wiegand (pitcher)

George Schmid (pitcher)

Bruce Haroldson (pitcher)

Dean Veal (pitcher)

Dayton Todd (catcher)

BASIN LEAGUE TOWNS 1957

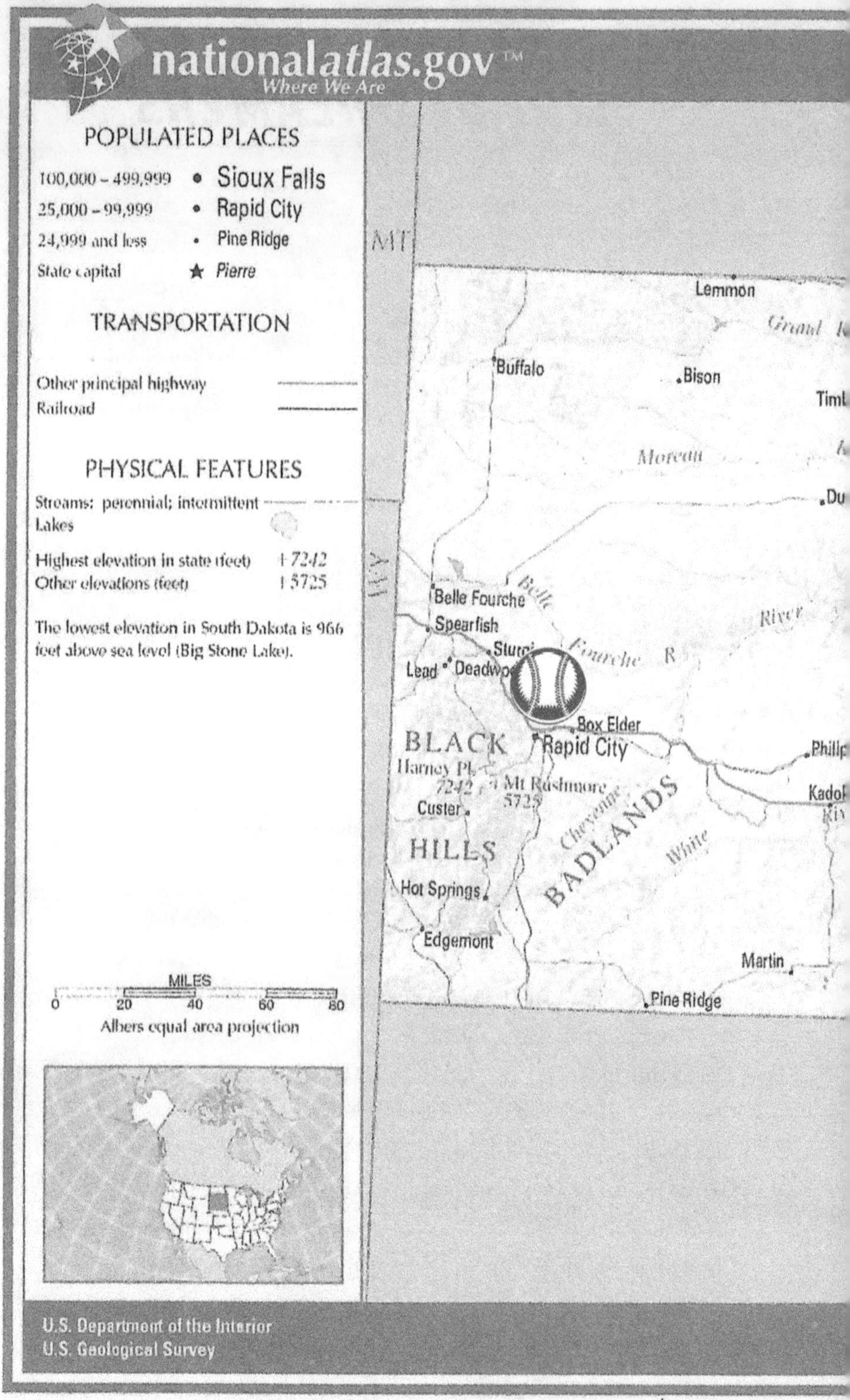
nationalatlas.gov™
Where We Are
POPULATED PLACES
100,000 – 499,999 Sioux Falls
25,000 – 99,999 Rapid City
24,999 and less Pine Ridge
State capital Pierre
TRANSPORTATION
Other principal highway
Railroad
PHYSICAL FEATURES
Streams: perennial; intermittent
Lakes
Highest elevation in state (feet) 7242
Other elevations (feet) 5725
The lowest elevation in South Dakota is 966 feet above sea level (Big Stone Lake).
MILES
0 20 40 60 80
Albers equal area projection
MT
WY
Lemmon
Grand
Buffalo
Bison
Moreau
Belle Fourche
Belle
Spearfish
Fourche R
River
Lead
Box Elder
Rapid City
BLACK
HILLS
Harney Pk
7242
Mt Rushmore
5725
Custer
Cheyenne
BADLANDS
White
Hot Springs
Edgemont
Martin
Pine Ridge
U.S. Department of the Interior
U.S. Geological Survey

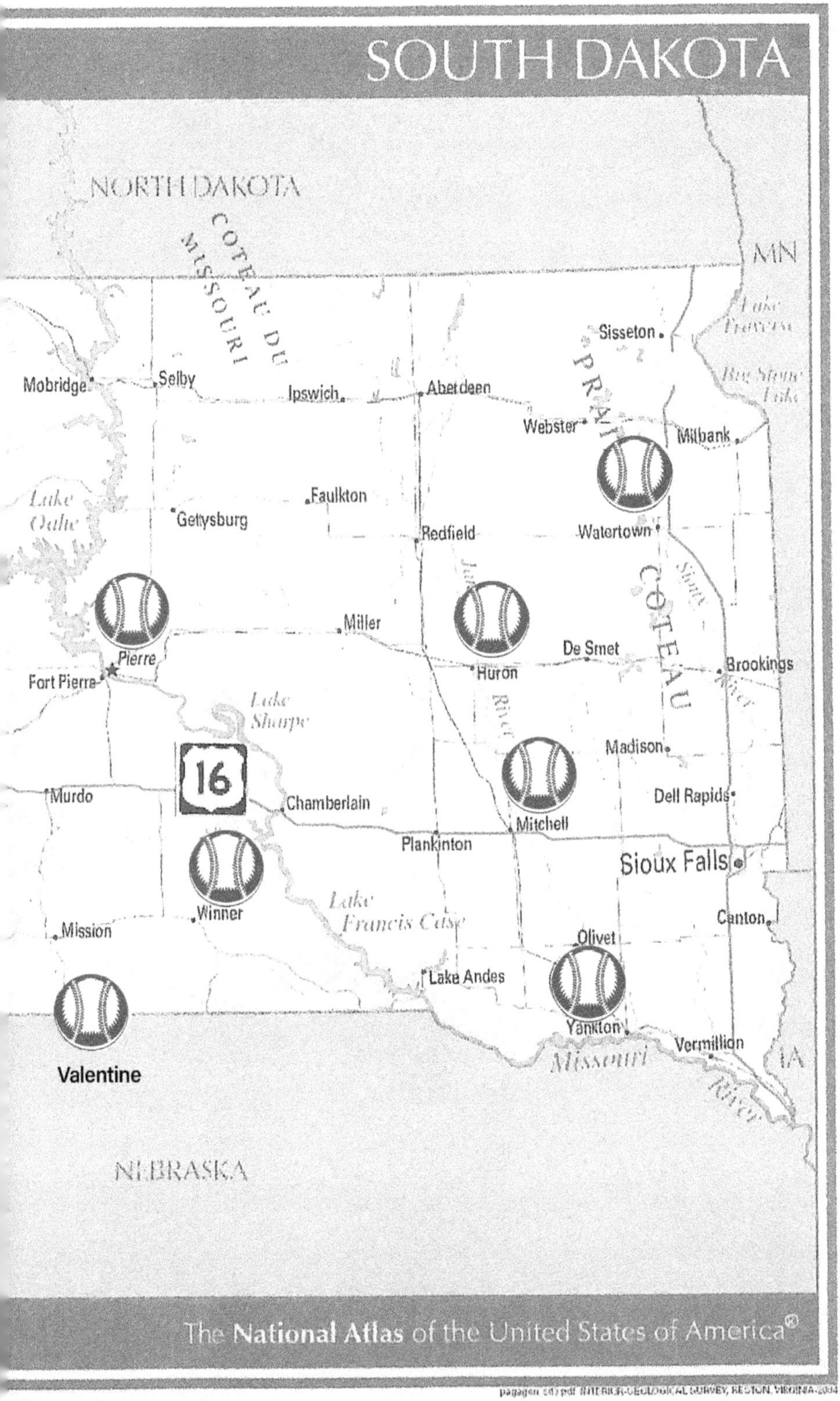
SOUTH DAKOTA
NORTH DAKOTA
COTEAU DU MISSOURI
MN
Lake Traverse
Big Stone Lake
Sisseton
PRAI
Mobridge
Selby
Ipswich
Aberdeen
Webster
Milbank
Lake Oahe
Faulkton
Gettysburg
Redfield
Watertown
COTEAU
Miller
De Smet
Huron
Brookings
Pierre
Fort Pierre
Lake Sharpe
River
Madison
16
Murdo
Chamberlain
Mitchell
Dell Rapids
Plankinton
Sioux Falls
Winner
Lake Francis Case
Canton
Mission
Olivet
Lake Andes
Yankton
Vermillion
Missouri
River
IA
Valentine
NEBRASKA
The National Atlas of the United States of America®

Chapter One

HE HEARD THEM BEFORE he could see them. He felt the house shake before he could hear them. They were coming, he knew, from a base down south—silver birds flying in formation, casting shadows like crosses on the rooftops and frozen yards of Rapid City, South Dakota.

Thirteen-year-old Billy Moran knew the planes were coming long before the newspaper announced their arrival. He'd heard about them from his mother, Jennie, who worked at Ellsworth Air Base teaching the children of the Air Force. Not that she'd ever told him about them. He found out the way he learned much of what he wasn't supposed to know—with an ear pressed to the bedroom wall he and his brother shared with their parents.

"The B-52s are coming." That's how his mother broke the night silence, moments after the bedsprings ceased to squeak and his father, James, choked out a "YES!" in a tone that reminded Billy of the climactic confessions on *Dragnet*, his favorite radio show.

"Hah!" His dad's laugh hit the wall like a blast. "Can't imagine what made you think of bombers, hon, but I'll take it as a compliment."

Billy didn't get the joke but listened hard to see if his mother had. He would have loved to hear her laugh, something she rarely did, at least when he was around.

"More planes." His mother sighed. "Now I'll never get the kids' attention."

Billy had hoped more secrets were forthcoming, but she merely droned on about the trials of teaching at the edge of a runway—the incessant whine of jet engines, the stifling smoke of takeoffs, the earsplitting roar that made the windows rattle and the blackboards shake.

Billy jumped out of bed as a squadron of bombers appeared over the Black Hills to the west. Their sound was rumbling like thunder and swelled to a single, deafening note.

Grabbing his binoculars, he stood on tiptoe to raise them above the window's frost line. Short for his age but sturdy and athletic, he'd grown strong from sports and a regimen of 'Dynamic Tension', the Charles Atlas Home Body Building Course he'd sent away for last summer, halfway across the continent to East 23rd Street in New York City.

Fiddling with the focus wheel, Billy gasped as the formation came into view. He'd seen commercial and military aircraft before, but they were faint arrows compared to the new B-52s, four-hundred-thousand-pound daggers that seemed to poke holes in the air.

A second squadron in a symmetrical 'V' passed over the Moran house. The *Rapid City Daily Journal* dubbed the B-52 Strato-Fortress the 'Shield and Sword of America'. Refueled in midair, the long-range bomber could carry its payload of nukes all the way to Moscow at close to the speed of sound.

"America's Sunday Punch," Billy's father called it, his voice brimming with pride. Billy trusted his father and had faith in what he read in his hometown newspaper. And while he still believed war was likely, he now felt safe. He'd not been made to feel safe before—not by cowering under his desk in the dumb 'duck and cover' drills practiced every week at school.

And there was something else. With the arrival of the B-52s, Rapid was no longer just a place that tourists passed through on the way to Mount Rushmore. Right here, in 1957, this Great Plains city of forty thousand stood ready to defend America against the 'Growing Red Menace'.

The alarm clock rang, and Billy's brother, John, age eighteen, leapt from his bunk. Fair-haired like Billy but much taller and thinner, he had features their mother described as "fine, like Alan Ladd's." While Billy's, she'd add without a smile, were "coarser, like his father's."

Casting a wary look at Billy's binoculars, John glanced across the way to the Rosen house. Seeing no sign of life, he set off to claim first dibs on the bathroom, limping a bit as he hurried from the room. Five years since the polio, he paid it no mind. The hitch in his gait would mostly work itself out by the time he reached school. As long as he didn't run, he was fine.

Billy sighed. With just one bathroom he'd learned long ago to hold it. And come fall, John would be heading off to college—maybe to a school called Yale, two thousand miles away.

Hearing a rush of water from the bathroom, Billy adjusted his binoculars. He was engaged now in a different kind of surveillance—of Dinah Rosen, the girl next door. A beautiful blonde sixteen-year-old who, as it happened, was his brother's girlfriend.

Dinah was new to the neighborhood. A year earlier, a man and a woman unlike any Billy had ever seen came to survey the empty lot along Silver Creek. Tall and swarthy, the man wore a brown bomber jacket and an Air Force cap. Blonde and glamorous in fur coat and heels, the woman seemed younger than her husband. They arrived in a shiny black Cadillac and walked the land, trailed by a nervous little man scribbling furiously on a clipboard.

A month later, construction began with the digging of a deep basement—an uncommon feature in a neighborhood of modest one-story homes, most built on slab. The Rosen house dwarfed the Morans' two-bedroom ranch and was as large as the stately mansions of West Boulevard in 'Old Rapid', where the town's gentry, the Yankee-Nordic elite, had long resided.

"Mongrel house," his mother called it, slandering both its style and occupants.

Dismayed, she watched it rise from the ground, stealing her cherished view of Silver Creek and the cottonwoods and willows that lined it and the fields and forests beyond. When the Moran men learned that Bernie Rosen had dammed the icy creek to make a goldfish pond, they couldn't wait to see this feat of engineering.

Jennie refused to go, though she'd dreamed of having one ever since she was a young girl growing up on the windswept prairie. Sneaking into the yard of a grand old Victorian in town, she'd knelt at water's edge and peered in wonder at its secret coves and darting firelight—a promise it seemed, in the boom years before the Dust Bowl, of a sparkling future and a life of limitless possibilities.

The smell of pancakes and bacon drifted into Billy's room, giving his stomach a puzzling flutter. Could this be Saturday—pancake day? No, he was sure it was a school day, and that Dinah Rosen would soon be getting out of bed. Shifting positions, he panned the binoculars past the Rosens' new evergreens, not yet tall enough to block his view—past the plaster lions guarding their driveway, to Bernie Rosen, in slacks and bomber jacket, exiting his sleek, black Cadillac.

Billy had never heard of the Rosens before they moved next door, though his parents and brother seemed to know who they were. Over the next few months, he'd gleaned that Bernie owned a supper club called the *New York Club*, where his wife, Lana, a singer, was the headliner; and a second night spot, a roadhouse down by Rapid Creek, called the Coney Island Club.

"A known trouble spot," his dad said. "Regular knife-and-gun club." His mom called it a "den of iniquity" and Billy could tell from her dusky tone that dark, indecent things took place there.

Then one day his grandma, visiting from Boise, referred to their new neighbors as *those Jews.* Billy was perplexed. How could there be any Jews in Rapid when he'd never met one or seen a Jewish church? Jews lived somewhere else, or in the Bible—not next door.

Still, he'd heard people say they'd been "Jew'd down," and somehow knew what that meant.

The next Sunday, after church, Billy asked his father about it. James explained that Jews had been in the Black Hills since Gold Rush days, and "quite a number" now lived in Rapid including Bernie Rosen who came west with the Air Force and stayed after leaving the Service. "Natural businessmen," James added with a smile that Billy wasn't sure was admiring, before citing their many enterprises—jewelry, clothing, advertising, Army Surplus, a supper club, a seed company, and the largest construction firm in the state. "They called themselves *The Five Families*," James said, though Billy counted seven. But in a city of 40,000, five or even seven families didn't seem like "quite a number."

Still, what puzzled Billy most was the different way his grandma said the word "Jews." And how neither of his parents said anything about it when she did.

A bit of light from the window across the way told Billy that his vigil had been rewarded.

Clad only in a sleeveless nightgown, Dinah Rosen raised her arms and stretched. Billy tingled.

"Don't let your brother catch you doin' that," his father said with mock sternness from the doorway. "Or, your mother," he added in a more serious tone.

"John still in the john?" Billy asked. James laughed. Physically, he'd once resembled Billy—stocky and strong. "Built like a brick shithouse," as his own father, a pioneer cow man, had proudly put it. Now, at forty, James had grown paunchy and soft. Folks new to Rapid never guessed that he'd once been an athlete, but Billy had seen photos of those days—James on a bucking bronco at the Belle Fourche Round-up and posing in his high school football uniform.

Sometimes Billy wondered how his father had been transformed into the man he now was. He suspected that his mom was to blame but couldn't imagine how or why she'd done it.

"Now, get a move on before your mother blows a gasket."

Billy loped toward the door, dribbling an imaginary basketball before springing to the seven-foot ceiling, marking it with another finger smudge. James smiled at his son, who never walked but ran—challenging the physical boundaries of his world and his pint-sized place in it.

Listening for the click of the bathroom door, James watched as another woman entered the bedroom across the way. Shapely like her daughter, but with a mature woman's fleshiness, Lana Rosen raised one leg onto a hassock and straightened the dark seam running up the back of her hose. James felt a rush of arousal followed by a shudder of conscience. Hearing footsteps in the hallway, he hurried to the kitchen. The table was set but his wife was nowhere to be seen. He took a sip of orange juice, then went to fetch the morning paper.

There, on the porch, stood Jennie in bathrobe and slippers, her eyes trained on the sky, where a parade of B-52s flew east toward Ellsworth Air Force Base, eight miles from the city.

James was surprised. He'd never seen his wife outside in anything but proper shoes and clothing. Putting his arm around her waist, he pulled her to him, and together they watched the bombers soar over the city—from the new western suburbs crawling up the forested foothills to the burgeoning eastern subdivisions sprawling across the treeless plains—passing along the way, the central business district, the county fairgrounds, Rapid Creek and the School of Mines and Technology—silver birds jetting into the brightening sky of a winter sunrise, and for a moment in their massing, casting a glint of shadow back towards the City.

"You OK, Jen?" Her eyes glazed, she looked for a moment as if she didn't know where she was. James held the door open and led her back into the kitchen. She was a couple inches taller and pencil thin, with soft, copper-brown hair and gold-flecked hazel eyes. Even in her bulky robe, they moved easily through the doorway together. "Are you sick?"

"Half day." She pointed to the *Journal*'s headline: ***ELLSWORTH WELCOMES THE B-52s!***

"Playing hooky this morning, hon?" James gave her waist a playful squeeze, but she pulled free. "I have an appointment," she said finally, her lips drawn tight.

James wondered what it could be but knew from her tone it was all she would say. Sitting down at the table, he opened the *Journal* to the sports section with its headline stretched across the page, ***WILL RAPID GET ITS STADIUM AND ITS TEAM?*** For James, this was a story of far greater moment than the arrival of Ellsworth's new jet bombers.

A year earlier, Rapid had applied for a minor league baseball franchise, hoping to join the Class "A" Western League. Nearly everyone in Rapid had rallied around the Morans' new neighbor, Bernie Rosen, who spearheaded the undertaking. Stirred to action by the chance to join Organized Baseball and assume its rightful place on America's Diamond Map—and proud of its forthcoming recognition as a city of regional importance—Rapid Citians were crestfallen when the franchise was awarded to Wichita, Kansas, a larger, better located city.

Undaunted, Bernie Rosen pressed on, petitioning the less prestigious, semi-professional Basin League for a team. A franchise was finally awarded but with one non-negotiable condition—Rapid would have to build a new stadium up to League standards. A fund drive had netted only thirty-five thousand dollars, just half the required capital, so tonight Rapid's voters were meeting to debate public funding to bridge the gap. James, a well-known schoolteacher, had been asked by one of his lodge brothers to speak on behalf of the 'Baseball Bond'.

Dressed in suit and tie, John strode into the kitchen and made a beeline for his mother. Resembling her to about the same degree that Billy took after his father, he was a young man of slender build and delicate features, including her distinctive front teeth—one slightly overlapping the other, like a mother shielding a child behind her skirts. Planting a kiss on his mom's cheek, he pinched a pancake from the griddle. Jennie lightly swatted her son's hand with the spatula and granted him a glimmer of a smile. Over his newspaper, James observed their affectionate exchange, and struggled to recall the last time he'd elicited such playful regard from his wife.

John eyeballed his mother's robe and slippers. "What's up, Mom? You get canned?"

Jennie blanched. Still in her probationary first year at Ellsworth Elementary, she seemed constantly on edge. On school nights, James would often discover her missing from bed, then find her at the kitchen table, grading papers or working on lesson plans.

"It's a half-holiday. There's a ceremony at the Base for the new B-52s," she explained.

"Wonder who's covering it for the paper," John mused.

"Someone who's already graduated high school, I'd imagine," James cracked.

Jennie wheeled around and glowered at James whose face now registered remorse. He knew that his son, a cub reporter at the *Journal*, was hungry for more meaty assignments.

"Billy Moran. NOW!" Carrying a platter to the table, Jennie let it drop with a thud, then walked to the sink where she stood eating a pancake with her back to the men.

John shifted the newspaper to read with his father. "Goin' to the meeting tonight, Pop?"

"Of course. I've been asked to speak. How 'bout yourself?"

John made a sour face. "Ladies Quilting Bee at the Methodist Church."

James clucked in mock sympathy, while Jennie, her face turning red, rushed to her son's defense. "Quilting's important, too!"

James and John exchanged conspiratorial smiles. "Yeah, Ma. Right."

Sensing her exclusion from an all-male alliance, Jennie scoured the griddle as if it were the most urgent task in the universe. "I need the Dodge. You'll have to drop John."

John's face fell and James laughed. "Sorry, Casanova. No nookie before school."

Jennie froze at James's quip about her firstborn's love life. John pointed to his camera.

"How 'bout I take the Chev after school, for my assignment?"

James grunted his assent, as Billy, his hair a riot of cowlicks, bounded into the kitchen.

Smiling, James gave the boy's shoulder a good-natured punch. Billy grabbed his arm in mock anguish, and glanced at his mom, hoping she'd be amused by his dramatics. Then, he noticed her robe and slippers—never allowed in the kitchen. Gray skirt, white blouse, and black oxfords was what she always wore, except at Christmas, when she'd add a red vest and a green rhinestone brooch which once belonged to her older sister, Florence, who died when Jennie was sixteen.

Hearing a knock at the kitchen door, John sprang from his chair. Making her entrance was Dinah Rosen, tall and fashionable in a camel-colored coat and fur-trimmed boots—her long blonde hair set off by a red chiffon scarf and matching lipstick. Recalling their earlier surveillance, Billy and his dad exchanged a guilty look as they rose from the table, welcoming her presence. Sparked by a receptive male audience,

Dinah threw the Moran men a high wattage smile. For years, she'd been aware of her effect when entering a room and relished it.

Through narrowed eyes Jennie watched James and Billy grin back at Dinah. "A matching pair of idiots," she thought. Giving the sash of her robe a cinch, she returned to the sink.

"Mahty cold out there," Dinah said in a mock southern drawl. "Better git goin', Johnny."

"Dinah, I didn't know you were from the South," Billy exclaimed.

"Why, Billy Moran, din't you know I was born and raised in *South* Dah . . . ko . . . tee?" The men laughed, while Jennie stood at the sink, her ramrod-posture a rebuke to the foolishness.

John grabbed his coat from a peg by the door. "We have to drive my dad," he said in apology. Dinah's blue eyes flashed, but her smile and accent never faltered. "Dee-lightful."

"Overshoes!" Jennie barked to no one in particular.

"I'll clean off the windows," John offered, holding the kitchen door for Dinah.

"It didn't snow last night!" Billy yelled after him in a practiced bratty tone. Bolting from the table, he grabbed his rubber boots and yanked them over his Buster Browns, while James struggled to reach around his ample girth to pull on his galoshes.

Jennie turned toward her husband of twenty years and felt a twinge of pity tinged with contempt. When he was young, he'd been stocky but fit—able to lift her onto a horse. Now he could hardly manage his boots and couldn't make it out the door without becoming untucked.

In the driveway, John grabbed Dinah's arm and pulled her to the far side of the car. The '53 Chevy was just tall enough to provide cover for the kiss he pressed on her. Dinah let him do it, but held her hand over her scarf, so he wouldn't muss her hair. Suddenly, she pulled back and adjusted her collar. "My dad . . ." she said in a low warning hiss.

Bernie Rosen strode across the driveway toward the disengaging couple. An inch or so under six feet and powerfully built, he moved with the assurance of a man who'd survived more than his share of tight scrapes. And there was something about his steely eyes that suggested he didn't miss much. Still, he nodded at the young couple as if he hadn't taken note of their smooching.

"Hi, Mr. Rosen." John wiped his hand across his mouth in case he'd been branded by Dinah's fiery gloss, while Billy chirped "Hi, Coach!"

Like an old-fashioned prize fighter, Bernie pummeled Billy's midsection, landing a few soft punches, while letting the boy score a couple of his own. Seeing Bernie horseplay with his son, James hurried to catch up while Bernie grabbed the boy's arms to bring the boxing to a halt.

Billy shot a glance at his father. Even a thick winter coat couldn't hide his big belly. More and more, he was aware of his dad's swollen figure. Sometimes, he feared that people thought he'd end up like that, too. Then he'd be struck by a terrible guilt and want to scream, "My dad's better'n your dad, and ten times smarter!" Turning his gaze back to Bernie, his face fell. Bernie—a man the same age as his father but still fit and trim.

"James," Bernie intoned, as the men shook hands with more formality than required.

"Hello, Bern. You'll be at the meeting tonight—right?" James's tone was meant to be casual but sounded forced.

"Whodja think called the meeting?" Then, his face clouded over. "But I'm gonna let folks like you do most of the talking."

James nodded, knowing that some Rapid Citians would never listen to Bernie because of who he was—a nightclub owner and a Jew—while others still blamed him for failing to win the vaunted Class "A" Western League franchise the year before. "Bond fight'll be a battle royale."

"Could be right," Bernie said, sounding more worried than James expected from a man who'd been a pilot in the War and faced far greater challenges than a bond fight over a ballfield.

"Dad, I'm coming too, aren't I?" Billy often accompanied his father to high school games—riding in the back seat of the Chevy, listening to the men up front dissecting strategy and tactics. Afterwards, they'd stop for burgers and fries, and for Billy, a chocolate malt, too.

James frowned. "Well, it won't be like going to a basketball game."

Bernie stepped forward and put a hand on his neighbor's shoulder. "Come on, James, it'd be a good civics lesson for him. That's your field, right?"

James bristled at Bernie's meddling. "OK, Billy . . . if you finish your chores first."

Billy beamed, while John sidled over, positioning himself between his father and Bernie. Dinah's eyes narrowed as she watched her beau join the menfolk.

"The stadium bond would cost each household just fifty cents a year, but letters to the editor are running three to one against," John offered.

James nodded. "Lot of folks 'round here remember when a dollar was a day's pay."

Bernie snorted. "They can't wallow in the Depression their whole damn lives. It's 1957!"

"Yeah, but some people are just aginners'."

Bernie looked perplexed. "Aginners?" he asked.

"That's what my dad used to say. No matter what it is, they're *agin* it."

"Contrary jackasses. This state's got more of 'em than the other forty-seven combined."

Billy and John turned to gauge their dad's reaction to Bernie's slander of his cherished Dakotaland, but James merely shrugged. He didn't rile easily, even when an outsider, like the Brooklyn-born Bernie Rosen, overstepped his bounds.

"Maybe that's what you need out here to survive," James countered.

"Penny-pinching be damned," Bernie cursed. "We gotta get that ball team."

Without warning, a snowball whizzed by Billy's ear. Forming his own icy sphere, he reared back and fired it straight at the chest of the laughing boy, toppling him like a bowling pin.

"Come by the Club sometime and I'll teach you the curve," Bernie yelled, as Billy sprinted to catch up to the classmate who'd launched the first strike.

Billy turned and waved. "Roger-wilko," as James and Bernie smiled and waved back.

"Great kid!" Bernie exulted, and James's smile faded. He'd always been pleased to hear his younger son praised, but there was something about Bernie's zeal—and his offer to teach the boy a new pitch—that put his teeth on edge.

John kicked a clump of snow and walked back to a scowling Dinah. He knew that Billy was his dad's favorite, just as he was his mom's, but it still stung, seeing his father and Bernie dote on his bratty little brother that way.

"Bye, Bye Dad-dee," Dinah said in her Dixie lilt, a bid for her dad's diverted attention.

"Bye, Princess. Learn something useful in school today."

"Why? Momma never did."

"Your momma didn't have to. She got me."

Bernie cast a backward glance at his driveway where his wife, Lana, dressed in a red wool coat and black high heels, was opening the front door of their Cadillac.

James saw that it was not the car Lana usually drove. "Where's the T-Bird?"

Bernie grunted. "In the shop."

"Need a lift tonight?" James asked, half hoping his neighbor would say no.

Bernie watched as Lana drove off with neither a honk nor a glance in his direction.

Then he shrugged and let out a bitter laugh. "Guess you could say I do."

Chapter Two

FINALLY, THE BIG DAY HAD arrived—the day Airman Clarence Williams and his fellow mechanics had long been preparing for. The new jet bombers—the B-52s—were coming to Ellsworth.

Waking before dawn, Clarence washed and dressed, taking care not to disturb Cherry Mae and their children, Clarence Jr., age twelve, and Violet, age nine, still asleep on a morning they had off from school. Tiptoeing around the small trailer, he drank his coffee cold, then grabbed the sack lunch Cherry had fixed the night before and headed for the Base.

A blast of cold air hit Clarence in the face as he broke into a jog. He wanted to catch the first bombers as they appeared over the horizon and greet in person what he and the other aircraft mechanics had only seen in diagrams and drawings.

He couldn't believe how excited he was. It was something he'd only ever felt at the start of a new baseball season. Every spring since coming north with his father, a widowed Mississippi sharecropper, he'd played on a ball team—first as a youth on the sandlots of Indianapolis, then as a young man catching for the Clowns of the Negro American League. From that time on, opening day marked the true beginning of his year—when setbacks and regrets were soon forgotten, and hopes and dreams stirred anew.

Clarence sprinted past Flyers' Field where his Ellsworth ball team played. Today the ground was frozen, and the grass laced with frost, but soon the field would thaw, and his Flyers would play again—with him, all six-feet-two and two hundred and ten pounds of him, stationed in his customary spot behind home plate.

Suddenly, as if sensing his unbridled excitement, his hip offered a cautionary rebuke. Sometimes it was the hip, more often his creaky knees. And yet, even at thirty-four—old for a catcher—he believed he still had plenty of good baseball left in him.

Clarence stopped for a moment to ease the ache. A thousand games behind the dish had taken their toll. Still, he wasn't ready to give it up. Baseball was what he lived for, and his fondest memories were of his days with the Clowns—the camaraderie of a close-knit band, a brotherhood of Black players barnstorming across the country, playing other

Negro League teams and plenty of white teams, too. In countless towns and cities, people paid good money to watch them play. And, to his surprise and relief, there was little taunting from the white crowds, though afterwards his team often had to eat and sleep on the bus.

Even the clowning was okay when it showed off their skill. But not when they wore whiteface. That was going too far.

Clarence clenched his jaw. He didn't like to think about his role in that shameful minstrel show. At least his father, killed years before in a streetcar accident, had never witnessed it. Though sadly, he never got to see the terrific ballplayer his son had become.

Clarence drew a breath and held it until it hurt. As a young man, he could take the bad with the good, swapping the hardships of the road for fame and respect at home. And more money than he could earn any other way—four hundred a month in the Negro Leagues' heyday during the War, when most folks, including Negroes, had steady jobs and came dressed in their finest to cheer on the Clowns.

Cherry Mae and the kids came too, when the team played at home in Indianapolis. And, with their rental house on Ransom Place and friends and family close by, she reveled in her status as wife of the hometown hero and didn't much mind his days on the road.

It was a good life, and he thought he'd live it forever.

Then along came Jackie. It was 1947 and Organized Baseball had finally embarked on its long, slow integration. Negro League attendance plummeted as fans stayed home, saving their money to see Jackie in the 'White Majors'—some making a pilgrimage of hundreds of miles to root for their hero, the man who broke the color bar and bore the burden of their dreams.

At the end of the '48 season, the Negro National League collapsed. By '51, the Negro American League had dwindled to six teams. Happily, for Clarence, it still included his Clowns.

Clarence never blamed the Black pioneers—Jackie, Satchel, Monte, and the others, whose signings with 'white baseball' had doomed the Negro Leagues. They'd done what anyone would—taking advantage of opportunity. He could only imagine how hard it had been for them. His Clowns were just fiddling on the ragged edge of that world—not, like Jackie and the others, striking at the very heart of it—competing against white teammates, taking their jobs, upsetting the whole damn apple cart.

And those white crowds? His Clowns had only to make them laugh and move on. Jackie and the other trailblazers had gotten their white teammates and the white fans to cheer for the Negro player—if only for what he could do for them. Clarence admired their courage and tried hard not to envy or begrudge them their success . . . that they, not him, were the chosen ones.

Still, he continued to hope that white baseball would one day reach down and pick him. After all, Jackie was twenty-eight and Monte Irvin thirty when they came up. Campy, a catcher like himself, had left half his career behind him in Black Baseball. They raised his sights, fired his ambition—for if the veteran Campanella, and Irvin at his advanced baseball age, could make it to 'The Show' well maybe he could make it, too.

Then, in '52, after the Clowns won their third straight Negro League title, Major League Baseball did sign a player from his team. But not him. It was his young teammate, Henry Aaron, age eighteen, who got the call. Disillusioned, Clarence could see that most of the signings now were like that—young, unseasoned Negroes with big potential.

Sometimes he regretted not lying about his age, like Clowns' outfielder Sam Jethroe, who claimed he was twenty-six, not thirty-one, when he signed with the Dodgers. Still, he couldn't deny that the scouts may have been right not to sign him—for after squatting countless hours behind the plate and suffering innumerable foul tips and collisions, his hands and knees were aged well beyond his twenty-nine years.

Bruised in body and spirit, he retired from the Clowns at the end of the season and came home to Indiana. Now he would work year-round as an auto mechanic, not just in the off-season. But the only ball he'd play was in pickup games on Sunday afternoons and in the backyard on summer evenings, having a catch with Clarence, Jr.

For the first year, it felt like a family honeymoon, and his aches and pains began to fade, but after a time, his days grew ever more routine. He thought again of his time with the Clowns and the spirited life of the road, the life he'd left behind. At the end of a grueling week, after crouching in the sludge of a grease pit, peering up at the underbellies of a hundred cars, he caught his reflection in the mirror. Smeared with grit and clots of oil, his face and hair were a caricature of the darkest Negro's—and not so very different from the hated whiteface of his days with the Clowns.

How far had he fallen, he asked himself. What kind of "clown" was he now?

Then one day he saw a poster in the window of a barber shop on Indiana Avenue. "***Uncle Sam Wants You! Join the Air Force and See the***

***World!*"** It said that the Air Force was now integrated and that men like him were wanted as airplane mechanics.

See The World! Thrilling words. Ripe for a change—and without consulting Cherry Mae—he joined up. His first assignment was at Bakalar Air Base, just an hour's bus ride from home and family. Not exactly *The World*, but at least in the Service he could play serious ball again since every base had a team.

In the spring of '56, it all changed. Expecting delivery of the B-52 Stratofortress, Ellsworth Air Force Base in South Dakota issued a requisition for engine mechanics. When it was discovered that Clarence was also an excellent ball player who could fill a critical need for a catcher, his fate was sealed. He and his family had to leave Indianapolis and its lively Black community for lily-white western South Dakota.

And though he starred for the baseball team, the Ellsworth Flyers, he found the competition—mostly town teams—weak and the level of play disappointing.

Which is why he'd asked Cherry Mae to speak to their son's teacher, Mrs. Moran, about the new semi-pro team forming in nearby Rapid City. A pitcher on the Flyers—a white mechanic—had a son at Rapid High and heard that Mr. Moran was a booster for the new team.

Just then, a pair of white Air Force Police slowed their jeep across from Flyers field and stared hard in Clarence's direction.

Hearing a sound like distant thunder, Clarence looked up and spotted the lead B-52 flying low toward the base. Ignoring the MPs' gaze and the clench in his gut, Clarence headed toward the hangar.

That horseshit, and baseball, would have to wait.

He had more important things to attend to.

Chapter Three

MARCH 22ND WAS A FRIDAY. At 1:00 p.m., Joel Meznik rose from his seat in Philosophy Hall and broke for the corridor. The Columbia College nine were playing Rutgers at Baker Field on Manhattan's northern tip. Bus Departure was 1:10. Game time, three o'clock sharp.

Joel glanced at the large oak clock above the door and pictured his father's reproachful face. Friday was a day he normally did not pitch, but this was the team's home opener, and as the sole senior pitcher and Ace of the Lions' staff, he was expected to get the 1957 season off to a strong start. Still, he wondered if he'd be able to begin a game at 3:00 and finish by 5:00—an hour and ten minutes before the 6:10 sunset, when Shabbos, the Jewish Sabbath, would begin.

The night before, Joel assured his father, Mordecai, that he'd look up sundown in the *Herald Tribune*, which he often found discarded on the subway between his home in Brownsville, Brooklyn, and Columbia's campus on Manhattan's Morningside Heights. This was not, however, a matter his father would leave to chance. Every Friday, Mordecai placed the *Jewish Morning Journal* at Joel's bedroom door with a circle drawn around the time of sunset.

Joel knew he had to be on the subway by 5:10 and off by 6:10 or be in violation of the Ninth Commandment, "*Remember the Sabbath day to keep it holy.*" On Fridays early in the season, he felt himself racing against an ancient Biblical clock, risking the wrath of both God and his Old Testament father.

Reaching the stairwell, Joel felt the knot in his gut tighten as a lecture emptied into the corridor. Muscling his way down the stairs, he reached the first-floor landing. Through the rain-streaked windows, dark clouds portended a downpour. The game might be rained out—a merciful act of providence. Or delayed—a catastrophe. The start of Shabbos, as immutable as his father's Torah, could not be postponed.

Finally free of the crowd, Joel sprinted past Rodin's *Thinker* and down the stairs from Low Library to the grassy lower campus. Darting west across Campus Walk, he weaved through Columbia boys in ties and tweeds and Barnard girls in pleated skirts and swing coats. Usually, he discreetly checked out the girls, knowing they checked him out, too. Tall, broad-shouldered, and blue-eyed, he belied the scholarly Jewish stereotype. His teammate Morrie Melton—short, wiry, and dark-eyed—joked that it must have been a marauding Cossack who bequeathed his friend's matinee-idol genes. Joel knew better. His maternal grandfather had been a bull of a man, a blacksmith in the Pale of Settlement—the sole part of Russia where Jews were allowed to live—before he fled to America on a dead man's passport.

"Where's the fire?" a pretty brunette yelled as Joel ducked his head. Overtures from girls always made him uneasy—wanting, though never giving in to the temptations laid before him.

1:10. Joel spotted Coach Balquist, arms folded across his chest. "Nice of you to show up, Meznik."

Offering a sheepish "Sorry, Coach," he boarded the bus. Morrie, in the second row, lifted a copy of the *Times* off the seat next to him.

"What took you so long?" Morrie whined. "Coach threatened to pitch *me* until I promised him your firstborn."

Joel smiled at his friend. The only son of a city attorney and a public-school teacher, Morrie was the Lions' star shortstop and base stealer. Short and slight, with a crooked nose and a goofy smile, he was also the team clown, and the only other Jew on the squad.

Reaching into his duffel, Joel pulled out his baseball cap and placed it on his head. His teammates sat bareheaded and would remain so until they changed into their uniforms. Morrie recalled the first time Joel wore the cap, revealing that he wasn't just a Jew, but an Orthodox Jew, required to cover his head at all times. Expecting Balquist to swat the cap off Joel's head, Morrie decided he must have shown enough promise as a pitcher to warrant such an exception.

In truth, Joel cheated now, eschewing a yarmulke and often a hat on campus. Once Morrie saw him slip off his skullcap as he ascended the subway stairs to the Columbia gate but never mentioned it, even in jest. He figured Joel had his reasons—perhaps the same as his own parents who long ago shed their orthodoxy to seem more American and live a modern life.

"So, you gonna usher in Shabbos with a win today, Ace?" Joel's face went dark. For a moment, he wondered if his friend was getting some malevolent pleasure in ribbing him. But Morrie's face was open and guileless. It was just schtick, one Jew to another.

"Sure," he answered, producing a paper sack with the lunch his mother had fixed the night before—kosher salami on rye and two half-sour pickles fished from an open barrel on Rockaway Avenue in

Brownsville. Lunch from home cost twenty-eight cents. At a kosher deli near school, it would have cost far more, an expense that Joel, son of a tailor, could not afford.

Morrie snatched a pickle and held it to his nose. "Ahhh . . . the fair fragrance of pushcart Brooklyn—the history of a people captured in one briny whiff."

Peering out the window as the bus drove north through Harlem, Joel spied the gray schist towers of City College, the renowned, free public college he'd once hoped to attend. Dubbed the *Jewish Harvard* for the countless Jewish doctors, lawyers, writers, and teachers educated there, *City* had lifted generations of Eastern European immigrants out of poverty. In the 1920s and '30s, when Columbia limited its Jewish enrollment to 10 percent, *City* opened its doors to all.

After the War, *City* became a power in college basketball. In 1950, its squad of Blacks and Jews became the only team ever to win both the NIT and NCAA titles in one season. It had made Joel proud that he might play ball at a school where Jewish athletes shone so bright. But a year later, a point-shaving scandal rocked the basketball world. For an athlete like Joel, *City*'s part in the scandal forever tarnished the golden patina of the *Castle on the Hill.*

And so, one spring day in '53, he rode the IRT from Brownsville to 116th Street and Broadway to try out on the great Quad before Columbia's baseball coach, John Balquist. Rising from the dank, subterranean darkness into the sunlight of a grand classical square, he was awestruck and vowed mightily to win the proffered scholarship. Rolling up his shirtsleeves, he pitched to Columbia's varsity catcher as Coach Balquist watched in stony silence, saying nothing until he dismissed him with a curt, "Thank you, son, that'll be enough."

Stunned by the tryout's sudden end, Joel turned for a last look at the fortress-like citadel of the great University—the majestic, colonnaded libraries anchoring the Quad and the broad, grassy expanse of South Field, Columbia's first arena, where Lou Gehrig got his start decades before, and where he, Joel Meznik, had strutted his stuff, sending the resounding thump of his fastball echoing across the storied ball yard. Joel knew that with his hopes and dreams raised high, he'd never be happy at City College. For how could he ride the subway past this stop, recalling the glorious Acropolis above, which for one splendid moment had been his?

Days later, Balquist called to offer a $900 scholarship, enough for tuition and books. Not an athletic scholarship per se—such were banned by the Ivy League—the expectation was for strikeouts and wins, not A's and B's, though in time Joel delivered both. But with no money for room and board, he joined Columbia's large straphanger underclass, young men from far-flung enclaves in Brooklyn, the Bronx, and Queens, making the long trip to college by subway.

His mother, Bertha, was thrilled that her only child would attend the famed University where General, now President, Eisenhower, the Liberator of Europe, once presided. His father, Mordecai, was not. "Is it for his mind or for slinging rocks past wooden clubs, like a caveman?"

Then he voiced his real concern. "Are there any Jews at Columbia . . . *real* Jews?"

Bertha shrugged. "So, he throws a couple balls, and gets a fancy sheepskin for his book learning. My father came to America on a dead man's passport. A life's path takes many turns."

Mordecai shook his head. "Six million of our people died—my parents, my sisters. Was I spared so Columbia could have a Jewish ball pitcher?" Scornful of America's obsession with a children's game, he never understood Joel's infatuation with Jewish sports idols, not even Hank Greenberg, the "Hebrew Hammer" who endured taunts of *sheenie* and *kike*, winning respect for Jews before the War as Jackie Robinson did for Negroes after it. To Mordecai's dismay, his only child revered Sid Luckman, Max Baer, Dolph Schayes, Al Rosen, Marty Glickman, and Brooklyn's own Sandy Koufax—praying that one day he might follow in the southpaw's footsteps and sign with the Dodgers.

"Maybe he'll show the goyim what Jews can do," Joel's mother asserted.

Mordecai was unswayed. "He will stop wearing his yarmulke. He will make friends. Some may be Jews, but he will not bring them home. And, what if he falls for a Gentile girl—a shiksa?"

Joel accepted the scholarship. But, as Mordecai predicted, he never wore his yarmulke on campus, and never brought anyone, Jew or Gentile, home to meet his parents.

"Nurses!" Morrie shouted, as they passed Columbia's hospital at 168th Street. The bus tilted a bit as the Lions rushed to its western flank to see the young women, their white winged caps catching the raindrops like thirsty petals.

"At least, I never fell for a shiksa," Joel thought, though he worshipped some from afar. Saturdays, after shul, he'd meet the comely, dark-eyed Rivkah, a student at Yeshiva University's women's college, but never did more than kiss her and feel her womanly softness through what seemed a dozen layers of fabric. At night, pleasuring himself, he kept his image of her pure, imagining instead a movie star like Marilyn Monroe, whose nude photo he'd seen—thanks to Morrie—in the centerfold of the racy men's magazine *Playboy.*

"Shoulda done pre-med like you, Joel—not pre-law." Morrie sighed.

Joel smiled. The promise of boundless nurses had never been a factor in his choice of studies. He was good at science, and medicine was what his father wanted him to pursue.

Picking up Morrie's newspaper, Joel skimmed an article about the campaign by Los Angeles to lure the Dodgers from Brooklyn. Simply reading the headline made his chest ache. The Dodgers were the heart and soul of his borough—the best Brooklyn had to offer.

The first time he saw his beloved *Bums* was in 1943 when a distant cousin took him to a game. Private Leo Kilimnick, soon to be shipped overseas, won two Dodgers tickets at a USO drawing. Thinking he'd take Joel's father, Leo quickly realized that to such a man, a game on the Sabbath was a grievous sin. So, he took Joel instead, sure that the spunky seven-year-old would relish an escape from the tedium of Orthodox Brooklyn life. "Just going to the park," Leo fibbed.

It was a day like no other. The stadium, glimpsed in the distance, looked to Joel like a picture of the Roman Colosseum from an old schoolbook. Inside, he gazed in awe at the domed rotunda, walled in marble and thirty feet to the ceiling, with a chandelier of gigantic baseball bats, and a mosaic floor—round like a baseball, and inlaid with the words, *Ebbets Field.*

Passing through the turnstile, Joel looked out on a joyous multitude and the greenest garden he could imagine. As the organ played a jaunty tune, the Dodgers romped in home-white jerseys as bright and billowy as the wings of angels he'd seen in store windows at Christmastime. And when the crowd rose like a mighty chorus to sing the National Anthem, it seemed like a religious service, and Ebbets, a temple for baseball.

Then the game began, and the mood abruptly changed. Thirty thousand men, women, and children turned boisterous and belligerent, transformed in an instant from parishioners to partisans, with the players turned zealots by the cry of "play ball," rallying to win 10-9—a team raised to victory by the will of the faithful, who now included him.

The game ran late, but they stayed until the end. "Baseball is a game that thumbs its nose at time," his cousin Leo intoned. Returning to

Brownsville, they said they'd toured the Botanic Garden, but they both smelled of cigars, not roses, and neither could name a single new flower or plant that they'd seen. When his father stared hard at him, Joel was afraid he'd break down and confess, but he'd promised Leo, his hero now, that he would never tell.

A year later Leo was killed at Normandy. The news arrived in a letter from Chicago. Mordecai read it silently, then spoke. "He was family. He made the supreme sacrifice to rid the world of evil, but he was not a good Jew." As he said it, he looked hard at his son. The letter had revealed their secret. Joel burst into tears and ran from the room. At that moment, he vowed to become a Dodger, dedicating his mission to the man who, on that sublime Saturday in Flatbush, had brought him to this hallowed game.

"Hey, Coach—we gonna play in the rain?" the Lions' catcher, a Californian, called out.

"Afraid of a little moisture, Loudin? You think Yogi worries about that?" Balquist, a diehard Yankee fan, often held up the pin-striped stars as models for his squad.

"Yogi's in Florida, Coach, playing in the sun." Loudin answered longingly.

"You think they don't got rain in Florida? Yogi wouldn't let nothin' disturb his mindset."

Joel turned to Morrie, forgetting that his friend was a Yankee fan, too. "Yogi Berra and mindset—now that's an oxymoron if I ever heard one."

"Who ya callin' a mow-ron, Meznik? Yah tink youse smardah den Yogi?" Morrie joked.

Coach Balquist glared at the two friends, and Joel stomped on Morrie's shoe.

Morrie crossed his leg and rubbed the assaulted foot. "They sure grow 'em mean in Brownsville. You moonlighting for Murder, Inc.?"

Joel laughed at the reference to the notorious Jewish and Italian mob, once based in his Brownsville neighborhood. "Yeah—mess with me and you'll sleep with the fishes."

"Gefilte fishes, I presume," Morrie added, then pointed to a photo in the *Times*. "You should sign with the Israeli Army this summer. Hear they need grenade throwers on the Suez."

"Not *this* summer. I'm gonna play ball." Joel looked over at Balquist, and in a rare burst of brash, called out, "Hey, Coach, find me a summer team yet?"

Startled, Balquist took an envelope from his pants pocket. "Was gonna give you this after the game." Joel turned the letter over in his hands to see where it was from, as Morrie leaned in to get a better look. "So, where you going? Cape Cod? Carolina?"

Looking puzzled, Joel read the address aloud, "Rapid City, South Dakota."

"What the hell league is that?" Morrie grabbed the letter as Joel looked over at Balquist.

"Basin League, different from Carolina or the Cape. Those leagues just take college kids. The Basin's a fast, semi-pro circuit with college boys and pros, some ex-Big Leaguers, too."

"So, what class is it?"

Balquist hesitated. "Not part of any major league farm system, but the level of play's higher than the Cape or Carolina because of the pros. They're saving you a roster spot. You'll pitch and learn the fine points of the game—pick up a little polish from the veterans."

Rapid City. Joel couldn't recall ever seeing that name on the map, and South Dakota—well, that was just one of those big boxy states out West. Though he knew that Custer's Last Stand and Wounded Knee were out there somewhere.

"So, who ya gonna pitch against—Sitting Bull? Crazy Horse?" Morrie joked.

Balquist ignored the jibe. "Club'll send you a bus ticket, line up a job for spending money, and board you with a local family. Had a kid in the Basin a couple years back. Pitched for the Pierre Cowboys and signed afterward with the Phillies. Not playing now, though."

"Oh." Joel wondered if Coach meant all that to be encouraging.

Balquist looked sternly at Joel. "It's a good opportunity, Meznik—you should take it."

Last spring, Balquist claimed he'd put in a word for him with the prestigious Cape Cod League, heavily scouted and popular among collegians for its ample beach time. But Joel never heard anything, finally accepting a job at Pfizer's Brooklyn lab, arranged by the faculty advisor to *Sawbones*, his pre-med society. For his father, the Pfizer job was evidence that his son was on the right path—at last growing up. Joel didn't disabuse him of the notion, though he mostly washed test tubes—and on Sundays, pitched for the company ball team in an industrial league.

Perhaps this Basin League in South Dakota was the best he could expect for the summer, and maybe his last chance to be seen by a Big League Club.

As Joel returned the letter to its envelope, he wondered how many miles separated Brooklyn from Rapid City. It was only fifteen miles from Brownsville to the Columbia campus, but that trip still felt like a border crossing—requiring no passport, but demanding new customs and attitudes, and practically a new language. How much stranger would it feel to cross half the continent to this place called Rapid City?

"Ya thank they got kosher buffalo out thar in Dakota?" Morrie teased in a cowboy twang.

Joel gave a start. Kosher buffalo? Could there be any Jews out there? Maybe descendants of Levi Strauss, who took his pushcart West to supply mining camps with sturdy work clothes. But kosher food? Still, he appreciated the offer, though he dreaded telling his parents. His mother, he figured, could be won over. Her observation, "A life's path takes many turns," ought to cover a summer detour to Dakota. His father, who never left Brooklyn and spent his one day off in temple, was another matter. He would never approve of him going to such a place.

Joel turned to Coach Balquist. "Thanks for this," he said, waving the envelope.

"You got a game now, Meznik," the coach growled. "Summer's a long way off."

In the locker room, Joel changed into his uniform with his back to the team. He always kept to himself on days he pitched—his teammates accepting it as part of his pre-game routine. Truth was, he still felt like an outsider, an observant Jew and scholarship kid who found it hard to join in the crude byplay and profanities of the locker room, which secretly he often enjoyed.

Today, with the weekend looming, players bantered about their Friday night plans which, because of the Sabbath, he could never be a part of—fraternity parties, a Barnard mixer, the spring play, movies showing around the City. As always, there was no coach's 'pep talk' and the players said nothing about the game—not when the unspoken goal was to avoid the adrenaline rush so useful in sports like football, but often disabling in the loose, soft-shoe of baseball.

At five minutes to two, Joel walked down the hill toward Baker Field. Pressed up against the Harlem River on Manhattan's northern tip, the field regularly flooded—and from the bluff above, the outfield fence looked like a dike holding back the river. A long shadow, cast by the hulking grandstand of the adjacent football stadium, ran parallel to the left field foul line. Late on a spring afternoon, the shadow extended halfway across the diamond—football at Columbia overshadowing baseball in more ways than one, Joel thought, with a sigh.

"Forty degrees, damp and drizzly: *Who could ask for anything more?*" Morrie brayed, aping Broadway belter Ethel Merman.

Joel cracked a smile but worried he couldn't stay loose or get a good grip on the ball.

Glancing at the rain-splashed grandstand, he didn't see the usual Columbia crowd. When the weather turned warm, they'd be back—classmates, girlfriends of the lucky few, and baseball nuts from the neighborhood. But never his parents or his girlfriend, Rivkah.

As the Lions took the field for infield drill, Joel checked his watch. Less than three hours until he had to board the train to Brooklyn. Why couldn't the game start now? He didn't need but ten minutes to get loose. From the bullpen he watched his third baseman slip in the mud and the left fielder fail to catch up to an easy pop-up. He couldn't count on his defense to make its usual number of assists, but then he'd often get half the required twenty-seven outs himself, especially early in the season, when most batters weren't up to speed facing a fireballer who'd been throwing all winter in the gym.

"Meznik. *Meznik!* Take the mound!"

Joel stripped off his windbreaker and strode to the mound. Squinting through the mist, he fired his first warm-up pitch. A few more throws and an adjustment or two and he found his groove, falling into a kind of trance, broken only by the umpire's cry of "Play ball!"

Drawing a breath, Joel rocked into his windup and delivered a fastball on the outside corner. Biting on the pitch, the Rutgers lead-off man lofted an easy fly to center.

Joel smiled. The first out. Often the hardest.

The next two batters struck out, unable to catch up to his early season heat.

In the dugout, Joel checked the time. Only six minutes had elapsed. He was on schedule.

Leading off for the Lions, Morrie worked a walk, then stole second. On the next pitch, he stole third, sliding headfirst through the mud. Rattled by the speedster's antics, the Rutgers hurler spiked a fastball past the catcher, and Morrie motored home with the game's first run. In the dugout, Joel gave his pal a playful punch and handed him a towel to wipe the mud off his chin. At the end of the first, Columbia led one-zip, but the two halves of the inning had taken fifteen minutes. At this rate, a full nine-inning game would not finish in time.

Joel frowned. The boundless game of baseball had become a contest of 'beat the clock'.

Neither team scored in the second or third innings, but Rutgers tied the game 1-1 in the fourth when a scorcher glanced off Morrie's glove and was followed by two ground outs, the second scoring the runner. "Should have been ruled a double," Joel thought, but it was judged a two-base error. E-6 on Morrie. Joel felt his gut clench. He couldn't fault his buddy for not making the play, though it extended the inning and put his Shabbos curfew in jeopardy.

It was already 4:02 when Joel took the mound in the fifth. Seeing his friend's tortured look, Morrie sidled over to offer counsel. "Guess your Sabbath train's about to leave the station. So, stop tryin' to strike 'em all out. Let 'em hit. In this soup, nobody's gonna jack one out."

Unpersuaded, Joel took ten pitches to record the first out—a strike-out—then turned to Morrie and nodded, as if to say, "OK, I'll try it your way." A grooved fast ball yielded a pop-up to short—just one pitch to bag the second out. Stifling a haughty smile, he moved quickly through the Rutgers lineup, needing only nine pitches to get three outs in the sixth, and a total of fifteen for the seventh and eighth.

In the dugout, Joel checked his watch. 4:40. A full ninety minutes before the start of Shabbos. Amazing. Never before had he outdueled the sun!

Joel tipped his hat to his buddy, then frowned. The game was still tied at 1-1. If the Lions failed to score now in the eighth, they'd have to bat again in the the ninth. Extra time. Disaster.

At the plate, Joel couldn't help his own cause. Batting with one out and a man on third, almost anything except a strike-out would score that go-ahead run. But after fouling off a fastball, he swung wildly at two curveballs breaking into the dirt. Two outs.

Then his spirits rallied as Morrie came to the plate and stroked a single to right, giving the Lions a 2-1 lead. But a badly rattled Rutgers squad couldn't get that final out to end the eighth. A high hopper to short was fielded cleanly, then thrown wildly to second. A pop-up to left was lost, it seemed, in the mist. A tapper back to the mound was fumbled as if covered in grease. And on and on it went—more Lions' walks and hits, more Rutgers' errors and miscues. When the eighth inning finally ended, the Lions led 10-1.

The game's outcome was virtually decided now. Columbia would win its home opener, and for that, Joel was glad. But the matter of the Sabbath on this drizzly March day had been decided against him. As he took the mound in the top of the ninth, Morrie came over to offer his condolences. "Sorry about the time, old buddy, but as they say, that's the beauty of baseball. By the way—didja know you got a no-hitter going?"

He did not. He'd forgotten that early Rutgers hit that skidded off Morrie's glove and was wrongly ruled an error. Buoyed by the prospect of a no-hitter, and with nothing left to lose, he took all the time he needed, bearing down on every pitch, and striking out the side.

When the final out was recorded, Morrie let out a roar and charged the mound, followed by the other exultant Lions.

Joel looked at his watch for a final reckoning—5:46. He'd pitched a no-hitter, his first in college, but he'd never make it home before the start of Shabbos. And now he was marooned on Manhattan Island, twenty miles from home. Surrounded by jubilant teammates, he closed his eyes. Morrie slapped him on the back. "No joy in Mudville? Don't worry. God will forgive your transgression."

Joel shook his head. At that moment he wished he could be Morrie, a liberated Jew.

Free to live in one world, not bound to live in two.

Chapter Four

JENNIE, STILL IN ROBE AND slippers, watched the cars drive off, leaving Bernie Rosen standing alone in her driveway. Spotting her at the window, he doffed his Stetson. Jennie turned away. A moment later she turned back, and he was gone. "Poof! Like magic," she thought, her spirits lifting. If only she could make all the Rosens disappear like that—or, at least, Dinah Rosen, that young hussy who'd bewitched her older son.

A cherry red Buick pulled into the Rosen driveway. Emerging from the house, Bernie climbed into the passenger seat and leaned across to kiss a striking brunette square on the mouth.

Jennie recoiled. Maybe people like the Rosens could lead such lives without being brought to account, but she knew all too well how decent folk could be destroyed by succumbing to temptation. Every time she laid eyes on Bernie's daughter, she felt a foreboding. Even now, when John seemed destined to go east to Yale, she feared Dinah would find a way to entrap him, and he'd end up part of the Rosen clan.

The Buick sped off, and Jennie finished washing the dishes. It was 8:15. Her appointment—the one she'd put off until she could wait no longer—was at 10:00. She thrust her hands into the pockets of her apron. Their momentary idleness felt like a reproach. She'd always worked with her hands—milking cows and laboring in the fields as a child and serving as a domestic in exchange for room and board during high school in Rapid. Then, in the little prairie towns where James had once taught and coached, she cooked and cleaned, gardened and canned, and sewed clothes for her boys and herself. And, when John came down with the polio, her potent fingers kneaded life and vigor back into his stricken limbs.

Jennie hung her apron on a hook behind the door. The kitchen was as clean as it could be, and she still had more than an hour until her appointment. Walking into the living room, she ran a diagnostic finger over the plastic-covered sofa—clean, as expected, for it was winter now, and the yards and fields were frozen, and the windows had been shut.

In summer, when windows were open, and the powdery topsoil of neighboring fields floated by, she would dust, though it was never a chore that calmed her. A child of the Dust Bowl, she harbored nightmares of black blizzards—of dust clouds so dark and dense they'd eclipsed the midday sun, with silt as fine as flour seeping through cracks around doors and windows. She recalled it all now—the unending cycle of shoveling, sweeping, and scrubbing—of always being thirsty and never feeling clean.

Worst of all was the sound of her precious calves suffocating before gauze bags could be hung over their snouts. They couldn't save them, she and her sister. They couldn't save them all.

Jennie walked to the window and parted the drapes that once framed her view of Silver Creek. During the construction of the Rosen house, she would watch the stream slowly disappear behind the rising edifice. James had tried to make her stop. "The creek was never ours, Jen," he'd say, though he knew its proximity was the very reason they moved here. How remarkable it was that they found their home, in a neighborhood called Canyon Lake, on a street named Evergreen. Some nights, after a storm, she'd lie awake listening to the creek's faint melody, lulling her to sleep like a remembered song. Now, she heard nothing, not even the wind in the trees, and all she could see was what had been lost.

Jennie's neck knotted up as a tingling crept up her spine. The sleeplessness had caught up to her. Night after night, she couldn't fall out, and now was afraid to try, because the nightmares had returned and were so real. They started when her sister Florence died and returned when she lost baby Lily, and when John got the polio. And now again, after he applied to Yale. Trapped in a ceaseless cycle of night-into-day-into-night, broken only by an hour or two of fitful sleep, all she could do was make a list, execute a task, and as a final recourse, do that furtive thing down there, which always soothed her but afterwards flooded her with shame.

Closing the drapes, Jennie turned to a photo of her and Florence in pigtails and gingham, savoring ice cream on a porch swing. In her mind she could see the blue and white check of their dresses, and the farmyard, lush and green, as it was in '26, the last year before the drought.

Sinking into the couch, she buried her face in her hands. Florence was gone now and the farm, too—lost in receivership, then reduced to rubble, its fields and garden reclaimed by a resurgent prairie. Jennie closed her eyes and tried to recapture it—the apple trees in the yard, the golden wheat bowing in the wind, the gentle roll of the land which was no longer theirs—but her mind would not submit, forced back inside its dark chamber.

She had not saved her sister. Found in the bed they shared—scalp and bone sprayed across the wall—their father's gun nestled by her shattered cheek.

Weeks before, Florence had begged her not to tell what she'd witnessed in the barn—Florence with her secret lover, Tommy Massey, the handsome young drifter who became their hired hand—kneeling behind Florence in the straw, his haunches pressed up against hers, his glistening penis slipping in and out of her, over and over again.

And again now—seen in Jennie's ravaged mind—her groin clenched. Hands shaking, she untied the belt of her robe and pulled the hem of her nightgown to her crotch. Crumpling the flannel into a rude ball, she pressed it to herself—kneading and rubbing, up and down, tilting her hips to meet her hand . . . her breath in gasps now, gasps of surprise, always the rising surprise, before the shudder and the shame.

Chapter Five

JOHN DROVE THE CHEVY TO the high school and handed his father the keys. They'd cut it close, and the parking lot was full—a somber sea of Fords, Chevys, Plymouths, and Nash-Ramblers. John's lip curled. Teachers' cars. Not a Pontiac or Buick in the bunch, and certainly no Cadillacs, despite the cunning placement of the dealership on Sixth Street, where students turned south to the high school and fathers, north to the business district. Today, the show window featured an Eldorado convertible, its pink-skinned contours a voluptuous vision for passing boys and men.

Jiggling the keys, James opened the Chevy's trunk and began assembling the day's history quiz from boxes of mimeographed sheets, while singing, kazoo-like, the School Pep Song.

Let's go, Rapid Cobblers, Give a cheer with a will,
Our hopes are all for Rapid, and our hearts are all a thrill.
We will shout for the big team, shout again and again,
Let's go! Let's go! For Rapid City's men.

Dinah rolled her eyes. "Does he have to sing?"

John flashed a look of *What can I do?* though he couldn't help but see the humor of it.

Finished with his task, James lumbered off toward the teachers' entrance laden with a stack of test papers. John's eyes followed his father's stout figure rocking side to side like a small carnival bear. Struck with poignant feeling, he couldn't imagine his dad owning any car other than the one he had—their reliable, no-nonsense '53 Chevy.

Suddenly Dinah's boot heel grazed his pants, sending a shiver up his leg. He'd never had a girlfriend or even a date before she came along. Maybe it was his slight limp or the awkward way he ran that held him back. He was seventeen when Dinah moved in next door. She was just fifteen—though he hadn't realized it when he first spotted her sunning herself in the backyard, one leg encased in a white plaster cast. Maybe it was the crutches lying next to her that emboldened him. He asked if she wanted to go for a ride "up in the Hills." Her parents didn't object—he was not like the reckless boys she'd dated before, the ones who took her on the joyride that broke her leg.

Bored by the backyard, she'd accepted his offer. Things took off from there. From *Cokes* after school to the Elks Theater balcony to their dark fumblings on Skyline Drive, they'd grown steadily more daring—inch-by-inch, button-by-button, ever charting new terrain. But while he'd become surer of himself and came to know her northern regions, he still hadn't braved that mysterious district south of the border, beyond the Great Divide of Blouse and Skirt.

For he'd never seen a woman naked, not even in a photograph. The drawings in a medical text at the library showed mostly the inside stuff—organs and arteries, not landmarks of living flesh. So, how could he know where to put it when the time came—find the right hole groping in the dark? Could he push through, or would he have to use his fingers to pop her cherry, whatever that was? And how would they match up down there? Would their connection be tight and dry, like a plug in a socket, or loose and slippery, like a greasy wiener in a buttered bun?

Who could he turn to for advice? No one he knew had ever done it. He couldn't ask his mom, and his dad said only, "A woman has a hole down there."

And, what if he was lucky enough to get inside her? Was it like what he did on his own, using her body to replace his hand? Or, like dogs in the street, though he couldn't imagine doing it like *that*. And would she move her body, too, so he'd have to time his movements to hers, as in a dance—one he'd never seen and couldn't practice, but with him expected to lead? He'd never been good at dancing, clumsy with his bad leg and slow to learn. Could he put the pedal to the metal and go all the way when the time came? He doubted that he could.

Putting the car into gear, he drove to their customary spot behind the equipment shed. Shielded from school windows, he turned off the defroster and let their warm breaths create a curtain of condensation on the windows. Sliding across the seat, he covered her lips with his and waited for her to return his kisses, but she remained inert.

"What's the matter, Di?"

"Your momma *hates* me. She acts like I'm invisible."

"You? Invisible? Not even to a blind man."

Dinah was not appeased. "Well, she wishes I *was*."

"Wishes you '*was*'?"

Dinah pulled away. "You're not listening—except to my *grammar*."

John held up his hands in mock surrender "You got me!"

Dinah pouted, her victory undercut by his faux assent. John smiled. Even angry, she was a sight to behold with her porcelain skin, shimmering blue eyes, and full red lips. And that sweet chin-dimple, which he traced with his finger until she batted it away. “Stop it!”

John caught her hand in his and held it to his mouth. “Is there something else I can do to make it better? Kiss your ring?” he fawned, planting his lips on the class ring that marked their status as ‘steadies’.

Dinah resisted the impulse to smile. John could usually jolly her out of her moods, but today she wasn’t of a mind to let him. “It would serve her right if we ran off and got married.”

“What?” John asked, caught off guard.

“Why not? I think that’s what my folks did.”

John was alarmed. “I’m sorry my mom gives you the cold shoulder. But that’s no reason to elope. You’re just a sophomore, and I’m going to Yale. At least I hope I am.”

Dinah tapped her boot on the floor. “So, what am I supposed to do, sit home and knit?”

“I dunno—finish high school, I guess.”

“While you’re going to dances in Boston?”

“New Haven, Dinah,” John corrected, then regretted it.

“Same difference,” she said, glaring at him.

John placed a hand on Dinah’s neck and began to knead it—something he’d seen his dad do when his mom had a bee in her bonnet. “Guess I haven’t thought about what you’d do.”

“Well, maybe you should. Four years is a long time to wait for somebody. Besides, what’s so bad about staying here? South Dakota has colleges, too.”

John’s head began to pound. He’d never imagined that Dinah didn’t share his dream of Yale. He assumed she was like his mom, wanting him to aim high. Dinah sounded more like his dad, who’d surprised him by arguing against his going East, urging him to enroll in the State University at Vermillion, a day’s drive from Rapid, and make a career for himself in South Dakota—in law and then in the State Legislature at Pierre.

“Daddy could give you a job at the Club,” Dinah added.

John almost hooted. He, a National Merit Finalist, working for Bernie, successful by Rapid City standards, but still, just a saloon keeper. Then he caught sight of Dinah’s face—not pouty or petulant, but hopeful and unsure, and in her vulnerability, never more alluring.

"Oh, baby, I know four years is a long time, but I'll come home every chance I get." Feeling heroic, like a soldier leaving for the front, he thought she'd respond in kind, saying something like, "I'll keep the home fires burning."

"I could go with you," she said finally.

John froze, then laughed nervously. Did anyone take his girlfriend to college? Or did she expect them to elope and come to New Haven as his bride? And if they got married, would they have children right away? How could they possibly be ready for kids?

"You could join the glee club."

Dinah jerked away. "That's real smart. You must be a genius."

"Well, it makes a lot more sense than eloping—you gotta admit that," he sputtered.

"Maybe to *you!*" Dinah yanked John's class ring from her finger and threw it in his lap. "And your mother."

Bolting from the car, Dinah slammed the door behind her.

A group of boys sneaking a smoke before Auto Shop gawked as she strode by, her chest heaving and face ablaze, like a dazzling peacock in a feathered huff. Aware of an audience of admirers, Dinah smiled and shifted gears into a full-throttle, hip-thumping sashay, which was quickly rewarded by a chorus of wolf whistles and cheers.

Striking the dashboard with his fist, John laid his head on the steering wheel as the late bell rang, signaling the start of another school day.

Chapter Six

JENNIE WAS LATE. SHE'D PASSED OUT on the couch and felt compelled to bathe, fearing that she smelled of her shameful act. Then the traffic stalled near the Gap, the narrow mountain pass through the hogback, the spiny ridge dividing Rapid City into halves—the new west, where the Morans and Rosens lived, and the old, established east.

The East was where everything Jennie deemed important was located: City Hall and the Courts; the Post Office and the Library; the hospital and High School, the *Journal* and YMCA, the mainline Protestant churches, and the Western South Dakota field office of the FBI.

It also included the affluent West Boulevard neighborhood with its lush yards and gardens and its stately homes, many in classical styles. This, she'd decided, was where John must live when he returned home after Yale. Her stomach lurched as the disquieting thought pushed its way in—*if* he returned home after Yale.

Arriving at the doctor's office, she was greeted warmly by the portly, middle-aged receptionist. "Why, Jennie Moran. Haven't seen you in ages. Yer boys must be gettin' big now. My Artie's a senior at the *School of Mines*. Studying metallurgy. Where's your oldest headed?"

Shell-shocked by the verbal barrage, Jennie blurted out "Yale," though the Admissions Office wouldn't be responding to John's application for another month or more.

"My! My!" the receptionist gushed. "You must be doing *well*, then."

Jennie frowned. The woman probably thought the Morans were flush—otherwise, how could they afford a famous, far-off university? Jennie considered telling her about the financial aid that schools like Yale provided now and the new National Merit Scholarship they hoped John would win. She'd learned about it in *Life* magazine, which described it as 'America's Big New Test' to identify the nation's smartest seniors and stay ahead of the Russians.

But it was too much to explain and none of her business anyway. Still, she'd rather have people think the Morans were struggling—provoking sympathy but posing less risk than envy.

"And all the way to Boston! My, that's a long way from home!" the woman continued.

Again, Jennie didn't know what to say. It seemed pointless to correct her when she was essentially right about Yale being in the East and so far from home.

Retreating to the back of the room, she picked up a copy of the *Saturday Evening Post* with a cover by Norman Rockwell. Jennie stared at the picture of a father, in farmer overalls, and his son, in suit and tie, waiting for a train. The son, with a State College sticker on his suitcase, looked brightly down the tracks, while his father sat slumped on the running board of his truck, gazing glumly at the ground.

Jennie traced the boy's face with her finger. Would he come home once he got his degree? She felt a lump in her throat though she knew she had only herself to blame. She'd set her sights high and believed that nurturing John's grand ambitions had been the right thing to do. After all, President Eisenhower had grown up on the plains of nearby Kansas, and Harry Truman hailed from a small city in Missouri. Still, at the end of the day, she couldn't get it out of her mind that Yale and the East might change her boy forever and break their special bond.

The door to Dr. Latham's office opened to a tall, dignified man with thinning gray hair. Quickly panning the room, he settled his gaze on Jennie, who sat on a deacon's bench staring straight ahead, like a truant waiting to see the principal.

"Good to see you, Jennie," he said as he ushered her into his office. "I see John taking pictures 'round town for the *Journal*. He sure got himself a nice-looking girl."

Jennie's face brightened with his first observation, faded with the second.

Dr. Latham took his seat and leafed through her chart. Jennie was not a patient he saw regularly, unlike women who showed up on schedule—like milk cows for servicing, he couldn't help thinking. His most vivid memory of her was how she'd held her newborn baby girl as she breathed her last breath, then handed the tiny, swaddled body to her husband and walked out of the hospital without so much as a look back. Some years later, he saw her again, when he treated John for polio at the Crippled Children's Hospital down in Hot Springs.

He studied her now at thirty-eight, plain and severe but still appealing, her face framed by soft, reddish-brown curls he was sure were natural, not from a permanent wave. Most striking were her hazel eyes, with that haunted look of certain country folk who'd lost everything—land

and livelihood, kith and kin—all evidence of the lives they led before the Great Depression. He called the look a 'scarring in the eyes'.

"What can I do for you, Jennie?"

Jennie swallowed hard. She'd never sought medical help for this or any other problem.

Days after her sister's death, she was back working with her boarder family. And when baby Lily died, she threw herself into gardening and caring for young Billy—and in the feverish first days of John's polio, she worked round-the-clock, applying woolen hot packs, and exercising his weakened limbs, putting her sleeplessness to good use.

"I need something to help me sleep, Doctor. I have a job."

Her request caught him by surprise. She'd never asked for anything before.

"How much are you sleeping?"

"An hour or two at a time—never more."

"Have you cut back on your coffee? Or tried warm milk and a bath before bed?"

"I don't drink coffee . . . or tea."

"Has this been a problem for you before, Jennie?"

"No," she lied.

He nodded. Though he sensed she was hiding something, he wouldn't pursue it. If she said she needed medicine, it meant she'd tried everything else and was at the end of her rope.

Picking up his prescription pad, he scribbled a few words on the top sheet.

"This will help. But you'll need a complete physical. It's been years since your last one."

Jennie turned pale at the doctor's suggestion. "Couldn't I make an appointment for later? I've got to get to work."

He knew she wouldn't return, suspecting it was the gynecological exam she was avoiding. "OK, Jennie. I'll take your blood pressure and listen to your heart, then you can go."

The phone rang as Dr. Latham handed Jennie the script. Turning in his swivel chair, he didn't see her slip away. By the time he hung up, she was behind the wheel of the Dodge, headed to the pharmacy. Stopping after work would make her late picking up James, and he'd want to know why. Then she'd have to lie to him, which she'd never done before and didn't think she could now.

Driving east on Kansas City Street—Rapid's 'Street of Churches'—Jennie felt the tug of the prescription, a small square of paper weighted by only a few lines of ink. She wondered if it was a prescription for sin, or proof of her lack of faith? Perhaps she should have turned first to prayer or sought her minister's counsel. Though neither had sustained her when her sister Florence was killed and after Lily passed.

Jennie pressed down on the gas and sped east to *Soderberg and Son, Druggists.* Hurrying inside, she hoped that Harry Soderberg, an old classmate, wouldn't ask too many questions.

At the sound of the entrance bell, a round-faced man with a gleaming bald head emerged from behind a curtain at the rear of the shop. Jennie recalled that Harry had been elected "Most Personable" the same year that James was elected "Most Likely to Succeed." She wasn't elected anything, except by James, who, a bit drunk at the Prom, dubbed her, "The One I'd Most Like to Succeed *With.*" When the dance ended, they drove north to Sturgis and watched the sun rise over the plains. There, in the front seat of James's Chevy, she let him slip down her panties and touch her—because, after Florence died, it was the one thing that made her feel good. Then, shutting her eyes tight, she touched him, too.

Harry grinned and held out his arms to her. "Hello Jennie. It's so good to see you."

Shrinking from his embrace, Jennie fished the prescription from her purse. "Hello, Harry. I need this filled in a hurry."

Harry glanced at the paper and frowned. At the recent convention of South Dakota Pharmacists, he'd been warned about drugs like this—potent central nervous system stimulants and depressants entering illicit channels through drugstores. While he would never fill an order without a prescription, even the legal dispensing of the drug put him on edge.

"Fine, Jennie. I'll have this for you in fifteen minutes."

"Please, Harry! I can't wait that long. I'm late for work."

"Sure, Jen, sure. Guess I'll be seeing James tonight," he added as he filled in the form.

Jennie blanched. She wondered if druggists, like doctors and lawyers, were obliged to keep their clients' business private—or would Harry tell James that he'd just filled his wife's prescription for a powerful barbiturate?

"The meeting . . . about the baseball stadium," Harry added, as clarification.

"I'm really very late, Harry," she repeated.

"Sorry, Jen—I'll see about that now. Hope I have it in stock. Lots of folks on this Seconal nowadays. Must be the Rooskies—this new hydrogen bomb makes people too nervous to sleep."

The doorbell tinkled as Lana Rosen burst into the store, a prairie fire in her red, fitted coat, with a mocking grin lit up by ruby-red lipstick.

Jennie was thunderstruck. What was *she* doing here—clear across town?

"My, my, wadda we have here—reunion, Future Farmers of America, Class of '36?"

"May I help you, Mrs. Rosen?" Harry's voice was formal and frosty.

"Now, Harry—I don't recall you being so all proper with me back in School Choir." Lana planted herself on a fountain stool and, pulling her knees up, propelled herself into a spin.

"I'll take care of it for you, Jen," Harry said, ignoring Lana's sarcastic tease. In the back room he handed the form to his son, Howie, a young man in his twenties who bore him a close likeness, except for a full head of carrot-red hair. Howie peeked furtively through the parted curtain, and Lana smiled back, pointing to her diamond wristwatch.

"*Some* recess, Jen. Playin' hooky today?"

Jennie looked away, refusing to acknowledge Lana's presence. Lana smirked, then grasped her chin between thumb and forefinger. "Hmm. Now why would Madam Schoolmarm be at Harry's drugstore in the middle of the day? She don't look sick. You think Jennie looks sick, Harry? And her precious boys both looked well this morning, 'specially that older one, smooching with my Dinah behind the car. Now he's *one healthy boy*—ain't that right, Jen?"

Shaking now, Jennie swung around and fixed Lana with a frigid glare.

"And James—nothing ailing that man 'cept too much home cookin'." Lana snapped her fingers. "I got it. You're here for those new pep pills I been readin' about—the ones some folks gotta have just to keep goin'."

Jennie felt her stomach clench as Harry reemerged from behind the curtain.

"It'll just be a minute, Jen. Howie's making it in the back."

Lana snickered. "That son of yours is always makin' it in the back . . . of something."

Harry glared at Lana sitting cross-legged at the fountain, her coat parting to reveal a tight skirt riding up her thigh. Then something occurred to Jennie—the cluster of cheap motels close by on East North Street—that, and Harry's handsome, unmarried son, Howie.

"That will be $3.50, Jennie. I know you're in a hurry."

Lana pulled out her compact and powdered her nose. "I'm in a bit of a hurry, *too*. Tell Howie I stopped by for my favorite *tonic*. He'll know what I'm talkin' about."

"Fine," Harry said curtly as Lana closed her compact with a self-satisfied snap and walked out of the shop laughing. Jennie shivered as a cold draft came rushing through the door.

Finally, Howie appeared with the prescription. Jennie hadn't seen the young man in years but couldn't look at him now without recalling that it was Howie—a camp counselor—who'd discovered John, febrile and delirious, that hot August morning when the polio struck. It was Howie who'd telephoned her to come as quickly as she could.

Howie brushed past Jennie, his eyes trained on the street. Harry stepped in front of his son, intending to block his exit. "Aren't you going to say hello to Mrs. Moran, Howie?"

"Oh, sure. Hi there, Mrs. Moran."

Jennie recoiled, hearing again the familiar timbre of the young man's voice—forever linked to that panicked phone call from Y-Camp. "Hello, Howie . . . Yes, thank you, Harry."

"See you in a month," Harry called as Jennie walked to the door. She wheeled around.

"If you'll be needin' a refill."

"Oh." Jennie hurried out of the store. Backing blindly out of the parking spot, she nearly struck a passing car. Looking up, she saw the Rosens' black Cadillac skidding around the corner, a man slumped in the front seat, his red hair ablaze like a comet in the sun.

Chapter Seven

THE ROOM WAS RANK WITH the sweat of a hundred pubescent boys after a day of hard-fought gym battles. Billy sat alone in front of his locker pretending not to listen, as Glen Merritt, Crown Prince of Canyon Lake Junior High, held court for an audience of eighth graders on the latest episode of the TV show *Dragnet*.

"So, Friday's hauling this guy off to the police station . . . " Glen repeated lines from last night's episode. Most of the boys—those with TVs—reveled in his account, while Billy and a few of the others—those without TV—stayed silent or forced vacant smiles.

Two years ago, he and Glen were best friends. He'd even been invited over when the Merritts brought home their 21-inch Philco. He remembered that first night on their living room rug, watching the strange, flickering images dance across the face of the mahogany console.

The next day, Billy was full of the wonders of TV and the nest-like feel of the Merritts' living room, so unlike the Morans', with his mom's spooky keepsakes from the farm and the plastic-covered furniture, which crunched in protest when he sat, and emitted strange sucking noises when he stood.

After two more nights of bliss, the invitations stopped. Billy showed up at the Merritts anyway. Glen's father, Augie, answered the bell, martini in hand. Peering down his nose at a bewildered Billy, he announced that the Merritts would not be watching TV that night, and he should "just run along." Billy saw the lie in Augie's mean eyes and in the flickering images reflecting off his bifocals.

Clearly, the Merritts had made a decision. They didn't want him coming around anymore.

When James got home from his lodge meeting, he found Billy in the backyard throwing rocks at the trash can, struggling to hold back tears. Later, he got the story out of him.

Despite disdaining TV, Jennie was furious. "They think they're so high and mighty now that they belong to the country club."

In the days that followed, Billy's worst fears were realized. Not only had he lost TV privileges at the Merritts', he'd also lost his friendship with Glen. Try as he might, he couldn't figure out why Glen ditched him, ignoring his invitations to ride bikes or play ball, and not even speaking to him at school when they passed in the hall.

Finally, Billy decided it had to be about TV.

Until two years ago there was no TV in Rapid. Everyone was in the same boat, listening to shows on the radio and reading about TV in *Time* and *Life* magazines. To Billy, television was like skyscrapers—something only a big city could have. Then, in 1955, Rapid answered the twin siren calls of *CBS* and *NBC*. Some of Billy's classmates got their sets that same year, but Jennie wouldn't hear of it. "There's nothing on TV you need to see," she said with finality.

For Billy, the advent of TV changed everything. Before its arrival, all the kids were pretty much equal. Sure, some had bigger houses or fancier cars, but every boy had a bike, a ball glove, baseball cards, and a radio, and could listen to *Gunsmoke* and *Dragnet*. No one was left out when the latest episode was talked about at school. Now, with TV, some kids were in the know and some, like him, were in the dark.

Billy looked around the locker room at the other eighth graders. Back when he and Glen were friends, they'd given classmates secret nicknames. The 'hicks' were the country kids, the 'sticks', those from the new subdivision closer in, and the 'slicks' were the city slickers, boys who walked to school from the older, settled neighborhoods close by, like Glen and him.

Still, Glen was a category unto himself, and not just because the Merritts were rich and lived in a mansion with an orchard and a yard big enough for a ball field. Or, that Glen had been to Disneyland in California, which just opened, and bragged that he'd seen Annette, the buxom Mouseketeer with the Italian last name. Glen seemed to have everything—even the highest IQ. Their homeroom teacher let it slip—Glen's was a hundred and forty-nine.

And there was no contesting Glen's physical superiority as the tallest, strongest, most athletic, and probably, the toughest of all the eighth-grade boys. At fourteen, he seemed a full-grown man and was the most popular boy, though Billy suspected that only the girls truly liked him. The guys just pretended to, because they feared him and needed to stay on his good side.

The showers were finished now, and most of the boys were done toweling off. Billy changed quickly, draping his shirttail over his crotch before swapping his jockstrap for briefs. He was grateful that gym was the last period of the day, so he didn't have to choose between a sweaty return to class or exposing himself to taunts and snickers in the shower.

For the locker room revealed his secret shame. Painfully, he'd watched his classmates acquire the valued markers of manhood—deepening voices, wiry hairs sprouting in telltale places. But not him. Would he always be low man on the totem pole—circus dwarf, squirt? He'd already slipped in the hierarchy of boys—friends pulling away as they spurted taller, their eyes and aims growing ever more distant from his own. Maybe that's why Glen tossed him aside.

It hadn't always been like this. He recalled a sun-blistering afternoon two summers before when he and Glen rode their bikes to a secluded stretch of Rapid Creek. On a weed-covered bank, Glen proposed a contest. Standing a few feet apart, each took his penis in hand and arched his stream up and out to the pool below. "Ready, aim, fire!" Glen ordered, and Billy obeyed. Sneaking a peek at his commander, Billy noted that their hoses were not all that different—ruddy fingers of comparable length, breadth, and range. "Saw you look, Billygoat!" Glen teased, bestowing his younger friend with a nickname, like dubbing him a knight. Billy blushed. It was the first nickname he'd ever been given. Then Glen cannonballed from the high bank into the pool below. Scared but excited, Billy waited for Glen to surface before following. Then they splashed and swam and took turns dunking each other in the cold, still water. Later, Billy wondered how Glen knew it was deep enough—deciding finally that he did not. Glen was just the bravest, craziest boy he'd ever met, someone he was sure would be his friend forever.

Slicking back his hair, Glen walked to his locker where a skinny towhead held out a copy of *Teen Screen* magazine like a sacrifice to a god. On the cover was Annette in a tight, white Mouseketeers tee shirt. Smiling at his acolyte, Glen took the magazine and traced the outlines of her breasts before popping his digit in his mouth as if licking cake frosting. "Mmm, Mmm, just like at Disneyland. Can't wait to see what Annette's cooking up today on the show."

Then Billy heard Glen's taunting voice behind him. "Hey, Billy *Moron*, no shower again today? Guess you don't care that you stink!"

Some boys snickered and all eyes turned to Billy who flushed in rage as Glen stood over him, his mean eyes gleaming like his father Augie's that night he dismissed him from the porch.

Slamming his locker shut, Billy stepped stiffly over the bench and started for the exit.

Glen stepped in front of him. “Not so fast, stinko. Got something for you.” Pointing to an ad inside the magazine’s back cover, he proceeded to read:

“Are you shy? Lacking in confidence? Ashamed to strip for sports? Don’t be half a man! Stinko, this is definitely you! Now here’s the pitch: *Dynamic Tension will turn the trick for you Fast. In just 15 minutes a day. Send for a free 32-page booklet, 115 East 23rd Street, New York.”*

Fighting back tears, Billy brushed by Glen and bolted for the door. Already a disciple of *Dynamic Tension*, Billy knew it wasn’t enough to fight the bigger boy. All he could do was make a vow. One day he’d get even with his tormentor . . . anyway he could.

Chapter Eight

JAMES SPOKE THE WORDS "CLASS Dismissed," but his voice was drowned out by his students bolting for the door. Watching the stampede, James, a rancher's son, playfully sorted them into stock categories. First, the stallions, vaunted athletes, and hard on their hooves, the cheerleaders, frolicsome fillies, their ponytails bobbing behind them. Then came the common herd, boys and girls who might have been popular had they been better looking or perhaps just more confident.

Next were the FFA boys, plow horses from the country who shouldered heavy burdens at home. James's heart went out to them, and the country girls, too, some handling jobs as domestics on top of schoolwork, as Jennie had done back in high school. Trailing behind were the Vo-Tech boys—refractory mules, prodded to plod on and finish school, rather than drop out and join the armed services or work full-time at the cement plant, lumberyard, or auto-body shop.

Last to leave were the Lakota, 10 percent of Rapid's population, but rare buffalo in his classroom. Present in the winter months, many would wander from kin to kin in fair weather, returning to school when it turned cold. James taught his class that South Dakota had once been Indian territory and was named for a band of the Great Sioux Nation. And, unlike some teachers, he praised their proud and valiant leaders: Red Cloud, Sitting Bull, and Crazy Horse.

Still, his efforts seemed only to make his Lakota students sullen—perhaps reminding them of all they'd lost—their Great Plains hunting grounds, their once abundant buffalo, and their sacred Paha Sapa, the Hills of Black, their exclusive domain until General Custer discovered gold there in 1874, spurring a rush of miners and merchants, outlaws and whores, and finally, homesteaders.

One Lakota student had stood out—Andrew Hanging Cloud, a class officer and star of both the basketball varsity and the American Legion baseball team. After graduation, Andrew vanished without a trace. Sometimes James wondered what had become of him.

"Excuse me, Mr. Moran." It was Martha Muffling, a slender Junior with a shy, endearing smile. Dressed in a baggy cardigan and shapeless plaid skirt, she always sat up front, doing well on tests but never raising her hand to offer an opinion or answer a question. Something seemed to hold her back, stopping her from being one of his best learners—a true thoroughbred.

"Will your son be debating this week?" Martha asked, in a halting whisper.

"Yes." James smiled, seeing now why such an awkward girl had joined the debate team. "He'll have a leg up on this one." The practice topic had been John's suggestion. "*Resolved: that City taxpayers fund a new baseball stadium with bonds financed by property assessments.*"

"Thanks, Mr. Moran." Martha's blemished face broke into a broad smile. Her hopeful spirit made James want good things for her, a shy country girl like Jennie at her age. Smiling, he watched her gambol out the door, a gangly filly who might one day blossom into a pretty mare.

James gathered his test papers and ambled into the hall, elbowing his way through a throng of boisterous teens until he reached the school trophy case, a glass-fronted cabinet harboring the hallowed relics of Rapid's athletic past: bronze plaques and silver loving cups; team photos and shrunken footballs inscribed with scores and dates. And, a faded photo of the '35 Cobbler football squad. Twenty-three young roughnecks in shoulder pads and knickers squinting into the low, November sun—and there he stood in the front row next to the legendary Coach Cobb, for whom the team was named.

He'd not been a star but was a starter on the kicking team, where he'd used his speed and agility to advantage. A transplant from the country, he found a home on the football varsity thanks to Cobb, who'd taken a shine to the eager young recruit, telling him, "There's always a place on the team for a man with 'desire' . . . a 'Good Little Man'."

And when he wasn't running after kicks, he stood with Coach Cobb on the sidelines as his proud, unofficial assistant learning the tactical twists and turns of the game from the master while dreaming that one day he would succeed him at the helm of the Cobblers.

But James was still in college when Coach Cobb retired from Rapid High. And so, he began his adult life as an itinerant coach and teacher, moving his family from town-to-town across the length and breadth of West River Country.

He was happy—when his team won. For in the little hill and prairie towns of western South Dakota, there was often more than one church, but never more than one coach or one school—with all twelve grades crowded inside. And on Friday nights in season all would congregate at the One True Church, whose crusaders were the heroes of hardcourt or gridiron, with Coach Moran, the Crusader King, bearing the town's standard throughout the countryside.

For Jennie, it was hell. Left alone with two young boys, she bore the brunt of their uprootings—some decreed by a losing record, others arising from James's restless ambition—his constant desire to move on, if only for a bigger school, a better team, or a bit more money. It was a lonely life—the late practices, the road trips, and at home, James's mind always turning to the game, like a compass seeking true north.

Jennie never shared in her husband's glory or appreciated the thrill and beauty of the games. For her, they were but frivolous contests meaning nothing in the larger scheme of things. But she never spoke her feelings, for he was the breadwinner and there were the boys to care for and always her need for him at day's end, no matter how late he came home.

Until one night in the small Plains town of Faith. Returning from a hard loss in a hard season, he found her crying in the dark of the yard, holding baby Billy in one arm, and pushing John on the swing with the other. Later, when he told her that he'd lost his job but would find another, she shut the door to the boys' bedroom and spoke in an icy tone he did not recognize.

"You want to keep coaching, James? First, it was Hill City—'the Rangers'—mountains, trees, streams. Then, it was Vale—the 'Beet-diggers'—irrigation country—trees and water getting scarce. Now, it's Faith—'the Longhorns'—the hot and dusty plains. Not a drop of water to be found and nothin' growin' 'cept weeds and grasshoppers. So, where to now, James? Maybe they'll let you coach in the Badlands, and our boys can play with the rattlesnakes."

It had been twelve years since she made him move the family to Rapid City, where no coaching job was available—only a position teaching history at the high school.

Sometimes he wondered if he could ever be in the running for a coaching position in a big town like Rapid. Was it his spotty record as a small-town coach that disqualified him, or did he somehow just not 'measure up?'

Finally, he settled for Team Scorekeeper.

James sighed, catching his shadowy reflection in the glass, his ample belly tugging the shirttail from his pants. Sucking in his gut, he stepped into the gym, taking a seat at midcourt as young men in white Converse sneakers and red practice jerseys frolicked in their last moments of freedom before their coach arrived.

They paid James no mind. They knew him as 'Scorer' and were used to seeing him at practices. Though James doubted that any of them understood why he came—to train his eye to discern through flailing limbs the one boy to rightly credit with the rebound, tip-in, or assist.

"Preparing myself to see," he called it, for he had learned early on that the unfamiliar or unanticipated is seen dimly, if at all.

Over time, James found that the numbers in his scorebook spoke to him. Studying the figures, he divined a kind of story—a whodunnit—which could be read over-and-over until, in a flash of insight, its characters, plot, and meaning became clear.

But in the locker room after the game, when James would hand the coach his scorebook, he'd give it only a glance and cast it aside—never asking for his analysis. And once, he found his 'book' lying face down in a puddle—hearing later that the coach had sniped, "Baskets win ball games, not statistics."

Suddenly, an errant basketball broke James's musings. Raising his arms, he had just enough time to stop the ball from striking his face.

Cradling it in his hands, he looked around the gym as the Cobblers' star forward called for the ball. "Mr. Moran."

James stood and gave the ball a backwards spin in his fingertips, sensing its weight and texture until it felt just right. Then grasping it in a firm, centered grip, he pushed it up past his chest—past his intentful gaze into a high, rising arc—the ball seeming to catch its breath at its peak before slipping down through the iron hoop, making a fine rustling sound as it paused for a hug in the basket's net skirt.

The slack-jawed Cobblers gaped in wonder as the man they knew only as 'Scorer' turned to hide his smile and strutted proudly from the gym.

Chapter Nine

JENNIE STOOD IN FRONT OF the class and raised her hands for silence. Without a word, she turned her palms upward and the children rose to face the flag in the corner of the room.

Sounding a sustained "*Ohh*," she listened for a moment of vocal consensus then dropped her arms, signaling the group to begin singing. "*O beautiful for spacious skies, for amber waves of grain.*"

This was how she ended every school day—with the singing of a patriotic anthem. And each morning she stood hand on heart with her class to recite the Pledge of Allegiance. Proud to do it, she considered it her civic duty.

Though one Monday morning, after Reverend Danvers devoted his Sunday sermon to the bus boycott and bombing of Negro churches down South, she wondered what her four colored students made of the words "with liberty and justice for all."

"*America! America! God shed his grace on thee.*" Before the song ended, a deafening roar of jet engines drowned out the children's voices. Jennie raised her hands again, and the children stood in practiced anticipation, waiting for the plane to complete its takeoff.

"*And crown thy good with brotherhood, from sea to shining sea.*" Jennie clapped her hands and the children filed out of the classroom, letting out a roar not unlike the one that had halted the singing. She ran a tight ship at Ellsworth Elementary, and the kids, like those vapors in the jets, couldn't wait to lose themselves in the wild blue yonder.

Jennie walked to the front of the room and erased the chalked numbers from the blackboard. Despite the frequent interruptions, she considered herself lucky to be teaching at the Base. For years, she had taught at a low-paying parochial school, unable to secure a position in Rapid's public system where, as a teacher's wife, she was forbidden to work. Then, unexpectedly, with the Cold War expansion of the Air Force, she was offered a position at Ellsworth Elementary where her starting salary was almost as much as James's.

Still, it wasn't an easy transition. The other teachers found her old-fashioned and aloof, and no one befriended her. The children of the military, frequently uprooted, could be restless and brash, knowing that this school, too, was just a bridge they could burn before moving on.

And there were the Negro children. She'd never met any Negroes before Ellsworth and worked hard to understand their accents and speech patterns, though they seemed to have no trouble with hers.

And yet, even in her most trying moments, Jennie never doubted her teaching methods. Still, she sometimes wondered if she could ever be beloved by her students—like Mr. Chips—or esteemed by her colleagues. All too often she imagined being fired at the end of the term.

It wasn't like that for James. Since moving to Rapid and giving up coaching, he'd settled into a complacent groove, with lesson plans reusable from year-to-year. His only preparation seemed to be reading *Time* magazine and the *Rapid City Journal*, leaving him free to pursue what she knew were his real interests—his men's clubs and scorekeeping, and the games of local college teams. It seemed to her that nothing had changed from the little hill and prairie towns where they'd once lived, except that James was now watching games instead of coaching them. Disheartened, she struggled to accept that her marriage would never be like her parents'—sharing a common purpose on the farm, and nearly every hour of their lives.

Jennie stumbled to her desk and laid her head on her arms. Though it was only a half day of school, she'd barely made it through.

Hearing the sharp clickity-clack of heels, Jennie looked up to find a short Negro woman dressed in white gloves and veiled hat as if for church. Trailing her was her son, Clarence, one of the more rambunctious boys in her class.

Forcing a smile, Jennie asked, "Can I help you, Mrs. Williams?"

The woman cast her eyes to the floor before slowly raising them to meet Jennie's. It was a gesture Jennie had observed before when speaking to the mothers of other Negro students. At first, she chalked it up to simple shyness. Later she figured it was something the women felt was expected of them—perhaps a habit picked up or required in domestic service, which she'd done herself back in high school.

Moved by Mrs. Williams' discomfort, Jennie broadened her smile, hoping it would put her at ease.

"I don't want to . . . uh, uh . . . disturb you, Mrs. Moran . . . " Mrs. Williams stammered.

"That's perfectly all right. What can I do for you?"

Mrs. Williams took a deep breath before continuing. "Clarence's father, Clarence Sr., wanted me to ask about this new ball team they be formin' in town."

Jennie's smile slipped a little. The boy pulled out of his mother's grasp and darted toward her desk. "My Daddy's base batting champ," he exulted. "He's good as Hank Aaron."

Mrs. Williams put a restraining arm around her son's shoulder and pulled him to her side.

"Hank Aaron?" Jennie asked.

A look of disbelief crossed Clarence Jr.'s face. "On the Braves. Don't you know 'bout baseball, Miz. Moran?" Mrs. Williams tightened the grip on her son's arm.

Suddenly weary, Jennie wished she were alone in the car, heading home with her bottle of pills. "Yes, of course, Clarence. He's just a player I'm not familiar with."

"He ain't just a player. He's a star. He hit 328!"

"Shush, Clarence. I'm sorry, Mrs. Moran, but Clarence's father heard your husband's helpin' get a team together and thought you might know somethin' 'bout tryouts . . . " Mrs. Williams took a step backward and glanced over her shoulder towards the door.

"It's all right, Mrs. Williams. I know how boys are about sports. I have two of my own."

Clarence Jr.'s eyes widened at this rare glimpse into the homelife of a teacher, and Mrs. Williams visibly relaxed. "Clarence Jr. and his Daddy jes' eat, drink, and sleep baseball. If it wasn't for my daughter, Violet, I'd never hear proper talk."

Jennie's face clouded over. "You have a daughter, too?"

"Yes. She's nine years old. Be in your class someday too, if we still here at the Base."

Shaken, Jennie stood to signal the end of the conversation. "I'll ask my husband about the tryouts," she said, forcing another smile.

"Thank you, M'am." Mrs. Williams took Clarence, Jr. by the hand and began a slow retreat toward the door.

Jennie walked to the closet and, slipping on her overcoat, felt for the vial in her pocket.

Her Lily, if she had lived, would have been nine this year, too.

Chapter Ten

JOHN BOLTED FROM SCHOOL the instant the bell rang. He couldn't wait to get away.

Dinah had snubbed him all day long and most humiliating of all, flirted at assembly with the captain of the football team, her beaming face turned upward as if inviting a kiss.

Peeling out of the parking lot, he arrived in a minute at the *Journal*, a quaint, Tudor-style structure with Olde English script above the entrance. *The Rapid City Daily Journal—The Newspaper of Western South Dakota*. John scoffed at the motto, thinking of his assignment to cover a church quilt show. Still, after a day like today, he was grateful to have a job to escape to. And he did respect the paper's wide circulation, covering an area larger than many states.

Certainly, it seemed vast to him when he manned the *Journal*'s sports phone, gathering scores and stories from throughout the West River. Sometimes he imagined he was reporting his own starring role, though he knew it was a fantasy. He could never have been a star athlete, not even in a small town. His stiff right leg, the polio leg, would have put the kibosh on that.

Yanking the door open, John stopped by the office of Paddy Olavson, Managing Editor. Cramped and lacking privacy, it was placed just inside the entrance—a location surely strategic—for no one could enter or leave the building, or take the stairs to the floor above, without Paddy knowing. Copy boys, secretaries, writers—all were known to him by the sound of their gait. He was said to have the ears of a blind man. Chafing under his thumb, they called him *Troll*.

Paddy sat with his feet on his desk, devouring the luncheon special from *Tally's*, a popular restaurant for *Journal* staff and Rapid's movers and shakers. Leaning back in his swivel chair, he wedged the plate between his chin and protruding belly and tipped the dish back ever so slightly, its rim resting on the wide spillway of his lower lip. A big, beefy man with a balding gray pate, he ate greedily, cutting large chunks of the meat loaf with his fork and pulling them to his gaping mouth through a swamp of mashed potatoes and brown gravy. Finishing, he wiped away bits of spill on his chin with the back of his hand and looked at his watch.

"Say, kid, you're early. Why aren't you home watching the fucking Mouseketeers?"

John smiled. Paddy and the *Journal* he could always count on. The shouts of reporters, the ringing of telephones, the vibration of the press down under, the mingled odor of ink, cigars, and newsprint never failed to lift his mood. And Paddy himself, who was always there to greet him, as he had greeted so many other cub reporters since coming to the *Journal* decades before.

"Paddy—even if I had a TV, I wouldn't watch that crap."

Paddy hooted, and John, warming to adult approval, felt his spirits rise.

"No TV? You come from fuckin' holy rollers?"

"Nope. Teachers."

"Oh! I knew that. A noble but doomed calling. TV will be the death of literacy in this great land. Libraries will crumble, books turned to dust, newspapers extinct in your lifetime. Damn shame they couldn't keep TV outta Rapid."

John threw Paddy a confused look. "Whatcha talkin' about, Paddy?"

"You mean you've never heard of 'The Meeting'? Couple years back, all the muckety-mucks in town—people who own theaters, radio stations, and the *Journal*, teachers and ministers, too—conspired to keep TV out of Rapid. After all the blowhards had their say, this woman in the back stands up. She don't mince words, 'If all you *men* think TV's a *bad* thing, it must be a good thing. I'm gonna bring TV to western South Dakota'.

"Know who it was? Helen Duhamel, owner of KOTA radio. And that's how TV came to Rapid." Paddy sighed. "What a dame!"

John heard a soft cough behind them and a brisk "Hello, Paddy."

R.W. Hitchcock, Publisher of the *Journal,* stood in topcoat and hat, poised to leave for the day. He shot Paddy a reproving glance. "Still telling tales of the 'Great Television Conspiracy'?"

Paddy chortled. "Don't let him confuse you, kid. It was real."

R.W. turned his sharp blue eyes on John. "R.W. Hitchcock. And you are?"

John extended his hand. "John Moran."

"Oh, yes. Heard you were with us. What is Paddy having you do?"

Paddy broke in. "He mans the phone on game nights, writes up the summaries for the little plains towns."

"Is that all? A smart boy like John should be doing more, don't you think?"

For a moment, John had a hopeful feeling. Then Paddy dashed his prospects.

"He's just a high school kid . . . "

R.W. took off his topcoat. "Son, come with me to the teletype. I'd like to show you how a newspaper works and how you might fit in here someday."

John followed R.W. up the stairs to a room where a big boxy machine stood alone in the center like a futuristic oracle. An automatic typewriter fed by a bolt of newsprint, the 19KRS generated a stream of news stories at a clangorous sixty words a minute. In spare moments, John often stood by the machine, feeling its link to the wider world and to the East, from which, like the morning sun, its reports seemed invariably to arise. Now he watched the broad ribbon of newsprint slip through R.W.'s hands as he read the headlines aloud.

IKE SAYS H-BOMBS ARE 96% FREE OF FALLOUT.

SHORTAGE OF POLIO SERUM EXPECTED—FEAR OF NEW EPIDEMIC.

Hearing the word 'polio', John's stomach clenched. Thrown back to the Crippled Children's Hospital and the dream that still haunted his nights—crawling through splits and clefts of a boundless cave, powerless to push through the rock jaws which trapped him. Jerking awake, soaked in sweat, he'd direct his thoughts to the first time Dinah touched him—a light stroke on his leg which he might never have felt if the polio had run its full crippling course.

"OK, John, here's where we get the stories for the first three *Journal* pages—national and international news, regional and local, too. "Here's a story that might interest you."

SOVIET REPORTS DEATH OF WORLD'S OLDEST MAN, 157.

"Says Egor was 'just one of many long-lived Russians'—point being, you live longer in the joyous Soviet system. We printed it but put in the counter claim. ***MAN EXAMINED BY NEW YORK HOSPITAL MAY BE 167 YEARS OLD.***" R.W. chuckled. "Same as Olympic medal counts. Silly comparisons when all that really matters is who gets the long-range missile first."

R.W. picked up a copy of that day's Journal. "And this item came from one of our reporters." NEGROES AND INDIANS FIND ALLEY FOR FIGHT.

"A different type of race riot Saturday night resulted in bloody noses and bruises for members of two minority groups. City police officers and air police dispersed the belligerent groups as the fracas threatened to grow into outsized proportions. According to police reports, about thirty Negro servicemen came into town in a group after one or more of their members were allegedly insulted and abused by two Indians outside the Coney Island Club."

"Bet you never heard that on TV. No one would come downtown ever again. We run this kind of story responsibly—on the bottom of page 3 where astute readers find what they need to know." John nodded pleasantly but wondered if Paddy would say R.W. had buried the story.

"Now, the local pages. Rapid City boy makes good—physicist at Los Alamos! Could be you someday." R.W. looked John square in the eye. "But, I hope you'll settle here after Harvard, or wherever you're headed for college. Hate to see our brightest leave and not come back."

John squirmed but managed to offer R.W. a weak smile.

"This is our Editorial Page. I write one every day. Today I endorsed a new water system—much needed but opposed by many taxpayers."

R.W. flipped to the sports section. "We print local people's names and pictures here, stars of high school and college games, winners of golf and bridge tourneys, bowling and softball champs. Readers love to see their names and pictures in the paper. TV can never match that.

"The women's pages, of course, are where we put the astrology guide and crossword, and ads for women's things—diet pills, clothes washers, and so on. Ann Landers is here, too. Today, she advises a woman whose husband fell in love with his secretary. Boy, is that an old story." R.W. pulled a handkerchief from his pocket and wiped his glasses, a faraway look in his eyes.

"That should make you proud of what we do here, John. For seventy-nine years we've been an important regional newspaper with a readership now of seventy-five thousand."

Folding the *Journal*, R.W. handed it to John, and strode from the room.

The paper felt heavy in John's hands, like he'd been entrusted with the sole surviving copy of the Magna Carta. Until now, he'd not understood all that the *Journal* meant to the community. And yet, he wondered if working here could ever be enough for him after going East. Would he be satisfied cutting and pasting the big national stories issuing from 19KRS's cold mouth—while waiting for some older man to die or retire, giving him a shot at writing editorials? Even then, would he be allowed to expound on important matters of the day, or be confined to mundane, local issues—like R.W.'s editorial on the need for larger gauge water pipe?

No, he didn't see the road to Yale leading back to Rapid. He'd only considered coming home to collect Dinah and take her wherever he was going. Now that prospect seemed gone.

A melody drifted up from the first floor, sung in a raspy tenor to the tune of 'Danny Boy'.

"Oh, Johnny Boy, the quilts, the quilts are calling thee."

John trudged down the stairs and grabbed his camera from Paddy's office. Out of the corner of his eye he spotted Paddy, his back to the door, taking a swig from a flask.

"Just 'cause they wear the fancy suits don't mean they ain't lyin' to ya."

John knew Paddy's comment was aimed at him, but he walked away without reply.

Chapter Eleven

JAMES WAS STILL SMILING about his basketball shot as Jennie pulled up to the side entrance of the gym. Swinging open the door of the Dodge, he pitched his test papers onto the back seat, where they landed in a neat stack. "Two for two!" he crowed.

Jennie threw him a look. "And if they'd fallen on the floor?"

"I would've picked them up," he said, jutting his chest forward like a preening rooster.

Jennie put the car into gear and left the lot, her mind fixed on what lay hidden in her coat. She had kept it there all day, thinking a pocket safer than her purse, which might have been searched by the Air Police. Luckily, she was waved through, and the pills stayed snug and still, except when she braked, and they stirred with a kind of rattle—like the lethal warning of a snake.

Their first stop was *Bob's Shoe Repair* on Main Street to have John's dress shoes re-soled. Waiting in the car, James gazed at the neon boot framed by the plate glass window. In '34, when he was seventeen, it was *Bob's Shoe Renewal*. That was the year his father lost the ranch and the two of them moved to Rapid, renting a room opposite the blinking *Renewal* sign. His dad found work at the lumberyard, and he washed dishes at a cowboy café on Main for a half dollar a day and his dinner besides. For a time, the sights and sounds of the "big town" were enough to dull the ache of losing their land and livelihood.

Then, along came Jennie—spotted standing under the blinking *Renewal* sign.

He didn't know her, but her face had a familiar plainness, and her figure spoke of the spare, hard life of a country girl. Yes, she was far too thin, but also tall and lithesome, with soft hazel eyes, curly red-brown hair, and countless freckles. Craving a bit of country, he rushed out to meet her, then walked with her to St. Joseph Street.

Just a block apart, Main and St. Joe formed the heart of the business district, though the streets were quite different—gritty Main with its pool halls and cowboy bars bordered by the city's blue-collar sectors to the north and east—stylish St. Joe with its dress shops and cocktail lounges skirted by the richer precincts to the south and west. Anchoring St. Joe was the Alex Johnson, a mountainous, eleven-story, stone-and-brick hotel in the style of an Alpine castle. The tallest and largest building in Rapid, it seemed to stand sentinel between the two streets, a towering fortress guarded by a garrison of 'soldiers'—young men in uniform that James had not yet learned were just bellboys. Halted by their formal bearing, he steered Jennie back towards Main, the only fit place, he thought, for a country boy like him.

Now solidly middle-class, James had widened his circle to include St. Joe—even making it inside the Alex Johnson on occasion—though he understood that as a mere classroom teacher, he'd never be part of St. Joe's true inner circle—the Rotary, which met once a week for breakfast at the Alex. A closed ring composed of the town's movers and shakers, the Rotary made all the important decisions in Rapid, including whether or not to back the building of a baseball stadium. Tonight, the Rotarians would be at the Bond Meeting and hear him speak. James swallowed hard. Suddenly, he felt nervous. Was he up to it? Would he impress?

"Open the door!" Jennie barked. James sighed. She wasn't always like this, he had to remind himself. Heading home, Jennie turned onto Jackson Boulevard, passing the *Flying V*, a dude ranch where a sorrel galloped hard along the fence line.

"We should go riding again, hon," James said, hoping the suggestion might please her and put her in a loving mood that would calm his nerves.

Jennie snuck a glance at her husband. He had a dreamy look, and she supposed he was recalling a ride decades earlier to a secluded spot on her folks' place, where under a canopy of cottonwoods, they'd made love for the first time. Placing a hand on Jennie's thigh, James confirmed her suspicion.

James was solidly built back then, and it pleased her—his weight pressing against her, an assurance of strength and stability. But now she felt crushed and couldn't wait for him to finish. Still, she'd never complain or refuse him, because their way was how God had prescribed it between husband and wife. And afterwards, he'd roll off her and always see to her need, and it didn't feel shameful, as when she attended to it herself, with sordid pictures of Florence and her deadly lover flickering across her eyes.

James feigned a yawn and spread his arms wide, then lightly kneaded Jennie's neck. "Sure could use a lie-down before the meeting tonight. How 'bout it, hon? Ya tired?"

Jennie made a sharp turn into the parking lot of Hermanson's Market. "We need coffee," she declared, though they had enough *Chase and Sanborn* for the week. Pivoting to open the door, she felt the bulge of the vial of Seconal against her hip.

She hadn't always been this prickly, but James reckoned he was the only one who knew it. Still, she might go along with him and do it before dinner—out of habit, if nothing else.

...

Forty-seven, forty-eight, forty-nine. James counted Jennie's thrusts against the heel of his hand. Rhythmic plunges forward, tremulous swings back. It wasn't long now. She seldom reached sixty. Fifty-one, fifty-two, her eyes nearly shut, her breath quickening, beads of sweat collecting between her shoulder blades. Fifty-five, fifty-six. Perhaps tonight she'd not make it, he thought. She was really wound up about something. Fifty-nine, Sixt . . . and then her breath and movement ceased, and her head jerked fitfully, lightly butting his chin.

James smiled, and removing his hand from under her, pulled her to him. Her flesh felt warm and flushed, as it always was after she came, which she reliably did after he pulled out of her and put his hand where she needed it. James turned toward Jennie and pressed his mouth against hers. He always loved the exchange of moist breath and kisses afterwards, but this time, she jerked her face away.

Sighing, James wrapped his arm around her waist and spooned his big belly into the scoop of her back. This was his favorite time to make love—before supper and his men's clubs, when it was still light enough to see the changes he made in her, the ruddy glow of her skin and her expression—seriousness changing to fright before giving way to rapturous calm.

He wished he could extend those moments of serenity for her, and that others could know that Jennie did escape, if only briefly, the fretful anxiousness that made her so hard to be around. If only he could tell them that the very best thing about their marriage was their intimate time together, and that in some odd way, her anxiety and his ability to 'fix' it, if just for a spell, was what bonded them and deepened their union.

James yawned. A snooze would make the interlude complete, but Jennie was restless, and he knew if she didn't settle after the first minute or two, his hopes for a nap would be dashed.

"I wish John would date other girls," Jennie interjected.

"Fat chance. He's got the prom queen." James cupped his hand over Jennie's bony hip.

"I'm serious. She'll use him as her ticket out. I won't have him saddled with her at Yale."

James gave Jennie's little belly a reassuring squeeze. "I wouldn't worry. Dinah's still in high school."

"She could make it impossible for him to go."

"Now, how's she gonna do that?"

Jennie scoffed. "The usual way—her momma's way."

"First, you're worried she's going with him to Yale. Then you're worried she's gonna keep him here. That won't happen. John's got a good, level head."

Jennie turned away from James and pulled the covers up to her neck. "There's a colored boy in my class, Clarence Williams, whose father wants to try out for the new ball team."

Surprised by the sudden change of subject, James was happy to follow her lead. "John and I saw him play in the tournament last summer at Ellsworth. He's named Clarence Williams, too. Solid catcher and a great hitter. Played in the Negro Leagues. Is the kid a good athlete?"

"I dunno. He's short, small for his age."

"Hell, so is Billy. But he's been knocking cans off fence posts since he was six." Pulling Jennie to him, he traced a figure eight on her bare back. "Would you consider doing it again?"

Jennie turned to face James and exclaimed. "What! Again?"

James laughed. "I mean, have another kid. Maybe we'd get a girl for you this time."

"We already had a girl."

James tightened his grip around Jennie, but she'd become rigid in his arms. "Oh God, I'm sorry, hon. Sometimes I forget. It was so long ago, and she only lived a few hours."

Jennie threw off his arms, and jackknifing out of bed, grabbed her robe. "Fine. You remember Billy practicing his pitching. I remember Lily."

Striding from the room, she let the door slam behind her.

James lay in bed for a moment staring at the ceiling. Then he got up and dressed—for Jennie's dinner and the Town Meeting.

Chapter Twelve

BERNIE SAT AT HIS DESK in the New York Club, waiting for James to pick him up. Running his eyes over a column of figures, he frowned. Receipts for the Coney Island Club were down. He'd have to get to the bottom of that. The Coney was just a dive bar to most, but for him it was a gold bar and the financial lifeline for the New York Club, the fancy showcase he'd built years back for Lana which bled red ink from the start.

Of course, his moneymaker could be a troublemaker, too. Like the fracas between Negro airmen and local Indians written up in today's *Journal*. Still, most nights Coney Island was just a lively joint where airmen could meet young women and drink, dance, flirt, and, yes, fuck.

Even before the War, he'd seen the need for a place like that in Rapid. More so after the Air Force integrated, and Negroes began arriving at Ellsworth. He knew that Black airmen were being refused service at some local bars and eateries. Just like when he was down South with the Air Force before the War. He'd seen the signs there—"No coloreds, no dogs, no Jews."

Bernie snorted, recalling the unlikely path that launched him, a Brooklyn Jew, first into the segregated South, then north by northwest to South Dakota. Raised solo by his mother after his father skipped out, he was recruited in his teens by Meyer Lansky, Murder, Inc.'s top Jew.

Kyping cars for Lansky's Jewish-Italian mob in Brooklyn, he was arrested in '37 with a gang of Jewish toughs for busting up a meeting of the German-American Bund—American Nazis in Yorkville, New York's 'Kraut-town' on Manhattan's Upper East Side.

Appearing before a Jewish judge—how Lansky arranged *that*, he never knew—he was given a choice. Jail or the military. Heeding his mother's plea to straighten up and fly right, he joined the Army where, as Lansky put it, he might get the chance to kill *real* Nazis. With 20/15 eyesight and a top score on the Army Air Force's Wonderlic Test, he found his way to flight school at Randolph Air Force Base in Texas. On a side trip north to Rapid, he met Lana.

Bernie hit a switch under his desk, and the blinds parted over the one-way mirror he'd installed between his office and the main room of the Club. Onstage, Lana stood under a spotlight, rehearsing the sultry standard, 'Fever'.

"Fee . . . vah in the mornin'. Fee . . . vah all through-oo the night."

Bernie felt Lana's voice resonate in his groin. Warm and dusky, and deeper in tone than her speaking voice, it seemed pitched to the lower register of a clarinet.

The first time he heard her, she brought down the house in a variety show with a rousing rendition of "Boogie Woogie Bugle Boy (of Company B)." "For our fine men in uniform," she purred, with a sly wink in his direction. From that moment on, he knew he had to have her, though he didn't exactly sweep her off her feet. Being a handsome flyboy helped and talk of New York and a fancy nightclub closed the deal, though it painted a false picture of what their life would be—and where—for he was smitten with the West and taking a woman like Lana back East was completely out of the question.

And that's why, on his way home after VE Day, he dropped in on his old boss, Meyer Lansky, in New York, to ask the notorious gangster to bankroll *two* ventures—a honky-tonk for Rapid's airmen and the classy supper club he'd promised his wife. Though dreading the long reach of the Mob if things didn't work out, he couldn't think of any other way to get the money.

Ushered into the racketeer's office, he was about to make his pitch when Lansky told him a story, better than a fairy tale, which led him to a pot of gold with no apparent strings attached.

"Rapid City? Yeah, I know it. Back in the twenties, Moe Annenberg built a place near there. Called it Ranch A—A for Annenberg." The dapper little man smiled sweetly as if reminiscing about a dearly departed uncle. "Moe was passing through on his way to Yellowstone and stopped at a little café that served the best trout he'd ever had. Owner said it was caught in a stream nearby, so Moe took a look, liked what he saw, and pulled $27,000 cash from his pocket. Bought that stream and the 650 acres around it on the spot. Built himself a big spread, deep in a canyon, miles from the highway. Wired it for bookies—direct line to every race-track and boxing ring in America. The perfect hideout if things got too hot back East." Lansky turned somber. "They got Moe anyway. Tax evasion. Spent his last years in the slammer. Lost Ranch A. Not sure who's got it now."

Ranch A—where Bernie found what he needed one moonlit night in '46, hidden in a boarded-up barn once owned by the man who made his fortune hawking the Daily Racing Form. He reckoned that if Moe Annenberg could pull twenty-seven thousand in cash from his pocket for a plate of fish, he might have stashed some in one of the horse stalls at Ranch A.

It was the best gamble he ever made, but for months afterward, he'd jerk awake with dreams of thugs from Murder, Inc. chasing him down Main Street firing Tommy guns.

Eventually, the nightmares stopped and now he rarely gave a thought to Ranch A or Moe Annenberg and how they fueled his lucky start here in the West.

Onstage, Lana turned and took a step toward the bass player. Bernie pushed back his desk chair and strode to the one-way mirror, his gaze locked on a billowing gap between the buttons of her blouse and a patch of ivory skin edged by a red brassiere.

Sure, he'd lied about his intentions—while Lana, to her credit, had been upfront about hers. Pregnant when they met, she asked only that Dinah never learn her real father's identity.

And so, he lassoed a mare and a foal, breech-birthed when he was in the service. All three survived the War, though Lana was ripped up real bad inside and could never bear another child.

Dinah, his only kin, shared his name, but not a single drop of his blood.

Chapter Thirteen

JOEL SAT AT THE END of the locker room bench, looking down at the floor. The thrill of his no-hitter against Rutgers had been short-lived—short-circuited by remorse for violating Shabbos and concern for his parents waiting, and surely worrying, back in Brooklyn. The sun had set, so he couldn't even make a phone call to reassure them, as that too was forbidden on the Sabbath.

"Come home with me, pal," Morrie offered. "Maybe I can talk Mom into lighting the Shabbos candles for you."

"She should have done it already."

"Oy, such a stickler."

"OK, but we should walk to your place."

Morrie grimaced. "Walk? That's six miles? Wait a second, Joel. You don't have to pay to get on the team bus, and the bus driver's not Jewish. Ask your Rabbi—bet he'll say it's all right."

"It's too late." Head down, Joel followed his friend onto the bus. "And I already know the answer."

Joel rode in silence, while Morrie, beginning to regret his offer, joined his raucous teammates celebrating the Lions' season-opening win. Dropped at the campus, the two walked to the Melton apartment on Riverside Drive. In the elegant, marbled lobby Joel eschewed the elevator, insisting on climbing the nine flights of stairs. Trailing behind, Morrie was muttering and cursing by the fifth landing. "What would you do if I lived on the sixteenth floor?" he asked.

"I'd take more time," Joel answered. Fumbling for his keys, Morrie opened the door—a Sabbath violation—then switched on the light—another breach, with others, Joel feared, sure to follow.

Looking around the large open room with its Danish modern furniture and abstract art, Joel saw that it bore scant resemblance to the cramped walk-up he shared with his parents in Brooklyn. "A stranger in a strange land . . . Manhattan of the secular Jews," he thought, as Morrie flipped on the radio to a station playing jazz.

Joel crossed the room to a picture window facing west to the Hudson River. Looking north he caught sight of a shimmering string of lights—the George Washington Bridge, linking Manhattan to that vast, unknown country he might soon explore. Again, he wondered—how much stranger would he feel out there in Dakota, halfway across the American continent?

In the kitchen, Morrie read a note Scotch-taped to the refrigerator. "Says they're at Hong Kong Gardens and I can join 'em." Noting Joel's pained expression, he added, "But let's eat here." Opening the fridge, he pulled out a roast chicken, a jar of pickles, and two bottles of Dr. Brown's Cel-Ray Tonic. Then he spied Joel staring at the bird, probably wondering if it was kosher. Or, perhaps he'd noticed that it was sitting next to a slab of bacon. Morrie flipped a loaf of braided challah to his friend, who caught it with one hand, smiling weakly. Within minutes they had picked the bird clean.

"So, you think you'll go to Dakota?"

Reluctant to reveal his concerns about his father, even to a friend, Joel said only, "I want to, but I've never been away that long. Or that far."

"Then, ya gotta go. Think of all those luscious farm girls you're gonna plow." Morrie drew an exaggerated hourglass shape in the air.

Joel laughed. "You mean the proverbial 'farmer's daughters'?"

"I mean this." With a lascivious grin, Morrie slid his right index finger back and forth through a ring formed by his left thumb and forefinger.

Joel, uneasy with the turn of the conversation, forced a laugh.

"You need to go out there and get some—like Henry Miller. You must know about him?"

Joel looked blankly at Morrie, trying to recall a randy classmate with that name.

"*Tropic of Cancer? Tropic of Capricorn?* His hot-to-trot tropics?" Morrie prodded.

Chagrined, Joel recouped. "Aren't his books banned in America?"

Morrie gestured to the hallway. "Follow me to the *sanctum sanctorum.*"

Frowning at Morrie's flip reference to the Biblical "Holy of Holies," Joel trailed him to a bedroom strewn with books and clothes, and on the wall an autographed photo of Jewish baseball hero Hank Greenberg. From behind a stack of books, Morrie pulled a red volume, its title spelled out along its spine, *'S E X U S'.* "Dad got it in Paris. It's Miller's latest, even dirtier than his first two."

Joel was astounded. "Your *dad* gave you a sex book?" And an illegal one at that.

Morrie shrugged. "I'm twenty-one. Easier to give me a book than talk about it." Letting the book fall open to a dog-eared page, he handed it to Joel with a grin. "Read, friend, and learn."

> *We got into a cab. Mara impulsively climbed over me and straddled me. We went into a blind fuck, with the cab lurching and careening, our teeth knocking, tongue bitten, and the juice pouring from her like hot soup. "Wait, wait," she begged, panting and clutching at me furiously, and with that she went into a prolonged orgasm in which I thought she would rub my cock off.*

Joel felt the blood pool in his groin. How could anyone think, let alone write, such things? Yet, he wondered—could girls really be like this? All he could say was, "Wow!"

He handed the book back to Morrie who skimmed the same passage. "You're so lucky going to Dakota. You can get away with murder there. Nobody'll know you."

Hearing the front door slam, Morrie shoved the book back into its hiding place.

"Where were you? We had eggrolls and chow mein!" Morrie's nine-year-old sister jumped into her brother's arms and stuck out her tongue at Joel, who looked down at his trouser-front, fearing it was still tented from *SEXUS*.

"You bring me back any?" Morrie asked, as he tickled her in the ribs.

"Maurice Melton, what have you done to my capon?" A slim, dark-haired woman in her late forties, dressed in a fitted tweed suit, walked into the room.

"Oh, hello. I didn't know you had company." She flashed a warm smile.

"Hi, Mom. This is Joel Meznik, the pitcher I told you about. He threw a no-hitter today. Masterful. Like Whitey Ford."

"Oh, yes, the stylish Yankee southpaw," she said as she shook Joel's hand.

Joel was impressed. He didn't know any women who followed baseball. Not his mother or even his girlfriend, Rivkah.

"Now you boys clean up your mess. On the Seventh Day, both God and I deserve a rest."

Joel's jaw dropped. He'd never heard anyone be so irreverent about the Commandments.

"Mom, Joel's staying here tonight. We're going out to celebrate the big win."

Joel wondered what Morrie had in mind—a wild night on the town, or a milkshake at the corner drug? Not that it mattered. Both would be violations of Sabbath law.

The two walked back to the kitchen and cleaned up, then Morrie excused himself to change, returning a moment later in a sports coat and cravat. Joel smiled at the affectation, wondering if this was his friend's standard Friday night attire.

"Where we goin'—the 'Darby' at Ascot?"

"Just trying to stand out from the crowd. Not everyone can look like Montgomery Clift."

Joel ducked his head. He knew he was good looking, but Montgomery Clift?

"So, where you wanna go, Joel? This is your big night on the town."

Joel swallowed hard. He should find the nearest synagogue or head for Low Library and let Morrie go out alone. But he was tempted. He might never get this chance again.

"Somewhere we can walk to," Joel said finally, thinking he'd circumscribe his sin.

"OK—let's see what's happening at the *West End*."

Joel knew the bar—he'd passed it many times and often wondered what it was like.

"Listen, Morrie, I can't handle money tonight, but I'll pay you back Monday."

Reaching the street, the two were met by a brisk wind off the Hudson powering them east to Broadway. Turning north toward campus, Morrie recapped the highlights of today's game, impressing Joel with his dead-on mimicry of Yankee broadcaster Mel Allen. Joel knew that Morrie, pressed by his parents, planned a career in law—just as he was expected to become a doctor. But now, he wondered if Morrie's manifest vocal talents would be wasted as a lawyer.

"Man," Morrie pouted, "you might as well be a thousand miles away."

"Sorry, Morr . . . that was great. If anything happens to Mel Allen, they can just slot you in." He paused before turning serious. "Maybe you *should* become a broadcaster."

Morrie beamed. "Thanks, Buddy. I've thought about it, but it'd mean starting out in Podunk, working my way up to Cedar Rapids, or Grand Rapids, or whatever rapids you're paddling to—then after ten or fifteen years, maybe reach the Big Leagues. What if I got stuck in the provinces? I'm a New Yorker. I break out in hives crossing the Hudson."

Joel was surprised. Could Morrie be a captive, too . . . tethered in his own way to New York Jewish culture—that modern variety found on the Upper West Side?

At 110th Street, Broadway became crowded with collegians and, it being Friday, most were dressed to impress. Morrie forged ahead, checking out the girls but failing to elicit a response, while Joel sensed that some were giving *him* the eye. But he couldn't allow himself to look back, fearing a betrayal of Rivkah, along with the Sabbath.

"Where's the dividend?" Morrie asked, with uncharacteristic bitterness.

"Dividend?"

"Yeah. If we were football players after a win like today, we'd be scoring here, too. But we're baseball players—so, my game-winning hit leaves me as unseen as the Invisible Man. At least *you* get a scholarship for your efforts. Me? Bupkus."

Shocked by his tirade, Joel saw that his doleful friend had joined the team to enhance his standing with girls as much as for his love of the game. He placed a hand on Morrie's shoulder.

"I know this isn't much consolation, but your teammates hold you in the highest esteem."

"And if I were looking to get laid by them that would make me feel a whole lot better."

At 113th Street they arrived at *The West End*, where a crowd of Barnard girls pressed toward the door. One regarded Joel in a way that was direct to the point of brazen. It was the striking young woman who'd shouted to him on the Quad that afternoon.

"Wait!" he whispered to Morrie, "There's a girl there . . . "

"Oh, her! Mona Solomon," Morrie said, his contempt palpable.

"You know her?"

"I do, and believe me, you don't want to. She's a tease and the worst type of intellectual snob. She'll lead you on, then dump you for a bullshit poet."

Joel guessed his friend had struck out with her. Still, he was intrigued.

The door opened, and Mona and a petite blonde walked up to Morrie, cornering him. "Hi there, Morrie," Mona said, overlooking his icy glare. "Who's your pal?"

"Hello, Mona," Morrie snarled, eyeing her friend. "I didn't notice you."

Ignoring the slight, Mona stared boldly at Joel, looking him up and down in a kind of challenge. No girl, and certainly not Rivkah, had ever appraised him that way, but he met her gaze, using the occasion to study her front-on—dark hair, blue eyes, full lips painted a deep red. Her bust, even blurred by her coat, was hard to ignore.

Mona offered her hand and Joel swallowed it in his pitcher's grip. "Joel Meznik," he said.

"Are you on the lam? You were in quite a rush this afternoon."

"Oh, I had to be somewhere," Joel said, unsure that his baseball connection would count for much with a Barnard girl.

Mona raised one eyebrow, something Joel had only seen before in the movies.

"We had a ball game. Joel's the Lions' Ace," Morrie interjected.

Joel knew it was intended as an endorsement, but it felt like Morrie was ratting him out.

"Do you know what that means, Mona?" Morrie added, meanly.

"The Ace of Diamonds, of course," she said. Morrie scowled, but Joel was charmed.

"Why haven't I seen you here before, Joel?" Mona continued.

Joel hesitated, wondering what he could truthfully say. "I'm Orthodox and shouldn't be here even now." Or "I have a girl in Brooklyn everyone expects me to marry." He started to sweat, as if the bases were loaded and he'd lost his control.

"We're celebrating his night of emancipation from Hebrew piety. Joel done sold his soul to beat the Damn Yankees." Morrie reached across Joel's back to give him a one-armed hug.

"You're Orthodox?" Mona asked, her eyes widening.

"Yep. Joel's here at the West End looking for a nice Jewish girl to light his candle."

Face reddening, Joel wanted to sock Morrie in the mouth but glowered at him instead.

Mona gave a snort, and the blonde giggled at the dirty jest.

Emboldened, Morrie pressed on. "As for myself, I don't require the girl who lights *my* candle to be either Jewish or nice. Let's find a table."

The foursome wended their way to the back of the room, passing a horseshoe bar and a steam table laden with pans of wilted cabbage and grayed corned beef that appeared left over from St. Patrick's Day. Joel pulled his friend to him. "Straighten up, Morrie, or I'll belt ya."

"It's working, Rabbi. I got a feeling we're gonna get lucky tonight."

"I'm not looking to get lucky."

"Suit yourself. Just don't blow it for me."

In a back corner of the room, a booth was being vacated. Led by Mona, they rushed past an empty table to stake their claim. "Why this booth—you hiding from the FBI?" Morrie snarled.

"It's the poet's corner. I met Allen Ginsberg here. Jack Kerouac, too." Mona's face flushed with her private memory of Kerouac, as Morrie reached past her to offer his hand to the blonde. "I'm Morrie Melton and I don't do rhyme. But I'm good for a couplet any old time."

Mona rolled her eyes, but her friend giggled and took his hand. "I'm Marcy Oberman, a nice Jewish girl, though I don't look it."

"Praise Jesus. I would have sworn you were Swedish gentility."

"Dutch on my mother's side—hence the fair hair."

"Nice!" Morrie said, and Marcy smiled. Shimmying into their seats, the girls sat next to each other on one side of the booth. Coatless in a cardigan, Mona faced Joel—her jutting bosom in a tug-of-war with three stressed buttons. Lifting his eyes to her face, he saw that she had followed his gaze and was relieved to see that she was smiling.

"Speaking of Ginsberg, has anyone read 'Howl'?" Joel asked, hoping to establish some intellectual clout.

Mona recited the poem's first line by heart. "I saw the best minds of my generation destroyed by madness, starving hysterical naked . . ."

Joel provided the second " . . . *dragging themselves through the negro streets at dawn looking for an angry fix.*" He hoped it was enough to impress. He couldn't go further, though he'd been captivated when a professor read parts of the poem aloud in class.

Mona flashed an approving smile, and Joel felt as if he'd passed some sort of test.

Striving for extra credit, he added, "Ginsberg won a scholarship to Columbia from the Young Men's Hebrew Association."

Morrie snickered. "Bet they're thrilled how that investment turned out—drug-addicted queer penning filthy poems."

Mona glared at Morrie and Joel cut in as a diversion. "Tell me about Kerouac. I don't know much about him." In truth, he'd never heard of the guy.

"You will someday," Mona asserted. "He's a Beat, too. He'll be as famous as Ginsberg."

"As what? Ginsberg's houseboy?" Morrie sneered.

"You know, Morrie, your fixation on homosexuality is a classic case of reaction formation. I'm sure your analyst would agree."

Joel frowned. Was Mona implying that Morrie was homosexual? And could his friend really have an analyst? He knew some rich Manhattanites had 'head shrinkers', and Morrie sometimes seemed a little cuckoo. But not handling problems on your own? Where he came from, that would be shameful.

"Reaction formation? So, when you fight with me, Mona, you really want to screw me?"

Mona reached across the table and slapped Morrie hard across the face. Standing, she grabbed Joel's arm. "Let's get out of here."

Joel's mouth dropped. He'd never seen a girl act like that—striking a man, taking command. It was scary but exciting, too, like swimming in the riptides off Coney Island.

"Joel can't go," Morrie said, rubbing his mouth.

"And why is that, Morrie?"

"Orthodox Law. You take him, you foot the bill. *Your* dough down the drain."

"Let's go, Joel," Mona repeated, her chest heaving.

For a moment Joel froze, unsure of what to do. Staying would make him the third wheel on Morrie's bicycle—but leaving might mean a night of temptation, and even sin and betrayal. And how could he possibly be ready for the likes of Mona Solomon?

"I'm staying," Marcy said, looking straight at Morrie, whose face broke into a grin.

Joel knew what he had to do. Taking Mona by the arm, he declared, "You're with me!"—a tough guy line he recalled from the movies.

Mona grabbed her coat and followed him out the door. "Where are you taking me?"

"Let's walk." He steered her across Broadway to the Columbia gate, then into the great Quad—dark except for a constellation of dorm lights on the east side of the square.

"So tell me, Mr. Pitcherman, what part of Brooklyn do you hail from?"

"How'd you guess," he asked, though he knew his accent was obvious.

Mona put a finger to her lips. "Let's see. Your mouth, your lips, your tongue . . . " He felt himself getting aroused as she ran her tongue along her lower lip. "And then, there's your accent—you might want to lose it," she added, breaking the spell.

Joel shrugged, hearing faint echoes of his home borough in her voice, too. "How long did it take to lose *yours*?"

"Had my eye on the Emerald City since I was a Munchkin. Couldn't get away fast enough. But I wasn't raised Orthodox. That's a rougher road, I imagine."

Joel turned away. He'd never spoken to anyone—even Rivka—of his road and his dream.

And, while it might feel good to let down his hair with Mona, he doubted he could trust her. She seemed like the kind of girl who'd betray a confidence as soon as she snagged a new suitor.

Suddenly a throng of young men streaked across the Quad, brandishing women's undergarments on sticks. "What was that?" Joel asked.

"Never heard of a panty raid? You *do* lead a sheltered life." Mona looked him straight in the eye. "Silly boys. If they knew how to ask for it, they'd get more than panties on a stick."

Joel swallowed hard, sensing the challenge in her words. Though he guessed what she might want, he didn't know how to ask for it, or even what to do with it, if it was handed to him.

"That where you live?" He pointed to a tall building on the Barnard campus.

"Yes, but I'd never get you past the beau parlor. Come. I know where we can go."

Joel fell quiet and she guessed he was nervous—that she would be his first. A first for her, too, as she'd never bedded a baseball player, or anyone Orthodox. Excited by the prospect, she saw it as her calling to take as many lovers as she could—men *and* women—then write an erotic novel, à la Henry Miller. If that made her a slut in the eyes of the world, so be it. Better that than her mother's drab life as a Brooklyn hausfrau.

Taking his arm, Mona led him to Claremont Avenue—Professor's Row. Joel's mind raced ahead to what he sensed was coming. He'd always believed it would be with Rivkah—both virgins on their wedding night, but now he was presented with an opportunity—a detour with a fast girl onto Claremont Avenue. "A life's path takes many turns," he thought, recalling his mother's sage advice, though he doubted this was what she had in mind.

Mona stopped in front of a five-story building and fished a key from her purse. An iron fire escape zee'd down its façade, and all the windows were lit except those on the top floor.

"Who lives here?" Joel asked.

Mona's smile was enigmatic. "A friend who's out of town. I study here sometimes."

"What floor is it?"

"Top. You don't mind stairs, do you?"

Joel hesitated. More stairs to remind him of the Sabbath.

Mona leaned against the door and fell forward as it gave way. Inside the foyer, she stood on tiptoe and kissed Joel on the mouth.

"Slow down," he told himself, fearing she could feel him get hard against her.

Mona started up the stairs, with Joel trailing, the two of them moving as in a conga line. If she was broadening her sway for his benefit, it was working, he thought.

On the fifth floor landing she pulled him to her for another kiss. This time, he held her head in his hands, entangling his fingers in her dark curls. Pushing inside the apartment, he was struck by the smell of stale tobacco and something sweet but cloying, a cooking herb he guessed. Mona flipped on a floor lamp and Joel saw that it was a railroad flat—with movement only from room to room as in a train. "Have a seat," Mona said, pointing to the sofa. "I'll be right back."

Joel placed his coat on the couch but continued to stand. Newspapers and books were strewn everywhere. He'd never seen so many outside a library or bookstore.

Mona returned with a bottle of wine and two juice glasses. "Le Chaim," she teased, raising her glass in the traditional Hebrew toast, 'To Life'.

Joel frowned, reminded again of his Sabbath violations, but drained the glass in a single swallow, hoping it would calm him. The wine tasted sharp, like vinegar, so unlike the sweet, ceremonial wine he would have had that evening at home in Brooklyn.

Mona walked across the room to a square cabinet and lifted the lid. "Jazz. Do you dig it?"

"Sure," he replied, though he knew little about it. At home he listened to ballgames mostly, while his parents played Heifitz or Stern—virtuoso Jewish violinists—on an old Victrola.

Crouching, Mona leafed through a stack of albums on the floor. Watching her skirt ride up the back of her thighs, Joel poured himself a second glass of wine, and downed it quickly. Mona set a record on the spindle. A plaintive trumpet filled the room. "Jazz is so liquid, don't you think—like Kahlúa and cream—warm and dark and thick." She threw her head back and swayed gently to the music. Sensing it was time to act, Joel started toward her.

"I really dig Miles's sound—caught him at the Vanguard. He was sublime," Mona opened her eyes. "Who do you like?"'

Joel froze. Even if the blood in his brain hadn't migrated south, he would have been hard pressed for an answer. "Louis Armstrong," he blurted, naming the only jazz musician he knew.

"Oh, sure . . . everyone likes him," Mona said dismissively.

Joel shrugged and walked to the bookcase to hide his embarrassment. "Whose books are these? Who lives here, anyway?"

"Yogi Berra," Mona answered in deadpan. "He's more cerebral than people realize."

Joel knew she was joking but didn't like being toyed with.

"OK, it's not Yogi." Mona kicked off her shoes and curled herself into a corner of the sofa—a dark triangle forming between her folded legs and the straight hemline of her skirt.

Despite his annoyance, he couldn't take his eyes off that shadowy portal.

"Guess again."

"No thanks."

Mona sighed. She enjoyed sparring but it wasn't sparking things. She traced a figure eight on the couch cushion. "Doesn't matter, the place is ours. I'll be good—I promise."

Joel moved next to Mona, who took his hand and turned it palm side up, as if to read his fortune. Tracing his pitcher's calluses with her fingertips, she turned it over and placed it above her knee, murmuring, "Take it nice and slow and we'll both enjoy it more."

Leaning forward, he kissed her, moving his fingers as she'd directed, ever so slowly up the smooth, warm skin of her inner thigh. Would she shudder like the girl in *Sexus?* he wondered. Would he shoot his wad if she did?

"Don't stop," she whispered. She wasn't wearing panties. Joel pulled back his hand—his heart pounding so hard he swore it would break through his chest. Mona smiled and began unbuttoning her sweater—from the bottom up, one pearlette at a time.

Then the front door burst open, and the room was flooded with light.

"Whoa there, young filly!" In leather coat, suitcase in hand, a tall, burly man of about forty stepped into the room.

Joel jumped off the sofa and stumbled over a steamer trunk.

Mona laughed nervously. "Harold, when did you get back?"

"Too soon, it seems." Shaking his head, yet smiling, he seemed more amused than angry.

Joel got up from the floor and squinted at the intruder. It was a Columbia professor he'd seen on campus. Grabbing his coat from the end of the sofa, Joel started for the door.

"You don't have to go, son, we haven't met."

Head down, Joel brushed past him.

"Wait a second—I know who you are. Didn't I see your picture in the *Spectator*? Aren't you the kid with the big fastball?"

Joel stopped—afraid the man could get him booted from the team. "Yes, sir."

"Senior? Set to graduate?"

"Yes." His voice cracked. A professor might have the authority to have him expelled.

"Anyone signing you?"

Joel sighed with relief—as Mona, her cardigan rebuttoned, sidled up to the older man.

"Well, I just got an offer today to play in the Basin League this summer."

"Don't know that one. Where is it?"

"South Dakota."

"Great place. Drove out there about ten years back when I was at Wisconsin. Man can hunt and fish there . . . make a life with his hands." The professor stopped his reverie. "So, you've been doing a little celebrating with our Mona here. Not that she cares a whit about baseball, do you, honey?" He slapped her butt hard, intending, it seemed, to reestablish his brand.

Mona glared at the man, but he was still studying Joel—though he now held her tenderly, one arm looped around her waist. "If memory serves, the Northern League had a South Dakota team called the *Pheasants*. Played some of our Wisconsin clubs. Don Larsen got his start there."

Joel's eyes brightened. Don Larsen, the only pitcher ever to throw a perfect game in the World Series, got his start in South Dakota! "I didn't know that, sir."

"Well, young man, it's a big country, with baseball tucked into every corner. And it sounds to me that you've got the ticket to explore it."

Knowing he'd been dismissed, Joel stepped forward and shook the older man's hand. "Thank you, Professor."

Outside, Joel bolted down the stairs and raced west toward the Hudson. Turning south, he ran until he could run no more—until the wine sweated from his body and his head cleared. Caught stealing home by a college don! He laughed out loud. Had he been robbed or rescued?

He checked his watch. Half past eleven. He could make it to the Bridge by one, and Brownsville before dawn.

Then, in a few short months, to a place beyond his imagining, where he might make a life with his hands, or his arm—Rapid City, South Dakota.

Chapter Fourteen

THE PARKING LOT OF THE Municipal Auditorium was almost full as James pulled the Chevy into the last row of cars. "Hard to think of baseball on a night like this," James offered, his face turned from the driving snow. Bernie chuckled, gesturing to the crowded lot.

"Oh, yeah? Looks like somebody's thinking 'bout it."

Racing ahead, Billy bounded up the steps of the auditorium and peered in, his mouth dropping at the sight of the huge gathering. Following close behind, James and Bernie searched for seats on the aisle, as a gust of wind blew snow down the necks of the crowd.

James took note of the men on the dais, which included several board members of Black Hills Sports. Scattered throughout the hall were town notables, including Mayor Baker, leading bankers and businessmen, heads of the fraternal organizations, and the Rotarians—all conspicuous by their absence from the stage. Did none want to be seen as supporting the Bond?

Earlier, Bernie confided to James that his own presence onstage might not help the cause. James wondered what worried Bernie more—the shame of losing the Western League franchise a year ago, or his notoriety as owner of the Coney Island Club, cited today in the Police Blotter for a brawl between Negro airmen and local Indians.

Or was it that he was a Jewish carpetbagger from the East, not even a respectable, homegrown Jew, like Sam Bober of Bober Seed or Stanford Adelstein of Northwestern Engineering, the grandson of a Jewish homesteader? Looking around, James noted that Adelstein was absent, though that might make sense, too, since he was the likely stadium contractor if the bond issue passed. The presence of another Jew, especially one with a vested interest, might not help the cause, either.

Rising to take the lectern was Carl Mueller, President of Black Hills Sports. Born in St. Louis, he moved to Rapid to take over the local Budweiser distributorship. A fellow Mason, he loved to regale James with stories of Branch Rickey and the Cardinals of the 1930s and '40s.

Carl rapped on the lectern with the gavel. "May I have your attention, please."

The crowd's low rumble slowly diminished as latecomers found their seats, with Bernie and James in the third row and Billy two rows behind. From his vantage point, Billy spotted Glen Merritt down front, yukking it up with the mayor's popular fourteen-year-old daughter. Sensing Billy's gaze, Glen turned and shot him a smirk. Billy clenched his fists and imagined pitching a bean ball squarely between Glen's mocking eyes.

Clearing his throat, Carl began. "My name is Carl Mueller, and I'm the President of Black Hills Sports. For years we tried to bring baseball to Rapid City, but our applications were always turned down. They said it was too cold here in the spring or too far from the other circuit cities. But now, for the first time, Rapid can enjoy top-notch baseball in the Basin League, a semi-professional summer league made up of outstanding collegians and former professional players, many of whom once played in the high minors and some in the Major Leagues. And all of the collegians are Big League prospects."

Carl looked up with a self-satisfied smile but received only a smattering of applause.

"Now, I want to report on the fundraising drive, which raised thirty-six thousand dollars." The mention of money woke the crowd like a thunderclap.

Carl pounded the lectern. "I know that sounds like a lot of money to many of you, but to build a stadium to Basin League standards, we'll need thirty-eight thousand dollars *more*, and *that* is the purpose of the Baseball Bond." The crowd responded in a disagreeable low rumble.

Ralph Sandstrom, a tall, weathered man of sixty-nine, rose to his feet. A former rancher, he once ran for mayor and lost by 108 votes. Denied a recount because the deficit was more than the statutory 100, he decided that this law, like most, was rigged against men like him. "Why in Judas Priest ya wanna build a *new* ballpark when we got two perfectly good ballfields already?"

"There's your 'aginner,'" James whispered to Bernie as Carl smirked from the podium.

"You mean Sioux San Field—where batters face into the sun? And Northside, with a broken backstop and knee-high weeds—little more than a cow pasture, really." Carl paused for his knockout punch. "You must know a cow pasture when you see one, Ralph."

The crowd guffawed, and for a moment, Carl seemed to have the audience on his side.

"Besides, the City is practically *giving* us the land for the new stadium in Sioux Park."

Ralph brandished a fist. "You mean you're gettin' free land and *still* need thirty-eight thousand US dollars? They jes' want to put *their* hand in *our* pocket. Now I ask you, who's got the most jingle, *us* or *them?*"

Switching sides again, the crowd bellowed its agreement with Ralph.

Carl pulled a handkerchief from his breast pocket and patted his brow, then called to a man in the first row. "Roy, come up here and explain how the money will be utilized."

A stocky young man in a National Guard uniform bounded up the stairs to the stage.

"For starters, we need heavy earth movers to skin and level the land. Then, we got to seed it, or if we get a late thaw, sod it—and build a high fence to keep out the moochers. Games are at night, so we'll need lights and steel stanchions. Then there's the scoreboard, press box, dugouts, men and women's, ah . . . facilities . . . a concession stand, ticket booth, and a parking lot big enough for a thousand cars. And maybe two hundred box seats and 2,000 grandstand seats. When we're through, we'll have the fanciest ballpark in all of South Dakota."

Ralph Sandstrom leapt to his feet. "*Fanciest,*" he exploded. "Why in tarnation do we need *fanciest? Plain* is good enough."

From the crowd's murmuring assent, James knew that for country people like Ralph, who'd lived hard, humble lives, plain was the best you dared wish for and all you professed to want. To strive for more—to want something fine or fancy and not merely practical—was believed foolhardy and vain, even sinful. "Plains Country sour grapes," James couldn't help thinking.

Billy looked around nervously. He'd never been in a crowd that got riled. And some of these people were his neighbors or the parents of friends, or town leaders he'd heard on the radio. He thought he knew them. He thought he knew his town.

Carl tried to make himself heard over the din. "Hear me out, everyone. It's always been my rule, 'Anything worth doing is worth doing well'."

The heavy rumble rippling through the crowd reminded James of a developing stampede. Sensing an urgent need for action, he rose by his seat and waved to Carl on the dais. Relieved to see a supporter entering the fray, Carl pointed to his fellow lodge mate. "Jim Moran!"

Glancing at Glen, Billy saw that he was looking directly back at him, a mean sneer spread across his face. Billy turned toward his father, a squat, rumpled figure in a boxy overcoat that couldn't quite close, looking nothing like the trim, dapper men on the stage.

James smiled, letting his eyes pan slowly over his audience, a teacher's gesture that seemed to calm it. Soon all eyes were trained on him, now standing erect and looking, to Billy's surprise and relief, confident.

"Carl, perhaps it would ease people's minds to hear exactly how much this bond would cost them."

"Why yes, Jim, I think it would. Do you have those figures with you?"

He did, thanks to John's analysis in that day's 'Sports Beat' column in the school paper.

"Yes, I have. Funding the new stadium would cost the average taxpayer forty cents a year, less than a half dollar per family. And, after ten years, the stadium will be paid for." James listened to the crowd's applause, sure that its ire had been assuaged. But a moment later, Ralph was back on his feet, firing bullets into the air, again riling the herd.

"Anybody remember what this here mayor promised us last 'lection?" Ralph paced the front of the hall, stopping right in front of Mayor Baker. "That's right. He promised to *cut* taxes, not *raise* 'em. So, I says unto you—make the people who *benefits* from this thing *pay* for it, 'stead of *shackling* the rest of us with another damned *bond*."

Joe Mahoney, owner of the Black Hills Kennel Club, seconded Ralph's concern. "He's right. They'll raise *our* taxes when *they* are gonna make the money. Think Carl up there will sell a little beer at a ballpark on a hot summer night? And Rosen, cocktails and floor shows after the game? Ever' last one of that bunch will make a cash dollar from this here ballpark."

The crowd responded to Mahoney with sustained applause, but James knew that Joe's real concern was that baseball would cut attendance and lower the gate at his greyhound dog track. Just like Ralph, whose wife ran 'Ancient City'—an odd sandstone formation suggesting that a prehistoric people once lived there. Many mocked its claims, but a lot of popular attractions—theaters, cave tours, the Reptile Gardens—stayed open late in summer and would be hurt by games played at the same time. James's throat tightened. Why would any of those people support the Bond? They'd all line up behind Ralph.

Norm Nordby, a Lutheran minister, rose from his seat. "Please forgive my crudeness, but how in God's name will we keep our kids' snouts out of the beer?"

As the crowd erupted with hoots and laughter, James held out his hands to Bernie as a plea to enter the fray. A moment later, Bernie stepped into the aisle and, tamping down his Brooklyn accent, began his defense. "Yes, folks, there will be beer but not for anyone under eighteen. And, sure, money will be made. But we are *all* going to make it—people with businesses and people who work for businesses—think that includes most everyone here tonight. Rapid is a tourist town. This can be another fine attraction for our community, one that will get tourists to stay longer and spend more. And people from farms and ranches and small towns—looking for something exciting *and* wholesome to do with the kids on a summer's evening—will drive into town, see a game, maybe stay the night. Remember, Rapid's got ninety-five motels and auto courts."

A man behind Billy turned to his wife and in a gruff whisper, quipped, "Bet Bernie's wife's been in evry' one of 'em." It was a comment Billy didn't miss but couldn't understand.

Still furious, Ralph Sandstrom reclaimed the floor. "See—that's the way it always is with these here . . . " Struggling to find the word, Ralph waved his cowboy hat toward Bernie—and for a moment James feared he might say 'Jews'." " . . . these businessmen. They git themselves a scheme for the profit motive and expect the rest of us to put up the seed money."

Worried, James spoke again, taking a different tack. "Our American Legion team hasn't had a home game in three years. No one will play us at our Sioux San or Northside fields. We owe our Legion kids a chance to play baseball here in Rapid on a decent field."

Baseball fans gave James a round of applause and Billy, proud of his dad, beamed. Until the man behind him wisecracked, "Sounds like James's youngest son is ready for Legion ball."

Hattie Phillips, a ruddy-faced woman in her forties, spoke in a high-pitched voice. "Never liked ball myself, but the Bible says an idle brain is the Devil's workshop. So, would you rather have our boys watch a ball game or thumb through smutty magazines down at Mills Drug?"

Amidst the gasps and chortles, a tall, gray-haired woman stood and raised her hand. It was Miss Moss, Rapid's head librarian. Her equine face took on a saintly glow. "A new stadium would be a wonderful addition to our community. Back before the War, all the towns in the Black Hills—even little Keystone with the men carving Mount Rushmore—had a team. On Sunday afternoons after church, we played town ball. It brought us all together."

Billy was shocked. The sourpuss librarian—who seemed to care only about shushing kids—boosting the new stadium!

Bernie, sensing an opening, called for the crowd's attention. "Beautifully put, Miss Moss. We must all remember how it was. And now, most of the big towns have Basin League teams to represent them. Mitchell's is called the Kernels. Pierre, the Cowboys. Winner, the Pheasants. Watertown, the Lake Sox. And Huron, the Elks. Yankton's team is the Terrys. And I'm sure you can guess what Valentine's team is called. The Hearts. Can't wait to break theirs!"

Bernie waited for the chuckles to subside. "Our team will be named in a contest open to all. Won't that be grand! A new stadium in Sioux Park and a team to pull for—to unite us as a community. What could be better than that—'specially for our kids?"

James was stunned—amazed that his neighbor, who just that morning had maligned his fellow Dakotans as contrary jackasses, was appealing to town pride and getting away with it.

The crowd responded with sustained applause, putting Bernie in a confident mood. When the cheering quieted, he went on—his voice slowly building to a crescendo.

"And so, I ask you. Do you remember how it was during the War? The sacrifices we all made—pulling together, doing our part? Farmers, ranchers, businessmen, teachers—men and women, and children, too—no one idle, everyone pitching in. That's how it can be again—coming together to strengthen our community and defend our youth—protecting Rapid against the twin scourges of Communism and juvenile delinquency. Baseball, the great American game, will save us. Yes, we need our team *and* our stadium. I urge all of you to go to the polls on April 15th and vote 'Yes' for the Baseball Bond. Good night and Godspeed."

The audience exploded with thunderous cheers and James had to admit that Bernie's impassioned appeal to hearth, home, and country, sacrifice and salvation, had worked, at least for the moment. Now, he regretted that he hadn't made a dramatic appeal of his own though he wondered if he had it in him to do something like that.

Carl, recognizing that Bernie had captured the high ground, pounded his gavel. "Thank you, Bernie. Understand the snow's startin' to pile up out there. So, you all better be gittin' on home before you have to put the chains on. Remember folks, tell your friends and neighbors to vote 'Yes' on election day. Good night, and thanks for comin'."

Swallowing his pride, James offered his congratulations to Bernie. "Good job, Bern, you sure hit that one out of the park."

Bernie smiled and clapped James on the shoulder, then motioned to Carl.

"Listen, James—Carl and I are stopping at the Club for a little nightcap and postmortem. You're welcome to come."

Flattered by the invitation, James realized it was a chance to become a starter on the Black Hills Sports team. Then he thought of Jennie alone at home and how she'd sat wordless through dinner without taking a bite. "Thanks, Bernie, but I'll pass. Gotta get the boy home."

"Suit yourself," Bernie snorted, guessing Jennie was the real reason James had said "No."

James and Billy headed for the exit, where Ralph Sandstrom stood shaking hands with his supporters. Billy could tell that a real battle was shaping up—his father and Bernie on one side, Ralph Sandstrom on the other. Billy beamed, thrilled to be aligned with the right side—the baseball side—with his two favorite grown-ups in the world.

Suddenly, he felt a sharp elbow in his ribs. Glen Merritt—an arm cinching the waist of the mayor's daughter, smirked as he brushed past on his way out. Whatever side Glen was on made no difference to Billy. They'd never be on the same side, in this or anything else.

Chapter Fifteen

JOHN PARKED THE CHEVY AND climbed the steps to the Methodist Church. It was a place he knew well. On Sundays, his mom sang in the choir, and he listened to stories of the minister's missionary work in India, imagining the wide world out there he might someday explore.

"Why, Johnny Moran? Is your mother with you?" A tiny, white-haired woman, looking like an aged pixie, beamed up at him. She was Winifred Goodsell, the late minister's widow.

"Just me," John said, patting his camera case. "I'm covering the show for the *Journal*."

"Really? Why not the baseball meeting at the Auditorium?"

John's face fell. "Just lucky, I guess. Now, tell me about the quilts, Mrs. Goodsell."

"Oh, well—isn't that nice. Let me ask you, John—do you know what quilting is?"

John hesitated at what he considered an elementary question. "Oh, sure. Blankets."

"Yes, yes—that, but much more. In different times and places, quilts were used for clothing, even armor. In the Middle Ages, quilted armor protected the Knights Templar."

"That's really interesting. I never imagined . . . "

John listened as Mrs. Goodsell described the methods and materials of the craft—jotting down terms like *appliquéd* and *batting*. She spoke ardently about her subject, like his dad did about sports, but there were no more references to Knights Templar, and he found himself checking his watch to see if he could still make it to the baseball meeting.

The widow continued her lecture for some minutes, not pausing even when she caught John stifling a yawn. Yanking his arm, she pulled him in front of a quilt with bright green designs on a cream-colored background. John gasped. The figures were swastikas.

"Thought that might get your attention. But it's not what you think. It's a Fly Foot. Or a Whirligig. Sometimes it's called the Battle Ax of Thor. It's an ancient symbol—goes back to the Egyptians. The Navajos use it, too. And the Sioux have something like it. You can see it on the lobby floor at the Alex Johnson. But no one uses it anymore, for good reason. My father got this one back in the twenties when he was ministering in New Mexico. It's not for sale, but I always bring it to the Quilt Show. Wakes up the husbands, the ex-servicemen, anyways."

She gave John a sharp look. "And cub reporters who should be paying attention."

John was truly embarrassed. "Sorry."

"Are you ready now to learn something worth writing about? 'Cause I'm too old to waste my time on some knucklehead who'd rather be somewhere else."

John nodded and lowered his eyes.

"Quilting bees aren't just silly gab fests, you know." Mrs. Goodsell led him around the room, pointing out the different patterns and symbols, explaining their meanings. "These are Temperance Quilts, sewn by the Women's Christian Temperance Union. See this design?" She pointed a gnarled finger at crisscrossing blue lines. "That's the Drunkard's Path—makes you think of a stagger. And those 'Ts' tucked into the design stand for teetotalers."

John took a photo of each quilt and copious notes. Soon, he had filled five pages and Mrs. Goodsell beamed at him in triumph. "We're more than a bunch of widows and spinsters sittin' around gossiping." She laughed in a naughty, delighted way. "Not that we don't do that, too."

John smiled, then stopped in front of a quilt with a repeating pattern of blue and white blocks—like an ascending staircase against a sky-blue background. "This looks familiar."

Mrs. Goodsell squeezed his arm. "Yes, I know. We made one for you."

There was a catch in her voice as she spoke the words. "It's Jacob's Ladder.

Jacob dreamed, and beheld a ladder set up on the earth that reached to heaven, and the angels of God ascending and descending. And the Lord said, Behold I am with thee and will keep thee whither thou goest, for I will not leave thee."

The old woman's eyes shimmered like distant planets. "When you got the polio, we sewed and prayed that God would set you upright on the path."

"Thank you, Mrs. Goodsell," he said when he was finally able to choke out the words. Then he closed his notebook and walked out of the church.

He never made it to the Town Meeting, though he might have caught the end of it. Heading west, he drove to the high school parking lot, empty at that late hour, and cut the engine. Jacob's Ladder was the quilt he lay under at the Crippled Children's Hospital when he caught the polio. Waking from a seemingly endless fever, he'd find his mother standing over him, applying hot cloths in a manner she called the Sister Kenny Method, massaging his legs, forcing them to move—willing them, and him, back to life. After his confinement, the quilt vanished, deemed infected perhaps, and thrown away.

John closed his eyes to stem the tears but still they surged—a dam breached by an old woman's story and the vision of Jacob's Ladder stitched in the language of quilts.

Just then, a police car on its evening rounds drove into the lot. Wiping his eyes on his sleeve, John turned on the ignition and headed home. Neither Bernie's Cadillac nor Lana's T-Bird was in the Rosen driveway. Another car was parked there instead. The captain of the football team's '56 Corvette. A soft light shone from Dinah's room. Her shade was pulled.

For an instant, John felt the urge to drive straight at Dinah's window. Glancing in his rearview, he saw that he'd been followed home by that patrol car. John turned right into his own driveway and watched as the patrolman passed by with a salute.

• • •

Jennie lay in bed, pretending that the red and black phantoms darting across her eyes were the dreams she no longer had.

She was alone again, quivery and charged, as if her body were throwing off sparks. Rolling onto her side, she opened the drawer of the bedside table. For the third time in the last half hour, she removed the bottle of Seconal and read its simple prescription, "Take one at bedtime." It was a reasonable command, but one she doubted she could follow. She'd never taken anything stronger than aspirin and believed that sleep should come naturally at the end of a productive workday, judging it a moral failing if it could not.

Twin beams of light swept across the bedroom ceiling, followed by a squeal of brakes.

Jennie's eyes snapped open. Tossing the pills back into the drawer, she sprang out of bed and peeked under the window shade. It was John, home earlier than expected, removing his snow boots on the back porch. Jennie pulled on her robe and hurried to the kitchen. She could hardly restrain herself from throwing open the door and wrapping her arms around him.

"My, my, this *is* early for you. I was about to make cocoa. How was the Quilting Show?"

John didn't say anything. Hanging his coat on the back of the door, he angled his body so she couldn't see his tear-stained face.

"You should be home this time every night, honey. You must take special care of your health. And you need to keep your grades up. A college can rescind its acceptance if your last semester's grades aren't up to the mark." She poured milk into a small saucepan and placed it on the burner.

"They don't give grades higher than mine, Ma." He started to walk out of the kitchen.

Jennie took a deep breath. "Wait a minute, John. I know you feel all grown-up and think you don't need your mother anymore, but I still know a thing or two . . . "

John thrust his chin forward. "I'm not doing anything wrong."

"Oh, no? What about the smoke. You come home every night reeking of it. You, who could have ended up in an iron lung . . . "

John winced at that image from the polio ward. "I don't smoke, Ma."

"So where does the smell come from? Does that girl of yours smoke? Sure looks like it."

"I don't have a girl."

"Really—then who was that in my kitchen this morning? The Queen of Sheba?"

"She . . . we broke up today."

Jennie felt a rush of relief. "Well, I never liked that girl."

"Then you're even."

"She said *that*? Nobody. Do you hear me—nobody says that about your mother."

John clenched his jaw. "I don't want to talk about it"

"Listen to me. That girl would have ruined everything. We're better off without her."

John struck the doorjamb with his fist.

Jennie gulped and looked at him pleadingly. "John!"

"At least when I'm in college, you can't run my life anymore!" Striding to his room, he slammed the door behind him.

Jennie felt the room swim around her and grabbed the table for support. Staggering to the bedroom, she reached into the night table drawer, opened the vial of Seconal, and holding it over her hand, gave it a shake. Two small ovals tumbled into her upturned palm. For a moment she stared at the pills and the directions on the bottle, "Take one at bedtime."

Placing both on her tongue, Jennie gagged a little as she swallowed them without water. And then she got into bed.

...

A howling wind buffeted James and Billy as they left the auditorium. At the car, James slid behind the wheel, and commanded Billy to find the scraper.

Out of the dark, a snowball whizzed by Billy's ear. Whirling around, he scooped a handful of snow from the car's hood, pressed it into a ball, and hurled it back into the darkness.

"You and Glen still not getting along?"

"He's a jerk," was all Billy said, for how could he possibly describe how Glen had shamed him in front of the guys in the locker room.

James didn't press for more. He might cast a line, but if Billy didn't bite, he'd just drop it.

Billy cleared the snow from the windshield, then swung the scraper like a Louisville Slugger before jumping into the car. Shifting into reverse, James joined the caravan slogging towards the exit. Then, without warning, a black sedan brushed by, cutting off a pickup truck at the head of the line. It was Carl's big Chrysler, with Bernie grinning next to him in the front seat. "Sure hope that pickup's not Ralph's," James said. "He'll have his shotgun with him in the cab."

Billy looked aghast. "He wouldn't shoot Mr. Rosen, would he?"

James felt a stab of jealousy at the concern in his son's voice. "I wouldn't worry about Bernie. He can take care of himself."

The car's heater made slow headway against the cold, and James, finally comfortable, reflected on the Bond Meeting and the brouhaha shaping up in the weeks ahead. It would not be the first he'd been a part of. In the small towns of the West River country where he'd coached and taught, fights over schools, taxes, budgets, or some other civic issue, were a favorite winter sport.

Billy switched on the radio to KOMA. a 50,000-watt station out of Oklahoma City that, with its skip signal, could be heard in the evenings when the sky wave came down.

A Kitty Wells hit from a couple years back was playing.

Makin' be-lieve, that you-oo still love me, It's leaving me alone aa-and so blue.

But I'll always dream—still I'll never own you, Makin' believe, it's all I can do.

"I think girls are unhappy 'cause they don't like sports," Billy pronounced solemnly.

James hooted and Billy protested. "I mean it. They don't play 'em. They don't watch 'em. You heard that lady. *"I don't like ball, but it keeps the boys away from smutty magazines."*

James punched Billy in the arm and laughed. "I'm not sure sports would make girls happy, Son, but they sure are a lot of fun for us guys." Billy grinned, then wondered if he meant sports or girls were fun. But he let it pass, proud of his man-to-man talk with his dad.

"And by the way, Mr. Man-of-the-World, what makes you think girls are unhappy?"

"Mom." Billy's one-word answer hung in the air like an icicle.

"Life's hard for women, Bill," James said finally. "And it's been real hard for your mother." James knew that Billy, who had lived most of his years in modern, prosperous Rapid City, could never understand the hardships of life on the unforgiving Plains—the droughts and dust storms, hail and grasshoppers, prairie fires and blizzards, and the desperate loneliness of snowbound winters. And for Jennie in particular, losing her sister the way she did. And recalling his blunder in bed that afternoon—their infant daughter, Lily. But he couldn't imagine sharing those stories with his young son—stories that were not his to share.

Billy looked down and murmured in a little voice. "I just thought Momma'd be happier if she came to some games."

James reached over and gave Billy's knee a reassuring squeeze. If only it were as simple as that. "Maybe you're right, Bill, maybe you're right."

When James and Billy arrived home, Jennie was sound asleep. John was in his bedroom with his record player turned up loud.

And, in the kitchen, the milk was blackening in the pot—just beginning to smoke.

Chapter Sixteen

ON THE WAY TO THE CLUB, Carl almost missed the turn as the driving snow got the better of his wipers. At nine thirty on a stormy night, the New York Club was practically abandoned. Only a dim light shone from inside and the lot was empty except for a few ghostly forms crouching under blankets of snow. From their muted outlines, Bernie recognized his Cadillac—which Lana had driven that day—his bouncer Buck's pickup, and the cook's panel truck. Then, his gaze fell upon a delicate little profile by the entrance—a sports car, clearly, but whose?

"Better let you go, Carl. Nothing we can do for a day or two anyway."

"That sonovabitch Sandstrom's spoiling for a fight. Gotta do something about him."

Bernie dismissed Carl's concern with a wave of his hand. "He'll make as much difference as a fart in a tornado. We're gonna get that ballpark and a team—one way or another. And I found a manager today, and a couple of ballplayers, too. A big slugger from Ohio State and a southpaw from Columbia University. Joel Meznik."

"All the way from New York. Gonna have a kinsman, huh?"

Bernie shrugged. "Nothin' to do with it. Heard good things about him—another Koufax."

"So, what about the manager?"

"Name's Guy Stockman. Catcher in the Dodger chain. Cup of coffee in the Big Leagues. Played winter ball in Havana this season. Early thirties. Should hit great in semi-pro. He'll catch and manage for us. He'll be here for the Base tryouts so he can pick out an airman from the Flyers team. Good for the gate and good for town-base relations."

Carl nodded. "A player-manager. That'll save us some dough, but I still think Ralph's gonna be a problem. Wish Mother Nature'd do us a favor and run him into the ditch."

Bernie lowered his voice and let his Brooklyn accent come through. "Ya want I should give the good Mother a hand?"

Carl's face blanched. "I was just kidding, Bern."

Bernie snorted, amused by his tough guy reputation. Though he never spoke of his past on the mean streets of Brooklyn, there had been rumors ever since he returned from the War and built the raucous

Coney Island Club and the classy New York Club with a grubstake that seemed pulled from thin air.

"Bern?" Carl repeated, his voice rising.

Bernie smiled. "Yeah, I was kidding, too. Look, if you're worried about Ralph, I'll get James to talk to the men's clubs and church groups. Not much doing after the school bell rings, and we won't have to twist his arm to get him to leave the little lady at home."

Carl chortled. He'd met Jennie Moran and couldn't agree more.

Bernie let himself out of the Chrysler and strode to the entrance, where Buck, a six-foot-five, full-blooded Oglala Sioux, held the door wide open. The two had met during the War when Bernie pulled him out from under a plane that crashed into a maintenance shed at the Air Base. Now Buck was Bernie's right-hand man, trusted without question.

Bernie brushed the snow from his topcoat and looked around the Club. The jukebox was playing "Moonglow," one of Lana's favorites. Peering into the murky darkness, he spotted her sitting at a table with someone he didn't recognize—a young man lighting her cigarette. He watched as she cupped the stranger's hand a moment too long to steady the flame.

He was on them in a heartbeat. Eyes widening in alarm, the man withdrew his hand. Lana took a drag on her cigarette, the tip glowing a fiery orange. If she knew her husband was behind her, her face didn't show it.

Bernie laid a hand on Lana's shoulder. "Having a little nightcap, are we?"

The man rose to his feet. "No crowd tonight, Mr. Rosen—the snow."

"Yeah, I been out in it."

Bernie spread his fingers across his wife's neck. "Slow night, huh, babe?"

Lana stood up and faced him. "Big crowd, small crowd—all the same to me."

"That's my girl, a real trouper."

The young man reached for his overcoat. "Well, guess I'd better be going."

Bernie eyes stayed locked on Lana. "Yeah, I'd say the show is over."

He listened for the sound of the man's footsteps and the front door closing behind him, "Speak to Dinah tonight?"

"No. Why?"

"She signed up for the school musical this afternoon. Damn Yankees—'bout baseball of all things. First time auditioning and she snagged the starring role. Lola, the femme fatale."

"No kiddin'. Didn't think she had it in her."

"First time's always the hardest—right, babe?"

Lana shrugged. "Can't remember. Been so many first times since then."

Bernie fingered a stray lock of her hair before securing it behind her ear. "You do 'Fever' tonight?" he asked in a low growl.

"Yeah—when there were still people to hear it."

"Do me an encore?" Bernie's tone fell somewhere between a query and a command.

Lana snuffed her cigarette in the crystal ashtray and lightly touched his arm.

"Later," she said, walking to her dressing room, knowing he was watching her every step of the way.

Chapter Seventeen

GUY STOCKMAN, VETERAN CATCHER, WALKED to the mound, knowing that all eyes were on him, every step of the way.

Gran Estadio de Cubano was packed that warm winter afternoon, with thirty-five thousand in the permanent seats and hundreds more standing behind ropes in the outfield. Flipping up his mask, Guy sneaked a peek at the crowd—a colorful Cuban cocktail of Spanish and Creole men in the box seats, darker-skinned workmen on numbered squares in the bleachers, and winter tourists—most of them white Americans—scattered like patches of snow in the grandstand. Flying in from the dark and cold of Chicago and New York or catching the steamship or ferry across the Florida Straits from Key West, they came to gamble or take in a show at the Tropicana or Sans Souci—or Meyer Lansky's Nacional—and catch a little beisbol on this, the last day of the 1956-1957 Cuban winter league season.

The feeling in the crowd was electric. Fans chanted and waved red and blue flags emblazoned with Lions or Scorpions. Roving vendors hawked medianoche, sandwiches of ham, butter, and cheese, and espresso in tiny paper cups. "*Caaa*fe, *caaa*fe," they cried. And gamblers trolled the crowd, trumpeting the game's ever-changing odds—making book, as a warm fog of cigar and cooking smoke drifted out over the playing field.

The game had reached its moment of truth—bottom of the ninth, two outs, bases loaded, and a full count on the Habana Reds' cleanup batter, Jorge Dominguez. The Almendares Blues, Guy's team, led by a single run. 4-3. Quatro-Tres.

It reminded Guy of the 1951 National League playoffs: his Brooklyn Dodgers against the New York Giants—an intense local rivalry like this one. Except that this game, the last regular-season contest between the Habana Reds and Almendares Blues, counted for nothing in Cuban League standings. It was but a showdown of honor in the frenzied, fervid world of Cuban winter baseball. And for Guy Stockman, his last chance to prove his mettle and revive his dream of returning to the American Major Leagues.

Chanting for the Blues, a chorus behind home plate shrieked "El Rubio," "El Rubio." 'The Blond', his nickname. Guy felt an agreeable chill. Fans hadn't shown him such fervor since his first Cuban League season, in '50-'51, when he was a young man with a batting average a hundred points higher. Guy frowned. That was the year he'd stalled out at Triple A, the highest rung of the Minor-League ladder, his final step to Brooklyn and the Big Leagues blocked by the Dodgers' established Negro catcher, Roy Campanella.

And then came Korea.

Blocking out the crowd, Guy scowled as he approached the mound. His pitcher, Roberto Garcia, had twice waved off his signal for the curve. When Guy gave a sign to a young pitcher, he expected him to deliver what he'd called for.

Roberto turned the ball over and over in his hand as he watched Guy approach. Only twenty years old, Garcia was on his way up in the baseball world and didn't give a damn what his over-the-hill catcher might want. After a solid season at Triple A in the States, he was headed to the Dodgers' spring training camp at Vero Beach and was slated to advance to the 'big club' in Brooklyn in late summer—joining a staff of Erskine, Labine, and their Negro Ace, Don Newcombe—pitchers Guy had caught in his brief sojourn with the Dodgers six years earlier.

Reaching the mound, Guy raised his mitt to shield his lips and called again for the hook. Roberto gripped the ball tight but wouldn't meet his gaze. "Bet he's worried I can't handle it if he bounces the curve," Guy thought. But all he said to Roberto was "Just keep it down. With two strikes, this guy'll swing at anything."

Resuming his position behind home plate, Guy winced as a knife-like pain shot through his left knee. Asking the umpire for time, he slowly loosened and retightened the straps, waiting for the pain to subside. Chased down a muddy hill by the Commies, he had injured his knee in Korea. Now, he mused, "It's the Habana Reds bearing down on me."

As Roberto lifted his stride leg, the crowd rose in a great wave. At home plate, Dominguez cocked his bat, waiting for the pitch. On the bases, all three runners broke from the gate, though only Aguilera at third and Amoros at second, the tying and winning runs, mattered.

As the ball left Garcia's hand, Guy saw it was the pitch he'd called for—a big sweeping curve. An instant later, he saw that the ball was trouble. Roberto had gripped it too hard or held it a bit too long, and now it was headed wide of home plate.

Dominguez lunged—missing the wild hook, as the umpire cried "Strike three!" Ball game over. Blues win 4-3—*if* Guy had caught the ball. But he had not, giving new life to the batter, who set off for first base. Frantic, Guy searched for the baseball, which struck the ground like a spinning top, wickedly whirling and snaking its way past him through the grass.

Knee screaming, vision blurring, Guy knew that the only chance for his Blues and for his redemption was to find the ball and throw it to first before the batter reached the base himself.

As Aguilera crossed home plate with the tying run, and the fleet-footed Amoros raced toward home with the game winner, Blues fans screamed "El Rubio, El Rubio" and pointed to the backstop. Reeling like a punch-drunk fighter, Guy ripped off his mask. Where had it gone? Where had the ball gone? Then hearing the triumphal cries of the Habanistas, Guy knew it no longer mattered. Amoros had scored, too, and Dominguez had reached first base.

The wild curve would remain lost as Guy made a mad dash for the dugout—with angry Almendaristas raining down debris upon his head.

• • •

Showered and dressed, Guy shoved his hands into his pockets and headed for the stadium exit—tensing as he passed two sideburned men wearing Amendares Blues jackets. The taller of the two spat on the ground and cursed. "La Blanca," Spanish for 'Whitey Girl,' not 'El Rubio,' Guy's admiring nickname. Nearby, a policeman showed no sign of interceding. After all, what was a Cuban sporting event without a little machismo run amok? Besides, he had more important things to watch for in Batista's Havana in 1957, including bombings by Castro's rebel army.

Pretending to ignore the men, Guy broke into a hobbled sprint for the nearest taxi. "Zanja Street, pronto," he ordered, as a beer bottle shattered against the side of the cab.

The driver stepped on the gas and the cab lurched forward along the sidewalk, skirting a line of taxis. Guy was impressed. "Nice move. Bueno. Guess you've done this before."

"Oh, yes. Someone always peeest after game. You make pass at mujeres?" Realizing the driver was fluent in pidgin English, Guy regretted starting a conversation. Now he couldn't brood in silence. "Worse than that."

The cabby turned and gave Guy a look of recognition. "El Rubio," he said solemnly.

In Havana, news traveled faster than a crushed fastball.

"You're not Almendares?" Guy asked, wondering if any place was safe for him now.

"Cienfuegos."

That was a relief. The Cienfuegos Elephants and the Marianao Tigers were the two other teams making up the Cuban League. Led by Orestes 'Minnie' Minoso and the young American pitcher Jim Bunning, the Tigers had captured the 1957 Cuban League pennant. But the Almendares Blues and Habana Reds were the Cuban League's most revered teams, battling each other since the 1860s, long before the nation gained independence from Spain. The oldest competitors in all of baseball, the Reds and Blues were hailed throughout the Caribbean as the 'Eternal Rivals." Almost as everlasting were the affections and loyalties of their fans—allegiances based less on geography than on who their fathers and forefathers had raised them to root for.

"On second thought," Guy interjected, "take me to the Malecon." Without slowing, the driver jerked the wheel, turning toward the grand boulevard and esplanade, which stretched along the city's northern shore. Unrolling the window, Guy filled his lungs with the moist salt air and imagined he could hear the soft suck of the tide. For a moment, his thoughts turned back to that first winter in '51, when he'd come to Cuba as a young Dodger prospect.

For Guy, Cuba was a revelation, a tropical isle with all that nature affords—sandy beaches and coral islands, rugged mountains and tropical forests, rolling plains and broad, fertile valleys. Columbus dubbed it "the loveliest land human eyes have beheld." Even that testimonial fell short, Guy thought, for how could Columbus possibly have imagined Havana, a man-made wonderland of grand boulevards and racetracks, ballparks and swanky hotels, fabulous floorshows and cabarets, gambling parlors and burlesque halls—along with what seemed a million beguiling young women in all their splendor? Under Batista, Havana had become a tourist mecca—a kind of wintertime Las Vegas for Americans eager to indulge itches they didn't dare scratch back home.

Seven hundred and fifty miles long—the narrow island was only a little larger than Guy's native Pennsylvania. A landlubber consigned to backwater towns of the minor leagues, he'd never felt a cool sea breeze or warm sand under his feet or the sweet air and dazzling light and color of tropical skies. And he'd never seen the immense, shimmering sea.

Guy had only known water that ran in streams or was confined to lakes and dams. At least, until the Conemaugh River Dam split, and spilt its waters down their narrow vale, drowning twenty-five souls, including his father, steelworker William Stockman. Big Bill had played catch with him, taught him to hit, and brought him to games of the Class 'C' Johnstown Johnnies—imparting the same love of baseball that *his* father had passed on to him, like a cherished family heirloom.

Arriving at the Malecon, Guy paid the fare and added a lavish dollar tip. In his salad days of '51, he would come to the Malecon to savor the Caribbean sunset and bask in his celebrity—sign a few autographs and maybe pick up a girl. This time around, it was to lick his wounds and make plans to drown his sorrows.

Guy gazed across the Straits of Florida to Key West, ninety miles away. Cuban baseball and Havana were over for him now. He'd get no offer to return. And there'd been no bites from the lines he'd cast up North. His dream of a future in baseball seemed over. Washed up at thirty—with no prospects, family, or wife. Could it get any worse? Could he possibly sink any lower?

Again, Guy felt his knee stiffen. "Damn Korea!" he cursed. Limping a few steps along the roadway, he was passed by a battered Chevy full of young toughs. A young man at the wheel recognized him and shouted as he passed, "Buenos noches, motherfucker."

Guy wondered if he could get through this last night in Havana without getting his head bashed in. What he needed now was a drink and a dirty fuck. He hailed a cab. "Zanja Street."

Deep into Barrio Chino, with its crooked streets and gaudy paper lanterns, Guy passed hawkers and whores and elderly torcedaros rolling cigars. Music—rhythmic and raw—pulsed from basement clubs like bands from Hell. Stumbling down four slick steps, he descended into a room packed with Saturday night revelers and uneasy tourists. On a raised platform, a Black piano player and a bongo drummer slapped out the beat, as a woman squeezed her maracas and warbled a song Guy remembered from his first Havana tour—an ode to second chances and the drug of corporeal comebacks:

I carry you from limb to limb as Tarzan carries Juanita
No longer love-sick I can say, because I took penicilina

Stockman muscled his way to the bar—"Double Cutty, straight."

"I lose mucho dinero today, Senor Stockman."

The voice came from behind—the accent Cuban, the tone low and menacing. Stockman turned to his accuser—recognizing a fearsome scar incised into the man's cheek—an "X," carved as if to mark the spot. Guy knew he'd seen the man before at the ballpark or a casino, or on the street, one of a hundred numbers sellers passed in the course of a week, though the menace he projected fit someone higher up the gaming hierarchy. Guy shrugged and raised his hands in a gesture of surrender. "You got me."

The man cocked his thumb and forefinger and pointed it at Stockman's head. Guy's fist shot straight for the "X." It was the only punch he landed before he blacked out.

Stockman awoke in an alley surrounded by garbage and rats—an angry lump rising like the tropical sun above his left eye. Staggering to his feet, he hobbled to the nearest wall. A mongrel dog nosed around his legs as he peed. Zipping up his fly, he limped onto the deserted street—lips cracked with blood and arms pitted with alley stones he didn't bother to brush off. His wallet was gone, and it was a long walk home, past shuttered shops and drunks sleeping it off in shadowed doorways, the heat of dawn already spoiling the night's coolness, and the brightly painted storefronts, garish green, blue, and yellow, assaulting his eyes as he trudged westward, on streets he'd never seen before.

As dawn broke over the low rooftops, he reached the travel agency next to his hotel—its windows ablaze with sunny optimism. Model airplanes dangled by threads over cardboard icons of America—the Empire State Building, the Golden Gate Bridge, Mount Rushmore. Guy averted his eyes and turned into the Hotel Roma. By the entrance, a tired table fan droned on, its limp streamers barely rustling in the breeze. The dozing night clerk raised his head from his arms.

"Senor Stockman. You OK?"

Guy grunted and headed toward the mechanical lift. A rotating fan cast flickering shadows on the floor. Guy thought he might vomit.

"Wait, Senor Stockman . . . a telegram—for you."

Guy turned and looked at the desk clerk, not sure he could traverse the few steps between them. "Where from?" he mumbled.

The desk clerk studied the address. "Rapide Citi?"

A smile tugged at Guy's swollen lips.

"Good news, Senor?"

Guy nodded. Spring was coming to America, and he was headed north. And, come summer—west, to South Dakota.

Chapter Eighteen

IN THE WEEKS FOLLOWING THE Town Meeting, James was rarely at home. By day, he taught at the high school. By night, he trolled the city's clubs, lodges, and service groups, angling for support of the Baseball Bond. He relished his campaign role and the chance to return to the spotlight after the Town Meeting—and this time, without Bernie Rosen around to upstage him.

James was uniquely suited for the role. Garrulous and gently humorous, he got along with everyone or, as he liked to say, "farmer, banker, minister, thief—cowboy, soldier, Indian chief."

And no one belonged to more organizations. Once, Billy caught his dad standing before his open closet, looking up at the shelf bearing his many headdresses—beanies; caps; dun and navy army hats; tassled fezzes in black, red, and gold. Where could he be going that night? Billy wondered. His father, staring a bit too long at the shelf, seemed unsure.

Meanwhile, James's opposite number, Ralph Sandstrom, railed *against* the Baseball Bond, though his targets were the town's factories and industrial works, its livestock barns and packing plants, bars and bowling alleys, pool halls and lunchrooms. And, instead of speaking to the owners and managers, Ralph sought out the workforce—laborers, clerks, bartenders, butchers, salesmen, secretaries, and waitresses—Rapid's humbler folk.

Well known from his failed mayoral campaign, Ralph just showed up unannounced at the rock pit at the Cement Plant, or the meat production line at Black Hills 'Pack', leaving with a powdery or blood-streaked hand. Stopping at Tally's or the Virginia Cafe, he'd mingle with the lunchtime crowd, then hail someone on the street, or walk into a tavern. His final stop was often a church, for a prayer meeting, or if he got lucky, a potluck supper.

Though both men regarded churches as worthwhile targets, they tacitly divided the city's 43 congregations into two great spheres of influence, with James calling on the upper Protestant hierarchy while Ralph claimed the less prestigious *Holy Rollers*. Both went after the Lutherans and the Catholics, too numerous to forfeit, though back in the '20s Ralph marched against the 'Papists' in a rally of 8,000 Klansmen, parading down St. Joe in his pointed hood and white robe.

One evening, James and Billy sat bolting down pot roast, while Jennie stood at the sink watching them eat. When would they leave? she agonized. She'd take a Seconal the moment they left, then slumber until the witching hour, when she'd pop a second to finish the night. After her fight with John, the only thing that calmed her came out of that amber vial.

Billy threw on his coat and ran outside to scrape the ice off the windshield. He was proud to be part of his father's mission and loved being with his dad—just the two of them in the front seat of the Chevy listening to the radio while James tapped out the beat on the steering wheel.

"We're heading to the YMCA tonight," James informed his son. "I might mention you in my pitch. When I do, I want you to look down at your shoes."

"Why?" Billy asked, curious, though not suspicious.

"You'll see," James said with a wink.

James parked the car, then pulled a pocket-sized book from the glove compartment.

Smiling, he replaced his fedora with John's old Boy Scout cap, a switch of headgear which puzzled Billy. Why was his dad wearing a Scout cap to the YMCA? And why was he taking *his* Boy Scout Handbook to the meeting?

Entering the Y, James and Billy were met by octogenarian Horace Miller, founder of one of Rapid's largest lumberyards.

"Bill, Mr. Miller served in the Spanish American War *and* World War I, then started American Legion Baseball, right here in South Dakota."

Putting his hand on Billy's shoulder, Horace cleared his throat for an oft-delivered history. "Back in the '20s, the Legion made it part of its Americanism Program to promote baseball. Kids were leavin' it for basketball and football—golf and tennis, too, some places." The corners of Horace's mouth turned down at the mention of the two country club sports. "So, my friend Frank McCormick and I starts Legion baseball. Been a great success 'cause it weren't just about baseball—'bout leadership, loyalty, an' fending off the Communist fiction."

James nodded. "Well, the Town Meeting showed that lots of people think like you, Horace. Remember Bernie Rosen's stirring speech at the end, and the applause he got?"

Horace's face clouded over. "Didn't like that much. Don't mean the words—believe *them*. Just don't believe *him*—a Jew, waving the flag. He's just in it for the money."

James swallowed hard. “You know, Horace—Rosen was a decorated soldier in World War II.”

Horace waved his hand in scorn. “Oh sure. Fought’n *that* one they did to save their own hides, but how many fought in the *Great* War? An’ look at ’em now—turned inta bunch o’ Commies, like them Rosenbergs. Got no loyalty ’cept to their own kind and their pocketbook.”

Billy’s jaw went slack at the old soldier’s attack on their neighbor. James might have suspected Horace felt that way, but he’d never heard him say it. But since Bernie was his only Jewish friend—if he could call him that—he couldn’t name any Jews in Rapid who might have fought in the First World War, though he figured there must have been at least one.

Still, he didn’t want to raise Horace’s ire by arguing. The Baseball Bond needed the support of his Legion. Besides, he didn’t feel he had standing to challenge a decorated veteran of two wars, when he’d never seen action in one. Stricken in boot camp by kidney stones, he was discharged and never felt the equal of the men who’d fought. Luckily, most vets didn’t talk about those years, busy as they were with jobs, cars, houses, and family.

James put an arm around Billy’s shoulder and led him into the meeting.

No, he’d not challenge Horace, though he didn’t miss the wounded look Billy threw him.

Inside the hall, Art Jones, Scoutmaster of Troop 55, greeted the Morans warmly. “Where ya been bivouacking, Billy Moran? Down by Rapid Crick?”

Billy turned away. He hadn’t imagined running into his old Scoutmaster at the Y.

“Teenagers!” James offered with a sheepish smile, hoping to excuse his son’s rudeness. He’d never asked Billy why he quit Scouts, figuring the reason was sports—playing them and accompanying him to the games of local teams—a choice he welcomed wholeheartedly.

Billy was glad his father never pressed him to stay in Scouting. For how could he explain that it was Scout Law that made him quit? Once, sick at home, he’d read the Handbook cover-to-cover and learned that he was not a true Scout if he couldn’t “resist temptation in thought, word, and deed.” And by ‘deed’ they meant the thing he’d done in secret as long as he could remember. He’d only been caught twice. Once by his grandma, on a visit from Boise, who called it ‘sinful’ and ‘self-abuse’ and said he'd go blind, and once by John, who warned, "Don't let Mom catch you." It was all the advice he ever got on the subject—the sum total of his sex education.

The day he quit Troop 55, he went down to Rapid Creek and shouted every curse word he could think of. After a minute, he felt light-headed and fell down laughing. It felt so good he never wanted to stop—the same way he felt about that deed, which to him felt nothing like abuse.

James pulled his note cards from his pocket and waited for Scoutmaster Jones to call him to the podium. Passing Billy on his way, he gave the boy's neck a gentle squeeze. Plucked from his funk, Billy smiled. He could always count on his dad to make things right.

Taking the stage, James took a moment to reorder his crib cards, as John, on a last-minute assignment, slipped into the hall and stood in the back of the room.

Finally, James cleared his throat and began his appeal. "I want to begin by thanking the Boy Scouts for all it's meant to my sons. My older son was a Scout for five years, achieving the rank of Star. And my younger son, Billy, advanced to the rank of Second Class until sports took up so much of his time."

Then he reached into his pocket and pulled out the Boy Scout Handbook.

Billy's eyes widened at the sight of that book. What was his father up to?

"I can tell from the thumbprints that this belonged to my youngest." James held the book before him, and pointed it towards Billy, who slumped in his seat. "This your book, Son?"

Speechless, Billy dropped his chin to his chest. Why was his father sounding like that holy roller preacher his grandma took him to after catching him in the act?

James smiled, thinking that Billy was following the directions he'd given him in the car.

"The Boy Scouts and YMCA understand that boys of Billy's age must be kept busy to stay out of trouble. I'm sure we can all remember what it was like to be a boy of thirteen."

Billy's heart pounded. Was his father taking over his mind, telegraphing his thoughts to the world? In the shadows, John felt a rare flash of sympathy for their father's favorite son who, to his great surprise, was not exempt from paternal exploitation.

James continued. "Now, what exactly does Scout Law say about teenagers? *A Scout is Thrifty. A Scout is Brave. A Scout is Clean.* He saves and conserves, both outside and *in*. He's brave in resisting temptations and the improper urgings of his fellows. And he's clean—clean in thought, speech, and *habit*. By habit, I think we all know what the Handbook is referring to."

John drew in his breath. He knew where his father was headed. Shocked by James's callous disregard—and by his own sheltering concern towards a brother who mostly vexed him—he wished he could grab Billy and whisk him from the room.

James cleared his throat and, assuming the tone of a preacher, read from the Handbook:

> *"A little soap and water will remove dirt from the outside of your body. But no soap will remove the dirt that gets inside your mind. Fellows who hang around street corners have time for dirty stories and thoughts. Those who keep busy with worthwhile things are also clean in their thoughts and actions . . .*

"Actions. Actions with others, and just as important, actions when alone," James paused to let his words sink in. Billy's face blazed and his stomach roiled. He hadn't expected to be used this way. He thought he might throw up.

John had heard enough. Hunching his shoulders, he turned and slipped from the room. When he wrote the story for the Journal, he'd edit all that out.

"There you have it," James continued, "the wisdom of the Boy Scout Handbook. Keep busy with work and worthwhile things. And what could be more worthwhile than a new baseball stadium and a team, and wholesome, summer fun for boys and their fathers—the whole family, too. So, I say unto you Scoutmasters, talk to your troops and urge them to tell their parents and friends to vote yes on April 15th for this vital, new community facility."

The crowd applauded warmly as James closed the Handbook, ending his speech.

Billy jumped from his seat and ran to the car without his coat and hat. Shivering in the back seat, he squeezed his fists into balls and crushed them into his eyes.

Flushed with triumph, James strode from the Y, Billy's parka slung over his arm. "That went well, don't you think?" Billy said nothing as James started the engine.

Removing the Boy Scout cap, James checked the rearview mirror for Billy's reflection. "Why you back there, Son? Don't you think it went well?"

Under the car's courtesy light, the bald spot on James's crown shone like a dome. A few straggly hairs sprouted from a mole usually concealed by a hat or strategic hair combing.

"OK," Billy muttered in a tinny voice.

He wondered why he'd never noticed that ugly mole before.

Chapter Nineteen

MARCH WAS THE WORST MONTH, but April could be deadly, too. Anyone might be caught off-guard by the killing snows of False Spring. At four thirty in the afternoon, Jennie slipped on her overcoat, and stepped outside for the first time since morning. Instantly, she was struck by the stillness around her—not a sound or a flicker of movement. Even the metal swings in the schoolyard—wind chimes in the ever-present prairie breeze—hung silent from their posts.

For Jennie, like anyone raised on the Northern Plains, weather was more than a casual concern. Last spring, a teacher's car stalled in a blizzard on her way home from school. She was found the next day frozen to death on the porch of her parents' farmhouse, six feet from the door.

And back in '33, Jennie's father was caught in a storm returning from town with their weekly provisions. Within minutes the temperature dropped to forty below, the wind-driven snow gusting to fifty miles an hour. Her dad would have perished if not for an abandoned homesteader's shack, which he buttressed against the wind with his coal-laden cart. Three days later, he trudged home, where he found Jennie, Florence, and their mother half-frozen beneath every blanket and garment they owned. They'd already burned anything that could serve as fuel—hay, cow chips, busted-up tables and chairs, and, finally, Jennie's beloved Montgomery Ward catalog, her mail-order wish book. Six pounds of paper, it could not be spared.

It was a lesson in survival she never forgot. Mother Nature could turn on you. The stillness before a storm—like a snake's rattle—should never paralyze but, instead, spur to action.

Jennie tensed. It was getting dark, and the wind had begun to stir. A few yards away, a gust lifted the lid of a trash can and sent it hurtling toward the hood of the Dodge. It struck with a clang, and she ran to survey the damage. The car seemed fine, but the right front tire was flat. It must have picked up something on the road that morning, or the tire, a retread, finally gave out.

Jennie's hands shook as she reached for her keys. It had been years since she'd changed a tire, and now she was racing against a storm. Opening the trunk, she peered inside. Tin placards promoting the Baseball Bond filled the space usually occupied by the spare. "Go to Bat for the Bond" they exhorted, along with a cartoon drawing of a paunchy little man hitting a baseball out of the park. Jennie frowned at the depiction, wondering why James had used his own likeness.

Hurrying, and a bit heedless, Jennie freed the jack but brushed the side of a placard, cutting herself on its metal edge. "Darnit," she swore, lifting her bloodied hand to her mouth.

"You all right, ma'am?" The voice came from behind her. It was deep and male with a slight Southern drawl—a bit hoarse and gritty, too. Whirling around, she saw him. Tall and broad-shouldered and dark—a Negro dressed in a navy-blue work jacket and dark khaki pants.

"You're bleeding," he said, pulling a folded white handkerchief from his pocket.

"It's really nothing," Jennie protested.

"May I?" Without waiting for a reply, the man took her hand to examine the cut. Caught off guard, Jennie flinched. "It's a nasty one—deeper than it looks," the man said.

Deftly, he shook out the folded handkerchief with his free hand.

"Not your handkerchief!" Jennie exclaimed.

The Negro threw her a questioning look. "It's clean."

Flustered, Jennie's words tumbled like potatoes from a split sack. "No, it's just too nice."

The Negro smiled—his teeth gleaming. "You need it, Mrs. Moran, that cut's a bleeder."

Jennie was taken aback. "You know me?"

"I'm Clarence's father," he said, pointing to the 'CW' monogram on the handkerchief. "Now let's fix that before it gets any worse."

Holding her pale hand, he proceeded to dress her wound.

With quick, sure movements he folded the cloth and wrapped it around the cut, tearing strips at the ends which he tied together to secure the bandage. Jennie stared at his long, black fingers and pink nails, luminous in the fading light. Her own hands were large for a woman—larger than her husband's. Not since her father's death had a man with such large hands held hers.

Finishing his handiwork, Clarence looked up and caught her staring. Jennie blushed—grateful for the cloak of dusk. "Mr. Williams? Did we meet at the PTA?"

"No. I was workin' that night. But, the boy, Clarence Jr., talks about you all the time. Described you once. Did a pretty good job of it, too, for a kid."

Jennie felt her temples pulse as blood rushed to her face in a way it hadn't in years.

"Now—tell me. Was you really fixin' to repair that flat yourself?"

Jennie bristled. "Yes. I was. I still am."

Clarence suppressed a smile. "I do believe you, Mrs. Moran. But now you don't have to."

"I can't ask you to do that, Mr. Williams," she said.

"With that hurt paw it'd be darned foolish. Anyways, you got a pro to help you now."

Jennie looked up at the sky. A few flakes of snow were beginning to fall. Her hand throbbing, she stepped away from the car.

Clarence's face broke into a triumphal smile, making him look a bit boyish and rather like his son. "Did Junior ever tell you where we was from, Mrs. Moran?"

Jennie recalled the boy's transcript from his last school. "Indianapolis, isn't it?"

"Yes, that's it. Well, you're an educated person. Let me ask what the town's known for."

Jennie hesitated for a moment until it came to her. "The auto race?"

"Right! I worked for Charlie Wiggins, famous race car driver. Owned his own garage. I spent many an hour changing a tire for old Charlie—when I didn't play ball for the Clowns."

Jennie threw him a confused look. Clowns? Had the man played ball in the circus?

"You got a watch, Mrs. Moran? Time me." Clarence leaned into the trunk and pulled out the jack, the spare tire, and the lug-nut wrench. "This'll take only two or three minutes 'cause we got a good surface with the concrete an' all. Never ever change a tire on soft ground or a slope."

Clarence blocked the wheels with stones, then pried off the hubcap and loosened the lug nuts. Moments later he'd jacked up the Dodge and with a few more turns, removed the flat.

Transfixed, Jennie watched him work. She should have been thinking about the storm or getting home to her family, but like a blinkered horse, she saw only what was in front of her—the swift, dexterous movements of a powerful man, a Black knight who'd come to her rescue.

"This here spare could use more air, Mrs. Moran. Been sittin' too long in the trunk." Clarence threw the spare onto the axle, fastened the lug nuts, and lowered the car to the ground. Popping on the hubcap, he cried "Time" and turned to Jennie. "How long, Mrs. Moran?"

Dazed, Jennie looked at her watch. "Oh, well, now, ah, let me see. Three, I think, or four."

Clarence grinned. "I'd say three. Your husband a big, strong man?"

"What?"

"I was thinkin' maybe I applied too much torque when I tightened the nuts. Can't count on me to be there next time your tire goes flat."

"Oh." Jennie's mind flashed to the caricature of James on the baseball poster. "Well, that's all right. I'll have the man at the filling station check it out. Thank you so much for your help, Mr. Williams . . . I guess I'd better go now, and try to beat the storm."

Without warning, Clarence reached out and took Jennie's bandaged hand. "It's bleeding through," he said with a frown, applying pressure with both thumbs. "You need a proper bandage when you get home, Mrs. Moran—maybe even a stitch."

Rattled by his touch, Jennie blurted, "Are you a doctor, too?"

Clarence beamed, pleased by Jennie's question. "Just for planes. I tend the B-52s, but my daddy used to say I coulda been one, always patchin' up stray dogs and kids on the block. Guess I got the hands for it." He smiled down at Jennie who struggled to regain her composure.

"Clarence . . . Clarence Jr. is good with his hands, too. He made a model of Custer's Last Stand with little horses he molded out of clay."

Clarence's smile widened. "He's really taken to school this year. Don't recall that happenin' before."

For the first time in a long time, Jennie flashed a smile—one she didn't need to force, one that made her eyes crinkle at the corners as if she were staring into the sun.

Clarence took a long look at Jennie's face and decided she was kinda pretty, as long as you could get her to smile. "Think that boy has a crush on his teacher . . ."

Jennie's smile faded as she withdrew her bandaged hand from his. "It stopped. The bleeding's stopped, I think."

Clarence stood for a moment, sorry that his teasing had cost him her hand. He'd made a mistake, thrown her a pitch she couldn't handle. Picking up the jack and wrench, he placed them under the placards in the trunk. "How's it look for the new stadium? Ain't they votin' tonight?"

Jennie now recalled that his wife had asked her about the tryouts for the new team. Could that be the reason for the man's solicitude? Suddenly, Jennie felt the cold wind through her coat.

"I'm sorry I never answered your wife's question."

"No matter. Commander talked to someone named Roseman, or somethin' like that. Says they'll be comin' to the base for tryouts once winter breaks."

Jennie frowned at the mention of Bernie Rosen, but Clarence didn't notice—he was looking at the sky. Near sunset now, the moon slipped in and out from behind a curtain of clouds. "Looks like we got lucky with that storm. You got far to go?"

"Just back to Rapid."

Clarence closed the trunk and turned to face Jennie. They stood for a moment regarding each other in awkward silence. Jennie looked down at her bandaged hand.

"I'll wash the handkerchief and return it to Clarence at school."

"That's OK. You can keep it."

"No, Mr. Williams. A little bleach will make it white as snow."

Clarence laughed, and Jennie wondered what she'd said that might be funny.

"Please, call me Clarence."

Jennie nodded but did not repeat his Christian name, or offer hers to him, though it was on the tip of her tongue. It wasn't his being a Negro that stopped her, though she knew some people in Rapid would think it improper for a white woman and a Black man to call each other by their given names. It was the act of saying them aloud—"Clarence," "Jennie"—exchanging names in the prairie twilight—acknowledging a bond that somehow felt wrong.

Jennie picked up her satchel and got into the car. Her warm breath clouded the windshield as she let the engine idle before driving to the exit.

At the stop sign, Jennie rolled down the window and put out her arm, reflexively signaling a turn. Clarence raised his arm—sure she was waving goodbye.

Catching it all in the rearview, she gripped the steering wheel and made the right turn, then trailed her headlights home to Rapid.

Chapter Twenty

BILLY TRUDGED UP EVERGREEN STREET, passing the modest frame houses that made up his block. He'd left a note saying he was going to see John at the Journal, but that was just to put his mom off his trail. It was election night, and without the note, she'd think he was with his father, waiting for the vote on the Baseball Bond. It's where he'd always expected to be, but ever since the Scout meeting at the Y, he'd avoided his dad as much as he could.

Evergreen was eerily quiet at that hour, with not a person to be seen or a sound to be heard except for the barking of a dog up by the highway. Every family except the Morans seemed to be home. Against the darkening sky, the lit windows made the houses swell and glow like jack-o'-lanterns. Pausing before the Johnsons' bungalow, Billy observed the TV flickering behind the living room drapes and Mrs. Johnson in the kitchen, in a kind of shadow play, fixing the family supper. He imagined he could see a pot roast on the stove and a pie in the oven. His slapped-together snack of Velveeta wrapped in white bread suddenly felt like a lump in his stomach.

While proud that his mother worked for the Air Force, he sometimes wished she stayed home and greeted him after school with cocoa and a plate of homemade cookies. Maybe if she didn't work she'd be more like his Cub Scout den mother years back, who'd wrap her arms around him as she guided his fingers to form a square knot. So different from his mom, whose touch always felt like a brake, stopping him from doing or getting what he wanted.

Billy loosened a stone from the hard clay beside the sidewalk. It seemed to be taking forever for spring and baseball to arrive—for him, one and the same thing. Every spring, when his instincts said it was time, he'd take out his baseball and throw it as high and as far as he could up the sidewalk, observing where it touched down. Then he'd count off the concrete squares and multiply by five, computing how many feet his throw had traveled and how much stronger his arm had grown over the winter . . . and how much closer he'd come to his dream of striking out Glen Merritt.

Billy cocked his arm and hurled the stone up the street. He'd have to throw faster to strike out Glen—or learn the curve. Sprinting to the bus stop, he grabbed the pole and spun himself in a circle. Breathless and dizzy, he finally stopped, waiting for his eyes to refocus.

"What ya doin', slugger?" Bernie Rosen asked, rolling to a stop in his big black Cadillac.

"Nothin', Coach." Billy blushed, fearing Bernie had seen him twirling like a little kid.

"Where you headed?"

Billy shrugged. "Downtown, I guess."

"Want a lift?" Bernie pushed the door open, and he jumped in. "Where's your dad—gettin' out the vote for the Bond?"

Billy shrugged. "Guess so."

Bernie gave Billy an appraising look. "Tell you what, ace. I've got a little time before I open the Club—suppose I teach you that curve I've been promising?"

"Gee, great!" But then he remembered. "I don't have my ball glove."

"Don't sweat it, kid. I've got one." Bernie pressed hard on the gas and the car sprang forward, clocking fifty in the thirty-mile-an-hour zone. And he drove with just one hand, holding a cigarette in the other. Billy was bowled over. His dad never challenged the speed limit and always kept both hands on the wheel. And Bernie took corners different. His dad braked before coasting around a turn. Bernie downshifted and sped up in the middle, pressing Billy back against the seat—like the rocket ship ride at the Range Days Carnival.

Bernie snuffed out his cigarette and turned on the radio.

"She touched my hand, what a chill I got—Her lips are like a volcano that's hot.

I'm proud to say she's my butter cup, I'm in love, mmm—I'm all shook up."

"You like Elvis, Bill?"

"Mom doesn't let me play rock'n'roll." He wasn't sure why he didn't tell Bernie that he and his Dad listened to Elvis in the car, when it was just the two of them.

"Could've figured." Bernie said, snapping his thick fingers to the beat.

Looking over at Bernie—cool as a cucumber, Billy could easily imagine him as the heroic fighter pilot he was during the War. Then he saw it—a dazzling blue neon with 'The New York Club' written in script across a silhouette of a city skyline. "All right, kid, we're here."

Billy looked around the dimly lit lot. "I don't know, Coach, it's pretty dark for baseball."

"Not outside, Bill—inside. You'll see."

They walked to the Club's entrance where a giant Indian swung open the castle-like door.

"Buck, this is Bill Moran, John's brother, and the next Bob Feller. We'll be downstairs. I'm gonna teach him the curve."

There were no customers yet, but inside the Club waiters were already dashing about, and at the bar, a man in a tuxedo was laughing with the bartender. It gave Billy a thrill to be in such a grown-up place.

"Wait here, Bill, I'll be right back." Bernie disappeared down a corridor and returned a moment later with a baseball and mitt. "Catch!" he yelled, tossing them to Billy.

The mitt was unlike any Billy'd ever seen—way bigger, with a huge trap and a deep, hinged pocket stitched all around. It was the Wilson *A2000*, an expensive new fielder's glove he recognized from the company's '57 catalog. When he hurled the ball hard into its pocket, the fingers of the glove seemed to close automatically around it. The A2000 was a *Super Sonic* ball glove, as amazing as Bernie's rocket-ship Cadillac.

And yet, something felt wrong. The glove was too big to mold to his small hand and it didn't require him to give it a pocket—it already had one as deep as the Grand Canyon. Two seasons ago, his dad helped him pick out a two-fingered Higgins, then taught him how to clean and condition it, and form a pocket using string to bind the mitt with a baseball wrapped inside.

Billy slipped off the A2000 and put it under his arm. His chest felt tight as he pictured his Higgins sitting alone on the shelf in his room—a ball bound in its pocket the way his father had showed him. Suddenly, he felt disloyal to his Higgins, and there was something else, which he couldn't quite name. For a moment he thought he might cry.

"This way, Bill." Bernie led them down a narrow staircase to the Club's cellar. Starting at the far wall, Bernie counted off twenty paces. "Sixty feet." He pulled a stick of chalk from his pocket and drew a line on the floor. "This is the rubber." Retracing his steps to the wall, Bernie drew a rectangle a foot and a half wide by three feet tall. "That's the strike zone."

"The main thing, Bill, is the grip. With the curve, your fingers aren't behind the ball. Your thumb's on the left side, between the seams, and your ring finger and pinkie are on the right, tucked under the ball. The index and middle finger grip the ball a little to the right of center, touching each other."

Billy pressed the two fingers together, making one fat finger.

"That's it. Now, make sure the seam is on the outside of your middle finger. It'll give it something to pull against when you snap your wrist."

Bernie raised Billy's arm to shoulder level and folded it into an 'L', then gave the boy's wrist a quarter turn. "Your palm and fingers face you now. That's how you gotta hold the ball when you snap your wrist. Now make your wrist stiff and throw hard. That'll give it a lot of spin."

Billy stood erect, his arm folded above his head in a twisted version of Lady Liberty. Bernie nudged him toward the makeshift rubber. "Let 'er rip, kid."

Nervously, Billy toed the line. It was a lot to remember, and he wanted to get it right. Winding up, he threw to the chalked target on the wall. The ball spun fast but didn't break. After two more tries, Bernie motioned for the ball. "You're not getting enough on it. Here, watch me!"

Bernie began to pitch with a rhythmic movement more like a dance step than any pitching motion Billy had ever seen. "Get your body into it—no 'short and choppy'. Start with your hips and chest turned away from the target. You can remember where the target is—it ain't gonna move. Take a long step forward and pick up the target as you pivot around. After you let the ball go, your hand comes down and across like this. It'll save your arm from getting hurt."

Billy watched in awe, though Bernie hadn't yet thrown a curve. Then, with no warning—at the very moment of the ball's release—Bernie turned his wrist and fingers to the right, and a pitch heading toward the top of the strike zone formed a kind of hump and looped down and to the left—raising a powdery cloud of white dust as it struck the bottom of the chalked outline.

"Strike three," Bernie said. "Fell right off the table—they call that a 'drop curve'."

"Wow!" Billy gushed. Where'd you learn that, Coach?"

"In the Air Force. Once faced Ted Williams in an exhibition game." Bernie lowered his voice to a conspiratorial whisper. "Just between us, he slammed me, but don't spread it around, OK? You learn this curve, you'll scare the bejesus out of batters. Turn their knees to jelly."

Billy laughed. He couldn't imagine what he'd done to inspire such confidence, but with all his heart, he wanted to throw Bernie's drop curve. He looked down at his feet, then up at Bernie, who smiled in a way he couldn't figure, but for some reason, reminded him of his dad.

Taking the ball and the A2000 from Bernie, Billy wound up and fired at the target. At the instant of its release, he knew the pitch was faster than any he'd ever thrown. And then, the ball formed a small loop and hooked down and away, striking the box's lower border and raising a tiny puff of its own. "It curved . . . it really curved," he exulted.

"Sure, kid—now do it again."

But this time his grip was too tight, and the ball struck the base of the wall and caromed past him. Running after it, he looked up to find Buck—the ball nestled like a walnut in his massive hand. "Somebody to see you, boss," he said.

Bernie looked at his watch. "Damnit. Listen, Billy, keep practicing. I'll be back in a jiff."

Billy nodded, though he felt let down. He wanted to break off a really big one but with Bernie there to see it. Lining up the target, he threw with all his might, but stumbled, sending the ball ricocheting off a steam pipe, and caroming across the room.

"Good thing Bernie wasn't here to see *that*," he thought, as the ball disappeared under a large table covered by a long white cloth.

In a moment he found it lodged behind two large packing crates. Crouching down, Billy squeezed his fingers between two wooden slats and pulled, until a foot-long fragment broke off into his hand. Replacing the piece, Billy's hand brushed against something cold and hard poking through the wood shavings. Crawling closer, he spotted one, then another and another—distinctive steel cylinders. Rifle barrels. Military type, like ones he'd seen in war movies.

Billy's heart pounded like a jackhammer. What in the world was Bernie doing with six crates of rifles? His dad said Bernie was in the National Guard, and their Camp was across the road. Was he storing them for the Air Force or Army? But why hide them under a table?

Billy wrapped his fingers around one of the gun barrels. It was hard and cold and sent a shiver up his spine. Maybe Bernie was the commander of a secret band who'd take to the Hills if the Commies tried to blow up Mount Rushmore? It was the most thrilling thing he'd ever imagined but real scary, too.

Billy traced an "X" on his shirt. "Cross my heart and hope to die," he swore. He'd never tell anybody what he found. Whatever Bernie's mission, he was with him all the way!

Grabbing the baseball, he pulled the shielding cloth over the crate. Backing away from the table, he spotted Bernie at the top of the stairs.

"This way, James. Wait till you see the drop curve I taught Bill."

James fought off a frown. While he appreciated all that was required to teach a new skill, he wished that someone else—anyone else—was teaching his boy.

Billy watched his father lumber down the steps behind Bernie. Why did he have to show up here, to this place that belonged to Bernie and, in a way now, to him, too?

Bernie put a hand on Billy's shoulder. "Hiya, kid, break off any big ones?"

"Billy, aren't you gonna say hello to your father?" James asked with a strained smile.

"Hi," Billy said quietly, without turning to him.

Bernie's sharp eyes moved from father to son. "OK, kid, show us your stuff."

Billy nodded, placing his right foot on the chalk rubber. Closing his eyes to block out the world, he recalled everything that Bernie had taught him, found his grip, wound up, and threw.

Both men saw it—the tight spin, the sweet little hump as the ball left his hand, and the arcing down as the ball neared the wall.

"Fell right off the table," Bernie whooped.

"A real 'twelve-to-sixer,'" James exulted.

Ignoring his father, Billy beamed at his coach and now, his secret ally in arms, as he scooped the rebounding baseball into his trusty new Wilson A2000.

Chapter Twenty-One

CLARENCE WILLIAMS STOMPED THE SNOW from his boots and climbed the metal steps of the mobile home he shared with his wife and children. A 1950 *Ironwood,* it was the first 'house' they'd ever owned. Thirty-two feet long and eight feet wide, it was a tight fit for a family of four, but he considered himself lucky to have found any decent, affordable dwelling this close to the Base.

Still, he wished he could have done better, but at the time no Base housing was available for new airmen with families. Investigating other options, he quickly discovered that most were in cabin camps, housing so cramped and ramshackle as to be threats to health and safety. Only one house fit the bill, a home for purchase in a new development in southeast Rapid. But after a go-around of some days with the project salesman, they were told that it was "just not available to you people."

"*You people?*" Clarence bristled. "You mean an airman in the United States Air Force?"

Still, they weren't terribly surprised, coming from segregated Indianapolis, long said to be the most southern city in the North and the most northern city in the South.

Despairing of ever finding decent conventional housing, they looked at trailer parks but found nothing of requisite size and quality. Two refused to rent to them at all. It seemed that Cherry Mae and the kids would have to return to Indiana. Finally, Clarence found a transferring Negro mechanic looking for a quick sale of his used Ironwood in a park not far from the Base.

To Clarence, the Ironwood had all their family really needed, though it was not a third as large as their rented house in Indianapolis, where both kids had their own rooms and Cherry Mae enjoyed a large kitchen and a root cellar for the vegetables she canned from her garden.

To Cherry Mae, it was just a temporary solution. She could never get used to the trailer's cramped quarters and the unsettling way its body trembled in the powerful prairie wind.

Clarence acknowledged her complaints but was secretly thrilled with his purchase. From his barnstorming days he'd come to value his freedom and the notion that if the mood ever struck or the need arose, they'd hitch it to the car and hit the open road, not leaving anything behind.

Crossing the threshold to their home, Clarence nearly stumbled over Violet, his chubby nine-year-old, planted on a rug, dressing her blonde baby doll in the colorful play-clothes Cherry Mae fashioned from scraps of old clothing. Smiling, he gave his daughter's braids a playful tug.

"Kiss baby," she demanded, holding the flaxen-haired doll over her head.

"No—I kiss *my* baby," Clarence said, covering Violet's face with noisy smooches.

Cherry Mae stood at the kitchen counter, hands on hips, scowling. A full head shorter than her husband, she had a heart-shaped face with brown eyes and fine, high cheekbones. She wore a plaid cook's apron over a flowered blue dress which she filled out nicely, top and bottom.

"How long do it take for a man to pick up a can of peas?" she asked, her eyes flashing.

Clarence placed the can on the table next to his son's history text, which was opened to a picture of a pioneer family heading West. A bonneted momma held the reins of an ox-drawn cart. In her pale, solemn face he saw echoes of Mrs. Moran. "Where's the boy?"

Cherry Mae threw Clarence a look. "He bedevil his sister, so I sent him to fetch *you*."

Clarence grunted. Since his transfer, she was always spoiling for a fight. South Dakota was not a bad assignment, and he liked being a B-52 mechanic. Was proud of it, too. But for her, cooped up on a remote outpost of the Cold War, it was no adventure. She missed her family, and she'd made only one friend, a Negro driver's wife who Cherry suspected was more interested in Clarence than in her.

Cherry Mae let the can of peas drop to the counter with a thud. From the beginning, she'd treated Clarence as suspect, never believing he'd been faithful on the road with the Clowns and not quite sure he'd ever fully retired from that life. Still, she'd never caught him stepping out. She'd only caught him looking, a complaint her momma dismissed with, "They be men," a logic that failed to mollify her, and made her wonder about her father, the preacher, too.

In fact, Clarence had been with other women in his years with the Clowns—though most were in his first time around the circuit. After being treated for the clap—a fact he kept hidden from Cherry Mae—he changed his ways and gave up the riotous roadhouse fun.

Cherry Mae rooted noisily in a drawer for a can opener and Clarence knew she was starting up with him again. Recognizing the signposts, he usually was happy to follow along, since the end of the road reliably came with reconciliation and the featherbed jig. But tonight, his heart just wasn't in it. Picking up the schoolbook, he studied the picture of the pioneer mother.

There had once been a white woman, a young whore in a Kansas roadhouse. An older teammate had egged him on. "Evry brotha's gotta taste Snow White once," was how he put it.

She had a room just wide enough for a bed and a side table and a lamp with a pleated red shade. On the wall next to the door hung a long oval mirror. To Clarence, the room was as stark and bare as a monk's cell. But then she removed her barrette, and letting her blonde hair hang down across her shoulders, lifted up her dress—up and over her head—revealing great pendulous breasts and a belly that compressed into thick, fleshy folds when she sat to remove her stockings.

"A fat beauty" was what Clarence thought, a woman with the largest expanse of pale skin he'd ever seen. When she shed her stockings, and he undressed, he lifted her to her feet and pulled her against him, kneading her soft belly and breasts with his thumbs and fingers.

"Makin' a pizza pie, Black boy?" she joshed, looking at their reflection in the mirror.

Clarence didn't laugh. He felt like a Negro God shaping the first white woman from milky clay. The memory of the whore reminded him now of Mrs. Moran. How her pale hand had looked against his in the twilight of the schoolyard.

Cherry Mae stabbed the can with the opener. "Chicken burned to a crisp when you were out there doin' somethin'." Normally, he'd bite when she baited him—first denying wrongdoing. Then, interposing his big body between her and the children, he'd reach around and murmur how beautiful she was and pinch her nipples gently through the fabric 'til they stiffened, setting the stage for later, when the dishes and homework were done, and the kids were asleep. A jealous game that seldom failed to work—in the end, giving each a measure of union and release.

"Well, you musta run into somebody—it don't take that long to get a can of peas."

Clarence felt a slight panic, as if Cherry Mae had read his thoughts or could smell the distant arousal of the school grounds. Clarence closed the textbook and laid it on the table.

"Nobody... nobody at all," he said, sidling up to begin their practiced routine, though feeling a peculiar remorse, as if he had in fact stepped out on his wife. Still, with her back turned to her husband's troubled face, it felt all right to Cherry Mae, and she let it *be* all right.

"Go find the boy. I bet he's pitchin' snowballs at some telephone pole."

Clarence grabbed his coat from the back of the chair. Retreating into the yard, he exhaled deeply then raised his eyes to the sky, searching for signs of the lingering storm. But the moon was shy and the sky, pitch black, and only a storm of emotion swept across his unmasked face.

...

The house was dark and empty, but Jennie was glad of it. She needed to be alone. The drive home had turned treacherous, with snow squalls and a wind so strong she had to tack into it to keep the car on the road. But weighing on her mind more than the weather or the road was Clarence Williams taking her hand and the surge of feeling which, like a powerful crosswind, threatened to sweep her off course.

Jennie winced as she opened the back door, the twisting motion pulling at the edges of her wound. Flipping on the light, she spotted a note on the table from Billy.

"Dear Mom, I'm taking the bus to see John at the Journal."

It seemed strange that Billy wanted to be with John tonight, instead of with his dad. For years it had been Billy with James, and John with her, a house divided, but somehow still strong. What if all the alliances broke apart, she wondered. Could the family survive if its foundation crumbled?

Suddenly, her hand began to throb. Raising it to her face, she examined Clarence's handiwork—his monogrammed bandage expertly tied but too bulky to fit into a glove.

The hankie proved hard to remove. The blood had dried, cementing the knot with a hard, rusty clot. Jennie walked to the bathroom and worked at the unyielding snarl with the fingers of one hand. Unable to make headway, she clenched the knot in her teeth, tasting the metallic tang of liquefying blood until it gave way. Leaning over the sink, she washed the gash with a fresh cake of Ivory, then pulled a roll of gauze and a bottle of iodine from the medicine cabinet. Steeling herself for the burn, she dabbed the raw flesh with the orange disinfectant, then dressed the wound—applying steady pressure, round and round, from wrist to palm to thumb and back to wrist again—muffling the pain, but not, for her, the memory—of strong, sure hands, darker than any she'd known, detonating a charge that coursed within her now, from breast to groin and back to breast again.

Jennie gasped, and the gauze slipped from her grip and tumbled to the floor . . . a cascade of white ribbon, unraveling as it fell.

Chapter Twenty-Two

BOND FAILURE ASSURES SUB-STANDARD PARK, the Journal headline announced.

The vote wasn't even close: 2,984 for, 3,837 against. But a cheery editorial asserted THEY DIDN'T VOTE US OUT OF A TEAM, which greatly puzzled James. If the new Basin League team required a new ballpark, it would have to be built now without public funding. Had Bernie pledged to fund it himself? A call to the man straightened him out.

"Don't sweat it, James. I had a backup plan. You know that summer opera company that went bust? I bought all their seats for a song. And that defunct drive-in, *The Starlight*? Got their concession stand, ticket booth, and projection shed. Dirt cheap. So, we already got most of what we need. Volunteers can put up the fence and do most of the other work. Only construction we need is the concrete retention wall, bathrooms, and dugouts."

James breathed a sigh of relief. Rapid would get its team after all. And Bernie's mention of a concession stand reminded him of something he'd been mulling over ever since the Bond Meeting. Running the concession stand was something he could do. He'd see all the home games—and for free—plus make some real money over the long summer recess. He did the math and figured he might clear as much as $2,500 for the season—half his annual teacher's salary!

He'd just have to play his cards right with Bernie Rosen.

• • •

James pounded on the boys' bedroom door. "Git a move on. We're leavin' for the Base in ten minutes!" Striding to the kitchen, he found the Journal at Jennie's spot, open to the sports page with the headline *BASEBALL TRYOUTS AT ELLSWORTH FOR LOCAL MEN*. Underneath was a photo of the Ellsworth Flyers team. He was surprised. Jennie never read about sports. Then he recognized catcher Clarence Williams—father of one of her students.

When Jennie walked into the kitchen dressed in her work-a-day clothes, James looked at her quizzically. "Are you going downtown?"

She cast her eyes down. "No, Ellsworth."

James's face brightened. That was where he and the boys were headed. "That's great, Jen. The tryouts will be fun."

She looked away. "I'm not going for the tryouts. I have papers to grade."

Alone in his bedroom, Billy glanced out the window at the Rosen driveway. He wished he could ride to the tryouts with Bernie, but the Caddy was gone. Picking up his binoculars, he trained them on Dinah's window just as John came to get his Leica.

"You little creep!" John yanked the binoculars from Billy's hands.

Billy spun around, landing a hard punch and down they went, flailing and cursing. Hearing the commotion, James rushed into the room just as Billy pointed in the direction of Dinah's bedroom. "You should see what she does with . . . "

Clapping a hand over Billy's mouth, it was as far as James would let him go. "Not another word—you hear me?"

Billy jerked his head free and swiped his mouth along his shirtsleeve, as if to erase all traces of his father's hand from his lips. James stared at Billy. How had it come to this—his beloved son recoiling from his touch?

"In the car, *now*!" he yelled as Billy ran from the room.

Alone with John, James collected Billy's jacket from the back of the door and his mitt from the bookcase. It was the *A2000*, the new mitt Bernie had given him. The old, two-fingered *Higgins* that he and Billy had picked out together was nowhere to be seen. Then, in the corner, he spotted another ball glove—stiff and cracked from neglect.

"You want your mitt, too, John—maybe you and Billy could have a catch."

John slammed the wall with his fist, and James placed a hand on his shoulder.

"I'm sorry, Son. First love is like that. But other girls will come along."

Instantly, he realized how hollow that sounded, like a cheer when your team is down twenty points. And false, too, when his first—and only—love was the woman he married.

"Right." John grabbed his camera and headed for the car, leaving his father alone in his sons' room, holding the brittle mitt in his hands.

• • •

The only sounds on the ride to Ellsworth were the mournful whine of the prairie wind and the cheerful croons of Bing Crosby and Pat Boone, which James thought Jennie might like. Staring out the side window, she appeared not to be listening, mesmerized instead by the same stark landscape she passed every day on her way to and from work.

In her coat pocket nestled Clarence's handkerchief—washed, mended, and folded to place the stitched "CW" on top. Scrubbed hard on a wooden washboard, it bore a faint, rusty stain—a shadowy trace of the wound he'd tended in the school parking lot. And though he'd told her to keep it, she'd been carrying it for weeks, ready to return it if ever she should spot him.

In the back seat, John and Billy sat slumped in their respective corners eyeing each other like wary prizefighters. But nearing the entrance to the Air Base, Billy sprang to attention, searching out the window for the new jet-bomber. Glimpsing his son's brightening face, James felt his own spirits rise.

"I wish I could see a B-52 up close," Billy said. "Maybe Bernie could take me."

John smirked. "Fat chance they'd let a snot nose like you near one of those babies."

James pounced. "Next one who opens his mouth spends the day in the car."

"Wha'd I do?" Billy protested, and James realized that the boy's only offense had been bringing up Bernie—the rival for his son's affection.

"Guess you're stuck in the car, little Willie," John said with relish.

"Forget about next week's allowance," James sputtered. "Both of you."

John shrugged, but Billy pouted, and James realized that again he'd unfairly targeted his younger son, who didn't have an after-school job to fall back on.

Pulling into the lot, Billy bolted from the car and ran toward the ballfield, while John slowly gathered his notebook and camera bag. With barely a glance at Jennie, James hurried towards the group of men gathered around home plate. He couldn't wait to get away from his squabbling sons and distant, confounding wife.

Jennie looked to the players on the field—men in pairs throwing baseballs back and forth in long, flat arcs. Many were Negroes, and her eyes darted from one to another, searching for a distinctive stance or feature. If Clarence was one of them, she couldn't tell.

Feeling foolish and ashamed, she grabbed her satchel and stepped out of the car. Then she heard the slap slap of shoes on concrete. Turning, she found her coat sleeve tugged by a small dark hand. "Miz Moran! Miz Moran!"

Jennie gasped, as the satchel slipped from her grip, spilling the week's homework onto the pavement. Frantically, she dropped to her knees, trapping the pages, all but one that danced off like a leaf in the wind, pinning itself against the hubcap of a car that had just pulled into the lot. Racing after the page, Clarence Jr. made a beeline for Bernie Rosen's shiny black Cadillac.

"Let me help you, Mrs. Moran." Clarence Williams, dressed in his Flyers uniform, squatted in front of her and slipped the fluttering papers out from under her knees. At ease in his catcher's crouch, he quickly gathered the sheets into a neat sheave.

Something pulsed inside Jennie, but she couldn't bring herself to look at Clarence's face. Still, she couldn't take her eyes off his hands, dark and long-fingered, just as she'd remembered.

Reaching for the satchel, Clarence tucked the pages inside and handed it to her. Then he placed a hand on each of her elbows and stood, raising her with him in a graceful unfolding.

"Here you go, Mrs. Moran. Seems like these parking lots always givin' you trouble."

Jennie took the satchel and without looking up, murmured, "Thank you, Mr. Williams."

Clarence watched a blush of color spread across Jennie's cheeks and felt emboldened. "You think if I come to your rescue one more time, you might start callin' me Clarence—and I might call you . . . ?"

"It's Jennie."

"Nice to meet you, Jennie. How's the mitt?"

For a moment she was thrown. "Oh," she said, turning her hand over. The tender new skin was hidden by a thick, rough scab, a few days shy of sloughing. "Much better . . . I . . . "

"Here, Miz Moran." A breathless Clarence Jr. thrust a muddy sheet at Jennie, then cast her a wary look. "It ain't a school day, is it?"

Jennie smiled weakly, grateful for the interruption. "No, it's not a school day."

Clarence laughed heartily and, releasing Jennie's elbow, gave young Clarence a mock punch to the shoulder. "I thought Miz Moran was our favorite teacher," he teased.

Jennie sneaked a peek at Clarence's face—manly, but full of boyish mischief. Her spirits soared. She wouldn't have missed him on the field. If he'd been there, she would have seen him.

"Not on Saturday," the boy protested. "You here to see my daddy?"

Jennie lowered her eyes. "No. I'm just catching up on some schoolwork while my husband and sons are at the tryouts."

Hearing the word "husband," Clarence turned his head for a quick scope of the area. Out of the corner of his eye he spotted a solid looking man in a bomber jacket standing in front of a Cadillac and staring hard at the three of them—Clarence, Jennie, and the boy. Clarence shifted his weight backwards and placed his hands on his son's shoulders.

"He trying out, too?" Clarence Jr. asked, looking a bit worried—as if his teacher's husband might have a better chance of making the team than his own father.

"No—he and my sons came to watch . . . maybe you can play catch with my younger son, Billy. He's here—somewhere."

"That your husband?" Clarence nodded toward Bernie while holding his eyes on Jennie.

Hearing the caution in his voice, Jennie glanced in the direction he indicated. There stood Bernie—smoking a cigarette and watching them like a hawk. She looked at Clarence's face—taut and hard, all playfulness gone. A face so different, she might not have recognized it on the field.

"Oh! No!" she said, her eyes darting nervously. "My husband—James—is . ." Jennie stopped, not sure of what she wanted to say.

"We will look for them, Mrs. Moran. Good morning to you." Clarence's voice was stripped of all familiarity as he placed his arm around his son's shoulders and headed to the field.

Jennie stood frozen to the spot. For a moment, everything seemed to rush toward her—planes, buildings, cars, trees. She had the sensation of being crushed—trampled—like a child caught in a stampede. Thrusting her hand into her pocket, she dug her fingernails into her palm until she felt the scab give way and the skin split open and begin again to bleed.

Then she turned—away from Bernie Rosen and away from the ballfield. Clutching Clarence's handkerchief, she crossed the lot to the school, the wound pulsing like a piston in her hand.

Chapter Twenty-Three

MANAGER GUY STOCKMAN CHECKED HIS watch. Two minutes until tryouts and still no Clarence Williams, the man he was told to watch for. Looking up from his clipboard, he saw a tall, muscular Negro with a small boy in tow. Williams, he thought. Finally. With his strong build and cocky, pigeon-toed walk, he did look like an athlete. Then the big Black man and the boy walked past without giving him a glance. "Damn. Where the hell's he going?" Guy muttered.

Clarence would have liked to leave his son in the bleachers and put everything that just happened out of his mind—how he felt seeing Jennie again and the stranger's hard gaze that shook him. But the boy pestered him about finding her son for a game of catch. To deny him that seemed unfair, though the thought of asking Jennie's husband for a favor made him uneasy.

Taking a deep breath, he approached the men gathered at home plate. As he got close, they stopped talking. He'd seen it before—white men gone mute when he came within earshot. He once thought they were afraid of him or had just said something defaming his race. Later, he concluded that they didn't want a Black man thinking he could be part of their conversation.

Clarence saluted the Base Commander. "Excuse me, sir, I'm looking for Mr. Moran."

James stepped away from the others and held out his hand. "Mr. Williams? I'm James. Moran. My wife told me you'd be trying out. I saw you play here last summer."

Clarence smiled weakly, wondering if Jennie had told her husband about the flat tire and the bandaged hand. "Nice to meet you."

"And this must be Clarence Jr. You look like a ballplayer, too, young man." The boy beamed and shook hands heartily with the jolly white man.

Clarence felt a pang of conscience. Jennie's husband seemed like a nice guy. "We—uh—just saw Mrs. Moran." Looking back toward the parking lot, he spotted the man in the bomber jacket—the witness—striding towards them. Every muscle in his body tensed and his voice hoarsened. "She said your son . . . might have a catch with my boy here . . . "

Arriving at home plate, Bernie offered his hand. "Clarence Williams, Bernie Rosen. I see you've met James Moran. Men, meet Clarence Williams, the pride of the Ellsworth Flyers."

Unsettled by the man's praise—which he wasn't sure was sincere—Clarence turned to the field and spotted the coach—a tall, blond, white man—glaring in his direction. James followed his gaze, then placed a hand on the boy's shoulder. "I'll find Billy. I'm sure he'd like a catch."

Mumbling "Thank you," Clarence jogged over to Coach Stockman, who greeted him with a smirk. "You got a problem punching a time clock? 'Cause I wait for no one. Now get out there and find someone to throw with."

Standing by the backstop, Clarence Jr. watched his father sprint to the outfield to join the other men. "Go Daddy!" he cried. All business now, Clarence didn't respond to his son's cheer.

Bernie turned to James. "Caught Jennie in the lot. Didn' know she was interested in ball."

"She has some schoolwork to catch up on."

"All work and no play, that wife of yours."

James laughed curtly, wondering from Bernie's tone what he might be driving at.

"Where's Billy?" Bernie asked. "I don't see him around."

Suddenly Billy appeared, and James's heart swelled at the sight of him racing toward them. Breathless, the boy took his place next to Bernie. "Hi, Coach," he said, ignoring his dad.

James's heart sank. Something had broken between them, something so deep-rooted he'd thought it indestructible.

"Carl," Bernie said, "you should have seen Billy at the Club the other day. Showed him the drop curve—picked it up just like that." Bernie snapped his fingers.

James stiffened. Would Bernie never let up?

Gripping Billy by the shoulders, he turned him toward the younger boy. "This is Clarence, the boy in Mom's class. Go have a catch with him."

Billy made a sour face. "Do I have to?" He didn't want to do anything his father wanted anymore, especially when he might stay with Bernie and bask in his praise.

James gave his son a stern look. "Yes, Billy, you do!" James gave Billy a shove and pointed to a spot along the backstop where the boys could throw and still watch the tryouts.

• • •

As he walked out to the eager prospects, Stockman recalled breakfast that morning at the hotel. "Find me an airman," Rosen ordered, "good for town-base relations."

Guy understood that a ball team paid for itself by attracting fans, but an airman couldn't do that if he didn't help his team win. As for the local college stars and town team heroes, could any be talented enough? He couldn't recall a single Big Leaguer from the Dakotas. After all, how many players could there be in this frigid, desolate place? You might as well look for a prospect in an Eskimo village.

Guy zipped up his windbreaker and turned up the collar. Then it occurred to him that a pitcher could be found anywhere. Bob Feller, an Iowa farm boy, developed his talent throwing at the side of a barn. And most airmen came from somewhere else, maybe someplace warm—Florida, Texas, California—where they might have grown up playing a lot of ball. So, maybe he *could* find a player in this bunch. Anyway, orders were orders. He'd give 'em all a look.

Approaching the players in the outfield, Guy saw that many were Negroes. They'd be the airmen, not the locals. Did Rosen really expect him to put one on the team and take him on the road? It was one thing to have colored players in Cuba, where he'd played two winters. All the teams there were mixed. But this was America's Heartland. Likely not a place that welcomed Negroes. Not as bad as the South, he figured, but maybe a close second.

A blast of cold air hit Guy in the face. He'd start with throwing. It would save him time in the winnowing, since few if any of these amateurs could possibly measure up to a professional standard for throwing a baseball, a rare and mysterious talent he believed could not be taught.

Walking steadily across the outfield, Guy watched each man throw—crossing off each name on his list until he came to the last pair of prospects. Transfixed, he confirmed what his eye had told him at a glance—that these two, unlike all the others, could throw. He'd never seen it so stark. Pros throwing side by side with amateurs. Graceful form, no straining, the ball exploding like a bullet from the hand of one and arriving at the head or chest of the other.

Guy checked his clipboard. Otis McNeeley and Clarence Williams, the one he'd been told to look out for. Judging both men to be in their thirties, Guy supposed they might be veterans of the dying Negro Leagues. Well, at least he'd found two in this bunch with professional arms. Now he'd see if either man could run or hit or show any other talent. Guy raised his hands to signal the players to stop. "All right, men," he shouted, "bring it in."

From behind the backstop Clarence Jr. swelled with pride. The manager of the new team had stopped only once as he crossed that wide field, and that was when he came to his father.

"That's my daddy he looked at," he said to Billy, pointing to the outfield.

Reminded of his own dad's shortcomings, Billy cut him off. "So what? Let's play catch."

On the mound, Guy Stockman stood with fungo in hand as a B-52 sliced down with a thunderous roar, its trailing squall flattening the few tufts of grass.

"Is your daddy a pilot?" Billy asked, looking up.

"He's a mechanic," Clarence Jr. replied.

"Oh," Billy said flatly.

"That plane don't fly without my daddy," the boy protested, pointing to the sky.

"Sure," Billy said without conviction, though he figured it might be true.

Clarence Jr. threw Billy a dirty look and walked to the backstop to hear what the coach was saying to the players. Billy followed a few steps behind.

"It's a cold day, so I'll keep it short. There are five tools to measure a prospect. Can he run, throw, field, hit, and hit with power? I seen you throw. Now I'm gonna see you run. 'Course, you don't need five tools to be a ballplayer, or make this club. Ted Williams has just two. Only a handful of players in the game today got all five. Mays, Mantle, Snider, Kaline, and now Aaron."

Turning to Billy, Clarence Jr. crowed, "My daddy played with Hank Aaron."

Billy flipped the ball behind his back and deftly caught it with his glove. "Sure he did,"

"He did—it's the truth."

"Right—your dad played on the Braves."

"No . . . the Clowns."

Billy's face broke into a mean smile. "That's a joke, right? No team's called the Clowns."

"Yes . . . there . . . *is*," Clarence Jr. insisted, his voice rising in frustration.

Billy squinted like the evil gunfighter in the movie *Shane*. "You're a low-down, stinkin' liar."

Clarence Jr. threw down his mitt and tackled Billy—and the two rolled around in a tangle of limbs. Caught by surprise, Billy took a punch in the gut before drawing on his know-how as a beleaguered younger brother to flip Clarence over and pin him to the ground.

"Say it," Billy ordered. "Go on . . . say it. 'I'm a liar'."

Clarence Jr. thrashed about helplessly trying to free his hands from Billy's grip.

By the time James and John and the other men arrived, Clarence Jr. had started to cry.

James grabbed Billy and yanked him off the younger boy. "What's going on here, Billy?"

"He said his daddy played with Hank Aaron."

Sputtering, Clarence Jr. scrambled to his feet. "He really did! On the Clowns."

"The Negro League," James said, tightening his grip on Billy's collar.

"He called me a liar!" Clarence Jr. was shaking, and tears streamed down his cheeks.

"You are so stupid," John said to his brother.

Billy charged at John and butted him in the stomach, toppling him. As the two brothers wrestled on the ground, Bernie stepped forward to break up the fight.

Bristling, James barked, "Stay out of it, Bernie. They're *my* sons."

Bernie raised his hands and backed away. "Poor bastard," he thought, recalling how Jennie and Clarence had looked at each other in the parking lot. The man had a much bigger problem than his squabbling boys.

James pulled Billy to his feet and pushed him against the backstop. "Stay put!"

"If you broke my camera . . . " John blustered as he stood and studied the lens, embarrassed that his younger brother had gotten the better of him in public.

James turned and put a hand on Clarence Jr.'s shoulder. "Your daddy played on that Clowns team with Hank Aaron. You must be so proud," James gave the boy's arm a squeeze and the boy stopped sobbing.

"Daddy, I'm sorry . . . " Billy mumbled.

"Not to me . . . say it to Clarence," James barked.

"Sorry." Billy muttered as Clarence Sr. rounded the backstop, shouting his son's name.

Guy shook his head as he watched his best prospect storm off, an arm around his son's shoulder. Looking down at the clipboard, he drew a line through the last name on his list—Airman Clarence Williams.

Chapter Twenty-Four

AT MIDNIGHT JAMES BACKED THE CAR down the driveway and headed for the New York Club. He needed to clear the air with Bernie. He wished he'd stayed calm—said "I can handle this, Bern," or just let his neighbor break up the fight between his sons at the tryouts. Instead, he showed his hand or, like a jealous woman, his heart. Now, if he had any hope of getting the ballpark concession, he'd have to swallow his pride and face the man.

On the way to the Club his thoughts turned to the day's trials—his sons' squabbles, Billy spurning him in front of Bernie, and worse yet, the fight between Billy and the Negro boy.

And then Jennie took to bed early and alone on a night when he longed for the comfort of her body. Looking in on her, he found her curled into a ball, a hankie clutched in her fist. For the first time in years, he craved a drink, a thought prompting a wry smile as he arrived at Bernie's club.

The door was untended as James let himself in. Looking at the dark stage, he wished he'd arrived in time for Lana's last show, then reminded himself he wasn't there to see her. Still, he tucked his shirt-tail firmly under his waistband before approaching the bar. There he felt a soft pressure on his arm. "James Moran! What a surprise!"

A rush of pleasure surged through him. "Oh! Hello there, Lana. I was looking for Bernie." Even to himself, his voice sounded strange.

Lana arched a curious eyebrow. Her arms were bare, and she wore a tight, sequined gown, which held her breasts in a way that even Jennie's brassieres didn't. "At this hour? Must be a matter of life or death to get you out past Jennie's curfew. Whadja want with Bern?"

"Did he tell you what happened today at the tryouts?"

"Really, Jim? What are the odds of that? I don't speak much to my jailer."

Shocked, James lowered his voice. "Is it as bad as all that, Lana?"

She shrugged. "Ignore me, Jimmy. I've always been dramatic. Remember *Showboat*?"

"I remember you being convincing." James smiled at Lana with a tenderness that made her look away. When she turned back, her expression was once again playful.

"You should have asked me out in high school, Jim. I would have gone in a second."

"Darn. If only I'd known," he said, warming to the banter.

"As if you ever would have stepped out on Jennie."

James's face turned solemn, and Lana nodded. "That's what I thought."

"Hey there, James. Heard you were lookin' for me." Bernie dropped a heavy hand on Lana's shoulder. "Found my wife instead, I see." His smile was casual, but his eyes flinty.

"Just wondering what happened at the tryouts." James's voice sounded tinny, and he was suddenly aware of his legs dangling from the barstool, his feet not quite reaching the floor.

"You don't mind if I steal our good neighbor, do you, babe?"

"'Course not, hon. Just talkin' 'bout old times at Rapid High," Lana said with an icy smile.

"Never had that pleasure myself. No reunions for the 'School of Hard Knocks,'" Bernie rumbled, and James wondered if hard knocks included hard time.

Bernie ushered James into his office. "Whadya wanna know, James?"

"Did the coach see enough of Clarence Williams to know how good he is?"

"Saw enough not to sign him. Said he was a hot-head and would be trouble on the road. The Base Commander and I tried to talk Stockman into it, but he just won't take him."

James's face fell. "Damnit."

Bernie leaned back in his chair. He figured James blamed himself, but the way he saw it, Clarence lost his cool, just like James had with him. "Tough break, but Stockman's got a point. Branch Rickey told Robinson to turn the other cheek. Guess someone should've told Williams that, too. Maybe Brooklyn in '47 and Rapid in '57 ain't all that different."

Bernie paused as another thought came to him. "'Course it was his kid. A man's always gonna put that first. Protecting his family."

Then he rose from his chair—a sign of dismissal James couldn't miss.

"Listen, Bern, about this afternoon—I'm sorry 'bout snapping at you. I know you were only trying to help."

"Forget it, Jim." Then he laughed a bit maliciously. "One helluva day for fathers and sons." For husbands and wives, too, he thought, recalling what he'd seen pass between Jennie and Clarence in the parking lot.

James's heart sank at the reference to his boys. The day had begun with high hopes about patching things up with Billy. Now things were worse than ever.

"But fight or no fight, I'm still gonna make Billy the batboy," Bernie added.

"Really!" James exclaimed. "John said something about an essay contest."

Bernie scoffed, "Yeah, sure, we'll have him write one of those." He held the door. "Good to see you, Jim—drop by any time."

James nodded and left the office. The air might have been cleared, but it didn't seem the right time to ask about the ballpark concession.

Bernie walked to the inside window and raised the blind. Through the one-way mirror, he watched James look back towards Lana, but she was otherwise engaged, chatting with a cowboy at the bar.

James yanked the door open and let himself out into the cold.

Bernie lowered the blind and grabbed his coat and hat. It was time to take his wife home.

Chapter Twenty-Five

IT WAS ALMOST MIDNIGHT, BUT Billy couldn't sleep. Glancing out the window, he saw his dad back the Chevy down the driveway. He suspected it had something to do with him.

On the ride home from the tryouts, no one said a word. His mom went straight to bed, his dad holed up in the living room, and John drove off somewhere and still wasn't home. No one fixed dinner, and finally he made a peanut butter sandwich, which he ate by himself in his room.

He didn't get it—all this fuss about the fight at the Base. He'd had fights before. A few weeks back, he'd bloodied Roger Eckholm's nose after church. When he explained how Roger hit him with a spitball in Sunday school, his dad laughed. But that was before the humiliation of the meeting at the Y when he could still count on his father to back him up no matter what.

Picking up a baseball, he fired it into his pillow. How was he supposed to know about a team called the *Clowns?* Who'd name a ball team something stupid like that anyway?

Then he remembered his dad saying something about the Negro League. Did Negroes have their own League somewhere—maybe in the South? And how come his brother knew about that, too? Could John have baseball cards from that League—the Negro League?

Racing to the closet, he reached up to John's special shelf and pulled down a battered shoe box plastered with handwritten warnings. "Keep out! Billy, THIS MEANS YOU!"

Billy was eight years old in 1952 when John came back from the Crippled Children's Hospital in Hot Springs and their Dad gave him ten packs of Topps baseball cards as a welcome home present. John already owned some of the earlier Bowman cards, but felt he'd been given a new lease on life with the handsome Topps series, introduced just that year. The cards became the germ of John's wide-ranging trading card empire, launched from a table in the Morans' front yard—an irresistible lure to neighborhood boys and a way for 'the polio kid'—victim of a disease whose cause and cure were still unknown—to break the ice with the most wary among them.

Billy still remembered how John had cried and his Mom yelled when she caught him opening the packs for the stale slabs of bubble gum inside. James, knowing the serious purpose of the cards, had been unusually stern, explaining that they were John's special possessions.

"Especially now," he'd added, turning away so Billy couldn't see his eyes fill with tears.

What James couldn't tell Billy was that John's life as an athlete was likely over and that the colorful cards might be all that remained of baseball, or any sport, for him.

Billy hadn't liked his father worrying more about John's feelings than his, though he didn't much care about baseball cards back then. That changed two years later when he saw slugger Eddie Mathews pictured on the first cover of *Sports Illustrated*. It was then that he began collecting cards of his own, including Matthews and Hank Aaron of the Braves.

Peering inside John's shoebox, Billy now discovered hundreds of cards meticulously sorted by team and year—each encircled with a thick rubber band and a strip of paper with the team's name and either the American or National League. None were labeled "Negro League."

Billy opened his dresser drawer and found his own set of cards. His favorite team, the Milwaukee Braves, was on top. Hank Aaron was the second card, right under Eddie Mathews, his idol. But the Aaron card said nothing about the Clowns. Maybe John had a different card, he thought.

Pulling John's Braves stack from the box, he flipped through it until he found all the Aaron cards. Then he picked out the other dark-skinned players—Bill Bruton, George Crowe, and Felix Mantilla. None of the backs of their cards mentioned the Clowns or a Negro League.

With a lump in his throat, he spread the four Negroes' cards across his desk. It was something he'd never done—separate the players by their skin color. It made him feel funny inside. Before, they'd all just been his Braves. Now he felt he didn't know them anymore.

He picked up Aaron's rookie card and studied it closely. The ballplayer had a smooth, baby face—a lot like the boy he fought today, the first Negro he'd ever seen up close.

He bit down hard on his lip. It wasn't like he'd thrown the first punch. Sure, he pinned the kid down, but he hadn't really hurt him. So, why did everyone come running and take his side—talking about some stupid ball team and a league he'd never heard of?

Was that why everybody got so mad at him? Were the rules for fighting different if a kid was a Negro? Or was it because the boy was younger and smaller than him?

Younger and smaller. He knew all too well what that was like.

His heart began to race. Suddenly he saw that what he did to Clarence was a lot like what Glen Merritt did to him. Taunting him with mean words. Calling him a low-down stinking liar.

Sticks and stones may break my bones but names will never hurt me. That's what everybody said. But he knew it wasn't true. And, Clarence didn't take it lying down—like he always did with Glen. He fought back. For that he had to give the kid credit.

Just then, he heard a car coming up the driveway. Springing into action, Billy swept the cards up with his hands, bringing his Braves back together as a team.

By the time John came in, his box of cards was up in the closet and Billy was back in bed—feigning, before finally falling asleep.

Chapter Twenty-Six

SUMMONED TO THE NEW YORK CLUB, Manager Guy Stockman expected a grilling. His refusal to sign Clarence Williams didn't sit well with the Brooklyn Boss Man. "Now it's your job to fill that last roster spot," Bernie snarled. "'Course, you only got 'til Monday."

Guy knew that the Negro catcher wasn't his only problem. Shown Bernie's roster, Guy was alarmed that nearly all the players were youngsters. And while he supposed that some of these college boys could play, he knew that only through experience came baseball know-how and the ability to handle the certain failure built into the game. He wished Bernie had signed men—tough, savvy veterans who'd once basked in the golden glow of promise themselves but went on to hone their skills in the professional leagues.

Of course, the college boys would play with more spirit and hustle and not chafe under the yoke of a rookie manager . . . him. But if his future as a manager depended upon winning, he needed his own men, not boys answering to Bernie Rosen.

Guy reckoned there were thousands of veteran ballplayers to choose from—men whose careers stalled out or were cut short by the shrinking of the Minor Leagues from fifty-nine in '49 to twenty-eight in '57. Gone now were the Lone Star, Wisconsin State, Sunset, and the K.O.M., which produced Mickey Mantle. Gone, too were four thousand pro ballplayers and two hundred teams and cities, including the Ponca City Dodgers, the Fond du Lac Panthers, the El Paso Banditos—all erased from the American Baseball Map. He'd seen the collapse around him. "Jackie Robinson killed the Negro Leagues, Jackie Gleason killed the Minors," a scout once joked. Pitchers, catchers, and sluggers—an army of ballplayers mustered out of service in the '50s by TV's lineup of comedy, game shows, and nationally broadcast Major League games.

Guy snorted, picturing them out there in TV Land—young vets slumped on couches, waiting for his call to re-up—dreamers hoping for the chance to play again in a serious league, one followed by Major League scouts, to show off the talent and grace that were no less wondrous for having been retired too soon. But could he assemble a team in just one day? And what would Carl and Bernie do when he presented his team as a fait accompli?

Shunning the allure of passing bar maids, Guy spent all day Sunday in a phone booth at the Alex Johnson seeking young vets still hanging on to 'the dream'. His first order of business was a shortstop, a pair of artful hands—Tony Schunot, his teammate from the Greenville *Spinners* of the 'Sally' League. A pesky hitter with little power, he was a wizard with the glove. Signed at eighteen, he rose steadily up the Dodgers ladder, from the Class D Olean *Oilers* in '46 to the Triple A Montreal *Royals* in '50. Close enough to smell the Big Leagues, his career stalled out behind Pee Wee Reese. It was a common minor league tale of riding the express from the basement to the penthouse, but not being allowed off. Barred by the Reserve Clause to leave the Dodgers for another team, Tony hung up his spikes.

Tony proved a hard sell. His son just had surgery and the bills left him broke. Guy offered him a princely six hundred a month and advanced him four hundred out of his own pocket, calling it "travel expenses." Now Tony could pay off his creditors and leave his wife and recovering son at home.

Next, Guy went after his center fielder, Clyde Kibbee. No one ever patrolled the 'outer garden' like Clyde. Closing his eyes, Guy could see the lanky Georgian with his long, erect stride gliding weightlessly across the field. In his dark-beaked cap and baggy road grays, he looked like a mighty hawk chasing a little white dove. At full tilt, he seemed to make time stand still as he reached up with a leathery claw and plucked the white bird from the sky.

Guy found Clyde coaching high school ball in Georgia. "The short summer season is perfect for you," Guy argued, "and semi-pro pays real good, better than the Minors ever did." The ex-Triple 'A' outfielder was unmoved. Then a comely waitress jiggled by, and Guy drawled, "You should see the girls up here, Clyde. Noo-bile country girls, ripe for the pickin'. They'll tap your derrick dry in Dakota, my friend." Clyde offered a protest. "You know, I've got a wife now." Guy continued in his playful drawl. "Waal, you ain't bringin' *her* up here, are ya?"

He now had the core of a team: a shortstop, a center fielder, and a catcher, his own savvy eyes behind the plate. Still, he needed a reliever to turn to when the game was on the line—a fireman, a stopper, a veteran to deliver wise counsel to young hurlers. Someone like Dick Quarles. Like many southpaws, Dick was an anomaly—a big man who threw soft, a pitcher who could hit, a self-educated egghead. Discovered on an Army Base, 'Q' became a top Dodger prospect. But after giving up a big homer in spring training, he struck the dugout roof with the heel of his hand and blew out his shoulder. Learning the knuckler, he attempted a comeback, but the call to the Majors never came. Guy found him playing for the Cardinals' Class 'A' Columbus Foxes. It was an easy sale.

"I know of your League, Guy. The Cards just signed a young Negro outta there—pitcher named Bob Gibson. He's gonna be a good one." Guy felt lucky to get Quarles. Even Big League clubs often didn't have a real pitching coach, just an ex-catcher or the manager's drinking buddy.

And so it went that Sunday—spinning out a web of dreams over the phone wires. By nightfall, Guy had his crew.

• • •

Arriving at the Club, Guy was hustled by Buck to Bernie's office, where he found Carl Mueller seated, smoking a cigarette. Carl pointed to the second chair, but Guy declined to sit.

"You remind me of a hungry coyote," Carl said, watching Guy pace back and forth. "I guess no luck finding a player to replace Williams?" he said with a smirk.

"Lots of luck," Guy answered, swinging his right leg across the corner of Bernie's desk.

Carl's eyes widened. Was he marking his territory right there on Bernie's rug?

Guy scanned the desktop—telephone, checkbook, rosewood clock, pearl-handled letter opener, brass desk set engraved with *Bernard I. Rosen, Prop.*, and a gold-hinged picture frame.

Guy reached across the desk for the frame and sounded a wolf whistle at the two blonde women pictured there. "So, who are the foxes?" he asked.

"Bernie's wife. She's the headliner here, and their sixteen-year-old daughter."

"No kiddin'," he said, thinking they didn't look like any Jewish women he'd ever seen.

Bernie burst into the room as Guy deftly passed the picture frame from hand-to-hand behind his back, returning it to the desk with his left hand while extending his right.

Spurning Guy's hand, Bernie restored the picture to its proper place, then ran his finger along the silver blade of the letter opener. "OK, Guy, let's see what you've got."

"I got a team," Guy said defiantly, "nine players, counting myself."

Bernie offered a sardonic smile. “Nine players? I thought you were only picking one.”

Ignoring the jibe, Guy pointed to a girlie calendar on the wall. “Mind if I borrow that?”

Not waiting for an answer, he flipped the calendar onto its blank backside and sketched a big diamond. At the bottom he wrote ‘Stockman,’ declaring, “I’m the catcher,” just in case they brought up Clarence Williams again. Quickly, he filled in his recruits, along with a thumbnail sketch of each. “Played with him in Triple-A, and believe me, he can go get ’em; hit .330 in the Texas League; woulda made it but broke his leg.” Then Guy smiled and pronounced, “That’s my team and it is good.”

Leaning back, Bernie offered his smirking assessment. “Well, Guy, that’s some team ya got, if you’re looking for a squad of has-beens and bush-leaguers.”

Guy’s face darkened as he stepped toward Bernie and raised his chin. Slowly, he spat out the words. “They . . . can . . . still . . . play.”

“So can collegians,” Bernie countered. “Watertown was League Champ last year with just four pros. Mitchell was runner-up with five.” Bernie neglected to mention that two of Mitchell’s five pros were ex-Major-Leaguers who led the Basin in home runs and RBIs.

Carl nodded his head. “Basin League teams use mostly college boys. Mitchell’s got a couple of all-stars from the Big Seven, Eddie Fisher and Don Schwall, and Jim O’Toole, a terrific southpaw from Wisconsin. Watertown signed a pair from Michigan State: Ron Perranowski and Dick Radatz, along with Dick Howser, All-American shortstop from Florida. Huron’s got Jerry Adair, a kid from Oklahoma State.”

Bernie nodded heartily. “And we signed Frank Hacker, an All-American from Ohio State, and Darren Hoades, a young catcher from Alabama, who’s highly regarded by the scouts.”

Stockman scowled. Why were they sniffin’ around for catchers? Had they heard about his bum knee or his dismal performance behind the dish this past winter in the Cuban League?

Bernie’s eyes flashed, and Carl held up his hand. “Bernie and I don’t mind you having a say, Guy, but there are considerations you as a ballplayer can’t appreciate.”

Bernie lit a Camel and exhaled. “Yeah, like money.”

“Look. I didn’t promise my guys any more than it took to get ’em here. Nine pros’ll cost you just seven grand for the whole season.”

Bernie snuffed out his cigarette. "College players won't cost us a penny. We'll find 'em jobs for their spending money and they'll bunk and board with local families."

Guy took a deep breath. He knew that Carl as President was the man who signed the checks, but figured it was Bernie, Vice President, and a Jew, who called the shots.

"Sure they won't cost you, but you can't count on greenhorns. Wanna win, you gotta sign men, not boys."

"And go broke. And don't forget, Williams will bring in a lot of fans from the Base."

Guy's voice dropped an octave and growled. "Look, I'm not taking a hothead Negro."

Bernie was surprised to hear Williams' race brought up by a man who'd just played in Cuba and on the Dodgers in '51 with Jackie Robinson. He hoped he hadn't hired a bigot.

Then he recalled that Stockman was a Dodger when Campanella owned the catching position. Maybe he resented all the talented Dodger transplants from the Negro Leagues—Campy, Newcombe, Jethro, Black, and Gilliam—who rose above white players like him. He probably feared competition from Williams—like Campy, another talented ex-Negro League catcher. "Hothead, eh? Seems to me Williams was just looking out for his kid."

"A ballplayer's gotta keep his mind on the game, not babysitting," Guy protested. "And, you got the Alabaman as my backup," figuring a green college kid would be easier to sideline than an angry, seasoned pro.

Though Stockman had a point, Bernie wasn't ready to give up on Williams yet. "So, put him in the outfield. He can hit and he won't cost us a red cent. Uncle Sam pays his way."

Guy took a close look at Bernie—solid build, around forty, with hard, sharp eyes that said he didn't take crap from anybody. Guy had met tough Jews before in Brooklyn and in Cuba: prizefighters, gamblers, mobsters. Bernie belonged to that crowd. But now he was a businessman, a Jew who somehow became a bigwig in a small western city. He needed to take a different tack. "Look, fans are front-runners. They won't show up if you lose, but you'll draw big if you win. It's that simple."

"Oh yeah?" Bernie sniped. "Who knows if these rubes will cough up even a dollar to watch a ball game? They voted down the Bond. That would've cost 'em only fifty cents a year. Maybe Rapid's just not a baseball town."

Guy turned to Carl. "Bet they wondered that in Milwaukee before the Braves moved from Boston. You've heard about those crowds. The *rubes* set records."

Carl nodded his assent. He'd never seen anyone stand up to Bernie before. "Man has a point, Bern. We can draw big if we win and promote it right. Maybe we should sign his pros."

Guy suppressed a smile. He was feeling confident. He had an ally.

"What about costs?" Bernie thundered. "Other league towns are close together—not many overnights for them. For us, it's The Long Bus League—hotels, meals, gasoline. Eight grand before we pay any pros. And wadda we tell the college boys we already signed? Get lost?"

Carl shrugged. "We only hold six signed contracts. Haven't yet heard from the others. Anyway, they were just promises over the phone."

"Which you'd renege on, just like that?" Bernie couldn't believe that he, and not stick-up-his-butt Carl Mueller, was the one with scruples. And what about the extra dough for Guy's pros? He couldn't just drop in at Ranch A, the former Annenberg spread, for another late night withdrawal from the horse stall. No chance there was a second pot-of-gold waiting for him there.

"Don't think there's a legal problem, Bern, and we've already signed the best of 'em, Hacker, Hoades, the Wisconsin pitcher, and that Jewish kid from New York, Meltzer."

"Meznik," Bernie corrected, scowling at his fickle partner.

Bernie turned his back on Carl and Stockman to riddle it out. He wanted a team that would win and draw big, and Stockman might be right that a team of mostly pros gave him the best shot. It could be worth it, seven grand for players only Stockman could deliver. But he'd make Carl cough up half—put his money where his mouth is. Only fair when Carl was gonna cash in big-time from his exclusive beer franchise at the Stadium.

"OK, OK, don't like it much, but I suppose there's no legal issue here, just a financial one, thanks to Mr. Stockman's free-spending ways."

Guy was elated. It looked like he'd prevail. It was time to close the deal. "Gentlemen, I guarantee you. This team, the men on that calendar, will bring you the Basin League flag."

Bernie smiled broadly at Carl. Picking up the letter opener, he ran his middle finger along the blade. "Guarantee? You guarantee the pennant? Hmm . . . I wonder what that's worth?"

Guy exhaled slowly. He could tell Bernie was angling for something—his pound of flesh. "I'll bet my last paycheck. We don't win, you don't pay me."

Carl looked eagerly at Bernie. "He's putting his money where his mouth is, Bern."

Bernie looked out to where Guy's red Pontiac convertible was parked next to his black Caddy. "Problem is—his mouth's bigger than his pocketbook. I want the Pontiac, too."

Guy swallowed hard. It would be a strong team, but no one could ever guarantee a pennant. He'd gone too far, set his own trap, but he couldn't back down. He'd have to risk the car—his Star Chief convertible. "OK, the car, too."

Bernie lifted his boot off the desk and stood to signal the end of the meeting.

"All right, Stockman, you've got your nine, counting you. I've got my six. That's the team for now. But from here on out, I run the show. If any of your pros screws up, I hire his replacement. And if you don't win the pennant, we keep the money and the car."

Chastened, but relieved that he'd got his way, Guy shook Bernie's hand. Then glancing over his shoulder, he stole a last look at the lush figure of Lana Rosen in the gold picture frame. No doubt about it, she was big league. One way or another, she'd play on his team, too.

And, somehow, Airman Clarence Williams was forgotten, passed over without further ado by all parties concerned.

Chapter Twenty-Seven

JENNIE STARED AT THE TOWER of report cards piled high on her desk. Grades and attendance reports were due, but all she wanted to do was sleep. Closing her eyes, she laid her head on her arms just as her supervisor, Mr. Dorgan, walked through the doorway.

"Are you ill, Mrs. Moran?" Despite her fog, Jennie heard the impatience in his question.

"Oh, no," she insisted. "Just a headache. I'm sure it will pass."

"I've come to speak to you about an attendance problem with one of your Negroes."

Jennie braced herself. She knew he meant Clarence Jr., often absent since the tryouts. James had called it a "little scuffle" when he picked her up that Saturday from her classroom. "How could Billy do that?" she'd blurted, her eyes ablaze, forcing James to make excuses for the boy that he didn't fully believe himself.

Dorgan folded his arms across his chest. "You may not have noticed, but the boy has been absent six times this month. Not six consecutive days—as with measles or influenza—but six days *scattered* throughout the month."

Jennie nodded. Of course, she'd noticed—and how sullen he'd become, slouching at his desk, throwing stones and kicking things at recess. Still, she couldn't bring herself to speak to him. James's account, along with her own memories of the day—the touch of Clarence's hand and the look of panic on his face as Bernie Rosen watched them—had left her frozen. Whenever Clarence Jr. failed to show up to class, she was relieved.

The supervisor went on. "I can't call them—they have no phone. Pay them a visit and get to the bottom of this. You are his teacher and a woman. Maybe they'll talk to you."

Jennie swallowed hard but couldn't find her voice. It was the last thing she wanted to do, but the implication was clear. Her probationary year was not up. She had no choice but to go.

Jennie stood trembling on the top step of the Williams' trailer. Could Clarence's father be home at this hour? Taking a deep breath, she knocked lightly on the metal door, half hoping no one would answer. Turning to leave, she heard voices inside. This time she knocked harder.

"Coming." Dressed in a flowered housecoat, Cherry Mae cracked open the door. "Why, Mrs. Moran, is somethin' the matter?" Her tone was strained, as if she already knew the answer.

Jennie managed a smile, which she hoped was reassuring. "I'm sorry to disturb you, Mrs. Williams, but is Clarence Jr. at home?"

Mrs. Williams' face clouded over. "No, I believe he playin' ball."

"Well . . . he wasn't in school today. He's missed six days already this month."

Mrs. Williams shuddered and cinched the collar of her housecoat. "Please, come in."

Jennie followed Cherry Mae into a narrow space with a frayed brown sofa and a lowboy supporting a radio blaring a soap opera. Cherry Mae hurried to flip off the program, then bustled about picking up crayons and smoothing the crocheted throws on the sofa arms.

Averting her gaze, Jennie raised her eyes to two sets of photos mounted on the wall, all of Clarence Sr. One set showed him in his Ellsworth *Flyers* uniform—batting, catching, posing with the team. The other pictured him in a baseball jersey inscribed with the name *Clowns*.

"I'm sorry, Mrs. Moran. I'll just get dressed and be back in a jiffy."

Cherry Mae's absence allowed Jennie to take a closer look at the photos of Clarence as champion ballplayer. The Clowns' pictures were clearly the earliest, showing him tall and lean, with a touch of shyness in his eyes. The Ellsworth group was the most recent—Clarence heavier now and with a hint of gray at the temples, but with a mature, confident gaze. Even in the team pictures, he stood out, with his broad smile and a certain lively, teasing look about the eyes—the same look that Jennie pictured in her dreams . . . and often in her waking hours, too.

Cherry Mae returned in a modest green dress and cardigan. "Can I get you somethin'? Soda pop?" Cherry Mae remained standing, fiddling with the buttons of her sweater.

"No, thank you." Jennie perched on the edge of the sofa. "Please, sit, Mrs. Williams."

Cherry Mae sat stiffly on one of the kitchen stools, her hands folded in her lap.

Jennie cleared her throat. She wished now that she'd accepted the offer of a soft drink.

"Perhaps I should have come sooner, but for the last few weeks, Clarence Jr.'s attendance and behavior have become . . . a problem."

Cherry Mae nodded and looked as if she might cry from Jennie's halting indictment.

"He just not the same since his daddy didn' make the team. Took it real hard, like it happened to him."

Then the front door opened, and Clarence Sr. walked in, stopping in his tracks when he caught sight of Jennie. "Is the boy all right?"

Cherry Mae sidled over to her husband and lightly touched his arm, an intimacy that made Jennie look away. "He played hooky from school today. Miz Moran says it been six times this month. I told her ever since the tryouts . . . "

Clarence shot Cherry Mae an angry look and she dropped her hand.

"Mr. Williams—I know about what happened there. I hope that . . . " Jennie stopped, searching for a term that wouldn't condemn her own son, though she feared he was to blame.

" . . . the unpleasantness . . . is not the cause of this."

Cherry Mae looked from Clarence to Jennie, confusion clouding her face. "What?"

For a moment, neither Jennie nor Clarence spoke—his face hardening into a stony mask.

"Just some rough play between Clarence and her boy. We seen it before."

Jennie inhaled sharply. Clearly, Clarence hadn't told his wife about the fight. Was it to spare a mother's pain or keep hidden what had passed between them earlier that day? Despite herself, she hoped it was because of her, more than concern for his wife.

Cherry Mae sighed. "Maybe the next base'll be better." She said the words with her chin held high, gazing off into the distance, as if imagining a better world with their next posting.

Jennie felt a panicky flutter in her chest. "You're leaving?" For the first time, she looked directly at Clarence, and the swell of feeling that rose from her gut almost made her reel.

"I'll be puttin' in for a transfer," he said coldly.

Jennie bit down hard on her lip as Cherry Mae turned to her. "You don't know what it's like here, Miz Moran. Not everybody is nice as you. Some shopkeepers here—they won't even touch my hand. They put the change on the counter and . . . "

"Mrs. Moran doesn't need to hear that, Cherry," Clarence broke in sternly.

Cherry Mae sighed. "No, 'spose not."

Clarence picked up Jennie's satchel and held it out to her in a way that ensured their hands wouldn't touch. "I'll talk to the boy."

Jennie took the satchel from Clarence's hand and, looking away, closed her eyes to picture the smiling, teasing Clarence of their chance meetings.

"I'm sorry . . . " she said, blinking back tears as she headed for the door.

Jaw clenched, Clarence strode from the room, saying nothing, and not looking back.

Chapter Twenty-Eight

"WE SIGNED PAUL BUNYAN!" Billy shouted from the kitchen, breaking his long silence at home. Ever since his fight at the tryouts with Clarence Jr., he'd gone mute, his utterances limited to "yes," "no," and "pass the potatoes"—that is, when he couldn't just point.

Hearing Billy's exuberance, James came running, followed by John. Looking over Billy's shoulder, they saw what had captured his fancy—the front page of a special afternoon edition of the *Journal*—actually, a wrapper, with its masthead and banner headline spread across the top, and filling the space below, the giant hand- and footprints of newly signed Chiefs slugger Frank Hacker.

6′7″ ALL-AMERICAN

"INKED" BY LOCAL TEAM

For those who've never seen a man as big as Ohio State All-American Frank Hacker up close, the Journal *provides these vital measures of a man's size.*

Billy removed his shoe and sock and placed his own hand and foot on top of the outsized prints. "He must be huge," Billy exulted, jumping up to fetch a piece of chalk. Watching Billy trace his hand and footprints inside Hacker's, James imagined it happening all over western South Dakota—fathers and sons seeing how they measured up.

Finishing his tracing, Billy pointed to the word "team" in the headline, and asked, "When they gonna pick a name?"

"Bernie's running a contest with kids mailing in names, Billy."

"Really? I could win that, too!"

James frowned. Bernie had promised Billy that he'd be the new team's batboy and now it seemed their neighbor could give him this as well.

"How about the *Cowboys*?" Billy suggested. "Or the *Bunyans*?" James and John suppressed a laugh. Clearly, Billy didn't know about the other word 'bunions'.

"Well, Cowboys would be a good name if the Pierre team didn't already have it."

James reached down to pat Billy on the back but halted a few inches from his shoulder.

He'd never had a falling out like this with his own dad and didn't know how to fix it.

"What do I get if I win?"

"Two season passes for all the home games."

Billy shrugged. "I don't need that. I'm gonna be batboy. Bernie says I'm a 'shoo-in'."

"Isn't there's an essay contest for that?" John interjected.

Billy threw John a dirty look. "It's in the bag."

John looked at his father who shrugged sheepishly. It had never been their way to use connections to get ahead. Sure, you could put in a good word for your kid, but only if he deserved it. "Yearn it? Then earn it!" was what he'd preached, but Billy seemed to be learning a different lesson, and James knew who was pitching it.

Still, he wanted his boys to have all they hoped for, and if someone like Bernie could help, then maybe he shouldn't stand in their way. And he was hoping to benefit from Bernie's largesse himself, with the ballpark concession.

"Maybe they'd give me free Cokes and popcorn instead."

James smiled ruefully. He hoped to be able to give the boy that himself if he got the concession.

Jennie shuffled into the kitchen—hair uncombed, blouse untucked, and without a word headed to the sink for a glass of water. It had been like this for weeks, though at least she was sleeping now. But as she continually tossed and turned, sometimes crying out, she'd jolt James awake, and now he was the one who couldn't fall out again. Worse still, their 'lie downs' either at night or before supper had ceased. After school, she'd head straight for the living room and pass out on the sofa, waking with the plastic cover's pattern stippled on her cheek.

In all his life, he never felt so alone. He never realized how much his sense of well-being depended on simple physical contact—fatherly hugs and playful punches with Billy and mutual intercourse with the woman he'd always been able to please, and who somehow had always managed to please him. He tried to drive his needful urges from his mind, but to no avail. But he could never take care of it himself, the way he had in bed or the bathroom before they married. It would be indecent, and cruel to Jennie. And while he'd always been faithful and believed he always would be, now half the women he passed seemed to possess an almost irresistible allure. Sometimes, unable to sleep, he'd remember Lana at the Club—the smell of her perfume and the feel of her hand on his arm.

"What's for dinner, Jen?" James asked, smoothing a strand of her hair. Hoping for a response, he let his hand linger on the nape of her neck, but it felt cold and stiff, like touching a mannequin, and she seemed not to notice that he'd touched or spoken to her at all.

"OK. I'm on chuck wagon duty. What would you boys like?" James asked with forced joviality.

"I ate at Tally's. I've got an assignment tonight," John said flatly.

"How about you, Billy? Steak OK?"

"I had one at the Club." Rising from the table, he started from the room.

James turned to hide his disappointment. He figured that Billy was practicing his curve at the New York Club, and now it seemed he was eating there, too.

"Well . . ." James glanced at Jennie, hoping she'd rouse herself and do what he couldn't do—forbid Billy from going to Bernie's club. But she said nothing.

"OK," James said as he folded and refolded the Journal's front page—the magic of the massive prints coming off in his empty hands.

Chapter Twenty-Nine

JAMES OPENED THE DOOR AND stole a peek—pastel streamers and a crepe paper arch with a papier-mâché pot o' gold at the end—the school gym transformed. *"And the dreams that you dare to dream really do come true!"* Hopeful words hanging like dewdrops from the rainbow.

Prom this weekend, graduation the next. It saddened him that John wouldn't be attending the dance or speaking at Commencement. After getting dumped by Dinah, he'd fallen to third in his class, below the ranks meriting public honors. Even his Yale admission failed to reinspire. He'd reported his acceptance to James with a simple, "I got in," depriving his mother, passed out on the living room couch, of hearing firsthand of her long-hoped-for triumph.

James took a seat in the bleachers. Soon the Basin League would be starting, but he still hadn't asked Bernie about running the ballpark concession. He seemed to have lost his nerve, with his neighbor giving Billy pitching lessons and awarding him the coveted batboy job.

James's face fell forward into his hands, his mind drifting to a wistful vision which often came to him in reflective moments. Thanksgiving Day, 1935. He and his Cobbler football teammates traveling by train to play the Minot Magicians for the historic *Championship of the Dakotas.*

It was a thrilling contest from start to finish, but with just two minutes left, neither team had managed to score. Stalled at midfield, the Cobblers were forced to punt. Pursuing the kick, James lowered his head and charged into the receiver's breadbasket.

James could see it all now, just as it happened on that cold November day—the pigskin bursting free, tumbling end-over-end toward the goal line. He had only to scoop it up and run with it for the touchdown. Then, he would be the star and, someday, one of Rapid High's immortals. But as he chased after the ball, he recalled Coach Cobb's words to his players before the game:

"Don't be the hero. You're all part of a team. Just do your job."

James fell on the ball. The game ended in a tie.

It was his life's greatest regret—falling on the ball, taking only what was given.

What was wrong with him, he wondered. Could he not smell pay dirt?

James again read the words, *And the dreams that you dare to dream really do come true.* Today he would do it, he vowed. Make his run for the goal line and get that ballpark concession!

. . .

"I'll drive," he said, as Jennie slid wordlessly to the passenger side and turned her face to the window. Glancing at his weary wife, he wondered how they'd ended up like this, bonded for twenty years by habit, history, and two fine sons, but stranded now in a silent, arid desert.

Without warning, a black Cadillac swung around them, the driver raising a hand in salute. It was Bernie headed for the ballpark site. Remembering his vow, James changed course and followed him to the field. "No more falling on the ball," he cautioned himself. Then he glanced at Jennie, now snoring softly, her mouth agape. With any luck, she'd sleep through it.

From the top of the rise, James spotted Bernie talking to a worker in a hard hat. Stepping out of the car, he gently pressed the door shut. Jennie stirred, then slumped back asleep.

The setting sun cast his bulky shadow before him as James lurched down the hill to the construction site. His pulse rising, his breath short, he waved to the men as he neared them.

Shading his eyes, Bernie called out to him. "James, what the hell! You get lost on your way home from school?"

James smiled and shouted, "Mind if we talk a minute, Bern—someplace quiet?"

"Sure—let's go up to my car."

James retraced his path up the hill, each labored step a reprimand for his girth.

Near the top, he felt a moment of panic when he couldn't catch his breath. Then he thought of a ruse. Looking down at the project, he let his eyes slowly pan the nascent ballfield, hoping this dawdling pantomime would be seen by Bernie as admiring his work.

Bernie took the bait. "Beautiful, ain't it, James? Shaping up real good. Used to ride horses here with Lana and knew it was perfect—a natural bowl, better'n flat ground. No need for a grandstand—just smooth out that slope there and lay down the seats."

James smiled broadly as if dazzled by Bernie's brilliance. Soon, he no longer felt his heart thump.

"So, tell me, James, what's this about—Billy?"

Irked by Bernie's assumption, James managed to force a smile. "No, no . . . it's about business—I want to propose taking on the Concession Stand."

"Whoa, James! Carl and I were thinking of running it ourselves—hiring a few people and feeling our way 'til we know the draw. You got any experience with this kind of thing?"

James began his pitch—an expedient mix of embellishment and fact. "As Superintendent of Schools in Faith and Hill City, I bought books, desks, sports gear and ran the concession. I negotiated with vendors and leaned how to get my money back when shorted. And my dad was a chuck wagon cowboy—taught me to make a damn good cup of coffee and left me his recipe for Sloppy Joes."

Bernie threw his head back and roared in delight. "James, you are a revelation!"

James grinned. "A bit of a businessman, anyway."

Bernie grew thoughtful. "One thing I know is that Carl and I would never worry about your hand in the till. Hell, I'm constantly on alert at my clubs. Especially Coney Island. But I've never seen you take a drink, James. You got any problem selling beer?"

James smiled. "I drink beer at the Legion Club and have a cocktail on occasion."

"Good. Never understood teetotalers. What about Jennie? She gonna be a part of this?"

James hesitated. It wasn't a question he'd anticipated, though maybe it would snap her out of her funk. "Yeah, sure, unless there's something for her at the base this summer."

Bernie couldn't help but smirk. "Yes, she might find something there. As for the beer, you'd have to agree to sell only Carl's Budweiser. That OK with you?"

"Sure. No *Beer That Made Milwaukee Famous* or *From the Land of Sky Blue Waters*."

Bernie laughed. "Well, this sounds good."

James wanted to shout. Bernie was handing him the ball, and this time he'd run with it.

Bernie furrowed his brow. "Now, as for compensation. We don't know how this will go, so I'd start you off with a small salary, and ten percent of the profits."

James swallowed hard before making his stand. "Well, twenty's twice as good as ten."

Bernie chuckled. He admired the man's moxie, and with the busy summer tourist season, he'd have more than he could handle with his two Clubs. "Fifteen and ya got yourself a deal."

Giddy, James walked back to the car. Awake now, Jennie sat bolt upright, her face a mixture of shock and alarm. Sliding across the seat, he touched her knee. "Jen, what's wrong?" Hesitating until Bernie drove past, she finally spoke. "Why were you talking to *him*?"

"I asked Bernie for the ballpark concession. Looks like I'll get it. I was thinking . . . hoping . . . maybe you might want to help out."

It was all she could do to keep from sobbing with relief. They'd not been talking about her and Clarence. "OK, I'll help."

It was not the response James had expected, and surely not so quick. "Gee, that's terrific, Jen. This is gonna be a great summer. I can tell."

Finally, he could smell the goal line and it smelled like popcorn, hot dogs, and beer.

Chapter Thirty

THE MORAN MEN SAT IN SILENCE, eating the pancakes James had cooked, while Jennie stared blankly out the window, her mind clouded by another two-Seconal night.

John ate quickly, eager to get to the Base to photograph the exhibition game between the *Flyers* and Rapid's newly christened *Chiefs*. The *Journal* had sponsored a 'Name the Team' contest, drawing 2,022 entries. The winner was Glen Merritt, son of Bernie Rosen's attorney.

Billy sat opposite his brother, glumly drawing circles with his fork in a puddle of syrup. He would not be at today's game, even though Bernie had given him the coveted batboy job.

"Can't risk another fight with the Williams boy," Bernie had told James.

"What's the matter, kid, got nothin' to do today?" John taunted.

James threw John a stern look, before turning to his younger son. "What *are* you planning to do, Bill?"

"I dunno. Everybody I know is going to the game at the Base."

"What game at the Base?" Jennie asked, with a faint tremor.

"It's an exhibition game, Jen—Flyers versus Chiefs."

"That man, Clarence Williams, is he still with the Ellsworth team?" It was summer now, and though Clarence Jr's attendance had improved by the end of the term, she didn't know if his family had moved on, or was still stationed at the Base.

"I'm sure he is. He was in the Flyers' team picture in the *Journal* today." John rose from his chair and headed for the door. "Gotta go. See you at the game, Dad."

James shook his head. "I'm not going. Got too much to do."

Both boys' jaws dropped. Their father never passed up a game as ballyhooed as this one.

James turned to Billy. "But I sure could use an assistant today, Bill. I'm ordering for the Stand. You can help me decide what to stock. We can only carry three pops. Should it be Coke, Pepsi, 7 Up, Orange, Root Beer, or Royal Crown? And which candy bars? Mounds, Hershey's, Mars, Baby Ruth? We got a job to do, Bill, and it won't get done watching a ball game."

Billy's face lost its doleful expression. "Will I get to eat some—before I choose?"

"Well . . . sure, if you need to have a taste before deciding what to get."

Billy broke into a smile like James had not seen since Hacker's prints appeared in the *Journal.* Then he waited for Jennie's sermon denouncing sweets, but she simply reached across Billy to wipe up a bit of spilled syrup. It made him wonder if she'd simply given up. In any case, something good was happening—he and Billy, father and son—going out on the road together.

• • •

James sat in the Chevy waiting for Billy to emerge from the house. Normally, he'd honk or yell something like "Git a move on, the candy's meltin'," but today he bided his time, afraid to say anything that might alter his son's promising mood.

He desperately wanted this trip to go well, to patch things up between them—though he still didn't understand why Billy got so upset at the Y. Couldn't he see it was just good-natured ribbing between buddies, the kind he always believed he and Billy were?

"This will be fun!" James exclaimed as Billy got in the car.

Billy shrugged, turning to the window, his prickly cowlicks aimed accusingly at his father. "Yep, yep," James said, as he headed to the warehouse district. But, distracted, he took a wrong turn onto an old tourist road. There they caught sight of a group of workmen and a massive Indian removing old bathroom fixtures from a shuttered motel.

"Isn't that Buck?" he and Billy said in unison.

Together they laughed, and James's heart soared. "What they doing?" Billy asked.

James figured this was Bernie's way of "getting it done," but he wouldn't speak his rival's name, afraid to remind Billy of his adult pal.

"Must be for the new stadium—cheaper to scavenge than to buy or pay full fare."

Seeing Buck scowl at them, James stepped on the gas and the car leapt forward, leaving a cloud of gravel dust in its wake. Billy yelled "Yahoo," and James knew he'd done the right thing, jump-starting the day's adventure in a way a boy like Billy could not resist.

Arriving at Black Hills Candy and Tobacco, Billy's eyes popped at the sweets piled high to the ceiling, each aisle marked by a colorful label. "It's Candy Land!" he exclaimed.

James beamed. "Yep. It sure is."

"No. I mean it's like *Candy Land.* It's this game. There's a path and each space is a different color, but some got names like Molasses Swamp and Gumdrop Pass, and they all got these neat pictures of candy—like Peppermint Sticks and Candy Hearts and Lollipops."

"Sounds fun. Where'd you play that?" It didn't sound to James like the kind of game Jennie would approve of, with her strict rules about candy and toothbrushing.

Billy's face darkened. "Glen's house."

"Oh . . . " James said, afraid that recollection might dampen Billy's spirits.

Billy approached a handmade sign and traced the letters formed from M & M's.

Just then a man appeared from behind the counter. "Like the sign? My daughters made it when they was little. Kept their hands off the stock—least, for a few hours."

James extended his hand. "James Moran, we spoke about the Chiefs' concession stand."

"Oh, sure. I'm Joe Stark. Played a little ball myself when I was young. You play, son?"

"I'm a pitcher," Billy said softly.

"Throws a mean curve," James crowed. "And he's gonna be the Chiefs' batboy."

Joe Stark cocked his head, though his smile remained steady. "No kiddin'. Won that essay contest, did ya? My grandson wrote somethin', too. I'll tell him I met the winner."

Billy squirmed. He hadn't thought about anybody else entering the contest—sitting down and actually writing an essay, only to get beat out by him.

A phone rang and Joe excused himself to answer it. "Look around. I'll be right back."

Truly, it was Candy Land, with whole shelves devoted to chocolate bars and chewy confections like Jujubes, Jujyfruits, Dots, and Tootsie Rolls, but the boy seemed less enthralled now, as if a cavity had messed up his sweet tooth.

"I guess a lot of kids wrote essays," Billy said finally, and James knew what was going through his mind, and what might be going through Joe Stark's mind, too.

Then, in a flash, James saw it, a chance to make it right with his son. Bending down, he whispered, "Ya know, Bill, the batboy shouldn't be someone who writes the best essay. It should be someone who knows and plays the game. And who's better at that than you?"

Billy wanted to believe his father, but his face reminded him of that night at the Y, when he tried to talk people into voting for the Bond. And he knew it wasn't right, either, that Glen Merritt won the Name the Team Contest for 'Chiefs', a name a lot of kids must have sent in.

James studied Billy's troubled expression. He'd hoped for more than a nod for his exoneration—one that quieted his own qualms, if not his son's.

Returning, Joe Stark held out a bag of broken candy bars. Billy took the treats and cracked a smile.

It wasn't the resolution James had envisioned, though maybe it was all he could expect.

Whether or not the season would be a sweet one remained to be seen.

Chapter Thirty-One

GUY STOCKMAN HAD NOT BEEN to Ellsworth since the tryout and didn't relish being back. But the new stadium in Sioux Park wasn't ready, and with the Chiefs' home opener less than a week away, he was desperate for a warm-up game to see his new team in action.

Turning to the stands, Guy saw that Bernie and Carl, like back-seat drivers, had taken seats behind the dugout. Cocking an ear, he overheard Carl praise the team's jersey, styled after those of the Braves and Cardinals, with 'Chiefs' emblazoned in red script across the front, underscored by a peace pipe. An odd symbol, Guy mused, for men going to battle, but that satiny pipe made him think that a certain woman had a hand in it. Guy smiled. He'd be sure to thank Mrs. Rosen for the handsome duds the first chance he got, in the very best way he could.

Just then Bernie strode down the aisle towards him. "Remember that kid the Braves offered a hundred grand? He signed with 'em, not us." Bernie took a drag on his cigarette. "Means you've got an unfilled roster spot. Perfect for Clarence Williams." Blowing smoke in Guy's direction, he turned on his heel and headed back to his seat.

Once out of earshot, Guy muttered, "Pushy, pushcart Jew."

Shifting his gaze, he studied his players limbering up on the field. Suddenly, Guy felt butterflies. His Chiefs were certainly more talented than this Air Force nine, but unless his team completely grounded the Flyers, Bernie and Carl might see it as a defeat. And he'd not caught or swung a bat himself since Cuba. That might bite him in the butt. A player-manager needed to lead by example—show the college boys how the game was meant to be played. But at least, as a catcher, he'd be stationed where any player-manager would love to be—behind home plate, calling the pitches, arranging the defense, and feeling in his hands when his hurler had lost his stuff—when a fastball lost its sting or a curveball, its bite.

Guy picked up his clipboard and studied the roster. Counting himself, just ten Chiefs were available today, since four players had not yet arrived, including Bernie's boy, the Jewish southpaw from New York. "Hell of a fastball, another Koufax," Bernie had bragged. Hearing the claim, Guy registered a mock smile. "Baloney on rye," he thought.

So, today, it was all hands on deck. But in the weeks ahead, Guy knew he'd make some of his men unhappy: a faltering starter shunted to the bullpen, an inconsistent infielder converted to utility man, a college star who spooked in a big spot and had to be sent home.

As the Flyers ran onto the field for their pre-game drill, Guy turned to watch Clarence Williams. Handling bunts and taking throws, he moved well for a man his size, though his pegs had a tail, like a low golf slice, putting his throws a bit off-line. And there was something about his footwork. Still, he was a better catcher than Guy expected, though he wondered if such a man could ever gain the respect of his teammates or accept direction from him as his manager.

Guy checked the time then waved for the team to come in.

"Listen up, guys, I'm not gonna preach, but this is my gospel, my Ten Commandments of Baseball. Batters . . . get a good pitch to hit, keep your eye on the ball, go with the pitch, follow through, run everything out. Fielders . . . charge the ball, stay low, use two hands, watch the ball into the glove, and back each other up."

"Amen, hallelujah, praise the Lord, brothers," Dick Quarles shouted, and the men all laughed.

Guy directed his crew to watch the Flyers' pre-game drill. "You can learn a lot from this. Are the catcher's pegs on target? Who's the weak arm in the outfield? Who are the speedsters?" Guy pointed to the two Negro outfielders. "Black man in center—lots of style but takes too long to get rid of the ball. Right fielder overthrows the cutoff. Look for the extra base with those two."

"Whadya expect from a coupla field hands," a voice dripping with Dixie syrup cracked. Several of the Chiefs laughed. Guy frowned. He might feel much the same way, but hearing it expressed out loud brought him up short. Though it also bolstered his belief that his team would never follow the commands of a Negro catcher barked out from behind the iron mask.

Then the Flyers' starter took the mound—a young right-hander with a follow-through that carried him a couple of steps toward first base. Guy smiled. He'd be slow to field a bunt along the third base line, and Tony Schunot, the Chiefs' lead-off hitter, was a pinpoint bunter. If he laid one down, it might start something. But how might that tactic reflect on him—a new manager—choosing to play 'small' right out of the box against amateurs?

Guy grimaced. It had started—the second-guessing, the ceaseless internal dialogue of the manager—for every situation, certain questions with no certain answers. Still, he buttonholed Tony in the on-deck circle, whispering, "First pitch—let's see if the third baseman's napping."

Tony grinned. "Sure, Chief. Love to put down the mouse and see 'em scramble."

As the umpire called "play ball," Tony took his place in the batter's box, and Clarence Williams signaled for a fastball with an index finger at his crotch. The pitch was down the pipe and, as Guy expected, the Flyer pitcher stumbled two steps toward first in his follow-through. At the last instant, Tony squared around and laid down a bunt, angling it neatly inside the third base line—out of reach of the pitcher and out of range of Clarence Williams behind the plate.

To Guy's surprise, the stocky third baseman, the Flyers hot corner man, fielded the bunt cleanly but failed to set his feet before throwing across the diamond. Sailing high and wide of first base, the ball bounded along the fence line toward the right field corner of the outfield.

Rounding second, Tony clutched the back of his left thigh, but gamely limped on as the right fielder uncorked a rainbow, arching over the infielders before bounding into the stands. Waved on by the umpire, Tony came home with the Chiefs' first run.

Guy smiled ruefully. The tactic had worked—Tony's wily 'mouse' had got things rolling.

But with his hamstring torn, Tony was done for the game and, likely, for the season. In a single play, the Chiefs had lost their leadoff man, shortstop, and best base-stealer. Guy's gut clenched. It would be hard for the team to recover from this critical blow.

At least, the Chiefs weren't done scoring. Casey walked, Hoades tomahawked a single to right, and Kibbee took first with a hit-by-pitch. That brought up Frank Hacker with the bases loaded. Guy tried to imagine what it would be like to pitch to a man that big. From sixty feet, six inches, he must seem to be standing too close. David vs. Goliath. It would give anyone the willies.

As the *Flyers* manager walked to the mound, Guy motioned for Hacker to join him up the line. "Listen, Bambino, this guy just plunked Kibbee with the curve. He's coming at you, first pitch, with the fastball. I don't wanna see that bat on your shoulder."

Scowling, Hacker returned to home plate and resumed his stance . . . feet spread wide, cleats pawing the dirt—lifting little spits of dust like a bull about to charge. Then he rocked his weight onto his hind foot and drew his bat down and back through the long, full arc of his swing. Struck by the fearsome display of leverage, Guy retreated out of the line of fire.

By the dugout, John Moran felt a rising tension. Lifting the Leica to his eye, he trained the lens on the massive slugger coiling his body to the cock point.

In his seat behind third base, Bernie turned to Carl. "This is gonna be good," he said.

When Hacker swung, Guy immediately recognized the sound—short, sharp, and faintly musical, the perfect meeting of ash and horsehide. "Oh my God!" he thought, as his eyes tracked the baseball, a tiny sphere rising in an arc through the sky, seeming to defy gravity, climbing still as it soared over an eighty-foot light tower four hundred feet from home plate. It was the longest home run Guy had ever seen, surpassing even what he'd thought possible before that moment.

In the stands, a thousand airmen and civilians sat in stunned silence as if they'd just witnessed Haley's Comet. On the mound, the young pitcher squatted hands-on-knees as Hacker circled the bases, his face bowed humbly to the ground. On the dugout steps, his slack-jawed teammates gazed up in awe, believing they might still see, in the darkening heavens, some trace of the hand of God. And by the backstop, John Moran lowered the Leica from his eye, knowing what he had seen, but wondering what the camera's eye had captured.

Bernie looked at Carl and grinned, "Christ, he really smote that one."

The Chiefs scored five runs in that first inning, but oddly, the game did not become a rout—not with Tony sidelined and four pitchers now playing positions in the field. *The ball always finds the hole.* Guy muttered the time-honored baseball maxim to himself. And it did.

As Guy strapped on his shin guards for the fifth, the Chiefs held a scant 5-4 lead. With rain now starting, he figured this was it—a five-inning game, enough to be official, but risky with the home-team Flyers getting last licks. Guy turned to his pitcher, Dick Quarles. "Hold 'em here, old buddy, and we get the win. Williams bats fourth. I don't wanna see him."

Quarles didn't need reminding about Clarence Williams, who'd homered for the Flyers in the first. If anyone got on base ahead of him, Williams could cop the win with one mighty swing.

And then the rain began to thicken. If the game was stopped, it wouldn't be restarted.

Dickie Butler, the Flyers' leadoff man, lifted a short pop fly to Hacker in right. Out number one, always the big one, Guy thought. The next Flyer batsman drilled Quarles's first pitch into the hole at short. Lee Casey, replacing the injured Tony Schunot, made a sliding, backhand stop and threw a perfect strike across the diamond. Two outs now, and Guy was feeling cocky.

Then Willard Hayes, the Flyers' number three hitter, came to the plate. Guy expected Hayes to swing, but the chunky infielder pushed a little roller toward third. With a jolt of adrenaline, Guy sprang from his crouch and sprinted after the well-placed bunt. Circling the ball, he seized it with his bare hand, then stopped. Dean Veal, the replacement first baseman, had started in when he saw Hayes square around, then slipped on the slick field and fell on his butt.

Guy stood holding the ball by his ear, as Veal scrambled to his feet and sprinted back toward first. Turning, he raised his glove to Guy, a target for the last out of the game. If Guy got the ball to him in time, Williams would not bat, and the Chiefs would claim the win.

Guy let it fly—a bullet to Veal's glove, then watched glumly as the umpire pointed to the ground. There'd been a collision. Hayes had knocked the ball free and rumbled on to second.

Carl turned to Bernie. "Wow! Did you see that Stockman move? Quick as a cat."

"Well, the cat lost his head, he should have held the ball. Now the tying run's on second."

On the mound, Quarles took a deep breath and wiped his brow. Guy called for time and walked out to his hurler. "Shake it off, Q—a real first baseman woulda held it."

"Yeah, I know. Just tell me what to do with *that* one," he said, nodding at Williams.

With first base open, caution dictated walking Williams and pitching to the next batter, but Guy couldn't bring himself to issue a free pass. He'd play small if he had to, but not here. The crowd might turn ugly if the hometown hero wasn't given a sporting chance.

Then he recalled that Williams was both a catcher *and* an outfielder. With Tony out, he could stick Williams in left and shuffle the rest around until he got a decent hand. But first he'd see how he fared in a big spot. Call it the tryout the big Negro never got. And if he managed a hit, he'd sign him.

Guy looked into Quarles' eyes. "Strike him out—that's what you do with him—feed him a diet of curves." Quarles grinned. It would be his finesse against Williams' power.

The count was full as Clarence reached out for a curve and lined it into right. Hacker, playing deep, got a good jump on the ball. Guy looked up the line to get a fix on Hayes rounding third, then watched as Hacker wheeled round to make the throw. Could the big man get the ball to him before Hayes ran ninety feet?

The throw came down the line—low and straight. Guy took a step toward third, blocking home plate. Would it carry on the fly or skip across the dirt? Two seconds was all it would take.

Thrown with a crow's hop as fast as Furillo's best—a thin white blur, carrying true to Stockman's mitt. On target and in time. All Guy could do was set himself for the blow he knew was coming. Grip the ball in the mitt with his meat hand and roll with the punch.

• • •

Williams had gotten his hit, but the Chiefs beat the Flyers, 5-4.

Carl and Bernie filed onto the field in the rain to congratulate the players.

Bernie, unsmiling, walked up to Guy and extended his hand. "Congratulations. I know you were shorthanded out there."

Guy decided to take care of things without further ado. "Let me come straight out with it. You weren't wrong. We can use Williams as backup catcher, and he can play left field until all our regulars get here."

You weren't wrong. Bernie repeated Guy's words in his head, knowing it was the closest he'd ever get to an apology from the man. Then, in a rare moment of restraint, he smiled. "Sure, Guy. I'll speak to the Colonel and get him signed."

Back on the bus, a couple of the younger Chiefs, exultant in victory, waved their sodden jerseys out the window. Hoades, naked except for his briefs, approached Guy. "Well, Skip, guess we sent them n*rs back to the cottonfield." Then he began whistling "Dixie."

Guy's smile froze. Like a man waking from a weeklong bender, he suddenly realized what he'd done signing Clarence Williams. And why it might come back to haunt him.

Chapter Thirty-Two

JOEL FELT A DULL ACHE in his back. For seventeen hundred miles he'd been bound to a Greyhound bus, sleeping fitfully and subsisting on the salami and loaf of rye his mother had packed for him. But now it was over, a cross-country trek that began at Port Authority in Times Square and ended in a bus station on Main Street in Rapid City, South Dakota.

His parents and girlfriend had seen him off—his father, Mordecai, tight-lipped and stoop-shouldered; his mother, Bertha, clutching her handbag and barely holding back tears; and Rivkah, smiling rather too broadly with her bravest face.

The trip had been long yet packed with wonders—his own discoveries as remarkable to him as Lewis and Clark's were to them more than a century before. Of course, he understood that their journey was through an uncharted wilderness and demanded great skill and courage, while his required only a bus ticket and the well-traveled roads of Rand McNally.

To Joel's surprise, Iowa was the most affecting. There the highway narrowed to practically a trail, with the young corn edging the pavement, refusing to yield to the road more than a strip of its precious soil. Every minute they seemed to pass another farm where fathers and sons toiled together in the fields and mothers and daughters in yards and gardens. The order and simple rootedness of the place enchanted him. This could be Jefferson's utopia, he thought, his dream of a nation of farmers, self-sufficient and proud, each with his own patch of ground.

Crossing into South Dakota, Joel sighted farms and fields much like the ones he'd just passed in Iowa. Was South Dakota a mere extension of that state, he wondered. His question was answered some hours later at a rest stop in Chamberlain, where he hiked to the top of a tall bluff and gazed out over a broad, yellow river banked by a nearly bare, treeless earth.

The Missouri River. On the far side, western South Dakota.

Could this be his river Jordan and his promised land?

As the bus rolled west from the river crossing, the prairie transformed into plains, with corn changing to wheat and wheat giving way to grass. Farmhouses flattened into ranch houses spaced miles apart.

For what seemed an hour, he saw not a single town or settlement in this hot, dry country, only a post office with a rusty gas pump out front and a pickup truck joining the highway at a dirt road junction. There was nothing to bound his sight now—not trees, towns, or people. As far as he could see, the views were always the same—with the world resolved into just two elements, the ceaseless plains below and the endless, vaulted sky above. With nothing standing tall—nothing tethered to the ground—Joel got an odd sensation of weightlessness, as if the bus at any moment might fall up into the sky, or off the end of the earth. Was this what the ancient mariners felt, he mused. The horizons of the Plains, like the horizons of the sea, appeared never to end. Flat and featureless, empty and silent, the Great Plains seemed a kind of desert.

Even the air he breathed now tasted strange—thin, dry, lacking in substance. He couldn't imagine night or winter in this barren land. Who could rescue them if the bus broke down? In a place like this, a man could disappear and never be found, or reappear as a new person.

He shivered at the thought, unsure if that prospect excited him or scared him more. Then he spotted a young man on a horse, racing alongside the bus. He waved his broad-brimmed hat and Joel waved back. His very first cowboy!

Then, the driver announced, "That thar in the distance is the Black Hills." Joel took a deep breath. Yes, there was a Black Hills and likely, a Rapid City, too.

That once distant prospect was finally within reach.

• • •

Rumpled and weary, Joel descended the steps of the bus and turned back to the driver. "Excuse me, sir. Can you tell me how to get to the Alex Johnson Hotel?"

The driver gave Joel a once-over, noting his wrinkled khakis and sweat-stained shirt. "See that tall building thar? That's the 'Alex'. Be sure'n ask for the Presidential Suite."

It was only a short jaunt to the hotel. Joel set his suitcase on the sidewalk and gazed up in surprise. Ten stories tall and decorated in a half-timbered, Tudor style, it reminded him of the grand hotels he'd seen in photos of the Swiss Alps. A bellboy appeared and carried Joel's duffel into the lobby—a fine, high-ceilinged room with a chandelier in the center and the great shaggy head of a buffalo mounted over a stone fireplace on the far wall.

And then, Joel saw it—a small detail in a room full of large, dramatic effects—a swastika baked into the terra cotta. He broke into a sweat, made dizzy by the symbol—repeated again and again across the lobby floor and high above on the circular chandelier, swirling like Nazi banners at a Nuremberg rally. Joel's hand jumped to his head, though he'd removed his yarmulke in the dark of the Lincoln Tunnel halfway between New York and New Jersey. Turning to the desk clerk, he choked out the words. "This design . . . "

The clerk leaned across the desk and looked down to where Joel was pointing. "Well . . . yes . . . guess I never noticed it before."

The bellboy suppressed a laugh. "Relax, mister. It's Injun, not Kraut."

Joel drew a deep breath and waited for his heart to stop pounding. Had he reached for his yarmulke only to hide it?

With a shaky smile, he took the key from the desk clerk and headed to his room for a badly needed shower and a good night's sleep.

Chapter Thirty-Three

JOHN WOKE EARLY AND RAN to the porch. Unfurling the Sunday *Journal*, he whooped. Under the headline ***HACKER HOMERS IN DEBUT AT BASE*** were his photographs—one, of the big slugger swinging, the second, a tiny white baseball set against a lead-colored sky. That was the shot he feared he'd missed—the home run ball suspended like a tiny moon over Flyers Field.

"Yahoo!" he yelled, bursting into the kitchen. "They put my photos on the front page."

"Terrific—let's see 'em," James said, clearing a spot on the kitchen table. Bending over the photos, he exclaimed, "These are impressive, John."

Binoculars around his neck, Billy ran from the bedroom to see what the fuss was about.

John glowered. "Look at this, you little peeping Tom. You won't need binoculars to see what talent looks like."

Scanning the front page, Billy's face broke into an impish grin. "Who's Ray Whitten?"

John scowled. "He's the *Journal*'s regular photographer—why?"

A smile curled the corners of Billy's mouth. He pointed to the name printed in tiny letters below each photo. "Looks like he took the pictures. Don't need binoculars to see that."

John peered at the photo credits, *Ray Whitten,* Journal *Photographer.* "What the hell!" he exploded. John's arm shot out, but Billy ducked the blow and John's fist hit the wall.

"Swing and a miss. You're no Hacker!" Billy taunted.

"I'm sure there's an explanation," James said, suspecting a drunken Paddy screwed up.

Raising his hand to his mouth, John sucked his throbbing knuckles. "I'm quitting."

"Don't do anything rash," James cautioned. "Call Paddy. Maybe he'll print a correction."

"What difference would it make? Who'd see it?" Retreating to his room, John tossed the newspaper on his desk and stared out the window. Dinah was in the driver's seat of the T-Bird with her dad next to her, pointing to the clutch. John crumpled the newspaper with his hand. Once, he'd hoped to be the one to teach her to drive.

He sunk into the chair. Maybe he'd leave town for a while. There wasn't anything to keep him here now—not Dinah, not his job, nothing. Turning to the map on the wall, his eyes landed on South Dakota, centered between the coasts. He was always proud to live in the heart of the country but now felt stuck in the middle of nowhere.

A moment later, the telephone rang, and James called out. "John—it's Paddy."

John trudged to the kitchen. Covering the mouthpiece, James added, "Hear him out, Son."

Turning away, John put the receiver to his ear. "Hello," he said in a low, flat voice.

"Did you see the paper today?" Paddy laughed nervously when John didn't respond. "It was a fuck-up by the typesetter. I'd run a correction, but folks would wonder. Tell you what—I'll send you on the Chiefs' first road trip. Make sure you get the photo credits this time."

John hesitated. He didn't believe Paddy. He likely got drunk and blew it, but at least the trip would get him out of Rapid and away from Dinah. "OK," he said without a "thank you."

John turned to his dad. "I'm going to Pierre with the team."

"That's good, John. See, I told you Paddy would make it up to you."

John shrugged and walked to his room, where he found his mother standing at his desk. Still in her bathrobe, she was smoothing the *Journal's* front page with her hands.

"Oh, John," she said, knowing without looking which of her two sons stood behind her. "These photos are wonderful!" She couldn't take her eyes off the photo of the ball, a lodestar, fixed in time, trapped between heaven and earth.

Without a word, John turned and headed for the bathroom. For now, at least, he'd not be going anywhere, except on the road with the Chiefs.

Chapter Thirty-Four

FINALLY ALONE IN THE HOUSE, Billy let it all out—his joy at being the first and only boy in town to sport the uniform of Rapid's new team. Cupping his hands around his mouth, he echoed out the announcement. "And wearing number forty-nine, the Chiefs' batboy, William F. Moran." The boys would all be green with envy, even Glen. The girls might take notice of him, too.

And at one o'clock, he and the Chiefs would board the bus to Pierre, the state capital, for their season opener against the Cowboys. It was a dream come true. One that almost didn't.

"Unthinkable," Jennie had declared, rousing herself from her stupor once she learned that Billy was expected to travel with the team.

James, too, had qualms, knowing how young men can misbehave far from home.

Still, he fondly recalled the time his father let him tag along with two older boys to the Bell Fourche Roundup. After the competition, the boys shared a pint of moonshine, then took turns with a seasoned rodeo whore in a horse stall. Just fourteen, he was the last to go. Maybe it shouldn't have surprised him, what he saw and heard, waiting his turn. On the ranch he'd seen livestock go at it, but how different it was for people, doing it face-to-face. He heard their pleasure in the sounds they made, and one boy even took a full minute. When his turn came, he wasn't sure he could do it. Asked if she was his first, he nodded, and the woman smiled, before feeling him through his Levi's until he was "good and ready." Then she pulled him to her on the horse blanket and, in ten seconds, he was done—his very first and last time . . . until Jennie.

James's face flushed with the memory. Surely Billy couldn't be ready for that. But if he didn't go on the road, the coach might have to replace him. Then, John got his assignment to cover the team's first road trip, and Jennie agreed to let Billy go with John as chaperone.

John was furious. The trip would not be the great escape he'd hoped for. Waylaying Billy, he threatened to take him home if he gave him guff or dared to mention Dinah's name.

Billy sputtered a protest, but John coldly replied, "Take it or leave it, squirt. They can always find another punk kid to fetch the bats—maybe someone who actually wrote the essay."

It was a crack that revived Billy's doubts about his worthiness, which only the arrival of his magical uniform had dispelled.

Hearing a car door slam, Billy looked out the window and spotted a young man exiting a taxi. Billy recognized him at once as the pitcher from New York, whose photo had appeared that morning in the *Journal*. "Hey, New York Chief!" Billy shouted as he raced to greet the ballplayer.

Joel smiled at the little guy in the Chiefs' jersey. "Howdy, Rapid City Brave!"

Tickled to meet a playful grown-up, Billy grinned. "I'm Billy the batboy!"

"Great to meet you, Batboy. I'm Joel. Hey, if you're Batboy, where's Bat Man?"

Billy couldn't believe his ears. "You read comic books?"

"Sure—sometimes. Bet you're a big fan."

"Yeah, but my brother says they're for dummies."

"Older brother, right?" While Joel had no experience with brothers, his sympathies naturally favored this lively young boy. "Well, he's just wrong."

Billy beamed. "Want to see my collection? I live right there."

Joel smiled. "I'm supposed to meet my host family—the Rosens—then report for work." He waved a piece of paper in his hand and laughed. "At the New York Club."

"They're not home. I just saw them leave in their cars."

"I guess I should find the *Club*. How do I get there?"

"We can ride bikes. You can borrow my brother's. You *can* ride, can't you?"

"What have they been telling you—that New Yorkers only ride around in limousines?"

"No, taxicabs and subways."

"Well, yeah, but we ride bikes, too. You sure your big brother won't mind?"

"Nah, he never uses it. And who's gonna tell him?"

Joel grinned. Nice kid—if a bit devious. "Can I leave my duffel? It's a lot to schlepp."

"Sure." Billy threw Joel a quizzical look. "What's *shlopp*?"

Joel took a deep breath. "*Schlepp*. It means 'to carry'. It's Yiddish . . . Jewish."

"Oh, sure. The Rosens are Jewish, too."

Joel exhaled. The kid, at least, seemed free of prejudice.

Billy turned to the New Yorker, a wary look in his eyes. "Are you a Dodger fan, too?"

"Oh? Are the Rosens Dodger fans?"

"Mr. Rosen is. He used to live in Brooklyn."

Joel smiled, pleased to discover he had things in common with his host. "What about you, Billy—what's your favorite team?" knowing that every American boy had one.

"The Braves."

Now he understood the boy's suspect look and tone. The Dodgers had won the National League pennant three of the last four years, and, each time, the Braves had finished second. "Well, Billy, they're a terrific team, and one of these years they just might beat my Dodgers."

Billy grabbed Joel's duffel and set it inside his back door. There, he had a devilish thought. If Joel was living with Bernie, he'd also be living with Dinah. That would demolish John for sure. Then, he recalled what his big brother had threatened if he even breathed Dinah's name on the trip. John would just have to find out for himself.

In the Club's dimly lit vestibule, Joel bumped against a standing cardboard cutout of Lana in a strapless evening gown. Then, a younger, taller likeness of the same woman brushed by on her way out the door.

Joel did a double take, and Billy blurted, "Dinah, wait, this is your ballplayer, Joel . . . "

"What?" Dinah stopped and looked from Billy to Joel.

"Joel Meznik," Joel said, trying not to gawk at her skimpy halter top. "And you are . . . "

"She's Dinah—you're going to live with her."

"Billy!"

"Pleased to meet you," Joel said, extending his hand to the striking, blue-eyed blonde.

Dinah gave Joel's tall, athletic physique a quick once-over. "Pleased to meet *you*," she replied with a genuine smile.

"Where's your dad?" Billy asked, not sure he liked the way Dinah and his new friend were talking.

"He's in the cellar," Dinah said. "Will you be working here, Joel?"

"So it seems. And you?"

"Sometimes, I help my dad with the coat check."

Joel let his eyes drift to Dinah's bra-like top and the long, deep cleft between her breasts. He'd never seen a woman so exposed except at the beach. And never Rivkah, not even at Coney Island. "Much call for coats this time of year?"

Dinah cocked her head. "Oh, you'd be surprised. It can get chilly here in the evening—even in summer. Everything's changeable in the West."

Billy scowled. "Come on, Joel. Let's find Bernie—you want to meet him, don't you?"

"Well, bye, bye, ballplayer. See you later at the house—just let yourself in."

As Dinah walked out of earshot, Joel gushed. "Wow! Whatta friendly town." And what a saucy Jewish girl, the last thing he expected to find in a place like Rapid City.

"Glad you think so . . . " A gruff male voice seemed to come out of nowhere.

Joel smiled, pleased by the familiar strains of Brooklyn issuing from a rugged-looking man in cowboy boots and a stylish, western suit. About six feet tall, with barrel chest, Bernie looked like a rich cattleman from the movies, except for his swarthy complexion and turquoise pinky ring, which made him look more like a gangster.

"Where you from, Meznik?"

"Brownsville, Brooklyn."

Bernie's eyes lit up. "No kiddin'. Me, too, but before you were born." Bernie clapped Joel's shoulder. "Dodger fan?"

"What else?"

Bernie let his eyes range over Joel, liking what he saw—a strapping young 'boychik', something he'd never seen before in Rapid. "So, how'd a member of the tribe end up at Columbia instead of City College?"

"High grades, low ERA."

Bernie laughed and then his voice acquired an edge. "Never went to college myself."

Joel looked around the Club—a bit gaudy but impressive, though he had no basis for comparison other than the movies. "Doesn't look like it held you back any, Mr. Rosen."

"You're gonna fit in just fine," Bernie guffawed, then motioned to Billy.

"Come on, kid. We've got to give New Yawk here his uniform."

• • •

Lana rolled onto her side, surveying the dirty bedspread, stained rug, and cracked ceiling.

"*The Royal Rest*, fit for a king," she snorted. "So, how come you're living in this dump? Bernie said you were at the 'Alex'."

Guy was taken aback hearing Lana invoke her husband's name right after they'd screwed. "You want to be doing this in the middle of town?"

"Why not? I like the bar there."

"And I like breathing. So why are you talking with your husband about my digs? Thinking of renting me a room down the hall?"

Lana threw back her head and laughed. "We're putting up the kid from New York, but we got room for one more. Bern says he likes the idea of having another man in the house."

Guy ran his hand along the soft turn of Lana's hip. "I was at the Alex for a week, but it's not cheap."

"Lively bar though. Plenty of action for a lonely ballplayer." To her surprise, Lana felt stirrings of possessiveness for her newest lover.

Guy snuffed out his cigarette, licked his middle finger, and eased it between her thighs. "Who's lonely? I got all the company I need right here at the Royal Rest."

After another go-round, Guy reached for his cigarettes and lit two. "How can I manage a ball club with you on my mind?"

Lana scoffed. She'd not slept with an athlete for years but recognized the smooth talk that often came with a hard body. "Tell me another one."

"You're a hard case, aren't you, babe?"

Lana took a long drag on her cigarette. "Never had any complaints before."

"Not complaining—it's easier this way."

A flicker of hurt crossed Lana's face. "Just passin' through, huh, Coach?"

Guy stared at the ceiling. "Hope so. Heard there might be an opening for a manager in the California League. Only Class 'C' and not much of a town, but if I win big here, then maybe . . . "

"Ah. California."

Lana's dreamy tone made Guy wonder if she thought he'd said *Hollywood*. He gave her a long searching look. "I've caught your act. You're big league. How come you're still here?"

Lana looked away. "Old story. Thought Bernie would take me back East with him, but he liked it out here. Probably figured he'd be small potatoes in New York."

Stockman nodded. "Star in the Minors, star dust in the Majors."

Lana smiled—a bitter one. "Promised I'd star in a New York Club. Didn't think it'd be in South Dakota. So, what's your story—how'd you end up in Rapid?"

"Bad luck. Signed out of high school with the Dodgers. Moved real steady up their ladder. Finally, got the call to the Big Leagues in '51. Brooklyn. Then, Uncle Sam gives me *his* call-up. Korea. Two years lost. Back in the States, I'm sent down to get my timing back. But I messed up my knee in the War, and this Campanella guy's ahead of me in Brooklyn."

"Campanella? Italian—huh? Bernie says you don't wanna mess with 'em."

A shiver ran down Guy's spine. When did Bernie Rosen mess with Italians? And when was she gonna stop bringing her husband to bed?

"Not Italian . . . he's a Negro." Guy's face clouded over. "Campy's a great catcher, but he never had to go to war. Just bad timing. Shoulda been born sooner."

Lana smiled at the man she knew was eight years her junior. Fondling his cock in one hand and cupping his balls in the other, she offered, "Oh, I'd say you're aged about right."

Guy groaned, "Oh, baby," and for the moment all thoughts of life's missed chances were dispelled—by the prospect at hand.

Chapter Thirty-Five

DINAH PULLED HER NEW CONVERTIBLE into the driveway of the Merritt house and honked. The car had been waiting for her at the Club when she and Bernie returned triumphant from her driving test. She didn't even mind that it was canary yellow. "Only car like it on the road," Bernie bragged—deliberately chosen to make it easier to track down if ever that was required.

School was over and Dinah was riding high. Her performance as Lola in *Damn Yankees* for the Spring Musical had been a triumph. Both the *Journal* and the school newspaper singled her out with rave reviews, and posters of her in scant costume brightened store windows throughout Rapid, assuring a full house both nights. All leading to an offer from the artistic director of the Mellerdrammer, an old-time melodrama theater, open every summer in the Black Hills. The director bought a ticket as soon as he saw Dinah's poster.

"Always pays to check out the local produce, 'specially when it's fresh."

Bernie wouldn't let her bunk with the troupe—"all those sex-crazed college boys"—so she had to learn to drive. "Can't be taking you every day. You want to do this—that's the deal."

And want it she did. To be onstage with all eyes on her lit her up inside, like liquor or necking, but ten times more. She hated to admit it, but the bug must have come from her mom.

Suddenly she felt a panic as a long buried memory came back to her: at age seven, on a trip to Brooklyn to bury Bernie's mother, Lana dragging her to a string of offices in Times Square where she read magazines while her mother talked to theater folk about what she called "our little secret"; Lana, singing and dancing like a grown-up Shirley Temple before a circle of ogling men; her father catching up to them in the theater, yanking her mother off the stage and whisking the two of them up the aisle, cursing all the way.

Dinah winced. Would her father one day pull her off the stage, too, just like her mother?

She thumped the horn again. Where the hell was that kid? She didn't know Glen Merritt—just that his dad was Bernie's lawyer and they lived in the other big house on the block. And that he was still in junior high but somehow landed a role in the Mellerdrammer. At first, she protested, not wanting to spend time with a snot-nosed brat, but Bernie's look zipped her lip. And how could she grouse when he'd given her a car and helped her pass her driver's test, 'persuading' the officer after she knocked down a traffic cone and signaled right while turning left? But then she'd always figured that was what fathers were for—to lift you over the rocks so you could swim in the stream.

At last, a well-built young man emerged from the house. About five-feet-eight, he wore a tight white tee shirt, cuffed Levi's, and sported a well-oiled ducktail, like the teen heartthrob James Dean. "Glen's older brother?" she wondered, as he bounded down the porch, letting out a long, low wolf-whistle, meant for her or the car, or both.

"Hi, I'm Glen Merritt," he said in a deep, manly voice.

Dinah needed a moment to respond. An early bloomer herself, she reckoned that her late-blooming neighbor, Billy Moran, had skewed her measuring stick for junior high school boys.

"Hi, I'm Dinah—hop in."

"Nice wheels," he said, panning the dashboard, before lowering his gaze to Dinah's legs.

"Just got it," she crowed. "Passed my road test this morning."

"Maybe you'll let me have a turn sometime."

She threw him a doubting look. "How old are you?"

"Fourteen," he said.

"They don't give licenses to fourteen-year-olds, unless you're a farm boy."

"I drive all the time. Licenses are a formality."

Dinah gave a snort. "Funny thing for *you* to say about licenses. Isn't your dad a lawyer?"

Glen shrugged. "They're just a way for the government to collect dough."

"Bet you heard that from your father."

Glen grinned. "Pretty *and* smart."

He slung his arm across the back of the seat, resting his palm on her shoulder. Dinah narrowed her eyes. She liked being called smart but not him taking license with his hands.

"Are you really fourteen?" she said, lifting his fingers from her bare skin.

"Next time I'll bring my birth certificate."

Dinah laughed, warming to the banter. "No need—I hear those are just a formality." Pulling a scarf from her bag, she took her time tying back her hair. Out of the corner of her eye, she caught Glen checking out her halter top.

"Oh, yeah, you really got it. I dug your act in *Damn Yankees*."

Dinah smiled and backed the car into the street. Two conquests—the ballplayer and Glen—and a new car, all in one day. What other triumphs might this day bring?

From the moment they arrived at the Mellerdrammer, Dinah and Glen were caught up in a whirlwind of activity. "You're our damsel in distress," Dick Irving, the long-jawed, middle-aged Director said, thrusting a script in Dinah's hands. "But you'll need the brunette wig tonight." Then he fingered a lock of her hair. "Does she or doesn't she?" he cackled, and Dinah flinched, sensing he didn't mean the Clairol hair-coloring treatment. Turning to Glen, he offered a curt appraisal. "James Dean, huh? Understudy. Hero and Villain."

"Understudy?" Glen sputtered. "What parts do I play?"

"Crowd scenes for now—and you can help our pretty ingenue here learn her lines. We're under the gun. Someone will be by with chow. Find your way to Costume by three. Dress rehearsal's at four, show's at seven. Outhouse is past the stage."

He placed a clammy hand on Dinah's bare back then slid his fingers down to her waist. "Hope you're a quick study, sweetheart."

Glen sulked all afternoon. "I gave up my summer at the lake for a couple of crowd scenes and a latrine?" He picked up a rock and sent it sailing into the woods.

"At least you didn't get pawed by that horrible man. Ick!"

Dinah gave a hard shudder, like a spaniel fresh out of a pond.

Glen laughed. "Well, I guess that's show biz, *sweetheart*."

At one o'clock their chow arrived, delivered by a portly young woman in a dirndl skirt. Introducing herself as Rhonda, she laid the tray of wieners and Cokes on a tree stump. "I play 'Ma,' she said, lingering for a bit as the attractive young couple ate.

"Well, Ma—you sure have a way—with wieners," Glen quipped.

Rhonda blushed, unaccustomed to flirty talk from a handsome young man.

"Is this your first summer, too?" Dinah asked, between bites.

"Oh no, this is my third season. I'll be a senior at South Dakota State."

"Are all the other actors in college, too?" Glen asked, suddenly aware of his lowly status.

"Yes . . . " she laughed, " . . . we come cheap—Will Act for Room and . . . " she did a sprightly vaudevillian skip and gestured toward the serving tray, " . . . Board."

"Isn't anybody else rehearsing?" Dinah asked, sipping her Coke.

"Nah! First production's pretty much the same every season." Rhonda threw Dinah a cryptic look. "Only the damsel changes."

At dress rehearsal, Dick Irving introduced Dinah to the troupe. Tossing back his cape, he draped a gangly arm around her shoulder.

"She's green but talented," he said. Dinah saw looks pass between cast members as his spindly fingers dangled over her breast.

At six, Dinah sat down to apply her makeup in the girls dressing room. "Make it thicker—they've got to see you from the back row," Rhonda advised.

"Thanks," Dinah said, as she went over her cheeks, lips, and eyes again. "How's that?"

"Better. Now the wig. Next time, do that first." Dinah pinned up her hair and donned the dark wig—a riot of black curls that swayed like a curtain fringe when she moved.

"You look like Scarlett O'Hara," Rhonda said with a touch of envy. "I can't believe you're just a junior in high school." She paused before asking what she really wanted to know.

"And your boyfriend, Glen? He's a senior—right?" A pink flush rose to her cheeks.

Dinah's face registered disbelief. "Glen? My boyfriend? Why, he's just . . . "

Then it hit her. Rhonda *liked* Glen. For a moment she was struck dumb. She seldom gave a thought to other girls' feelings, but there was something about Rhonda that moved her. Still, would a boy like Glen ever go for a girl who looked like Rhonda? Of course, she was older, and Glen might dig that. "Glen's not my boyfriend, just a family friend."

Rhonda's broad face lit up, and Dinah felt a strange but pleasing glow. She'd never stepped aside for another girl, but it might be nice to have a female friend. Other girls had them, even some of the pretty ones—though she didn't think her mother did.

Rhonda leaned down and lowered her voice to a whisper. "Listen, Dinah, a few years ago, the girl who played your part was in high school, too, and Mr. Irving—you know he's married—his wife cooks and runs the ticket booth—well, she had to leave in the middle of the summer."

"His wife left?" Dinah asked, baffled by Rhonda's breathy account.

"No!" Rhonda said. "The ingenue! The last week she was here, she threw up all the time. She was only sixteen. He could have been charged with statutory rape."

Dinah nodded. She'd never heard that term but got the drift. "Don't worry, Rhonda. I wouldn't let that old goat near me with a ten-foot pole."

Rhonda gasped, and the two girls burst into peals of laughter, loud enough to be heard in the men's dressing room next door.

"Save the laughs for the show!" Dick Irving's voice boomed through the thin wall as the girls collapsed into each other's arms, shaking with suppressed hilarity.

Chapter Thirty-Six

GUY'S RED PONTIAC BARRELED INTO the parking lot and screeched to a halt. His last go-round with Lana had made him late. Grabbing clothes clean and dirty, and his Panama hat from his Cuban days, he raced to meet the bus, an old excursion coach shaped like a loaf of bread with the word 'PIERRE' posted like a crusty eyebrow above the windshield. Out of the corner of his eye, he spotted Bernie Rosen making a show of checking his watch. "Screw him," Guy said, pleased at keeping the boss-man waiting while he fucked and re-fucked his wife.

Scanning the lot, Guy tallied his players—fourteen—all accounted for, except Clarence Williams, late once more. Guy was again reminded that he may have made a mistake in signing the Negro. The only person in uniform was the stocky young batboy, standing next to a new ballplayer with dark, wiry hair—Rosen's Jewish pitcher from New York, he supposed.

Throwing the equipment bag over his shoulder, Guy's step quickened as he felt a familiar thrill—a new season, a new team, a fresh chance.

"Give you a hand, Coach?" Rosen's pitcher approached, trailed by the batboy.

"Meznik—see you finally decided to join us." Guy handed Joel the equipment bag, threw Bernie a perfunctory nod, and strode to the bus.

Taken aback by the sarcasm, Joel wondered if it was his late arrival—or something else—that prompted his brusque welcome.

Just then, a black '51 Ford, spit-waxed shiny, pulled into the lot. Clarence Jr. darted from the back seat and made a dash for Jennie, standing under a cottonwood tree with James and John.

"Miz Moran, Miz Moran. My daddy made the team!"

Jennie braced herself against the tree trunk, her face gone ashen. "Yes," she said in a high, thin voice. James threw her a questioning look before turning to the boy.

"That's great, son. The team's lucky to have your dad." James was glad things had worked out and relieved that he could now put the ugly incident between their sons behind him.

Then, Clarence Jr. caught sight of Billy in uniform by the bus. "How come *he* gets to go?"

"Clarence! Hush!" Cherry Mae, catching up to her son, swatted his butt. "I'm sorry, Mrs. Moran. Just wanted to say hello and tell you we be staying on in Rapid for a bit."

Staring past them across the lot, Jennie locked eyes with Clarence's father. After a moment, he dropped his gaze, directing his sight line to take in only his wife and son.

James turned and saw Billy buzzing about a lanky, dark-haired Chief. "So, who's Billy bird-dogging out there?"

John shrugged. "The new guy from New York. He wasn't at the exhibition game."

Jennie roused herself. "I don't want Billy talking to players. Get seats near the driver."

John scowled. "What do you expect me to do, cover his ears when anyone speaks?"

"Do what your mother says," James ordered, though he knew John was right.

John slung his camera over his shoulder and headed towards Billy, while James put a hand on the nape of Jennie's neck. "You all right, Jen? Too much heat?"

Jennie shrugged off his touch. "Sweaty," she said.

James pulled his hand away and rubbed it dry against his leg. This would be the first time in years that the two of them would be alone in the house. He'd even thought about picking up a bottle of Cold Duck to celebrate and get Jennie in the mood—for she still wasn't herself. Lately she'd taken to undressing in the bathroom, depriving him of even the sight of her.

"Come on, Billy, grab your stuff. We've gotta get on the bus."

Joel put out his hand. "You must be Billy's brother. I'm Joel Meznik. I just graduted Columbia. Billy said you're headed for Yale. It's a beautiful campus. Impressive architecture in the neo-Gothic style."

John hesitated, then extended his hand. Scholar or pompous windbag, he wondered. Either way, he was not impressed. "You must have majored in architecture," John said coldly.

"No." Chagrined, Joel realized he'd come off as pedantic. "Just an interest of mine."

Billy felt a tightening in his stomach. What if Joel liked talking to John more than him?

"Come on, Joel," Billy said, "let's get our seats."

John grabbed Billy's arm. "Mom and Dad said you have to sit with me." Billy pulled free from his brother's grasp and John walked away from the bus. "Fine, we're staying home."

"OK, OK." Billy threw Joel a beseeching look. "Can you sit across from me?"

"Sure, Bill. I'd like that." Though caught off guard by Billy's desperate appeal, he was relieved to have someone to sit with. The last Chief to arrive, he was nervous about breaking into the group. He knew he'd have to prove himself all over again—compete against collegians with big reputations and seasoned professionals, grown men who might have even fought in Korea.

And he was a Jew. Most likely, few of these guys ever had a Jewish teammate before.

Billy grinned, and with John on his tail, darted to the bus.

Reaching for his duffel, Joel spotted a tall, husky Negro standing cross-armed by a black car. At first, Joel thought he might be the bus driver, until he noticed the cleats slung over his shoulder.

He was shocked. At Columbia, he'd never had a Black teammate, though his Dodgers now had six Negroes. And, he'd never had a Negro friend. When he was a kid, Brownsville was mostly Jewish with so many synagogues it was dubbed "Little Jerusalem." Though in the last few years many more Negroes had moved to the neighborhood. Recently, in his father's tailor shop, he heard a customer lament: "Brownsville's turning." Turning . . . like milk going sour. Mordecai merely shrugged. Now Joel wondered if his father—who never expressed racial animus at home—secretly agreed with that sentiment. Or was he just reluctant to challenge a paying customer?

Joel frowned. He hadn't spoken up either. Was it concern for his father's business? Or the respect he believed was due any older adult? Whatever the reason, recalling it now made him feel ashamed.

Joel returned his gaze to the Negro ballplayer. This was the last thing he expected to find in South Dakota. Where could he have come from? The man was too old to be a collegian.

A team in the hinterlands with both a Negro *and* a Jew? Who would have thunk it?

"Southpaw, right?" A tall, tanned man with a crooked nose approached Joel, smiling.

"How'd you know?"

"Elementary, my dear Watson. Yer left arm hangs lower than your right and you've got the cockeyed look of a pitcher. I'm Dick Quarles, king of the junk-ballers. You can call me Q."

Joel shook his hand. "Joel Meznik, fastballer."

"Meznik, huh? What's that? Bohunk? Kraut?"

"Brooklyn . . . " Joel said. And then—his neck muscles tightening—added " . . . Jewish."

Quarles smiled. "Koufax's cousin, then."

"I wish!" Joel said, his body relaxing.

"Don't sell yourself short—good summer in the Basin and you can be a bonus baby, too."

The bus driver gave a honk and Q slapped Joel on the back. "There's our shift whistle—better git in before the foreman locks us out."

Grateful for Q's welcome, Joel arrived at the bus the same moment as the Negro. Letting him go first, Joel heard a voice behind him. "After you, sir. No, after you, *boy*." Both Joel and Clarence jerked around. On the top step of the bus, Q placed his hands on his hips and scolded in school-marm falsetto. "No pushing and shoving, you'll all get to see the naked lady."

Everyone laughed except Billy, who looked around to see if what Quarles said was true. John worried that their mother might have overheard the quip.

Staring straight ahead—not turning to wave to his wife and kids—Clarence filed onto the bus and took a seat halfway down the aisle. Recalling Rosa Parks, Joel felt ashamed by his own trifling worries about fitting in, compared to a Negro trying to find a place on his own team bus.

"Here, Joel," Billy called, pointing to a seat across the aisle.

Joel hesitated. Should he join the Black man, demonstrating the solidarity he felt?

"What's the matter, Joel?" Billy persisted.

"Yeah, Joel, what's the matter?" The mocking voice came from behind him, and Quarles wagged his finger at the heckler. "Next time, I'm gonna assign seats."

Joel settled in across from Billy, fearing he'd already drawn too much attention. And maybe, the Negro wanted to sit alone. He wondered which of the ballplayers had done the mocking, but figured he'd find out soon enough—the man had a decided southern accent.

From a few rows back, Guy witnessed it all—Hoades, the Alabama bigot, Meznik, the Negro-loving kike, and Clarence Williams, burning a hole through the window with his fiery gaze. And he wondered how many times Quarles might be called upon to play the jester—and defuse the charge before it blew up in their face.

. . .

As the bus pulled out of the lot, Joel reached behind Billy and tapped John on the shoulder. "How far is it to Pierre?"

"I don't know, ask the driver," John said curtly. On cue, the ruddy-faced man behind the wheel turned to Joel. "Hundred eighty-nine miles as the crow flies, a little longer on the road."

Joel thanked him but wondered why Billy's brother was so frosty. Had his little display of erudition put him off? Turning to the back of the bus he observed the Negro reading a magazine, the manager dozing, and the rest of the Chiefs talking, smoking, and playing cards. A radio played a Western ballad, accompanied by a player on a harmonica. *Oh Lord I'm tired, tired of living this ole way.* Sung in a sour warble, the mournful refrain made him feel as if he'd stepped into a Steinbeck novel—until a player called out, "Change the station, damnit! That Country-Western hillbilly shit's depressing the hell out of me!"

Dick Quarles rose from his seat in the back of the bus and pivoted to the middle of the aisle. "Tsk, Tsk," he chided, hitching his thumbs onto imaginary suspenders. "You can't be lumpin' Country and Western together. There's a world of difference between 'em. And don't be callin' this fine music 'hillbilly shit'. You wouldn't call Beethoven 'Kraut crap,' would you?"

"You tell 'em, Dick!" Darren Hoades jumped in. Joel, hearing that distinctive drawl, wondered if this was the guy who'd mocked him when he boarded the bus.

"All sounds the same to me," George Schmid insisted in a flat Midwestern tone.

"To the untrained ear that might be true. Now take out your pencil and paper—there's gonna be a test. They all harken back to English, Irish, and Scots folk music. Country's got strings—guitar, banjo, fiddle. Western music's more for dancin'—saxes and horns, and . . . "

"This is too much fun to miss," Joel thought, heading for the back of the bus, with Billy just behind and then, reluctantly, John. Other players followed, drawn like iron filings to a powerful magnet. Only Clarence Williams and Guy remained in their seats.

"What about Elvis—ain't he Country *and* Rock'n'Roll?" Lee Casey chimed in.

"He's just Rock'n'Roll," said Andy Richkas, owner of the radio.

"Nah—he's country—started out as the Hillbilly Cat," argued Kibbee.

"First time my momma heard Elvis, she swore he was a n*r," Hoades drawled.

Joel looked long and hard at the speaker, a muscular, crew-cut blond. He was the one. Glancing back at the Negro ballplayer, Joel wondered if he'd heard the slur, but he sat ramrod straight, staring out the window. Then he looked at Billy and John Moran, but neither seemed to respond to that word uttered aloud. Was it only him, a Jew, who found it and the Southerner offensive?

"Elvis grew up in Tupelo and Memphis—heard a lot of Blues there," Quarles interjected.

"OK—enough lecture. What about the music? I'm gonna slit my throat if I have to listen to that crap all the time," Hank Paskiewicz whined. "I want Rock'n'Roll."

"But it's *my* radio—I should have the biggest say," Richkas protested.

"Yes," Joel conceded, "but when it's loud enough for everyone to hear, it's a communal issue. Maybe, we should vote on what to listen to."

"We need more radios!" someone shouted.

"Save your nickels! That's what I did. Took me a year to get this baby," Andy bragged.

"Guess I'll have to skip the whores in Pierre if I want my own," Hoades said.

"*Fort* Pierre," the bus driver corrected from up front. "Pierre's the capital—Fort Pierre's across the river, where the politicians go for an extra hour of drinkin' and fornicatin'. You might say Fort Pierre is Pierre's Sister City—if yer sister was a whore."

The men all laughed, but not Billy, and John hoped he wouldn't ask what a whore was.

"OK," Quarles said. "Let's put it to a vote—Rock'n'Roll or Country—majority wins."

"Then we'll have to listen to the same music all the time," Paskiewicz cried.

Joel put up his hand. "There's going to be a lot of bus time. Maybe everybody should get a turn picking the music. Equal time for every Chief."

"Are you kidding? What are you—a Commie?" objected Richkas.

"Whadya expect from a New York Jew? Probably gonna pick up military secrets from Williams over there." Hoades jerked a thumb in Clarence's direction, "and sell 'em to Moscow."

Instantly, it felt like the air had been sucked from the bus. Joel curled his fist as Clarence lunged down the aisle. Coach Stockman opened his eyes and swung a leg across his path—while John, heart racing, yanked Billy into an empty row.

Hoades, his eyes flashing, rose to meet the Negro's challenge, but Quarles and Hacker quickly stepped in front of the young Alabaman to block him.

"Taking turns don't make you a Commie, Hoades. You'll see when we pass the whores around in Ft. Pierre," Quarles quipped. Some of the Chiefs laughed nervously, then an awkward stillness set in, like the pause between the lightning flash and the thunder that follows.

"Speaking of whores, you know Charlotte the Harlot?" The harmonica player, Harlan Dalluge, broke into song in a hillbilly twang that sounded to Joel like the *Hallelujah Chorus*.

Charlotte the Harlot the girl we adore.
The pride of the prairie, The cowpuncher's whore.
She's dirty, she's vulgar, she spits in the street.
Whenever you see her, she's always in heat.
One day in the canyon, no pants on her quim,
A rattlesnake saw her and flung himself in.
Charlotte the Harlot gave cowboys the frights,
The only vagina that rattles and bites.

Everyone hooted, and to Joel it seemed that the team had exhaled all at once. John laughed, too, but not Billy, who sported the kind of off-kilter smile that meant he didn't get it but wanted everyone to think he did. John sighed. Their mother was right about the road trip. An hour out of Rapid and Billy was getting an earful. Thankfully, it all seemed to sail over his head.

"Good one, Harlan," Q interjected. "You hear about the Platex Living Bra? . . . It bit her."

"How about the Playtex Living Girdle," Joel added, courtesy of his Columbia teammate Morrie, who kept him current with the latest dirty jokes. " . . . It ate her."

The Chiefs exploded in guffaws and Quarles slapped Joel on the back. "I move we accept New York's proposal and take turns. Hoades picks first. I'm guessin' some soulful R & B."

Hoades glared at Joel and Clarence, then at Hacker, towering over him like a guard dog.

"You're a riot, Quarles," he snarled, returning to his seat.

"Here's to dirty ditties and off-color jests," Joel thought with a sigh of relief. Still, he couldn't help noticing that everyone passing Clarence averted his eyes.

"Cut the colored or the bigot?" Stockman wondered, as he settled back under his Panama. "Either way, the Jew stays in the picture . . . for now."

Chapter Thirty-Seven

THE CHIEFS' BUS MADE GOOD TIME on US 16, a two-lane blacktop rolling east across the dun-colored prairie. At regular intervals, signs appeared beside the road for Wall Drug. "Forty miles to Wall Drug," "Thirty miles to Wall Drug," and, finally, "Free Ice Water at Wall Drug."

Joel laughed at the last. "What's the big deal with the drugstore and free ice water?"

"Well, it's free and it's cold and most important out here, it's water," John explained, deciding that after Hoades' defamatory attack, Joel deserved some cordiality.

Joel nodded. He'd read about the Dust Bowl and seen photos of that time—stark depictions of despairing farmers, their dry, powdery topsoil swept up into great clouds of dust.

Returning his gaze to the road, he noted the passing towns: Box Elder, 56; Wasta, 196; New Underwood, 462—each with a post office, general store, and a church, with the largest boasting a second church, café, feed store, bank, and a tavern. And always, in the town center, soaring high above and visible for miles, was 'The Tower', a massive, swollen water tank on metal stanchions, a beacon of hope and promise, Joel figured, to travelers on the rain-starved Dakota plains.

Then, beside the road, Joel saw a gaping cleft—the earth's skin torn away to reveal a viscera of riven rock. "What's that?" he exclaimed.

"Erosion," John explained. "It's part of the Badlands. We won't see much of them today. You'll have to make a special trip, but it's worth it."

"I will, thanks," Joel said, pleased that John's hard crust might be eroding, too.

As the bus rolled on, Joel watched the prairie grass ripple and sway like waves in the wind. Was that why covered wagons were called prairie schooners ferrying homesteaders across a sea of grass? Could this bus be his schooner, carrying him to his new life as a ballplayer?

When the bus reached Wall, US 16 became Main Street, and was choked with cars, trucks, motorcycles, and tourists bound for Wall Drug, a block-long assemblage of shops and stores selling food, drink, and souvenirs.

Stockman dashed up the aisle. "This place is famous all over the world," he whooped, recalling a sign that had made it all the way to

Korea. Planted by another American GI, it read "6,050 miles to Wall Drug"—a bittersweet reminder of home in that godforsaken Army post.

Leaping from the bus, Guy vaulted onto the boardwalk and charged through the swinging double doors of what appeared to be a saloon. "Thirty minutes, guys," he shouted.

Joel threw a quick look at Clarence, who showed no sign of leaving his seat. Though he hadn't expected to find a Negro on the Chiefs, he was more surprised that having one sparked a racial clash. He'd long assumed that Jackie Robinson and the Negro stars who came after him had changed the game forever and that fans and teammates rooted for Willie, Campy, and Hank as hard as they did for Mickey, Yogi, and the Duke. Still, he knew that some college teams in the South remained segregated. Maybe the guy with the drawl played for one of them.

"Here, get two cones." John flipped a quarter to Billy, who caught it one-handed.

Joel smiled wistfully at the pair, recalling his lifelong wish for a brother—especially an older one to help bear the brunt of his father's expectations. He'd gleaned that there'd been other attempts—his mother sick and holed up in her room and sadness in the house, but no babies.

"Hey, Joel, want some ice cream?" Billy yelled from the line at the soda fountain.

"No thank you, Billy." That morning he'd finished the last of his salami and loaf of rye, and kosher dietary law dictated that he wait six hours before consuming dairy. Then out of the corner of his eye, he spotted the Southerner shooting him a dirty look as he passed into the store.

"What's his story?" he asked John, nodding his head toward the surly teammate.

"Darren Hoades, catcher and outfielder, from the University of Alabama."

"And the Negro player?"

"Clarence Williams. Also a catcher and outfielder. He's an airman, an aviation mechanic at the Base—Ellsworth Air Force Base, east of Rapid."

"Ah! Now I get what the Southerner meant by 'stealing military secrets'."

"He's an asshole." John gave Joel a cold look. "But the Rosenbergs *were* traitors."

Joel swallowed hard. Did John think this because they were Communists or because they were Jewish Communists? Most people in New York saw the Rosenbergs as innocent scapegoats, but out here in the West, who knew what people thought of them, or why?

Joel forced a shrug. "They mean nothing to me," he said, a quaver in his voice. Looking away, he pointed to the owner of the contentious radio. "What's his name?"

"Radio man? That's Andy Richkas, first baseman from a Junior College in Omaha."

"And the guy with the long neck and goofy face, who sang and played the harmonica?"

"Harlan Dalluge. One of the pros, I think. Sidearm pitcher from Indiana."

"And the guy with the flattop and the one who looks like Tab Hunter?"

"Dave Wiegand, another pitcher. The blond is George Schmid, tonight's starter."

Joel laughed "And the tall fellow with the glasses—looks like a professor?"

"Bruce Haroldson, a fastballer from Augustana College in Sioux Falls. And next to him's Dean Veal, a pitcher, too. He's from 'State'."

Joel looked puzzled. "State?" he asked.

John chortled. "No, not the state penitentiary—the State College at Brookings, the Morrill Act, Land-Grant college for agricultural and engineering studies."

"John, you are a veritable font of knowledge." Clever, too, Joel thought. For a moment, Joel flashed on Morrie. Maybe this Ivy-bound westerner could be his summertime stand-in.

"Font of knowledge?" John wondered if the collegian was mocking him, but searching Joel's face, he saw only sincerity. Flushed with pride, John turned away, fearing discovery.

"So what's the story with Q, who broke up the fight and acts like the team captain?"

"Dick Quarles. Pitcher-first baseman. Played with Stockman in the Dodger chain. Gonna be the pitching coach. You've picked out all the pitchers, Joel. You got radar or something?"

Joel laughed. "Takes one to know one," though he was concerned at how many there were. He counted seven, including himself. A lot of competition for a starting role.

Then, without thinking, Joel extended his hand, as if this were their true introduction or at least a fresh start. "You're a natural born reporter, John. You could be the Chiefs' publicist."

John shook Joel's hand and smiled. Maybe he'd misjudged the Ivy Leaguer. He'd also been known to show off when nervous. And truth be told, Joel looked like the only Chief he had anything in common with and the greatest potential as a friend.

Back on the bus, Guy spotted Williams reading his Bible. He hoped it was the part about turning the other cheek—the gospel Jackie Robinson abided by his first two years in the Bigs.

"Listen up, men! We lose an hour crossing the Missouri at Pierre, so we'll drive straight to the ballfield. Change into uniform now. I don't wanna put on a strip show in the parking lot."

"Why not, Chief? Ain't Pierre famous for 'em?"

"Thought it was famous for Lewis and Clark and fur trading."

"Like I said—famous for beaver!"

"I don't get it." Billy whispered to Joel.

"You will in a couple of years," Joel said, exchanging knowing smiles with John.

Turning the bus into a rolling locker room, the players pulled their kits from the overhead rack and began changing. Billy, already in uniform, watched in wonder as the young men, with startling nonchalance, dropped their pants and skivvies and exchanged them for jockstraps—each man tugging at the wide waistband, drawing the elastic leg straps high and tight under his butt cheeks, then pulling at the pouch to raise cock and balls snug against the pelvis.

Just this year, Billy was given a jockstrap by his dad but couldn't see how a thin cloth undergarment could protect him on a direct hit. Not yet hung, his 'stuff' lacked mature size and dangle. But viewing the spectacle on the bus, he saw in a flash that the jock was there to keep a grown man's cock and balls away from the grinding scissors of the thighs.

And what thighs they were. Two of the Chiefs looked like the Greek sculptures in the *World Book*, with arms and chests subdivided into hard, bulging parts, and hair growing out of unexpected places. His father and brother had only scant hair, and he had none.

Suddenly, Billy felt funny, like when he watched Dinah through the binoculars. Then, some of the Chiefs started a chant, whooping and hollering like the cartoon Indians he'd seen at the movies. Billy leapt from his seat to join the men, dancing and swinging from row to row. It was the most astonishing thing he'd ever done, and he'd never felt happier.

Guy looked on from his seat, smirking as he spotted one of the men checking out big Frank's 'equipment'. Clarence Williams, Guy noted, donned his armor where he sat. Not that he blamed the man. Big or small there was no winning for a lone Negro baring it all in *that* game.

John kept his eyes straight ahead. It made him uneasy, these men stripping, and he felt out of place, left out of what seemed a tribal rite—a band of warriors preparing for battle.

He tapped the bus driver on the shoulder. "Are we going to pass the big dam on this route?"

"Oahe? Nah, that's five miles upriver."

"What's that?" Joel asked, pulling off his khakis. Thinking it awkward in front of Billy—and doubting he'd play tonight anyway, he didn't strip to change from briefs to jock.

"It's going to be one of the largest rolled-earth dams in the world. Big as Rhode Island."

"Wow! How are they doing that?" Joel asked.

"They just drown the town," the driver interjected, laughing at his rhyme. "It were mostly Injun squatters. They had no claim to it, 'specially when it's fer the good of the people."

Joel looked at John to check his reaction to the driver's slur, but John just nodded in agreement. Was this how people thought out here, even someone headed for Yale?

Crossing the Missouri, the bus entered Ft. Pierre. To the east, the dome of the State Capitol gleamed in the late afternoon sun. Stockman, like a modern-day trailblazer, stood by the driver, his eyes trained forward, as if directing the party's crossing. "How far to the ballfield?"

"You see the Capitol? You can read the scoreboard from there. Whorehouses and a ballfield—Pierre's a lawmaker's dream."

"Balls, bills, and strikes," John quipped, and Joel laughed.

Billy scowled. His brother and Joel were getting far too chummy. Then he recalled that Joel would be living in Dinah's house. That would put the kibosh on their friendship, for sure.

Standing in the middle of the aisle, Stockman called for the team's attention. "All right men, we've had our fun, now it's time to get serious. Tonight, we're facing Hank Hamrich, a veteran lefty. Word is, he comes three quarters with a decent heater but has trouble getting the curveball over. So, we'll sit 'dead red' till I say otherwise."

"Hey Coach," Hacker interrupted. "What's the name of the Pierre team?"

"The Cowboys," Guy answered, and everyone hooted.

"Just a game of cowboys and Indians, boys," Quarles crowed. "And this time, I swear, the Indians are gonna win."

Chapter Thirty-Eight

BERNIE SAT AT HIS DESK and frowned. It irked him that he'd have to wait for Carl's postgame call for details of the Chiefs' first contest in Pierre. None of the Basin League teams were broadcasting their games on the radio, believing it tantamount to giving the product away. Still, he continued to push for it—knowing that back in the '30s, radio boosted attendance in the Major Leagues, luring new fans to the ballpark for all three New York teams.

He threw a sour look at the Zenith on his credenza. He hated missing the season opener in Pierre, but it was simply out of the question. He might have given it a shot, hightailing it across the prairie in his big Caddy—but there'd still be the long drive back, the late arrival home, and missing Lana's two sets at the Club. He fingered the framed photo of his wife. Staying overnight in Pierre was simply out of the question.

He hit the switch for the one-way mirror. At rehearsal Lana had never been better, slowing her songs to a seductive purr. Something was up. He'd felt it all week. Could something be someone she'd be singing to in the crowd tonight? It's not like it hadn't happened before.

"When's Dinah gettin' home from the Mellerdrammer?" Lana breezed into the office in a sequined gown cut low front and back—twin 'Vs' drawing his eye down to tantalizing shadows.

"Should be back by eleven."

"How'd she like the car?" Lana took a compact from her bag and, pursing her lips, ran her tongue around the reddened oval as Bernie looked on, his engine revving higher with each lap.

"Loved it." Placing his hand on his wife's bare back, he slipped his fingers down to the top of her lacy garter belt. "How was your day, babe?"

Lana stiffened. "Fine—nothing special."

"Came by the house 'round noon, thought you might be home . . . "

Lana's face reddened, recalling what she'd been doing at that hour with Guy at the motel.

"Later, Bern—I've got my face on."

Bernie let her go. Her restraint might be professionalism, or it could mean something else. "Knock 'em dead, baby. That Patsy Cline medley's gonna leave 'em howling."

Lana pecked his cheek. "Will do, Daddy."

Bernie watched as she walked to the bar. "Catch a tiger by the tail and you can never let go," he thought. It had been years since he'd roamed more than a couple hours' ride from Rapid. The family's last real trip was eight years back when they flew to New York for his mother's funeral. That was when Lana tried to jump ship, sneaking off to audition in a Broadway theater.

Returning to his desk, Bernie searched for the insurance papers for Dinah's new car. He wondered how she was faring at the Mellerdrammer—slapping on the greasepaint like her mama. Reaching down, he unlocked the bottom drawer. Inside lay his WWII service revolver and a jumble of pictures—mementos of his life as a husband and father. Rifling through the clutter, he found the photo—he in flyboy uniform, Lana in a loose-fitting pink suit, her telltale bump mostly hidden by strategic draping. Yes, Dinah was there, too—front row center.

Replacing the photo, his hand brushed against another frame—one constructed from popsicle sticks and paste, the word DAD spelled out in shiny half marbles. He ran his fingers over the letters, reflecting on his day with Dinah. How he'd dazzled her with her dream car, helped her pass her driver's test, then laid the groundwork for a promising shidduch—a match with a smart Jewish boy so she wouldn't get knocked-up by a shiftless bronco-buster, like Lana had, just months before their own wedding.

Bernie turned his gaze to the stealth mirror, as Lana stepped to the mic, mouthing the word—courtesy of Patsy Cline—that summed up his life as well as any word could. "*Crazy.*"

Chapter Thirty-Nine

THE RAPID CITY CHIEFS, FIRED UP and ready for battle, filed off the bus and strode briskly towards Pierre's Hyde Stadium. John held back, framing the scene through his Leica—fifteen uniformed men and their little drummer boy, Billy, marching off to war—sun on their shoulders, air filled with tension and, as he lowered his camera, a storm of white fluff filling the sky. "What the hell!" he thought. He'd seen cottonwood seeds before but never like this—a summer squall of wispy pods wafting about and collecting on the ground like snow.

John raised the Leica to his eye and clicked. Then, in the blink of an eye, the players changed from resolute soldiers to children, swatting at the puffs or catching them in their caps, pressing them into balls and firing them at each other in mock battle. He half expected the Chiefs to stick out their tongues to capture them, the way he had as a child with real snowflakes.

"Uh-oh!" Big Frank Hacker said. "Cottonwoods must be seeding."

"Something to worry about?" Stockman asked.

"Nooo. Usually stops after a while," Hacker said with a twinkle in his eye.

• • •

The last player to leave the bus was Clarence Williams. He needed a moment to think. Before the Base tryouts, he'd expected that both he and his pal, Otis, would make the cut. He had no interest being the only colored man on a traveling ball team. Still, he'd been in the Air Force long enough to distinguish an offer from a command. And Cherry Mae was tickled pink, and Clarence Jr.—proud as a peacock—had snapped out of his funk. Then came this rotten bus trip and the white cracker questioning his patriotism. Now, he saw how it was going to be.

The bus driver cleared his throat. Clarence, squaring his shoulders, left without acknowledging the nudge. He'd not disembarked in Wall and was desperate for a men's room. Under the grandstand, he found one and opened the door with such force that it banged against the wall. Startled by the noise and the unexpected appearance of a Negro, an old man at the urinal halted his business and, buttoning his urine-darkened trousers, made a hasty exit.

No stranger to such reactions, Clarence turned his mind to his assignment with the new team. Left field, not catcher. It had been years since he'd played outfield and even then, only a handful of times. Still, as a catcher, he knew the game better than any outfielder ever could. Smart positioning and his powerful throwing arm could make up for his inexperience and lack of speed. And if he got a hit tonight in a big spot, then Coach'd just have to let him play regular.

Clarence buttoned his fly and walked to the sink. But if he fucked up in the field, he'd only pinch-hit and they'd never let him catch. Playing *whiteball* for The Man was bad enough, but when the The Man himself played the same position you did, there wasn't much chance you'd get a shot. Then he thought of Clarence Jr., waiting at home for the report of his dad's first game. He couldn't let him down. "Don't press," he told himself, "Don't mess this up for Junior."

• • •

Guy wiped his damp palms on his jersey. After ten seasons as a player, this was his first as a manager in a game that counted, and he wasn't at all sure he'd be any good at it. Could he handle the headstrong veterans? Give heart to the nervous young collegians? Bring out the talents of all his men?

Guy reached into his duffel for the scouting report, which was little more than a list of each Cowboy's college, or the top level of Organized Baseball reached by each pro. Nine of the twenty men on Pierre's early season roster had pro experience. One had a 'cup of coffee' in the 'Bigs', two had played at Double A, two at A, three at C, and one at D. Was this how it was, Guy wondered, in a so-called "fast semi-pro league"—players of the widest-ranging skills and experience, with the pitching and quality of play ranging greatly from night to night?

For his Chiefs, the big unknown was defense. After Tony Schunot blew out his hammy, he was forced to move everyone around. Casey would be okay at short, but Hoades was a dubious second baseman, and Clarence Williams was not an outfielder. And in right was the slow-footed Hacker. Only Kibbee in center and Paskiewicz at third were solid fielders.

Still, it was hard to predict how anyone would perform based on practice drills. In time he'd know who was good, not just cocky, and who choked when the pressure was on. Guy looked over at Bernie's boy, Joel Meznik. Late arriving, he was the biggest mystery of all.

Down on the field Joel and Billy lugged the canvas bat bag to the visiting team dugout. Billy grabbed Joel's arm. "Joel, I've . . . I've never been a batboy before."

Joel placed a hand on Billy's shoulder. "I can help. I doubt I'll even warm up tonight."

Unloading the Louisville Sluggers into the bat rack, Joel pointed to the lineup card on the wall. "Check that to arrange the bats in the right order. See what each man uses. Note the model number stamped into the knob. By the way, the K-55 is Mantle's bat, the R-43 is Yogi's. The 'R' stands for Babe Ruth, who used this model first—a longer, heavier version of the same shape."

"That's amazing," Billy exclaimed. "Who uses this S-2?" he asked, fingering the knob.

"Willie Mays and Eddie Mathews."

Billy beamed. Eddie Mathews, his hero. With Eddie's bat in his hands, he had the odd feeling that their lives had finally come together. Later, when Joel wasn't looking, he took a swing with the S-2, imagining it was bottom of the ninth with bases loaded, and this was the home run that would finally win the National League pennant for his beloved Milwaukee Braves.

When Guy announced batting practice, he turned to Joel. "Meznik, get Hoades and warm up in the bullpen. You'll pitch BP third, after Wiegand and Q. Nice and easy now—just five hitters, six-four-two." Joel was glad to brush off his cobwebs in batting practice but wished that Stockman had told him to throw to Clarence Williams instead of the Alabama bigot.

Joel jogged out to left field where Hoades was playing pepper. "Warm me up," he said flatly. Darren didn't answer but sauntered back to the dugout for his mitt. Waiting for his return, Joel checked out his new teammates in the batting cage—men he would depend upon to support him at bat, and in the field when it was his turn as starting pitcher.

Then Frank Hacker stepped into the three-sided cage, and everyone stopped what they were doing to watch the big slugger as he fired a line drive toward short. For an instant, it seemed that Casey might spear it with a well-timed leap, but it quickly disappeared over the left field wall. Joel looked across the field and saw jaws gone slack. Never had he seen a ball hit that low, that far, that fast. On the bus, Frank seemed awkward, frustrated perhaps by the bounded physical space, but in the cage his movements were expansive and joyous, as he rocketed baseballs into the heavens.

For Billy, it felt as if he'd died and gone to heaven when Stockman barked, "Kid! You are Captain of the Ball Bag. Get behind the pitcher and take the return throws from the fielders." Handling the bats, filling the watercooler, and running errands he had expected, but not this—being *on* the field *with* the team, performing a vital function.

Between pitches, Billy scanned the Chiefs spread out across the stadium. The starting pitcher, Schmid, was stretching in the bullpen while Veal ran wind sprints in the outfield. Hacker chased fly balls struck from the left field corner. And Stockman, between home and first, fungo'd grounders to the infielders on the off beats between Wiegand's batting practice offerings.

Then Paskiewicz dove for a hot smash behind third, tumbled to his feet, and fired the ball to second, where Hoades juggled it a moment before rocketing a strike to first where Quarles stretched for the throw like a rubber-limbed contortionist. Tumblers, jugglers, contortionists! He couldn't believe his good fortune. It was as if he'd run away from home and joined the circus!

While much impressed by the Chiefs' gymnastic feats, Billy was truly awed by the way all the Chiefs could throw—Casey, the slender shortstop, fielding a grounder moving toward third, then whipping the ball all the way back across the diamond to first. And Hank, the stocky third baseman, firing the baseball like it was shot out of a cannon. It was mysterious, even miraculous. Was there some trick to it? Or was it something about the baseballs, smooth and white as pearls with thick red stitches, unlike any he'd ever seen on the playground? All he could come up with was a fisherman he once saw, who just flicked his wrist and cast his worm halfway across the pond. Whatever it was—this knack they all possessed—he vowed to get it.

John was there to take pictures. Paddy had told him he needed to get close to get good shots. So he positioned himself behind the bullpen screen, a mere two feet behind the catcher. But despite the protective barrier, he was more nervous than excited, and when a pitch sailed over the catcher's glove and struck the screen, he was shaken. Looking across the field, he saw Billy with a beatific smile on his face, shagging balls in the very center of the action. Eyes cast down, John fiddled with his Leica. Even *with* protection, he preferred his action through a lens, distanced from a game he truly loved.

Guy waved for the Chiefs to come in. Pacing back and forth he looked from man to man. "We haven't practiced much, so we'll be ragged at times, but I expect you always to hustle—run everything out, back each other up. On pop-ups, if the shortstop calls it, it's his. Fly balls to the outfield, it's the center fielder's call. In-between stuff, if the outfielder wants it, the infielder backs off. Outfielders, if I stand up and rub my chest, move in. Rub the back of my head, move out. As for a scouting report, I wish I had the dope, but we're just as big a mystery to them."

"Elementary, my dear Watson," Quarles quipped. "We'll crack this mystery but good!"

The team chuckled, but Guy merely nodded, too tense to smile. "Batting order's posted. Signs come from Dalluge, third base coach tonight. First thing's the indicator. If Dalluge don't do this . . . " Guy brushed his hand across the "Chiefs" on his jersey. " . . . nothing's on. He may do other stuff, but it don't mean nothin' lest he rubs across the "Chiefs" first. If he does that, look for what comes next. If he touches his belt, you bunt. Touches his hat, hit and run. Touches his leg, steal. If he holds up one finger, that's the take. Don't swing on the next pitch no matter what. If he rubs down his arm like this, the sign's off. Simple signs tonight, so no fuckups."

Billy's mouth was agape. Simple? How could anyone keep all that straight?

"Now comes the tricky part. When the count goes to 3 and 0, you always take the next pitch, *unless* Dalluge does this . . . " Again, Guy held up his right pointer. "Then, it's *not* the take. So, if the Cowboys swallow the bait and lay one down the pipe on 3 and 0, we want you to take a rip at it. We'll only do this when the game is on the line. So, let me repeat. If Dalluge gives you the finger on 3 and 0, you take a cut if you get a good pitch."

"Dalluge gives *me* the finger, I'll punch him out," Quarles joked. The Chiefs all laughed.

"Now, the sign for the suicide." The atmosphere in the dugout grew tense. "We have no safety squeeze, only the suicide. So, the batter's *got* to get the bunt down. Now the sign for the suicide is two fists together with a swing." Guy put his hands together and swung as if holding a bat. "Makes it look like you're supposed to hit away. But it means bunt. Now, you batters got to show you got the sign. Give your nuts a tug, like you're adjusting your jock. Runner on third, answer back same way. Ya payin' attention, Hacker? Ya miss *this* sign, you'll knock Hoades' head into the River." The Chiefs, except Hoades, laughed again but nervously this time.

"A word for you college boys. You wanna go pro? Then think like one. Ask what's this guy hit? Where's he hit it? How's his arm? This is your chance, the scouts are watching."

Joel frowned. If Stockman was serious about the scouts, he wished he was the one pitching, but this was the Chiefs' season opener and Stockman hadn't seen his stuff.

"Now let's jump on top and get Schmidy some runs. See there . . . that's the Governor, so there'll be the usual speeches and the national anthem—then he'll throw out the first pitch. Time enough for a dump." The men laughed as Hoades got up and headed for the men's room.

• • •

Much later, after the incident in the ninth inning, Guy realized he should have insisted that the groundskeeper remove that pile of cottonwood seed before the game. But after all the pomp and ceremony, Guy was anxious to get started and decided to let it go.

And so, it sat there the entire game—outside of fair territory, but still on the playing field—a pile of cottonwood fluff, like a snowdrift in the right field corner.

For most of the contest, it didn't matter. No ball came close. Then, in the ninth, Hoades hit a grounder down the right field foul line that angled into the pile and disappeared. He was nearing second base when he realized where his ball had gone.

Seizing the moment, Hoades completed his circuit of the bases—backwards! Prancing like a show pony while pointing to the corner as the hapless outfielder—down on all fours, dug like a dog, raising a spew of white dust searching for the buried bone. As Hoades finished his mocking jog, the frenzied crowd booed and threw bottles on the field.

And yet, Hoades' inside-the-park home run mattered little in Rapid's 9-4 victory.

When the game ended, the team made a hasty exit from Pierre's Hyde Stadium.

Coach Stockman just hoped that Hoades' hot-dogging wouldn't come back to bite his Chiefs in the butt.

Chapter Forty

"FIRST A DRUBBIN', THEN A rubbin' in," the bus driver quipped, hailing Stockman at the gate.

"We're here to win ball games, not make friends," Guy snapped.

"I'm not complainin', mind you—most times I'm stuck takin' tourists to see the stone faces or the big hole in the ground. So, where we headin' now?"

"Sportsman's Lodge, Ft. Pierre?"

"Well, there's a ball o' fun to be had there, though some of your boys may not be in the best shape come the morrow."

Tired of the man's prattle, Guy turned away. His players could sleep it off on the road.

Trailed by Stockman and the team, the driver cursed as he boarded the bus. "What the hell!" A thick layer of cottonwood seed covered the steps, the aisle, and half the seats, with suitcases and duffels pulled from the luggage rack, their contents strewn across the floor.

"Crap!" Guy called to the team. "Haul ass, men, we're leaving on the double!"

"Look over there!" Billy turned to a group of men on the hillside, laughing and pointing at the bus. Casey and Richkas gave chase, but the local jokesters had a head start.

"Forget it!" Guy yelled. "Get back here and clean up."

Like a town hit by a hop-scotching tornado, some sections of the bus were completely untouched, while others were smothered in fluff.

Clarence Williams' seat had been spared. Brushing away a few tufts, he slid over to the window. He felt good. He'd played a good game—delivered a run-producing double and made a fine catch—though only the Jewish pitcher offered a compliment.

Hoades' row was one of the hardest hit. Starting up the aisle with an armload of seed, he stopped when he reached Clarence who sat reading a magazine, ignoring his teammates' efforts.

"Of all the . . . " Hoades sputtered, then dropped his load onto Clarence's lap.

"Here you go, ya lazy cotton picker."

Clarence sprang, catching Hoades under the chin with an uppercut that sent him reeling. The bus fell silent as Quarles and Hacker quickly formed a cordon between the two men. Both John and Joel stepped in front of Billy to shield him, while Guy jerked his thumb toward the front of the bus. "Williams . . . up front . . . now!"

Clarence balked, then stormed forward and took a seat behind Joel. Stockman grabbed Hoades and shouted. "Hacker! Give me a hand!" The big man came forward and tossed Hoades over his shoulder, then dumped him onto a seat at the back.

"Sportsman's Lodge. Let's get going," Stockman barked.

The driver turned the ignition key, eliciting only a sour, high-pitched whimper, like a dog having a bad dream. He turned the key again, but the sound just grew fainter. Bolting down the steps, he charged to the rear of the bus. A moment later, the mystery was solved—the engine block had been drowned in 'cotton'.

"Fuckin' yokels—can it be fixed?" Stockman asked the driver.

"Damned if I know, never seen anything like it."

Stockman strode to the door of the bus and yelled, "Williams, get out here."

Clarence remained in his seat, stone silent.

"You're a mechanic, right? Engine's fucked."

Clarence stood and, without a word, followed Stockman outside.

"Can you fix it?

"Dunno. They mighta swiped a part, too."

Stockman looked at his watch. It was late. "How far is the motel?"

"Couple miles, I reckon," the driver answered.

"Well, we can walk. You two stay and fix the bus."

The driver nodded "yes." Clarence shook his head. "No, I don't do this work for free."

Guy seethed. "Fine, I'll pay you. *If* you fix it."

Filing out of the bus, duffels in hand, the Chiefs trekked westward to the bridge across the Missouri. Most of the players were in high spirits, undampened by the scuffle minutes before. They'd won their season opener and were about to celebrate in a wide-open western town.

Only Joel and the Moran boys were quiet, troubled by what they'd just seen. John worried that he might not be able to protect Billy if something like this happened again. Joel was disturbed by the racial aspect of the clash. He wondered if this would get worse as the season wore on, forcing teammates to take sides, ripping the fabric of this patchwork team.

Billy was excited by seeing grownups fight but confused by it, too. Coach Stockman seemed to side with Mr. Williams, though he was the only one who didn't help clean up the bus. And he said he wouldn't fix the motor unless he got paid. Was he so mad at Hoades that he wouldn't help his own team?

Walking across the bridge, Guy had an uneasy feeling. He'd played on a lot of teams, but this was the biggest collection of oddballs he'd ever seen. And yet, now Hoades was sharing a laugh with Hacker and Quarles. Maybe Williams was the problem. Without the Negro on board, the Alabaman would probably get along just fine. He might ride the Jew, but Meznik seemed like the kind who could take it. Williams, it appeared, could not.

As the team crossed into Ft. Pierre, a police car pulled over and motioned for the men to stop. "Headed for another game?" the officer asked with a straight face.

"No," Stockman said. "We just played."

"I know, I was there." The officer gave Guy the once over. "You the manager?"

"Yeah . . . don't suppose you saw who messed up our bus? Engine won't start."

"Can't say I did," the cop said flatly, making Guy wonder if he couldn't say, or wouldn't.

"So that's why you're crossin' Big Mo on foot. Where you headed?"

"Sportsman's Lodge."

The policeman nodded. "You'll be happy there." Then he looked over the group of players. "Where's the colored guy who hit the big double?"

Stockman was surprised by the question. "He stayed with the bus to fix the motor."

"Maybe I'll drive by and see how he's doing."

Immediately, Guy felt uneasy. Despite being furious with Clarence, he knew about cops beating up Negroes in the South. "Oh, that's not necessary, officer."

"You manage your team. I'll decide what's necessary in my town." Then, the policeman gestured toward Billy. "Kid's too young to be out at this hour. Come here, son."

Billy stepped forward, a look of panic on his face. John followed, a step behind.

"And you are . . . ?" the officer said, addressing John.

"I'm his brother—I'm responsible for him."

"Then, be responsible—stay with him at the motel. No hitting the bars or strip clubs with the boy, and don't leave him in the room alone. Understand?"

“Yes, sir.” John put an arm around Billy, dumbstruck by his first brush with the law.

The patrol car did a U-turn and headed back in the direction of the stadium while the team gathered around Stockman, all buzzing at once. “Shit. What was that all about?”

“Probably giving us a hard time because we beat his Cowboys.”

Suddenly Joel spoke up, his tone serious. “Maybe we should all go back to the bus.”

Stockman figured he knew what was bothering Joel. The cop. And the Negro. But going back made no sense. “He’ll be all right. The driver’s there. And the cop’s gonna check on them.”

“A little roughing up would do that n*r some good,” Hoades said and spat.

“You Neanderthal,” Joel hissed, glaring at Hoades. Then Joel turned on his heel and started back across the bridge to the stadium. Billy darted after him, and John grabbed their suitcases and hurried to catch up.

“Must be the kiddies’ bedtime,” Kibbee said with a smirk.

Stockman scoffed. *Neanderthal*? What kind of asshole says that?

“Let’s get a move on, Chief,” Quarles shouted. “Before it’s the whores’ bedtime, too!”

• • •

With the capitol dome as their guide, Joel and the Morans retraced their steps through the deserted streets of Pierre. Already weary, John wondered why he hadn’t grabbed Billy and stayed on the bridge with the team. Sure, Hoades was a bigot, but Clarence seemed a hothead. Still, he recognized that Joel had done something courageous—sticking up for the underdog in his odd fashion. *Neanderthal*! John chortled, imagining using that same epithet himself.

With nothing open on the Capitol side of the river, John began to worry. What if they got back to the stadium and the bus was gone? Maybe Clarence fixed it and drove to the motel. And his bad leg was starting to throb. Despite the coolness of the night, John broke into a sweat. He didn’t think he could make it if they had to reverse course and walk all the way to the motel.

“Hold on a minute.” John sat on the steps of a large gray building and rubbed his calf.

“You OK?” Joel asked.

“He had polio,” Billy blurted. John shot him a murderous stare.

"Really? Gosh, I'm sorry." Joel said.

"No, I think I stepped off the curb wrong, pulled something . . ."

Joel nodded, but he could tell John was fibbing. He recalled the polio scares in Brooklyn, confined to the apartment on stifling summer afternoons, barred by his parents from the beach, movies, and ballfields. One boy he played with caught it—came to the field just once after that, his withered legs girded in metal braces. Leaving after the first inning, he never returned.

"I could use a rest myself," Joel said, sitting down next to John.

Billy looked at the two of them. "I'm hungry," he said.

John shrugged, though he felt a twinge of guilt. Like it or not, he was responsible for Billy's welfare and that included seeing he got fed.

Joel poked Billy in the stomach. "After all those hot dogs I saw you eat at the stadium?"

"Only two," Billy protested. "The other seven were for Hacker." Then he yawned. It was way past his bedtime, and now that he'd stopped moving, the long day was catching up to him.

John stood and pulled Billy to his feet. There was no way he could carry him. And they couldn't sleep on the steps of a building. "Let's go!"

"Why are we going back to the bus anyway?" Billy asked.

John and Joel exchanged a look, then burst out laughing.

"Some rescue mission," Joel said, shaking his head.

"Who we rescuing?" Billy asked, confused.

"At this point, maybe just ourselves," John said.

They trudged on—Billy dragging his feet and John limping, with Joel, a walker in the City, the only stalwart. Then, as they passed the statehouse, John noticed a single light on an upper floor. Pointing, he joked, "If worse comes to worst, we can always call on the Governor."

Joel winked at John. "Wonder what he could be up to at this hour?"

"Probably the same thing as the team," John quipped. "Guess that makes you the biggest hero, Joel. Giving that up for a noble cause."

"No great sacrifice—got my eye on someone in Rapid."

"Really? Who?" John asked, worried that Joel had already run into Dinah.

Billy held his breath. It was the moment he'd been waiting for, when Joel would crush John's hopes with a single word "Dinah." But now he wasn't so sure. He liked being one of the *Three Musketeers*—sharing adventures, avenging wrongs, getting in and out of scrapes.

Something in John's tone made Joel cagey. Dinah was, after all, the Morans' next-door neighbor and seemed about John's age. "Just some girl I met at the hotel," he replied.

Billy exhaled, their happy trio safe, at least, for the moment.

"Found someone already? How long you been in town? One day?"

Joel grinned. "I'm known to be impulsive," though nothing was further from the truth. But maybe that was why he'd come West—to be rash and reckless, throw caution to the wind.

"Hey look, we made it." Billy darted across the parking lot towards the darkened bus.

"Hold on, partner, we don't wanna scare 'em." Joel grabbed Billy, slowing him to a trot.

Tapping on the bus door, Joel got no response. Finally, he yelled. "Open up, it's Joel Meznik!" The door hissed, then parted, and at the top of the steps stood the driver with a flashlight, and Clarence, a baseball bat. The driver shone the beam into Joel's eyes, blinding him for an instant.

"You forget something?" the driver croaked in a voice thick with sleep as Clarence tromped back to his seat.

"No, we . . . " Joel stammered, "There was this cop . . . we just wanted to make sure . . . "

John looked at his shoes—also at a loss to describe what had transpired on the bridge.

"Oh yeah, he came by. Nice guy. Said he'd send a tow truck in the morning."

Joel glanced towards the back of the bus to see if Clarence had something to add, but he was silent. All he could make out were the Negro's long legs, dangling across the armrest into the aisle. Following Joel's gaze, the driver wondered if Clarence might have ended up sleeping on the bus regardless. He wasn't sure if any motel in Pierre would have taken him in.

"Well, hop aboard. Plenty of room at the Inn."

"Got any food?" Billy asked. The driver hesitated. He'd stashed a can of Spam in his duffel but was saving it for breakfast. Then a Hershey bar came sailing towards them, barely discernible in the dim light. Reaching out, Joel caught it before it hit the windshield.

"Wow! Gee thanks, Mr. Williams," Billy shouted, surprised it had come from him. Clearing his throat, John threw Billy a look. "OK, OK. I was gonna share it."

The bus driver declined his portion and Joel divided the bar evenly into three sections.

"There's a water fountain round back of the stadium. Here, take this . . . " The driver handed Joel the flashlight, " . . . and you might want to piss while you're out there."

Back on the bus, the driver showed Billy how to make a small pillow by stuffing his change of underpants inside a T-shirt. Joel offered his jersey as a blanket for the boy. Happily swaddled, Billy wedged his body against the seatback and curled himself into a contented 'C'.

At 6'2," Joel knew he couldn't achieve Billy's comfort on the seat and wouldn't be happy stretched out like Williams. Yet, he couldn't spend the night sitting up. He'd done that on the bus from New York and woke with a painful crick in his neck. What if Coach called on him to pitch tomorrow against Huron?

Gauging the narrow aisle between the seats, he found that his best bet.

John chose Clarence's technique, draping his body along the seat like a wave. Once settled in, he listened to the sounds of sleep around him. Joel, he could tell, was still awake, squirming to get comfortable on the hard bus floor.

"*Psst.* Joel, you up? I wanted to ask—how'd you end up out here anyway?"

Joel laughed. "Coach at Columbia set it up—said semi-pro was a good opportunity."

"Are you looking to go pro?"

"Maybe. I'm supposed to start medical school in the fall . . . guess it depends on how things go out here." Joel propped himself up on one elbow. "Now, can I ask *you* something? How come you came down with polio and Billy didn't? I thought it was real contagious."

John hesitated—no one ever asked him about the polio anymore. He hardly ever limped, and the family didn't mention it. Of course, big mouth Billy had to spill it to a stranger.

The words came slowly at first, like hauling up an anchor. "We were both at Y Camp—different barracks. It was our first night, so I must have caught it somewhere else. Counselor found me shivering and sweating at bed check. Next morning, I couldn't move my legs. An ambulance from Rapid rushed me to the hospital. All the parents came to get their kids—emptied the camp in an hour. No one else got it." John shuddered, reliving the moment he woke up paralyzed, not knowing if he'd ever walk again.

"God! You must have been terrified."

John remained silent. He'd not told the story in years and now he remembered why.

Afraid he'd probed too much, Joel added, "Thank God we have the vaccine now."

"Yeah . . . now all we have to worry about is nuclear annihilation and Commie spies."

Joel stared into the darkness. He couldn't see John's face but thought his tone more facetious than accusatory—not another reference to the Rosenbergs. Deciding their budding friendship deserved the benefit of the doubt, Joel signed off as he might have with his friend Morrie.

"And on that happy note, I bid you good night and good luck."

Chapter Forty-One

THE POLICE CAR ARRIVED at Hyde Stadium followed by a tow truck. Rousing the sleeping men with a honk, he drove the ballplayers and the Moran boys to the Capitol Café while Fred stayed behind to help the tow truck operator and breakfast on his squirreled-away can of Spam.

Billy darted into the café first, taking the nearest stool. He couldn't believe his great luck. First a ride in a police car, then breakfast at a big café. John and Joel joined him at the counter and Clarence followed, turning customers' heads as he entered. Stealing a look, Joel saw that Clarence seemed unaware of the attention he caused. Or maybe just unconcerned.

Twirling on the red vinyl stool, Billy extended his legs like the blades of a propeller and shouting "lift-off," caught John smack dab in the knee.

"Cut it out!" John swatted his brother and leaned down to rub his bad leg. Sleeping on the bus and the long walk the night before hadn't done it any good—and now this.

Glancing up, John noticed the waitress, a slender blonde with a ponytail, staring straight at him. Putting a hand to his chin, he felt a patch of stubble. At least he'd put on a clean shirt, so he'd not look like a hobo. He smiled sheepishly at the girl who was already staring past him to Joel who, with his dark, day-old beard, looked more like a swarthy pirate than a bum.

The waitress dealt out the menus then waited until Joel was seated to fill his cup with coffee. John scowled, figuring that without Joel, he'd be the likely object of the girl's favor.

"You take it barefoot." The waitress said, as Joel lifted the cup to his mouth.

"Huh?" Joel replied.

"Horned," she added with a sly smile. Joel blushed, though unsure of her point.

"She means black, strong, no milk," John said curtly, as the girl filled Clarence's cup then headed back to the kitchen. "Oh Miss," John called after her, but she didn't seem to hear.

"You sure that what she meant by 'horned'?" Clarence joshed. Joel and John stared at him. He'd not said a word all morning even in the patrol car on the way over.

Joel turned to the menu and studied its many potential transgressions. Since leaving New York he'd subsisted on the hard salami and loaf of rye his mother had packed for him, but now he had to figure out how to keep kosher in Dakota—while keeping it on the QT.

Turning to John, he pointed to the Special Breakfasts section. The Representative simply offered eggs and toast, while The Senator added orange juice and a choice of sausage or bacon, and The Governor provided eggs, toast, orange juice, flapjacks, and *both* bacon and sausage.

"Figures that a Governor's breakfast would have plenty of pork," Joel quipped.

Not to be outdone, John replied, "What about a 'Filibuster'—fare to fill and bust yer gut."

Joel hooted, "Good one." And John felt proud for holding his own with the Ivy Leaguer.

The waitress appeared again and stood before Joel with pencil and pad.

"I'll have six eggs over easy and four slices of toast with jam."

Amused by Joel's order, the waitress smiled. "Bacon or ham with them eggs?"

Joel needed more to sustain him but had vowed not to eat pork out here. "No thank you."

"You seem awful hungry. Sure you don't want meat? There's some on the lunch menu."

Joel scanned the lunchtime fare. "What's a walleye?"

"You're kiddin', right? You don't know 'bout walleye?" the waitress exclaimed.

"It's fish," John fumed. At this rate, he figured, only Joel would get served.

"OK, but how is it prepared?" Joel persisted.

"They drown it in a lake of lard, like everything else around here," John said.

The waitress glared at John. "You got complaints, I'll git my Daddy. He's the cook."

"I'm sure it's delicious." Joel flashed an ingratiating smile. "I'd love some."

The waitress took their orders, but again walked away without pouring John any coffee.

"So, am I gonna regret this, John?" Joel asked.

"Nah, it'll be all right," John said, though he expected *his* eggs to be overcooked and his toast burnt. "But, if you're worried, get the pork."

"Don't you like bacon, Joel?" Billy asked. He'd never met anyone who didn't love it.

Joel hesitated, doubting he could explain anything so complicated as Jewish dietary laws.

"I just wanted to try something I've never had before. Is walleye caught around here?"

"Right here on the Missouri. It's like trout, only bigger," John explained.

"Have you ever caught one?" Joel asked.

Butting in, Billy extended his arms as far as he could. "Sure! It was this big!"

John rolled his eyes. It was the one time their dad took them fishing—right before he got the polio. Twice they had one on the line, but couldn't reel 'em in. "You did not."

"Almost did." Billy poured sugar direct from the dispenser into his mouth and wondered what had happened to the "all for one and one for all" of last night's *Three Musketeers.*

The waitress returned with the carafe and topped off Joel's coffee—again ignoring John's gesture towards his empty cup.

"They're smart fish," Clarence interjected, "will snatch yer bait and not get hooked."

"Sounds like alotta guys I know," the waitress purred.

Joel looked over at Clarence and exchanged a knowing look.

"Mr. Williams, have you ever caught one?" Billy asked.

"Uh-huh. So has Clarence Jr.—a big one last summer."

"Oh!" Billy frowned, startled by Clarence's mention of his son, sparking memories of their fight at the base tryout and his mixed-up feelings afterwards.

"My mom doesn't like fish anyway. Says they stink up the kitchen."

Clarence didn't respond. It had slipped his mind that the brothers were Jennie's sons.

Deftly balancing plates on each arm, the waitress dealt out the four breakfasts. "Here ya are—three Guvners and one Pres . . . ah . . . den . . . tay." The waitress stared at Joel as he ate, then sashayed back to the kitchen once she caught his eye. Watching her, he had the odd feeling he was in a movie—cast as the hapless hero who loses his head over a truck stop dame.

John, noting the ballplayer's distraction, switched his empty cup with Joel's full one, figuring it was the only way he'd get any 'joe' in this joint.

The waitress returned with a bottle of ketchup. "Some folks like this with their fish."

"Thank you, miss . . . " Joel peered at her name tag as he slapped the bottle's bottom. "I have a question . . . Dottie. What would you recommend we do today in your beautiful Capital City?"

"I don't get off until after lunch," she said, her mouth curling into a saucy smile.

"Oh, no . . . well, that's too bad," Joel stammered, "but we leave town at noon. I mean—what can we do here that's fun for a couple of hours this morning?"

Dottie shot the four of them a doubtful look—her eyes lingering on Clarence. "Maybe somebody could take you out on the river."

"Could we rent fishing poles and fish for walleye?" Joel winked at Billy who stopped shoveling flapjacks, sensing that something mysterious was going on between Joel and the girl.

Dottie furrowed her brow. "Rent? Folks 'round here got their own poles."

"What do you think?" Joel looked at Clarence.

Clarence shrugged. "Might go down to the river—bet someone's rentin'."

Dottie slid Joel's check toward him, grazing the back of his hand with her fingernail.

"Bring back your catch and I'll cook it up for you real nice."

"Uh, sure," he said, swallowing hard as he paid the bill, adding a generous forty-cent tip.

Dottie pocketed the money and gave Joel a broad smile. "Guess you liked my walleye."

"Yes—my compliments to your father in the kitchen."

"Daddy—in the kitchen? He don't work here."

"What?" Joel asked. "I thought you said . . . ?"

Dottie shrugged. "More fun than tellin' you it's ma husband."

On the street Clarence clapped Joel on the back. "Gotta hand it to you, boy. That'd been me, I'da high-tailed it outta there. But you took your sweet time, finished them eggs, paid a visit to the necessary. That cook coulda slit your throat the way you was making time with his cooze."

Joel grinned. It felt good to have Clarence praise him—he was glad he'd stood up for him on the bridge. Though he suspected a proud man like Clarence would rather fight his own battles—not be championed in his absence by a white man. Still, he hoped they could be friends.

"Back in Brooklyn the guys who ran always got caught. The ones who played it cool got away with murder," Joel offered.

Clarence nodded solemnly as if Joel had quoted Scripture. "Same way everywhere."

Wide-eyed, Billy watched the two men and said a silent prayer. "Please, God, when I grow up, let me be as cool as them." Then, remembering the fight with Clarence Jr., he added, "And please don't let Mr. Williams hold that against me."

• • •

Stockman woke early, thinking about the bus and Lana—the one giving him a headache, the other a hard-on. Up late the night before, he partook of the burgers and striptease but skipped the sweet temptations of the 'dessert course'—foregoing a quick coupling with a dimpled blonde who appealed to him some. He just couldn't get his mind off Lana, feelings he'd not had in years. But could it last with him just passing through and her a married woman with a kid?

Suddenly he remembered—the bus! If it was still sidelined, they'd have to hire one, and hustle so the team could eat and have a full batting practice before the game. And so his starter, Joel Meznik, would have enough time to warm up properly for his Basin League debut.

Stockman gnawed at a callus on his thumb. What kind of guy was this Meznik character anyway? He'd never seen anything like that stunt on the bridge. Oh, sure, he'd stood up for a teammate, but defending a Negro you barely knew who wasn't even there to hear the slurs?

Guy called for a taxi to take him to the stadium. There he spotted the garrulous bus driver gabbing with two workmen in overalls. Guy wanted to call out to him but didn't know his name.

"Hey there, Chief. These fellas were just sayin' how they're gettin' TV here next month."

"Yep, it's true," said one of the mechanics in a mournful drawl. "Yankton's got TV, Sioux Falls's got TV, Rapid's got TV, even Aberdeen and Watertown got TV."

Stockman snorted, wondering if he was about to hear a list of every village and town in the state that got television before the Capital City. "How's the bus?" he interjected.

“Purrin’ like a stroked pussy. Just needed a plug.” The mechanics hooted their delight.

Stockman nodded, then settled-up and took a seat near the driver for the short jaunt back to the motel. “You know those guys? You were pretty chummy.”

The driver shrugged. “Just bein’ friendly, Chief. It’s the way folks are ’round here.”

Guy turned to the window as the bus crossed the Missouri. In the distance, three men and a boy floated in a rowboat—a red speck on the wide, brown river.

No, he wasn’t here to make friends with the locals. As Lana put it, he was just passing through. Being called ‘Chief suited him just fine.

Chapter Forty-Two

IT WASN'T UNTIL THE BUS reached Huron that Guy told Joel he would start. Instantly, Joel felt queasy, regretting that he'd taken Quarles' advice to "try the chicken fried, always good at a truck stop." To his surprise the dish wasn't chicken at all, but a gristly, gravy-smothered, low-grade slab of beef, fried in God knows what.

He knew he'd be nervous in any case, for nothing he'd ever done was like this—pitching against a lineup of pros—men who'd played in the high minors, even a couple in the Major Leagues—and star-studded collegians, certified professional prospects. Of course, he'd never pitched *for* such a talented team either and that made him nervous, too.

The rest of the Chiefs seemed loose and high spirited, reveling in their season-opening win and their wild night afterwards in Ft. Pierre. Stockman, feigning sleep, smiled under his Panama. For the very first time, he felt the stirrings of a team.

From the back, a plaintive drawl called out. "Hey, Coach. What'm ah gonna do—I gotta piss real bad!" Joel tensed. It was Darren Hoades, his antagonist. Guy tilted up the brim of his Panama and grinned. On every ball club he'd known, every winning one at least, there was always a jester, and clearly Hoades was making his bid for that role on the Chiefs.

"Just pinch it, man, squeeze it—we'll be there in five minutes."

Guy's josh produced a chorus of laughter, encouraging the Alabaman. Holding his crotch, Hoades stepped into the aisle. "Ah don't think ah kin make it, Coach. The piss is up to ma eyeballs . . . ma molars is havin' motorboat races." The Chiefs again broke into guffaws, and Billy, hearing grown-ups making pee-pee jokes, was beside himself with joy.

"Just hang it out the window, Hoades . . . it's long enough, ain't it?"

"Oh, you bet it is, Coach . . . it's long . . . like Ted Williams' bat."

"Long, like Ted Williams' bat?" chided Quarles. "Ain't what your whore told me last night in Pierre. Had a nickname for you, Hoades. Now, who's that plays shortstop for the Dodgers . . . *Pee Wee!* Yeah! That's it. Said she didn't want a Pee Wee at her wiener roast."

Darren didn't wait for the laughter to die down. "Very funny, Dickie *Queers*. Your whore said your weenie's so tiny you couldn't get arrested fer exposin' yerself." The Chiefs, including Quarles, hooted at Hoades' retort—but not Clarence, silent at the window, or Joel, who refused to grant even a smile.

When the bus reached the stadium, the Chiefs filed out, but Joel remained in his seat. His face pale, his legs beginning to shake, he tried to recall every fear he'd ever faced, every trial he'd ever met—attempting to draw from his shallow well of experience the few moments of triumph or glory that might replenish his evaporating self-confidence.

His biggest concern was the crowd. At Columbia he pitched before small gatherings of students and fans from the neighborhood—like dress rehearsals before an empty theater, he thought. But tonight, he'd be performing before a real, live audience, a noisy partisan one. He hoped it wouldn't rattle him and cause him to rush, because his delivery was a finely coordinated thing—an acceleration in place, a kind of muscular dance—more Gene Kelly than Fred Astaire. Anything disrupting that quickening flow, forcing him from his fragile groove, would be trouble.

In the bullpen before the game, he finally stopped shaking. Warming up, his fastball really popped, the sound echoing throughout the stadium. He'd never heard it so loud—like a gun going off or a car backfiring. It must be the adrenaline, he thought—that, and the way Guy caught the ball flush in the pocket with his hard, practiced hands. His catcher at Columbia wasn't so precise, often receiving the ball off-center, or quietly in the glove's trap.

And Guy caught or blocked every pitch. With a pro behind the plate, he felt free to throw his big curve, his twelve-to-sixer, which broke straight down, sometimes bouncing in the dirt.

Afterward, Guy told him what to expect. "I'll keep it simple. We're bringin' the heat—fastballs high and tight, fastballs low and away. Just rear back and throw the shit out of the ball." Joel eyes widened—his college coach could never have said that! "And forget your slider . . . it ain't workin'. I won't call for the curve 'cept when they ain't lookin' for it. And don't try to be cute. Don't shoot for the corners. Just keep it down." Then he made a cutting motion across his Adam's apple. "This is the cue for the brushback—chin music. That'll back 'em off the plate. One more thing." He said it slow, looking into Joel's eyes, "No . . . thinking . . . tonight."

Guy's talk calmed him. Taking the mound, he felt composed. It was familiar ground, a plot whose bounds and measures scarcely varied—a low hill with a gentle slope all around and a hard rubber slab marking its summit—a dirt circle in a grassy square, raised and lit like a stage, and framed on three sides by a grandstand, the familiar confines of a pitcher's domain.

Crouching to tighten his laces, Joel snuck a peek up at the crowd. It was the largest he'd ever played before, surely more than a thousand. Nearing twilight, the infield was in shadow, the outfield bathed in brilliant sunlight. Until sunset, batters would find it hard picking up the path of his pitches as they moved from light to shadow. For a time, he'd have the advantage.

"LEADING OFF FOR THE ELKS, NUMBER TWELVE, SECOND BASEMAN, ED BOWMAN."

The boom of the announcer jarred him from his unsanctioned thinking.

"Come on, Eddie, get it started," the home crowd cheered.

As Joel peered in for the sign, Guy spread two fingers against his crotch to signal for the curve, a big surprise. Joel took a deep breath. He'd hoped Guy would ask for the fastball, his best pitch, and a better release for the adrenaline rush he was feeling, but he couldn't shake off his catcher and manager. He'd follow his order, "No . . . thinking . . . tonight."

Feeling for a seam, Joel gave a slight nod to show that he'd gotten the signal, then delivered a big hook that broke across the center of home plate. "Stee . . . rye . . . ick!" the umpire brayed, throwing his right fist in the air. Shaking his head in surprise, the batter had taken the pitch. Stockman was right—when he called for the curve, the Elks wouldn't be looking for it.

The second pitch, a fastball, was thrown as hard as he could throw one. Delivered to the right spot, he believed it was unhittable, but riding out over home plate, it missed its target by more than a foot, and the batter reached out and served the ball into right. Turning to follow the hit, Joel watched as Frank Hacker got a late start, letting the ball get past him.

Elks fans rose from their seats as little Eddie raced around the bases while big Frank chased after the ball. Recovering it at the fence, he unleashed a mighty throw, carrying to third on one bounce, but too late to catch Eddie. Two pitches, and already a man on third. Joel slammed the ball into his glove. A decent outfielder would have made the catch.

Guy signaled for another fastball, and Joel fired the ball straight at the target, but Jerry Adair, the Elks' shortstop, slapped a grounder through the hole between first and second, scoring Bowman from third, giving the Elks a 1-0 lead.

Joel fumed. Richkas, the first baseman, had made no real effort on the ball and Hoades at second was slow to react, lunging at the grounder as it scooted past him. Joel wiped his sweaty hand on his shirt front. One run in, a man on first, and still no outs.

Then it all changed. Guy threw out Adair stealing second, and Kibbee ran down a long fly in left center. He'd made the catch look easy, but Joel thought it should have been Clarence's ball, then wondered if any outfielder as slow as Hacker or Clarence could ever make a good catch, let alone a great one. So what use were they if they let balls get by them, turning outs into triples? Might as well station the two elephants on their respective foul lines and deed over the entire outfield to the speedster, Kibbee. Then Joel realized what he'd been doing. Thinking.

"Stop it," he told himself. Just "throw the shit out of the ball."

And so he did, fanning the Elks' cleanup hitter on three fastballs to end the first inning.

Taking a seat in the dugout, Joel felt buoyant. Still, none of the Chiefs managed to get on base, and the inning ended with the Elks leading 1-0.

And so it went for six innings, as Andy Swota, the Elks' ace, served up a puzzling gumbo of curves, sliders, and screwballs, spiced with a 'something else', a pitch Joel had never seen before. Not a knuckleball floating and fluttering like a butterfly, but a mystery pitch masquerading as a fastball but dipping unpredictably at the end of its flight.

"You see the spit flying off it? Like Preacher Roe's," Quarles said, amused.

"What the hell!" Stockman exclaimed about the outlawed spitball. But when the umpire demanded the ball for inspection, the Elks' catcher nodded politely, then fumbled it into the dirt before giving it a good rub and handing it to the man in blue along with his apologies and a shit-eating grin. Recognizing the catcher's craft, Guy couldn't help but offer an admiring smirk.

With the Elks holding a scant 1-0 lead through six, Joel supposed that someone who'd heard only the score might think that he and Swota were locked in a pitchers' duel. But in truth, Swota had continued to baffle the Chiefs, while the Elks were figuring *him* out—passing up his unreliable curve and waiting for his straight fastball, which by their third time up, they'd learned to time. Joel tugged at his cap and took a deep breath. His legs were losing their life and he knew why—his fitful night on the floor of the bus and his morning spent fishing on the broiling Missouri. Under Clarence's tutelage, he and Billy each caught a walleye, which Clarence gutted with a switchblade pulled from his back pocket. Then they'd built a driftwood fire and ate the roasted fish with their fingers. He'd never done anything like it and wouldn't have missed it for the world, but now he worried that it might cost him his first chance to shine with his new team.

Then, with two out in the seventh, he surrendered back-to-back singles and a walk to load the bases. The next batter blasted a fastball up the gap into right center. Joel's heart sank. If the ball dropped it would clear the bases and give the Elks a decisive 4-0 lead. Only Kibbee had any real chance for it, but as Joel tracked the ball's flight, he feared that not even the Chiefs' fleet center fielder could catch up to it. He figured the game was pretty much lost right there.

And then, Kibbee caught it. With a burst of speed and a desperate lunge along the grass, he'd snagged the monster fly mere inches from the ground. The hometown crowd, after a groan, acknowledged the feat with scattered applause.

Steadied by Clyde's heroics, Joel believed he could still win, but in the top of the eighth, the Chiefs' bats remained stubbornly silent. The night before, they'd handed George Schmid three runs to work with before he even set foot on the mound. Joel wondered if there was something about himself that failed to spark his teammates. All game long, no one spoke to him except Quarles, saying "Atta boy Joely. Lookin' good out there," and Stockman, barking, "Get the curveball down," and later, "Pick up the pace, boy, you're putting your infield to sleep."

Only two more innings—six outs—and his night would be done. But did he have enough gas left in the tank? A fastball, his first pitch in the eighth, was hammered like a bullet. It was the best fastball he could muster at the moment, but it was creamed—though Kibbee, continuing to shine, knew just where to station himself and gathered it in. The next batter then ripped a blistering grounder over the bag at third. Paskiewicz, playing deep, made a diving stop and, jackknifing to his feet, fired the ball across the diamond to nip the batter by a step.

At least, his teammates were picking him up in the field, and he had only one more out to get. Joel took a deep breath. What he needed now was a skinny little Princeton shortstop, a Classics major, say, who couldn't hit his way out of a book bag.

Instead, he got slugger Verne McKee, who'd already delivered two hits in his previous at bats. Working the count full, McKee fouled a fastball into Guy's mitt. If he'd held it, it would have been strike three and the final out in the eighth. But undercut by a vicious swing, the ball spun with wicked English and Guy dropped it. Joel didn't fault him. No catcher could count on holding a foul tip. Like catching a bee in your bare hands, someone once said.

Given life by the dropped third strike, McKee crushed a double off the wall in right. Then a liner past Joel's ear advanced McKee to third, bringing the crowd to its feet, screaming "Let's go Elks!" As rowdy first-rowers stood and pressed themselves against the chain-link backstop, Joel felt like an animal in a cage. Then he saw Andy Swota, the Elks' pitcher and number nine hitter, approach the batter's box—the very man he most wanted to see at that moment—his own little Princeton shortstop.

Joel breathed a sigh of relief. He'd ring up Swota, and that would take care of the eighth. Guy's sign was for a high inside fastball, his bread and butter all night. The pitch was straight to the target, but the umpire called "Ball one!" Peeved, he toed the rubber and fired another fastball. Slipping a bit in his moist fingers, the pitch faded, but he believed it caught the outside corner. "Ball two!" the umpire cried.

Removing his hat, Joel ran his sleeve across his forehead. On the dugout steps, an Elks player hollered, "Hey brillo head, they call that a strike in New York?"

'Brillo head'? 'New York'? A double-edged gibe, but only the epithet hurt. He suddenly felt dizzy. Was that what he looked like to these people? A white Negro, or a Jew?

His third offering was a waist-high fastball over the middle of the plate, and Swota failed to check his swing. Either way, it had to be a strike, but the umpire roared, "Ball three!"

Infuriated by the call and the 3-0 count on the hapless Swota, Joel stomped forward and swung his glove hand in a boxer's roundhouse to take Guy's return throw. The hot-headed gesture brought a round of catcalls from the Elks' dugout and a coarse growl from the crowd.

To catch his breath, he called for a fresh baseball. Unmarked and smooth, the new ball was harder to grip than the last. Turning to the resin bag, he hoped the fine yellow dust would absorb the sweat in his hand and give him a grip. It was no use. His curveball was gone.

Joel's fourth offering to Swota sailed high and wide of the strike zone. Ball four. Guy had to leap from his crouch to save a wild pitch. The umpire waved Swota to first, loading the bases.

The hometown crowd responded with a roar, while a chorus of Elks bench jockeys moved to the top steps of the dugout. Flanked on three sides by a thousand fiery throats, Joel dropped to a squat, hands on knees, eyes turned to the ground.

Signaling for time, Guy walked slowly out to the mound. "Listen kid, ya got two outs and they haven't scored. I don't give a shit about the crowd. I don't give a rusty fuck about the umpire. I don't wanna see temper out here. Just focus on the mitt and fire the ball."

Joel nodded. He'd give it everything he had, hoping his teammates would help. But he couldn't help thinking that Swota never could have hit his way on base, and now, with the bases loaded, he'd face the top of the Elks' batting order again. They'd seen all he had to offer, and with his curveball gone AWOL, what had been a guessing game of fastball or curve became the much simpler game of see the ball, hit the ball. Pow! Pow! Pow! Like cannon fire on the Brooklyn Parade Grounds—five more runs plated before he ended the inning on a groundout.

In the top of the ninth, Guy tried to rally his team, but only Hoades delivered, lining a double to right before Kibbee struck out and Hacker skyed to center to end the game.

Joel had lost his first start. It was the team's first loss too, and that made it hurt more. He was surprised that Stockman said nothing to him afterwards and sent Quarles instead. On the walk to the bus, Q offered a bit of wisdom. "Joely, in baseball, yer gonna have good days and bad. Put this one behind you and get ready for your next start. You have every physical gift of a big-time pitcher. You just gotta work on your head. And we'll find you a better breaking ball."

On the bus, Joel pressed an icy Coke against his aching shoulder and stared into the darkness. From conversations he couldn't quite make out, he imagined teammates blamed him for the loss and for Stockman's pronouncement banning beer on the long bus ride home. Was Coach signaling that they'd all had a hand in it? Joel doubted that anyone saw it that way—even Clarence, who passed by without a word on the way to his seat. And John Moran averted his eyes when he boarded, though Joel couldn't say what he expected of him—not a teammate and not yet a friend.

Joel sighed. At a time like this it would be nice to have a friend.

Only Billy, with his brother asleep, cast his lot with Joel, crossing the aisle and taking the seat beside him.

Chapter Forty-Three

"WHERE YA GOING, JOEL?" John asked when the pitcher followed the brothers off the bus at their stop on Evergreen Street. For a moment John thought that Billy had offered to put the ballplayer up for the night, something he knew their mother would not allow.

"I'm bunking next door with the Rosens," Joel said, slinging his duffel over his shoulder.

Without a word, John turned and went straight to bed, but unlike Billy, who collapsed the moment he hit the mattress, he found it impossible to sleep. The thought of Joel living next door, and maybe even sleeping in a bedroom down the hall from Dinah, was simply too much to bear. How could he possibly compete with a college grad, star athlete, and handsome Jew planning to be a doctor? It was easy to imagine Joel taking her back East with him at the end of the summer—not to Yale's New Haven, but to glamorous New York City.

He was out the door before breakfast, disappointing James who was hoping for a full account of the road trip from his cub-reporter son. "Gotta get the photos to Paddy," John wrote in a note, determined to avoid seeing Dinah and Joel together next door.

As soon as Billy woke, he raced outside to see if Joel was up, and that's when he saw it.

Dinah's new yellow Skyliner convertible gleaming like a gold brick in the morning sun. Billy ran back to the kitchen where his dad was reading the Sports Section. "When did they get *that* car?"

"Yesterday. Dinah must have passed her road test. So, how was the trip?" James patted the back of the chair next to him. "Grab a seat, Son, and tell me all about it."

James sighed as Billy darted out the door to circle the incandescent car. Spotting the boy from the window, Bernie strode out to greet him. "Snazzy, huh?"

"Better than the T-Bird! Bet it's fast!"

"Not really. The T-Bird's the hare, but a pretty turtle's better for Dinah up in the hills."

Billy ran a hand along the car's golden flank. "What's she doin'up there?"

"She's working at the Mellerdrammer. With a school chum of yours. Glen Merritt."

"Glen?" Billy's heart sank.

"Yeah. Dinah drives him."

"In the Skyliner?" Billy practically wailed.

"Yes, Bill. It's her car."

"Every day?"

Bernie frowned. The conversation was beginning to irritate him. "So, how was the trip?" Bernie asked. "Havin' fun as batboy?"

Billy shrugged, and Bernie started back towards the house shaking his head. He expected more from Billy, especially since he'd given him the job. "OK, kid."

Billy trudged up Evergreen, muttering to himself. Finally, he let loose. "Damn you, Glen Merritt!" Collapsing to the curb, he sat knees to chin. He'd lost Dinah to his arch enemy. Not that he ever expected to be her boyfriend—he knew he was too young—but she'd been his in a secret way, and now she belonged to Glen—seeing her every day, sitting next to her in the car, close enough to even touch her sometimes. The thought of it made his chest ache.

Just then, James' Chevy pulled up to the curb. "You ran out so fast, I didn't get to tell you. You got a ball game this afternoon at the schoolyard. And tonight's the home opener at Sioux Park. What a great summer. Baseball—morning, noon, and night."

Baseball? What did it matter now that Glen was in the Mellerdrammer and wouldn't be around for him to strike out? He'd learned the curve for nothing.

On the ride home, Billy averted his eyes as they passed the Merritt house. Glen with Dinah. What a summer, he thought to himself. What a sucky summer.

Chapter Forty-Four

CHERRY MAE DROPPED CLARENCE AT the ballfield before heading for Rapid's public library.

Clarence Jr. grumbled, "I don't wanna go to no library. Why can't I come to practice with you?"

"The game don't start for three hours. There'd be nothing for you to do."

"I can watch you warm up."

Clarence felt his jaw tighten. He never intended to bring his family to the home opener. But the base commander had practically ordered him to take them, saying it was good for "town-base relations." Still, he worried. What if they were the only Negro family there? People might stare and point, or worse. To bigots like Hoades they'd be like crows on snow. If that cracker said anything about his wife or his kids, there'd be no holding back.

And he needed to get loose without worry or distraction. He didn't think Billy Moran would pick another fight, but his own son might be looking to get even. During the game, his boy wouldn't have the opportunity, but beforehand, in an empty stadium, he might.

"You've seen me warm up plenty of times. You better off readin' a book."

Cherry Mae parked across from the pink sandstone building with ***PVBLIC LIBRARY*** carved above the columned entrance. She'd not been in a library since leaving Indianapolis. Clarence Jr. wasn't much of a reader and Violet brought books home from school—tales of pasty-faced blondes and freckled redheads in pinafores and sailor suits and girls with names like Pippi and Beezus, sounding like they might be colored, but never were. Once, thumbing through *The Bobbsey Twins in the Country*, Cherry Mae came upon a line that stopped her cold—a Negro maid saying she'd hoe the corn, then "steal de watermelons."

It had been that way for her as a child too, reading about beautiful white princesses and Little Black Sambo and Little Brown Koko with his "flat brown nose" and "big fat black Mammy." Back then she hadn't thought anything of it. That was just how colored people were portrayed in books and movies—lazy, silly, shiftless, sneaky—with thick ruby lips and bug eyes, or in whiteface, like clowns. It wasn't until she was a teenager at all-Black Crispus Attucks High School that she began to question what she was given to read.

"Why we only read about white folks' troubles?" she complained to a friend about Upton Sinclair's *The Jungle*. She was shocked when her teacher, a bespectacled young graduate of Ohio's all-Black Wilberforce University, took her aside and handed her a book called *Native Son*.

"Richard Wright, the author, is a Negro, and the book concerns a Negro and . . . " she added, with a sly smile " . . . *his* troubles."

But her preacher father made her give it back. "Tell your teacher not to be giving you any more agitatin' books puttin' colored people in a bad light."

"But Daddy," Cherry Mae protested, "it's written by a Negro." Then she pointed to the book's cover and it's Book of the Month Club stamp. "Ain't that a white people's club?"

"Colored boy kills a white woman? How's that good for our people? A Negro writer should know how things get twisted. We've got to show we're good Christians, no matter our station. White folk, even the nice ones, don't like us to get uppity. Don't you ever forget that."

She returned the book the next day. "I liked it—what I read, but my daddy didn't approve."

In truth, the book frightened her. Especially when Bigger Thomas said white folks owned the world and that they filled his chest and throat "like fire" so he couldn't breathe.

She'd had those feelings, too, at times—though never that strong. But from then on, Bigger's words came back to her whenever she ventured into the white world of Indianapolis, away from the familiar streets of the segregated north side. And sometimes now in Rapid with saleswomen, the few times she came into town to shop.

"I don't see why I couldn't watch Daddy," Clarence Jr. persisted. "That white boy, Billy Moran—bet he gets to do everything. His Daddy's not even on the team."

Cherry Mae didn't know what to say. This is how it happens—you let your children mix in the white world and soon enough they learn who runs the show.

Mounting the library steps, Clarence Jr. made a game of it—darting up, then leaping down—while Violet climbed slowly, her arms folded tight against her chest. Cherry Mae reckoned that her daughter's tender breasts, budding just that spring, were the reason.

Cherry Mae clucked her tongue. It was hard to believe that her baby girl was already knocking at the door of womanhood. She felt a pang of envy, like when she passed new mothers on the street pushing prams. She didn't know why there'd been no more babies after Vi when there'd been plenty of baby-making fun. She thought by now she'd have at least four kids, maybe even half a dozen, like her mother and two of her sisters. And a proper house, too—not a trailer on the barren Dakota plains, far from home.

Clarence Sr. comforted her when she fretted about being struck barren. "I love our little brood," he'd say, adding, "Why we need more than two? We don't have a farm."

Neither suspected that he was the one who'd put an end to his wife's fruitfulness. Treated for the clap on a road trip with the Clowns, his 'drip' had cleared, and afterwards he'd always been faithful, but she'd already caught it on an earlier furlough home. The assault was silent, the damage irreversible. She could never bear another child.

Clarence Jr. slid down the railing then bounded back up the stairs to do a cartwheel on the landing. Cherry Mae scowled. She questioned her husband's plan to kill time here when he wasn't around to help. She hoped the librarian would be like the boy's teacher, Mrs. Moran—stern but kind and able to harness his boundless energy, or at least, help keep him occupied.

Violet, she knew, would not be a problem. In the trailer, she'd while away the hours reading books and paging through Cherry Mae's *Jet* magazines, a subscription her sisters had bought her for Christmas. "So you won't have to look in the mirror to see another colored woman out there in Dakotee," they wrote in the card.

Cherry Mae loved the pocket-sized tabloid—a potlatch of celebrity gossip, photos, and lurid articles, like "White Film Producer Denies Fathering Negro Extra's Baby." Serious news, too—bus boycotts and lunch counter sit-ins—brave Negroes standing up for their race. Accounts that thrilled her but alarmed her, too, though less so than Bigger Thomas, because these heroes were always proper—the Reverend King, resolute yet calm in church-suit and tie, and Rosa Parks, steadfast and serene in somber skirt and prim hat—at peace, like a Christian martyr. She couldn't imagine herself ever being so composed while saying "No!" in the white man's world.

Violet's favorite *Jet* feature was 'Beauty of the Week', a contest open to anyone sending in a photo of herself in a bathing suit. Violet would line up the photos of the weekly winners, her eyes brightening at the sight of the stunning Negro women. "They're so pretty," she'd gush. But once, she held the winner's face next to her own dark hand, and Cherry Mae knew just what she was thinking. Watching Violet's eyes dart between hand and picture, she feared she'd done the wrong thing, bringing this feature, with so many 'high yeller' beauties, to her daughter's mind.

Then, a week ago, Clarence came home to find Violet sitting on the floor looking at an article captioned, *White Mother Calls Negro Children Embarrassing.* Snatching the magazine from her hand, he scanned the story of a white woman who put her Negro children up for adoption after marrying a white man and bearing his child.

"What you givin' this child to read?" he yelled at Cherry Mae.

"I didn't give it to her. She musta found it on the bed stand."

"It don't belong in this house," he bellowed. "Bad enough *you* read this trash."

Cherry Mae jabbed the spatula at her husband's chest. "Don't you go actin' all high and mighty. I know you read it in the morning when you do your business."

Clarence gave a snort. With a sharp-eyed wife and a small trailer, it was hard to get away with anything. "I'm a grown-up. This is nothing a colored child should be reading."

Cherry Mae grabbed the magazine from his hand and skimmed the article, her face clouding over as she reached the final line, "*She played with her two Negro children outside the courtroom but left without a backward glance at them after the ruling.*"

"Well . . . " she murmured , almost like a prayer. "She can't know what it means."

Violet scowled and looked up at her parents, hovering above her like sheltering trees.

"I do *so*," she insisted, banging her thigh with a balled-up fist. "But why do that white woman have colored children? Did the stork make a mistake?"

Clarence and Cherry Mae gaped in shocked silence, then burst out laughing. Violet's face broke into a wide grin. She had no idea why her question had cleared away the storm clouds but was glad to have provided the happy wind that did it.

Later, Cherry Mae hid the *Jets* at the back of the bedroom closet. Now, she wondered if Clarence had picked the library as a rebuke.

"Tuck in your shirt, Clarence," she ordered as she patted her own hair in place.

Suddenly, she felt the fire in her chest and wished her husband had not left her with only Bigger Thomas's words to face the white world inside. Yanking open the library door, she grabbed the childrens' hands—as much to steady herself as to guide them.

Ida Moss, Head Librarian for forty years, stood behind the circulation desk, watching the family approach. Tall and big-boned with long, yellow buckteeth, she'd never been much for smiling. Yet, even with perfect teeth, she would not have greeted the Williams family with a smile. That was for salesmen and supper club hostesses, not for the guardian of the library. The fact that Cherry Mae and her children were Negroes was irrelevant. Whites, Indians, and Negroes from the airbase were all met with the same forbidding countenance.

Cherry Mae approached the desk, tilting her head to the side so as not to face the cheerless librarian straight on. "Afternoon, ma'am."

"Good afternoon." Miss Moss responded, observing that all three were suitably dressed for town and all had beautiful straight white teeth.

"My children and I would like to pass some time in your library, if that's all right."

Miss Moss was surprised by the request for permission, then supposed that they came from the South, where libraries might still be segregated. "Of course. This is the Public Library."

Violet raised her hand and Miss Moss nodded in her direction, amused that the child had mistaken her for a teacher. "How come it's spelled with a 'V', Violet asked, pointing in the direction of the door. "Outside. Ain't it supposed to be a 'U'?"

Cherry Mae stiffened. The girl could be cheeky, and she never could tell how people would take her. She was relieved to see a smile flitting at the corner of the librarian's mouth.

"It's the traditional way of representing the letter 'U' when carving in stone. Seen on older buildings, it's called a convention and reminds us of how things were done in the past."

"But how do you say it? PVBLIC?" Violet made a cartoonish "pffv" sound, puffing up her cheeks. Clarence Jr. burst out laughing and gave his sister a jab.

Miss Moss jerked her head in his direction, as Cherry Mae snagged his hand.

"No. It's still pronounced 'public,'" Miss Moss explained.

"Why?" Violet persisted and Cherry Mae gave her daughter's hand a thwartive squeeze.

Miss Moss frowned, feeling the strain of conversation with this lively young girl. Raising her hand to signal the end of the discussion, she pointed to a wall of books at the back of the room. "That is the children's section." She did not disclose where the periodicals or adult fiction were located, expecting the mother to remain with her children—the bright, bothersome girl and the rambunctious boy who'd likely require close minding.

"Thank you, ma'am." Still holding her children's hands, Cherry Mae steered them as directed. Suddenly, Clarence Jr. let out a shout, which turned the heads of readers and propelled Miss Moss across the room, an admonishing finger pressed to her lips.

"Look! It's Daddy!"

And there he was, in the Chiefs' team photo on a small oak table in the center of the room. Miss Moss had worked long into the night on the display celebrating the *Chiefs'* home opener with books devoted to baseball, including *The Jackie Robinson Story*, and magazines with ballplayers on their covers—Willie Mays on *Look*, Mickey Mantle on *Life*, and Roy Campanella and a smiling Jackie, his head popping out of a cluster of oversized baseballs on *Time*.

At the Town Meeting, she'd spoken in favor of the Bond, surprising many that the elderly librarian cared at all about baseball. They didn't know that her brothers had played on the Sturgis town team and both had died in the Great War, along with the team's gangly first baseman, who'd made it his mission to get her to smile for him. She finally did on the night he shipped out, and was rewarded with a kiss—her first, and the only one she was ever to receive, a memory Miss Moss conjured every night, dreaming that the ballplayer had come home to her.

"You are Clarence Williams' family," she pronounced, her eyes softening and the corners of her mouth rising slightly, changes that did not go unnoticed by Cherry Mae.

"He's my Daddy," Clarence Jr. said proudly, and Violet piped up, "Mine, too."

"You must be excited about tonight's game."

Clarence Jr. beamed. "You goin', too?"

"Well . . . yes . . . I am."

Cherry Mae studied the collection of books and magazines on the table. She never knew there was so much written about baseball. About Negro ball players, too. "Are they for reading?"

Miss Moss hesitated. She'd conceived it more as an exhibit. *Look but don't touch.*

"Um, yes, of course."

Cherry Mae picked up the book about Jackie Robinson and all the magazines with Negro players on their covers and handed them to her son. "Now sit yourself down and look at them."

Miss Moss's face fell as she viewed the dismantling of her shrine. "There are several young adult books about sports in the children's section which might be more suitable."

Cherry Mae looked at the librarian. She wanted to ask if those books were about Negro players but couldn't imagine saying the word "Negro" or "colored" to a white person.

"Thank you. These are fine. They got pictures, don't they?"

"Yes, but you could get a library card and check out those other books."

Suddenly, Cherry Mae realized Violet was no longer with them. Whipping around, she spotted her sitting at a wooden table in the back of the children's section, absorbed in a book.

"I'll make sure he returns these," Cherry Mae said, hurrying to her daughter.

Violet looked up, her eyes bright with delight. "Look, Momma. They got a new Pippi Longstocking book." She held it out for her mother to see. On the cover was a drawing of a mirthful white girl swinging from a tree limb under the title, *Pippi and the South Sea*. Cherry Mae nodded. She knew her daughter would not want to read about Negro ballplayers, so this would have to do.

"There are colored people in it, Momma. And they're not wearing shirts!"

Alarmed, Cherry Mae took the book and riffled through the pages until she found the illustration—a drawing of wide-eyed, topless natives with thick lips and kinky hair, bowing before Pippi and a fat white king, both seated on thrones, and both fully dressed.

Cherry Mae swallowed hard before scanning the text, while Violet stood on tiptoe and read silently along with her mother.

Violet laughed. "It's funny. Pippi is funny."

Cherry Mae studied the picture, struggling to find something to say.

"What's wrong, Momma? Don't you think it's funny?"

"It sure is . . . funny," she finally replied, holding tight to the book.

Violet put her hand on its cloth spine and gave it a tug. "Momma! I was reading it!"

Cherry Mae resisted then relinquished the book to her daughter. "Read it quick. We're leaving soon." Violet looked downcast, then brightened. "Can't we take it home, like at school?"

Cherry Mae could easily imagine her husband coming across the offensive illustration and the fight that was sure to follow. "No! Read it here!"

Cherry Mae began circling the room. So many books. Was there nothing here her daughter could safely read? Again, Cherry Mae found herself at the checkout desk.

"Excuse me, ma'am. I was wondering if you had a certain book. It's for me."

"Did you check the card catalogue?" Miss Moss asked, impatient now with this family, which had taken so much of her time and plundered her display.

Cherry Mae had a vague notion of what Miss Moss was talking about, but she'd not used one since high school. "Oh! Where would that be?" she asked, eyes darting around the room.

Realizing it would take Mrs. Williams farther from her children, Miss Moss waved her hand to dismiss the question. "What is the name of the book?"

"*Native Son*, but I don't recollect who wrote it."

Miss Moss frowned, recalling the story; a kindly young white woman smothered to death by an angry Negro and a Communist-inspired defense of the crime. "Yes. I remember the title. We may have had it once, a long time ago, but not now," she added, a decided edge to her voice.

"It was the Book of the Month," Cherry Mae pressed, though she wasn't sure why.

Miss Moss knew that. Outraged by the content, she'd written a letter to Clifton Fadiman and the Panel of Judges to protest the book's selection. "If I recall, that was a long time ago."

"Back in forty," Cherry Mae said, remembering her teacher and father, and the vortex that had roiled her after merely dipping a toe in the book's swirling currents.

Miss Moss narrowed her eyes. Why was the woman so intent on reading a book like that?

"You sure you don't have it?" Cherry Mae pushed.

Taken aback by the woman's insistence, the librarian assumed a softer tone.

"A long time ago, but much has changed since then, don't you agree, Mrs. Williams?"

To Cherry Mae's ears, the librarian's words were oddly singsong, like the lilting croon her Aunt Rayna summoned when calming her simple-minded son.

Cherry Mae looked straight at Miss Moss's unsightly mouth—the white woman's words blazing in her ears, her own raging hot in the pit of her throat.

"No ma'am.. No! I cannot say it be so."

Chapter Forty-Five

SEEING THE NEW STADIUM FOR the first time, Joel was less concerned with its features than the position of the setting sun in the western sky. It was late Friday afternoon, and he was about to spend the Jewish Sabbath, his first since leaving New York, in a ballpark, not a synagogue, which he'd learned from the phone book did not exist in Rapid City.

In truth, he'd already lost track of the days. The only reason he knew it was Friday—Erev Shabbos—was that he'd finally unpacked his duffel and discovered his tefillin—two small leather boxes, each containing a tiny scroll of Biblical verse—along with this note from his father: "It will be difficult to follow all the Commandments, but this one I know you can keep."

Sitting on the edge of his bed, Joel had cupped the twin boxes in his hands, letting the leather bands slip through his fingers. Every morning since his Bar Mitzvah, he'd strap on the boxes—the shel rosh to his forehead, the shel yad to his left arm next to his heart—and pray before leaving for school. Identical cubes, each the size of a ring box, they were reminders that God and his teachings should never be far from his mind and heart and that he was now a full-fledged member of the Jewish community, able to participate in all the rituals of the faith.

And yet, when it came time to pack for Dakota, he purposely left them in a drawer, only to be discovered by his father and slipped into his gear with the admonishing note.

Joel shook his head. Did his father expect him to don them in a motel room shared with Gentiles? How shocked he'd be to know how far he'd already fallen. First, the forsaken yarmulke, then the food he'd eaten on the road, perhaps fried in bacon grease, or prepared where milk and meat had been mixed, rendering it *trafe*—unkosher, unclean.

Cradling the sacred boxes in his hands, the history of his people broke over him like a wave—all the prejudice and persecution they'd endured for thousands of years, and the extreme measures taken to stay true to the rites and Commandments.

Now, as he headed for the Chiefs' dugout the sun was still high above the ridgeline of the Black Hills. It was 5 p.m., three hours at most until sundown, when he might again break the Fourth Commandment: "Remember the Sabbath Day to keep it Holy."

He furrowed his brow. His limitations had been mostly manageable at Columbia. There everyone understood that he was an observant Jew, not a creature from an alien planet. But he couldn't ask Coach Stockman to tailor the rotation so he'd never pitch on Shabbos, which began at sundown on Friday. And Coach wanted him to keep the 'book' which he shouldn't do either. Pitching and a task like scorekeeping were deemed work and thus forbidden on the Sabbath.

At least there was no chance he'd be called on to pitch tonight after his disappointing debut in Huron the night before.

Just then the wind shifted, carrying with it the smell of fresh popcorn from the concession stand. Joel's stomach growled. In Brooklyn, the sun would have already set on his home and family. Pivoting, he fixed his eyes on the dusky silhouette of the Black Hills to the west, where the sun held a longer lease on time. He could buy himself a bag of popcorn and a Coke before sundown. That, he told himself, would surely be kosher enough.

. . .

Jennie was alone in the concession stand waiting for James to return with ice. The stadium wasn't open yet, but already a few ballplayers had dropped by for something to eat, and James had told her they should be served. "Who knows how many customers we'll get tonight." Jennie agreed for a different reason. She wanted to be open in case Clarence Williams came by.

Looking up, she saw a tall, well-built Chief approaching the Stand. "May I help you?"

Joel flashed a smile. He recalled now that she was Billy and John's mother and was eager to meet her. "Hello, Mrs. Moran. I'm Joel Meznik. I met your sons on the trip to Pierre."

Jennie gave a start. The young man had an accent like Bernie Rosen's, and with his dark hair and olive complexion, looked a bit like him, too.

"I'm staying next door with the Rosens," Joel continued.

"What can I get you?" she asked curtly.

Joel was puzzled. Billy was friendly and outgoing, but his mother seemed grim and forbidding. Frosty, like John when they first met. Then Joel recalled that he was the reason Billy ended up sleeping on the bus in Pierre. Perhaps she knew about that and hadn't approved.

"I'm sorry. I'm sure you have plenty to do. I'd like a Hershey bar and a Coke, please."

"The Coke's not cold."

"Do you have seltzer? I mean fizzy water. I can drink that warm." Joel felt a pang recalling the blue spritzer bottles delivered weekly to their Brooklyn apartment. His father, in a rare moment of levity, had dubbed it *Jewish champagne*. "And a popcorn, please, if it's ready."

Without a word, Jennie drew him a small cup and grabbed a candy bar and a box of corn. "Forty cents," she said, charging him the same for plain soda water as for a cola.

Joel reached into his pocket for two quarters, all the money he'd brought with him because of the Sabbath. After sundown, he'd no longer be allowed to carry cash or coin, which raised the matter of the dime he'd get back as change. He decided that leaving a tip would take care of the problem. "Thank you, Mrs. Moran. Please keep the change."

Jennie pressed her lips together. She was a merchant, not a waitress. Staring at the dime for a long moment, she dropped it in the cash drawer then turned her back to the counter.

"It was nice meeting you," Joel said in a last stab at comity, but Jennie didn't respond.

This was not the ballplayer she had hoped to see.

And any friend of the Rosens was no friend of hers.

Chapter Forty-Six

MANAGER GUY STOCKMAN ARRIVED EARLY at Sioux Park Stadium. He needed to walk the field before his players arrived—map out the slick spots from last night's rain and gauge the sun angles for the early innings of the game. For tonight was his Chiefs' home opener and opening night for the new ballpark, too. How would they play, he wondered. How would *it* play?

Minutes earlier, lost in thought, he'd almost missed the turnoff. From the passing motorway there was little to suggest a stadium—only the tips of the light towers rising above the low-lying field and the wooden fence, revealing but a glimpse of the ball grounds within.

Guy had to laugh. It took a lot of gall to call this a stadium. For starters, it had no clubhouse, no locker rooms for the players and umpires, and no bleachers or grandstand. It was merely an open-air ballpark with rows and rows of wooden benches hugging the prairie ground. At least every seat was a good one. Every fan would sit near the infield with a close, unobstructed view of the diamond, where baseball's action begins.

Then Guy heard the faint strains of Sousa and spied a pack of pretty girls on horseback, American flags holstered in their saddles, stepping their ponies through a rehearsal for the evening's color guard. Straight out of small-town America! It felt grand to be part of it—still playing the game he'd learned as a boy when his father first tossed him a baseball outside the Bethlehem Steel Works in Johnstown, PA.

Guy charged down the hill towards the field. There might be nothing grand about this new Stadium, but he knew it wouldn't matter if his team played well. For if the action was good—thrilling in the way only baseball can be—Rapid's fans would catch the 'fever' and, together with his Chiefs, transform this plain little prairie ballpark into the grandest in the land.

• • •

James did a quick count of the wieners. Everywhere he went that week, the size of the opening night crowd was a matter of speculation. James hoped for fifteen hundred, the regular turnout at high school basketball games, but because of the bond failure, he feared the gate wouldn't break a thousand. In his dreams, he envisioned a big, hungry crowd, drinking his beer, eating his wieners, cheering his Chiefs, laughing, maybe getting a little drunk, like a raucous yard party, the kind he'd longed for but knew Jennie would never let him have.

Boldly, Bernie had predicted a crowd of two thousand. James wasn't persuaded, but he had to prepare for the boss's number and so he set about stocking the little stand with every wiener and bun, every bottle of beer and box of candy he could cram into it. Already, it was so jammed with inventory that he found it hard to squeeze his ample girth past the stacked boxes to the coffee maker or soda dispenser or the electric hot plate with its pot of boiling wieners.

James's throat tightened. If the crowd were small, what would happen to his wieners? He knew he'd have to dump them and that he, not Bernie Rosen, would suffer the loss. His mind reeled. Yes, he wanted the Chiefs to win, but more important, they had to out-compete the other attractions in the area that night—the Rapid Valley Speedway and the Black Hills Dog Track, the town's two supper clubs, the picture shows downtown showing respectable movies, and the passion-pit drive-ins on the outskirts luring customers with tawdry come-ons like *Female on the Beach* and its sensational ad, "She was too hungry for love to care where she found it!"

And the carnival at the County Fairgrounds and Dinah Rosen's Mellerdrammer, along with the Black Hills Playhouse in Custer State Park and the lighting ceremony at Mount Rushmore, a powerful magnet for tourists and local folk alike. With all that going on, who would go to a ball game? As an ex-coach, he knew that a team could bring a town together, but that was when it was made up of its own young men. Could folks feel the same way about a squad of imported strangers?

And then, dark clouds rolled in, casting the field in shadow. He'd forgotten about the weather. What if a hailstorm struck, or the game got rained out? Even that threat could keep people away from an outdoor event, especially farm folk coming from afar. He shivered as if a cold front had set in. "What will happen to me" he wondered. "Who will buy my thawing wieners?"

• • •

Billy was awestruck. Just weeks before, Sioux Park Stadium was little more than two acres of dirt with stakes and strings marking its boundaries and two mud holes where the dugouts would go. Now he beheld a finished ballpark with a great green outfield, and a perfect grass infield ruled in chalk, and eight soaring light towers. It all happened so fast it seemed like magic.

Billy lifted his eyes beyond the fence to a grove of cottonwood lining the swift little stream that had given Rapid City its name. He had never seen Rapid Creek from this height before but recognized at once the spot where he and Glen, when they were still friends, swung from a rope, plunging naked into its chilly waters on blistering summer afternoons, and hunted for arrowheads in the little meadow now transformed into this ballfield.

His chest tightened. He'd never imagined that the opening of a wonderful new stadium could mean the closing of a place and a time he once loved.

• • •

"I did it," Bernie shouted as he pounded the Caddy's steering wheel. Created a team and built a ballpark—christened "one of the state's finest" by the *Rapid City Journal*. It wasn't easy. Every promotion he came up with had failed—speakers bureau, radio-TV telethon, rally at the City Auditorium, appeals to civic pride, cash solicitations in exchange for good citizen pins. And finally, in desperation, a Postcard Campaign utilizing schoolchildren. Nothing worked. Despite his rousing speech at the Town Meeting, Rapid's voters had failed him. Bernie's teeth clenched. Maybe he and Carl were the problem, a Jewish nightclub owner and a beer salesman trying to exact tithings from a town of good Christians.

Still, he had gotten it done—built a ballpark without building much of anything. The wooden sheds, the grandstand benches, the lumber for the fence—all were spoils of his and Buck's scavenger hunts or were acquired secondhand from local enterprises that failed . . . a defunct drive-in, a shuttered tourist court, an aborted summer opera company.

In the distance, Bernie glimpsed the shining stadium light towers. He couldn't wait until the crowd saw their effect. And what would Billy think, he wondered, when he saw how much faster and more magical it seemed—baseball under the lights? "He'll be wowed!"

Bernie parked the car by the entrance and broke into a smile when he saw the freshly painted outfield fence. But something was missing. Signs! He recalled the Ebbets Field of his youth and the fence ad for Abe Stark's Clothing—Hit Sign, Win Suit!—making Abe rich and getting him elected to the City Council. Hit Sign, Win Steak! Bernie whooped, then realized that without a ball hawk like Dodger right fielder Carl Furillo to guard his sign, it might happen too much. Hit *Homer*, Win Steak!

Yes, that was it, he crowed. He could just see it, a painting of a luscious T-Bone—pink in the center and sparkling in its juices, with carrots and mashed potatoes—a tableau in pink, orange, and brown. "The Home Run Special," he'd call it—and fans would flock to the Club for a steak and to see the players, like Toots Shor's in New York. He'd get rich and be elected to the City Council. "City Council, hell!" he roared. "I'll be mayor one day!"

...

The threatening clouds had indeed made the fans late, but when they came, they came in droves—with the business and professional crowd claiming their box seats along the backstop, and the City's robust middle class assuming its rightful place behind them in the grandstand, and the late-arriving farmers and ranchers, workmen and tradesmen, stationing themselves along the flanks, and the 'Knothole Gang', young boys, most fanatical of all, seizing their nickel seats by the bullpen near their new heroes, and on the hill, the young colleens, teenage social queens, separating from parents to roam the broad, graveled concourse behind the seats, trailed by an entourage of teenage boys with one eye fixed on the game and the other on them.

James was too busy with the onslaught of customers to hear the short speeches by local luminaries or watch the horse parade of the Cowgirl Color Guard, but he stopped and stood with Jennie to sing the National Anthem and watch the mayor christen Sioux Park Stadium by throwing out the ceremonial first pitch.

In the game that followed, the Rapid City Chiefs overpowered the Hearts of Valentine, 12-7. For the sportswriters in the press box, the loosely played contest offered little drama.

The many fans in attendance scarcely noticed, thrilled as they were by the new stadium and their new team, especially the herculean exploits of Frank Hacker who, inspired by the large, ardent crowd, produced fireworks the likes of which they'd never seen, featuring a fence-splitting two-bagger and a towering home run that sailed out of sight.

Witnessed by 2,352 joyful fans—more even than Bernie Rosen had predicted, but with Ralph Sandstrom, the 'aginner', not among them—Sioux Park's inaugural game generated the largest crowd ever in Rapid

City for a ball game of any kind. A shared community spectacle, it augured well for the Chiefs and their Basin League season ahead.

And, at the concession stand, two unending lines had formed, one tended by Jennie, the other by James, who jingled about in his change apron, feeling a lot less burdened and a whole lot lighter with every thawed wiener sold.

Chapter Forty-Seven

JENNIE RAKED THE POPPED CORN over the warmer's pierced bottom and listened for the ping of virgin kernels as they dropped into the Old Maids Drawer. In little more than an hour, she had popped and boxed twenty kettles of corn, steamed two hundred wieners, and warmed eight dozen buns. It was a lot to prepare, but she knew from last night's home opener that they'd need it. Now, all that remained was to brew a big batch of coffee once James returned with the urn.

Jennie pulled the plug on the popper, which was starting to smoke. Down on the field, the shouts and whistles of young men signaled that the Chiefs had begun what James called their 'infield' drill, though Jennie knew that the outfielders were involved, too.

Grabbing a wet dish rag, she lifted the countertop along its hinge and passed through to the gravel apron bordering the Stand. Moving to the end of the counter, she turned to face the ballfield. From her vantage point, she could wipe the counter and still have a clear view of the outfield where the Chiefs' left fielder, Clarence Williams, plied his trade.

Never before had she behaved in such a manner, devising ways to glimpse a man or listening in on her men-folks' banter, her heart thrilling at the mention of his name. It was a crush, pure and simple, though she didn't recognize it as such. Her sister's death had foreclosed that part of her girlhood. Thereafter, all men were suspect and only James ever breached her defenses. Patiently, he pursued her and in the end she did yield, though she'd never truly yearned for him. He'd just been there and always would be, to give her children and a grown-up life.

Jennie dabbed at the countertop as Clarence, in the drill, dove for a long fly ball.

That he was a Negro and she was white—that he'd not sought her, or come to the Stand like the other Chiefs, made no difference. He was her reason for getting up in the morning and her reason for falling asleep—without pills or nightmares now—and with dreams only of him, which made her reach for James last night, and they'd made love—he to her and she to him—to Clarence, that is—in a kind of haunted trance.

Jennie shifted the condiments on the counter, prolonging her lookout. Warm-ups offered the best chance to see him before she got busy with customers, including Clarence's wife and children when they dropped by the Stand at the home opener the night before. Luckily, the long line confined their chat to pleasantries, "Hello, nice to see you," though the last was a lie, for Jennie hoped they'd no longer make the trip from the Air Base to see Clarence play.

Jennie watched the routine—one man hitting the ball to each of the others, who caught or trapped it, then threw it to a teammate waiting motionless at his station 'til the arriving baseball, like a spark, jolted him into action. Working in pairs and triplets, weaving in and out, running, jumping, twisting, turning, flying through the air, as in a Cossack dance or a western hoedown.

Again, Clarence took his turn in the drill—chasing an arcing fly that went all the way to the fence. Falling backwards into a slide, he speared the ball just inches from the ground. Then, with his right leg bent under him, levered himself to his feet and pivoted for the return throw to the infield. To Jennie, he looked like a cat righting itself with a turn of its tail.

"Wow, he's really something—moves like a gymnast."

Jolted from her reverie, Jennie spun around. It was the Jewish ballplayer from next door.

"What a great place to watch. I'm usually in the bullpen or the dugout, a worm's-eye view. The patterns, the rhythms, poetry in motion. You can see it all from up here."

Without a word, Jennie retreated inside the Stand.

Joel was taken aback. At Columbia, he'd seemed almost mute compared to motor mouths like his pal, Morrie, but with Mrs. Moran, a tight-lipped Westerner, he felt like an open faucet.

"Are you buying anything?" Jennie asked coldly.

Joel looked longingly at the popcorn. It was Saturday—Shabbos—and he wasn't carrying any money. "Not today, thank you, Mrs. Moran." Joel turned and headed back to the dugout.

Down on the field, Clarence, with an arm raised high, leapt to make a stabbing catch. Jennie ripped the cover off a candy box, and using a wax crayon, wrote in letters as small as she could manage:

Dark limbs soar

Branches of a towering tree

Naked in winter

Reaching for a fiery orb.

Jennie stared at the words. She'd not written a poem since her sister died. It was a word game that Florence, a natural teacher, had devised to pass the long winter evenings on the farm. Taking turns, they'd trade rhymes—concocting nonsense poems that had them squealing in delight and sometimes, to their surprise, made them proud.

Jennie folded the cardboard into a small, hard nut and walked to the garbage pail. The verse didn't rhyme and didn't seem worthy of pride. Staring for a moment at the trash in the bin, she rolled the poem between her fingers, then squirreled it deep inside the pocket of her apron.

...

"Fenski couldn't fix ours in time, so he lent us this." James deposited the coffee urn on the counter as Jennie grumbled, "You should have made him give us a new one."

Normally, James would be irked by his wife's reproach, but today he was floating on cloud nine. Last night, they'd been constantly on the move—the cash register jingling like Christmas in June. Then hours after passing out from exhaustion, they'd made love for the first time in over a month—initiated by Jennie, and without protection or any holding back.

James reached across the counter and touched Jennie's hand. "You're right, hon, tomorrow I'll tell him we want a new one." Turning, he surveyed his new domain, a testament to his initiative and hard work. "Looks like everything's 'bout ready to go." Lifting the pass-through, he squeezed into the Stand and wound his arm around Jennie's narrow waist.

"Last night was wonderful," he murmured.

Jennie dipped a tin cup into the drum of corn oil. If only he'd not talk about last night. Wriggling out of his grasp, she glanced at his beaming face. Could he not see the truth?

Smiling, James fiddled with the dial of the radio he'd just bought for the Stand. At last night's home opener, with patrons lined up six-deep, he couldn't pop out to catch even a moment of live action. It was agonizing—like a blind man at a silent movie, thrilled by the audience's outcries but unsure of their meaning. And he could make no sense of the stories that Stockman and others told when they dropped by the Stand afterwards. Last night he felt like an outsider. Tonight, he'd be able to speak knowledgeably to his sons and cronies after the game.

Turning back to the counter, James smiled broadly as a trio of teenage girls approached. "Hello there, Miss Martha," he chirped, recognizing Martha Muffling, his shy American History student. "What can I get for you girls?"

The night before, three of his male students had come by and he'd had a very different response. One was a Vo-Tech boy, a wiseacre he regularly sent to the Principal's office. James had braced himself for a crack about his mustard-stained shirt or the change apron that barely circled his belly, but the boy put out his hand and said, "Hello, Mr. Moran, heard you were in charge." Then he asked for a job. Chest swelling, James saw that his status among certain high school boys had been elevated from teacher to businessman—someone who could put money in their pockets and now deemed worthy of respect. James invited the boys to drop by after the game to hear about the excellent prospects for a ballpark hawker. Pouring Cokes for all three, he added a casual, "It's on the house."

Standing by the counter, Martha surveyed the cluttered Stand. "John's not working here," she said flatly. Undeceived by Martha's nonchalance, her companions exchanged knowing looks, and Jennie jerked around to see which female had shown an interest in her firstborn.

"He's taking photos for the Journal's Sunday Edition," James said, with a sympathetic smile. "If you go down to the field, you might still catch him."

As the group walked away, Jennie asked, "Who was that girl?"

"Martha Muffling, a good student and a debater, too. I think she has a crush on John."

Jennie flinched at the word "crush." Was that all it was, this crushing spell she'd fallen under, an infatuation like the one this teenager had for her son? But she was a grown woman—a teacher, a mother, a wife. She looked down at her shoes. "Crush." The belittling label stung. And yet, she doubted she could stop, even if she wanted to. Just as she hadn't been able to will herself to sleep all those weeks before Clarence Williams came into her life.

And then, the National Anthem boomed from the loudspeaker. Turning towards the center field flagpole, James placed his hand over his heart, and Jennie, glad for the diversion, followed suit and sang, too. Then, with the last strains of the music fading, James turned up the radio and heard the announcer echo the umpire's cry of "Play Ball!"

Knowing that the Chiefs started in the field, Jennie inched towards the counter pass-through. If she wanted to catch Clarence, she had to position herself outside at the top of each inning. When the Chiefs batted, it wouldn't matter where she stood. She couldn't see the batter's box from her counter outpost, so she might as well be inside following him on the radio.

Grabbing a wet rag, she ducked out of the Stand, muttering something about spilled soda. James merely nodded and began spooning coffee into the urn's outsized basket.

"Howdy, neighbors. Keepin' busy I see, James. You too, Jennie."

Jennie spun around to find Bernie Rosen standing behind her, lowering his head in an apparent attempt to see what lay along her sight line. "Well, looky here, where Jennie's standing you get a clear shot of left field, and our very own Negro star, Clarence Williams."

Jennie froze, recalling how Bernie had stared at them in the parking lot at the Base. How this must have looked to him—a strapping Negro man kneeling at her hem. Turning her back, she scoured a spot of dried mustard.

Bernie looked on, amused. "Sharp as a teacher's pointer you are, Jennie." Pulling a cigar from his breast pocket, he added. "Bet you've got the cleanest counter in the Basin League, too."

James forced a smile, but wished his neighbor, and now, his boss, would lay off Jennie.

"Can you see it, Jennie?" Bernie continued, "Out there on the center field fence, under the flagpole, just to the right of our favorite outfielder?" Jennie blanched as James squeezed through the pass-through to have a look, his curiosity piqued by Bernie's outstretched arm.

"What, Bern?"

"My latest brainchild. 'Hit Homer, Win Steak! Bernie Rosen's New York Club'. Something to inspire our troops," he said smugly.

"Oh, is it just for the Chiefs?" James peered across the field to read the sign again. "I'm not sure that's clear from the wording, Bern."

Jennie couldn't suppress a snort, as Bernie chomped down hard on his cigar.

"Chiefs or visitors—all good for business. People like to hang around young studs, especially women. Don't you agree, James?" Bernie flashed a smile at Jennie and James couldn't wait for him to finish his beer and leave. He hadn't figured on Bernie's nightly presence at the Stand, or his sarcastic jibes aimed, it seemed, more at Jennie than him.

Jennie pressed her thighs together. Brushing by her tormentor, she headed for the Ladies' room, as James's sticky seepage flowed like warmed honey into the web of her panties.

Chapter Forty-Eight

BERNIE STOOD AT THE SIOUX PARK gate, steak coupons in hand, waiting for the Chiefs to pass by after their 20-10 drubbing by the Kernels. It wasn't a task he relished, dishing out three free dinners for home runs that had not produced a win. Worse yet, he'd already delivered seven coupons to the Kernels sluggers, honoring the rash promise of his center field sign.

Bernie riffled the wad of coupons against his palm. What if his Chiefs weren't as good as he thought? With so many pros and extra travel costs, he needed a big gate to cover. If it looked like they'd finish out of the money, would fans turn out for a long slog to September?

And what about the fences? Had he set them too close—395 in center, 330 down the lines? But Ebbets' right field line ran just 297 feet. The Polo Grounds' fences were even closer—250 in right and 280 in left. Bobby Thomson's 'shot heard round the world,' which won the '51 playoffs, traveled only 300 feet or so. At Sioux Park, not a home run at all!

Then he recalled playing ball at the Air Base in New Mexico—how his drives had soared in the thin, dry air of the High Plains. Sioux Park's elevation of 3,200 feet was almost as high.

Yes, he'd give out a lot of free meat this season—steaks pulled out of thin air.

In the dugout, the Chiefs tried to fathom how they could hit three homers, score ten runs, and still lose. The answer was their pitching, which yielded twenty hits, thirteen for extra bases. Watching Dean Veal falter, Joel felt better about his own rough outing two nights before—and a bit guilty for finding comfort in a teammate's travails.

"Hey Dickie, you wanna collect on our steaks?" Frank Hacker, who'd had a good night at the plate, asked Quarles, who'd hit a solo homer.

Clarence, who'd also homered, was left off Frank's invitation. Joel wondered if it was intentional or just an oversight. Hack didn't seem prejudiced. Twice he'd stepped in to stop Hoades in dustups on the bus, though he stayed silent on the bridge in Pierre, like everyone else. Did it take violence, the proverbial sticks and stones, to goad him to action? Packing up his gear, Clarence didn't look up, and Joel wasn't sure he'd heard the proposal, or just chose to ignore it.

"Nah. It's bad form to celebrate after a loss," Quarles declared.

"But a man's gotta eat." Hacker's plea sounded as plaintive as a kitten's mewl for milk.

Hoades chortled. "Ya think that cheap kike's gonna pay off when we got butchered?"

Joel swallowed hard. In Brooklyn he'd never let something like that slide, but here, he had to play it cool, like Jackie Robinson or Hank Greenberg. Or Clarence Williams.

"The New York Club's not a short-sleeve kind of place," Joel said as calmly as he could. "You'll need a sports jacket or a suit. Go tomorrow—after we win."

Quarles slapped Joel on the back. "Tomorrow I pitch—we win, we eat steak. Hacker, me, Williams, anyone who homers, or wants to check out the Club's Class Act."

Stockman smiled to himself. He'd checked out the Club's Class Act himself that very afternoon—served up rare and juicy, just the way he liked it.

• • •

"Hey, Rosen, ya gonna pay up on all ten steaks—Chiefs *and* Kernels?" It was Paddy Olavson, *Journal* Managing Editor.

Bernie narrowed his eyes. The very question was an insult, not worthy of reply.

"So, what was the trouble tonight—Kernels' corncobs scalping your sitting bulls?"

"Guess they were hungrier, wanted it more."

Paddy grinned and scribbled something in his notebook, and Bernie frowned, wondering what tasty morsel he'd just fed Rapid's town crier.

Chapter Forty-Nine

LANA REACHED ACROSS THE TABLE for the phone. "Bernie!" she yelled, "It's Carl—says it's important." Bernie took the receiver and pressed it to his ear. "What's up, Carl?" A moment later, he grabbed the *Journal* and flipped to Paddy Olavson's column on the *Journal*'s Editorial Page.

Chiefs Not Hungry 'Nuff, Says Big Chief Rosen

Such were the few, choice words of New York Club owner and Chiefs' Sachem, Bernie Rosen, when asked about his promise of a free steak dinner to anyone hitting a home run at Sioux Park Stadium. In last night's rocket show between Rapid and Mitchell, a grand total of ten four-baggers were blasted through the thin mountain air, aided and abetted by some charitable chuckin' from both the Chiefs and Kernels, including the center-cut offerings of a milk-fed young Chief named Dean Veal, who tenderly served up four of the dinners.

The crowd loved the pyrotechnics, though only three of the rockets were fired off by the hometown boys. The other seven circuit-masters were powdered by the visiting Kernels. Which makes us wonder if this League has arms to match its bats, and if Black Hills Sports Inc., viz, Bernie Rosen, has built us a professional baseball stadium or a horsehide-missile launching pad.

Still, if last night's fireworks prove anything, it is that these toothless Chiefs cannot live by steak alone, though it may be too early to write off our hometown heroes, so we'll bide our time and see what the future holds—more slugfests and steaks, or a better-balanced diet of singles, stolen bases, and double plays. But if the latter don't prevail, Chief Rosen can't complain, 'cause his vegetable gummers are the tribe of his own choosing. So, for now, as your big sign swears, you'll just have to pay up, though it can't be much fun serving steaks with all the trimmings to traveling trenchermen and dare we say it, feeding the mouth that bites you. OUCH! So don't be an Indian Giver, Chief Rosen, LET THEM EAT STEAK!

"Sonovabitch!" Bernie hit the counter with his fist. Joel, entering the kitchen, stopped in his tracks—but seen by Lana, it was too late to retreat to the basement.

"Sit, honey. Don't pay his temper tantrum no mind—happens all the time 'round here."

"That bastard!" Bernie didn't mind the *Journal* drawing attention to his steak offer—but mocking him for not laying out a bigger ballpark? What got to him most, though, was the insinuation that he was an 'Indian Giver'. He couldn't help substituting 'Cheap Kike' for the slur. Seeing Joel, Bernie thrust the paper at the ballplayer. "Never trust newspapers."

Lana laughed. "See? He's all right now he's figured out who to blame."

Joel squirmed in his seat. His own parents never raised their voices, and sarcasm was as foreign to them as pork chops. Quickly, he skimmed the column. While he found it clever, he knew he had to support his boss and benefactor. "Sorry, Bernie—this isn't fair to you."

Lana laid a hand on Bernie's shoulder, but when she spoke, her tone was more acid than sweet. "When you're the big Jew in town they always got the cross ready for ya. At least they mentioned the Club, Bern. Might be good for business."

"Truth is, and don't you repeat this, kid, what's got me worried is my college boys screwing up, while Stockman's pros get the job done."

Joel nodded. He had wondered how the Chiefs were assembled. Now he knew. Two distinct factions—one Bernie's, one Stockman's—welded together with lots of sparks.

Hearing Bernie speak Guy's name, Lana flushed. Distracted, Bernie studied the roll of Lana's bottom as she moved from table to stove. Joel averted his eyes. It was hard not to respond to her physical charms. And there was the imminent arrival of the other half of the bewitching mother-daughter duo—Dinah.

Bernie turned back to Joel. "I called Quarles this morning and you're meeting him at the field in half an hour. He'll work with you on your slider. You might pitch tonight in relief."

When Joel finished breakfast, Bernie hustled him out the door, then picked up Billy to serve as Joel's catcher. Catching a glimpse of Dinah in her baby-doll pajamas, Joel wondered if Bernie had purposely scheduled this early session to minimize their contact. Last night, he'd lingered in the kitchen hoping to see Dinah, but she'd not come home. Finally, he complied with Bernie's command, "Time for bed, boy," something he hadn't heard since he was thirteen.

• • •

Arriving at Sioux Park, Joel was afraid that Bernie would hang around to supervise, but he didn't get out of the car. Billy, on the other hand, stuck close by his side. Scanning the outfield, Joel dispatched his little shadow to look for balls along the fence line so he could speak to Quarles alone. "Sorry about Bernie calling you, Q. Was going to ask you myself but . . ."

Quarles smiled. "Rosen don't need an invitation. He signs the checks. He's not the only owner with meddlin' ways. You just have the added misfortune of sleeping under his roof."

Joel laughed. "Hope you didn't tell Coach about this. Don't want him to think I'm taking orders from Bernie, too."

"Mum's the word. Now, let's talk about pitching." Q turned to Billy who'd returned from his ball hunt. "You listen too, kiddo, this'll come in handy when you try out for the Braves."

Billy grinned, pleased that Quarles had remembered his favorite team.

"I'll be blunt. I'm here to break up your romance with the curve. For a lefty who mostly faces right-hand batters, a curve is ofttimes not a great pitch. Now I'm not sayin' you have to ditch her—just date her in the eastern ballparks, where you're closer to sea level and the air's thick as soup. Here in Rapid, with the high altitude, she don't give you much action, just spins a little and dances up there, and 'boom'—air-lifted right out of this sweet little ballpark. Now, tell me, Joely, what pitch is most often hit for a home run in the late innings?"

"I suppose it's the curve."

"Bingo—at least when it's a big one like yours and the batter knows it's coming the instant it leaves your hand. The curve's a problem for just about everybody, 'cept the great Maglie. It's a big, sweeping pitch, hard to control early on, then settles down in the middle innings and gets the job done. But in the late innings when yer fastball's losing steam and you really need a breaking ball, you press a little and hang it—big as a piñata—waist high, middle of the strike zone." Quarles' voice rose to a whimpering falsetto. "And the ball cries, 'whip me, hurt me, beat me'."

Joel and Billy laughed as Q smacked his hands together, miming a ball flying off into space.

"And on the road, late, with the home crowd screaming in his ears, the ump won't call it a strike if it'd go against the local boys. And a big bender don't look like a strike to the yokels in the cheap seats. Been that way since time immemorial, Joely, and it ain't gonna change. Yer gonna get jobbed on the close ones. So don't get rattled, say nothing, and smile at human nature."

Joel nodded, recalling his display of temper toward the end of his disastrous Huron debut.

"Well, that about does it for the curve, so let me ask you—what type of pitch, of all the pitches you *could* throw, would put the most doubt in the hitter's mind?"

"I don't know—do I have one?"

"What pitch drove DiMaggio nuts after he came back from the War?"

"Must have been the pitch Feller and some others started throwing back then, the slider."

"Joely, you *are* a smart boy. Some call it a slide ball, others, a nickel curve, but whatever you call it, it's a great pitch 'cause it comes in straight and true—looks like a fastball 'till the last moment, then jams on the brakes and does a little juke, dodging the fat of the bat."

"You know, I already throw a slider," Joel offered in his defense.

"Yeah, but your bat-dodger don't always break, and you hang it high. And when it don't break, it's just a cock-high fastball at batting practice speed. I'll give you a slider that works."

Quarles held the baseball at arm's length in front of his nose. "Start with a fastball grip, then move your first two fingers a little to the side, so you're holding the ball in the middle with your thumb and pointer finger, like this."

Waiting for Joel to get his fingers into position, Quarles spotted Billy positioning his own fingers around a ball and smiled.

"That's it, Joely." Quarles signaled to Billy to put on the catcher's gear and get down behind home plate. "Warm up slow—just fastballs 'til you get loose. Then, go with the slider. Aim it over the plate so it'll look like a strike coming in. That'll get the batter to swing. Then, when it breaks, it'll miss the bat barrel or break out of the strike zone. Now, if you throw it and just miss your spot, throw it again next pitch, while you still got some feel for it. Don't go changin' to a fastball or curve. But, if the first slider's awful and misses by a lot, throw somethin' else next pitch."

Joel could hardly contain his excitement. He'd never had a pitching tutorial like this, not even at Columbia. His curve and his justly maligned slider—along with his pitch selection—he mostly had to work out on his own.

After a few minutes, he got the green light to air it out, and the payoff was quick, a pitch that reliably broke six inches or more, darting sideways and down. In less than an hour, he'd gained a new tool—an effective third pitch—making it harder for batters to guess what was coming. Like a kid with a new toy, he wanted to go on throwing, but Quarles knew the younger man might be called on that night and made him stop.

"Another thing, New Yawk. You're a nice, clean-cut young man. Mom and Dad are to be congratulated. But, if you're gonna sign a professional contract and earn your bread and butter in the Big Leagues, you're gonna have to act a little. Put a scowl on your face and let your black beard grow—and buzz that good hummer of yours straight at the batter's Adam's apple now and then. Give him a close shave like Sal 'the Barber' Maglie."

Joel chuckled. "Yeah, I got it. Be a sonovabitch."

"No! *Look* like a sonovabitch. By the way, I hear Maglie's a nice guy off the mound."

Quarles turned to Billy. "I think you may have missed a couple o' balls in right field. Find 'em and they're yours."

With Billy out of earshot, Quarles continued. "Couldn't say this in front of the kid—but in baseball, you never want to think too much or try too hard. It messes with your wiring. We're all like that—not just ballplayers. Suppose you got a date with Marilyn Monroe. You might not be able to get it up 'cause you want it too bad. So, you gotta trick yourself to not give a damn. One of the cruelest things about baseball. They call it irony."

Quarles gave Joel a wry smile and gazed across the field at Billy, gamboling in, a grass-stained baseball held aloft in triumph. The veteran's smile turned wistful. A couple more summers in the Basin was all he could hope for, but Joel and Billy—they were still young--young enough to dream.

Chapter Fifty

FLUSHED WITH SUCCESS, JOEL AND CLARENCE, along with Guy, Hacker, and Quarles, headed to the New York Club to claim their free steaks. Joel was flying high. Riding his peerless new slider, he'd pitched four innings of scoreless relief, copping the win after Guy homered in the eighth with two aboard.

In the dugout after his win, Joel changed into a dress shirt and sports jacket as Bernie had advised that morning. "Gotta feed you somewhere, might as well be at the Club." Clarence had also come prepared, carrying a dark blue suit, white shirt, and a red-and-blue repp tie.

Joel was surprised that Clarence was joining the celebration at all. He was the only ballplayer with a family to go home to, and he'd likely be the only Negro at the Club. Joel wondered if he felt he had something to prove—to the team or to himself.

"Did your family come to tonight's game, Clarence? I didn't see them."

"No," he answered curtly. While there'd been no trouble at last night's game, afterwards Clarence Jr. griped about Billy being batboy, and Cherry Mae said she'd chatted with Jennie Moran at the concession stand, which unleashed a storm of emotion Clarence barely managed to hide.

And, when Cherry described her oddly disconcerting encounter with the town librarian, they decided that she and the kids should stay home and listen to the games on the radio now that KOTA was carrying them. It was a decision offering him relief but sparked the guilty sense he wanted it more to protect himself than his children.

"I'm under strict orders to bring home leftovers," Clarence added, waving the folded sheet of tinfoil Cherry Mae had pressed on him as he headed out the door.

Joel chortled and Clarence was glad he didn't repeat his wife's last bit of advice. "Get that steak before the Jew-man change his mind." Though he had laughed out loud when she said it.

At the Club, Buck met each car in the convoy. "All together," he commanded, carrying out Bernie's order to insure a dramatic entrance for the packed house.

The five ballplayers trooped in, lingering in the vestibule to admire Lana's life-sized cardboard cutout. Only Clarence hung back, feigning indifference. It had been only two years since young Emmett Till was lynched for whistling at a white woman down South. And while he and Joel were friendly—perhaps becoming friends—he doubted even a do-gooder like Joel would excuse him for ogling a sexy white woman, even a cardboard replica of one.

Frank Hacker let out a long trailing whistle. Stockman jerked his head angrily towards the big collegian.

"That's Rosen's wife," Joel interjected, thinking it was the reason for Guy's response.

"No kidding?" Quarles said, looking around the big amphitheater. "You gotta hand it to the guy. He sure makes the most of small-town life."

Guy checked out the stage. Lana was nowhere to be seen. Recalling his hot reaction to Hacker's wolf whistle he was surprised by the proprietary feelings he didn't realize he had.

Out of the crowd, Dinah sidled up to Joel, playfully bumping him with her cigarette tray.

"Cigars, cigarettes, mints?"

Joel's jaw dropped. He hadn't imagined she'd be here, and never in his wildest dreams in this skimpy outfit—stiletto heels, fishnet stockings, and a black corset scarcely bounding her.

"What are you doing here?" he sputtered, as his teammates zeroed in—but not Clarence, who took a quick look at the girl, then angled his body away.

"Mah daddy owns the place, case you forgot."

"No, I mean, didn't you have a show tonight up in the Hills?"

"Cigarette girl called in sick. I came after the show." Dinah surveyed the players who, like a pack of hungry wolves, had formed a circle around her. Her eye caught Guy's, but he looked away, excited yet disturbed by the illicit prospect—a mother *and* a daughter. That would be a first.

"Aren't you gonna introduce me to your friends?" Dinah purred.

"Uh, well, no, I don't think so," Joel stammered, wishing he could throw a sheet over her.

"Come on, Joel, be a sport," his teammates protested, spurred by Dinah's theatrical pout.

Joel had never been in this kind of pickle before, having to fend off rivals for a girl. "OK. This is Dinah Rosen, Bernie's daughter." Hacker's and Quarles's mouths dropped as Bernie's family tree bloomed before their eyes. Then, the man himself swooped down.

"Great game, Chiefs," he said in a booming voice, in case anyone had missed their grand entrance. "Let's get you a table so you can sign autographs." Placing a hand on Dinah's back, he lowered his voice. "Customers could use some smokes." Gently, he pushed her toward the outer ring of tables, far from the Chiefs' hungry eyes.

Looking back, she drawled, "See ya later, Joel."

Joel beamed, pleased she had acknowledged his special status among the men.

"This way, fellas." Bernie led the Chiefs down to a table near the stage.

As they passed through the crowd, patrons slapped them on the back, though no one touched Clarence—some staring at him instead, a few with hard faces that made Joel uneasy. Looking around the big room, he saw that Clarence was in fact the only Negro there. Could Jim Crow have roosted this far north, he wondered, or was it merely an unwritten code? Or maybe there weren't any Negroes in Rapid or at the Air Base who could afford a pricey place like this.

Bernie motioned to the waiter. "Five T-Bones with all the trimmings. Tell 'im how you want 'em cooked, boys."

Joel hesitated. In his excitement, he'd forgotten about the meat and couldn't recall the kosher cuts his mother served. Not that Bernie had given them any choice. Still, there was no chance that the steaks were butchered in the prescribed kosher manner. But he missed good beef. Maybe if they cooked the hell out of it, got rid of all the blood, it wouldn't be so sinful.

"Medium." "Well done." "Medium." "Medium." "Charred and rare."

"Burnt and bloody, huh Stockman?" Bernie remarked.

"Long as it don't moo, I'm happy."

Leaving the table, Bernie declared "Budweisers all around," and not in a way that invited contradiction.

Hacker leaned across toward Joel. "Does he pick out your clothes for you, too?"

"Maybe that pussycat in the French maid getup does it, or his sexy house mom."

Quarles' comment about Lana again raised Stockman's hackles.

"You got it made, Meznik," Hacker groused. "I'm bunking with a kid who pops his pimples at the breakfast table."

Joel laughed. "You think I got the Life of Riley, but they've locked me in the cellar."

"Break out, man, break out!" Hack yelled, pounding the table with his water glass.

"Maybe the cigarette girl will bake you a pie with a file in it," Quarles said.

"Apple pie, or peach?" Hacker sighed. "She sure got nice peaches."

"Call me if you need help opening her crate," Quarles offered. "Another pair of hands."

Joel snorted. "Thanks, Dicky-boy, but I can handle her fruit just fine." Everyone at the table, including Clarence, exploded with laughter.

Just then, the lights were doused and a moment later, a single beam illuminated the center of the stage. And there, in a bright circle of light, appeared Lana, dressed in high heels and a skintight Chiefs' uniform—half unbuttoned—and leaning on a baseball bat.

The crowd howled like hyenas as Lana doffed her cap and tossed her head, letting her hair tumble down around her shoulders. Stockman and the other Chiefs, sprouting like spring bulbs through the snow, were grateful for the room's dim light and concealing tabletop.

The band played the lead-in three times before the bedlam could subside. Stepping off the stage, Lana walked to the ballplayers and, extending the bat, touched each man on the shoulders like a queen conferring knighthood. The last to be dubbed was Stockman, who was happy to play along, humbly bowing his head. But when she was done, he raised his eyes to meet hers, and they locked in a way not lost on Bernie. Pivoting from her lover, Lana held out the bat to her husband, then returned to the stage, where she began to sing, purring out the words, punctuated with sweet, soft sighs—"Take me . . . out . . . to the ball . . . game."

It took five minutes for the hoots and hollers to die down. Bernie sat mesmerized as his wife delivered a performance the likes of which had never been seen in Rapid, or for that matter, anywhere between Kansas City and Denver. Gripping the bat, he made a mental note—day clerk at the Royal Rest goes on the payroll. Lana's T-Bird would be easy to spot.

• • •

John removed the film from his Leica and handed it to the darkroom technician. He wasn't sure what he'd caught at the game but figured that one shot at least would find its way into the Sunday Sports Section. Most of all, he hoped it wasn't a photo of Joel on the mound. He had no interest in helping him become the local hero and boosting his stock with Dinah. Surely, it was only a matter of time before he made his move on her. Hadn't he said as much in Pierre?

Then Paddy walked up and gave John's shoe a friendly kick. "Thought I was the only one 'round here who got paid for loafing."

John jerked a thumb at the darkroom door. "They're working on my game pictures."

"OK, but then ya gotta check out the New York Club. Rosen's been running ads all day about his big steak giveaway. Thinks the Chiefs can draw enough to fill his white elephant."

The technician emerged from the darkroom. "They're over the sink."

John looked at his watch. He'd have to rush to make it to the Club before the last show. Placing the film strips on the light table, he examined each with a magnifying glass. The first was a series taken during the Chiefs' initial at bat, but no one swung the moment he snapped the picture. Next, he focused on fielding plays, but again, none of the shots were dramatic.

Finally, he came to the last strip of acetate, photos taken merely to finish off the roll. It was there that he found it—Joel on the mound frozen into a position John had never seen—back arched, chest bulled, long legs striding, pitching arm bent backward like a bowstring at what seemed an impossible angle. The camera had caught the moment of greatest stretch, fixing the instant when a pitcher's contorted arm and body begin to rotate forward to the point of the ball's release, perhaps the key to throwing a baseball at such a remarkable speed. John knew the picture was special—like Hacker's home run—a unique moment captured on a mere inch of acetate.

Through the magnifier, he studied Joel's face. His grimace wasn't flattering, but sports fans would be struck by his intensity and his posture, a cross between Superman and a sideshow freak. The photo would make Joel the talk of the town, but with a snip of the scissors, he could bury Joel's shot at instant fame. With an angel on one shoulder and the devil on the other, he marked the picture with a red pencil and walked it down to Paddy.

It was almost midnight when he pulled into the Club's parking lot. He'd never seen it so packed. Elbowing his way through the throng, his attention was drawn to the stage, lit by a yellow spot, and the words of a familiar song, "*You gotta have heart,*" delivered in a sultry croon. For an agonizing moment, he thought it might be Dinah reprising her star-turn from *Damn Yankees*. Then someone moved aside, and he saw that it was Lana, dressed in a body-hugging *Chiefs* uniform, her lips brushing the mic as she sang, "*All you really need is heart.*"

When the applause died down, she stepped off the stage.

"Don't go anywhere, folks—just gonna help myself to a little firewater."

John looked around the crowded supper club, so different from when he'd come in fall and winter when Dinah worked coat check. Doing homework at a table in the back, he'd enjoy a free meal and one drink—all that Bernie allowed. "Vodka. Your mother won't smell it on you."

Most nights business was slow, and Dinah sat with him. Bernie would bring her a Shirley Temple, which she'd spike with John's vodka, and then, warmed by drink and desire, they'd detour on the way home to Skyline Drive, his hands slipping under her blouse, and hers, along his thigh. That was all gone now, but being here brought it all back, as if it were yesterday.

"Damn," he swore. He should have refused Paddy's assignment to check out the Club.

Returning to the stage, Lana announced her next number: "A little change of pace—something a bit blue. Also from *Damn Yankees*. 'A Man Doesn't Know'."

The lyrics cut through him like a blade.

A man doesn't know what he has until he loses it.
When a man has the love of a woman he abuses it.
I didn't know what I had when I had my old love."

He couldn't take any more. Pushing his way to the entrance, he spotted her as soon as he charged through the door. Dinah—sobbing against the side of the building, the cigarette caddy hanging from her neck. He froze at the sight of her. Shouldn't she be at the Mellerdrammer?

And why was she crying? All at once, he was sure he understood—she'd heard Lana's song and felt as he did, stricken with regret for what the two of them once had.

John placed a hand on her bare shoulder. "I'm here, Dinah."

Dinah sloughed off his touch. "That bitch stole my songs! No one will remember I sang them first."

John's heart sank. Turning on his heel, he strode to the Dodge and sped back to the *Journal*. Swiping Paddy's bottle of Four Roses, he jumped back into the car and roared east across the prairie, as Jerry Lee Lewis wailed on the radio, "Whole Lotta Shakin' Goin' On."

It wasn't until morning that he learned what had transpired at the Club after he left.

"You're lucky I liked the shot of the pitcher, or I woulda had you canned," Paddy blazed.

Hungover, John couldn't look him in the eye. He'd stayed out until dawn, stumbling home at first light, and slept only a few hours before Billy woke him, waving the *Journal* with his photo of Joel on the sports page. This time his name was printed under it.

Standing before Paddy like a truant schoolboy, John abandoned his search for an alibi. "I'm sorry, it won't happen again." He pulled a dollar from his pocket and handed it to Paddy.

"What the hell is that for?"

John was brought up short. Paddy hadn't checked his liquor cabinet.

"There was a ruckus at the Club," Paddy continued. "The Black ballplayer and a couple of cowboys got into it. So, I jumped in my car to check it out and no one's seen you and no one's talkin' either. Were you even at the Club last night?"

John looked down at the floor. How could he explain why he'd left? He'd look like a crybaby or a lovesick fool. Paddy would lose all respect for him. And he'd be right.

The lie came to him in a flash. "I'm sorry. I wanted a drink. I knew they wouldn't serve me at the Club, so I helped myself to your Four Roses on my way out. Drank too fast, got sick, and had to go home. But I'm friendly with one of the pitchers and with Clarence Williams, too. They'll clue me in. I'll get you the story tonight."

Paddy's eyes twinkled with delight. "No Boy Scout after all, eh Johnny boy? Don't matter now. Got a call from R.W. to kill the story. Rosen musta threatened to pull his *Journal* ads. By the way, the Sports Editor liked the photo of the pitcher. Thinks you got talent."

• • •

In the fracas at the Club, the leftover steak had been lost. That's what bothered Clarence the most driving back to the Base. By filling up on rolls, he'd saved half his T-Bone for Cherry Mae, and Joel cut a line down the middle of his own steak and deposited half onto his plate.

Clarence didn't know what lay behind Joel's gesture—half a steak, half a sin, and that half, mitigated by Sudukkah—charity—for someone who might need it more.

And so, before the waiter could take his plate, Clarence pulled the tinfoil from his pocket, spread it on his lap, and began wrapping the steak. But it leaked in the transfer and a few drops of grease fell onto his lap. “Take care of spills right away ’lest you live with ’em forever,” Cherry Mae always said, so he headed for the Men’s Room, clutching his wrapped steak and drawing the attention of two drunken cowboys at the bar.

Balancing the steak on the edge of the sink, Clarence soaped a corner of his handkerchief and dabbled at the stain. Then, the two men sauntered in. He knew at once they were trouble. Smirking, one pointed to Clarence’s hand suspended over his crotch, while the other planted himself between the ballplayer and the door.

“If you gonna do that, boy, you should go to Coney Island with the other coons.”

Clarence never asked why Joel, Hacker, and Quarles happened upon the scene, but when they did, he knew he’d have backup when he threw the first punch.

And so, the steak got lost or tossed. When Bernie sent in his dishwasher to mop up, none of the blood belonged to the ballplayers, or even to the meat.

Chapter Fifty-One

AS SOON AS BERNIE WALKED into the kitchen he started in on Dinah. "You gonna cut out? See me first. I was worried sick 'til Buck said you left."

Dinah kicked the table leg with her slipper. How could she possibly explain how she felt watching her mother perform her songs from *Damn Yankees*? And, better than she could herself.

"Sorry," she muttered, sounding anything but.

Entering the room, Lana kissed Bernie on the cheek. "What are you apologizing for, Di?"

Ignoring her mother, Dinah shoveled a spoonful of corn flakes into her mouth.

Bernie looked from his wife to his daughter. "I told her to let me know when she leaves the Club." Bernie put a gentle hand on Dinah's shoulder. "Why'd you leave anyway?"

Dinah shrugged. "I felt sick. I did a full show yesterday before I came to the Club."

Lana snorted. "When I was your age, I could do three shows a day. Right, Bern?"

Dinah clanged her spoon against the cereal bowl. "Well, you're just Superwoman. I'm a mere mortal."

Bernie let out a deep guffaw. "Mere mortal, I love it. Where'd you pick that up?"

Dinah couldn't help but smile at her dad's approval. "I read it somewhere," she said, while Lana mouthed "comic book" as she brushed by Bernie on the way to the percolator.

"So, what you got planned today, kitten? Theater's dark tonight, right?"

Just then Joel bounded into the kitchen, all charged up from backing up Clarence in the men's room at the Club. He felt like Pee Wee Reese standing up for Jackie Robinson in '47.

"Why not take Joel for a tour of the Hills? He's got the day off, too," Bernie added.

Dinah hesitated, wondering if she should continue to sulk or take her father's suggestion, which she had to admit appealed to her. "What would you like to see, Joel?" she asked.

"Whatever you'd like to show me."

Bernie threw him a censuring look, but Dinah felt a tingle. "Well, you gotta see Rushmore, Needles Highway, and Sylvan Lake. You got a swimsuit?"

"No, sorry, didn't think I'd need one."

Bernie turned to his daughter. "All right, Dinah, make a quick stop at Olson's Men's Store, then head out on US 16. You got cash, Joel?"

Joel hesitated. He didn't want to take money from Bernie, at least not in front of Dinah.

"Tell Olson to put it on my tab. You did good last night, kid, and not just on the mound."

As Dinah, dressed in halter top and shorts, drove north on Evergreen, Joel was hard pressed to keep his eyes on the road. With Rivkah, he'd rarely seen even her bare feet, let alone anything more revealing. Then he felt a pang. Why had he thought of Rivkah, and why her feet? Stop it, he told himself. You're out West. There'd be plenty of time to feel guilty later.

At mid-block, Dinah hit the brake. "What did Daddy mean by 'you did good last night'?" The question surprised Joel. He thought she was there at the Club when the fight took place.

Regardless, he couldn't answer. Bernie had sworn the Chiefs to secrecy. "Bad for the team, bad for the New York Club. No one wins if this gets out."

"I pitched well last night," Joel said, hoping to satisfy Dinah's curiosity.

Dinah laid on her best drawl. "Ah believes that only covahs the 'mound' part of the evenin'." Joel smiled, charmed by her accent and impressed that she'd seen through his ruse.

"I'm not sure what your dad meant. Maybe you should ask him."

Dinah pulled the car to the curb. She had no patience for a game where she didn't know the score. "Tell me, or I'll let you out here."

Joel was shocked. No girl had ever spoken to him that way. Not even Mona Solomon.

"Your dad said not to tell anyone, so promise to keep it to yourself."

Dinah made a face but raised her right hand. "I won't tell, scout's honor."

"OK, Clarence Williams, our Negro outfielder, went to the men's room and a couple of cowboys followed him in. We saw it and figured there'd be trouble and went to help him out. Then, Buck dragged them to the back exit and gave 'em the boot."

"Oh," Dinah said in a way that conveyed indifference. "There are fights like that at the Coney Island Club all the time. The Indians and Negroes get drunk and get into it."

Joel was disappointed by Dinah's reaction. Either she wasn't impressed by what he'd done or had some fixed notion of how these fights happened and who was to blame. "They were white. And Clarence wasn't drunk. Those guys had it in for him."

Dinah shrugged and stepped on the gas. "So tell me, who else defended the colored guy?"

"The big guy, Hacker, and Quarles, one of the other pitchers."

"Oh! Not the older man—the blond?"

There was something in her voice that baited him. He'd noticed the look that passed between her and Stockman when they were introduced. As his competitive instincts kicked in, all annoyance with her take on the men's room fight flew out of his head.

"No, he stayed at the table. Wasn't in on the fight."

"What's his name again?"

"Stockman," Joel said flatly.

"What position does he play?"

"Catcher, but he's pretty old now."

"Really? How old?"

"I'd say forty," Joel inflated.

"No kidding. I would have guessed thirty."

"His knees are shot, all that squatting in the dirt. Probably get arthritis in ten years." Joel smirked at the image he'd planted in her mind of a hobbled ballplayer bent over his cane.

"Ten years is a long way off," Dinah chirped, sensing what Joel was up to. Then she parked the Skyliner in front of Olson's Men's Store and waited as Joel ran inside. Aware of her alone in the convertible and a lure to any passing male, he grabbed the simplest swimsuit he could find, a pair of white trunks he didn't try on. As he strode to the cashier, a man stepped in front of him.

"Your money's no good here, Mr. Meznik."

For a moment Joel was puzzled. Would he not sell him the suit? Was this some kind of prejudice toward him? Then he recalled that Rapid City merchants were offering the Chiefs free meals, haircuts, and other stuff on the house. Perhaps his brush with bigotry out here—Hoades' kike slur and the 'brillo head' crack in Huron—had made him touchy.

"Just send me an autographed picture. We'll put it up with the others," Olson said, pointing to the lineup of 8 x 10 photos behind the cash register—Stockman, Kibbee, Quarles, Casey, Hoades, and Hacker. All had cashed in their chits for fancy duds.

When Joel returned to the car, Dinah was gone. Searching the broad thoroughfare, a jealous fantasy played out in his mind—Stockman happening along, charming her out of the convertible and, at that very moment, having his way with her in his Alex Johnson lair.

Then she appeared, carrying a paper sack. "See what I've got," she said with a self-satisfied smile. "I thought we could picnic at Sylvan Lake."

A minute later, they were barreling south, running a gauntlet of motels with signs touting pools, air-conditioning, and TV. At the city limits, the highway rose steeply, lifting them in circles up the mountain, from the plains of southeast Rapid to the higher elevations of the Black Hills.

Then, the tourist signs appeared. Petrified Forest, Reptile Gardens, Sitting Bull Cave.

"The Petrified Forest is in the Black Hills?" Joel asked. "I thought that was in Arizona."

Dinah scoffed, "We got two, but this one's a fake. The owner trucked in some logs and scattered them beside the road. Daddy says he wished he'd thought of it first."

Joel laughed. "Is that cave a fake, too?"

"No. But the cave's owner claims Sitting Bull spent his winters there. Daddy says the Indians never lived in the Black Hills 'cause they're sacred. Only came in for teepee poles and deer. But the Sioux put on a terrific pageant here every year."

"Cave's owner?" Joel was incredulous. "People out here own caves?"

"Sure. Why not? People own land, don't they? If they own a mountain with a cave in it, they own that, too."

"Own a mountain? I thought only the government owned mountains."

"Not all of 'em. This guy Korczak bought one and he's carving a statue of Crazy Horse on it. An Indian Chief got him to do it after he saw Rushmore. Korczak charges the tourists just to watch him work. Daddy says he makes a bundle every time he blasts a little rock off the hill."

Joel was amazed. Was there nothing you weren't allowed to do out here in the West?

Turning south onto US 16, the Skyliner passed through a broad valley with cattle and rolls of hay that looked like great shaggy beasts. Then, he saw a sign with a leering caricature of a Villain in a black cape and top hat, fingering a handlebar mustache.

"Say, isn't that the Mellerdrammer where you work? Can we stop?"

Dinah made a face. She didn't want to visit Rockerville and run into her boss. But maybe seeing her with a big strapping man would curb his roving hands and ogling eyes. She cut the wheel, and Joel almost toppled into her lap. "OK, but we won't stop," she said, laughing.

Passing through Rockerville, Joel was charmed by the re-created frontier town with its wooden sidewalks and false-fronted buildings—saloon, dance hall, bank, and livery—just like in the movies. "What a great place. I'd love to come see your show."

"How can you? You don't drive, and you play ball most nights."

"Couldn't I tag along with your folks sometime?"

"They never come. They're always at the Club," Dinah said flatly.

Joel studied Dinah's impassive face, wondering what she was feeling. His own parents never made it to his games, offering no explanation, but he always suspected that if he'd been playing the piano or violin or starring in a science fair they would have come. But how could it be the same for Dinah, following in her mother's footsteps?

Continuing in silence onto Rushmore, they wound their way down the mountain through the little tourist town of Keystone. Pointing to the right, Dinah announced, "Won't be long now, keep your eyes peeled." A moment later, Joel let out a shout. "I see it!" he exclaimed, catching a glimpse of the stone faces through a break in the timber. A second later, he was crestfallen.

"They're gone," he cried, sounding like a child who believed that an object moved out of sight had ceased to exist.

"Wait," Dinah said, "just around this curve."

And there they were again—the massive faces of Washington, Jefferson, Teddy Roosevelt, and Lincoln. Carved from solid gray granite, they glowed in the soft morning light.

Choked up, all Joel could say was "wow." He'd not expected to be so moved. Some of his Columbia teammates scoffed when he said he was excited about seeing Rushmore. He supposed they didn't think it was cool, wanting to view the famous monument to the nation's founding fathers.

Dinah pulled off the road and stopped the car. Born and raised in the Black Hills, she couldn't remember the first time she'd seen Rushmore, but was pleased by Joel's wonderment.

Joel darted from the car and gazed up at the giant sculptures. Then, unexpectedly, he thought of his father who would never see this, never venture beyond his self-imposed ghetto in Brownsville to learn about the country that had saved him from the storms of the Old World.

Dinah gave the horn a tap. "Hey, get in, they sell postcards at the gift shop."

Arriving at the entrance to the monument, Joel vaulted from his seat and motioned for Dinah to follow.

"Can we get close?"

Dinah smiled at him slyly. "How close do you want to get?"

"Inside George Washington's nose," he said.

"*Eeew!*" She laughed. "All right, follow me." Together, they skipped off to the observation deck to join a group of tourists listening to a park ranger. "Took fourteen years to build. Same number of years as to build the Brooklyn Bridge." Dinah touched Joel's bare arm and smiled as if they now shared a special connection—Brooklyn.

The Ranger went on. "Rushmore is the largest carving of hard stone in all recorded history. Took four hundred men to remove the 450,000 tons of rock from the mountain. Done with dynamite, where the smallest slip might ruin the entire memorial. And, despite the obvious peril of hanging off a mountain and sculpting with explosives, none died or were seriously injured. Rushmore even had its own ball team made up of carvers, hired for prowess with bat and ball as much as their skill with hammer and chisel."

Dinah stifled a yawn. She'd heard it all before. Rain or shine, her father had brought them to the mountain every Decoration Day on an annual family pilgrimage. It was one of the few holidays they celebrated together, and Bernie always let her buy something at the gift shop.

"Let's go." Dinah took Joel's hand and pulled him past a "No Trespassing" sign up to the base of the monument. Looking up at Washington's nose, Joel could see that Dinah had delivered on her promise.

He took a deep breath and looked down at their hands—still locked together. "Do you think they can see us?" Joel asked.

"If we can't see them, they can't see us," she said smugly.

Joel was astounded by her moxie. “Do you often go around breaking rules like this?”

Dinah smiled slyly. “Don’t you want to know if I ever get caught?”

Secretly thrilled, Joel could only shake his head. The girl was trouble, maybe more than he could handle, and she was, he had to remind himself, only sixteen years old.

Joel studied the heads up close and was even more impressed by the carving—effects created by smoothing some rough surfaces while letting others remain untouched, or creating a detail like TR’s glasses with a tracery of stone or leaving a polished bit of rock in each eye socket to catch the sun, adding a spark of life. And most of all, how distinct expressions of mood and character were created in each countenance—Washington thoughtful, Lincoln brooding, TR resolute, Jefferson dreamy with a distant look in his eye as if charting the course of the Republic.

“Let’s go.” Dinah jerked Joel’s arm and they began their retreat, darting from tree to tree, like kids playing Peter Pan in the forest. Back on the observation deck, Joel pulled her into the gift shop. “I want to get my parents a postcard.” While Dinah browsed for jewelry, he stood at the card rack, examining each one. As he handed the cashier four cards, Dinah appeared behind him. “Who else you sending cards to?”

“My friend Morrie and this one’s for me.” He held up the last card in triumph, having found a shot of the four faces taken from the spot on the road where he’d first seen them.

“That leaves one,” Dinah observed. “Who’s that for?”

“My folks, different views.” Joel lied, slipping the bag of cards, including Rivkah’s, into the pocket of his chinos. “Who’s your favorite President, Dinah?” he said, changing the subject.

“Washington, I guess—Father of our Country and all, but my dad’s favorite is Polk.”

“Really? James K. Polk. That’s kind of an odd choice.”

“Daddy says he’s an unsung hero—knew what he wanted to do, got it done fast, and when he was through, the whole country was ours.”

Joel nodded. It made perfect sense for someone like Bernie to admire the President who’d bluffed the British and won Oregon, then beat Mexico for the rest of the West.

“Well, mine’s FDR. He belongs up there as much as his cousin Teddy.”

"Daddy likes Teddy, too. Says he came out here a sickly boy and the West made a man of him." Dinah threw Joel a coquettish look. "Guess that's why alotta people come out West, huh?"

"Never sick a day in my life, ma'am," Joel said, feeling suddenly bold as he wrapped an arm around her waist. "Let's go swimming."

On the winding road to the lake, the Skyliner climbed, then descended the mountain, each hairpin curve producing a squeal of tires and a skid, with only a low metal guard standing between them and the abyss. Silently, Joel recited the 23rd Psalm, King David's expression of faith and plea for divine protection. "*The Lord is my shepherd: I shall not want . . .* "

After what seemed like an eternity, the car came to a stop. Joel's eyes snapped open.

"You can stop praying now," Dinah said, laughing. "Saw your lips move."

Blushing, he looked out the window and saw a green meadow, and buffalo, a hundred or more, their honey-brown calves roaming the pasture foraging for grass. Joel gulped.

"I didn't think you'd want to miss this," Dinah said shyly.

Joel grabbed her hand and gave it a squeeze. "You're the best. Can we get close?"

Together they ran across the road to the fence corralling the animals. Dinah stopped a few feet from the barrier, but Joel strode up to it, extending his hand through the wooden slats. A lone bull swatting flies with his tail spotted him and plodded over.

"Not that close," Dinah cautioned. "Daddy says they can leap this fence if they get riled."

Joel studied the old bison—nearly ten feet in length and six feet tall at the hump, with a huge head and chest and outsized forequarters tapering to lean, muscled loins. Reaching into his pocket, he extracted a nickel and compared the image on the coin to the silhouette of the animal before him. "Not a bad likeness. Wonder if the engraver used this guy as his model." Joel flipped the nickel, plucked it from the air, and offered it to Dinah.

"A tip for a terrific tour guide. I never imagined I'd get this close to a real live buffalo. Thought they were all killed off to starve out the Indians."

"I don't know about that, but they've been in Custer State Park since I was a kid."

"So, this park's named for General Custer. I imagine he's a big hero out here."

Dinah threw him a confused look. "Where isn't he a hero?"

"Well, on the Indian Reservations, for sure."

"Oh! There!"

Joel winced at her dismissive tone; the same one she'd used when he told her about the incident with Clarence at the Club. It made him want to challenge her, but he held his tongue.

"That reminds me, where *are* you hiding the Indians? Heard there were thousands here."

"Didn't you stay at the Alex? There's always a bunch hanging around the bars on Main Street. You should steer clear of them."

Joel couldn't let that slide. "Wait a minute, Dinah. Indians have had it rough. We forced them onto reservations. Gave them the worst land we could find."

Dinah waved off Joel's argument. "They lost fair and square."

"Treaties were broken. Innocent women and children massacred."

Dinah glared. "They attacked white settlers. Scalped 'em, too. Everybody knows that."

Joel felt his blood rising. Didn't she know about the Trail of Tears or the Wounded Knee Massacre, right here in South Dakota? He looked at Dinah's face, stormy and petulant. Maybe he was being too hard on her. Before entering Columbia, he hadn't known that history either and saw things the way she did—the same way it was presented in movies he'd seen. And, as a kid, in games of *Cowboys and Indians*, when you tossed the coin, the loser had to play the Indian.

He'd never really thought about what that meant before.

"I guess it was a bloody history on both sides," he offered flatly.

Dinah didn't say anything, but her blue eyes flashed as she stared across the pasture.

To Joel, the magic of the day was slipping away. Even the old bull seemed to sense the change as he turned back to the herd. "That old boy must be their patriarch."

Dinah's puzzled expression told Joel that he needed a simpler word.

"Their leader, their daddy," he corrected.

Then a dark-coated cow arched its tail and let forth a spill of cloudy urine as wide as Niagara. When she'd finished, the old bull bellowed and ambled over. Sticking his nose in her arse, he nuzzled it for a time, then gave it a long lick, bottom to top, with his thick, silvery tongue, lingering as if savoring a rare liqueur. Stunned, Joel felt the color rise in his face.

Dinah hooted. “Been around animals much, Joel?” and he burst out laughing.

Grateful for the unabashed candor of a beast he thought was extinct.

Chapter Fifty-Two

LANA DID NOT REPRISE THE entire baseball anthem—she only got as far as "Take me . . . " and Guy was on her and in her, and minutes later, they did it all again. Spooning her afterwards, they fell out, their moist skin sticking, so that when he stirred, they both felt the breach and woke.

Guy reached around and cupped a breast with his hand. "Ever float these in the ocean?"

"Fresh water only," Lana said. "Never seen the Pacific and didn't make it to the beach in New York. It was too cold anyway—that one time."

"Come with me, baby, and I'll get them good and salty."

Lana turned to face him, resting on one elbow. "Is that a real offer?"

"Could be." Looking more serious than Lana had ever seen him, Guy took her face in his hands. "Listen. Something happened last night. I walked into the Club and thought, *I'm gonna see my girl.* And when Hacker whistled at your picture, I almost belted him. I haven't felt that way in years—maybe never."

Lana looked away. She'd cheated before—with hard-bitten bronco-busters and sweet soft boys like the pharmacist's son, but no one ever said anything like that to her, or offered to take her away. "I'm too old to start over."

"You? Too old? What are you—twenty-nine?"

"Hah! With a sixteen-year-old daughter?"

"OK. Don't matter. Listen. If things work out here, I could get a job in the Pacific Coast League. Big towns—San Francisco, Los Angeles, San Diego, *even* Hollywood has a team. I wouldn't be a manager at first, just a coach, but the Dodgers might make the big move to California, and I could end up in LA before long."

Lana fingered her wedding band. "I'm not looking to get married again. And I can't have any more kids, even if I wanted to."

"I don't care about kids—marriage either."

From his smile, she might have thought life had always gone his way, but she saw it for what it was—post-coital hubris. Big man, big plans. A modern-day Samson boasting of the lions he'd slay before his locks got caught in the scissors' blades.

Her face darkened. Bernie seemed to be growing suspicious. Last night's show, and the attention she'd paid Guy, had been a mistake. Afterwards, she went to Bernie to throw him off the scent, and he'd fucked her hard—a warning, claiming fuck—but despite a long shower and douche beforehand, she still feared he could sniff out the interloper.

There'd be no escaping Bernie. He'd come after them with both barrels blazing.

Misreading Lana's silence, Guy put his arms around her. "We don't need to get married. Being hitched to that sonovabitch would sour anyone on that."

• • •

Ten minutes earlier, Bernie would have caught Lana leaving Stockman's room at the Royal Rest. Five minutes earlier, he might have spotted her walking to the market where she'd parked the car, or seen her in the T-bird, heading west as he drove east toward Guy's motel.

When Guy sighted Bernie's Cadillac by the Manager's office, he hustled back to the room, flushed away a tissue branded with a red lip print and swept the sink and tub of stray strands of Lana's blonde hair. By the time the heavy knock came, he was ready for the man.

"Hello, Bernie. What brings you to my neck of the woods?" Guy moved inside the frame to block the man's advance.

"Heard you left the Alex. Wanted to make sure your new accommodations were up to snuff," Bernie said, with a cold smile.

"Yeah, fine, don't like to spend money just to sleep."

"Speaking of sleep, I called around to the other Basin League towns and found out which motels let the coloreds in. Cafés, too. They got something called the *Green Book* for that. Don't want Clarence sleeping on the bus again, or a repeat of that nasty business at the Club."

Guy shrugged. Clarence Williams was Bernie's boy, and it only seemed right that *he* should be saddled with the burden of figuring that out.

Bernie peered over Guy's shoulder into the room. "Passed this dump plenty of times but never been inside."

"Not much to see, Bern."

Bernie tapped his boot heel on the metal doorsill. "Yeah, well, gotta take a piss."

Brushing by Guy, Bernie glanced at the rumpled bed as he walked to the bathroom. Guy racked his brain to recall if Lana said Bernie packed a gun. While he was sure he could take the older man in a fair fight, he feared Bernie was a no-holds-barred kind of guy.

Bernie emerged from the bathroom, drying his hands on a small white towel. "Guess living in this dive makes back the money you gave Tony Schunot to get him out here."

Guy was surprised that Bernie knew about the deal he'd cut with the shortstop who'd blown out his hamstring in the exhibition game and decamped back to Florida.

"Yeah, I hear things." Bernie gave Guy a look as sharp as the silver-tipped toes of his custom-made boots. "All sorts of things."

Bernie chucked the towel against Stockman's chest and walked out the door.

Watching his cuckold stride to his Caddy, Guy knew it was the last time he and Lana would make love at the Royal Rest. But not the last time they'd make love.

That, he vowed, pitching Bernie's towel across the room, they'd do for a lifetime.

Chapter Fifty-Three

SYLVAN LAKE WAS UNLIKE ANY BODY of water Joel had ever seen. "Is it glacial?" he asked. Dinah shrugged, handing him the brochure the park ranger had given them at the entrance.

"I can't believe it. It's a man-made dam—not a lake at all!" What a wonder was the West, he thought—a place where you could mold nature to your desires—carve faces on a mountain or dam a prosaic little creek to make an enchanting sylvan 'lake'.

Dinah drove along the water's eastern edge and parked in a small lot. Reaching into the back seat, she tossed Joel his shopping bag and grabbed the grocery sack.

"You change, then we'll eat down on the beach."

"Don't you need to change?" Joel asked.

Without a word Dinah laid the bags on top of the trunk and shimmied her shorts to the ground. A polka dot bikini! The sight of her was better than he'd imagined, better than the Black Hills and Rushmore combined—better even than that randy old buffalo.

Joel grabbed the shopping bag and headed for the changing room. Standing in a bathroom stall, he stripped off his chinos and BVDs and prayed for his hard-on to subside, but the persistent memory of Dinah in her bikini kept him hard. Joel pulled his new swim trunks out of the bag and wriggled into them. Yanking them up to his navel, he found they fit tighter than he expected—with no room to hide his state of mind.

Joel began to sweat. He couldn't leave the bathroom like this, and he was taking too long to change. Lifting the toilet seat, he tried to pee, but the effort was fruitless. Briefly, he considered jacking off, but he'd never done it in a public place and certainly couldn't do it now. Then he thought of his parents, imagining them in the stall with him, and Rivka, too—how disapproving they'd all be of what he was up to with Dinah. And, how hurt.

Joel grimaced. This was the last thing he wanted to think about, but it worked. His hard-on drooped like a flower in the sun, and like a faucet turned on, his pee gushed forth in a long, hard stream. Then he washed his hands and splashed cold water on his face.

When he emerged from the bathroom, Dinah was sitting atop a log fence with two handsome park rangers circling around her. Spotting

Joel, she slid from her perch and waved 'toodeloo' to her newest conquests. Joel fought off a frown, recalling what a biology professor once said after passing a Barnard girl surrounded by admirers. "Ever wonder what a flower looks like to a bee?"

Being Dinah's boyfriend, he realized, would entail many such encounters and eternal vigilance, though he certainly couldn't blame the Rangers, or any man, for trying. Still, he wondered if she ever did anything to discourage male buzz.

"Don't those guys have forest fires to put out," he quipped.

Dinah hooted and Joel, glancing back, observed that the Rangers were keeping a watchful eye on the girl in the polka dot bikini. "I may have to set one myself to keep them occupied."

He took the bags from her and gave the Rangers a mocking salute.

Dinah was impressed. At least Joel could joke about it, unlike John who'd sulk, acting as if she'd gone out of her way to make him jealous. And Joel certainly looked good in those white swim trunks. For the first time all day, she felt the kick of anticipated pleasure as, hand in hand, they followed the winding trail down to the water. As they neared the white sand beach, they passed several families picnicking on blankets spread on the ground.

"How about somewhere less crowded?" Dinah suggested, and Joel smiled, sensing it was only a matter of time until he'd get at least a kiss from this alluring girl. Turning from the beach, Dinah led the way uphill to a flat slab of granite projecting from the side of the mountain. There she set out the food and soda pop.

"What's for lunch?" he said, picking up a sandwich wrapped in wax paper.

Dinah smiled. "Ham on rye."

His face fell.

"You don't like ham?" Dinah's voice cracked with disappointment. "I asked at Tally's what would keep best on a hot day and they said ham, because it's cured."

Joel nodded and turned away. What she'd done was well-intentioned, but it surprised him that Bernie Rosen's daughter didn't know the most basic tenet of a kosher diet—no pork. Then again, his friend Morrie ate bacon all the time, despite having a Jewish deli on practically every corner in New York. So, what could he expect in South Dakota—a kosher tongue sandwich?

Gingerly, he lifted the top piece of bread and examined the strange square of shiny pink meat. His throat tightened. Then, he remembered their salacious bull buffalo, and he rocked with laughter. If he could eat pickled tongue after seeing what that beast had done, then maybe he could try the ham.

"What's so funny?" Dinah asked, puzzled by his reaction.

"Ham is fine, Dinah—a smart choice, really."

Dinah beamed and pulled a bottle opener out of her bag and Joel, seeing the effect of his compliment, offered another. "And you remembered the opener. You deserve a merit badge!"

"Too bad I'm no Girl Scout." She wedged a Coke between her knees to pry the cap.

As Joel bent over to lend a hand, the cap popped and the warmed contents exploded, dousing them both in a shower of sticky brown fluid. "Damn it!" Dinah swore.

And Joel, looking down at the dark stain on his white trunks, declared, "We're going into the water," thinking God may have intervened to save him from a ham sandwich.

"This is better anyway," he added. "If we'd eaten all that, we'd have to wait to swim. You can cramp up when all the blood rushes to your stomach."

As soon as he said it, he realized it couldn't be true. All one's blood never went anywhere—except maybe to a penis, like back in the changing room. Just an old wives' tale, passed down through the ages—maybe not that different from an ancient proscription against pork.

"My mom never waits and she's never had a cramp," Dinah argued.

"It's a matter of probability," Joel said, then wished he'd picked a less pedantic term.

"Like odds in gambling," Dinah said, and Joel smiled, relieved. She was Bernie Rosen's daughter—she would know something about odds.

The water was icy cold, but Dinah dived right in, then popped up for a peek at Joel, standing shirtless onshore, revealing a thick matt of dark chest hair and powerful shoulders—a lot like her father. Finally taking the plunge, he swam to Dinah, who glided smoothly through the still water in a fluid breaststroke. Silently, they moved side by side toward a line of granite boulders jutting up from the depths like the knees and shoulders of a half-submerged colossus.

Motioning with her arm, Dinah directed Joel to the far side of the rocks, out of sight of the other swimmers and picnickers. With one hand wedged into a crevice, Dinah teased the stain from the bikini top with the fingernails of her other hand. Joel did the same, grateful that his work was underwater, since the biggest stain was over his crotch. Finally, she hauled herself up, impressing Joel with the strength in her arms and the ease with which she moved. Extending his arms to the top of a crag, he chinned himself out of the water, joining her on the rock.

Examining her handiwork, Dinah frowned. "We'll have to bleach our suits at home." Joel shook his head. "I'm not crazy about mine anyway."

"Why not? I think it looks good on you."

Joel didn't know what to say. He wasn't used to anyone remarking on his clothes.

Still, he'd heard it was smart to notice what a date was wearing. "Your suit is swell."

"It's a bikini, you know. They don't sell them in Rapid. My mom ordered it from Frederick's of Hollywood, where the movie stars shop."

"Is that where your mom's from—Hollywood?"

Dinah snorted. "Are you kidding? She was born and raised here, just like me."

"Oh, I thought . . . she's really talented . . . she's got a great voice."

Dinah made a face. "Yeah, she's got a good voice."

Joel sensed this was a sensitive subject—best avoided. "Do you sing, too?"

"A little," she said coyly.

"Sing something for me. I bet you're terrific."

Dinah hesitated. Joel had heard her mother at the Club. What if she didn't measure up?

Joel leaned back, grazing her shoulder. "Come on, Dinah, I'd love to hear you sing."

"Well, OK." Dinah stood and turning her back to Joel, bowed her head. Choosing the only song from *Damn Yankees* that her mother hadn't stolen for her own act, she raised her chin and turned to face him, her face rapturous in a way Joel had only seen before in religious art and Morrie's *Playboy* magazine. Staring straight at him, she began to sing.

Whatever Lola wants . . . Lola gets . . . And, little man, Little Lola wants you.

On the far side of the rocks, bathers and picnickers stopped their frolicking and searched for the source of the husky-voiced torch song caroming off the canyon walls.

I always get . . . what I aim for. And your heart and soul . . . is what I came for.

You're no exception to the rule. I'm irresistible, you fool. Give in! Give in! Give in!

When she finished, Joel reached up for her. "You're terrific, even better than your mom."

Dinah took his outstretched hand and let him pull her down to him. Then he murmured, "I give in," though she was the first to part her lips, and take him in.

Chapter Fifty-Four

THE SUN HAD SCARCELY CLEARED the horizon as the Chiefs boarded the bus for their game across the state against the Yankton Terrys.

Greeting each Chief as he climbed aboard, Fred, the bus driver, saved his warmest welcomes for Joel, Clarence, and the Moran boys, asking, with a wink, if they'd brought their K-Rations and bedrolls for bunking on the bus. And though he knew Joel's name, he called him "Freako," referring to John's now famous photo of Joel's contorted arm, caught in mid-pitch.

Head down, John tinkered with his Leica, hoping that Joel would board without noting his presence. He'd been avoiding the ballplayer all week, fearing he'd tell him what a great gal he was seeing—the same gal who'd once been *his* great gal. He almost refused the assignment to cover the Yankton trip, imagining what it would be like when the Chiefs swapped stories about their romantic conquests. Would Joel chime in about Dinah, John wondered—turning his private pain into public shame—or was the New Yorker the honorable sort?

Still, he felt better when two of the ballplayers stopped to praise his *Journal* photo, and he smiled, despite himself, when Joel slapped him on the back, dubbing him the "Kodak Kid."

Settling in for the long road trip, most of the men shut their eyes as they took their seats. Some were sleepy, others hung over from a night of carousing. Frank Hacker had returned to the New York Club to catch Lana Rosen's act a second time. Quarles went to the track and won the daily double with a pair of greyhounds named Dirty Rooski and Enola Grey. And Hoades and Kibbee got crocked at the Coney Island Club where they'd gone seeking a "strange piece of ass."

Clarence Williams spent his day off playing catch with Clarence Jr. and manning the barbeque—burgers for the kids and a replacement steak for Cherry Mae. Later, he was rewarded with the best lovemaking they'd had since coming to Dakota. Clarence figured it was the steak that accounted for his wife's ardor but having seen his bruised knuckles when he'd returned from the Club, she was elated merely to have her husband alive and home in one piece.

Joel spent his night in a rolling dream, constantly waking with a hard-on. "Somewhere in this house sleeps the girl of my dreams," he thought, then laughed since her exact whereabouts were unknown to him, confined as he was to kitchen and basement by Bernie's decree.

Aroused anew by the thought of her, Joel crossed his legs and stared out the bus window. In the distance, he saw the long, ragged outline of pastel-colored cliffs, a silhouette not unlike the New York skyline seen from the Jersey Palisades. Immense cloud shadows drifted across the stark surfaces, an image of Creation, he thought—the hand of God passing over the void.

"I call this the back door of the Badlands," Fred interjected, as if reading Joel's mind. "Not where you'd welcome company, but good enough for kin—and Injuns. We'll be passing through their land soon." Fred turned to Billy. "Be ready to circle the wagons."

Billy grinned, but Joel's jaw clenched. Was this how it would be for him in South Dakota—someone always making a prejudiced remark? He looked at Clarence across the aisle reading *Popular Mechanics*. Shouldn't he be offended at this swipe at Indians—like Negroes, stuck to the bottom of America's melting pot? Or maybe he just had enough of his own battles to fight.

Turning off the main highway, the bus bumped along a road that had turned rocky. Fred pointed to a road sign shaped like an arrowhead. "Tribal road. Rough ride for us ahead."

What bothered Joel most was biased talk from people he liked, not just jerks like Hoades. He recalled Dinah's warning to steer clear of the Indians on Main Street. He wondered if she'd been harassed by them. He knew from experience that was hard to forgive and forget. As a kid he'd been called a kike and roughed up by Negro toughs from neighboring Bed-Stuy—had his bus money stolen and yarmulke tossed about in a mean game of keep-away. White kids from the local Catholic school did that, too. They were painful memories, but what was he supposed to do? Hate all Black people? All Catholics? How could he be like that—be like Hoades?

"What's the matter, Joel?" Billy asked. Taken aback by the scrutiny, Joel realized he'd better perfect his poker face, or spend the entire summer explaining himself to the boy.

"So, when am I gonna see the *real* Badlands?" Joel asked, trying to sidetrack Billy.

"You coulda yesterday," Billy noted. "Whadya do all day?"

"Mount Rushmore and Sylvan Lake." Across the aisle, John steeled himself for what was coming. The Lake had been one of his and Dinah's favorite haunts, where it had all started for them.

"How? You don't drive," Billy asked.

"Took a tour," Joel lied, then quickly pivoted. "Ever drive a tour bus, Fred? Must be big business around here."

Setting forth a tale of his circuit days, Fred unknowingly provided cover for Joel's expedient fib while John stewed, suspecting that Joel was dissembling—either as a chivalrous attempt to keep Dinah's name out of the team's dirty patter, or simply to keep her all to himself.

"Drive anyone famous?" Joel continued.

"Well, they was said to be famous. Politicians and newspaper men, the summer Coolidge moved the White House out here. Never made so much money ferrying swells and baby kissers."

"Hey, driver, where's that restaurant you told us about? I'm starved," Stockman boomed.

"Comin' right up, Boss," Fred crowed, turning off the road into Pinky's, a ramshackle wooden café with a massive dead cottonwood out front. Joel half expected to see a buzzard on a limb, and a sign reading, *Dead Man's Gulch*, like in a Bugs Bunny cartoon.

"Whatta dump," Hoades interjected, as a bone-thin hound ambled by, dragging her teats through the dirt.

"Don't judge a cookbook by its cover," Fred countered. "If this ain't the best chili you ever 'et, I'll eat my Stetson."

"I played ball in Louisiana and nothing beats Cajun chili," Hoades protested.

"Are you kiddin'? Texas chili's tops," claimed Kibbee.

"Nope. Kansas City's best," added Quarles.

"Tally's!" Billy chimed in. Joel smiled, relishing the verbal chili war, but John stayed silent recalling the great buffalo chili he and Dinah shared last summer at a café in Custer.

Fred cranked open the door and the team trooped out, crossing the dusty lot to the café.

"Hey there, Big Bear, brought the whole team."

Big Bear smiled, exposing a broken hedgerow of yellowed teeth. "Good thing, or I woulda made you eat it all yerself."

Then he waved for Fred to move closer. "Who's the boss?" he whispered.

"Yellow hair, white hat."

Big Bear grunted "Custer" and spat on the floor,

The chili was hot and spicy and Joel dug in, having decided that morning to eat what was offered. Now he'd shun only pork, bacon, and dairy with meat. And he'd thrown away his internal calendar alerting him to his sin when he played ball on the Sabbath. None of his teammates knew he was Orthodox—and wouldn't get what that meant anyway. And he was sure that God had more pressing concerns than a fallen Jewish pitcher's transgressions out West.

Big Bear lumbered over to Stockman's table and stood over him for a long moment.

"Great grub," Stockman said, reaching for his wallet. "Whadda I owe ya?"

"Come outside, please."

Stockman glanced over at Fred, rising from the table, sporting a shit-eating grin. "He's got something to show ya, Coach. Ya won't be sorry."

"Why do I get the feeling this stop wasn't for the chili."

Sensing a story, John followed the men, with Joel and Billy close behind as Fred led them to a weed-choked field where a young Indian stood on a makeshift mound. He was about six feet tall but couldn't have weighed more than a hundred and thirty pounds.

When he saw the skinny Indian, Stockman turned on his heel and started back toward the café. Fred hurried over and blocked his path. "You got to be kidding!" Stockman growled.

"He's a terrific pitcher," Fred argued, "You'll see."

"He'd better be Allie Reynolds, but it don't matter 'cause our roster's full."

Joel knew about Reynolds, the all-star Yankee pitcher dubbed 'Super Chief' for his heritage and the speed of his fastball—likened to the famous train that ran between Chicago and California. Surveying the neglected ballfield and the weathered, defeated-looking men gathering around, he wondered if Reynolds, an Oklahoman, could have come from a place like this, too.

John recognized the young pitcher as Andrew Hanging Cloud, onetime ace of Rapid's American Legion team and, according to James, the greatest basketball player the State ever produced. John had seen him make the game-winning basket in the State Sectional Tournament, a soaring 'rainbow' from behind the half-court line. Afterward, all the boys in Rapid imitated him, aiming high-arching shots at hoops mounted over garage doors. His disappearance after graduation was a big disappointment to John and James, who'd hoped to follow his promising athletic career. Turning to Billy, who'd never seen him play, but had heard the stories, John supplied the name. "That's Andrew Hanging Cloud." Billy's mouth gaped. "Really? Wow!"

"Who is this kid?" Stockman asked. Big Bear didn't answer but Guy noticed the growing crowd of solemn men appearing as if out of nowhere. He figured that if he didn't give the young Indian a look, there might be trouble. He turned to Joel.

"Meznik, we need a catcher. Tell Hoades to get out here."

Joel jogged back to Pinky's—returning a minute later with most of the Chiefs in tow, but with Clarence Williams holding the catcher's mitt, not Hoades.

"I told him, but . . . " Joel could never repeat Hoades' stated refusal to touch the same ball as a "dirty Injun."

Guy looked at Clarence. He didn't want to stoke the Negro's desire to catch but couldn't waste any more time. Turning to Hanging Cloud, he said, "OK, let's see what you got."

Clarence appreciated the irony—that the bigot Hoades had given him the chance to show Stockman what he could do at his natural position. Warming up, Clarence quickly branded Hanging Cloud a 'slinger', powering his pitches not by cocking his arm at an angle and snapping the ball but by reaching all the way back with a nearly straight arm and whipping it across his body as he strode forward. By his sixth or seventh offering, Hanging Cloud seemed ready, but his pitches—all thrown sidearm—cruised in at a similar, unimpressive speed.

Standing behind Clarence, Stockman decided the tryout shouldn't take long. There was no getting around that sorry fastball.

Then, Hanging Cloud made a gesture with his glove, and in the same motion as for his heater, broke off a big, sweeping curve. Failing to pick up the Indian's signal, Clarence only managed to tip the ball, which to his chagrin, ricocheted onto Guy's shin. Grimacing, Guy ordered, "Do that again," and Hanging Cloud broke off another big bender.

"Is that it?" Stockman asked, ready to end the tryout.

Wagging his glove at Clarence, the skinny Indian offered another curve, but this time from an arm angle below sidearm, while stepping well to his right before releasing the ball. The pitch, like the curve before it, rose a bit before breaking sideways, but with that long starboard step and crossfire delivery, it seemed to come from third base. Guy at once saw the potential of such a pitch. In a big spot, against a right-handed slugger, it would be a devastating weapon.

"HACKER," he called out. "Grab a bat and get in there."

As Frank assumed his stance at home plate, a low murmur spread through the crowd, imagining a showdown between the sequoia-sized slugger and the reed-thin pitcher. Sensing danger, Stockman held up his hands. “He ain’t gonna swing. He’s just standing in as a target.” Then, he approached Hacker and said in a low voice. “Listen, Bambino, whatever you do, don’t swing your bat. I don’t want a repeat of the Little Big Horn.”

Turning to the Indian, Guy commanded, “Throw that last one again. The sidewinder.”

Striding to his right, his upper body angled nearly parallel to the ground, Hanging Cloud released a wide, flat curve that started toward Hacker’s hip before sweeping across home plate. Thinking the ball might hit him, Frank’s knees buckled and the big man stumbled to the ground. Enraged by the ululating whoops, Hack scrambled to his feet, brandishing his bat like a club.

Stockman stepped in front of his big slugger. “Ain’t ‘Geronimo’s’ fault you fell on your ass. That was a strike. If you wanna stick in the Big Leagues, you gotta learn to hit that pitch.”

Stockman jerked his thumb toward the parking lot. “All right, men, mount up.”

As the Chiefs filed slowly to the bus, Billy darted toward Hanging Cloud, arriving at the same moment as a pocked-faced young woman cradling an infant in her arms while a dark-eyed toddler tugged at her skirt. “I’m Billy Moran. My dad was your teacher. He told me about you.”

John approached and put out a hand. “It’s an honor to meet you. Saw you make the shot.”

Hanging Cloud didn’t respond. Picking up the toddler, he walked to his pickup with his family, leaving John to wonder what could have happened to him since high school.

Billy was mystified. If he’d made that legendary shot, he’d still be bragging about it.

Before boarding the bus, Guy pulled Fred aside. “Don’t ever do that again.”

The bus driver’s smile was ingratiating. “But ain’t he good?”

Stockman was not having it. “Wanna keep your job, stick to driving.”

Fred’s smile faded, and Stockman felt a twinge of regret. The man was a good driver and the kid had a special pitch. If another team picked him up and the Chiefs had to face him, he might regret his decision. “So why go to so much trouble for Big Bear? He *your* kin, too?”

"Me and Bear were bunker buddies on Saipan."

Like a skeleton key that opens all locks, their shared history of service turned the tumblers of Guy's heart. "Maybe, if someone's arm goes bad . . . right now, the roster's full."

"Thanks, Skip. I'll tell Bear."

"OK, long as he don't have the medicine man put a spell on our pitchers."

"Too late, the spell were in the chili," Fred added with a chortle.

A moment later, the Chiefs were back on the bus heading for Yankton. Then, it struck—full bellies transformed into agonizing crocks of flatulence.

"Hey, Fred, what the hell did Big Bear put in that chili?"

"Dunno, differnt ever' time." Fred ticked off the ingredients. "Beans o' course—rabbit or squirrel, antelope or buffalo when he can get 'em, and, o' course, rattlesnake."

The Chiefs erupted in groans. "Rattlesnake? I think I been poisoned."

"You guys are a bunch of sissies. Wouldn't last a day on Bataan. Hell, rats *was* Sunday dinner." Fred rubbed his belly with gusto.

"Yeah, snake ain't nothin'. We used to eat alligator gumbo," Hoades bragged.

"Alligator? What's it taste like?" Casey asked.

"Once you pick off the scales, I'd say chicken."

"All critters taste like chicken," offered Kibbee.

"Dog don't," interjected Quarles, with authority.

"You eat dog?" Hacker asked, a pained look on his face.

"Well, yes, once. Some Indians do, too. Never bring Fido to an Indian rally, big man. You might go home with an empty leash."

"Is that really true?" Hacker asked, begging Q to say it ain't so.

"Bye, bye, bow-wow at the pow-wow," Quarles quipped.

Joel frowned. He couldn't believe Q could make a joke about Indians after seeing the bleak conditions on the reservation.

Hacker groaned. "That's not why they call 'em hot dogs, is it?"

Casey and Paskiewicz hooted at the big man's innocence. Quarles turned toward Fred with an impish look and shouted. "Hey Fred, Big Bear put dog in the chili?"

"Nah. Dog a delicacy to the Sioux. He don't give it to strangers, saves it for hisself. 'Course, he might give it to the White Man if he wanted somepin' special, like a favor."

Quarles probed. "Like signing one of their braves to a contract?"

"Well . . . dunno . . . guess so . . . maybe," Fred hedged.

"Not *this* white man, Fred," Stockman rejoined, using Fred's name for the very first time.

The Chiefs broke out in guffaws, without Joel joining in, though something other than the chili and the jokes was troubling his gut. Would Stockman have signed Hanging Cloud if the roster wasn't full? Or would he cut one of his pitchers later to make room for a man who offered a special kind of weapon, the confounding 'sidewinder', a nearly unhittable pitch to a right-handed batter?

Joel's mouth went dry. He had pitched well in relief, but he didn't want to just be a reliever—he was better than that. To secure his place on the team and to impress the scouts, he needed to return to the starting rotation. And he needed to win. There were no two ways about it.

Chapter Fifty-Five

FRED HAD TO GUN IT to make up for time lost on the reservation checking out Hanging Cloud. Crossing the Missouri in the late afternoon, he pulled into Riverside Park, where Billy took note of the sign: "Home of the Yankton Terrys."

"Why'd they pick a guy's name like Terry?"

"Maybe it's short for terriers, those scrappy little Scottish dogs," Joel offered.

John set them straight. "The team's full name is the 'Territorials'. Yankton was the capital of Dakota Territory until 1890, and Yankton's the name of a tribe of the Great Sioux Nation—means *village at the end of the line*—the place where they made their winter camp."

"Interesting, Moran!" Joel was impressed.

John smiled, then looked away, peeved with himself for being cheered by his romantic rival. "Damn that girl," he swore. If not for her, he might have been friends with Joel.

Exiting the bus, John decided on a few pre-game shots from Riverside Field. Built along the riverbank, the grandstand offered splendid views of the Missouri and the grasslands beyond. Gazing at the broad ribbon of water, he imagined himself transported downstream all the way to New Orleans. He really should go. Dinah was lost to him anyway, and the thought of her and Joel together made him want to scream.

"Hey 'Jimmy Olson'. The action's this-a-way."

John turned to find a squat, ruddy-faced man leaning on a pair of crutches. Who was he, John wondered, and why had he called him *Jimmy*? Then, he remembered. Jimmy Olson was the cub reporter in Billy's Superman comics.

Tucking one crutch into his armpit and leaning on his left leg, he extended an open hand.

"Don Bierle, Sports Editor, *Yankton Press & Dakotan*. Paddy said to keep an eye out for you."

John introduced himself but tried not to stare at the man's legs. He assumed that Bierle had suffered polio—a much worse case than his own—though he wore no leg braces.

"Need any dope on the Terrys? Us newshounds gotta stick together. All part of the same kennel club." The man laughed. "Of course, I'd expect as much from you."

Caught off guard, John wasn't sure what he might ask or reveal in exchange.

Bierle went on. "How'r things going with your colored ballplayer? Any problems there?"

John's mind flashed on Hoades and the ugly confrontation over the cottonwood fluff. And the incident in the New York Club bathroom. His guard rose like a shield. "No real problems there," he lied, protecting—as he thought he must—his town and team.

"Really? He's the only Negro in the league this summer. Can't be easy."

John frowned. He fancied himself a reporter but never considered writing about a serious issue like race relations on the Chiefs. Did he have the guts to put the team in a bad light or air the town's dirty laundry? And would the *Journal* even print it? They'd squelched the story about the fracas at the Club. Why would this story be any different?

Bierle laughed and touched a finger to his nose. "That's OK, kid—if there's a story, I'll sniff it out. Here's some free advice. When I'm working out of town, I always get the local paper. You can learn a lot that way—see what's on people's minds." Balancing on a crutch, he reached into his pocket for a copy of the *Yankton Daily Press*. "Just happened to have . . . "

John took the newspaper. "Thanks, Mr. Bierle. Guess if I had the *Journal*, we'd be even." Bierle jammed his crutch into his armpit and slapped the side of his neck with his hand.

"Damn bugs. If mosquitoes were a cash crop, Yankton would be swarming with millionaires."

Watching him hobble away, John felt a prick of shame. Things had turned out so much better for him with the polio, but he was nowhere near as cheerful as this man.

Finding a seat in the grandstand, John turned to Bierle's column. Then a headline about a local high school boy caught his eye.

"Tom Brokaw and Governor Foss to be on National TV Show"

Two South Dakota governors will appear on the television show Two for the Money, *Saturday, August 3—Gov. Joe Foss and Boys State Governor, Tom Brokaw, a 17 year old Yankton high school student. The appearances will be in connection with Boys State and Boys Nation, concluding in Washington, DC.*

John's envy swelled with each line of the story. A year ago, he'd held office at Boys State, too, but only as Lieutenant Governor. It made him wonder why he'd not vied for the top spot. Then he, not Brokaw, might be paired with Governor Foss and get a chance like that.

The TV people have arranged for his all-expense paid trip via airline from Rochester, Minn. to New York and for several days stay at the Hotel Abbey there.

John hit the seat beside him with the newspaper. A headline and story like this about him would make Dinah sit up and take notice again. And who could tell where this kind of fame might lead. John rose from his seat and tossed the newspaper into a nearby garbage can. He'd learned enough about what was on the minds of the people of Yankton.

• • •

Heading north on US 81, the Chiefs were in high spirits after their dramatic come-from-behind win over the Terrys. And no one on the bus was happier than Billy, but not just because of the victory. For they were on their way to something he'd heard about all his life and seen in countless photos and postcards, the world-famous Corn Palace of Mitchell, South Dakota.

Joel could not share in the merriment. He'd been the Chiefs' starter and had put the team in a deep hole, surrendering four runs to the Terrys before being yanked in the second inning.

Clarence tried to console him by blaming the hometown umpire, but Joel knew it was the specter of Andrew Hanging Cloud that threw him off kilter—along with the looming roster deadline. Stockman had to decide soon if he wanted to cut someone to make room for the 'Lakota Sidewinder', and that someone just might be him.

As Joel brooded on his fate, Billy jabbered on, speculating about the theme of this year's Corn Palace display. In years past, the huge exterior murals had depicted events of South Dakota history, agricultural tableaux, indigenous wildlife, and during the War, scenes of Allied victories. "They use corn in all these different colors—red, brown, purple—not just yellow!" Billy crowed.

"Can't wait," John said about the State's third-most famous attraction after Rushmore and the Badlands. His mood, which plumbed new depths after reading about Tom Brokaw and the quiz show, soared when he saw Stockman take the ball from Joel's hand in Yankton. Now, he figured Hanging Cloud might hasten Joel's exit from both the team and Rapid.

"Look, it's sports," Billy cried with delight as the Corn Palace came into view—a massive, fortress-like building the size of a city block, covered by murals made of varied colors of corn, grain, and straw.

Fred chuckled, recognizing that season's theme. "Kid, somebody up there must like you 'cause I don't recall the palace ever doin' sports before."

"This is great!" Stockman yelled. "Better'n Wall Drug. Everyone out—twenty minutes."

Billy took off like a shot, determined to see the murals on all four sides. John grudgingly followed. He would have preferred to stay back and exchange observations with an educated person like Joel but felt deceitful after reveling in the collegian's recent failure.

"Looks like the Kremlin," Joel mused to himself, noting the several onion domes crowning the roof. Then recalling Hoades' slur about Commie Jews, and John's claim that the Rosenbergs were Russian spies, he was glad he hadn't uttered his impressions aloud. Though sharing the rooftop were sixteen American flags. Joel wondered if they'd been added to nullify any Communist associations that tourists might otherwise make to those Kremlin-like domes.

On the sidewalk, Stockman spoke to Joel for the first time since he'd relieved him of the ball the night before. "Hey, Meznik—isn't there a Jew word for this? Heard it in Coney Island about the pavilions."

Joel's throat tightened. For a moment he couldn't speak. Stockman might have said "Jewish" and avoided offense, but there it was—the 'Jew' slur—slipping off his tongue so easily that Joel suspected it lived there always, right on the tip. Still, this was the man who held his future in his hands.

"Kitsch," Joel answered flatly though he knew the word was German, not Yiddish.

Stockman nodded. "Yeah—that's it—kitschy," then placed a hand on the wall of colorful cobs. "How did they do this?" he asked with childlike wonder.

Joel studied the mosaic. "Looks like they split the cobs in half and nailed them to the wall."

Stockman nodded. "Well, it's just amazing."

Joel snorted at Stockman's unintended pun. "An . . . *ah* . . . *maz* . . . *ing* monument to *maize*."

Stockman slapped Joel on the back. "You're one smart . . . kid. If only you can get control of your breaking ball. Think you're smart enough for that?"

Joel swallowed hard. So, time wasn't yet up for this one smart Jew. And Stockman was right. Control was key, and not just in pitching.

• • •

The Mitchell *Kernels* played ball on flat prairie ground which had once been a cornfield and could easily be turned back into one. John found it lackluster, expecting more from a town boasting the colorful Corn Palace. Maybe it was the setting. The Terrys had Big Muddy, the Cowboys, the Capitol dome, and the Chiefs, a grand view of the Black Hills.

Shifting his gaze, John noticed a tall, smiling man surrounded by a crowd of admirers. Moving closer, he recognized George McGovern, the first Democrat elected to Congress from South Dakota in twenty years, representing the rich farming area east of the Missouri.

"That's right," McGovern was saying, "my father played ball in the Cardinals' chain, but wasn't keen on the seedy pastimes of the sport back then, so he became a preacher—which I'd planned to be too, until I discovered I didn't have the temperament. Not sure what he would have made of my going into politics instead—with all the wheeling and dealing in Washington."

"Maybe he'd say you were just looking for a bigger pulpit, George," a man called out, and McGovern laughed, his eyes twinkling merrily.

Close-up, John measured the lanky politician with interest. His manner was easy and his eyes steadfast and sincere—though squinty, like a farmer gazing across a cornfield, or the war hero he'd been, piloting a B-24 Liberator on more than thirty missions over Germany.

John sensed something else, that he'd also observed in Governor Foss, another war hero—a humble confidence and manly demeanor which made them seem older than their years. John wondered if leading men into battle—delivering some home but others not—made them what they were. He feared it was something that, because of his infirmity, he could never know himself.

McGovern looked over the crowd and caught sight of John with his camera. "Hello there, young man—were you sent from the *Daily Republic*? Need a picture?"

"No. The *Journal*—Rapid City. But I *would* like a photo."

"Ah—a delegate from the West River—not my constituency but welcome all the same."

"Not your constituency *yet*, George," someone added, referring to a possible statewide run for the US Senate.

"Let's not get ahead of ourselves; it's only the first inning," McGovern quipped, before returning his attention to John. "Your people—are they farmers or ranchers?"

"Farmers on my mother's side, ranchers on my dad's."

"Hmm—a mixed marriage." McGovern's jest drew a knowing laugh from the crowd and a nod of assent from John, who'd learned from his dad the bitter history of their state, cleaved eternally into rivalrous halves by the Mighty Missouri cutting north-south through its heart.

"Rugged individualism crossed with communal rootedness—the sturdy American character." McGovern went on in a flat, prairie accent, enunciating each syllable as if it were part of a campaign speech. "I see you're interested in journalism—are you going to college, son?"

John nodded. "Yes, I'm starting in the fall," neglecting to mention Yale.

"Brookings? Vermillion? Maybe my alma mater, Dakota Wesleyan?"

"I'm going East."

McGovern nodded, recognizing the modesty in John's response. Turning, he addressed the group in summation. "But there's nothing like coming home to Mitchell, walking the streets, talking to folks, watching a ball game with old friends and a couple of new ones." He held out his hand to John. "Good luck to you . . . " His pause conveyed a request and John responded.

"I'm John Moran, Congressman."

"John Moran, a fine Irish name." McGovern clasped John's hand between his. "If you get down to DC, drop by and see me. We can always use another bright young Dakotan."

John nodded, pleased by the man's solicitude, and heartened by the turn of events. Ever since the polio, he'd dreaded the vagaries of life. It seemed that no good ever came of them, but with Joel edging closer to his exit and his own horizons broadening, perhaps this summer in South Dakota would prove that wrong. "I will, sir. Yes, I certainly will."

Chapter Fifty-Six

DINAH OPENED THE DOOR of the Skyliner and tossed a book onto the back seat.

Glen reached back and read the title. *Gidget, the Little Girl with Big Ideas.*

"She's a California surfer girl." Dinah sighed. "Boy, I'd love to go there."

"I'd love to go . . . back." He gazed dreamily at the sky and Dinah socked him in the shoulder. "You're such a jerk—you've already been there!"

Glen lightly touched Dinah's arm. This was the chance he'd been waiting for—to become more than just her theater buddy—maybe even her boyfriend. For despite getting some action from college-girl Rhonda, Dinah was the girl who fueled his fantasies and dreams.

"Why don't we go? We can audition for the Mousekeeters. You've got wheels and I know where my folks stash their cash."

Dinah hooted. "Are you kidding? You're only fourteen and I just turned sixteen."

Though hurt by her putdown, he pressed on. "You think Annette and Cubby are eighteen? You gotta start young in Hollywood."

"Come on, Glen—didn't you agree to work here all summer? I know I did."

"So, all that griping 'bout cornpone and the Director's pawing was just talk, huh?"

"No. I do want to go. And I'd love to audition for the Mouse Club. Just not now."

"Must be that ballplayer," he shot back. "I saw the two of you drive off yesterday."

Dinah didn't say anything. Oddly, Joel hadn't crossed her mind. Their thrilling moment at Sylvan Lake had been interrupted by a bunch of bratty boys in a rowboat. Later, when they made out in Dark Canyon, it wasn't all that different from necking with John Moran, or the boys she'd known since him. She wondered what made that kiss on the rock so magical. Was it the beauty of the lake, or would she have to sing for him every time to get that special feeling—be that other Dinah, the one she became onstage?

"I'm right. I can see it from your face. It's him." Glen began cracking his knuckles, a succession of pops that set Dinah's teeth on edge.

"My father would kill me—and you, too."

Glen swallowed hard. He'd only met Bernie Rosen once but knew the man's reputation and suspected it might be true. "Just forget it."

Sulking, he tossed *Gidget* into the back seat while Dinah brooded. Could Glen be right? Should she be in Hollywood, getting discovered before she got too old?

One thing she knew for sure—her dad would never let her go. The look on his face when he yanked her mom off the stage in New York was something she'd never forget.

• • •

It was 2 a.m. and the Chiefs were headed back to Rapid after another shellacking by the Mitchell Kernels. This time it was Haroldson who'd pitched badly, giving Joel a measure of guilty comfort. At least, he wasn't the only Chiefs hurler to get bombed on the trip.

All the Chiefs were asleep except Joel, plucked from a dream about Dinah by a lightning storm that split the sky with sharp, spidery bolts. Waiting for his pulse to quiet, he wondered if she was dreaming of him, too, or even thinking of him at all. Recalling the park rangers at Sylvan Lake and his teammates ogling her at the Club, he feared she might already have found someone else to take his place.

Not that he hadn't had his temptations, too—local girls waiting at the stadium gate. But he couldn't imagine chatting up a new girl when all he could think of was that first kiss at Sylvan Lake. For the first time in his life, he understood the meaning of 'besotted'.

Arriving at the Rosens', he flipped on the kitchen light and looked for a sign he'd been missed—like a note from Dinah or a plate of homemade cookies. Then he saw the envelope addressed in his mother's hand propped against the napkin caddy. Behind it lay a second letter—this one from Rivkah.

Who had arranged the mail like this, he wondered. He recalled how Dinah had counted his postcards at Rushmore and questioned him about their recipients. How might she react to a girl from home writing *him*? Surely, she was more accustomed to inciting jealousy than suffering it.

Joel stuffed the letters into his pocket and opened the fridge. Foraging for peanut butter, he didn't hear the footsteps behind him. "Find what you're looking for?" It was Lana, in a sleeveless pink peignoir. Startled, he almost dropped the jar of Skippy. What kind of mother paraded around like that? Certainly not his own mother back in Brownsville.

"Bread's in the breadbox—jelly, refrigerator door," she said, taking a seat at the table.

"Thanks," Joel said, struck dumb.

Lana pointed to the napkin cannister with her cigarette. "Find the letters? Both of 'em?"

Joel detected an edge to her voice. "Yes, thank you, Mrs. Rosen," he said, relieved that Lana, not Dinah, had put them there.

"I see you're from Brooklyn. You goin' back there in the fall?"

Joel stopped his sandwich making, unsure of where she was headed. "I expect so."

"Fine. Just don't leave a bundle on my doorstep after you're gone."

Stunned, Joel stammered, "Wh . . . what? But . . . we're not . . . "

"Oh sure. Have it your way. But when you do, be a good boy scout and be prepared."

Joel blanched. He couldn't decide what was more shocking—that Lana thought he and Dinah were doing it or that she was brazen enough to talk about contraception. "OK."

"OK—what? You know where to get 'em?"

Joel hesitated. "I can find out."

"I'll save you the trouble. Mills Drug. Downtown. Across from the Post Office."

Joel returned the milk to the refrigerator, wishing he could climb in with it and shut the door behind him. He'd fantasized about going all the way with Dinah, but knowing that Lana anticipated it, maybe even condoned it, made it seem sordid.

Lana took a drag on her cigarette, then gazed out the window to the Moran house. "Can't promise you'll be her first, though. The neighbor boy may have beat you to it."

• • •

Dinah charged down the steps and threw herself on Joel's bed. "Wake up, sleepyhead!"

Joel opened his eyes and smiled, but only for a second, as his doubts about her came barreling back with a vengeance. "What time is it?" he asked.

"Almost noon. I thought for sure you'd be up by now."

Joel leaned back against the cushion. After what Lana had alluded to, he expected to find Dinah less alluring, but she was as appealing as ever. "I got in really late."

"That's OK—we still have time." With that, Dinah lifted her skirt and straddled Joel, her thighs sandwiching his. Bending forward, she let her blouse brush against his bare chest as she kissed him full on the mouth, her tongue tickling his lips.

"Dinah—your folks." Joel grabbed her shoulders to restrain her.

"They left." Smiling, she moved herself slightly against his groin.

Joel groaned despite himself and Dinah wedged her fingers under the band of his BVDs.

"No . . . Dinah." He grabbed her hand and held it tight, so she couldn't go any further.

"I want to see it," she said with a sly smile.

He was both excited and repelled. What kind of girl demanded to see a penis? Was she a sex fiend? Or did she want to compare him with John Moran?

Above them, they heard a door slam.

"Oh, God," Joel cried, pushing her away. "What if it's your dad?"

Dinah put a finger to her lips and, grabbing Joel's hand, pulled him off the bed. In the dim cellar light, she led him across the room through an arched doorway, past a small bathroom and laundry to a steel door painted an inky black.

"You're kidding me, right?" Joel's eyes widened as they entered what he'd read about but never seen—a cinderblock, A-Bomb fallout shelter, complete with cots, card table, flashlights, shelves stacked with Fiestaware, canned goods, and six cases of Coke.

"Yep," Dinah said proudly, locking the door. "Daddy says it's the only one on the block, maybe the whole neighborhood." Grabbing his hand, she pulled him to a cot under a poster of Marlon Brando on a motorcycle. "Let's pretend it's the end of the world," she whispered, wrapping her arms around him.

At that moment, Joel could have killed Lana Rosen. If she'd not turned over Dinah's rock, exposing the grubs and slugs of her past—he might have been able to join in her game, maybe not all the way, but far enough. Now, all he could see was John Moran and could barely remember how he'd felt about her on that glorious day at Sylvan Lake.

He grabbed her arms and pulled them from his neck. "No, Dinah. I can't."

Dinah's face fell. "You met someone on the road, didn't you?"

The hurt in her voice stirred him more than all her sexy appeals. "No!"

"Then, why not?"

"Somebody's upstairs. And your car's still in the driveway. They'll be looking for you."

"That's not the reason. I can tell."

Joel sat down on the cot and held his head in his hands. "You're too young."

Dinah folded her arms across her chest. "I wasn't too young in Dark Canyon."

"We only made out," Joel protested.

"So, what did you think we were going to do here?"

"You asked to see my . . . "

"I've never seen one."

Joel snorted. "Oh, sure. What about John Moran?"

"Who said that . . . that little snitch Billy?"

"So, it *is* true. You did it with John Moran."

"I did not. Billy's a liar if he said that."

"Billy didn't tell me."

"Then who . . . John? He's a bigger jerk than I thought."

Just then, there was a loud pounding on the shelter door. Dinah and Joel froze, as a male voice called out. "I know you're in there. I can hear you talking." It wasn't Bernie.

"Go away, Glen," Dinah yelled.

"We're going to be late!" he shouted.

Dinah beat on the door. "Screw the Mellerdrammer!" she cried back.

Joel looked at Dinah, then around the room, with all the provisions Bernie had stockpiled for Armageddon. Fiesta in the fallout. Brando in the bomb shelter. The absurdity of it made him giddy. He lunged at the door and cupped his mouth against the steel divide.

"Screw you, whoever you are! We're waiting for the end of the world. So, scram!"

Dinah looked at Joel and Joel at her and their laughter rang through the shelter like a shock wave.

Chapter Fifty-Seven

AT 6 A.M., CLARENCE STRETCHED out his hand to silence the alarm. He'd been asleep for only three hours, falling out after making love to Cherry Mae on his return from Mitchell. Miffed at being awakened mid-dream, she soon sparked to his advance, then fell back asleep.

Clarence wished he could have caught a little more shut-eye, but knew he had to report at the regular time. Sometimes it rankled him that he was the only Chief who had to work. The other pros got paid just to play ball, and the collegians had their sham jobs. And he couldn't just go through the motions either. He and the other engine mechanics were responsible for keeping the B-52s in the air. It was tricky, working out the kinks in the new bird, but he was proud to do it. At times, he even loved his job, a feeling he never had working on earthbound vehicles.

Dragging himself from bed, he showered for a quick wake-up. Over coffee he read an account of the Flyers' exploits in the town team league, a 13-2 walloping of Swanson's Bread. Clarence chuckled. The 'Loafers'—always a soft spot on the schedule. He recalled the summer before—playing with his buddies—whites *and* Blacks on the Air Force team. Never having to worry about being cut or shunted off to left field, or getting beaned, as he just was in Yankton.

Still, he was grateful that Stockman told the Chiefs not to talk about that. Cherry Mae already had her suspicions about what transpired when he went to collect his free steak at the New York Club. Another unexplained incident and she might ask him to quit.

And, despite everything, he didn't want to quit. The fast competition of the Basin League was bringing out the best in him. He'd got his stroke back, and he might yet get a chance to catch. He liked Joel and Quarles and got along well enough with Stockman, at least for now. And he'd be lying to say he wasn't pleased when his teammates charged the mound on his behalf after the beaning. A week before, he wouldn't have believed it was possible. Of course, Hoades and his sidekick, Kibbee, weren't part of the avenging band, but that was simply too much to expect. He wished he could lure those two crackers to the Coney Island Club—let a couple of Negro airmen he knew work 'em over good.

Clarence returned the milk to the fridge and grabbed the sack lunch he found there, leaving his dirty dishes on the counter. Cherry

Mae would get on him for that, but he figured it was just sowing a seed he'd reap later—a little tiff, with the makeup ending sweetly between the sheets. That part of his life was better now, too. Being on the road with the Chiefs was like recess had always been, the best way to blow off steam and duck some of life's tedium.

Maybe that's what Jennie Moran was about—a way to beat the boredom of a dull Dakota winter. Then he remembered how her eyes sought his, like nothing he'd ever seen from Cherry Mae. Three times it was, and always in a parking lot, like a plea to take her away.

Suddenly drained, he stepped from the trailer. He felt the sun on his face and the wind at his back, a stiff gust which caught his jacket like a sail and sped him on his way. For a moment, his fatigue ebbed, letting him reflect on the blessings in his life—his job, his kids, his cozy mobile home, his season with the Chiefs, imperfect though promising, and most of all, his Cherry Mae, who made him coffee, packed his lunch, and let him make love to her in the middle of the night. What kind of fool would risk all that?

Then, a pair of white Air Force Police drove by in a jeep, their expressions a mix of scorn and derision. Clarence shrugged. Some things, he figured, never change, and likely never would. But some, he now believed, really could.

Chapter Fifty-Eight

JAMES WAS WAITING IN THE KITCHEN for his sons to report on the Chiefs' eastern road trip when Jennie walked through the door, grocery sack in arms. "I thought we might have some French toast before we go to the ballpark."

James smiled, heartened to see Jennie up and dressed and enthused about something.

"No game today, Jen. Just a practice this afternoon."

"Oh . . . " Jennie turned from her husband and pulled the egg carton from the sack.

Hearing the letdown in her voice, James realized how much the Stand meant to her. On game days she became her old self again. Even better than her old self, he thought with a flush of heat, with that exciting, post-game dividend, their middle-of-the-night lovemaking. It was the only time they had relations now as she'd taken to the living room sofa most other nights.

John sat down at the table and James reached over and clapped him on the shoulder. "So, tell me about the Chiefs' skirmishes on the Eastern Front."

"We're not supposed to talk about it, but a Terrys' pitcher threw at Clarence's head."

The eggs slipped from Jennie's hand and fell to the floor.

"Mom!" John jumped to avoid the splatter and James grabbed a dishrag from the sink.

Jennie knelt to clean up the spill. "Is Mr. Williams all right?"

"He's fine, Mom." Billy stood, excited to relate the tale. "The pitcher tried to bean him, but Clarence got out of the way. The next time he tried it, the whole team charged the mound."

"Not Hoades or Kibbee," John corrected. "A decade since Jackie Robinson and nothing's changed here."

James frowned. "Don't be so hard on your home state, John. Those two players are Southerners."

"There was an earlier incident at the Club with Clarence. Local guys," John added.

"What!" Billy and James said together, and Jennie let out a soft groan.

"He wasn't hurt, Mom. And Bernie killed the story. Said it would be bad for the town."

"Bad for his business, more likely," Jennie countered.

James chortled, amused by her taking a swing at Bernie from her knees.

"I'm not sure it's the right thing to do, covering this up and pretending it doesn't happen here," John insisted. "Some things are more important than this stupid ball team."

James glowered. "Most boys would give their eye teeth to travel with the Chiefs like you do. Plus, all the good things it's doing for Rapid." And family finances too, he added to himself.

Jennie shook her head. "No, John. If Mr. Williams doesn't want to make a fuss, then you shouldn't either. You don't want to make life harder for him."

"Maybe Rosa Parks should have given up her seat on the bus, too!" John shot back.

James bristled. "As a journalist, you can't make half-baked cracks like that. What would you write? Pitchers brush back *white* hitters all the time. They call it 'chin music'."

"Who's Rosa Parks? Does she live downtown?" Billy asked, figuring that anyone who had to take the bus didn't own a car and lived downtown.

John scoffed. "I'm going to the *Journal*." Turning on his heel, he slipped on a splash of egg white before catching himself. "Damnit!" he yelled.

James grabbed John's arm. "Help clean up this mess. And clean up your mouth, too."

Frowning, John hesitated, then took the rag from his mother and got down on the floor. Jennie dumped the eggshells in the trash and walked from the room.

With a sigh, James pulled a box of Cheerios from the cupboard. Somehow, it had turned into another cold cereal morning.

Chapter Fifty-Nine

GUY STOCKMAN'S DAY BEGAN WITH the phone ringing by his bedside. It was Lana, calling from a booth at *Safeway* grocery. "Where are you?" she asked. "We said noon at Safeway."

Picking the sand from his eyes, Guy remembered now. At noon he was to drive to the rear of the big supermarket, wait for her to lose the T-Bird in the crowded lot, then slip through the busy aisles to the back door, where she'd jump into his Pontiac for the short drive to their hideaway. He hadn't forgotten but was too beat to hear the alarm. All he could do now was apologize and hope for Lana's mercy. "Sorry, babe. Guess I overslept."

For a moment Lana didn't respond. She was piqued, though not really hurt. She knew the Chiefs' bus had gotten in very late. Softening her voice to a throaty whisper, she offered forgiveness. "It's all right, Guy. You can make it up to me. Come fetch!"

Guy's cock rose to attention at her command, which sounded a lot like "Come fuck!" "I'll be there in twenty minutes, just need to shave and shower."

"How long if I take you dirty?"

Guy cupped his balls in his free hand. "OK, babe. Back of *Safeway* in ten. And bring me a sandwich—a ham sandwich—or any other lunchmeat if ham's a problem."

Lana stared at the receiver. "Why would ham be a problem?"

"Well," Guy stammered, "... I, uh, thought, because you're Jewish?"

Lana hooted. "Me, a Jew? I'm a South Dakota shiksa. What else you got wrong about me?"

When Guy drove up to the back of the store, Lana was waiting.

"Hi!" she said, as she stepped from the shadows and produced from behind her back the ham sandwich he'd asked for and a red apple with a single leaf on top. "Wanna bite?"

Guy laughed and took the apple, thinking it couldn't hurt to freshen his breath.

The hideaway was named Verna's Cabin Court, which Guy had spotted with the cunning of a private dick. Six snug little cabins, well-separated and concealed from passing motorists by thick veils of pine and spruce. "You could hide an eighteen-wheeler behind those trees," he thought. His red Pontiac convertible? No problem.

When they arrived at Verna's, Lana stayed in the car while he went inside for the key. When he stepped outside, the Pontiac was gone. He assumed she'd moved it to cabin #5, the one he told her he'd reserved, and there he found it, now with the top down, parked between a tall hedge and a thick stand of pine, with the cabin closing off a third side. Lana was nowhere to be seen until he got close and saw her lying in the backseat, naked as the jaybirds flitting in the trees above. "Get in, Guy," she whispered. "They can't see us."

At half past noon on a summer's day there was indeed little chance of being seen. The tourists were up in the Hills seeing the sites, the maid had gone home, and the old couple who ran the place were in their office sharing a ruminant lunch. And so, he stepped into the back seat of the car and there, amidst the dappled light of a piney bower, she gave him the ride of his life.

"Now *that's* my idea of nature," he thought afterwards, gazing at Lana's rosy cheeks and amber locks, framed by a robin's-egg blue sky. Thirty years old and he'd never fucked outdoors before, not in broad daylight anyway and not joined by birdsong. He was thunderstruck.

Guy pulled on his jeans and walked around the corner to the door of the cabin. Following his signal, Lana clutched her dress in front of her. Inside, Guy ate his ham sandwich as Lana stretched out on the bed smoking a cigarette. "Enjoying your pig sandwich, big guy?" she asked.

His mouth full, Guy could only smile and grunt.

"This is fascinating, watching a man chew. 'Course, I can get that at home." She was peeved, but Guy needed his sandwich. It was all he'd eaten since the night before in Mitchell. He grunted again, this time in an exaggerated attempt at humor. "Can't speak, Alley Oop? Then come here and show Oola what you can *do*." Lana snuffed out her cigarette and fell back onto the bed, opening her arms to him. Guy hooted, delighted by his funny, sexy girl.

Bone hard again, Guy followed his bobbing cock to her. He gazed at her for a long moment. She looked, he thought, like two different people at once. Her face, lined and shadowed by makeup, spoke of the chic, mature beauty she was, but her body was more like a young woman's, bearing few marks of motherhood. Guy lay down on the bed and let her have it the way *she* liked best—with her on top, setting the rhythm, dictating the pace, making her pitch, and him underneath—her catcher, her receiver, her battery mate.

When Guy woke, Lana was gone. He looked around for evidence she'd been there . . . a rumpled bed, its bunched sheets ripe with the cheesy smell they'd cooked up together and the lingering, illicit scent of stale tobacco mixed with strong perfume, which he supposed she donned to mask where she'd been and what she'd been up to.

She'd left behind a copy of the *Journal*. Steeling himself, Guy turned to the account of the Chiefs' loss to the Mitchell Kernels the night before. "CHIEFS BLOW CHANCE FOR BASIN LOOP LEAD," screamed the headline. Of course, he knew it. A victory against the Kernels would have moved the Chiefs into a tie with them for the League lead. And for much of the game, Mitchell seemed to be helping—committing errors, issuing walks, blundering on the base paths. But the Chiefs played still worse, booting the ball six times and issuing twelve walks.

Guy leaned back in his chair. The Kernels were shaping up as the Chiefs' strongest rival, with pitchers Jim O'Toole, Eddie Fisher, and Don Schwall. But the Elks and Lake Sox also boasted strong staffs, especially the Lake Sox with Dick Radatz and Ron Perranoski.

As for his own ball club, it was not the one he thought he'd have—a team with an air-tight infield and an aggressive running game. After the slick-fielding Schunot went lame, players were forced to play out of position in both the infield and outfield, and only Casey and Kibbee could run. At least, with Hacker and the other sluggers, they'd enjoyed the power game—better suited for a hitters' league like the Basin anyway, and especially for Sioux Park with its high elevation. And with Quarles' help, the pitching was coming along. But, for the Chiefs to stay in the thick of the pennant race, the defense would have to gel, and the collegians play with more poise. Against the Kernels, they'd had a comfortable lead after seven innings, but with victory and the League lead within their grasp, they couldn't handle it.

Guy laughed at how the word 'hands' kept coming up in his thinking. But hitting, fielding, and pitching truly were about hands—strong, sure hands and 'soft' hands for handling the hot smash and the trickling bunt—or having the touch, or feel, to spin a curve or a slider for a strike when you absolutely had to have one.

But was he tough enough to handle his players? Or his team confident enough to handle prosperity? It was a bit too early to tell, but with the League's roster deadline looming, he'd have to make changes, and this seemed as good a time as any to riddle it out. Finding a piece of motel stationery, he began making notes on where each Chief stood. Who to keep and who to cut.

The pros, Lee Casey at short and Hank Paskiewicz at third, were easy to rate. Solid in both the field and at bat. Nothing got by them, and Hank hit for power. +2 for each.

Kibbee, another pro, was a great outfielder but hadn't hit much, though he'd steal a base when he got on. A ball hawk, he covered ground for the outfield lead-foots, Hacker and Williams. He just hoped that Clyde would come around with the stick in the stretch run. +2.

Darren Hoades, at second base, was error prone. Signed as a catcher-left fielder, the muscular Alabaman was frustrated by the tricky footwork around the keystone on steals and double-plays. And as a catcher who'd mostly thrown overhand from an erect position, he hadn't yet learned the wide assortment of throws required of a second baseman. Guy doubted he'd become even an average second baseman by summer's end.

And yet, the Alabaman's struggles in the field hadn't hurt him at the plate. A tough kid, he was ready to kill on every pitch. Tough kid, hell! Darren was a dick really—but his cocky, hard-headed attitude only helped him at bat. "Give me a bastard every time," Guy thought. +1

Hacker. With a .370 average, he was one of the League's top hitters. He'd also shown Ruthian power but often hit blistering ground balls or line drives failing to clear outfield fences. Pitchers fed the towering outfielder a steady diet of low balls. His own worst enemy, Frank seemed duty-bound to swing at every strike, breaking Babe Ruth's First Commandment, "Get a good ball to hit." Still, Guy knew it was foolish to tinker with Hack's batting. Just convince him to lay off that first, tempting strike at the knees. Or accept Hercules for who he was, a fence-busting singles hitter who occasionally clobbered one five hundred feet. +2.

Clarence Williams in left hit for power and high average. Slow afoot but strong of arm, he'd handled most balls by smart positioning and never threw to the wrong base. Guy caught himself. Would he have made that last basic point about a white guy? +1½, or +2.

Andy Richkas, first base. The collegian with the contentious radio. No 'handy Andy' in the field, and a low-powered 'banjo' hitter at the plate, he was one to cut. -2.

And himself. He'd been good behind the plate, better than the other League catchers, but his bat had been quiet, except for a couple of home runs.

Guy rose from the desk and lit a cigarette. At least he'd hit in the Mitchell games. But only because he'd 'cheated' after spotting a 'tell'—the Kernels' shortstop stepping toward third when the catcher called for a slower pitch, like a curve or a change-of-pace to a right-handed batter like himself. When the shortstop didn't take that step, he knew a faster pitch was coming. Against the Kernels, he was 'tipped off' on the type of pitch to expect and had never struck out.

Guy felt an odd flutter in his chest. A tell could change the outcome of a game—may have even turned the tide in last night's loss to the Kernels—if he'd shared it with the team.

Guy chewed his lip. A player-manager had to hit, not just manage and play defense—for how could his men respect him if they thought he was washed up at the plate, or needed that tell? Until he got his timing back, he'd keep that edge for himself. +2.

Finally, the hurlers, always the linchpin. Quarles, Schmid, Wiegand, Haroldson, and Dalluge had not been overpowering, but they'd usually been reliable. One exception was a local collegian, Dean Veal. Guy chuckled. "Not prime beef." Another easy cut.

Guy scribbled a note to sign another righty. Maybe that Indian with the name like 'bad weather'. Guy cackled, imagining Rosen busing in the whole tribe to boost the gate.

Which brought him to Bernie's boy—Joel Meznik, Riddle #1. Pitchers were always the hardest to figure, and especially southpaws, who often had a screw loose. At Huron, in his first start, he was terrific early on, but got spooked at the end. In his last start, he came unglued in the third inning. Still, of all the Chiefs' pitchers, Meznik had the best fastball and the best slider, and the biggest curve. And the most pro potential, though in Guy's experience, potential only meant that you hadn't done it yet and maybe never would. +1/-1.

To be sure, the kid needed toughening up, but he'd never get Bernie's OK for that—not when Meznik was the team's sole Jew, who by no coincidence was living under the boss man's roof. Maybe the boy just needed to grow up a little, become a man—get laid—and for that he was sitting pretty, "in the catbird's seat," as Red Barber, the Dodger announcer, used to say.

"But he'll have to screw the Rosen Princess," Guy hooted. "The red-hot Queen is mine."

Chapter Sixty

DINAH SETTLED INTO HER SEAT, the one Joel had picked out for her next to the Chiefs' dugout. It was her night off from the Mellerdrammer, and she was thrilled by the prospect of watching him pitch. Not that she expected to understand all she'd be seeing, for despite her dad's zeal, she'd only ever been to one baseball game, and that was when she was just seven years old.

But now she was Joel Meznik's girl—a big-time pitcher's girl, she thought, a badge of distinction for anyone, let alone a high schooler. And for that, she had the bomb shelter and Glen Merritt to thank. For in that cramped basement space, with Glen caterwauling at the door, she and Joel had cleared the air.

And later that night, with her parents still at the Club, they'd gotten hot and steamy down there. Peeling away her robe, she exposed her mother's sheer pink peignoir with the feathery trim. And, when it slipped from her shoulders, Joel got to see it all, and as he rose from the cot, for a moment she saw all of him, too. Then, neither saw much of anything as they kissed and felt each other all over. For a second, he thought of the rubbers he'd just bought—but before he could reach for one, Dinah climbed on top and began to rub against him, as she did when alone with a pillow or stuffed toy. And, in a moment he came, spurting a milky stripe along his bare stomach as she moved against him. A minute later, she came, too, holding her breath until she felt the familiar clench, and with a soft cry, pitched forward onto his chest, her bottom slowing but still moving, as she slid forward and back along his softening penis, smearing the line of spilt seed.

When Joel felt her go limp, he wondered if that was it. All he'd known of how it worked was what he'd read in Morrie's banned copy of Henry Miller. It never occurred to him that a girl might do it that way, without a man insider her—coming on her own, like what he'd done himself most every night for as long as he could remember.

Still, it puzzled him, even frightened him, the way she looked at that moment. He'd expected a smile, but what he saw instead was a look of agony, and then he felt the shudder and her body gone soft on top of him. "Are you all right?" he whispered.

She didn't answer, but a slow smile spread across her face as she lifted her head and planted a moist kiss on his open mouth. No question about it, she had come. And, normal or not, she was happy, and he was over the moon. Bomb shelter it might be, but for Joel it was the Garden of Eden, and he was Adam . . . and she, of course, his Eve.

• • •

Joel hurdled the gate next to the Chiefs' dugout and walked a few steps before waving back to her. Smiling broadly, Dinah blew him a kiss and Joel doffed his cap.

"OK, lover boy." Dick Quarles slapped Joel on the butt and turned him toward the bullpen. "I see you've been gettin' some home cooking, but we got a ball game to play."

Joel laughed at the ribbing, pleased that Quarles recognized something had changed. Metamorphosed into a man by a beautiful girl, he couldn't believe how confident and powerful he felt. And tonight, he'd been given the start in front of a big home crowd . . . and with his girl in the stands. What could be better than that? He couldn't lose!

• • •

Alone in the press box, John prepared for his first stint as Official Score Keeper. He was excited to do it until he spotted Dinah seated next to the home team dugout. He hadn't figured that she'd be there—she'd never made it to a Chiefs game before. He wished it was because she'd caught the 'fever' that had spread through town, infecting Rapid Citians with pride and joy in their new team. But he knew that wasn't the reason. The 'reason' was warming up in the bullpen down the left field line.

In a curious reversal of custom, the home team dugout at Sioux Park lay along the third base line, as did the press box, giving John a sight line so cruelly perfect that if he raised his eyes from his scorebook he'd see Dinah by the dugout, and raising them a bit more, Joel on the mound. And that was how he feared it would go for him that evening—eyes shifting from scorebook to Dinah to Joel and back again, like the needle on a scratched record. How could he stand it? How could he do his job?

And, he had a bad case of nerves. He'd never been Official Scorer before, and tonight, he'd be the final authority on all rulings of hits, errors, RBIs, and earned runs. Fortunately, he was well acquainted with the *Official Rules of Baseball* and had apprenticed at Air Force games with his father, an experienced scorekeeper. He'd proved a natural to the trade—alert and quick-sighted and possessed of a fine, small hand—disdaining, as did James, a pencil and eraser for a ballpoint pen. And he delighted in the shorthand of scoring—the signs and symbols—and the ascribing of credit and blame—invoking his father's cheery optimism for the one and his mother's fault-finding pessimism for the other.

James had taught him that the primary purpose of charging an error is to protect the pitcher from unfair blame when, through no fault of his own, he'd allowed a base runner or surrendered a run. And, to deny the batter undue credit when he reached base or scored a run through the complicity of an erring fielder. Charging the perpetrator, defending the innocent, dismissing the alibi—the Scorer's call meant Baseball Justice for All.

But no matter the righteousness of his decision, he knew that certain people would be critical of his judgment. His father told him to expect second-guessers on calls that could have gone either way. "Every batted ball is different," James counseled, "struck a little harder or a little softer or with more or less 'English' or with the fielder receiving it in a different spot."

John felt dizzy, his mind grappling with the sheer randomness of it all, which seemed to mirror the events of his life—the polio skipping over the other campers and landing on him alone, or a rare girl like Dinah wondrously appearing next door, or Joel Meznik surfacing in Dinah's basement, undermining his fondest dreams of reunion.

Still, he was relieved that nothing he could do as Scorer would impact the game's outcome. For unlike the pronouncements of umpires—Fair! Foul! Ball! Strike! Safe! Out!—his rulings would not affect the scoring or which team won or lost. His judgments would only shape the statistics, the measures by which players and teams might be remembered and compared. Or, as his father put it, "Umpires affect outcomes; scorers only egos." James then cautioned him that players who had something to gain from a ruling—a higher batting average or a lower ERA—might complain bitterly or even become belligerent if his call went against them.

John's stomach flipped. A riled player could come after him. Hoades had once cornered Bob Romaker, the *Journal* Sports Editor in the men's room, blocking his path and spraying his jacket with chaw-spittle after Romaker as Scorer saddled him with an error. The call seemed right, but hotheads like Hoades were always spoiling for a fight. John figured that was why Romaker gave him his Scorer's job.

His mouth went dry. Only thirty-five minutes to game time, but time enough for a Coke and a question or two for his dad. At the Stand, James smiled warmly at him, proud to have his son follow in his scorekeeping footsteps. "Good to see you, John. What can I get you?"

"Just a Coke, Dad, but I've got a question."

"Shoot, Mr. Official Scorer." James grabbed a hot dog to go with his son's soda.

For a moment, John allowed himself to bask in his father's solicitude. Since the polio, he could never impress with his athletic prowess like Billy often did, but at least they could always talk sports. And now scorekeeping. "Is there a custom in scoring when it could be either a hit or an error, something like *the tie goes to the runner?*"

James responded in a low, confiding tone as if sharing a trade secret. "You're right to call it custom, John—*tie goes to the runner* is not a rule—but scorers are stingy with errors 'cause you make two people unhappy, the batter *and* the fielder. Call it a hit and only the pitcher gets irked."

John laughed nervously. Was his dad making a joke or indicting scorers for low ethics? Or, perhaps just warning him. Before, he'd always preached that scorers and umpires, too, were charged with protecting the moral integrity of the game, and the right thing to do was to just call it as you see it. Now James added, "Never make a ruling to please someone or dodge a fight. And remember—all that's ever required of the fielder is ordinary effort. That's your standard for a hit or an error."

Returning to the press box, John found four large men sitting butt-to-butt on the wooden bench: KOTA radio's Verne Sheppard; former Mayor Baker, the public address announcer; Bob Romaker, *Journal* Sports Editor and ex-official Scorer; and a newsman from Valentine—all dressed, like John, in sport coats and slacks. Each man, except Baker, had a scorebook. Yes, he might be *official* Scorer tonight, but there'd be no shortage of second-guessers in the press box.

Baker patted the wooden box in front of him. "I'll wait for your ruling before posting, John, but don't make me wait too long. The natives get restless waiting for the public shaming." The men laughed as Baker pointed to the right field fence and a large metal scoreboard with light bulbs spelling out 'HOME', 'VISITOR' and 'H', 'R', and 'E' for hits, runs, and errors.

As the game began, no one could have imagined it would be a very special night for Joel after he walked the leadoff man and beaned the batter who followed. Still, for a pitcher who led the team in both walks and hit batters, it was not an unexpected beginning.

Mayor Baker covered the microphone with his beefy hands and issued a prediction. "Betcha Columbia don't make it out of the inning."

The men laughed, and John—taken aback by the branding of Joel as "Columbia"—wondered if they'd call him "Yale" when he came back from the East.

Continuing to struggle, Joel walked the next batter to load the bases. But then, the Hearts' big cleanup hitter pulled a sharp grounder to first base, triggering a first-to-home-to-first double play, and Kibbee ran down a long fly for the third out. John drew a line on his scorecard to mark the path of the fly and circled his scoring symbol, F8, noting the play as an early game highlight. The line score for the Hearts' first at bat was 3 goose eggs—0 0 0—no hits, no runs, no errors.

Joel strode from the mound to the cheers of the crowd and John scoffed. If the defense hadn't made great plays behind him, Joel might have been knocked out of the game. Then *he* wouldn't have to watch the strapping southpaw make goo-goo eyes at Dinah on his way to the dugout.

In the hometown half of the first, the Chiefs exploded for three runs—with Hacker clouting a mammoth home run over the flagpole in center. On KOTA radio, Sheppard, with glee in his voice, called it "a tape measure job the mighty Mantle might be proud of." And both Baker and Romaker clapped and cheered along with the crowd. John pretended to be busy recording the play. He couldn't be a fan tonight—not as a journalist, and certainly not with Joel on the mound.

Joel began the second inning as he had the first, walking the leadoff batter, then bouncing a third strike under Stockman's mitt, allowing the batter to advance to first. Fidgety, Joel broke his hands as he started his delivery to the third Valentine batter and was called for a balk—the umpire advancing the runners to second and third. With no outs and two men now in scoring position, Stockman walked to the mound to talk to his young pitcher. John used the break to sneak a peek at Dinah leaning forward in her seat, one hand covering her mouth. Heartsick, he glanced down the line to the Chiefs' bullpen but saw no one warming up. In any case, whatever Stockman said worked well enough, as Joel retired the next two Hearts batters on weak grounders to the right side, and the third on a pop-up to Quarles at first base.

Still, the Hearts' two groundouts had produced two runs, narrowing the Chiefs' lead to 3-2. And this, for a moment, lifted John's spirits. Dinah's knight in shining armor looked tarnished, and if he didn't turn things around soon, he'd be knocked off his high horse.

In the bottom of the second, Clarence Williams got things started for the Chiefs with a sharp single to left. Quarles then struck out, but Joel laid down a well-placed bunt—intended as a sacrifice—which John rightly ruled a hit when no one could handle it. Casey plated both runners with a blistering double to right center, widening the Chiefs lead to 5-2. John chewed on the click-end of his ballpoint. Could the Hearts still rise up and drive Joel from the mound?

But like a machine whose gears mesh better when their edges wear down a bit, Joel's delivery became smoother and faster as he ground away on the Sioux Park mound.

Then, he went to his new pitch—the nickel curve, or slider, that Quarles had taught him—fast and wickedly sharp, sending dispirited Hearts back to their dugout muttering to themselves.

In the third, the Chiefs didn't score, but a play at first base got the booth talking. Hacker hit a grounder between first and second that the Hearts' first baseman, Big Bill White, lunged for and missed, but which their second baseman, Frisina, managed to scoop. A foot race then ensued between the massive Hacker and the mountainous White, who'd picked himself out of the dirt and lumbered back toward first base to receive Frisina's throw. To the men in the press box, it looked like a looming train wreck—a collision of five hundred pounds of plodding pig iron.

Through the shrouding cloud of dust, John saw that Hacker got to the base first but only because White never got there at all, his foot stabbing blindly for the canvas bag behind him.

Was it a hit or an error on White, who'd reached the first base junction well before Hack, but failed to locate the base with his foot? "What'll it be, John, hit or an error?" Baker asked.

His first test. John's hands began to sweat. White had got the ball in time to tag the base but clearly had not. Was it a fear of being trampled by Hercules or clumsy footwork that botched the play? Was it fair to charge White with an error for not being graceful or nimble-footed? Would the average first baseman be expected to find the bag behind him when he had to turn on the run to take the throw? And did it matter that the Hearts' pitcher could have easily made the putout himself if he'd remembered his duty to cover first base on grounders hit wide of the bag?

In the Air Force Tournament, his dad ruled an error on just such a play. Yes, he'd go with his pop on that. White would get an error, while Hacker, hometown hero, would not get a hit.

When the error call was posted, the fans surprised John with a low-pitched groan. He had expected the players to care about his rulings, but not the fans, too. It was a bit unnerving, but at least he was nameless and out of sight, the 'man behind the curtain', not an actor on the stage.

Romaker leaned toward John and whispered his advice. "Let me give you a tip, Johnny—don't let Hack catch you with that scorebook after the game." John grimaced and turned away.

The Chiefs did not score in the inning, but it seemed not to matter to Joel, who jogged to the mound, eager to pitch to the Hearts in the top of the fourth.

Then, the Hearts' Frisina grounded the first pitch into the hole between third and short, and John was back on the hot seat. Casey may have looked away before bobbling the ball but John, too, was looking away at the same instant—his eyes on Dinah, whose eyes were on Joel.

"So, what's this one, young man, hit or error?" Baker asked.

John had seen only the end of the play. He'd looked up too late to measure how hard the grounder was hit and how long it had taken to reach Casey. And he was too flustered to look at the batter sprinting to first base, to gauge his speed and the odds he would have beaten a throw across the diamond if the ball been fielded cleanly. "Hit or error?" Mayor Baker asked again.

"Damn that girl," John hissed to himself. He couldn't ask the other men to tell him what he should have observed himself. "It's an error," he said, trying to sound confident.

"Yeah, Rizzuto would have made that play, Pee Wee, too," Romaker interjected, playfully squeezing John's neck. "And Aparicio," added the man from Valentine. "'Course, none of 'em's playing shortstop in the semi-pro Basin League."

Hearing the men's comments, John knew that he had booted it.

As Baker pressed the button lighting the scoreboard under 'E', John's face turned red. "Baseball Justice?" he asked himself. "More like 'Blind Justice'." This was the Basin League, not the Big Leagues. To get the calls right, he'd have to apply a lower standard for "ordinary effort." But how could he know what that was when he'd seen only a handful of Basin League contests? He had to be more vigilant now, paying rapt attention. Take the game one pitch at a time. Not let his eyes drift off to Dinah, even if he couldn't keep his mind off her.

As Joel took the mound in the top of the fifth, a murmur spread through the crowd. Was it just the close score, or had it occurred to Chiefs' fans that Joel still had not surrendered a hit?

Joel ended the inning on a called third strike, and Mayor Baker updated the Scoreboard,

3-0-1. Three Valentine runs, no hits, and one error—with that goose egg in the center of the Hearts' line score a galling reminder of John's own error and growing heartache.

Baker, pointing to the scoreboard, let out a low whistle. "You see what I see?" He wouldn't let a no-hitter get jinxed by speaking of it.

By the top of the sixth, the prospect of a no-hitter seemed real to everyone in Sioux Park. On edge in the early innings, Joel now appeared calm, cool, and collected—stylishly snatching Guy's return throws and wasting little time between pitches. Ten was all it took to strike out Hammond and Shoemaker and induce Frisina to fly out to Kibbee.

Three more innings and Joel would have it, a glorious no-hitter. John knew the numbers. Since 1901, there'd been only ninety-three no-hitters in the Major Leagues, though last year there'd been four, including Don Larsen's—also the only perfect game in World Series history.

Of course, there'd been many no-hitters in the Minors and semi-pro leagues, even perfect games—but no-hitters would be scarce in the Basin League, with its short season, and rarer still in high-altitude Rapid City, where fly balls seemed to sprout wings and soar out of the ballpark. But tonight, because of John's faulty scoring, Joel might claim one of those precious gems for himself.

John stole a glance at Dinah, jumping up and down like a puppet on a string as Joel passed her on his way to the dugout. She turned just long enough to show her face—suffused with happiness—or was it jubilation or rapture even, a look he'd dreamed one day she'd show to him. John whispered an unkind prayer. "Please, God, give the Hearts a hit, and make it a clean one."

He didn't care anymore about Joel winning the game. He wouldn't deny him that. But his ripening no-hitter was already a phony—from that distracted moment in the fourth inning when, with a touch of his ballpoint, he'd magically transformed a hit to deep short into an error.

By the top of the seventh, Joel was cruising. Every batter had been up three times, but instead of getting smarter and figuring him out, each batter seemed more perplexed than ever as if confronting a new pitcher each time. And in a way it was true. Facing Joel the fireballer in the early innings, Joel the slider-master in the middle of the game, and now, in the seventh, Joel the old pro, with a bag full of tricks. John felt doomed. Two more innings, six outs, and he'd have it.

Glancing down at Dinah, John saw Bernie sitting next to her, smiling broadly, like a feudal lord ready to bestow his damsel daughter on the dashing knight-errant.

In the top of the eighth, the Chiefs had a comfortable 8-3 lead. Now, the Sioux Park faithful cheered Joel's every pitch, caught up as they were in the mounting drama of a young pitcher who'd somehow found the form of a veteran and was hurling the game of his life.

Then Hoades at second base dove to his left to snare a hot grounder and jackknifed to his feet to make the throw to first for the third out. If Darren had not thrown wildly, pulling the first baseman off the bag, it might have been the play of the game. "Safe!" the umpire called.

John panicked, then recalled what his dad once said about the two halves of a play. "A great stop doesn't give the fielder license to make a wild throw if he has time to make a good one." When John's error call was posted, the crowd let out a cheer, and for a moment, he felt that the cheering was for him. While he knew that the fans didn't realize he'd made the right call—only that it preserved Joel's no-hitter—he couldn't help feeling that he deserved their applause, for he'd risen above petty jealousy and rendered true judgment, honoring the role of the Scorer, the Guardian, whose rulings make up the Official Record, the true chronicle, of the game.

Romaker took issue with the call. "John, this Meznik fellow, he a friend of yours?"

Was Romaker razing him, he wondered, or did he truly believe Hoades lacked the time for an accurate throw? John smiled feebly, marking the play down as an E-4t, a throwing error.

When the eighth inning ended, Joel was greeted with rousing applause, while Dinah stood at her seat clapping wildly, her blonde ponytail bobbing up and down like a yo-yo.

John wanted to throw up. One more inning and he could leave the lovebirds to their celebration, drop off the Scorebook at the *Journal*, and grab a shot or two of Paddy's Four Roses.

In the top of the ninth a pinch-hitter laid down a bunt. Joel, and Paskiewicz from third, converged on the ball halfway up the line from home plate. Taking charge, Joel speared the ball cleanly and, whirling around, fired a strike across the diamond. It appeared too late to catch the speedy Heart. John heaved a sigh. The no-hitter was over and this time he'd not have to rule.

But as John looked down at his scorebook, poised to record the play as a hit, he heard the exultant roar of the crowd. The umpire's call had been slow in coming, but glancing up, John saw the Man-in-Blue stabbing his thumb in the air like a hitchhiker. "Out!" he'd brayed.

John was stunned. The Hearts' manager sprang from the dugout to protest the call. Clearly, Joel's throw was late. The runner was safe at first and deserved to be credited with a hit. Had the umpire not seen it? Or was a hit not a hit in the ninth inning of a no-hitter if the play was close and the game was on the pitcher's home field?

Could this be the way it was with certain no-hitters, aided and abetted by an umpire who craved the applause of the crowd? Where was the integrity his dad spoke of?

When play resumed, Joel, who'd waited out the lengthy squabble in the cool mountain air, had trouble finding the strike zone and fell behind the Hearts' next hitter, Charlie Shoemaker.

Then, on a 2-0 pitch, Shoemaker ripped a liner to Hoades' left, giving him only an instant to lunge and put up his glove. The ball glanced off the webbing and trickled into right field.

John's mind reeled. He knew how he should rule. But the crowd would recall the ball Hoades fielded the inning before—one struck as hard as this one and in the same direction—which he managed to glove, before throwing wide to first, earning Hoades his error. So, what was different this time, Chiefs' fans would ask. How could he rule an error on *that* ball, but a hit on *this* one?

His head throbbed. He was alone. No one could help him. Closing his eyes, he reviewed the two plays in his mind, seeing them as if he could reenact them.

Hoades had played 'deep' the inning before, so the ball took longer to reach him, giving him more time to react—to snag it and keep it from passing into the outfield for a hit. But this inning—playing 'in' on the speedy Shoemaker—he had little chance to glove the hot smash.

Different situations, but in any case, Hoades' heroic stop in the eighth had not established a higher standard for him in the ninth. Ordinary effort was all that was ever required.

And yet, when Mayor Baker asked him the question, John could not at first utter the word. Baker's voice sounded as if it came from another room or another planet. John took a long moment to collect himself, recalling his father's advice to trust his first impression. Yes, that clinched it. Shoemaker's liner was a rocket, and Hoades did everything required of him.

"Come on, John!" Baker's words were half plea, half command. "What's your verdict?"

John was hot. His shirt and jacket were soaked through, but his mind was clear, He would not lose his nerve and give in to the passions of the mob. Turning to Baker, "Hit" was all he said.

Smiling, Baker gave him two thumbs up and posted the call on the big scoreboard—the Hearts' line score now read . . . 3 . . . 1 . . . 2 . . . three runs, one hit, two errors. The crowd let out a cry at the sudden end of their soul-stirring drama. Joel's no-hitter was over.

John felt proud, even thrilled, by what he'd done. Still, he couldn't resist a look at Joel, smiling sheepishly, who tipped his cap to the crowd, which was standing now and applauding.

But the game was not yet over. There were two more outs to get. John marked the hit in his scorebook, then glanced over to Dinah to see what her reaction might be.

She was nowhere to be seen.

A minute later, he heard footsteps on the stairs outside the press box and then the door swung open, banging loudly against the wall. And there she was in all her glory, standing behind the bench of startled men—Dinah Rosen, arms akimbo, her face flushed and full of fury.

"*John Moran! You bastard!*"

Neither Mayor Baker, the public address announcer, nor Vern Sheppard, on KOTA radio, had time to cover his microphone. Dinah's explosive charge was broadcast to the Sioux Park faithful—all two thousand five hundred and sixty-four of them, and thousands more throughout the region who'd caught the slander on the 5,000 WATT radio station.

He'd been publicly shamed in both his hometown and parts of four states. Turning to face her, his hands balled into fists, his body trembling, he cried, "Get the hell out of here!"

This time both microphones were covered, but saying it still felt like sweet justice—though John already knew the call . . . that he, not Dinah, would get the hell out of there—out of town, that is—ditching Rapid at dawn for parts unknown.

Chapter Sixty-One

MORE EMBARRASSED THAN EXULTANT for his near no-hitter, Joel returned to the dugout expecting a ribbing for Dinah's outburst. What he got instead was a dirty razzing.

"Some wildcat you got there, Meznik. Better watch out for her claws," Hoades quipped. "Looks like pussy, growls like tiger. I'd chain her to the bed if she was *mine*."

Joel lunged at Hoades, but Clarence yanked him back enough to duck Darren's fist.

Stockman put a stop to it. "Sure you want to say that 'bout the boss's daughter, Darren?"

Joel scanned the Stadium lot for Dinah's yellow Skyliner, always easy to spot, even in a sea of cars, but it was nowhere to be seen. Earlier they'd agreed to leave right after the game and steal a little time together in the shelter before Bernie and Lana got home from the Club. He wondered if Bernie had scolded her or she'd hightailed it out of there before he got the chance.

He'd never known a girl so impulsive—or so exciting. But he'd mostly lived in a world of men—on ball teams and at synagogue. Still, what man would want to be seen as someone who couldn't control his girlfriend? With someone like Dinah, wouldn't that always be a problem?

Then Clarence pulled up in his car. "My, my, that was some performance," he teased.

Joel laughed as he hopped into the passenger side. "Clarence . . . ?" Joel started. He needed advice, but would a mature Negro man's experience apply to an unworldly Jew like him?

"You lookin' for a little love counsel from a sportin' man," Clarence said with a wink.

"Yeah, somethin' like that."

"Well—she's young and spirited—a mite wild, but that's what makes it fun. Right? And her heart's in the right place—standing up for her man like that—even if her mouth's too big."

"Should I say something to her?"

"Tell her she's a tiger and you want to tame her pussy!"

"What? Hoades' line? I could never say that!"

"Why not? It's pretty good—plan on usin' it myself tonight."

Suddenly, Joel felt ravenous, but didn't relish the prospect of more peanut butter from the Rosen kitchen. And he wasn't ready to face Dinah yet. "Say, Clare, you hungry? I know a joint that's got something called a 'turkey steak'."

"Steak?" Clarence shook his head. "Not sure I like the way they fix it in this town."

Joel stiffened. Clearly, the man was recalling the fight at the Club—an incident he'd reveled in—throwing a punch against prejudice. He'd forgotten that it would mean something entirely different to Clarence—a stark demonstration of the risk a Negro faced eating out in Rapid. "It's a drive-in—you can get a burger instead," he offered.

Clarence clapped Joel on the shoulder. "I'm joshin' you, man. Turkey steak sounds good . . . long as they hold the Crackers."

• • •

John sat alone in the press box until the field went dark. Last to leave was Verne Sheppard of KOTA radio, who signed off reminding his audience that the word 'fan' was short for fanatic. "And tonight, we learned just how apt that word is."

John heard his father call his name from the foot of the stairs—too steep and narrow for James to mount. John held his breath as he had as a young boy, hiding under the bed when a spanking was coming. Pity, he knew from his polio days, could sting as much as a whuppin'.

Earlier, Bernie stood in the exact same spot as James—speaking to each man as he left the press box, trying to make light of things. "Guess that filly of mine needs reining in." He didn't wait for John to emerge—the young man was still too raw. And he'd found someone else for his daughter. Someone better—in Joel.

Dinah knew her dad would be livid—the faces of the men in the booth reflected the gravity of her offense. Head down, she lost herself in the swirl of exiting fans and made a dash for her car. Racing east across the prairie flats, she put distance between herself and the punishment she feared was coming. Ten miles out, she decided to turn back and face her father's wrath—get it over with and maybe salvage the evening with Joel.

At home, Bernie gave Dinah a hard slap on the butt before offering a peek into the male mind. "You wanna stand by your man? Keep your mouth shut. No guy wants a girl to fight his battles for him—makes him look like a *pussy*." Then Buck called to warn him that Stockman and some other Chiefs had arrived at the Club for Lana's second show.

Bernie frowned. Not a good time to be AWOL from the Club, even for a critical paternal duty. "I'll be right there."

Dinah turned to hide a smirk. There'd be no penalty for her outburst. When Bernie left, she caught a quick shower and dabbed on a little of her mother's French perfume. Bathed and buoyant, she again donned her mother's pink peignoir.

Whatever punishment Joel might dish out, she was sure she could handle it.

Chapter Sixty-Two

JENNIE COULDN'T STOP WORRYING about John—missing since his humiliating encounter with Dinah Rosen in the broadcast booth the night before. Twice she called home from the ballpark but there was no answer. Finally, she threatened to call the police, but James said it was too soon to report a missing person. He offered to ask around though he already knew John had skipped town. Paddy had called that morning after finding John's camera and a note saying simply, "Taking a trip."

Exiting the Stand James counted to a hundred. How could he tell her? He didn't want to think about what she might do. He could have been as worried about John as he was about her, but something told him his firstborn would be okay. The boy had a level head and came from pioneer stock, men and women not afraid to pull up stakes and seek their fortune elsewhere. James suspected west was the direction John had taken, but how far he'd go he couldn't guess.

Returning to the Stand, he told Jennie—as if it were fresh news—that John had left town. Then a collective gasp rose from the stadium followed by a sustained "Boo." In a tone usually reserved for condolences, KOTA radio announced that Clarence Williams had been beaned, speculating that "Hoskins may have deliberately aimed at Williams' head."

Bernie, about to order a beer, heard the announcement and the dull clunk behind him as Jennie's head struck the counter.

James sank to his knees, and Bernie, seeing Clarence rise to his feet and amble toward first, hurdled the counter to be at his neighbor's side. There he watched with contempt and pity, as James stroked Jennie's brow, whispering, "He'll be back, Jen. John will come back."

When Jennie came to, she was in an ambulance, demanding to be returned to the stadium.

"Sorry, ma'am," the ambulance attendant said as he shone a penlight into her eyes. "Once you're here, you got to go to the Emergency Room. That's the rule."

"But I'm fine now," Jennie insisted.

"Jennie! You were out cold," James protested.

"What about Mr. Williams—is he all right?"

James, who'd not heard the public address announcement, took Jennie's hand and patted it. "I think you're confused, hon. That happened back in Yankton."

Jennie pulled her hand away and said coldly. "No. It was just now. I heard it."

James threw an anxious look at the ambulance attendant, who seemed taken aback by Jennie's tone. "Just lie back, ma'am. You'll go home real soon."

But Jennie's doctor was delivering a baby, and she was moved upstairs to the women's ward. The nurse took Jennie's vital signs and left a hospital gown for her, along with instructions not to get up unless another nurse was present. Jennie sat on the bed staring in alarm at the shapeless gown she'd been handed. The last time she'd worn one was when baby Lily died.

Mumbling something about "giving you privacy," James left to warn the nurse that Jennie might try to sneak out in the middle of the night. "My wife hates hospitals. Maybe you should lock up her shoes and clothes."

The nurse was surprised. Jennie hadn't seemed agitated or disoriented. "This isn't the psychiatric ward. I can't restrain her, but I'll keep an eye on her."

"Oh, and please tell the doctor that my wife may be pregnant," James added in a low voice.

The nurse cocked her head. "Won't Mrs. Moran tell the doctor herself?"

"She doesn't know," James said.

The nurse threw him a quizzical look. "And you do?"

He hadn't figured someone might find that strange. But they'd made love several times without protection and she'd only ever fainted before when she was pregnant. "It may be why she fainted."

The nurse nodded. "I'll be sure to tell him."

Tiptoeing back into her room, James was careful not to wake the other patients, tucked in for the night between starched white sheets. Even the traction apparatus of the woman across the room was draped in white. He recalled Billy's pup tents, pitched in the backyard, fashioned from clothesline and old sheets. Smiling at the memory, he whispered a prayer that Jennie was indeed pregnant and that the baby would be another boy, like Billy. Then he crept to Jennie's bedside. She was asleep, her hands clasped under her cheek like an angelic child. For a moment he was reassured by her quiescence until her foot shot forward, grazing the bed's side rail. James sighed—her body, like a tightly wound spring, bore the marks of its tensions, even unspooled.

...

When James arrived home, Billy was in the kitchen wolfing down leftovers with unwashed hands. James told him that his mom was okay but had to spend the night in the hospital. Billy just nodded and plucked another chunk of cold meatloaf from a pool of ketchup.

Then, James told him that John had left town and without his older brother to chaperone, he couldn't go with the Chiefs on their road trip in the morning.

"Why not? I don't need John to watch me. Joel can do it," Billy protested.

James shook his head, looking more solemn than Billy had seen him in years. "This isn't the time to upset your mother. She'd want you here."

Billy ran to the bedroom and slammed the door behind him.

The next morning, he watched mournfully from his window as Bernie and Joel set off to meet the team bus. Then it struck him. His dad's face when he said his mom would want him here. What if she was sick enough to die? Was that why his dad wanted him here? He ran to the kitchen where James sat reading in his underwear, which he never did when she was home.

"Is Mom OK, Dad?"

James looked up from the newspaper, struck by the concern in his son's voice.

"I'm sure she'll be fine, Bill. I'm calling the hospital in a minute to get a report."

"Why did she faint? She never did that before."

James wished he could tell Billy that his mother might be pregnant—how she'd fainted early on in all her previous pregnancies. But that would raise the matter of sex and they'd not yet had 'the talk'. He'd been waiting for just the right moment, which never seemed to arrive.

"I'll ask the doctor when I telephone." James pointed to a box score on the *Journal* sports page. "Hey, Billy boy. Eddie Mathews hit another homer yesterday."

Billy could tell that his dad was trying to put him off. Something *was* wrong. But during the call he couldn't hear enough or read his father's face, which was turned to the wall.

When the call ended, James turned to Billy. "The doctor hasn't seen her yet, but she seems fine. Eating breakfast just like us."

"Did they tell you what was wrong with her?"

James shrugged. "No, but it sounds like it wasn't much of anything."

Billy wanted to believe him, but it might be the kind of thing parents kept from kids. Last year, Danny Cook's mom died from cancer, but Danny never acted like his mom was sick. Maybe he didn't know until she croaked. Then, he recalled that since then, Danny often came to school in dirty clothes and smelled bad, even on assembly days.

"Want to come with me when I get her?" James asked.

Billy stared into his cereal bowl. He hated hospitals. That was where his baby sister had died, and where John was taken when he was struck down by polio. He remembered it all—the masked attendants, the white ambulance with its blood-red cross, John being carried out on a stretcher from his bunk at Y Camp Tamaha. And, most of all, his brother's eyes, crazed with fear—how he held his hand out to him as he passed, until a gloved attendant slapped it away.

"I'll stay home and wash the dishes," he offered.

James smiled, surprised by his son's thoughtfulness. "Mom will appreciate that."

When James left, Billy quickly dispensed with the chore and returned to his room. Pulling himself onto John's top bunk, he felt under the mattress for a hard lump. It was *Peyton Place*—a book Glen Merritt once bragged was about a town like Rapid, "but a whole lot dirtier!"

Billy let the book fall open to a well-worn page and a bigger surprise, a snapshot of Dinah in a skimpy swimsuit. Holding the photo in front of him, Billy felt his soft cock through his underpants. Afraid to get caught, he often exercised this precaution. A soft penis never mattered. It always felt good and never failed to produce a sweet tremble in the end.

But this time something different happened . . . a milky, viscous flow, right into his briefs. It was just a bit of liquid, but he felt the spurt and he felt even better than usual. So, what was this stuff? Penis spit? Or some magic potion only a girl like Dinah could conjure up?

Billy lifted the waistband to see how much goo had come out. Was this the way it was gonna be from now on? Could he blot it all up with a Kleenex? Would it leave a telltale stain? Would his mother discover it when she did the laundry? Was there any chance she wouldn't?

Billy broke into a sweat. Why did he have to think of his mom again right after he'd made such a big discovery? Returning Dinah's photo to *Peyton Place*, he stuffed the book back under the mattress. Now all he could think of was Danny Cook and his stinky trousers.

And how he wanted his mom to be around to do his wash. And, at the same time, didn't.

Chapter Sixty-Three

THE NEXT MORNING, JENNIE WAS asked to pee into a cup. Pulled from a dream, she thought she was still at Sioux Park, watching Clarence chase down a long fly ball—the sun radiating off his face in a corona of spectral colors, like light dispersed from a diamond.

"We need it for testing," the nurse said. Jennie sat up slowly. Her left temple throbbed with every breath. Gently, she felt the lump with her fingers, imagining that she, not Clarence, had been the one hit by the errant pitch.

Jennie took the cup and walked barefoot to the bathroom. Squatting over the bowl, she closed her eyes and the poem came to her. Taking the wax pencil for labeling specimens, she tore a sheet off the clipboard at the end of her bed and wrote in thick black script.

Buried deep and far from eyes unseen

Soft and dark it gives itself

To heat and time and earthly pressure

Transformed to a brilliance

Unwitnessed it dazzles

and blinds the eye

to everything around it.

It took the weight of the world to make it

this hard

this way.

Black Diamond.

Jennie folded the paper and tucked it into the pocket of her gown. Returning to her bed, she waited for Dr. Latham. When he hadn't arrived by eleven, she decided she'd waited long enough. But where were her clothes and shoes? Frantic, she searched the night table and locker and between the beds of her roommates. Next to the door, the woman in traction spoke up. "Nurse took 'em in the middle of the night. Maybe gettin' 'em laundered for ya."

Jennie grunted, doubting the woman's explanation. Drawing her thin gown tight around her, she left the room, determined to track down the nurse and her clothing.

The corridor was empty, except for a janitor mopping the floor, spreading the stink of ammonia she'd always associated with hospitals. In the distance, she heard the rumble of gurneys and meal carts, sounds still painfully familiar from John's stay in the Crippled Children's Hospital and the time here before that, when baby Lily died.

Jennie's eyes darted up the hallway. She was tempted to walk out as she was, but doubted she'd get far barefoot. Then a troubling thought came to her. What if they kept her against her will? Quickening her pace, she arrived at the end of the corridor just as a nurse stormed out of the solarium lounge. "Oh. There you are, Mrs. Moran. Dr. Latham is looking for you."

Then she glanced at Jennie's feet and frowned. "I'll find your shoes."

Jennie nodded, relieved. One way or another she'd walk out of this house of ghosts.

...

Heading for the hospital, James backed the Chevy down the driveway, surveying the lawn as he passed. He remembered how it once had been—a happy patch of crab grass and dirt, strewn with balls and bats, trikes and trucks, a red Radio Flyer, and a BB gun. It could be that way again, he thought, if Jennie were pregnant again—with a boy.

James imagined time flipping backwards—not to the trying days of diapers and no sleep but later to the boyhood years, when John and Billy would run to greet him, arms spread wide, faces beaming, crying "Daddy, Daddy," as if he were a war hero or Superman.

Smiling, he let the car idle as he grabbed the mail from the postal box. "Bills," he groaned. Gazing at the Rosen house, he was struck by the contrast—four bedrooms and three baths for one child—two bedrooms and one bath for his two, and now, possibly three. And, while John would be off to Yale in the fall, Billy could never share a room with a wailing baby.

And he didn't want a crib in his and Jennie's bedroom either. Once the baby could hoist himself, he might see things that no child should ever see. He wasn't even sure he could do it with a baby there. And he wouldn't want to spoil the special bond he shared with Jennie.

An addition to the house would solve the problem, but would a bank lend him money for construction? Maybe, if he showed enough income from the concession stand. But last night, he lost a hundred dollars in sales when he was at the hospital with Jennie. Later Bernie called, ordering him to hire more help, even if she returned. He knew Bernie was right. The Stand wasn't doing the volume it should. Long lines discouraged fans from leaving their seats.

Tossing the mail onto the passenger seat, he watched the envelopes spread wide like a lady's fan. One letter, addressed in a feminine hand, stood out. Curious, he opened it and read:

Dear Mr. Moran,

I came by the concession stand last night to ask if you would consider hiring me. As you know, I am a hard worker. As the oldest of four, I do most of the cooking and cleaning at home, and I cook every week at the Church of the Nazarene, preparing the Sunday supper. Yours very truly, Martha Muffling.

James looked for a return address. There was none. And no stamp either.

Martha must have dropped it off that morning to insure a speedy delivery. He pictured his sweet, shy student—with a crush on John—carrying the hopeful missive in her pocketbook.

Was she really keen on working, he wondered, or just hoping to rub shoulders with his son? With John gone, she'd be disappointed in that, but her eagerness boded well for the Stand.

And he wouldn't have to pay her all that much. Faster service would mean more customers, more profit.

James's heart raced. Jennie might oppose hiring the girl even if it made good financial sense. You could never tell with Jennie. But for the moment, at least, she was in no position to say no. His best bet was to get it all in place—then at least she'd have to give Martha a chance.

James put the letter back into its envelope and slipped it into the side pocket of his trousers. His first step was to hire Martha Muffling.

Chapter Sixty-Four

WHEN DINAH SCREAMED, HER PARENTS came running—Bernie from the kitchen brandishing a knife, and Lana from her vanity, her face looking lopsided with just one eye lined and shadowed.

"What happened?" Bernie sputtered, spotting his daughter on the couch, her hands pressed against her cheeks. Speechless, Dinah pointed to the TV.

"It's John Moran!" Lana said, "On TV, with Groucho Marx. It's *You Bet Your Life*."

Groucho puffed on his cigar as he turned to the contestants—John and a young blonde in a tight white cardigan and hip-hugging gray skirt. *"So, you're Peggy Knecht. Pronounced* KAH . . . NECT, *right? Like, what this young man might say to the switchboard operator—*'KAH NECT *me to Miss Knecht'*." The female contestant giggled as John looked on admiringly.

"This is very interesting," Bernie said, joining Dinah and Lana on the couch.

"I'm told you're also Miss North Dakota. What was your talent . . . or can I guess?"

"I played the organ."

Groucho hiked his eyebrows a couple of times and wagged his cigar at the audience.

Bernie chuckled. "Not even Groucho's gonna touch that one."

"Daddee—shush!" Dinah groused.

Groucho turned to John. *"And you're John Moran, from South Dakota. Doesn't that put you right under Miss Knecht?"* Groucho's eyebrows again broke into a dance.

"That's right, Groucho, geographically speaking," John answered, sliding his right hand under his left. Lana hooted, as the audience responded in a chorus of guffaws.

"Not bad," Bernie said while Dinah stewed, stone-faced.

Groucho smirked. *"Somethin' tells me he'll be a winner tonight one way or the other."*

Bernie threw back his head and snorted.

"So, what do you do in South Dakota, John?"

"I'm a reporter for the Rapid City Journal."

"Rapid City, huh? So tell me, what makes Rapid City so fast?"

John looked over at Peggy. *"Gee. I don't know. The girls, maybe?"*

Lana gave Dinah a long, hard look. "Looks like your Johnny boy's making a name for himself in Hollywood."

Steaming, Dinah felt the urge to throw an ashtray at the TV—or at her mother.

"So, what's the big attraction in Rapid City, other than fast girls?"

"Well, we've got Mount Rushmore."

"Oh, yes. The stone heads of the Presidents. Remind me—who's up there?"

"Well, let's see . . . There's Harpo . . . Chico . . . Zeppo . . . and who's the last one?"

"Hah!" Lana exclaimed, as Dinah scowled.

"I wonder if James knows this is on?" Bernie asked.

Lana threw Bernie an incredulous look. "You think 'Johnny Be Good' would forget to tell his mommy he was on TV?"

"They don't have a TV," Bernie said.

Lana shrugged. "That's not our problem now, is it?"

Dismissing his wife with a wave of the hand, Bernie walked to the kitchen and dialed the Morans. No one picked up, though he doubted Jennie would have darkened his doorstep even for this. He snorted, imagining Jennie running on winged feet if Clarence Williams was on TV.

People could be as entertaining as television, he mused, with a grin. Then he got his camera.

"That won't work." Dinah scoffed as he took a photo of the screen.

"You want to put money on that, little girl? It won't be a good picture, but I bet it ends up on the front page of tomorrow's *Journal.*"

And it did. For not only had John appeared on the popular TV show, but he and Miss Knecht won—sharing the top prize of $10,000, plus $100 for guessing the secret word—*tree.*

• • •

The Morans learned about John's triumph from Bernie's grainy photo splashed across the front page of the next day's *Journal.* "Local Boy Wins Big" was the headline. Later, John called home—for the first time since he'd left town—promising to return to Rapid in a week or so.

On her way out the door, Dinah saw the photo and fumed. If only she'd taken Glen up on his scheme to go west and audition for the Mouseketeers. Then it could have been her on the front page of the *Journal*, and on a show broadcast to millions of viewers across America.

She remained in a foul mood all day. Even a new part couldn't pull her out of her funk. Glen listened to her rant as she practiced her lines. "John Moran on coast-to-coast TV, while I'm stuck in the woods with this damsel-in-distress hokum."

Smirking, it took all of Glen's self-control not to pelt her with 'I told you so's'. Finally, she commanded him to "Say it and get it over with." In reply, Glen whistled Groucho's theme song, "Hooray for Captain Spaulding," then ducked the script she hurled at his head.

And though the Director played the perfect gentleman in the show's dress rehearsal—that night he circled Dinah like a spider, coiling his rope around her, and with his cape blocking the audience view, but in full view of the cast, ran his fingernail across her nipples while murmuring, "Lovely, lovely."

When the show ended, Dinah bolted from the theater and ran to the car sobbing.

Glen offered what he hoped were comforting words. "He's just an old pervert!"

After a few minutes, she wiped her nose on her sleeve and, still sniffling, turned to him.

"We're going to California. Tomorrow, but don't let anyone know."

Chapter Sixty-Five

BACK FROM THE CHIEFS' EASTERN road trip, Joel expected Dinah to jump into his arms as soon as she could sneak downstairs. But the morning passed, and she never came.

When she hadn't appeared by ten, he came upstairs. "She left early," Lana said.

He only learned of John's TV triumph when he saw the *Journal*'s front page but didn't make the connection to Dinah's absence. Instead, he worried that he'd simply been too long out of sight and out of mind. With that thought, he set off for the New York Club with a plan to see her that night at the Mellerdrammer. But for that he'd need Bernie's help.

Bernie watched through his one-way mirror as the ballplayer entered the Club. He had to hand it to his daughter. Once she switched from the hot-rodding high school crowd, she'd shown good taste in boyfriends—John and now, Joel—smart, ambitious young men, with more on their minds than just chasing tail. Until last night, he'd written off John as a contender for Dinah's hand, but his appearance on *Groucho* may have signaled a comeback for the boy next door.

"Come in," Bernie yelled in response to Joel's knock. "No one to play with today, kid?" he teased, motioning for Joel to sit.

"Yeah, no practice and . . . well . . . "

"Yeah, she's got the Mellerdrammer tonight."

"I suppose you've already seen the show."

"Nah. When you run a business, you can't duck out any time you like."

Joel nodded, though he'd seen Bernie at every Chiefs' home game. "Maybe you'd like to go tonight. There's no game."

Bernie narrowed his eyes. "What's your angle, kid?"

Joel laughed. "I thought if you wanted to catch it, I could ride up with you."

Bernie grunted. The Chiefs' night off was no time to leave Lana alone at the club.

"You got teammates. Get one of 'em to take you."

"That's an idea. Do you know how I can get in touch with Dick Quarles?"

"Do I look like your social secretary? Ask Stockman. He's at the Royal Rest on North Street. Buck can give you directions."

Joel mounted his bike and headed east to find Stockman and, hopefully, Quarles, the only man he felt he could trust to go with him to the show. He hadn't forgotten how Dinah looked at Guy at the Club and it crossed his mind that she might prefer dating an experienced man.

Especially after the last time they'd gotten together—in the bomb shelter after her outburst in the broadcast booth. Slipping out of her pink nightie, she stood on tiptoe and kissed his sweaty neck. Fearing he might come then and there, Joel yanked off his uniform and lay down on the cot, expecting they'd do what they'd done before. But this time, instead of rubbing against him, she knelt beside him, took his cock in her hand, and gave it a long lick. He came in an instant and she recoiled, shocked by the sudden eruption. He was mortified. "Gosh, Dinah, did I get you?"

She patted her face and hair. "Nope. Missed me." Then she started to laugh. "You could take an eye out with that thing." He couldn't join in her merriment. Having no control wasn't something to be proud of.

"No one ever did that to me before," he said, as a kind of explanation.

"Well, I never did that either. It just looked like a candy pop. You ever taste it? Cum?"

"Are you kidding?" In fact, he *had* tasted it once, off his hand. It didn't taste like anything else—faintly saline, but not salty like tears, was as close as he could come to describing it, but it smelled nice and fresh, not acrid like urine or sweat.

Dinah stuck out her tongue and licked the tip, where a small drop of semen still adhered.

"Dinah!" Joel yelled, but his cock jumped with delight.

"*Eeew . . .* " She wiped her tongue on her arm. "It's not sweet, I can tell you that. But it sure is fun to make it dance." Then, like a magician, she passed her hand back and forth over it, tapping it lightly, watching it rise and fall like a puppet on a string.

Unamused, Joel grabbed her hand, sure that Old Faithful would once again blow. "Wait." He took the corner of the sheet and wiped his penis dry, then pulled her toward him.

"Now let's do it like we did it before." He wanted to see that look on her face—now that he had a word for it. Ecstasy. And she happily obliged.

Joel sighed as he turned onto North Street. No doubt about it—he had to see her tonight.

...

Joel never made it to Dinah's show, or even to Stockman's motel. He only made it as far as Safeway where he picked up salami and a roll and slapped together a sandwich. Wolfing down his lunch, he walked out the back of the store and sat on the loading dock, where he could enjoy a bit of shade and a view of Rapid Creek. A moment later, he got a clear view of Lana Rosen giving Guy Stockman a long, open-mouth kiss in the front seat of his fiery red Pontiac.

It was like a blindfold had been torn from his face. As Guy's Pontiac pulled out of the lot, Joel blinked at the harsh new light, and cried out, "Shit!" And then he ran—across a rock-strewn field and then back along the creek, until he felt as if his heart would burst.

Everything was mixed up now—a blur of air, land, water, and trees. Finally, he collapsed under a cottonwood and lay there panting in the heat. Lana, he now saw, was a common slut, and Stockman, a vile seducer, and Bernie, a pitiable cuckold. How could he go on living in the Rosen house knowing what he did? How could he face any of them again?

And Dinah. Was she just an apple of temptation not fallen far from her mother's tree?

Every qualm he had about her came crashing down in an avalanche of doubt and disgust as his eyes were opened to the hard, new facts of life in Rapid City.

...

Bernie was home when the call came in from the Mellerdrammer. Dinah and Glen never showed for work. Panicked, he called the police. No accidents involving a yellow Skyliner. He phoned Glen's dad who seemed unconcerned. "Maybe they went for a swim at the lake."

Something was wrong. He could feel it in his gut. Dinah, like her mother, would not skip a show. But last night, she came home still dressed in her costume, looking like she'd been crying. And that morning, she left with a small valise. When he joked about her running off to join the circus, she smiled nervously and said her costume was inside.

In her bedroom, drawers were open and clothes strewn across the floor. But he couldn't be sure this was unusual. On the nightstand he found a framed photo of him and Dinah at Rushmore, looking like they were sharing a joke. Bernie felt a tug in his chest. Dinah might not be his blood, but she surely was his daughter and he'd do anything to protect her.

Next to the photo was a booklet entitled *Family Life Education for Girls*. Flipping through it he found chapters on pregnancy and venereal disease. His alarm redoubled.

And then he spotted it—Dinah's costume from the night before, peeking out from under her bed—not, as she'd claimed, in her suitcase. The 'sex' booklet, the lie about the costume, ditching work, and her tearstained face last night. What if Dinah were pregnant? She'd had a lot of boyfriends, but he didn't think she'd gone that far with any of them. Now he feared she had.

Who could the father be, he wondered. He doubted it was Glen, the youngest of the lot.

Most likely, it was Joel. He barreled down the basement stairs. If the baby was Joel's, they might have run off to get married and his duffel would be gone.

Bursting into Joel's room, he yanked open the doors of the wooden armoire. On the pole hung a sports coat and slacks, and under it, his duffel, unzipped, with two packets of rubbers on top. Bernie stared at the foil-wrapped squares. The boychik had come prepared.

So, maybe it *was* Glen Merritt. Last night Joel came home stinking of booze. Maybe he'd discovered Dinah was two-timing him with her handsome young passenger. A cold shudder ran through him. Glen was too young to marry, but what if they went to get an abortion—in some back room up in Deadwood, like Lana had when she was Dinah's age? The thought of his daughter going through that made him gag.

Then he started to laugh. How could he be so stupid? Dinah wasn't pregnant. Or, if she were, there was no way to know this soon. Joel had been in Rapid just a few weeks, and she'd only known Glen about as long. Maybe they really had gone off for a swim and a little nookie.

Heading toward the staircase, Bernie spotted a light radiating from the fallout shelter. "What the hell!" he cursed. The bomb shelter was off-limits. Rushing to the room, he found one cot unmade, its sheets rumpled. Blood rushed to his temples. How dare Dinah thumb her nose at the sanctuary he'd built to shield their family from nuclear disaster.

Then, he saw it—a pink negligee, wedged between the mattress and the wall. Bernie grabbed the feathered nightie and scanned the label, though he already knew what was printed there. Frederick's of Hollywood—Lana's brand. Crouching, he buried his nose in the sheets and inhaled the faint scent of L'Air du Temps, his wife's favorite perfume.

"That fucking little kike!" Joel had played him for a fool, pretending to pursue his daughter while shtupping his wife. Throwing back his head, Bernie ripped the peignoir to pieces—his howl tearing through the shelter like a bomb blast.

Chapter Sixty-Six

NURSING A HANGOVER, JOEL sat in the Chiefs' dugout puzzling over the tangled mess he'd stumbled onto. Adultery, lust, coveting thy neighbor's wife—commandments that were once mere abstractions now involved people he knew, some he wanted to respect. He didn't know what to do. Turn a blind eye to Guy's betrayal of Bernie? Bernie was his host, but Guy was the man who directly controlled his future as a ballplayer. He could imagine what Stockman might do to him if he snitched. Cut him from the team entirely or at the very least never pitch him.

And, what about Dinah, the girl he'd fallen hard for? Before coming West, the only women he knew well were his mother and Rivkah—both faithful and honorable. That other kind of woman—Bathsheba, Helen of Troy, Cleopatra—femme fatales who drove men wild and inspired betrayal, even bloodshed—he knew only from the Bible or the movies.

Joel trudged to the water cooler and filled his cup. Downing his drink in a single gulp, he followed with another and another, hoping to reverse the effects of yesterday's therapeutic poisoning—a pint of bourbon from a package store on East Main.

Luckily, Dick Wiegand still looked strong, pitching in the seventh, ending the inning with a strikeout to maintain the Chiefs' 7-2 lead. For that, Joel was grateful. It was his turn to relieve if the day's starter faltered, but on this day, he wasn't sure he could deliver a single strike.

Just then Stockman jogged to the dugout and helped himself at the water cooler before anyone else could have a turn. "Greedy bastard," Joel muttered under his breath. The man just takes what he wants. He slumped forward, head in hands as Guy stripped off his gear.

"You sick or somethin', Meznik?"

Joel raised his bloodshot eyes. "Yeah . . . something."

"Been dicking around in the liquor cabinet with Bernie's little party doll?"

The words spewed out before Joel could stop them. "Go to hell, Stockman."

Everyone in the dugout turned toward Joel, wondering if their ears had deceived them. They'd never heard him swear, even when he'd challenged Hoades on the bridge in Pierre.

"Whoa there, bud. Go home and sleep it off. We won't be needin' ya tonight."

Stockman grabbed his Louisville Slugger and headed for the batter's box. He was a player now. He'd manage Meznik later.

• • •

The Cadillac braked to a stop a foot from Joel, pinning him hard against the stadium wall. Bernie stuck his head out the side window. "Get in the car, Meznik!"

For a moment, Joel stood stock-still, staring blindly into the windshield.

"*In the car!*" Bernie barked, and Joel's knees went weak. "*Now!*"

Joel raised his hands as if Bernie were pointing a gun. "OK, OK. I'm getting in."

"What's wrong?" he asked, his heart racing.

Bernie threw a scrap of a pink peignoir onto Joel's lap. "Don't touch it!" he growled.

Joel's hands froze in midair. "Oh, well . . . " he stammered.

"Oh, well?" Bernie's scornful mimic was chilling.

"I'm sorry, Bernie. We were just foolin' around, making out. I swear, nothing more."

"You call 'making out' nothing?"

"Just necking, Bernie. I swear. Dinah and I . . . "

"Not Dinah, you little shit." His finger stabbed the air above Joel's lap. "That's my wife's nightgown."

"But Dinah wore it that day in the shelter! Ask her. She'll tell you."

For a moment, Bernie went quiet. "I can't. She ran off with Glen Merritt."

Joel couldn't believe it. "Dinah ran off with that kid she drives? That's a laugh!"

Bernie slammed the dashboard with his fist. "Well, she's laughing at you now, the same way you're laughing at me."

Joel threw up his hands. "I swear on my mother's life, Bernie. I did not do it with your wife. Or your daughter."

"What about the rubbers, the ones in your duffel?"

Joel swallowed hard. "Lana told me to get them in case I went all the way with Dinah."

"Lana told you *that*? Mother of the Year, that woman. *Time* magazine should put her on the cover." Slumped in his seat, Bernie covered his face with his hands.

"Women," he said finally, breaking his long pause.

Joel hesitated, then asked his own question. "Did Dinah really run off with Glen?"

"Well, they didn't show up for work. They took off somewhere."

"I don't think she'd do that, Bernie. We were going together."

Bernie shrugged. "Women lie. Men, too. That door swings both ways."

Joel thought about Stockman and Lana and how right Bernie was.

"What's that look for?" Bernie's eyes narrowed, fixing on Joel's face. "You're hiding something. I can tell. Let's have it."

Joel cursed his scrutable face and Bernie's sharp eye. If he didn't come clean, he was finished—with Bernie, the Chiefs, with Dinah, too, whatever that was worth now. He'd either spill the beans or have to leave town. Drawing a deep breath, he forced himself to speak.

"I saw Lana get into Guy's car yesterday behind the Safeway grocery store."

For a long time, Bernie just sat there, saying nothing. Joel stared straight ahead, the scrap of pink peignoir resting in his lap. Suddenly, there rose a thunderous roar from the ballpark.

"Sounds like we're winning," Bernie said flatly.

Joel turned to look at Bernie. "Bernie, I'm sor . . . "

"Forget it, kid. You didn't do nothin' wrong."

• • •

The next morning, the highway patrol picked up Dinah and Glen outside the Wyoming town of Little America. Back in Rapid, she told her father of the abuse she'd suffered at the hands of the Mellerdrammer's director and that the plan to go to California had been "all Glen's idea," inspired by John's phenomenal success on Groucho's *You Bet Your Life*.

Bernie sent Buck to straighten out the Director whose arm was more than a little crooked after he left. Stepping down, he was replaced by Dinah's high school drama teacher who, she assured her dad, never got fresh with her or anyone else directing *Damn Yankees*.

Joel remained in his digs down the hall from the bomb shelter. He'd delivered bad news but was deemed all right by Bernie. And he'd bought the condoms, which Bernie had to admit was good advice on Lana's part, though a shotgun shidduch—Dinah knocked up and hitched to a smart Brooklyn Jewish boy—would suit him just fine.

Joel kept his mouth shut when Stockman showed up the next day with a bandaged hand, announcing that Clarence Williams would get his long-awaited chance behind the plate.

"Caught it in a car door," Guy told the team, alluding to the digit snapped like a chicken wing at the spot where palm meets thumb. "Hands off the missus," Buck told Guy when he waylaid him at the Royal Rest, adding, "Boss says let the colored guy catch."

Billy, taking out the garbage that night, saw Bernie slap Lana across the cheek and, a moment later, push her face against the tabletop, folding her body at the waist like a half-open jackknife. With Bernie pressing from behind, her head jerked in a rhythmic way that Billy did not understand. A minute later, he saw Lana smooth her skirt, pin back a stray lock of hair, and reach into the fridge for a bottle of beer.

Passed out downstairs, Joel heard the rhythmic thumping overhead as in a dream. Exhausted, he pressed the pillow against his ear and fell into a blessed, numbing sleep.

• • •

Stockman never put it together, Joel's outburst in the dugout and Bernie's discovery of the affair. Libertine Havana and his time in the blind-eyed East had made him reckless.

When Lana called, he was in bed at the Royal Rest, a fifth of Jim Beam on the nightstand. Fingering his cock, he laughed bitterly. At least he'd been spared his wangin' hand.

"It's me," Lana whispered, though her husband was halfway across town collecting Dinah at the police station. Hearing her voice for what he feared was the very last time, Guy responded with an agonized groan. "You all right?"

Lana snorted. "He can't maim the headliner. Anyway, sounds like he got you worse."

"Your husband sure knows how to get his point across."

There was a lull in the conversation as each waited for the other to end it.

"I think this is where you offer to knock him off for the insurance money," Lana quipped.

"Oh, baby. I wish . . . I . . . "

"Guess I won't be going to California. Had my heart set on seeing the ocean 'fore I die."

"Not this time," he said as gently as he could.

Lana hung up first. Guy stared at the phone, then flung it against the wall.

Halfway up the stairs, Joel heard enough of the call to know it was over between them.

His own situation, with Dinah, was less clear. One thing was certain—the Chiefs were leaving in the morning for Valentine to play the Hearts, and this time he couldn't wait to get out of town.

Chapter Sixty-Seven

BILLY WAS IN A FUNK. Yesterday he'd been ecstatic when his mom agreed to let Joel be his chaperone, but now he looked glumly out the bus window, an unread comic book in his lap.

An hour out of Rapid, Quarles rose from his seat to address his teammates. "OK, guys—let's play a game."

"Like animal, mineral, vegetable. Or twenty questions?" asked an eager Frank Hacker.

"Something like that. Only this one's about geography."

Joel nudged Billy. "Sounds like fun, right, Bill?"

Billy shrugged. "Guess so," and Joel frowned. Billy's mood seemed out of character for the usually light-hearted lad. When he'd agreed to watch the boy, he looked forward to a cheerful distraction from the Rosens' Borgian treacheries, not an echo of his own low spirits.

"I'm in!" Joel yelled, hoping a game would provide the desired diversion.

"You would be," Hoades muttered. The Alabaman had just learned that Clarence, not he, would replace Stockman as catcher. Pulling Guy aside, he protested. "That broken down old coon?" Guy shrugged. Bernie's command, delivered persuasively by Buck, could not be defied.

"What are the rules?" Joel asked, ignoring Hoades' crack.

"Remind me again, Kibb, what are the rules? The college boy wants it spelled out."

"Rules . . . duh . . . we never talked about no rules, Dickie."

"Professor Kibbee is correct. We never *talked* about rules, but that don't mean there ain't none—just that the rules are for us to know and you to find out."

"That's not fair," Hacker complained.

Quarles shrugged. "Sorry, big man. Life's not fair. Take it or leave it."

"This is stupid," Hoades protested. "You and Meznik play."

Stockman, his thumb throbbing and in no mood for Quarles' falderol, spoke up from beneath his Panama. "Just start the damn game, Q."

"Our brave leader, Chief One Thumb, rises from his sickbed to quell mutiny on the bus."

"Heard he hurt his thumb laying pipe in a tight place," uttered a low voice from the back. The cheeky comment made Joel wonder if the entire team knew about Stockman's affair.

"Now, follow along, guys . . . It's called 'Game of the States'. There are forty-eight of 'em for those who forgot. I'll start it with Michigan and, ahh . . . Maine."

"Hey, that's what I was gonna say," Kibbee griped. "All right, here's another one . . . New York and, ahh . . . New Jersey."

"Excellent, Clyde. That's a double for you."

"How about Massachusetts and Minnesota," Joel offered.

"Close, but not quite. Fly-out to the warning track."

"California and Carolina?" Lee Casey, the shortstop, proposed.

"Carolina ain't really the name of a state, Lee, but even if it was, you'd be wrong. E-6."

"Mon . . . tan . . . a and Lou . . . is . . . i . . . an . . . a," posed Haroldson in exaggerated rhyme.

"Good job, Bruce. A Dakotan connecting with the Louisiana Purchase. But that's not it."

Joel was perplexed. Same first letter did it sometimes, but not every time. Same last letter didn't do it at all. Montana and Louisiana rhymed but that wasn't it, either.

Kibbee laughed. "Here's a hint. North Carolina and, . . . ahh . . . South Carolina."

"Don't give it away like that, Kibb," Quarles warned.

Joel cupped his hands. "I think I've got it. Nebraska and ahh . . . South Dakota."

"Home run, Freako! Give an 'A' to the Ivy Leaguer."

Joel turned to Billy. "You get it? Just listen to every syllable when a person gets it right. I'll tell you later if you haven't figured it out. You could drive kids crazy with this at school."

Hoades, to Joel's surprise, was next to score. "Alabama and, aahh . . . Miss . . . i . . . sipp . . . i."

"And you didn't want to play," teased Quarles. "Chalk one up for the Crimson Tide."

Hoades grinned and thrust his arm in the air, chanting, "*Rollll, tide, roll!*"

"Nothing worse than a sore winner," Hacker grumbled.

"OK, big fella. When you get it, we'll let you sing the Buckeye fight song."

Harlen Dalluge, enunciating clearly, offered "Id . . . ah . . . ho and, ah, Ill . . . i . . . nois."

"Dalluge, that's brilliant. Using your home state to advantage. Like Hoades."

"Oh, I get it now," Hacker responded. "Ok . . . la . . . ho . . . ma and O . . . hi . . . o."

"No, no. Sorry, big guy, still way off base. Two pitchers and one catcher got it so far. Guess pitchers are twice as smart as catchers," Quarles said slyly.

Hoades grunted. "Catcher? Me? Since when? We got an old Clown for a catcher now."

Joel glanced at Clarence. He'd not had a chance to congratulate him for taking over from Stockman but couldn't do it now, not within earshot of the disgruntled Hoades.

Eyes closed, Clarence just smiled to himself. Let him grouse. On the first road trip he'd sparked to the Southerner's slurs, but now that Stockman made him the catcher there was no way he was going to jeopardize his new post by confronting Johnny Reb. Though he was sure he could beat the living daylights outta him anytime, anyplace if given the chance.

The pitcher, Dave Wiegand, tried again, "New Hampshire and New Mexico."

"Some broad strike zone you got there, Wig, but you whiffed. Thought you overheard us at the Alex concocting our little game, but I guess that cute little redhead balled up your brain."

Joel imagined the scene at the bar—his teammates drinking and joking and picking up girls. Maybe he had it wrong, just sticking to Dinah, and thanks to Lana, he carried protection in the bag by his feet. But could he do it with a stranger picked up at a bar? Did he even want to?

Fred pulled off the main highway and stopped in front of Wall Drug. "Everybody out for the free ice water," he yelled.

"Come on, Bill. I'll buy you an ice cream," Joel offered. Billy shook his head, "No."

"What's the matter? Your Mom OK? I know she was in the hospital."

Billy shrugged. "Yeah." Searching her bedroom, he'd found only a half-empty pill bottle and an appointment card for a month away—much too distant for anyone just about to die.

"You car sick?" Joel asked.

"No . . . it's . . . " Billy lowered his voice. "Did you ever hit a girl?"

"No. Did *you* hit a girl?"

Billy looked aghast. "I'd never do that." He hesitated for a moment as if afraid to go on. "I saw Bernie hit Lana. Hard. On the face. Like this." Billy made a sharp swing with his hand.

"When was that?" Joel asked, though he suspected he already knew.

"Last night. I think he spanked her, too. She had her head on the table." Billy bent forward turning his neck to the side. "He held her down. But I couldn't hear if she cried."

"Oh God!" Joel turned pale, guessing what had transpired, something Billy couldn't possibly have understood. And now the boy's bewildered expression pleaded for an explanation.

He had to say something. "All parents fight, Bill. I know mine do."

"My Dad would never hit my Mom!" He thrust out his chin. "I hate Bernie."

"Hate's a strong word," Joel countered, though he knew this was a feeble response.

Billy shook his head. Bernie had violated a hallowed honor code: *Never hit a girl!*

Joel appreciated the boy's principled certitude, but how could anyone as young as Billy understand what could drive a man to do such a thing when he didn't understand it himself—how a wife's betrayal could make a man do something so violent to even the score, and that a woman might accept it and remain with him afterwards.

"If I wanted to, I could get Bernie in trouble," Billy added, a mean edge in his voice.

"What do you mean, Bill?"

"I could go to the police. I know something . . . something else. About Bernie."

Joel wished Billy would shut up. He'd already seen what Bernie was capable of when the man pinned him to the stadium wall with his car. "Come on, kiddo. Let's get a cone."

Billy scowled. "You're not taking me serious."

Joel was worried. Billy was itching to tell someone. What if he told the wrong person, or worse yet, went directly to Bernie with his accusation, whatever it was. "OK, Bill. Tell me."

Billy cupped a hand at his mouth and whispered into Joel's ear. "He's got guns hidden in the basement at the Club. Army rifles. Hundreds of 'em."

Joel gasped. Guns. Bernie. Billy might be wrong about the number or type, but could he be wrong about seeing a cache of weapons at the Club? He took Billy by the shoulders.

"Don't say anything about this. Ever. To anyone. You hear me?"

Billy looked like he could cry. "What are they for?" he asked in a small, frightened voice. "I have no idea." Joel said, wishing that the Rosens' kitchen shades had been drawn.

And that Bernie Rosen wasn't a Jew with a name so much like Rosenberg.

Chapter Sixty-Eight

BACK ON THE ROAD, no one took up the game again except the hapless Hacker.

"Ne . . . bras . . . ka and A . . . las . . . ka."

"Sorry, Hack. Alaska's not a state yet, though they sure are trying up there."

Ignoring the chatter, Joel tried to make sense of Billy's discovery. Bernie didn't strike him as a Communist plotting to overthrow the government. More of a capitalist out to make a buck. But wasn't he exactly the sort of person who *could* be a spy—posing as a businessman, knowing everyone in town through his nightclub and baseball connections—the last person you'd suspect, like those Englishmen, Burgess and MacLean, Cambridge educated agents who defected to the Soviet Union a few years back.

Shutting his eyes, he tried to quiet his racing thoughts as the bus continued east, passing through the tiny town of Phillip Junction. Fred announced that it was named for a Scotsman who'd come to America in gold rush days, hoping to strike it rich. When mining didn't pan out, he married a Sioux woman and started a ranch on reservation land, which he could do "only 'cause he married an Injun, just like me."

Fred married to an Indian? Joel found that almost as shocking as Bernie's guns.

"How 'bout this? Kan . . . zas and R . . . Kan . . . zas?" Hacker's booming voice startled the dozing men. Quarles yawned. "Never woulda thought of that, Hack, maybe 'cause it's wrong."

Joel gnawed at his thumbnail. Maybe he figured it wrong. He'd thought Fred was prejudiced toward Indians, then learned he was married to one. And weren't those Rosen family pilgrimages to Mount Rushmore evidence of Bernie's patriotism? Now he felt ashamed for jumping to a conclusion that someone like Hoades would make about a New York Jew stockpiling weapons in his basement.

Back home, everyone he knew believed in the Rosenbergs' innocence. So, what was it that made him presume Bernie's guilt?

He looked at Billy dozing in his seat. Maybe he could tell the boy that the guns were for defending Rapid City—better still, Rushmore—in case the Reds ever made it this far west.

Closing his eyes, he could finally sleep. It was a story he could almost believe himself.

• • •

When the bus arrived in Valentine, Hack gave it one last try. "Mississippi and Missouri?"

"Miss-take," was all Quarles said as the big outfielder stormed off the bus.

Hoades and Kibbee shared a laugh. "Think the big guy's gonna erupt."

"Yep, sure is fun, winding him up like that." Quarles twirled his index finger skyward, then plunged it down in a wailing crescendo. "Like watching a twister toss a two-ton trailer."

Joel forced a smile. He'd never liked pranks or practical jokes—meanness masquerading as fun. He was grateful there'd been little of that on the Columbia squad. Still, he chose to go along. "I dunno, it might backfire at the plate. I think we need to make it up to him."

Quarles shrugged. "So tell him the trick. I'm tired of it anyhow."

"I'm not sure that's enough to square things," Joel countered.

A smile spread across Quarles's face. "Let's treat him to some hot dogs. Buy him a dozen."

Joel hesitated. Stockman wouldn't like his big slugger stuffed full of wieners right before the game. "What about Coach? Don't think he'd approve."

Quarles's eyes danced with delight. "Don't worry. He won't find out. Big Chief pow-wows with the other manager before the game. We'll feed Hack the dogs when they're trading lineups. Bet he can polish off the whole dozen before Coach gets back to the dugout." Quarles reached into his pocket. "Are you in, New Yawk? Here's a buck for the weenies and another for the bet."

Joel was taken aback. He couldn't believe Quarles would risk sidelining their best hitter, possibly cost them the game, for a practical joke. Still, he didn't want a reputation as a stick in the mud, especially with Quarles. "I'm in. But our two bucks won't buy a dozen dogs."

Quarles grabbed Kibbee in a half nelson. "Hey, piker, cough up that deuce you owe me."

Dragging the bat bag, Billy couldn't stop thinking about Bernie. His mom always said he was bad. Now it looked like she was right. Then he recalled what the old man at the Scout meeting said about Jews not being patriots and Jewish traitors named Rosenberg. He stopped in his tracks. What if Bernie's real name was Rosenberg? Spies used fake names all the time.

"Hey, hold on a minute." Joel caught up to Billy and handed him four dollars. "I'll take the bats. Get a dozen hot dogs and two Cokes. Bring 'em to me, and don't let Coach see you."

"Are you treatin' the team?"

"No, they're a surprise for Hacker."

"All of them? Is it his birthday?"

Joel laughed, wondering if the concession stand had a candle to stick in one of the dogs. Then he chided himself, abashed by how easily he'd succumbed to having fun at Hacker's expense. "No. It's for being a good sport. Get yourself one while you're at it, on me."

The concession stand was manned by a pretty teenager stirring a pot of wieners with a long, pronged fork. Distracted from thoughts of Bernie's treachery, Billy stood at the counter flipping through his new bank roll while sneaking a peek at the comely concessionaire. Dressed in blue jeans and a plaid shirt, she was slender with strawberry blonde hair plaited in two long braids. Billy pictured her riding a pony, her braids bouncing up and down against her back.

"Can I help you?" The girl wiped her hands on her jeans and smiled.

"I need twelve wieners, no thirteen, and two Cokes," he said, his voice cracking a bit.

The girl glanced at Billy's uniform. "You buyin' for the whole team?"

"No. They're for our outfielder."

"Thirteen hot dogs for just one guy?"

"Only twelve, the other one's for me."

"Only twelve. Hmm, well then it's OK." Her eyes crinkled as she laughed.

"He's a really big guy, six-seven and two-forty-five." Instantly, he kicked himself for calling attention to Hacker's size when the girl appeared to be a couple inches taller than he was.

"Sounds like Paul Bunyan to me. He'll grow even bigger after he eats a dozen."

"I once ate six," he fibbed. "My parents run the concession stand in Rapid."

"That's funny, this is my folks' Stand, too. Do you work there?"

"I'm batboy for the Chiefs but I help out in the Stand before the game." He lied again.

"Batboy. Wow! Let me ask you a question. Do your folks pay you?"

"Two cents a box." A third lie.

"Really? I only get a penny. About a dollar a game."

"I usually make ten dollars! Once we sold a thousand boxes." Emboldened by each triumphant fib, he upped the ante, hoping the girl wouldn't call his bluff.

"Wow! You're so lucky living in a big city like Rapid."

Billy glanced nervously at the Chiefs' dugout across the way. "I have to get back."

"Oh, I'm sorry. I should have been laying out the buns." She whirled around and grabbed a package from the shelf.

"I can help." Ducking under the counter, Billy spread open a bun as the young woman speared a wiener from the steaming pot. Then to his delight, she sped up the pace, giving hm the chance to show off his reflexes. Soon, twelve wieners were stacked in a box.

"Where are your folks?" he asked as he watched her pour the drinks.

"They're at the café. We own Parkers on Heart Street. I'm the waitress at lunch. You can come by and see me tomorrow."

Billy beamed at the invitation until Joel's stern voice broke in. "Tomorrow? You'll be on the next bus home if I don't get you back to the dugout . . . NOW."

Joel took the box from Billy's hands. "Come on!"

The girl handed Billy another wiener. "Your thirteenth."

"Gee, thanks," he said, celebrating with a bite as Joel steered him toward the dugout.

"Looks like you were picking up more than just frankfurters," Joel teased, relieved that the boy's mind was occupied by something other than Bernie Rosen's guns.

"Hey, batboy, what's your name?" the girl called after him.

"Bill," he yelled back. "What's yours?"

"Ginny."

Billy choked on his wiener. "Did you say 'Jennie?' He hoped he'd heard it wrong.

"No, *Ginny*!"

Joel slapped him on the back to stop the coughing.

"Gotta get you back, kid. Stockman says I'm screwing up the bats."

"Wheredja tell him I was?"

"In the bathroom, puking. So, eat fast and try to look a little green when you get back."

Billy punched Joel in the arm. "Thanks a lot."

Joel squeezed the back of Billy's neck. "Anytime, little buddy. Anytime."

Billy smiled. For the first time in his life, he didn't mind being called "little."

Chapter Sixty-Nine

JOEL COULDN'T SLEEP—still thinking about Bernie and the guns, and when he closed his eyes, of Dinah singing to him on the rock at Sylvan Lake. Rolling onto his side, he reckoned what he really needed was a moment of privacy in the bathroom, but the door had no lock and he wasn't sure that Clarence and Billy were both asleep.

Counting sheep, Joel's mind drifted to that night's loss. Dalluge, the pitcher, was in trouble from the start and told he might relieve, he sat on pins and needles all game. While not called on to pitch, he'd not calmed down enough hours later to fall asleep.

On days like this, Joel wished he played another position—first base, maybe, or the outfield. Then he'd be a regular part of the action, instead of anxiously waiting for his next start. Or being asked to relieve, which involved far more pressure than what he felt as a starter when he'd be given ample time to warm up and get his head on straight before taking the mound.

And yet, he felt blessed having the ability to propel the little sphere ninety miles an hour, and he loved the righteous duel with opposing batsmen. And while the fielders had to wait for something to happen in this slow game, he relished being on the front line—the initiator who got it all going, if only every fourth day. It gave him a heroic feeling that he wasn't ready to give up.

Joel turned to face the window and thought about stepping outside to gaze at the stars. Never were so many visible as here on the Plains. Back in Brooklyn, with its streetlamps always bright, even a single pinprick in the night sky was cause for excitement.

He recalled one summer when a blackout plunged Brooklyn into darkness and he and Rivkah saw the Big Dipper for the first time. It was the night of their very first kiss, after a good-natured tiff about the name of the constellation, with him arguing that the arrangement of stars and size of the handle made it look more like a pot than a 'dipper'.

"You want to rename it 'The Big Pot'? Very poetic," Rivkah teased.

"Hey, I'm as poetic as the next guy!" he'd insisted.

Taking her face in his hands, he kissed her—not deeply, but long, on a street corner as dark as ink, lit only by a ladle of stars. Then the lights came back on and the look she gave him, adoration mingled with trust, was like nothing he'd ever seen from a girl before, or since.

Joel heard Billy stumble out of bed and make his way to the bathroom. He likely had a lot rattling around in his head, too. After the game, he'd hung back to ask a question. Fearing it concerned Bernie's guns, Joel was relieved it was about the girl at the concession stand. Stricken by jitters, Billy asked Joel to go with him to the café the next day. Then he pulled a paperback from his back pocket. It was the racy best seller, *Peyton Place*. "Where'd you get that, Bill?"

"It's John's. Did you read it?"

"No, but I know about it." He didn't tell Billy how the entire Columbia squad had thumbed through the book on a long bus trip to Cornell.

"Can I ask you somethin'? Is there a letter down there"—Billy pointed to his crotch, " . . . on girls?"

Joel stifled a laugh. "A letter. You mean, an envelope with a stamp?"

"No. Not that kind of letter. A 'V'." With that, Billy formed a V with his fingers.

Joel tried to hide his shock. "Where's it say that?"

Billy opened the book to a dog-eared section. "On page 203, it says 'his hand found the 'V' of her crotch'. See, my brother circled the 'V'. Is there a 'V' down there, like a tattoo?"

Joel sputtered. "I don't know, Bill, maybe you should ask your brother about that."

"He's not here. I thought you knew about this stuff."

"Yes, but I just can't . . . but I'll come to lunch with you tomorrow."

"Fine," Billy said, sounding like it was anything but.

Joel looked over at Billy's empty cot. He had to give the kid credit for asking. He'd been equally in the dark at his age. And, with no older brother, all he could do was pay close attention to racy scenes in movies. Though even that wouldn't have solved the riddle of the 'V'.

Billy emerged from the bathroom and felt his way back to his cot. Based on the length of his visit, Joel suspected he might have done the same thing he wanted to do to get to sleep.

Crouching low, Joel crept by the head of Billy's bed and whispered, "On women and mature girls, there's hair down there and it forms a triangle—a sort of 'V' pointing down."

"Gee, thanks!" Billy grinned as Joel headed for the bathroom where the lack of malodorous vapors confirmed that Billy was indeed old enough for the information he'd just received.

"Horny white boys," Clarence Williams thought, making a mental note to speak to Clarence Jr. about the shape of things down there.

Missing Cherry Mae, he closed his eyes and counted backwards from a hundred, figuring he'd either be asleep by the time Joel finished, or take his own turn in the common bedtime ritual.

Chapter Seventy

THE NEXT MORNING, JOEL AND Billy walked to Ginny's café on Heart Street. Jumpier than usual, Billy kept patting down his hair, sure that his cowlicks stood out like porcupine quills.

"Did you have trouble finding it?" Ginny asked as she came from behind the cash register to greet them. Wearing lipstick and in a sleeveless dress with her hair loose, she seemed older than Billy remembered, and, to his dismay, her wedge-shaped heels made her even taller.

"No . . . the sign." Billy pointed to a wooden heart inscribed with the words "Parker's Café."

"I made it," Ginny said, her face glowing with pride.

"Wow!" Billy, exclaimed. "With a jigsaw?"

The girl's face fell. "No. I painted it."

"Well, that's one beautiful sign!" Joel interjected.

Billy didn't appreciate Joel's butting in—particularly when Ginny, her face brightening, turned in his direction and introduced herself. And when Joel extended his hand, getting to touch her first, Billy regretted bringing along a good-looking man who towered over him by a foot.

"This way, gentlemen." As soon as Ginny left to get menus, Billy scowled at Joel.

Guessing what was bothering him, Joel lightly punched his arm. "She likes you!"

"She likes *you*," Billy muttered through clenched teeth.

Joel's smile was sympathetic. "OK, but she likes you, too, and I'm way too old for her. I'm not trying to steal your girl. I came to help."

Abashed, Billy nodded. "I know." Then Ginny breezed by, and Billy sat up ramrod straight, as if he'd been poked in the ribs.

Maybe that was the crux of his problem, Joel thought. Billy was cute but short for his age, and completely boyish looking—a real late bloomer.

"Ya gotta relax, buddy," Joel whispered. Then, echoing Quarles's prescription for pitchers, added, "Pretend you don't care what happens."

"Whadya mean?" Billy asked, looking bewildered.

Joel frowned. It was hard to explain to a kid. "Like when you play ball, you've got to be loose as a goose. Best way to mess up is to try too hard, so tell yourself you don't care."

Billy looked incredulous. "You think Eddie Mathews doesn't care?"

"I said *pretend*, Billy. It works. Be cool as a cat and you're more likely to score."

Billy looked stricken. "But what do I say when she comes back?"

"Say something nice, like what you'd say to a friend."

Billy was baffled. He never said anything nice to a friend, except about a new bike or ball glove or if he did something terrific in a game. Anything else he'd ignore, like all the guys did.

When Ginny returned, Billy offered her a French fry instead.

She demurred. "Thanks, but they don't let me eat on the job," then added, "I get off in half an hour." When Billy didn't respond, Joel kicked him under the table, but the boy remained mute, like a batter watching the perfect pitch float across home plate, unable to pull the trigger.

"Gotta go," Joel said. "Promised my girl a postcard, but you can stay, Bill." Brought in to pinch-hit, he'd made solid contact, but would the ball fall in for a hit to advance his little buddy?

Ginny looked from Joel to Billy, then furrowed her brow. Joel could see her working it out in her head, the basic math of it, a simple subtraction, and the rightness of the reconfigured difference. Finally, she touched Billy's sleeve and smiled. "OK."

True to his word, Joel left after paying the bill and slipping Billy a quarter for the tip.

Billy finished his burger and fries and at half past one, Ginny sidled up to him. "We can go now. Come meet my mom."

At the register, a tall woman with a hound-dog face was counting the day's receipts.

"Mom, this is Bill. His parents run the concession stand in Rapid."

The woman grunted, without looking up. With her grim set of mouth and unwelcoming manner, she reminded Billy of his own mother. "Be back by four to set up for supper," she said curtly. Ginny grabbed his arm and pulled him out the door, into the bright sunlight.

"She's such a pill!" Ginny shouted as they ran side by side down the narrow sidewalk.

"So's mine," Billy hollered back. Thrilled, he wanted to leap at his good fortune—two and a half hours with a real live girl, one prettier and bolder than any he'd known.

Passing the bank, Ginny brushed an old farmer who looked back, chiding her by name. Singing out a loud "Sorr-ree!" she led Billy into a narrow alley. "Shortcut!" she cried.

A few blocks farther, she stopped before a small clapboard house with a yard of patchy brown grass. Two beat-up bikes leaned against the house. Breathless, Ginny pointed to the boy's model. "You can use my brother's. He's in the Army."

Billy nodded and walked to the bike. Instantly deflated, he almost cursed. The seat was set at the highest level and the bolt rusted tight.

"Oh," Ginny said after a pause. "We don't have to go. I really don't care."

Pretend not to care. Billy recalled Joel's advice. "It's not a big deal. I can fix it. All I need is a wrench."

Ginny darted into the house and returned waving one above her head. Adjusting the tool's jaws around the nut, Billy pushed down hard, praying it would turn. The nut refused to yield. Trying again with no success, he opened his hand, claw stiff from the strain, and blew on his palm. Afraid to look up, he was sure she'd see how close he was to tears and how much he really *did* care.

"Gosh, that sure is tight," Ginny sighed.

Inspired by her gentle tone, Billy gave it another try. Holding her breath, Ginny watched as it held firm, then slowly gave way. "You did it!"

Shimmying the seat to the right level, Billy said in his deepest voice, "Let's go!"

Leading the way, Ginny turned onto a two-lane blacktop, deserted except for a swarm of grasshoppers in a field of sunflowers. West of town, she turned onto a dirt road.

"This is what I wanted to show you," she said, pointing to an abandoned farmhouse.

Suddenly, she turned somber. "My best friend lived here before they lost the farm. Now she lives in Rapid. I miss her so much."

Ginny motioned for him to follow her to the barn, devoid of livestock except for the lingering smell. On a crossbeam over the entrance, a single, scrawny chicken paced back and forth, emitting a loud protest of tortured squawks. Transfixed, Billy followed the ceaseless march of the agitated bird. "What's wrong with it?"

"Nothing, it's just tryin' to lay an egg. You never seen that?"

"Gosh no! Wonder if havin' a baby's that hard?"

"I guess, but that's how it is for every egg you eat."

Restless, Billy wandered through the barn, gathering eggs from nooks and crannies, depositing them in his baseball cap. Ginny noticed what he was doing and frowned. "I don't think that's a good idea. Those eggs are rotten. My friend's been gone a while."

"I wasn't gonna eat 'em. I need 'em for target practice." He looked around the barn and pitched an egg through the open bay of the hayloft. "I'm gonna be a pitcher in the Big Leagues," he boasted. "Coach said to grip the ball like it's an egg."

Ginny laughed. "Better not squeeze it or you'll find out it really *is* an egg."

With that, he fired the second egg through the open bay. "Strike two!" he crowed.

Seeking a greater challenge, he spotted a gap between two wall planks. Pointing to the hole, he fired another missile, but this time, an old wagon wheel hanging by a chain intercepted the egg in mid-flight, showering them with a gooey, putrid shampoo.

"Oh my gosh!" Ginny exclaimed, examining her dress. "What am I gonna do? This is my only work dress. And I gotta go back to the café."

"Damn, I'm sorry, Ginny," Billy cursed, sure that his showing off had ruined the day.

Ginny studied the frock with an anxious look. "Guess I can try to wash it out." Running to the pump in the yard, she pushed down on the handle over and over, but not a drop of water emerged.

"I can do it," he said, recalling his triumph with the bicycle seat. Pumping up and down, never losing heart, he still couldn't raise a drop.

"*Eew.*" Ginny pointed to the back of Billy's shirt and made a face. "You got hit, too."

Billy pulled off his shirt and laid it on a flagstone near the pump. Ginny snuck an admiring look at his broad back and chest as he worked. Though short in stature, he had the contours of a boy who'd someday be a muscular man--aided and abetted by his regimen of 'Dynamic Tension', the Charles Atlas Home Body Building Course.

Finally, a trickle of liquid fell from the spigot to the dry ground. "Told yah!"

Ginny ran to the house for a metal pail and watched as Billy filled it. Then, without warning, she lifted her dress over her head, exposing white cotton panties, bra, and expanses of freckled, cream-colored flesh. Staggered by the sight of her, he grabbed the pump for balance.

"Keep pumping," she ordered, plunging the dress in and out of the water, splashing her bra and panties and slowly revealing the outlines of her breasts and the dark triangle below.

Awestruck, Billy couldn't turn away from the most beautiful sight he'd ever seen—the great mystery of Peyton Place answered in a most natural way. Inside his pocket, he formed a triumphant "V" with his index and middle fingers.

Ginny pulled her dress out of the bucket, wrung it out, and placed it by the pump. "Your turn," she said, grabbing the handle. Crouching, he scrubbed the egg-stained collar between his knuckles, then stuck his face under the pump and whooped as cold water cascaded down his neck. Standing up, he pounded his chest, letting out a Tarzan yell.

Ginny answered, "Now me!" Leaning back, she let the water stream through her long red mane. To Billy, it looked like a waterfall lit by fire.

Ginny stood up. Breathing quickly, they faced each other as rivulets of water sluiced paths down their chests. "There's a line." She pointed to the top of the little hill, where a long white cord dotted with clothespins stretched between two wooden poles. Side by side, they pinned their wet garments to the clothesline, then took a step back and watched them billow in the warm prairie wind—her dress and his shirt flapping and fluttering, like partners in a country dance, sometimes touching, sometimes breaking apart.

Ginny took Billy's hand in hers and closed her eyes as she leaned in for a kiss. It was exactly how he'd imagined it, and then, when she opened her mouth a little, even better.

• • •

Billy may have forgotten about Bernie's basement arsenal, but Joel had not.

Leaving the café, he walked down Heart Street, onto the weed-strewn tracks of the Chicago and Northwestern rail line. For the first time since leaving New York, he wished he could talk to Rivkah. But what would he say? That he lived with a Jewish thug, a Meyer Lansky in cowboy boots and possibly a traitor? That his wife cheated with the team's manager, then was brutalized by her husband? That he'd gone further with a sixteen-year-old than he ever had with her?

What could she advise him other than to leave this Sodom of Dakota and not look back?

Joel stepped over the rail and stood in the center of the track. Never could he have imagined what he'd encountered on the Plains, a place he'd expected to be as straight and true as the tracks that lay before him. Once back in Rapid, would he dare investigate Billy's claim about the guns? And if he were right, would he report Bernie to the FBI or confront him instead—a man who almost mowed him down with his car?

And there was Dinah. He trusted her once when she swore she'd not done it with John Moran, but he'd be a chump to take her back after she went on the lam with that Merritt kid.

With the sun on his back, Joel trained his eyes east across the yawning prairie to the unseen canyons of New York and the life that awaited him there—marriage to Rivkah and medical school, kids and a house in the suburbs, and perhaps a summer bungalow in the Catskills. The familiar confines of a life drawn too close. Turning west, he imagined a different future, one bright with ballpark lights and cheering crowds and roads yet untraveled.

Joel picked up a rock and hurled it up the tracks. Everyone back home thought this was just a lark, a last fling at baseball before settling down. They didn't know about the clippings in his wallet: a *Brooklyn Eagle* feature on his high school career and, from the *Times*, the news of Sandy Koufax signing with the Dodgers for a big bonus.

Joel braced his feet against the rails and stretched his arms beyond the track as far as they could reach. This was no pipe dream. It was his life's dream, ever since he first saw Ebbets Field.

Pretend not to care? He just couldn't do it. Scheduled to pitch that night, he was determined to put everything out of his mind. Everything but winning.

Chapter Seventy-One

JOHN OPENED HIS EYES AND GROANED. Waking in a strange bed, the air thick with perfume, he knew he wasn't alone. The room clearly belonged to a woman. But who could she be?

He pressed his temples with his thumbs. The last thing he remembered was sitting at a bar with a pretty brunette discussing the future of television in Rapid City.

He covered his face with a pillow. Either the room was spinning, or he was, but one had to stop. Slowly, he slipped the pillow off his eyes and scanned the trail of jettisoned clothes leading from door to bed. Thrusting a hand under the covers, he felt his penis. It was bare and sticky. Shocked, he never imagined it would happen like this. His fantasy was always of Dinah.

"I thought I heard stirrings." Coffee cup in one hand, cigarette in the other, it was the brunette from the bar, in a black peignoir. John felt the blood rush to his face.

"I'm sorry. I don't recall your name," he stammered.

"Shirley . . . Randolph." She set the coffee on the nightstand. "Let me reintroduce myself." Assuming a dramatic pose, she extended her arm in a grand sweep. "On behalf of the good folks at Plymouth-DeSoto I'd like to present you with a check for five thousand and fifty dollars."

Now, he remembered. The check—hopefully still in the breast pocket of his sports jacket, strewn somewhere on the floor. "You work for the sponsor?"

"Yes—public relations."

John snorted. "Guess that makes me John Q. Public."

Smiling, she snuffed out her cigarette and slipped back into bed.

"So whatcha gonna to do with your winnings, Mr. Moran?"

John's dick stiffened as she ran her finger down the lacy plunge of her nightie. He could barely manage an answer. "College, I suppose."

"Oh, yes—Yale, right? Awfully far from Rapid City. How will you get there?"

"The bus, I guess."

"You should buy a car. Celebrate your TV triumph. Impress your girl back home." Shirley slipped a hand under the cover and commenced a five-finger exercise with his cock. "I can get you a great deal on a '57 Belvedere. Like new. Want to test drive it . . . later?"

John closed his eyes and let out a soft moan. "Oh . . . yes . . . please . . . later."

Later, on the drive back to Rapid in his Sand-Dune-White and Desert-Gold Belvedere Sports Coupe, John realized that Shirley had only been doing her job—recouping a sweet piece of the sponsor's stake. But with the top down and the scent of the sea off the Pacific, John had no doubt he'd cut a great deal. Turning off Highway 1, he steered the car into the morning sun toward Route 66 and the first leg of his journey home. Now he was ready, equipped in every way, to win back Dinah Rosen.

• • •

Shod in fluffy, pink mules, Dinah stared out the kitchen window at her Skyliner—top up, doors locked, keys squirreled away somewhere by her father.

It was her day off from the Mellerdrammer and she'd slept in, catching up for the night she'd spent with Glen Merritt under the stars in Wyoming. The house was quiet—her folks had gone to the Club. Not like yesterday when her dad tailed her all the way to Rockerville. "Got my eye on you, little girl," he'd said.

Dinah thumbed through *Seventeen,* a movie magazine with a cover story about a fresh-faced ingenue named Carol Lynley. She scrutinized the photo of the young star—blonde, like her, but unremarkable of figure, almost boyish. And yet, there she was, a movie star at age fifteen, while she was stuck in Rapid, hamming it up for tourists and local yokels.

Dinah grabbed her hairbrush and attacked her blonde mane with a flurry of angry strokes. Glen was right. Opportunity was passing her by every day. John had left town and became a celebrity overnight. She'd driven him out of Rapid, and now she couldn't drive herself to the corner. But he was eighteen and a guy. He could slip away, hitch rides. She'd never get into a car with a stranger, even to escape her dad's dragnet.

Just then she heard a car pull into the driveway. Running to the door, she spotted a cream-colored convertible and a familiar figure emerging from the driver's side.

Dinah flung open the screen door and darted outside.

John could scarcely believe his eyes. Before him stood the vision he'd conjured over and over on the long ride home from California—Dinah, greeting him with open arms upon his triumphal return.

"What are you doing back here?" she blurted, taking a step towards him. Something in her eyes mirrored back to him, the look he'd always longed for, making him throw all caution to the wind, and deliver the line he'd rehearsed for a thousand miles between Hollywood and home.

"I came back for you."

• • •

It all happened in a flash. Throwing herself into his arms, Dinah kissed John long and full as he carried her into her room where, thanks to Shirley Randolph, he knew exactly what to do to satisfy the girl next door—and himself, too.

As they lay in stunned silence, John reached for his trousers and dug a small velvet box from his pocket. Placing it on her belly, he uttered the first words he'd spoken since she'd leapt into his arms. "Dinah Rosen, will you marry me?"

• • •

"What about Yale?" James asked, when John told his parents he was marrying Dinah.

John shrugged. "I don't need Yale anymore. There are opportunities right here in Rapid."

When Jennie bolted from the table, no one tried to stop her. James knew that nothing he could say would make things right. In time, she'd get used to the idea. And John no longer cared what his mother thought. Dinah was his woman now. Pleasing her was all that mattered.

James was happy to hear his son speak so highly of remaining in Rapid. Unlike Jennie, he'd never been sold on John's going East, believing he could forge a fine future here in South Dakota. "What's your thinking, John?"

John rose from the table. "Keep this on the QT, Dad. I'm talking television. Rapid has one sleepy little station broadcasting just a few hours a day. Bernie could bring in another one that goes full-time. I'd get in on the ground floor. Be a newsman or a producer."

James nodded. John's plan made sense, and he'd have a powerful backer in Bernie.

"Does Dinah know you intend to stay in Rapid?"

"What difference does that make? Bernie's not going anywhere, so neither is she."

James snorted. "You're right about Bernie, but I guess she didn't tell you about her break for California? She and Glen Merritt ran off one morning, maybe following your trail. Bernie sent the highway patrol after them."

"She took off with Glen Merritt? He's just Billy's age, isn't he?"

"A year older," James said, then realized it wouldn't make John feel any better. "Better you should know now—the girl's got itchy feet and may think you're her ticket out."

John's face darkened. "She'll be my wife—she'll have to stay with me."

James didn't respond. Though his own marriage had held, he knew how easily the bridle of matrimony could slip . . . or break. He supposed it was something John had to learn on his own.

"She's only sixteen. You'll need Bernie's OK."

John's face brightened. "That works in my favor, don't you think?"

Later that afternoon he drove down Evergreen Street and stopped across from the Merritt house where a shirtless Glen arched a shot at a hoop over his garage door. Broad-shouldered and muscular, he possessed the physique John always wished he had.

"Goddamn her," he cursed. Earlier he'd been floating on air. Now he felt himself crashing to earth. He thought he'd finally won Dinah because he was the man of her dreams, not just her ticket out of Rapid. Now he wondered if any of it had been real.

Suddenly, he heard the sound of running footsteps and the high-pitched shrieks of children. Turning, he spotted a pack of young boys chasing a huge soap bubble up the street. Stalling above the hood of the Belvedere, the fragile sphere hung for a moment and then vanished. One boy slammed a hand against the hood and raised his arms in triumph, as if he'd popped it himself. "Get the hell outta here," John yelled, pumping the horn to disperse them.

Hearing the ruckus, Glen Merritt turned to watch the odd sight—a cream-colored convertible streaking up Evergreen with a band of screaming kids racing after it.

• • •

Dinah sat at her vanity, admiring her diamond. As soon as John left, she called her father with the news. She didn't tell him what happened before the proposal—she could hardly believe it herself. With all her boyfriends, even Joel, she'd set the pace, then hit the brakes before going all the way. But today, with John, she didn't want to stop. She let him in and he did the rest. And she liked it—the feel of a man on her and in her, the pounding energy out of her control.

Opening her diary, she wrote *Mrs. John Moran* over-and-over-again beneath the word *HOLLYWOOD*—its letters arched like the sign she'd seen high on that hill in the movies.

Then she wrote Dinah Moran—a solid stage name, and not a bit Jewy either. Not like Rosen, she thought, before suffering a sting of guilt about her father.

Yes, she could be happily married to John Moran, chasing her dream of stardom together, in California.

• • •

It was Lana who broke the news to Joel when he returned late that night from Winner.

Highball in hand, she said it straight out as he walked through the door. "She got herself engaged to John Moran." Joel looked out at the Moran driveway and the cream-colored convertible gleaming in the moonlight. "Right," he said, heading for the basement.

"Wait!" Lana picked up a plate and held it out to him—a comestible prepared to soften the blow. Without a word, he grabbed the peanut butter sandwich and started down the stairs.

Lana lit a cigarette. She wasn't surprised by Joel's flat response. A few nights back, he came home drunk so she figured Dinah must have dumped him. Later, she wondered if Dinah asked him to take her west, but harboring dreams of his own—baseball dreams—he'd refused.

Like her and Guy, she thought, though he seemed to believe they were in perfect sync.

Oh sure, they might have ridden off into the sunset together, but they'd be chasing *his* star—not hers. That was how it always was, she mused, settling in with her drink and cozy cynicism. A lesson learned the hard way from a lifetime of Bernie's broken promises.

If a woman had a dream, she had to go it alone.

• • •

Joel sat on his bed and took a bite of his sandwich. Lana's news about Dinah and John had left him oddly calm. His problems with the Rosens . . . the faithless girlfriend, the seductive mother, the cache of guns in the New York Club basement . . . no longer seemed to matter. The West had no claim on him now—not when he was just passing through for a summer of baseball.

And yet, he couldn't help wondering how he'd feel when he saw John and Dinah together—sparking bittersweet memories of his sublime moments with her. Was winning a big prize on a game show all it took to claim such a girl? Then it came to him—Dinah and California. First, she tried to run away to Hollywood and now she was marrying a man who'd just been there and had the means to take her back.

If that's what it took to win Dinah, he had two strikes against him—he couldn't drive, and he didn't have a car—no way to win back a girl whose dream was to get out of town.

Joel kicked off his khakis and lay down on the bed. Fingering his cock, he struggled to conjure a serviceable image to arouse himself and get the release he needed to sleep. Finally, he decided it would have to be an angry jerk-off. Yanking, then stroking harder and faster, he came at last, then drifted off to a land of scattershot dreams and slurred destinations—Califor-dinah.

...

James didn't tell Billy about John and Dinah, but if he had, Billy might not have heard him—smitten as he was by the new convertible, spotted the instant the Chiefs' bus dropped him on Evergreen. Shimmering like a spaceship in the porchlight, it appeared ghostly, like a mirage, and Billy ran to it, sliding his hands over its sleek sides as if to convince himself it was real.

At breakfast, John informed Billy of his engagement. Jennie was nowhere to be seen.

"Mom's sleeping in," James explained, though in fact, she'd passed out after popping two more pills at the first glimmer of dawn. John's news had sent her spinning out of control—leaving her no place to turn except the amber bottle stashed months before in her bedside table.

"Wow, that's terrific!" Billy gushed at John's news. Still basking in the glow of his own special moment with Ginny of Valentine, he gave John a hearty slap on the back—the cheerful gesture inspiring the older boy to offer his brother a spin in his new car.

"Stop in front of Glen's house," Billy ordered. "I wanna see his face."

John balked, certain that Glen had witnessed the embarrassing soap bubble incident the day before. But a moment later, they arrived at the Merritts', and he eased his foot off the gas.

"They're not up," John said, noting that the living room curtains were still drawn.

Billy scooted across the seat and pressed down hard on the car horn. Startled, John pushed back against his brother, but not before the front door swung open and Glen appeared on the stoop, staring at them in the open convertible. John hit the gas and the car peeled off, leaving a rubber trail on the concrete. Billy let out a whoop until John flung out his arm and hit him in the chest. "When are you going to grow up!"

Billy scowled. "Why are you so mad? Glen's a jerk."

"You want me to take you straight home? 'Cause I will."

Billy sulked. "Who cares. You're no fun anyway."

John took a deep breath. He had to admit that Billy wasn't off base. Ever since the polio, he'd never risked getting in trouble. But this summer he'd learned that playing it safe was for suckers. Sometimes you had to swing for the fences.

Glancing in the rear-view mirror, he saw that Glen had left the porch and was standing, hands-on-hips defiant, in the middle of the street.

"Sonovabitch," John muttered, then yelled "Hold on!" Shifting the car into reverse, he roared back down Evergreen, straight for the handsome youth.

As Glen leapt into the ditch, Billy yelled, "My brother's marrying Dinah Rosen!"

The very point the brothers Moran wanted to make all along.

Chapter Seventy-Two

JOEL JERKED AWAKE IN A cold sweat. In the nightmare that woke him, John's Belvedere roared past him into the sunset with John at the wheel and Dinah next to him—her head thrown back, mouth a riot of laughter, stretching wider and wider until it swallowed him whole. To Joel, the meaning was clear. John Moran wasn't just marrying Dinah. He was taking her to Hollywood. If he had any hope of reclaiming her, he'd have to learn to drive. And quick.

Squaring his shoulders, he prepared to face the Rosens upstairs.

"Mazel tov, Bernie. I hear congratulations are in order," he said, striding toward the table. Dinah's mouth gaped open, as if she'd forgotten that Joel still lived in her house.

Bernie grunted, and Lana rolled her eyes. Dinah fingered her diamond, then quickly moved her hand to her lap as Joel smirked, pleased by the discomfort he'd caused her.

"*Journal* says you almost lost it in the ninth," Bernie said, pointing to the paper's account. "If it hadn't been for Kibbee's catch we would have dropped another game behind the Kernels."

"Yep. Funny how that can happen. Ya think you've got everything under control and suddenly, in the blink of an eye, it all changes . . . " Joel thrust his long arm across the table and snapped his fingers under Dinah's nose " . . . just like that."

Dinah flinched, as if she'd been slapped, and Lana snorted. Dinah looked to her dad to come to her defense, but he just shrugged. Dinah pushed back from the table and bolted from the kitchen.

"No appetite?" Joel taunted. "Hear that's common for blushing brides."

"OK, kid," Bernie growled. "Got that out of your system?"

Joel's smile was shaky. He wasn't usually sarcastic but couldn't deny how good it made him feel. "Sorry, Bernie, but I got a question. Where can I go today to learn how to drive?"

"Today? What's the rush? You skippin' town?" Bernie's tone was light, his eyes hard.

"No. It's my day off, so, unless you've got some work for me at the Club. . ." *Like unpacking armaments,* Joel thought, still troubled by suspicions about their purpose.

Bernie waved off Joel's suggestion. "Ever been behind the wheel of a car, New Yawk?"

"Only the bumper cars at Coney Island."

Bernie turned nostalgic. "Yeah, that was a great ride."

"Now you got your own Coney Island, Bern. Just a different kind of ride," Lana quipped, rolling her hips in a playful display of bump and grind. Bernie laughed and Joel looked away as she brushed against her husband on her way to the stove. Clearly, they'd patched things up, though he couldn't himself imagine ever forgiving a betrayal like Lana's.

"That's the difference between us. Both Brooklyn, born and bred, but the Boy Scout here studied and played ball while I hot-wired cars and played hooky."

"Not so different, Bern. I stole bases, you stole cars."

Bernie hooted, reminded of how much he liked the young man. He would have made a fine son-in-law, too, he thought. And a lot more laughs than John Moran.

"I'm not busy, hon . . . " Lana offered, pouring a cup of coffee. "I could give Joel a lesson."

Bernie grunted. No more Chiefs for her. "No, doll, got something else in mind. Fred once gave driving lessons to officers' wives at Ellsworth. Really got those base broads shifting gears."

Lana roared and Joel couldn't resist a smile. "More fun than driving around ballplayers."

Bernie guffawed. "You got that right, kid. Fred'll teach you good. My treat."

• • •

Joel leaned against the plaster lion guarding the Rosen driveway, waiting for Fred. The heady feeling he'd enjoyed from his attack on Dinah at breakfast had worn off. Now he felt foolish, thinking he could so easily be done with her, the only girl he'd ever made love to and the inspiration for his near no-hitter.

The last thing surprised him. He'd never been one to harbor baseball superstitions—the devotion to unlaundered socks to extend a batting streak or the ancient proscription barring sex on game day. He'd proved that one wrong big-time—enjoying the first sex of his twenty-one years in the afternoon, then pitching brilliantly that night.

Then she took off with Glen Merritt. And despite his oath on the railroad tracks, he'd faltered that night on the mound in Winner. Only a big lead and a game-saving catch had saved him.

Did he love her, he wondered. Certainly, he didn't trust her, but she made him feel he could do anything—both on and off the mound.

Then, out of the corner of his eye, he spied Fred driving up the street—not in a Ford or a Cadillac, or any regular kind of car, but behind the wheel of a long black hearse. Joel stared at the massive, solemn Chevy—like a coffin on wheels, with an interior of red satin and window panels draped in black. Was Bernie playing a joke on him? "Hey, Fred. What's all this?"

"The wife took the pickup to the rez, so it was either the team bus or this here hearse. I drives it for the Jolley Funeral Home up in Sturgis when it needs an extra vehicle. You know—house fire or head-on collision, multiple fatality, more than one corpse."

Joel coughed into his hand to hide his urge to gag. "I'm not sure I can learn on a hearse."

"Drivin's drivin', son. You learn on this, you can drive anything."

Looking around, Joel spotted Lana at the window, dabbing at her eyes with a tissue and shaking with laughter. "OK, Fred, but can we go someplace we won't be seen?"

"Guess yer embarrassed, not knowin' how to drive at yer age. So, we'll keep her off the main roads, take her over to Robbinsdale. Streets there are empty all day. Hubby's got the car at work. Only the little wifey's at home." Fred's eyes twinkled, and Joel could swear he heard a confession there.

Fred did a three-point turn into the Moran driveway. "Been meaning to ask ya—whatever happened to Billy's brother? Never heard 'bout why he stopped comin' on the trips."

Joel forced a smile. "Went to California, got on Groucho Marx and won a ton of money."

"No kiddin'! Missed that. No TV in the trailer. Smart kid. Book smart, like you. Wasn't surprised when you two hit it off."

Joel swallowed hard. Fred must have heard them talking that first night on the bus.

"So, how much he win?" Fred continued.

"About five thousand."

Fred let out a whistle. "Can buy a new house with that. What's he doin' with the dough?"

"Bought himself a convertible. Drove all the way home from California."

"So, that why you wanna drive—figure John'll let you borrow it?"

Fred's question caught him by surprise. He could never explain his plan to use a driver's license to compete with John and reclaim Dinah.

But there was something else, too. Crossing Iowa, and later—on the team bus—he'd glimpsed the highways and byways of America and felt the freedom he'd come to believe was his birthright. "You know I love your tours, Fred, but at some point, ya gotta get off the bus and explore the country for yourself."

"I know what ya mean. War did it fer me—took me lotsa new places."

Joel nodded, then wondered if Fred might be an old war buddy of Bernie's. Maybe he could shed some light on the basement arsenal. "Were you in the service with Bernie?"

"Nope. Buck were—he's my wife's brother."

"Really! So, you're friends. What do you think of him?"

"Buck? Somebody you don't want to mess with, that's for sure."

"No, I mean Bernie."

"No complaint there—treats me good."

"Is he involved in politics here?"

"You mean . . . guvment? Don't think so. Too busy makin' money."

"No, I mean . . . " Joel paused, knowing what he wanted to ask, but unsure of how to put it.

Even thinking the word 'Communist' made him sweat. "Is he a Republican or a Democrat or—don't know if you have this party here—Socialist?"

Fred cocked his head and looked at Joel as if he'd never seen him before. "Don't think we got those kind of people out here, but one thing I know for sure, the man's a patriot."

"What does that mean to you, Fred—'patriot'?"

Fred narrowed his eyes. "Never had to explain that before."

Joel jumped in, nervously. "A man who loves his country, right?"

"Man who'd die for his country."

Joel nodded, sorry he'd brought it up. "Yes. Of course. That's what I think, too."

In strained silence, they arrived in Robbinsdale, and as Fred had promised, there were hardly any signs of life and not a vehicle to be seen. And some of the roads were cul-de-sacs or curved, without aggravating thru-traffic and busy four-way crossings, most dreaded by Joel, struggling with the tricky rhythm of clutch-shift-release and intersection stall-outs, a mortal peril.

Then, Joel spotted them—John and Billy, walking out of a little frame box with a 'For Sale' sign staked on its grassless front yard. Joel started to laugh—a full-throated laugh, leaving him light-headed and giddy with newfound hope. John wasn't whisking Dinah off to Hollywood after all. He had other, more domestic plans for his prospective bride.

Fred turned to him. "Looks like your friend's aimin' to buy a house with his winnin's after all. Wanna go on another street, so they don't see us?"

"Nah, let 'em see. We have no secrets from each other."

Billy spotted them first and, grabbing John's arm, pointed at the hearse.

Joel honked twice, so there'd be no question in John's mind that he'd seen what he was up to. Now all that remained of the secret was the telling.

• • •

"So . . . I hear you're interested in politics," Bernie asked Joel who was behind the wheel of the Caddy, practicing his driving while ferrying them both to the Stadium.

Joel stiffened, wondering what Bernie was getting at, but afraid to search his face for a clue. "No more than the next guy, I imagine."

"Then why the hell'd ya ask Fred if I was a Socialist? You workin' for Karl Mundt?"

Startled, Joel lost the rhythm of the clutch and stalled out in the middle of the road.

Bernie reached across and slammed Joel's left thigh. "Clutch in, turn the key, give it some gas." With a lurch, the Caddy shot forward—the rising engine noise signaling time to shift.

"Karl who?" Joel asked, afraid Bernie might have said "Marx."

"Karl Mundt, South Dakota Senator—HOUSE UN-AMERICAN ACTIVITIES COMMITTEE. Ever hear of that?"

Joel took his foot off the gas and the car soon began to shudder. "Clutch in—shift down."

As the car spasmed, Bernie grabbed the wheel and steered the Caddy onto the shoulder. "Lesson over. I want your attention." He fixed Joel with a hard, appraising stare.

"That was a joke about Mundt, but this isn't. Out here, you got two strikes against you—you're an outsider and a Jew—so don't go talking politics if you know what's good for you."

Joel blanched. Trapped in the car with Bernie, he was again on the hot seat. But this time he knew it was his own fault. He'd warned Billy that loose lips sink ships, then raised a red flag with motormouth Fred, asking about Bernie's politics. And for what—to be reassured about Bernie's basement arsenal? Frantic, he riffled through his mind for a distraction, a red herring.

"I saw John Moran looking at houses out in Robbinsdale."

"Yeah . . . so what?"

"Come on, Bern. Bet Dinah thinks John's taking her to California. I mean, isn't it odd that she accepted his proposal just a week after she lit out for the West Coast with that kid Glen—and right after John appeared on a TV show in Hollywood?"

"So, what's it to you?"

"Well, this may come as a surprise, but I'm not exactly a disinterested party when it comes to your daughter's impending marriage."

"OK, Sherlock. So, what if she thinks he's taking her to Hollywood? She's too young for that, and not talented enough."

"I beg to differ. She sang for me up in the Hills."

Bernie snorted. "So, what are you? Her agent? Take it from me, young man—a dick's no judge of talent."

Joel fumed. While relieved that Bernie had fallen for his diversion—the way he demeaned his daughter reminded him of his own father belittling his baseball talent and the hard work that went into developing it. An endeavor, like acting, worthy of recognition and respect and the chance to succeed.

"But it's wrong, Bernie, to trick her like that. Marrying her off at sixteen, before she even has a chance to see if she's got what it takes. She could go to acting school, or college."

"So, now you're her guidance counselor? What next—her daddy? She's already got one."

"You should let her try—like my parents are doing this summer with me." A half-truth, as his father had declared it "a complete waste of time and a great disappointment."

Bernie scoffed. "You're twenty-one. Any man who lets his parents brake his train at twenty-one is no man to speak of. Dinah's only sixteen."

"But you're willing to marry her off at sixteen!"

"Sure. To a nice, smart boy like Moran. I'd have married her off to you, too. But now that he's here to stay, I like him even better. She ain't ready for LA or New York." His face darkened. "Couple years back she fell in with a fast crowd—beer parties, drinkin' and drivin' up on Rimrock Highway. One night the car she was in flipped over and she got thrown.

We were lucky—just a concussion and a broken leg. But the night I got the call—sittin' in the emergency room before she came out of it—was the longest night of my life."

Joel sat in silence, stunned by the peek into Bernie's tender heart.

"So, I don't want you queering the deal. She's gonna marry Moran—give me a grandson, make me a zayda. And she's gonna do it right here in Rapid, where I can keep an eye on her."

Joel nodded. His ploy had worked but he hardly felt triumphant. His defense of Dinah and her dream only made him feel closer to her and worse about losing her to John Moran.

• • •

"So what!" John said, after dropping Billy at the ballfield. So what if Joel saw him coming out of that house in Robbinsdale? He'd already warned Billy not to let it slip—his plan to buy the house and surprise Dinah by carrying her across the threshold. Unimpressed, Billy's sole concern was would they get a TV, and could he come by to watch. "Sure, sometimes," John muttered. Then, as insurance, he slipped Billy five bucks hush money. "Mum's the word. OK?"

John parked the Belvedere in the driveway and looked over at the Rosens'. All their cars were gone. Dinah must have left for the Mellerdrammer, and Joel, well, John knew where he was at that moment, though God only knows why he was driving a hearse with Fred.

His spirits flagging, John felt a powerful need to see Dinah—to do it again, to listen for the tempo of her breath and the small sounds she made when he touched her just right. And soon, they'd be able to do all those things in the privacy of their own little home, with no parents or snoopy little brother, or jilted boyfriend, listening in.

First, he had to buy the house. Though after the car, the ring, and taxes, his quiz-show winnings came up short. Even with a half mortgage he'd have to empty his college fund. Which saddened him some, for despite his plan to forego Yale, his savings represented years of after-school and summertime jobs and the embodiment of his long-held dream of college.

Now, with regular mortgage payments looming, he realized it was time to get a grown-up job—at KOTA TV, while his Groucho stint was still fresh in people's minds. John dialed the station and just as he expected, was put straight through with an appointment for later that day.

Then Bernie called. "Moran—I gotta talk to you. Now. At the Club."

• • •

John sat across the desk from Bernie, wondering why he'd been summoned. Bernie's eyes were sparking. "Got this great idea. Yer gonna get a job at KOTA TV—now, before your quiz-show fame's yesterday's news."

John grinned broadly. "I have an appointment there this afternoon."

"Good. Take whatever's offered and learn all you can. But don't let KOTA catch wind of what you're up to. And don't worry about pay. I'll slip you a few bucks if you're short. I know you're gonna get hit with mortgage payments. Yeah, news travels fast, but I'm silent as the sphinx. And the ballplayer in my basement ain't gonna squeal either. I made sure of that."

John couldn't believe it. Bernie knew about the house and had KO'd Joel as a threat. The man certainly worked in mysterious ways. But what exactly was his idea?

Bernie did a drum roll on the top of the desk. "Hang onto your hat, kid. I'm opening a second TV station in Rapid. Just applied for the FCC license. Starting out, we can shoot right here on the nightclub stage—news programs, bands and variety acts, and maybe a mother and daughter duo, too. We've got the two foxiest broads in Rapid, and we should capitalize on it."

John felt his gut clinch. Bernie had beat him to the punch—came up with the identical idea and had already set the wheels in motion. "You might not believe this, Bern, but I had the same thought. That's why I made the appointment at KOTA. To get my foot in the door."

Bernie pulled a cigar from his humidor and lit up, drawing a few priming puffs before a long, self-satisfied suck. "Great minds think alike, huh? Well, I'm gonna do it, so if you want in, I'll give you a piece. But I want you *all* in."

John gulped. He knew a venture like this cost real money, and he now had less than half his Hollywood winnings to invest. If he bought the house, he'd be broke. He could still work for Bernie, taking whatever he offered—be a salaryman like his father, but the new station was the opportunity of a lifetime—*if* he got a piece of the action as Bernie's partner.

John fingered the wad of hundred-dollar bills in his pocket which he was supposed to hand over for the sweet, little Robbinsdale nest. "If I let the house go, I'd have twenty-five hundred to invest. That's everything, including my college fund."

Bernie shrugged. "Well then, let it go. Live with us. We got plenty of room for you and Dinah, even a couple of kids."

John swallowed hard. This was not his dream, living under the Rosen roof, next door to his own family. And, with Joel just downstairs, they'd have to put off getting married until after the Basin League season. Even then, he'd feel funny doing it with her folks just down the hall.

Bernie puffed on his Corona and watched John wrestle with his predicament. He knew that some men in his position would be more generous with a future son-in-law and make the house a wedding present, but no one had done that for him.

John felt a trickle of sweat run down his back. He wished he could ask someone for advice, but the best person for that was sitting across the desk from him, nursing his cigar between Cheshire cat grins. He'd have to decide on his own—as he had on Groucho's show when he had but seconds to wager it all or walk away. A big risk that paid off big.

Unmoved by John's dilemma, Bernie let his mind drift—imagining a grandson growing up under his roof . . . taking his first step, babbling his first word. He'd missed out on family life during the War, and Lana hadn't been much for sending snapshots. In truth, he'd never pined for home-front photos of a baby not his own. But, upon his return he found a child who'd been walking and talking for years—a veritable chatterbox—and he proved an easy mark, won over the first time the tow-headed curlytop climbed onto his lap and called him "Poppy."

Leaning back, Bernie reached the part of his recurring fantasy where he teaches his grandson to throw a baseball, and later the curve, like what he'd done with Billy.

"Elbow up, reach back, snap it forward, follow through."

John slipped a hand into his trouser pocket and pulled out the wad of hundreds.

"OK, Bernie. It's a deal."

Chapter Seventy-Three

WITH JOEL ON HIS WAY to Yankton, Dinah could finally relax. Whenever he was in the house, she felt on edge. At night she'd started to dream of him. She wasn't sure how, but he seemed to have gained the upper hand—almost as if *he'd* dumped *her*.

Finally, she'd asked her dad to evict him. "He's so mean, Daddy. Remember how he almost hit me at the kitchen table." She mimicked Joel's finger snap under her father's nose.

Bernie just laughed. "Grow up, little girl. He's hardly ever here and when he is, he stays out of your way." In truth, Bernie felt more sympathy than he expressed. He had never been torn between two loves. Despite the odd dalliance, no dame but Lana ever vied for his heart.

Bernie strode into the kitchen and took a last gulp of coffee. "Hey there, Princess, shouldn't you be heading for work?"

"Told 'em I'd be late. I need to talk to John about the wedding."

"Well, you're wasting your tardy pass. John just got a job at KOTA."

Dinah was shocked that he'd done that without telling her. "What? Why?"

"Takes a lot of dough to support a wife. He's smart to strike while the iron is hot."

"But he won all that money on *Groucho*."

"Ever hear of taxes? And those wheels weren't free, or the rock on your finger. But I'm springing for the wedding so don't bother John 'bout that. You and your mother can plan it."

Dinah threw him an incredulous look. "Mom plan a wedding? Did she even have a wedding dress? I never saw any wedding pictures."

Bernie checked his watch. "There's one around here somewhere. Anyway, it was war time. We had bigger things to worry about. But I bet she'll get a kick out of planning yours. We'll do it all at the Club. Our waiters and our band. Flowers, a big 'ole cake, decorations. Sky's the limit. Just do me a favor and ask Mom to help."

Excited by the prospect of a big party with her as centerpiece, Dinah threw her arms around her father. "Thank you, Poppy! I will."

Bernie welled up at the sound of his old nickname. Locked in his daughter's embrace, he wiped his eyes, but not so quick that it went unnoticed by Lana, entering the room.

"So, what were you two talkin' 'bout?" she asked Dinah after Bernie left for the Club.

"The wedding. Daddy thought we could plan it together."

"Not sure I know much about that. Didn't even get a wedding dress for mine."

Dinah burst out laughing. "That's what I guessed!"

Lana lit a cigarette. "Well it was the War . . . "

"And you had bigger things on your mind," Dinah chirped, in singsong.

"OK," Lana said—not caring what lay behind her daughter's mocking tone. Even before her terrible teens, the girl could be sassy and they'd steered clear of each other, engaging only in periodic skirmishes with never a reconciling 'heart-to-heart'.

When Bernie returned from the War, she let him take over the discipline, though mostly he just spoiled her. Still, nothing Dinah pulled so far was as bad as what *she'd* done at her age—taking up with married men and rodeo roughnecks, and a backroom abortion in Deadwood that almost killed her. When she met Bernie, she was pregnant again, this time by her bronco-busting husband—killed weeks earlier, driving drunk in his girlfriend's pickup. Bernie knew all about it but swore he'd rather raise another man's child than risk losing her in a botched abortion—magic words that made her say "yes." Lana didn't have to wonder what magic John Moran used on Dinah. Any line that included "California" would have done the trick.

"Dad says you have a wedding photo from yours."

Lana turned away to light a cigarette, a move Dinah read as evasion. "Well, he's wrong."

"Not even one picture?" Dinah persisted.

"Nope."

"Well—what *did* you wear?"

"A tailored suit, I suppose. But you know, Dinah, I got things to do—so if you want to talk about *your* wedding—that's fine. But . . . "

Dinah couldn't imagine why her questions made her mother so testy, but she thought it best to stop. "Daddy says we'll have it all at the Club."

"Really? That's not how it's usually done here. People in Rapid get hitched in church."

"But we never go to church. Don't you have to go to a church to get married there?"

Lana's eyes sparkled with mischief. "Could use your mother-in-law's. Think she's a Methodist." Lana primly folded her hands in the lap of her peignoir. "Or a Presbyterian."

Dinah made a face. She'd not given Jennie Moran a thought since she and John got engaged. "She doesn't have a say-so, does she?"

Lana shrugged. She wondered how much influence Jennie might still have with a son who proposed as soon as he got his own wheels and a little jingle in his pocket.

"Did you and Daddy get married in a church?" Dinah asked.

"No . . . City Hall."

"Because Daddy's Jewish?"

"Because it was the War, and he was shipping out the next day."

Dinah couldn't believe she knew almost nothing about her parents' wedding. "So, you never had a honeymoon?"

"We went down to Blue Bell Lodge in Custer State Park for a night."

The thought, too quick to censure, pierced her brain like a dart. "So that's when you musta gotten pregnant with me."

Reaching for the ashtray, Lana brushed Bernie's coffee cup with her elbow. "Could be," was all she said, but Dinah caught the lie, just before the cup hit the floor.

. . .

She'd never given it a thought—why her parents didn't display any wedding photos or celebrate their anniversary. But now she figured she knew why—to hide that she'd been there from the get-go, tucked beneath her mother's bridal suit.

Dinah paced her bedroom. The wedding portrait Bernie spoke of—whose existence her mom denied—would hold the proof. But could a posed picture answer a more important question—how they felt about *her*, the uninvited wedding guest and likely the reason they had to get hitched? She was almost afraid to know.

Dinah reached for the photo of her and her dad at Mount Rushmore—standing side by side with no space between them. And today in the kitchen he'd held her as if he never wanted to let go. But her mother? She couldn't remember the last time they'd hugged.

Slumping at her vanity, she began to cry. Then she gave her arm a hard pinch to stanch the tears. Crying made her face blotchy, and she had a show tonight. Wiping her eyes with a tissue, she studied her complexion in the mirror. Blue-eyed and fair of hair and skin, she much resembled her mother, not at all her dark-eyed, swarthy father. Though neither parent had her little chin dimple, which John liked to trace when they necked.

And then it hit her. The very real chance that she could end up like her mother, pregnant at the altar, her dreams of stardom waylaid by the birth of a child. All it had taken was a spark—five little words. *"I came back for you"* . . . and boom.

Was that how it had been for her parents? An unexpected flash of heat and then *her*?

Dinah heard the screen door slam and her mother's car backing down the driveway. Running to her parents' bedroom, she riffled through the dresser drawers searching for that photo but found nothing she'd not seen before on forays for jewelry and lingerie. Stepping into her mother's closet, she flinched as a feathery boa brushed her cheek. Flooded by memories, she recalled playing dress-up as a child, wrapped in theatrical props and tottering about in Lana's glittering hi-heels.

Then she spotted a trunk hidden behind a rack of silky gowns. Raising the lid, she coughed as a scent of mothballs rose from a stack of sweaters. Then something shiny caught her eye. Reaching inside, she pulled out a white rodeo vest dotted with silvery studs, a pair of ivory colored cowboy boots, and a red buckskin skirt with a fringed hem. Dinah's mouth dropped.

"*My Rodeo Queen*." Sometimes Bernie called Lana that, but she always acted like it was a joke. But here in the trunk lay the proof, and beneath it—the mother lode—a thick leather album with the word *SCRAPBOOK* notched in gold foil across its cover. Pulse racing, Dinah braced herself for the secrets that lay inside about the life Lana gave up to be her mom.

"MY RODEO ALBUM" was written in a flowery script on the flyleaf. Under the heading was the date July 4, 1931, and the words *Belle Fourche*, which her dad once explained was French for "beautiful fork." Below the inscription was a photo of a beaming young girl sitting tall in the saddle holding a ribbon with *1st PLACE* written on it.

Surrounding her were a smiling, middle-aged couple and a teenaged boy—all sharing the same fine features and light-colored hair. Clearly, it was her mom's family, but all Dinah knew of them was what her dad once told her—the brother killed in the War, the father in a farm accident, and the mother, from an unremembered cause—all strangers, seen now for the very first time.

Trembling, Dinah couldn't take her eyes off the photo. Why had her mom hidden it from her? Had her family been mean to her? Did she hate them? It didn't seem so from their proud expressions or from Lana's smile, the most genuine one she'd ever seen her display.

Dinah took a deep breath and turned to a page of newspaper clippings naming the contest winners from that year's roundup. Running her finger down the column she found her mother's name—Lana Hansen, All-Around Girls Junior Rodeo Champ.

Had Lana's mother saved it for the scrapbook, or had Lana done it herself, as Dinah had to do when the *Journal* reviewed *Damn Yankees*? Neither of her parents had bothered to clip the articles. She wasn't surprised when only her dad showed up on opening night.

Turning the page, she found her mother's blue ribbon. Next to it lay a pressed pink rose and the words, "From Momma," written in Lana's florid hand. Dinah burst into tears.

It was through that shimmering veil that she finally found it. Not the wedding picture she'd been searching for, but a photo from a later Roundup—of Lana, now a shapely knockout, posed with a group of cowboys smiling at the camera—all except one, a lanky, fair-haired man grinning directly at her mom. Even through her tears, Dinah couldn't miss it—the deep, circular hollow in the man's chin, a brand neither Lana nor Bernie, nor any of Lana's kin, possessed. Shared only by her and her real father—the grinning bronco buster at the beautiful fork of Belle Fourche.

...

Dinah didn't know how she got through that evening. The discovery of her mother's secret staggered her. Still, she turned in a memorable performance, which did not go unnoticed by her new director. "Tears! Honest to goodness tears! A first, I'm sure, for the Mellerdrammer."

Now, driving down the mountain with Glen, she brooded. It was clear that her mother had tricked Bernie into marrying her. Though she probably wished she'd dropped her on a church doorstep, like a character in one of her melodramas. Or done away with her all together, so she could chase her own dream of stardom—and not in a two-bit nightclub in Rapid City, South Dakota.

A sob caught in her throat. Her mother didn't love her. Only Bernie did. Everything he said and did, even the bossy things, proved it. But would he still love her if he knew she wasn't his flesh and blood?

Without a word, she dropped Glen at his house then pinched her thigh hard, hoping to quell her tears. She couldn't face her parents looking like this, knowing what she did.

Then she remembered a quote from drama class. "*All the world's a stage and all the men and women merely players.*" She was an actress. She could pull this off. And for that she had her mother to thank—the great pretender she'd been understudying all her life.

She glanced in the direction of the Moran house. John's car wasn't there. She had to speak to him—tell him to get time off for a long honeymoon—somewhere out West, where she'd talk him into pushing on to Hollywood. Or slip away while he was asleep and drive there herself. All she'd have to do was wear him out first.

If a star performance was called for, she knew she could deliver.

Of that, she had no doubt.

Chapter Seventy-Four

ON THE LONG RIDE TO Yankton, Joel was finally able to forget the Rosens and focus on his pitching. Just one other hurler was struggling—Dean Veal. Lately, both he and Dean warmed up together in the bullpen with neither getting the nod. Like death row inmates, they seldom spoke, knowing that friendship was a losing proposition when only one might get the Governor's call.

Joel looked up as Quarles in a gay party hat coughed to signal the start of a major address. "Four score and seven—I mean one score and twelve years ago—my blessed mother brought forth on this continent a new ballplayer, conceived in liberty, or in the back seat of a Chevy—dedicated to the proposition that all ballplayers are created equal in the pursuit of pussy."

Though amused, Joel gestured towards a grinning Billy with his thumb. "I believe the phrase is 'pursuit of happiness', Q."

"Happiness . . . pussy . . . same difference." Quarles threw a mock punch at Billy's shoulder and winked broadly. "Right, little man?"

A delighted Billy answered back, "Yup," causing Joel to wonder how far he'd gone with the girl from Valentine and why Quarles seemed to know about the matter. To his surprise, he was peeved that there might be a rival for his little buddy's affection.

Fred turned on the ignition and looked over at Stockman. "Everybody on board?"

"Wait!" Joel cried. "Where's Dean Veal?"

"Back home by now, I'd guess," Stockman answered back. "Let's go."

"Calf to the slaughter—Veal on the plate—or off it, like his pitches," Kibbee joked meanly, as Joel realized that his quiet rival had at last been cut from the squad. A guilty sense of relief washed over him. Dean, not he, was headed for the guillotine.

Then Guy raised his cleaver for a second swipe. "Who's up for more chili?"

Joel whipped around and glared at Stockman, who met his gaze head-on. Clearly, they were on the way to the Reservation to pick up Andrew Hanging Cloud.

"You droppin' Veal for a dirty Injun?" Hoades protested. "Are you nuts?"

Stockman shrugged. "What's it to you, Hoades? Williams is gonna catch him."

Hoades jerked himself back into his seat. "Lock up your stuff. That's all I have to say."

Billy looked at Joel. His folks warned him to avoid the Indians on Main Street—but he expected Joel to stand up to Hoades for a crack like that. It was just the kind of thing he did.

Across the aisle, Clarence knew why Joel kept silent—the fear that the Indian might keep him out of the rotation. He hoped it wouldn't happen to his pal but looked forward to once again catching Hanging Cloud's sweeping sidewinder.

Finally, Billy put it together—his mind leapfrogging to what it would mean if Joel, like Veal, was cut from the Chiefs. Without Joel as chaperone, there'd be no more road trips for him, and he'd never see Ginny of Valentine again. Reaching across the aisle, he touched Joel's left arm, as if to reassure himself that Joel still had one.

Struck by the gesture and the boy's concern, Joel gave him the thumbs-up, though it was hard to pretend he didn't care about his fate. At least he had one person in his corner.

Arriving at Pinky's, Quarles stood up to make an announcement. "The Chiefs in the back of the bus had a council fire and voted to pass on Big Bear's chili. We hear there's a café cross the border that makes chili from a known source. Like a cow."

Fred parked the bus by the entrance, returning a few minutes later with a metal dinner pail and Andrew Hanging Cloud. "Eat your hearts out, guys," Fred barked, holding the pail aloft.

"Hearts, brains, scalps—Injun specialty," Hoades growled.

Andrew Hanging Cloud, starting down the aisle, caught Hoades' gaze as he took a seat next to Clarence, across from Joel and Billy near the front of the bus.

"Nobody's gonna boycott where the coloreds sit on *our* bus," Hoades added, and someone laughed. Joel turned to look at Clarence and Hanging Cloud. Then, swallowing hard, he reached across the aisle and extended his hand in welcome to the newest member of the team.

• • •

Joel wiped his brow. It was the bottom of the ninth and his Chiefs led the Terry's 2-1. On a night when he lacked his best fastball, he was proud that he'd stayed calm and held the Terrys to just one run over eight innings. But with the top of their order due up, he needed to get three troublesome outs to secure the win. In the bullpen, two young pitchers waited to relieve him if he faltered. One was Hanging Cloud. Joel saw Andrew get up and begin to throw. Was Stockman like a kid with a new toy—eager to try out his recent acquisition?

• • •

After the win, the Chiefs were in high spirits boarding the bus for Quarles' birthday celebration. Joel wished he could join in, but his heart wasn't in it. Relieved with two outs in the ninth, he was troubled by Stockman's flagging faith in his ability to work out of a jam and nail down the win. He'd given up two hits in the 9th, putting the tying and winning runs on base, but one was just a little squib over first, and the other, a short pop down the line that an average outfielder, but not Hacker, would have caught for the third out, giving him the win. And yet, there was Stockman, marching to the mound, calling for the ball and waving to the bullpen for Hanging Cloud.

• • •

"Here we are," Fred announced, stopping at a stately old hotel in downtown Yankton.

The Charles Gurney was not the Chiefs' usual economy motel on the outskirts of town. A modest indulgence, it was touted as a place for good food, a lively bar, and comely companionship for the randy young Chiefs. Which now included Guy, who'd decided it was high time to forget Lana Rosen and get back on the horse—or whore, as the case might be.

As Guy spoke to the desk clerk, Joel wondered how the addition of Hanging Cloud might affect room assignments. The Indian could bunk with Veal's roommate now that Dean was gone—or with him and Clarence in a kind of minority cluster that Hoades and Kibbee would surely find fitting and proper. And that would have been okay with him, too, if Andrew wasn't shaping up as his direct rival. A constant reminder of his precarious place in the pitching rotation--and on the team-- was the last thing he needed. Then he spotted Billy surveying the hotel lobby and recalled, with relief, that the boy made for three in their room—too many to add another.

Exploring the lobby's Wild West curios, Billy discovered a plaque that read "Site of the Trial of Jack McCall, the man who shot Wild Bill Hickok in 1876." And the hotel bar was called Aces and Eights, Hickok's legendary 'dead man's hand'. Whooping, he ran to tell Joel. Then, the saloon doors swung open and two striking blondes in sleeveless cocktail sheaths wound their way through the young men. Thirteen pairs of hungry eyes followed their sinuous path across the lobby. Only Clarence, after a glance, turned away.

"Ask me what I want for my birthday!" Quarles exclaimed. Everyone laughed, and Stockman added, "Funny thing, it's *my* birthday, too." Quickly, the other Chiefs all declared it their birthdays, including Joel, who decided to treat this night as his *re*-birthday, the day he'd finally stop pining for Dinah.

"Hey, Coach, hurry up with them room keys!" Kibbee shouted, as Joel turned to Clarence, and whispered, "Can you keep an eye on Billy tonight?"

Billy narrowed his eyes, then reminded Joel that Yankton had two TV stations with programs never seen in Rapid. Joel shot a look at Clarence, who chimed in. "Can't wait to see what's on," and Joel was grateful to be bunking with a married man with kids, who, unlike Quarles, took his vows seriously.

The Chiefs returned to the bar in two waves, depending upon which roommate grabbed the shower first. Broad-shouldered and tanned, even the homeliest looked appealing. But with the two women the only females in sight, the birthday boy and Guy moved in to claim them. Hoping to mollify his men, Guy threw a bit of red meat their way. "Order steaks, chops—anything you want—all free tonight!" On Bernie Rosen's tab, he added to himself with a smirk.

"They're whores," Hoades drawled, sidling up to Joel, seated at the bar, staring at Q's honey-blonde catch. Joel was surprised that Darren had sought him out. They hadn't spoken since Hoades' "pussy" crack about Dinah. Still, he was intrigued. The only whores he'd ever seen were the crusty prostitutes who accosted sports fans after events at Madison Square Garden.

"How can you tell?" Joel asked, signaling the bartender for another bourbon.

Hoades shrugged, then fessed up. "Kibbee told me. Got down here first to check their price tags. He's taking up a collection for Quarles."

Joel turned to the pool table where the prankish center fielder was soliciting for the cause.

"A buck for Q's birthday bang. Student discount. Two bucks for you pros. Tonight, Ol' Quarrelsome's gonna get a present he'll love to unwrap."

Smiling, Joel reached into his pocket and made a move toward Kibbee, but Hoades stopped him with a hand on his shoulder. "Wait a minute, Meznik. I got somethin' for you."

Joel stiffened. The Alabaman's tone put him on guard. "And what might that be?"

"Kinda humiliating being shown up by an Injun, ain't it?"

"We all do our part . . . " Joel said, flatly, " . . . for the good of the team."

"Yeah, right—for the good of the team." Hoades' mocking smile was triumphant.

Joel blanched at his unmasking. Was he really that easy to read?

"Didya know he's got a 'tell'." Hoades continued. "Does it every time he throws that killer pitch of his."

"I know what a tell is," Joel bristled, recalling a Yale pitcher who spread his glove to hide his grip for his baffling change-of-pace. Once spotted, his Columbia Lions knew when it was coming.

"Oh yeah?" Hoades smirked. "Did you happen to notice what it was?"

Joel had not but wasn't going to admit it to Hoades.

"That's what I thought," Hoades gloated, rightly interpreting Joel's silence. "'Cause if you had, you would have already told the Redman. For the good of the team, right?"

Joel reached for his drink and signaled the bartender for another.

"Just imagine, Freako, if I let this get 'round the League. No more surprises with that killer pitch. And the Injun gets a one-way ticket back to the Reservation."

Darren grabbed a fistful of pretzels from the bar and started towards the team's party table. "Of course, I'd expect you to return the favor. Right, Kemosabe?"

Chapter Seventy-Five

THE TV BROKE IN THE MIDDLE of *Dragnet.* And there wasn't any room service and the hotel's café was closed. Still, Clarence didn't feel right taking Billy down to the lobby bar for a meal. That could put a crimp in Joel's style and expose the boy to something his momma wouldn't want him to see.

Clarence took a good, long look at Billy slumped in his chair, staring crestfallen at the darkened picture tube. For weeks they'd been together on the bus and in the dugout—even shared a motel room—but somehow, he'd dodged the connection between the boy and his mother. But there he sat, Jennie's child, though he little resembled that lean, long-limbed woman, save for his forlorn, half-moon eyes.

Clarence turned away, pained by the memory of her visit to his trailer and that time they'd spotted each other across the parking lot. Since then, he'd steered clear of her, skirting the concession stand and ducking her congenial husband, too, for all their sakes. And yet, at this moment he was responsible for her son's welfare and nourishment.

"Come on. Let's go get something to eat. Gotta be a place still open 'round here.

Crossing the lobby, Billy looked longingly at the entrance to the bar, and Clarence almost relented, but then the door burst open and a drunk staggered out—his arm draped around a heavily rouged woman in a low-cut dress. Clearly, Aces and Eights wouldn't do.

The desk clerk supplied the name of a nearby tavern known for its bratwurst and slaw.

Clarence had hoped for a café or diner, not another bar serving food, but he figured Billy would at least be spared the spectacle of his Chiefs heroes' drunken carousing.

"What's this tavern like? Is it OK for a kid?"

The desk clerk hesitated as he studied the unlikely pair—the tall, rugged Negro and the stocky young white boy. "Tell Shorty that Marcus from the Gurney sent you, and you're with the ball team. He'll treat you right."

And Shorty did, greeting them cordially and serving them quickly. The place was nearly empty, just a couple of workmen at the bar, who glanced in their direction when they entered, then seemed to pay them no mind.

Shorty proved a talkative host, which Clarence welcomed at first, since Billy seemed deep in thought. Even questions about the Braves, his favorite ball team, had failed to spark his interest. Clarence wasn't sure if it was hunger, exhaustion, the broken TV, or being ditched by Joel, but whatever the reason, the boy was in a funk, so he gave up trying to draw him out.

"We don't get many coloreds in here . . . " The barkeep set a Coke by Billy's plate and a stein of Grain Belt before Clarence. "But we got quite a few Negroes in Yankton."

Clarence felt his guard go up at the reference to his race. Billy looked away. This was the first time he'd been alone with Mr. Williams, and while they'd had fun at the diner and fishing on the Missouri with John and Joel, he'd been nervous since they left the hotel. What if he brought up the fight from the tryouts? What if he thought he'd started it because his son was a Negro?

Shorty continued. "The coloreds got their own bar, just a stone's throw from here."

Clarence froze. What was the man getting at? Was he saying he should have gone there?

"Hell, they even got their own church. Longest name I ever heard—African, Episcopal, Methodist." Shorty laughed in a friendly way. "Never knew the Episcopals and Methodists were so chummy. Freed slaves came up the Missouri and built it. Been here since the last century."

Clarence nodded curtly, though Shorty got the name wrong, switching the order of the denominations of the AME church. Still, he'd never correct him—couldn't imagine talking about Negroes or slavery with a white man. Certainly not in front of Billy, who sat with bowed head, looking like he'd just received a scolding.

"Thanks. I'll check it out," Clarence said, hoping to put an end to the race talk.

Billy yawned and his eyes began to close. It was way past the boy's bedtime and maybe past closing time, too, since they were the last remaining customers. Nudging the boy, they headed out the door into the moist cushion of air drifting off Big Muddy.

A block from the tavern, they were set upon—Billy, shoved against the door of a dress shop, and Clarence, pinned down by two men, while a third punched his face and gut.

"Next time take your Black ass to the n*r bar."

Then came two more men, and the flash of a knife, and the men who'd held Clarence fled up an alley, while the one beating him screamed as the knife struck deep. Clarence groaned and rolled over, out of harm's way, while Fred yelled, "Run, Andrew, run!"

And Hanging Cloud and his knife vanished back into the heart of the Great Sioux Nation.

. . .

Billy didn't know how he ended up in Sacred Heart Hospital. And he couldn't recall Fred happening upon the scene or his being carried to the police car for the ride to the emergency room. He was conscious for the exam and his first ever X-ray, which he might have thought cool if circumstances had been different. But nothing seemed cool to Billy now, lying flat on his back in the stark-white emergency room, surrounded by grim-faced nuns in white robes.

Diagnosed with a mild concussion, he was moved upstairs to a room with a gold crucifix mounted over every bed. Fred accompanied him, and while tucking the starched coverlet under Billy's chin, whispered, "Mum's the word 'bout Andrew. He warn't there." A timely admonition, since it had all started coming back to Billy—the sound of running feet, the flash of a knife blade, and the face of the man wielding it.

"What about Mr. Williams—is he all right?" Billy asked.

"They're workin' on him now, but there warn't much blood. Should be OK by mornin'."

One officer stayed to question Billy. Another took Fred to a room off the chapel where he gave his statement, putting his storytelling gifts to good use. "I was lookin' for a place to get a beer and saw Billy lying on the sidewalk and a guy maulin' the Negro. There was two more guys, but one ran away. Pulled the one off Clarence, but the other guy came at me with a knife and got his pal instead. Then *he* ran away. Happened fast. I yelled 'Police!' and you showed up."

Later, the sheriff made Fred go through the story again. "You're telling me you were able to scare off one man, and outfox two others, all by yourself?"

Fred shrugged, "Learned to fight on Saipan." The sheriff, a vet himself, was persuaded.

Clarence, who'd suffered facial lacerations, a black eye, and two broken ribs, added little other than his suspicion that two of the men were at the bar when he and Billy were eating.

"Never saw him before last night," Shorty, the barkeep, told the police when asked the next day about the dead man. His lie went unchallenged. The corpse—a transient day worker with no ties to the community—couldn't contradict him from the grave.

Clarence didn't mention Hanging Cloud in his account of the fight. And, since Fred wasn't an Indian, the police never bothered checking out the Thunderbird Bar, where he and Andrew had stopped earlier for a beer.

As for Billy, he understood that what happened to Clarence was the worst kind of bullying—three against one—and for no reason other than the color of his skin.

And that Hanging Cloud, an Indian, had been more heroic than anyone he'd ever known—not the brutal savage he'd seen in the movies.

"No, I didn't see who had the knife," Billy said, turning onto his side, away from the gaze of the golden Jesus. Could God ever forgive such a lie, he wondered, even to save a hero?

Chapter Seventy-Six

JOEL DOWNED HIS BOURBON AND ordered another. He couldn't even pretend he was having a good time. Watching Q canoodle with the blonde harlot only reminded him of Dinah's duplicity. And now he had another cloud hanging over him, Andrew Hanging Cloud, albeit with a possible silver lining—the 'tell', which if broadcast throughout the League might chase that cloud away.

If conscience allowed it, he might exploit that information—but what could Hoades possibly want in return? Clearly, Darren didn't offer the tell just because he despised Indians or to help him, a "Commie Jew." He wanted something more—something big. But what could it be?

Then he recalled what Hoades had said in Quarles' bus game. "*Me a catcher? Since When?*" It was right after Stockman chose Clarence, a Black man, not the Alabaman, as his replacement. Joel supposed that for a bigot like Hoades there was no greater insult.

And now with Clarence doing all the catching, and Hoades still stuck at second base, the Alabaman would never be able to show the scouts what he could do at his natural position. Despite himself, Joel sympathized a bit with Darren. His own situation was much the same. He, too, wanted to be seen by Big League scouts.

And then it hit him—what Hoades meant by "return the favor." In exchange for a tell that could lead to Andrew's ruin, Darren wanted him to convince Stockman to let Darren be his "personal catcher" whenever he pitched. With Andrew gone from the team, he would surely start every fourth day, insuring Hoades a regular appearance behind the dish.

But could Stockman be persuaded by a demand for a personal catcher from him, a college hurler competing for a regular spot in the rotation? And could shunting aside Clarence every fourth day ever be a conscionable exchange for ridding himself of the talented Indian? Could he do such a thing to a friend to further his own dream? He hated to admit it, but he was tempted.

And then, Joel spotted Hoades across the room playing poker. With his ramrod-straight posture and blond crew cut, he seemed ready for a Hollywood casting call as a Nazi stormtrooper.

Joel shook his head. He could never do that to Clarence. And tomorrow he'd let Hanging Cloud know that he had a 'tell'. He didn't think he could live with himself if he didn't.

Joel slid from the barstool and headed for his room. It was late, but Clarence and Billy might still be up. A bit wobbly, he arrived at the elevator the same time as Q and his 'birthday gift', already partly unwrapped, her slip straps looping from her shoulders like party ribbons.

"Did you meet Joely? He's from New York, but don't ya go running off with him, 'cause it's *my* birthday." The girl shot Joel a sly smile as the three of them stumbled onto the elevator. Pushing the button for the fourth floor, she caught Joel staring at her.

"Where do you get off?" she asked Joel, and Q gave her waist a hard squeeze.

"Babe, you and I will get off together, but Joely will have to get off all by himself."

As the elevator opened onto the fourth floor, a teetering Quarles came face-to-face with a slender redhead in a belted sun dress. Without batting an eye, Q dropped his arm from the hooker's waist and pushed her toward Joel. "Peggy, sweetheart, baby! What ya doin' here?"

The woman's eyes flashed as she glared at her husband. "What are *you* doing—with *her*?"

"I'm . . . uh, helping my friend Joel here." Dick cupped his hand over his wife's ear. "He's a virgin and the team bought him a girl. I was just protecting our investment."

Hands on hips, Peggy scowled. "Sure she's not *your* present?"

"You're my present, babe, and the best a guy could ask for—driving all the way out here to surprise me. What a gal!" Q put his arm around his wife's waist and pulling her toward him, started down the hall. "Have fun, kids," he yelled back at Joel and the blonde.

Joel stood in the hallway, stunned by the sudden turn of events.

"You really a virgin?" the girl asked, sizing up the handsome ballplayer.

"Well," Joel fairly stuttered, "I've got a girlfriend."

"She around here, too, somewhere?"

"No."

"Then it's your lucky day. You got yourself the party favor. Bought and paid for."

. . .

"Get up," the girl ordered, giving Joel a shove. "You can't stay here."

Joel groaned. Looking across the bed, he watched her put on a starched white uniform, not the black cocktail dress of the night before. Was she a nurse, he wondered.

Feeling a renewal of desire, it came back to him—how she sat him on the bed, sucked his cock, mounted him, and slowly guided him inside her. He'd come lickety-split, making her think he truly was a virgin, but she withheld comment, knowing that even nice guys can turn rattler mean if teased about their manhood. Besides, he'd been sweet—lightly stroking her hair afterward.

Watching her now, Joel had the odd notion that the striptease and all that followed had happened to someone else. He expected to feel terrific—going all the way for the first time—but instead he felt dirty. Sitting up, he slipped on his watch. The change of position released a salvo of musk and bourbon-scented sweat from his privates. He couldn't go back to the room he shared with Billy and Clarence smelling like that. "I need to take a shower."

"Not here," she snapped. "Shower in your own room." Stung by her tone, Joel turned to her. She was about his own age, and he wondered if she still lived at home. He imagined she told her parents that she worked the night shift at the hospital, then came to the hotel to pick up men for money. The thought that she had a family troubled him.

"Do you need me to walk you to work?" he asked.

It was an offer she'd never gotten before, though she'd had lots of less chivalrous ones. "You're sweet, but I work here."

"Aren't you a nurse?" he blurted.

Her face clouded over. "No."

Then, Joel realized that she might be a hotel maid. Fearing that he had embarrassed her, he felt a wave of remorse. "I'll be out of your way in a minute," he said, picking his clothes off the floor. In the bathroom, he peed and washed his hands and face, drying them on toilet paper so as not to dirty a towel. Then he swiped his genitals and again washed his hands. Finally, he wiped the sink, tossed the paper into the toilet, and flushed it down. Heading for the door he didn't know what to say. It wasn't her fault he felt let down. She'd done her part, and more.

"Goodbye," was all he could offer as she passed by him on her way to the bathroom. He hoped she'd notice that he'd left it tidy, as clean as when he'd entered.

...

Joel slipped into his room and felt his way in the dark. Instantly, he sensed an unnatural quiet. No soft snores from Clarence or restless rustlings from Billy. Nudging the door for light, he drew in his breath. Billy and Clarence were missing.

It was four in the morning. Where in the world could they be? Heart racing, he tried to calm himself. Perhaps they went out to eat—but surely, they would have returned by now. Maybe they'd found another room, so he could have the place to himself if he got lucky. But their things were still here—Clarence's pajamas folded neatly on his bed, and Billy's odd, straw valise plopped like a giant shredded wheat biscuit on top of his cot.

What if Billy was sick or had an accident? Joel grabbed the phone and called the desk clerk. "No. I didn't see no Negro and white boy leave the hotel," he said, his voice thick with sleep. A minute later, the clerk called back to report that a call had come in around 1 a.m. from the emergency room. Joel barreled down the staircase for directions to Sacred Heart Hospital.

"It's by Mount Marty College, next to a stone church. Big 'ole steeple. Ya can't miss it!"

Training his eyes on a tall gray spire, Joel raced through the deserted streets of Yankton, arriving breathless and shaken at a squat, brick building tucked into the shadow of the cathedral. The front door was unlocked, and the lobby deserted, but a bright light shone at the end of the hallway and Joel ran to it, past portraits of priests and statues of saints, and a robed Jesus, his pierced crimson heart wrapped in a wrestle of thorns jutting like a fist from the Savior's chest.

A nun in a white habit put an admonishing finger to her lips. "It is too late for visitors."

Joel swallowed hard, suddenly aware of his rumpled clothes, his sweat-slicked face, and his breath reeking of bourbon—his body, of worse. "Please, Sister, I'm a friend of Mr. Williams and Billy Moran—the Negro ballplayer and the white boy."

The nun furrowed her brow. "Oh, yes. They are both resting comfortably." She returned to her charting, as if the matter were closed.

"Can I see the boy? His parents asked me to keep an eye on him." Then his voice cracked—as his and Billy's night converged in one plaintive truth. "He's so far from home."

When the nun nodded, Joel almost cried with relief. He'd let Billy down. The knowledge of what he'd been doing, possibly at the exact moment Clarence and Billy had been injured, tore at him. "Do you know what happened? Is the boy badly hurt?"

The nun's face was impassive. She'd overheard the police questioning Billy but would not divulge what she'd learned. "He has a bump on his head. He's having a restless night and called out in his sleep for someone named John. Is that you?"

"No. That's his older brother, back in Rapid City."

"Once he cried out—something about polio. Was he afflicted?"

"No. His brother had it, but he recovered."

"Thank the Lord," she said and crossed herself. Entering the children's ward, she pointed to a hardback chair, then whispered, "Please come and get me if he becomes agitated."

Joel waited until the nun left, then moved the chair so he'd not have to look at the crucifix on the wall. Watching Billy, he was soothed by the soft rush of the boy's rhythmic breathing, and the peaceful look on his face. "Baruch atah Adonai. Blessed be the Lord," Joel whispered, praying that the boy would be spared further harm.

Billy's piercing wail jolted Joel awake along with several of the children on the ward. "Where were you, Joel," he sobbed, his eyes filled with confusion. "Where were you?"

• • •

Early that morning, Fred repeated his version of the attack to Stockman, adding that Hanging Cloud got word his son was sick and caught the first bus back to the Reservation. Guy wasn't surprised that Williams got jumped. He'd always expected it would happen somewhere sooner or later. But he didn't buy Fred's story about Hanging Cloud—likely concocted to make his nephew seem less shiftless. He imagined the Indian just got drunk and took off.

"Whadya mean he got word? They send up smoke signals from the Reservation?"

Fred had anticipated Guy's biased skepticism. "His mother called her sister—my wife—and she told me when I called her."

"Right." Stockman rolled his eyes—as if anyone ever called his wife from the road.

Checking his watch, he dispatched Fred to the hospital to collect the three roommates—a battered and bandaged Clarence, a bleary-eyed Billy, and a weary Joel. On the bus, several Chiefs approached Joel with grins and outstretched hands, demanding their "whore money" back. "It weren't your birthday." Joel took the razzing as he knew he must, but it saddened him that such a private experience, now tainted with so many dark associations, had become just another spool in the team's ceaseless joke mill.

Between the ribbing and his exhaustion, Joel didn't notice that Andrew Hanging Cloud was AWOL until the bus was an hour out of Yankton. Leaning forward, he tapped Fred on the shoulder. "Say, Fred, where's Andrew?"

Fred repeated the story—phone call, sick child, the first bus back to the reservation.

"I hope the baby's OK," Joel said flatly, and Fred grunted.

Behind Joel's back, Billy and Clarence exchanged a look, then turned away, letting the roll of the bus lull them to sleep. And Joel, too, succumbed to the rhythm of the road and the urgent need to forget.

• • •

There was no way for Clarence to hide from Cherry Mae what had happened. His face and body said it all. Bruises on top of bruises, two broken ribs, both eyes blackened and one swollen shut, injuries that couldn't be ascribed to a mishap or a collision at home plate, though that was the story they told the children.

In all his years barnstorming with the Clowns, as a grease monkey in Indianapolis and now as an Air Force mechanic, he'd never been laid up for more than a day or two. But here he was, captive in a hot, cramped trailer, too hobbled even to play catch in the yard with Clarence Jr. or twirl a jump rope for Violet. Every movement—bending, reaching, breathing—hurt like hell. The Ironwood he'd always loved now felt like a prison cell.

But it wasn't just his body that hurt. Each wince became a reminder of the attack—the shock and shame of it. For he'd never been taken down before. His sixth sense and sheer size had always protected him. Why had he let down his guard, he wondered. Had working with white mechanics at the Base and buddying up with Joel made him color-blind to the threat still out there—at a bar, on the street, in the men's room?

And there was the lie they'd told the children about home plate. Was it wrong not to prepare them—warn them the way his father had warned him when they came north to Indiana?

He didn't want them to be fearful of whites—the way Cherry Mae sometimes seemed to be. But he didn't ever want them blindsided, either.

Cherry Mae's response was strangely calm—no wailing or "I told you so's"—just sighs and nods as she bandaged his ribs and prepared poultices for his face. She'd been expecting something like this as far back as his days with the Clowns. Whenever he went on the road, her chest got tight. Finally, she could breathe. Her husband had been attacked but survived, so now, without her having to make a scene, she might get him to put in for a transfer back home to their people.

In the meantime, she chided him only for taking a youngster out late in a strange city, especially Billy Moran. "How we gonna face that nice Mrs. Moran after this?"

Mrs. Moran. Jennie. Clarence turned to hide his face when his wife said her name.

At first, he thought it was the shame he felt for not protecting her son. But in the days that followed—long, idle days, unable to work and banned from the ballpark, he thought about her more and more. In the old way—the way he did when they first met in the parking lot at the Base. It made him feel better, though he wasn't sure why.

Maybe he just didn't like the way Cherry Mae looked at him now—her worried stares, which made him feel helpless, and her tight-lipped darts of disapproval when he started drinking to dull the pain that filled his hours. Whatever it was, it was Jennie's face he saw when he closed his eyes at night. And when he woke in the mornings, too.

Chapter Seventy-Seven

STOCKMAN STOOD AT THE SINK in the *Royal Rest* and swept his thumb back and forth under the faucet. Finally, the swelling was down, and the doctor said he'd regain its full use in time—for tiddlywinks, Guy thought ruefully, if not for catching.

The Chiefs' dearth of catchers was something he never expected. They'd started the season with three. Then he went down with the broken thumb and Williams with busted ribs. Which left only Hoades, a nineteen-year-old with just a couple dozen college games under his belt. To snag the pennant, they'd need a veteran catcher, and soon. Like it or not, he'd have to ask Rosen. According to their deal, it was the boss man's pick to make.

He reached Bernie at the Club. It was the first time they'd spoken since Buck rearranged his thumb, and to his surprise, the man was cordial and businesslike. Said he knew of a catcher from the Cleveland chain who might be available. Then, he asked about Hanging Cloud.

"Pitched good. But he's gone now, too. Went back to the rez. Sick kid or something."

Bernie snorted, spotting a tall tale, but figured he'd get the skinny later from Fred or Buck. "Any other disasters I should know about—droughts, cyclones, earthquakes?"

Stockman laughed. He didn't mention Billy's night in the hospital or his doubts about Joel's pitching. He figured the man had a vested interest in Joel that was stronger than his attachment to Williams. Probably a clannish thing. Jew for Jew, but Jew for a Negro? What was that about? Maybe it was the Air Force connection.

"I'll get this guy here pronto," Bernie promised. "Williams can't suit up until his face heals. No reason to parade him around in public or get his picture in the paper."

Guy hung up the phone. His chat went okay but triggered memories of Lana. When the break was fresh and he was on the road, it was easier not to think of her, but nearly recovered now and back in town, he wasn't sure he could stay away. He forced the thumb backwards, producing a sharp pain. Maybe that's what was needed to remind him that Bernie's woman remained off limits. Still, he doubted it would work. Liquor and road girls could take the edge off, but Lana had gotten under his skin. For where could a man go after scaling Everest, breaking the sound barrier, hitting for the cycle? It was hard to find words for how he felt.

Maybe he just loved her.

...

Standing in the shower in the Rosen basement, Joel raised his face to the spray and let it rain down on him. He felt dirtier than he'd ever felt. And homesick. He missed Rivkah and Morrie and New York. He wondered if he'd made a mistake coming to South Dakota to play ball.

Everything he'd once believed about the West was proving a fraud—the reputed warmheartedness of small-town life, the vaunted honesty and decency of its people—attested to by the covers of the *Saturday Evening Post* and the sentimentalities of *Our Town*, a play which had moved him to tears. Now it all seemed like fibs and fables—like the come-ons of the 19th-century rail barons, luring homesteaders west with false promises of fertile farmland.

And the Chiefs, he was beginning to believe, were a team in name only. Where was the fraternity and solidarity of a true ball club? All he saw were cliques and schisms and cruel teasing that passed as camaraderie.

Maybe it was Stockman's leadership fostering an atmosphere of insecurity . . . three catchers vying for one starting job, pitchers haunted by the threat of a bus ticket home. But mostly, he hated what this was doing to his character—reveling in the failures of his fellow hurlers, secretly pleased when a child fell sick and swept away a rival, being tempted to undermine a friend to secure his place as a starter.

He recoiled at the revelation of his bitter core, the poison lurking in his pit, like cyanide in apple seeds. Grabbing the bar of soap, he scrubbed his armpits and groin. He'd not showered since his sprint through the dark streets of Yankton and could still smell the stink of panic and the ripe odor from his turn with the nameless whore.

Yes, he'd hoped for new experiences out West, and no one could say he hadn't found them. And yet, so many had turned sour. Dumped by Dinah, threatened by Bernie, condemned by Billy, dismissed by the young whore as if she were a parking meter and his time had expired. Even when he'd finally gone all the way, instead of euphoria or, at least, a degree of satisfaction, all he felt was a compulsion to bathe and remove all traces of the act and its aftermath.

And so, he pulled a picture postcard from his chinos and wrote "I miss you" on the back of a drawing of Mount Marty Cathedral, bought in the hospital gift shop while waiting for Billy's discharge. Addressed to Rivkah, it was received in Brooklyn as a cry from the wilderness—an SOS—which Joel never considered might also be read as a confession.

• • •

Joel was late for practice. He'd waited for Billy to bike with him, but the boy never showed. Arriving at Sioux Park, Joel was heartened to see him fetching batting practice balls, showing no ill effects of his concussion. Then his heart sank. At the end of the dugout bench sat a new ballplayer lacing up his spikes.

Joel kicked a clump of clay. Hanging Cloud was scarcely gone and already a new storm cloud had gathered. Was it just a matter of time before he'd have to pack up and go home?

Then, the man pulled shin guards and a chest protector from his duffel. Never had the tools of ignorance looked so bright.

Best of all, the new catcher was Hoades' problem, not his.

Chapter Seventy-Eight

JAMES WAS AFRAID TO TELL Jennie he'd hired Martha Muffling to work in the Stand though he was sure it was the right thing to do. Finally, he had no choice. "Who is she?" Jennie snapped.

Oddly, her prickly response gladdened James. For the first time in weeks, she seemed her irascible old self. John's engagement and cold indifference had driven her into a deep freeze. Every night she paced the narrow hallway of their house, then slept all day on the couch until they left for the Stand. At least he could count on her for that, though he worried about her being on her feet for hours, especially if she proved to be pregnant.

"Martha Muffling, one of my best students. She came by the Stand a couple of weeks ago asking about John. Nice country girl, from a ranch down by Hermosa."

Jennie shrugged, but James remained hopeful. Perhaps this sweet, earnest girl could lift her out of her woeful state.

Waiting at the stadium entrance, Martha was dressed in a dirndl skirt that fell well below her knees and a white-collared, long-sleeved blouse. With her modest costume and mouse-brown hair, she looked a lot like Jennie at that age and James thought that might appease, maybe even please her.

Smiling shyly, Martha held out her hand to Jennie. "Thank you for this opportunity," she said, as James looked on like a proud papa. Jennie brushed by her without a word, anxious to get to her lookout before the Chiefs finished their pre-game warm-ups.

"How did you get here, Martha?" James asked, hoping to divert her from Jennie's cold response. Martha's eyes darted. "Uh . . . well . . . my . . . mother," she stammered.

Martha wasn't sure why she lied. Her stepfather, Daryl, insisted on driving and collecting her, though she could have driven herself. "Can't have you roamin' 'round after the game. Might attract a rough crowd—them coloreds from the Base."

Daryl had been her father's right-hand man and stayed on after he died, marrying her mother and siring three sons. He'd started up with Martha when she was just ten. Never putting it in her—only in her hand or mouth—assuring her that it was okay "'cause we ain't kin and you won't get preggers." Now, she dreaded the long ride home from the ballpark—the turnoff onto a side road, out of sight of car, house, or barn.

James was baffled. He knew Martha was shy, but he'd never seen her this nervous. It pained him to see Jennie snub this gentle girl he'd helped break out of her shell. Hoping to reassure her, he put an arm around her shoulder, but she flinched, and he quickly let go. He couldn't recall ever touching a female student before—or any woman other than Jennie, except to shake hands. For a long moment, he stood helpless, arms at his side. Finally, he clapped his hands together and assumed a jovial tone. "All right. Lots to do before the crowd arrives. Ever popped corn, Martha? We make a mountain of it here."

Martha managed a weak smile as she followed James to the Stand. She was grateful to her teacher, who had always been kind to her and had given her this job where she might get to see his son John. And just as important, provide an excuse to escape the ranch and the long summer twilight when her mom was occupied by her brothers' baths and bedtimes, and it was hard to elude her stepfather's traps.

"I manned the popcorn machine at the church fair last spring," she offered shyly.

"Hear that, Jen? She knows how to pop."

Jennie said nothing as she peered down at the field. She'd arrived too late and missed Clarence in the drills. Shooting Martha a cold look, she ducked under the pass-through and began filling pots with water.

James sighed as he ushered Martha inside, careful now to keep an arm's length between them. With Jennie engaged, he helped Martha with the popper. She was an apt pupil, but he was reluctant to praise her, fearing it might darken his wife's mood. Maybe it was a mistake hiring Martha without running it by Jennie first. If only he could say it was for her welfare and that of the baby—if there was one.

He regarded the two women, working wordlessly, side by side, and for the first time in a long time, thought about baby Lily and what it might have meant if Jennie had a daughter in her life. On impulse, he bowed his head and silently prayed, "Let this one be a girl," but when he looked up, Jennie was staring at him, making him fear that he'd spoken the prayer aloud.

"Hello, Mr. Moran." Approaching the Stand, Joel looked past James, who offered a smile, to Jennie who did not. A split decision but enough to afford him some relief. Clearly, they hadn't learned what had happened to Billy in Yankton. "Don't tell my parents," the boy snarled in the hospital—the only words he said to him since leaving Yankton.

Joel caught the eye of Martha behind the popper. "Hello," he said, more out of courtesy than interest, for the girl was plain, though her eyes were softly brown and soulful.

James looked from Joel to Martha and smiled. Perhaps he could make up for Jennie's rude treatment by helping the sweet, unassuming girl. "Joel, this is Martha Muffling, one of my best students and a prize debater. Martha, Joel is a college graduate and future Major Leaguer."

Martha blushed and looked down at the floor and Joel forced a smile. He'd come for a snack, not to be reminded of his dubious baseball future.

"I'll take a Hershey bar and a Coke, please." Then, to acknowledge the girl's presence, added, "And a box of your best popcorn."

As Martha approached the counter with the popcorn, Joel did a double take. In her modest skirt and hi-necked, long-sleeved blouse, she could pass for a Brownsville 'shul' girl, like Rivkah. "Thank you, Miss Muffling," he said, as Martha set the popcorn on the counter, her eyes brightening. James beamed, delighted that he'd done right by the girl.

With snacks in hand, Joel started toward the field. Maybe he could ask Martha out after the game, date a modest girl in the time-honored way. Glancing back at the Stand, he saw that Martha was still looking at him. No! To play with the feelings of a sweet, shy girl would be a greater transgression than what he'd done drunk in Yankton.

Then, out of the corner of his eye, he spotted Bernie and another man striding toward the Stand. It took only an instant to recognize him—not by name but by vocation. Tall and lanky, with a deeply lined, tanned face, he was dressed in khakis, windbreaker, baseball cap, and sunglasses, and walked with a cocky, athletic gait. He was, no doubt, a Major League Scout.

He'd seen them before at Columbia games, watching intently, some scribbling in a notebook, others more guarded, hiding their reactions, recording only mental notes. At times he thought one was there to see him—though none ever approached him or contacted him at home.

And he'd never gotten an offer to play ball from any of the highly touted East Coast summer leagues either, like Cape Cod, swarmed by scouts from all the big eastern baseball cities.

Was he not up to snuff, or did they doubt that a Columbia ballplayer could cut it in the Big Leagues? The last player to do that was Lou Gehrig in the 1930s. Maybe they thought Ivy Leaguers were soft. Or was a different prejudice operating? Could word have gotten out that he was an observant Jew requiring special accommodation, an encumbrance not worth the bother?

Joel broke into a sweat. He needed to pitch while the scout was in town but wasn't due to start until the next road trip. Tonight's starter was Schmid and tomorrow it was Dave Wiegand, though the scout wouldn't hang around to see an old pro like Dave. He'd only be interested in the collegians, and once he saw Schmidy, the most successful of the Chiefs' younger pitchers, he might never return to Rapid. If only the Scout had seen him throw his one-hitter. Now, his only chance was to persuade Stockman to let him pitch tomorrow instead of Wiegand.

Arriving at the counter, Bernie made the introductions: "'Red' Hughes. James Moran. And that woman with the wieners is James's wife, one of the Chiefs' most passionate fans."

With that, Jennie ducked under the pass-through and headed for the restroom.

Standing on the gravel path, Joel looked to the dugout where Stockman stood talking to Schmid. He had to get back before he was missed, but first he needed to speak to that Scout. Ambling up to the counter, he positioned himself next to the man and muttered, "Salt."

Without a word, Martha handed him the shaker, which he shook vigorously over his popcorn—a motion that drew both Bernie's and the Scout's attention.

"Hey there, Meznik. Guess you're not chucking tonight."

"Not tonight, but . . . " and the lie just popped out " . . . I'm starting tomorrow."

Bernie threw Joel a look. He knew the pitching rotation but guessed what his boychik was up to. Admiring his chutzpah—his nerve—he played along. "Red, this is Joel Meznik, the Brooklyn southpaw I told you about. Could be the next Koufax. Red is with the Dodgers, Joel."

Joel swallowed hard. His beloved Dodgers. "It's a real honor, sir."

"You stayin' tomorrow, Red?" Bernie asked.

"If I got reason to."

Bernie smiled benevolently. "Why don't you come to the Club tonight and meet my wife, Lana. She's the headliner, and believe you me, she can belt one out better than Frank Hacker. And you'll get the best T-Bone west of Kansas City, on the house."

The scout slapped Bernie on the back. "Don't have to twist my arm, Rosen. I've heard about your wife. Now point me to the little boys' room. I've got a game to watch."

When the Scout was out of earshot, Joel gushed his gratitude. "Thanks, Bernie, but you know I'm not scheduled to pitch tomorrow."

"No kidding, but I'll talk to Stockman. So, have your slider working."

Joel wanted to throw his arms around the man, for doing what his own father never could—or would.

James handed Joel another Hershey bar. "On the house. Good luck to you, son."

Joel's smile was shaky. The enormity of what was at stake began to sink in.

"Thanks, Mr. Moran. I might need it," he said, as he headed toward the Chiefs' dugout.

"Good luck," Martha called after him. Turning, Joel caught her look—shy but admiring, giving him a surge of confidence. He could do this. Pitch another great game. He didn't need Dinah rooting from the stands.

And wouldn't it just slay her if he signed with the Dodgers and ended up in LA while she was stuck in Rapid, keeping house for John Moran!

Abandoning his pledge not to toy with a plain girl's heart, he waved the box of popcorn in Martha's direction. "Martha Muffling, you are my good luck charm. If I win tomorrow, we'll paint the town red!"

Martha lowered her eyes and smiled. And James, glancing back at his new clerk, saw the hopeful smile spread across her face, as beautiful as the dawning of a new day.

Chapter Seventy-Nine

A STATICKY SPUTTERING from the public address system told Jennie it was time. Depositing the hot dog platter next to James, she ducked under the pass-through. She wanted to see Clarence stand for the National Anthem, his hand raised to his brow, saluting the Stars and Stripes as the only member of the Chiefs serving in the Armed Forces. But he wasn't there.

Perplexed, she waited for the lineup to be announced. She knew it by heart or, at least, the Chiefs' first five batters. At night, she'd often recite it to herself until she fell asleep—*Casey, Hoades, Paskiewicz, Hacker, and Williams. Casey, Hoades, Paskiewicz, Hacker, and Williams.*

Now it boomed over the stadium loudspeaker: "*Leading off for the hometown Chiefs and playing shortstop, number three, Lee Casey—Casey, number three, leading off. Batting second and playing second, number eight, Darren Hoades—Hoades, number eight, batting second.*"

Then Paskiewicz and Hacker were announced with the same prolix patter. Now, she thought, comes Clarence. "*And, batting fifth tonight, in his Chiefs' debut, number twenty-eight, the catcher, Dayton Todd—Todd, number twenty-eight, batting fifth.*"

Another man in Clarence's spot. And none of the remaining batters was Clarence, either.

"What's wrong, Jen?" James shouted, as she darted down the gravel path.

When she didn't answer, he started after her, thinking it might be morning sickness, or God forbid, a miscarriage. Following her toward the Ladies Room, he stopped as she made a sharp turn and charged down the aisle to the Chiefs' dugout, calling out Billy's name.

Billy's mouth dropped. His mom had never sought him out in the dugout—never embarrassed him that way. Had someone told her he'd been in the hospital in Yankton? He'd made Joel promise not to say anything. And Clarence wasn't at the ballpark tonight.

"Where is Mr. Williams? Why didn't they announce his name?"

Billy's stomach flipped, until he realized she hadn't mentioned Yankton and must still be in the dark about that. "I dunno. Maybe he's sick."

She could tell he was lying. "Tell me the truth!"

Billy swallowed hard. "He got hurt."

Her face went ashen. "What do you mean? What happened?"

"He broke a couple ribs," then recalling Clarence's face, added "His nose, too, I think."

Jennie gasped and Billy paused. The easiest lie was to say it happened in a game. But if his mom learned he'd lied to her twice, he'd be punished for sure—maybe even grounded and miss the road trip back to Valentine to see Ginny. He had to say something true, even if it wasn't the whole truth. "He got beat up in Yankton, Ma. But he's OK—just can't play ball for a while."

"Who did it? Another player?"

"No, it was in town, after the game . . . "

"Oh, no!" she said, in a voice that frightened him.

"Mom! What is it?"

"Where is he now?"

"At his house, I guess. He came back on the bus. He was OK then, Mom, I swear."

Abruptly, she turned and strode up the aisle to the Stand. Watching her from behind the counter, James was baffled by the distant pantomime between his wife and son. What could Billy have done to upset her that much?

"I need the car." Palm up, Jennie extended her hand to her husband.

The way she said it, James knew he wouldn't get any more out of her.

"Will you come get me after the game?" James asked, pulling the keys from his pocket.

Jennie didn't answer.

"My stepfather can drive Mr. Moran home," Martha offered, forgetting her earlier fib that her mother would be picking her up.

Jennie simply said, "There."

"OK." He handed over the car keys and watched as she hurried to the exit.

"Is everything OK, Mr. Moran?" Martha asked with real concern.

"I have no idea," was all he could honestly say. "No idea at all."

• • •

Jennie pulled the car off the road and sat for a moment in the Chevy. She remembered how it had been that cold spring day when she came to speak to the Williamses about their son. The trees were bare then and the road could be seen from the steps of the trailer. Now, the leaves were dense and lustrous, a curtain of green shielding the Ironwood, so only pulses of light glinted off its sun-struck metal.

Stepping from the car, she slipped silently through the grove, until she came to a large tree not far from the trailer. All was quiet and Clarence's car was nowhere to be seen. Then the trailer door opened, and Clarence stepped outside, beer bottle in hand. He wore boxer shorts but no shirt, and his chest was swathed in thick bands of white tape below a breastplate of hard muscle and tight coils of black hair.

Jennie drew her limbs in close. Squeezing her slender figure within the borders of the cottonwood, she fixed her gaze on Clarence's face—bruised and bloated, with one eye swollen shut beneath a jagged, sutured cut.

Standing on the stoop, Clarence chugged the beer and let the bottle drop to the ground, where it shattered on a pile of empties. Then he paced the tiny yard, kicking at clumps of switch grass. Finally, he walked to the edge of the lot and stopped at a scraggly bush. Reaching through his fly, he pulled out his penis and let go in a long, arching stream directed back and forth as if watering a lawn. Jennie squeezed her eyes shut, then opened them.

With a tug, Clarence gave his penis a couple of good shakes, then cradled it like a tuber about to be peeled. With a quick glance about, he cupped his balls with one hand and stroked himself with the other, first slowly, then faster and faster with an urgent raw energy.

Clapping her hand over her mouth, Jennie pressed hard against the tree, and spasmed herself a moment after he came. By the time she opened her eyes, he was gone.

Jennie ran to her car and sped home. Stumbling from the car, she staggered across the lawn, past the Rosens' stone lions and the nursery-bought trees, to the rear of the house where her creek had once run. Breaking the surface, she stepped into the pool and let the coldness engulf her in the dammed, icy water of Bernie Rosen's pond.

• • •

"That mother-in-law of yours is having one helluva nervous breakdown," Lana announced, depositing a bowl of oatmeal in front of her daughter.

"Huh?" Dinah glanced nervously at the basement stairs. The Chiefs were back in town, and she never knew when Joel might appear, sarcastic and smoldering and muddling her mind.

"Last night I came home between shows to get a fresh gown . . . "

"Fresh is right!" Bernie interrupted with a lascivious grin. "Your Momma let it rip all the way from Bear Butt to Twin Peaks." He gave his wife's backside a playful slap. "Do that every show, babe—a little extra skin to boost the gate."

Appetite gone, Dinah dropped her cereal bowl in the sink. Still reeling from the truth about her parents, she couldn't watch their bawdy little game without wanting to scream.

"I stepped on my train!" Lana explained, merrily. "Never did that before. So, I'm comin' out of my closet, and I see this crazy woman streaking across our yard . . ."

Dinah froze at the sink. Lana's show gowns were hung in the same closet as the trunk with the scrapbook. Had her mother noticed something amiss?

"Dinah!" Lana exclaimed. "Are you listening? This is rich!"

"Yes," she replied, but her voice sounded strained, and Bernie placed a hand on her shoulder. "Anything wrong, Princess?"

Dinah managed a wan smile. "I'm fine. Go on with your story, Mother."

"So, it's Jennie Moran, runnin' like Chicken Little, you know, the sky's a fallin', the sky's a fallin', and the next thing I know, she's jumping into our goldfish pond with all her clothes on!"

Bernie hooted, "What a stitch," then threw a look at Dinah to see her reaction to this crazy tale of her future in-law.

Dinah shrugged, though for the first time she felt an odd kinship with Jennie Moran.

But the show, she reminded herself, must go on. "Didn't she melt?" she quipped. Raising her arms over her head, she slowly shimmied into a heap on the kitchen floor in a perfect mime of the watery end of the Wicked Witch of the West.

Even Lana had to smile at her daughter's devilish performance, and Bernie roared, thinking Joel might be right. The girl had talent.

Tossing a look of parental pride in Lana's direction, he missed the icy glare Dinah shot her mother as she exited, stage right, from the room.

Chapter Eighty

"LONG DISTANCE, PLEASE. I'd like to place a collect call to Indianapolis."

Cherry Mae made her decision in the middle of the night, right after Clarence cried out "Jennie!" in his sleep.

That was when she figured he must have stepped out, most likely on the road, as there were no colored women at Ellsworth by that name. Maybe that was the real reason he got beat up in Yankton—a jealous husband or boyfriend and not, as he claimed, by white men when he was out getting food with the Moran boy.

For Cherry Mae it was the last straw—time to throw in the towel, or at least on their life in Dakota. Clarence would have to give up the team and get a transfer home to Indiana if he wanted his family back.

Tiptoeing around the trailer, she gathered what she needed, including all the cash from his wallet, then woke the children with a cautionary finger to her lips. "Don't be wakin' your father," she said, though she doubted that anything could rouse the man these days—often passed out drunk and reeking of dried blood and beer.

Waking at noon to a quiet trailer, Clarence found no coffee on the stove and no car out front. When they hadn't returned by nightfall, he knew his family was gone. He wasn't surprised. He'd always figured it was just a matter of time before Cherry Mae ran home to Indiana.

But when he checked his wallet and found his pay missing, he felt at peace. They'd be all right for a time, and he could heal on his own, the way nature intended. When he was whole again and sober, he'd come to fetch them, and she'd have to take him back, because he'd done nothing wrong—been faithful on the road and until he got hurt, was a good husband and father.

Crawling into bed, he lay flat on his back, the only position that quieted his ribs. The next afternoon he downed three aspirin, gave himself a farmer's shower and shave, and donning his airman's blues, walked to the Commander's office to put in for a transfer back home.

"Could have happened anywhere," the Commander declared, figuring that was the reason for the request. Seeing Clarence's battered face, he ordered him not to talk about the attack or return to work until he was completely healed. With all the boycotts and marches going on down South, he didn't want the other colored airmen riled.

"Yes, sir," Clarence said, adding to himself—could happen *anywhere* a colored man lets his guard down 'round white folk. "My wife took the kids and went home to Indianapolis."

The Commander grunted, resisting the urge to say, "So what?" A real airman knew his home was wherever the Air Force sent him. A wife who didn't understand that had no business marrying a serviceman.

"I'll see what I can do," he said curtly, and Clarence, recognizing his dismissal, saluted, and pivoted to the door.

Outside, he slumped against the side of the building, his head pounding and ribs ablaze. His plan to rejoin his family no longer felt like a sure thing. But, in a day or two he'd phone his father-in-law and tell Cherry Mae he'd put in for a transfer, to show her at least he was trying.

"Hey, Williams. What the hell happened to you?" Otis McNeeley, his old Flyers teammate, pulled up in his '52 Plymouth. "Your face, man. Whadja do, walk into a propeller?"

"Worst slide I ever had." It was the lie he'd prepared for those unconnected to the Chiefs.

"You can say that again. Hell, I was about to drive into Rapid to watch you play."

Clarence hesitated. He was sick of being cooped up and told what to do. Opening the car door, he slowly lowered himself into the passenger seat. "Let's go, man!"

• • •

Martha pulled her school satchel from her closet and slipped a floral sundress inside. It was her favorite frock—sleeveless, with a scalloped neck, cinched waist, and a flared skirt falling just below the knee. She'd sewn it in Home Economics Class but had never worn it. Even on the hottest days, she kept her arms and legs covered. And her blue jeans, from Sears, were purposely ordered a size too large—saggy in the thighs and butt.

Not that any of this mattered to her stepfather, Daryl. He wanted it regardless of how she dressed, and on a side road heading home after her first Chiefs game, he got it the way he'd taught her, starting with her hand and finishing with her mouth, so as to "make no mess."

It had been years since he first followed her to the barn and made her kneel in a corner stall, ordering her to milk it like a teat, then suckle it like one of her beloved calves. Terrified, she'd complied, closing her ears to his frightening grunts, hearing only the complaints of the milk cows, waiting for her gentle, discharging hands.

Long ago she realized that she could never tell on Daryl, who said they'd lose the ranch without him. And what might it do to her mother to learn what he'd been up to all those years—if she even believed her. At least, her modest mode of dress showed she'd not invited his advances.

Still, when a classmate sewed a pretty frock, Martha borrowed the pattern and fashioned the only item in her wardrobe that flattered her spare figure. Smuggling it home, she stashed it under her bed, ready, she hoped, for John Moran. And, while it wasn't John who'd asked her out, she brought the dress to Sioux Park, so Joel might see her at her best and be inspired to win.

On the way into Rapid, she told her stepfather that a girlfriend would bring her home that night. Daryl looked at her hard. "Sure it's not that fat old teacher we gave a ride to last night?"

Arriving at Sioux Park, Martha made a beeline for the ladies' room to scrub her hands and rinse Daryl from her mouth. Then, she donned her special dress and shook out her hair, letting it fall in waves across her shoulders. Frowning, she yanked the side strands into a half ponytail and secured it with a rubber band, so Mrs. Moran couldn't grouse about hair getting into the food. As a final touch she pulled a dented lipstick from her satchel and outlined her lips with a nubbin of pink paste. It was all that remained of a tube rescued from her mother's waste basket. Puckering her mouth like a movie star, she felt a tingling. Tonight, she might finally kiss a boy.

Flushed and beaming, she hurried to the Stand. James drew in his breath. He'd never seen Martha look like this, and the effect was automatic. Lowering his eyes, he fussed with the beer bottles in the ice chest. "Boy, it's a hot one tonight. Guess we're gonna need some more ice," though the chest was nearly full. Grabbing the counter, he remarked in his best offhand manner, "Oh, hi, Martha. My, my, don't you look nice." A shy smile crossed the girl's lips, which he noticed were pink and shimmery.

He turned to look at Jennie. Last night, when Martha's stepfather dropped him at home, Jennie's car was in the driveway—door open, keys still in the ignition. Rushing into the house, he found her passed out on the bed in the same dress she'd worn to the Stand, now dripping wet. Panicked, he turned her onto her side, and she opened her eyes, barely noting his presence. Asleep all morning, she never changed out of her dress—now dry but patterned with a web of fine creases. And when they left for the stadium, her hair was still matted, and was only put right when he pressed a comb into her hand at a stoplight.

Now she seemed herself, or what passed for herself these days, robotically removing buns from their packaging, and slipping the wieners one-by-one into the boiling water. Her work routines reassured him, but when Martha brushed by him, grazing his bare arm, he handed his change apron to Jennie. "Take over, please, we need more ice." He had to get away.

Once in the Chevy, James gripped the steering wheel with both hands. If only he and Jennie could be intimate again—like before John left town—his thoughts might not twist into a senseless spiral about his student, sending him on a diversionary goose chase for ice.

"Jennie better be pregnant," James swore as he turned into the New York Club lot.

At least there, the ice would be free.

• • •

On the ride into Rapid, Clarence was able to relax for the first time since he was jumped. He enjoyed hearing Otis's account of his season with the Base Flyers and looked forward to seeing a ball game with his old pal and sharing a couple of beers. Then he realized where they'd be buying those beers—Jennie's Stand. A charge shot through him, and he winced.

"Sorry, man. Bump in the road. You're really beat up, huh?"

"Only hurts when I breathe."

Otis laughed. "War hero. Maybe they'll give you a medal."

When they arrived at the Stadium, the lot was nearly full. "Let's grab a beer," Otis said as they passed through the gate and Clarence thought, "What the hell." Odds were that Jennie's husband would be there to remind him of his folly.

But James wasn't there—only Jennie, filling orders and making change, along with a plain-looking white girl darting from popper to cooktop. In his airman's garb with his cap pulled down, it wasn't until he moved up the line and was standing right before her that Jennie saw him, then heard him speak her name in a gravelly whisper. "Hello, Jennie."

Jennie gasped. Reaching up, she touched his bruised cheek with her fingertips. Otis's jaw dropped, as did Martha's. The girl had never seen the look of love in person—only at the picture show—but she knew it when she saw it now, and so did Otis, who figured his friend was in the worst kind of trouble a Black man could get into here in the West.

Nudging Clarence aside, Otis addressed the white woman in his most deferential tone. "Evenin', ma'am—two hot dogs and two beers, please."

Seeing Jennie fixed to the spot, Martha handed the wieners to the airman, then said with pointed emphasis, "*Mrs.* Moran, there's cold beer in the ice chest." Then, louder, "*Mister* Moran said he'd be back with more ice real soon."

Otis paid for the food as Clarence moved a few steps down the counter, his eyes never leaving Jennie's. "Let's go," Otis said, grabbing his friend's arm. But instead of heading toward the grandstand, he started for the exit, with Clarence trailing after him.

"You nuts, Williams? What the hell you doin'? You're a married man and she's a married woman, not to mention she's Snow White! This ain't New York or Chicago. Hell, this shit don't fly there, neither. Maybe Germany after the War, but not here, man, not here."

With his thumbnail, Clarence stripped the paper label from his beer bottle. "Cherry Mae left me. Took the kids and car and split back to Indianapolis."

"She leave because of her? Hit you with a frypan first? That how you got your face?"

"Nah, she don't know about her. Nothin' to know . . . haven't done nothin'."

Otis snorted. "Yeah? Ain't how it looked to *me*—white girl saw it, too. She her daughter?"

"She doesn't have a daughter. Just sons. One's the Chiefs' batboy."

"Well, she got a husband, don't she?"

"Yeah. I know him, too."

"So why you messin' with her, Clarence?"

"I don't know. Maybe she got under my skin."

Otis snorted. "Skin, huh? Sure a funny way to put it. That your flavor? You a vanilla man?"

Clarence shrugged, trying to remember if he'd told Otis about that time he went off with the soft, white whore. "I dunno, maybe, but this one's different."

"You can say that again. Shit, I'm takin' you to Coney Island. Get you a nice Indian girl. You gotta fuck that white witch outta you."

"I can't. I'm beat up real bad. Everything hurts."

"Your dick hurt, too?"

Clarence recalled the last time he'd worked it—out back behind the trailer, picturing Jennie's face, imagining more.

"Sorry, Otis, take me home. Comin' here was a bad idea."

But that was a lie. Because it turned out better even than he'd dreamed . . . the look in Jennie's eyes and the feel of her fingers on his face. It felt like a promise.

• • •

John didn't know where he was going. He had the night off from KOTA and longed to see Dinah, but she wouldn't be home from the Meller-drammer for hours.

He missed her—missed it. They'd only done it that once, but he couldn't wait to do it again, and not just for the thrill of it. In the back of his mind, he hoped she'd get pregnant, binding her to him and Rapid forever.

John slammed on the brakes as the light turned red, and a thick folder pitched onto the floor. It was full of notes about TV—technical stuff, along with his ideas for new shows, reserved for his and Bernie's big venture to break KOTA's chokehold on West River airwaves.

He checked his watch. This was as good a time as any to report to Bernie what he'd been learning on KOTA's dime. Entering the Club's lot, he was surprised to see his father's car by the entrance. Inside, Buck jerked his thumb towards the bar where James sat, highball in hand.

"Hi, Dad—whatcha doin' here?"

Chagrined, James patted the side of a metal washtub the bartender was filling from an ice chest under the counter. "Howdy, Son. You're just in time to give me a hand with the ice."

"Uh, well, I came by to talk to Bernie, but I'll help you put it in the car."

James gulped his bourbon and signaled for another. What was it with Bernie—always having first call on his sons?

John was taken aback. He'd never seen his dad drink anything stronger than beer.

The bartender turned to him. "Boss left for the ballpark before your father came in."

"OK, Dad, I'll help you get it to the Stand and look for Bernie there."

"Thanks *a lot,* John," he snarled. "And you might say 'hello' to your mother there, too."

John frowned. He and his mom hadn't spoken since he announced his engagement to Dinah. And while it pained him to see her wandering the house like a ghost, he believed it was up to her, not him, to cut the cord.

Then a worrisome thought hit him. "You left Mom at the Stand by herself?"

"No. I hired someone to help. Martha Muffling."

"Martha? No kidding. How's she doing?"

James's face reddened, recalling why he'd come to the Club in the first place. Finishing his second drink, he said, "She's fine. Let's get back. Thanks for the ice, Joe."

John cocked his head, intrigued by his father's flushed face and strained voice. "Wow! That's a helluva lot of ice. Sure you need all that?"

"Yes, John. Hot night, no one wants warm beer. And watch your mouth."

John's lips tightened. "Helluva" wasn't a curse, and it wasn't his dad's job to monitor his speech anymore. For an instant he regretted not buying the Robbinsdale place, so he'd not be under anyone's thumb. But if his capital got tied up in a house, he'd only be a salary man like his dad, not Bernie's partner. Looking at his dad now, he was sure he'd made the right choice.

Loading the ice into the Chevy, James and John drove caravan style to the Stadium where they were met by a disturbing scene—grumbling customers crowding the Stand, and a frazzled Martha Muffling, armpits stained, bangs hanging lank against her forehead. And no sign of Jennie. "Where's Mrs. Moran?" James barked.

Seeing John, Martha tucked a sweaty lock of hair behind her ear. "She went to the Ladies Room."

"John, take over the counter," James ordered. "Martha, go see if Mrs. Moran is all right."

John's eyes followed Martha as she raced to the restroom—a long, appraising look that aroused a jealous eruption in James's gut. "Stop it," he snapped, "We've got work to do."

John's eyes widened. What was it with his father? Was he drunk?

In the bathroom, Martha found Jennie staring at the mirror. Water dripped from her face and the faucet flowed unchecked. Martha was shocked. She'd seen it with her own eyes. Mrs. Moran and that Negro from the Base two-timing her favorite teacher. Pulling Jennie away from the sink, she cried, "Mrs. Moran! Your husband's back. He needs you."

"What the hell's going on here?" Leaning over the counter, Bernie seethed. "Came for a beer and found this poor girl manning the booth all alone. This how you run a business, James?"

Stung by Bernie's reproach, James bristled. "Everything's under control now, Bern."

Bernie turned to John. "And why aren't you at the TV station?"

James glowered at Bernie. Who the hell was *he* to tell his son where he should be?

John looked from Bernie to his dad and back again, then untied the change apron from around his waist and laid it on the counter. "Just helping with the ice," he said, as he ducked under the divider and joined Bernie on the other side.

...

For the rest of the night, James kept his back to the women—making change and speaking just to customers. Shaken by John's betrayal and his unbidden feelings toward his student, only the coins in his hands kept him from punching the wall.

Martha was the only one in the Stand listening to the game. Though Joel hadn't dropped by beforehand, she didn't lose heart. Darting back and forth, ferrying popcorn and hot dogs, she couldn't keep still, hearing her future mapped out by the flights and fancies of a small white ball in a game she scarcely understood.

The radio announcer seemed as involved in Joel's pitching as she was, as if he knew what was at stake for her. And while his comment about a dropped third strike mystified her, the roaring crowd told her that Joel had prevailed in the end. Bowing her head, she whispered, "He won," then waited for him to come and claim her. But there were customers needing a last beer, and the usual cleanup of pots and pans, and the unused buns to be wrapped and stored.

Martha checked her watch. The game was long over, but still no sign of Joel. Neither James, counting the night's take, nor Jennie, gazing at the deserted diamond, noticed when she ducked out, soda in one hand, popcorn in the other. Hurrying down the aisle to the Chiefs' dugout, she thought that Joel might have been detained while the coach reviewed the game, like after a debate match. Then, she spotted him leaving the stadium with the red-haired man he'd met the day before at the Stand.

Just then John rushed past on his way to the exit and Martha lurched to her left, spilling the popcorn as the Coke lapped over the lip of the cup, splashing her dress.

"John . . . " she called after him.

He stopped and looked at Martha in her cola-stained frock, damp hair plastered against her face. "Oh! Hi, Martha, didn't see you."

Martha's eyes filled with tears. "I don't have a ride home, John."

He looked away. Any minute now, Dinah would be getting back from work. "Sorry, Martha. I gotta be somewhere. Maybe my dad could take you"—a suggestion made on the fly as he dashed for the exit.

• • •

Looking back, James couldn't remember Martha asking for a ride, or Jennie stumbling from the Chevy to the house. Or Martha coming around to the front seat, taking Jennie's place next to him. He never turned on the radio or attempted small talk. He just drove, speeding into the cool dark night, like he'd done as a restless teen on the ranch, sneaking out for a wild ride in the pickup, while his father sat hunched over his ledger, trying to salvage their future from numbers that could never add up.

Martha cried softly into her hands. James didn't know how long she'd been crying when he reached over and patted her arm. Turning, she leaned against his shoulder and put her hand on his thigh. He glanced at the girl, and she gave him a look, stricken and pleading—one he'd only ever seen once before—from Jennie, after her sister was killed.

That was his last true thought as he pulled the car off the road, took her face in his hands, and kissed her. And when she moved her hand to his crotch, he didn't grab her wrist to stop her—until it was too late to stop himself.

Chapter Eighty-One

CLARENCE WAS READY FOR HER. Sponge-bathed and shaved and all aspirin'd up . . . with bed linens changed and the top sheet turned down, like he'd once seen in an old-fashioned hotel. Then he sat at the kitchen table in his freshly pressed khakis, bare-chested except for his rib corset, waiting for her gentle tap on the door.

Without a word, he took her by the hand, though he would have loved to gather her in his arms and carry her to the little bedroom at the back of the trailer. She couldn't stop shaking as he unbuttoned her dress, then unhooked her bra and pulled down her panties, both white as hankies, and ran his hands up her freckled arms, across her breasts, and through her red-tinged bush until she spasmed. Then he kissed her deep, pulled off his trousers and briefs, and lay down on the bed, motioning for her to mount him, not wanting to crush her or worsen his pain.

"Like this," was all he said, and she stared at him and his upright member, then climbed on the bed and straddled him, like she'd seen her tussling boys do when one gained the upper hand in a fight. Hoisting her hips, he eased her down, then bucked her up—once, twice, three times before stopping, so she could know the pace on this unmarked trail, until she clambered off and, crouching on all fours, echoed his command.

"Like this."

Stumbling to his feet, he pulled her hips to the bed's edge and slipped back inside her. She closed her eyes and saw it—her sister with her lover in the barn . . . and she clenched again until he was done. Then, she stuffed her fist into her groin and pounded to climax one last time.

From the bed, he watched as she dressed, her back to him, her eyes fixed on the floor. Neither spoke, and he didn't try to get her to, knowing there were no words for this and believing she would return.

• • •

Stripping off her clothes, Jennie stepped into the shower of a cabin court just outside of Rapid and watched the water trickle down her thighs, mixing with Clarence's first drippings—with more to follow, she knew, in the days to come. Then she wrapped herself in a towel and passed out on top of the bed cover.

By the time she arrived home, a chill had settled on the town. Through the dense hedgerows, fireflies signaled their intentions, while moths thrashed wildly against the porchlight.

Passing through the kitchen, she said nothing, and James, slumped behind a wall of beer bottles, didn't ask where she'd been. It was that way, too, as they passed their night, alone together, with only the walls as witness to the scenes playing out across their open eyes.

Chapter Eighty-Two

DINAH WOKE WITH A HEADACHE, but for a moment, couldn't figure out why. Then she remembered—her head bumping against the armrest of John's Belvedere when they parked in Dark Canyon. Again, it just happened, and it felt great at the time, though afterwards her thoughts had drifted elsewhere. "I'd love to do it on a beach," she mused, her fingers trolling the floorboards for her discarded panties. "Did you see the ocean when you were in California?"

California. John froze at the word. Would only a baby stop her? "*Shhhh*," he whispered, pulling her to him. "Tide's coming in. Gotta do this before you turn back into a mermaid."

For that bit of whimsy, she let him take another dip, his surging tide driving her backward, her head crashing against the armrest's rocky shelf.

Dinah opened a bottle of aspirin. She expected to feel terrific, but something felt terribly wrong. And not just her throbbing head. It was John, twice taking her without precaution. She thought she'd told him to take care of that. Surely, he didn't want a baby either. A baby would mess up everything—just like it had for her mother.

Dinah slumped at the vanity. Through the bedroom door, she heard Bernie and Joel sharing a hearty laugh in the kitchen. It infuriated her that she was the one holed up in her room while Joel was treated like Bernie's long-lost son. She could easily imagine Bernie shifting his love to the Jewish ballplayer if he ever learned she wasn't his own blood.

Stifling a sob, Dinah changed into the white shorts and polka dot halter top she'd worn when she and Joel picnicked at Sylvan Lake. Girded for battle, she squared her shoulders and marched into the kitchen.

"Morning, gorgeous!" Bernie took in his daughter's sassy outfit as did Joel, recalling that special time they'd shared in the Hills. He wished she had stayed in her room as she'd done most mornings since announcing her engagement to John.

Dinah poured herself a glass of juice. "What were you two laughing about?"

Bernie smiled. "I was just saying how funny it was that a boy from Brooklyn had to come out to South Dakota to be seen by a Dodger Scout."

For the first time, she looked directly at Joel. "That's like a talent scout, right?"

"Pretty much—yes."

"Did you get the job?"

"Not yet."

"You mean, no?"

"I mean, not yet. You get your call from the Mouse Club—yet? How's that song go. 'California, here I come' . . . and yet, you're still here." He pushed back from the table. It would serve her right to marry Moran and spend the rest of her days raising a passel of brats in the boondocks. "Gotta go. Bus to catch. Bon voyage, Annette. Give my regards to Mickey!"

Dinah bolted from the room, leaving Bernie to wonder why these charged-up young thoroughbreds weren't the ones getting hitched instead of her and the plow horse next door.

• • •

"You're here, so I guess you're not the Bums' latest bonus baby."

On the bus to Valentine, Stockman's jibe caught Joel by surprise. He thought he'd pitched well for the Scout—at least after a nervous first inning when he hit a batter, walked the next, and gave up a windblown homer that barely cleared the close fence in right. After that, he settled down and in the middle innings, he was overpowering, retiring nine in a row, six on strikeouts.

Of course, it helped to know that Stockman wasn't going to pull him at first falter. Bernie had taken care of that beforehand. "Gave Stockman his marching orders," he assured Joel.

Before the game, Quarles offered his sage advice: "With the scout here, we're goin' with the heat—fastballs, top of the zone. Swings are slower up there. Can't catch up. Stay away from the low pitches, Joely. They get crushed 'cause gravity speeds the bat—like when you swing the ax down to fell a tree. Hear you got one growing in Brooklyn."

And for seven innings, Joel dominated—his ten strikeouts evidence of a pitcher with a bright future. Then, in the eighth he walked two, and his teammates let him down in the field, with Casey booting a double-play grounder and Hacker misjudging a soft liner, giving the Lake Sox a 5-4 lead.

But in the bottom of the inning, the Chiefs rallied, as Hoades smoked the first pitch he saw over the scoreboard in right, and Hacker, after apologizing for his earlier miscue in the field, one-handed a home run to give the Chiefs a 6-5 advantage.

In the ninth, Joel again felt strong and steady, retiring the Sox one-two-three while recording his eleventh and twelfth strikeouts. He hoped the Scout would remember how he'd overcome a bout of wildness, a feather in the cap for a young fireballer like himself. A lot like Sandy Koufax, he thought, another Brooklyn southpaw with big potential but erratic control.

Still, Stockman was right. He'd not gotten an offer, though the Scout sounded encouraging—said he'd seen some things he liked, and would keep an eye on him, which Joel hoped wasn't just a nice way of saying, *Don't call us, we'll call you*, or a sop to Bernie for his hospitality at the Club the night before.

Now, on the bus, hearing his teammates' snickers, he wondered why Coach went out of his way to put him in his place after he'd won a critical game, keeping the Chiefs within spitting distance of the first-place Kernels. Maybe he resented Bernie telling him who to pitch.

"I'm just holding out for a bigger bonus," Joel finally quipped in response to Stockman's crack about Bonus Babies. Quarles snorted his approval as Hoades cracked, "Spoken like a true Jew." Swallowing his pride, Joel ignored the slur, though he would have loved to deck the bastard. Still, he couldn't risk hurting his hands—critical tools of the trade for a pitcher or a surgeon . . . whichever path he ended up taking.

• • •

"Girls *like* that?" Billy exclaimed from the back of the bus. As soon as Billy boarded, he gave Joel the cold shoulder, moving to the rear, across from Hoades and Kibbee, companions Joel knew his parents would never approve of. But he wouldn't risk a scene by making Billy move up front—not when the boy hadn't said a word to him since Yankton.

At least, Fred hailed him with a smile. "Ya did good, Freako. Showed real grit out there. Struck out a dozen and only gave up four hits."

Joel appreciated that he didn't mention the eight walks. "Thanks, Fred. It went all right."

"Better'n all right. So, what'd you do to celebrate?"

Like a cattle prod, the word 'celebrate' triggered a forgotten promise. "Oh, hell. Martha!"

"Martha? Name's kinda plain, but lots of fun things come in plain brown wrappers." Fred chortled, recalling how his latest girlie magazine had arrived in the mail.

Joel heard Billy giggle again. Tilting his head, he strained to hear what Kibbee was saying, with Billy all ears on this trip back to Valentine and to Ginny, his young lady love.

"Ever' year, I'm gittin' more pussy 'cause I got a kinda baby face, so the younger girls don't think I'm too old and the older gals—housewives—are goin' for me, too, now. I'm haulin' down amazin' 'mounts of ass, my friend—at home and on the road," Kibbee bragged.

Joel shook his head. This had to be more than any young boy could handle.

"No details, New York? 'Bout Martha in the plain brown wrapper?" Fred persisted.

"Sorry, Fred. Nothing to tell," Joel said as raucous laughter burst from the back of the bus. Fred jerked his thumb in that direction. "Guess I'll have to lasso Quarles or Kibb for my jollies."

Joel slumped in his seat. Even those he considered friends seemed to tire of him. Yesterday, he'd felt so hopeful—confident he'd ride the small, white orb across this broad land. Now his big break was behind him, and nothing had changed—no Dinah, no real friends on the team, and with only a dubious future in baseball. And he'd blown his chance with Martha. He looked back at Hacker and Schmid playing gin rummy and laughing as if they didn't have a care in the world. Didn't they realize that the Scout had passed on them, too? Though both men still had a season of college ball ahead of them, while he only had a few weeks left in Dakota to show his stuff . . . if any other scouts showed up to see it.

Again, he heard Billy exclaim "Wow!" He closed his eyes and sighed. Nothing he could do. Sooner or later the kid would learn it all. Who was he to say that later was better?

In Valentine, Billy was first off the bus and first through the gates of Hearts Field. But in less than a minute his heart was broken by the sight of the Hearts' second baseman planting a kiss on the lips of Ginny, the young concessionaire. Joel—expecting to witness a happy reunion—saw it all but wasn't quick enough to intercept the boy racing back to the exit.

When Kibbee called out, "Where's the fire, kid?" Joel hesitated, unsure if he should follow. He couldn't imagine Billy landing in real trouble. He wouldn't get drunk, like a grown man might, or fall into a river. The terrain was as dry as a bone. He'd likely just end up brooding.

Waiting until the Hearts' second baseman left, Joel approached Ginny. Scooping popcorn, she reminded him of Martha—though this saucy girl couldn't be more different, decked out in tight shorts, sleeveless knit shell, and cowboy boots. He imagined suitors buzzing around her all summer—boys, men, ballplayers—anyone with a pair of eyes and a working dick.

"A pretty girl is like a melody everyone wants to hum," he improvised. Maybe he'd say that to Billy, along with the advice that if you mine the Hope Diamond, you'd better be willing to spend your life guarding it. It was something he told himself now to feel better about losing Dinah.

"Hi there, Ginny. Remember me?"

"'Course I remember you." Ginny craned her neck in both directions. "Where's Billy?"

Joel couldn't believe the girl's nerve. "Why? From what I saw, you weren't exactly waiting for him with open arms."

Ginny's eyes flashed. "Waiting? Now let me see. Schedule says you come down here three times a summer. Pretty exciting for me, now, ain't it?"

Joel imagined that in a tiny town like Valentine, summer might feel interminable, but he wasn't going to let Ginny off that easy. "Does your mother know you're seeing a college man?"

Ginny shrugged. "Don't bother Momma none. It's what she likes best about him. Says he has prospects."

Joel had to smile—echoes of a Jewish mother, here in the heartland.

Spotting the shift in Joel's expression, Ginny relaxed. "Sure hope Billy stops by."

"Well . . . I'll tell him. But I wouldn't count on it. He saw you two smooching."

Ginny sucked her lower lip between her teeth. "He's a freshman at Chadron State. It's close by." Joel could tell that it wasn't just Ginny's mother who was weighing her prospects.

"That's convenient," Joel conceded.

Later, that night in the motel, he told Billy that Ginny said "hi."

"She can go to hell," Billy spat, and Joel recognized which track the boy had taken after bolting from the ballpark. The same one he was taking with Dinah.

Chapter Eighty-Three

JAMES COULDN'T BELIEVE HIS EYES. Martha Muffling waiting in front of the concession stand as if nothing had happened. No longer wearing lipstick or a dress that flattered, she'd reverted to the shapeless skirt and blouse she wore her first day at the Stand. For that, James was grateful, though it wasn't enough to stem the flood of emotions released at the sight of her.

For three days, the Chiefs had been on the road, and she'd haunted his every thought.

In the Chevy, after his shameful act, he couldn't utter a word and the girl was silent as well. Dropping her at the ranch gate, he'd sped away, stopping at the first open establishment he saw, a tavern south of town. Head spinning, he lurched inside a bathroom stall and vomited bourbon along with the bile his actions had naturally produced.

Slumping against the side of the stall, he broke into a cold sweat. What Martha had done was her idea, not his, but did it matter? He'd kissed her first, and while he never expected what happened next—especially from a plain, shy girl like Martha—he went along. What if she had scooted back against the car door and hiked up her skirt? Could he have stopped himself then? He shuddered—the ruination of his marriage, his career, his reputation—everything that knocking up a student would mean flashed before him.

And yet, the memory of her hand down there aroused him still.

He slammed his fist against the door of the roadhouse stall. What kind of man was he? A teacher and a father who'd almost had a daughter of his own.

That night, and every night after, he hardly slept. He wanted to call Martha to apologize, but was afraid her stepfather would pick up or listen in. A man like that might come gunning for him. And who could blame him? That's what he'd do if Martha were *his* daughter.

Now all he could trust himself to say was, "Hello, Martha."

"Hello, Mr. Moran . . . Mrs. Moran," Martha muttered as she ducked under the counter.

James stared across the counter at the empty stands. He couldn't wait for the crowds to arrive and take his mind off her, but his first customer was the one person who offered no relief—Joel—whose broken promise had led him to that dark country road with Martha.

Glaring at the ballplayer, he saw that Joel was holding a bouquet of flowers at his side. Instantly, James knew how it would go. Joel would apologize, and Martha would forgive him, and they'd share a malted and a kiss and likely more.

His head pounded. He knew he should be happy for the girl, or at least relieved, but all he felt was empty. They, too, had shared a kiss, and while also sinful, it felt pure in the moment, and he couldn't bear to think of it any other way. "What can I get you?" he growled at Joel.

Perplexed by James's harsh tone, Joel recalled that he was the one who'd introduced him to Martha, praising her like a proud papa. He pictured Mr. Moran and the girl waiting for him to collect her at the Stand. He hoped he could make it up to them. Stretching his arm across the counter, he offered Martha the bouquet. "Miss Martha, if you can forgive me, I'd like to take you for a soda after the game. And if Mr. Moran would lend me his car, I'll drive you home, too."

James fixed his eyes on Martha, but she was staring past him to the ballplayer. When she held out her hand for the flowers, he saw the light of hope return to the girl's eyes. Then he turned to look at Jennie, who stood gazing into the pot of boiling water as if it held the secret to all life's mysteries. That's when he knew he had struck bottom.

• • •

It had all started with a kiss after a lovely date sharing fried chicken and Cokes at the Daisy Dell and chatting for an hour—Joel about college and New York, and Martha, in response to his playful questioning, about growing up on a ranch. "Sure, I can ride a horse."

"But can you ride a subway? That takes skill, too," he teased.

Then, she excused herself, and when she returned from the ladies' room, her hair was freshly brushed and her lips shiny with pink gloss, which he took as a sign that she'd made up her mind about him, and he'd get a chance to see what a nice girl in South Dakota had to offer.

Second base, he discovered--or at least what his friend Morrie once told him was second base. All in the front seat of Mr. Moran's Chevy on a dark country road serenaded by a chorus of crickets.

Dropping Martha at the ranch house gate, he kissed her again and asked if he could see her the next night. "Yes," she answered, leaning in to kiss him one last time.

At home on Evergreen Street, James saw the headlights as soon as the Chevy turned up the driveway. Handing over the keys, Joel declared, "What a great girl," because it was true, and he believed it was what her patron wanted to hear. But if the light had been better and he'd seen James's stricken face, he might have realized it was not.

The next morning, James was asleep when John took the call and jotted down the message. "*Martha's mother called. She broke her arm and can't work anymore.*"

James read the note three times. And suddenly he knew. It was the stepfather. The other night, on the ride home from Sioux Park, the man had been stone-faced and silent, rebuffing all attempts at conversation, ignoring even his praise of Martha's academic prowess and work ethic. Then, as soon as James exited the pickup, he snapped his fingers and Martha scrambled over the tailgate to take James's place in the front seat. Like a trained bird dog.

Heart racing, James strode to the garage. Wedging an arm between the wall and Jennie's garden cabinet, he freed his shotgun, wrapped it in a towel, and stuffed it in the trunk of the Chevy.

He was ready, but for what he wasn't exactly sure.

• • •

Joel slept better than he had in a month. Finally, things were working out with a sweet, wholesome girl. And while he wasn't smitten, as with Dinah, dating Martha seemed less fraught.

He might even learn to ride a horse this summer, among other things.

With that thought, he reached into his duffel bag to get a condom for his wallet.

Then it clicked. Martha, like Dinah, was still in high school. Likely just fifteen or sixteen.

Joel grimaced. What was the matter with him? There were lots of girls his age in Rapid. He'd see them stationed on the aisles near the dugout where they could flirt with the players as they passed. So how did he end up with two high school girls? Was he some kind of pervert?

In his defense, he hadn't sought them out. Circumstance had thrown him together with Dinah, a girl whose father encouraged his interest and mother lectured him about condoms.

And Mr. Moran had sung the praises of his plain, shy student.

Still, he felt uneasy. Martha's parents—likely God-fearing farm folk—might not feel the same way about them dating. Worse yet, if she were a minor in the eyes of the law, he could be charged with a crime if they went any further. Maybe even for what they'd already done.

Joel chucked the condom back into the duffel. He had to find out the age of consent here in Dakota and do it without raising suspicion.

• • •

For days, Clarence waited for Jennie to return. Worried that he might miss her, he never left the trailer before dark. After three days he became frantic. Had her husband found them out? Surely, he would smell the stink of another man on his Cherry Mae. Still, what white man would ever think his wife could have taken up with a Black man? And wouldn't Mr. Moran have already come after him if he suspected?

Maybe she'd fallen ill or had an accident? His chest tightened at the thought.

He had to be sure she was all right—then convince her to come back to him. But how could he just walk up to her front door and ring the bell? Maybe he could pretend to visit Joel, who lived next door with the Rosens. Then, he recalled how Bernie had stared at him and Jennie in the parking lot at the tryouts, as if he knew what was going to happen even before they did.

He would have to call her. Go to Rapid and find a phone book and a place to meet where no one would spot them. Stepping outside, he pictured Jennie coming through the grove of cottonwoods into his arms. It was a wild, desperate thing they'd had together. Different from any sex he'd ever had before. He couldn't imagine not doing it again. Could she?

With that, he walked to the road and put out his thumb. It took a half hour before a truck from the PX stopped for him. The driver, a Korean War vet, drove him into the city, and dropped him in front of the library.

• • •

Climbing the steps of the library, Joel felt a shock of recognition. Despite the passersby in cowboy boots and hats, it was like entering the Brownsville branch of the New York Public Library, where he and Rivkah spent hours holding hands beneath the long oak tables, before sneaking off for a chaste kiss between sheltering rows of books.

Joel drew a breath of dry Dakota air, to reset his compass. The irony was not lost on him—thinking of faithful Rivkah while researching the legality of her summer stand-in.

Approaching the circulation desk, he noted the librarian's double-take. Given the favored reading material of his teammates—girlie magazines and the like—he supposed he might be the first ballplayer to cross her threshold. "Excuse me, ma'am—is there a section with law books?"

Miss Moss pointed to the reference section. "We have a few. What are you researching?"

Then he spotted Clarence, seated at the back of the room staring straight ahead, showing no sign of seeing him.

"Excuse me." Grinning broadly, Joel made straight for his friend. "What the heck you doin' here, Clare? You with your family?"

Clarence flinched. Surprised by Joel, he'd not thought of Cherry Mae or his kids since his friend Otis scolded him in the stadium parking lot. His family hardly existed in his new world—now shrunk to the boundaries of his trailer and those few moments Jennie had shared his bed.

"Yeah. They 'sposed to meet me here." Clarence seemed jumpy, and his voice oddly flat as his eyes darted to the entrance.

Joel placed his hand lightly on Clarence's shoulder. "How've you been, Clarence? Enjoying your time off with the kids?"

Clarence shrugged, and Joel was again surprised by his friend's reticence. He hadn't seen him this aloof since the first time they met—on the bus to Pierre.

"We miss you, man. Can't wait to get you back behind the plate."

"Thanks," Clarence muttered, hardly registering Joel's praise. Joel let his hand drop, as a disturbing thought dawned on him. What if Clarence, like Billy, blamed *him* for what happened in Yankton—that his quest for sex had ruined the man's summer, maybe even his health?

He felt hollow, worse than he had after losing Dinah to John Moran. Clarence was more than just his favorite battery mate. He was his one true friend in Rapid and on the team. "Clare, I hope that . . . "

In a single jolt, Clarence sprang from his seat, sending the heavy chair toppling backwards to the floor. Startled, Joel followed his friend's gaze to the library entrance in time to see a woman—or, at least, her slender white legs and the hem of her blue dress—as she darted back through the doorway toward the stairs.

Joel glanced at the librarian, who stood staring at the fleeing figure. He could practically hear her clucks of disapproval from across the hushed room. Turning, he looked at Clarence as a smile broke across the catcher's battered face.

Jennie had come.

Chapter Eighty-Four

BILLY STARED BLANKLY AT THE *Journal* Sports Page. Normally he enjoyed reading accounts of the Chiefs' games, but today all he could think of was Ginny Parker kissing the Hearts' second baseman at the concession stand.

Glancing out the window, he spotted Joel behind the wheel of Bernie's Cadillac. In Valentine, Joel had told him that he'd passed his driver's test—one of several stabs at conversation that Billy ignored. And not just because Joel had deserted him in Yankton. In truth, that grudge was fading, pushed aside by something even more hurtful—Joel witnessing the pretty concessionaire's betrayal. Now every time Billy looked at him, he felt his heartache and shame all over again.

If only some other Chief could look after him and take his mind off the girl. Those guys always seemed to have fun, playing cards, and doing crazy things. Like the time Hacker ripped the sleeves off his shirt, pumped his biceps, and bragged, "These guns too damn big for holsters."

Smiling at that memory, he could finally turn to the box score of his Braves, now in first place in the National League. Then the phone rang in the kitchen. Hardly anyone ever called their house. What if it was an emergency—like his mom in the hospital again? But it was a man talking in a serious, grown-up voice. "May I speak to Billy Moran?"

Billy tensed, reminded of Yankton and the sheriff who'd questioned him after he and Clarence were attacked. His voiced cracked. "Who are you?"

"Jack Cannon, Features Editor for the *Journal*. I'd like to interview you for a story."

Billy's cry was a mixture of relief and exhilaration. "Wow!"

"Of course, we'll need to take a picture of you in your batboy uniform. I'll drop by the dugout after the game tonight. OK?"

"Yes, sir!" Whooping, he ran to his room to change into his uniform, then to the bathroom to practice his smile in the mirror. Rolling up his sleeves, he flexed his arms. "Too damn big for holsters," he crowed, knowing that the whole town would see him in the *Journal*.

Maybe Ginny of Valentine, too.

• • •

Joel was feeling cocky. After 'riding the pine' in Valentine and Winner, he'd been given the start against the Pierre Cowboys and made the most of it, pitching a rare Sioux Park shutout. If only the Scout had been there to see *this* performance, he thought—one which Stockman praised without his usual sarcasm, adding that he'd like to work with him on his pickoff move.

Surprised, he wondered what might account for Stockman's change in attitude. Could the Scout have said something that made Coach see him in a different light? Until now, Stockman only made time for Hacker and Schmid, the team's two top prospects. Could his newfound interest mean that he was a prospect now, too?

"Nice job, Joely." Quarles clapped him on the shoulder. "You back with Rosen's foxy daughter? You pitched with finesse out there, like a man gettin' some."

"Yeah, but this time, not from the boss's daughter."

"Well, whoever she is, it's working."

Joel smiled. Sex as the magic bullet. He'd subscribed to that notion himself after he pitched his one-hitter. Now he saw that his newfound craftiness owed more to studying Quarles and the Chiefs' other veteran southpaw, Dave Wiegand.

Though he had to admit that gettin' some was a whole lot better than getting none.

Bounding up the dugout stairs, he caught sight of Billy, head cocked to the side, grinning from ear to ear for a photographer.

Hoping to thaw the ice, Joel waited for Billy to finish, then asked what was going on.

Forgetting himself, Billy crowed, "They're writing a story about me!"

"That's great, Bill. What about?"

Billy turned his head and spat on the ground. "I'm the batboy," and Joel could swear he heard the boy mutter "dummy" under his breath.

"I mean what did the reporter ask you?"

Billy shrugged. "I dunno."

"Come on, Bill. I'd like to know."

Reluctantly, Billy replied. He'd been hoping that one of the other Chiefs would take notice, but no one had. Just Joel. "They asked me my most favorite thing."

"Whadya say?"

"Corn Palace."

"Yeah, that was terrific. What else?"

"What was the worst."

Joel laughed. "I bet I know. A bus full of chili farts? Right?"

Billy fixed Joel with a squint-eyed stare, then turned away.

Joel swallowed hard. The boy could really hold a grudge, but he wouldn't let it ruin his mood. He'd had a great game and Stockman now seemed to be in his corner. Even his chance meeting at the library with Clarence had turned congenial. In the end, they'd chatted so long he never got around to researching his question about Martha.

Heading for the Stand, he hoped James would let him borrow the Chevy again. He still didn't know if what had happened with Martha was legal, though they'd had a proper date first—dinner, conversation, and a few modest kisses. Perhaps he needed to meet her parents—make sure they were okay with her dating a twenty-one-year-old.

"Hello, Mr. Moran, Mrs. Moran. Is Martha around?"

James grabbed the counter and recited the line he'd practiced for this exact moment.

"Sorry, Joel. She broke her arm and won't be working here anymore."

"Oh gosh! Really? What happened?"

"I don't know. Her mother called and left a message with John."

"I'd like to go see her tomorrow if I might. Could I borrow the car again?"

James fingered the coins in his change apron. He hadn't anticipated this request. "They're country people, Joel. She has chores during the day."

"She can do chores with a broken arm?"

"There's always something to do on a ranch."

"Maybe I can help out."

James snorted. "Ever milk a cow? Pitch hay? Round up cattle? Sorry, son. You'd probably be in the way. And don't you have a game tomorrow?"

"Yes, but they won't use me again so soon. I could see her in the morning."

James frowned. A throbbing pain pulsed his temples. Why couldn't the young man just drop it? "This is no time for visitors."

Joel was plumb out of arguments, and while he wasn't sure why Mr. Moran was so discouraging, he believed the schoolteacher must have Martha's best interests at heart.

"I'll just call her, then. Do you have her phone number?"

"At home. Listen, son, there's no rush. She's with her family. She's not going anywhere."

"OK, sir. I'll drop by tomorrow for her number." Joel picked up his duffel and headed for the exit. He'd won an important start, but it was hard to celebrate knowing that Martha was hurt and that their promising new relationship was likely sidelined. Maybe for good.

Chapter Eighty-Five

DR. LATHAM READ JENNIE MORAN'S lab report and frowned. Not because Jennie was pregnant—which she was—but because the results had sat on his desk unread for far too long.

It wasn't like him to slip up this way, though he'd been distracted—called out of town for the difficult birth of his first grandchild in Denver. And James Moran had never contacted him for the results. Still, he couldn't completely excuse his oversight.

Prepared to apologize, he called James but quickly realized there was no need, when his "Thank you, Doctor!" was so exultant it could have launched a spaceship to the moon.

Hanging up the phone, James let out a whoop, then bowed his head in grateful prayer. God had not forsaken him. A baby was what he'd most hoped for, the one thing that would make Jennie whole and right the family ship.

Everything was changing and he needed a plan. She'd have to stop teaching—that was the pregnancy policy at all schools. And no more working at the ballpark—standing for hours over a steaming kettle. He shuddered to think what she might do if she miscarried again. She'd have to stay home, and he'd have to find a way to make up for her lost salary.

Grabbing a pad and pencil, he drew up a list of family expenses—present and future—all the things they'd have to get for the new baby—and all they'd have to give up.

Immersed in his calculations, he failed to register the knock on the door. "Anyone home?"

It was Joel in his Chiefs uniform, appearing like an apparition through the screen door.

Annoyed, James muttered, "It's open," before resuming his reckonings.

"Hello, Mr. Moran. I came for Martha's phone number. Did you speak to her today?"

James turned pale. He'd forgotten about Martha. The news about the baby had swept all thoughts of her from his mind. "No," he said flatly. "I'll get it." He grabbed a shoebox from the counter. Inside was the fateful letter she'd delivered weeks before. His hands began to shake. He'd only been trying to help a plain, lovelorn girl earn some money and lend Jennie a hand. Where had his good intentions landed him? On that country road to hell.

Head pounding, he scribbled Martha's phone number at the bottom of his budget. For a moment he studied the figures he'd compiled—the accounting of his family's future, and below it, the number of the girl who could ruin it all just by opening her mouth. "God help me," he swore as he ripped her number from the page and thrust it at Joel. "Take it," he growled.

Joel flinched. First cold and now angry. Did Mr. Moran think he was merely trifling with the girl? "Thank you, sir. I really do care about Martha's well-being."

James took one look at Joel's earnest face, and it came to him—a young, single man with no wife, family, or concerns beyond his next ball game. The pitcher could relieve him—be the hero and rescue the girl. "I'm sorry, son. You should phone her. She'll appreciate that."

Then he said he had a business call to make, so Joel wouldn't ask to use his phone.

After he left, James dialed a retired policeman he knew, and hired him to take Martha's place in the Stand. Striding to the garage, he took the shotgun from the trunk of the Chevy and restored it to its hiding place behind Jennie's garden cabinet.

He'd wipe Martha from his mind, along with those wild nights he'd had with Jennie—the stuff of dreams and the root of nightmares. And the memory of that kiss on the country road, too.

Now, all that mattered was the baby.

...

Joel stood in the Rosen kitchen and dialed the number Mr. Moran had given him.

"Who's this?" A man with a raspy voice picked up on the fourth ring.

Joel drew a deep breath. "I'm Joel Meznik, a friend of Martha's. I heard she broke her arm. I wanted to see how she's doing."

There was a long silence on the other end—then words that brought Joel up short.

"Yer that Jew pitcher from New York. Ain't ya twenty-one? Girl's just sixteen."

Joel stared at the receiver as the line cut out, his wishes for Martha's speedy recovery conveyed to a deadly silence. A jarring buzz, like a trapped hornet, blared in his ear.

A signal, loud and clear, that he must cut out, too.

• • •

James drove to the store and bought two thick rib eyes, potatoes for mashing, and a quart of strawberry ice cream, Jennie's favorite in her last pregnancy. Then he waited to give her the good news. But hours passed before she pulled into the driveway. Frantic and famished, he had to remind himself that her behavior was no longer wholly within her control. And who was he to criticize when he'd been so reckless himself? Still, when she walked through the door, he couldn't stop his harangue. "Where have you been? I've been waiting dinner for hours."

Without a word Jennie started for the living room. She'd not been anywhere to speak of. Just alone in the Hills sorting through those jumbled moments in Clarence's trailer—scenes circling in her mind like slides in a view-master. Rapture, release, renewal. Words she'd never known for feelings she'd never had.

Now overshadowed by fear—fear that the ballplayer might tell what he'd seen at the library.

It wasn't what she wanted to be left with, but the one thing she knew she could never abide was the shame she would suffer if Bernie Rosen learned he'd been right about her all along.

James placed a gentle hand on his wife's arm. "Please come back to the kitchen, Jen. I have something to tell you. I planned a nice dinner. It's not too late. We can still make it."

Later, he kicked himself for not sitting her down for the news.

But this time, at least, he caught her before she hit the floor.

Chapter Eighty-Six

POSTMARKED INDIANAPOLIS, CHERRY MAE'S letter lay unopened for a week. For three days after its arrival, Clarence telephoned the Moran house from a pay phone at the Base. Once, Billy picked up, and once, James. Both times Clarence hung up. The other time the phone just rang and rang. "Come on, Jennie—pick up, pick up," he whispered—just as he had when he'd called her to meet him at the library. Then he took his pal Otis's advice to "fuck that witch outta ya," bedding a raven-haired whore at the Coney Island Club until Jennie's ghost had fled.

The next afternoon he jogged to the base field and laced up his cleats. Finally, his body was healing—ribs knitting, scabs sloughing, pooled blood receding like floodwaters after a storm.

Running, throwing, swinging—blood pumping through his whole body, not just the wounds. Sodden with sweat as when a fever breaks, he returned to the trailer. Only then did he open the letter from his wife. It was written in perfect Palmer Method cursive, a talent that once won her a blue ribbon in her youth. He smiled, recalling her showing the prize to the children when they fussed about practicing their penmanship.

Dear Clarence,

I know you be mad at me for taking the money and car. I guess thats why you don't call or write, but I couldn't take Dakota no more.

We're staying at Daddy's. I got a job at the library on Meridian Street. Just two days a week and Violet likes to come with me. We take the bus.

Clarence stopped reading, his eyes stuck on the word 'library'. Not because he'd been to that library in Indianapolis, or that Cherry Mae had found work in one, but because he couldn't see that word anymore, without thinking of Jennie.

Juniors playing baseball at Flanner House. Remember Paul Terry from church? He's the coach.

Clarence threw the letter on the floor. Who was this man making time with his boy and, maybe, his woman, too? Then he laughed out loud. Maybe there was a Paul Terry or maybe there wasn't, but he had to hand it to Cherry Mae for the ploy. He picked up the letter and read on.

We not coming back but we miss you. Maybe you can get a transfer back home.

Your loving wife Cherry Mae

Grabbing a coloring book from the table, he ripped a blank page from the back.

My dear sweet Cherry.

I already put in for a transfer. I miss you too and the kids so much it hurts. I'll be home soon. Just hold on a little longer okay? And you tell that Paul Terry I'm coming back to coach my boy myself.

Reviewing what he'd written, he couldn't bring himself to mention her new job at the library. He hoped in time a scab would form and shield that tender wound. Tomorrow he'd post the letter and again put in for a transfer. Then, he'd call Coach Stockman. He might not be healed enough to catch, but the Chiefs could use an outfielder, and another big bat. His.

Chapter Eighty-Seven

THE HOUR WAS LATE, and the bus quiet, but Guy couldn't sleep. The road trip to Watertown had put him in a funk. The Chiefs had enjoyed first place for only a day, winning the first game of the series, then losing the second to the Lake Sox's towering moundsman, Dick Radatz.

Adding insult to injury, Clyde Kibbee turned his ankle jumping off the dock at Lake Kempeska and would be lost to the Chiefs for a good long while. More serious still, Hacker badly misjudged a fly ball, letting in two runs. This, in the presence of Red, the vaunted Dodger Scout.

"Didn't think much of 'im," Red said afterwards. "Can't judge a fly ball, can't hit the curve, and runs like a Mack truck backing uphill."

Guy wasn't surprised by the Scout's remark about Frank's speed. As a longtime Dodger farmhand, he knew it was practically Gospel—the first and greatest Commandment of "The Dodger Way"—that "Thou shalt be fleet of foot." Branch Rickey had etched it in stone, and his scouts fanned out across the country seeking prospects who could run. It was no accident that Jackie Robinson, Rickey's greatest protégé, was once a college track star.

Guy gazed upon the sleeping giant two rows back. If only Red had seen Frank on a good day—his glorious throwing arm and the power to smite a baseball a country mile.

For it was Guy's dream—or scheme—to steer big Frank to Brooklyn, then claim as his reward a coach's job on one of the Dodgers' fourteen minor league teams—like the Dodgers' Class "C" team in Reno, which Red mentioned might have an opening. It only seemed his due as a good soldier on the Dodger chain gang for almost a decade and now as a proven manager of young players on the Chiefs. Yes, that was the plan—to ride Hacker's coattails to Reno and beyond.

Then Guy had a troubling thought. Another club might be a better fit for Hacker. The other day a Red Sox Scout saw Hack and quipped, "Could be a spot in Bean Town for your Bunyan."

And it was true. Fenway Park in Boston with its close left field wall offered Frank, a right-handed pull-hitter, a most inviting home run target, much better than the Dodgers' Ebbetts Field. Hell, Hack might slug fifty homers a year for the Red Sox. And Fenway had only a small left field for him to cover. By the time he worked his way up through the

Red Sox minors, he'd be ready to take over in left field for Boston's aging, slow-footed slugger, Ted Williams, now thirty-eight.

Still, there was no comparing the two organizations. The Dodgers regularly contended for the pennant—while the Red Sox seemed perpetually stuck in fourth place behind the Yankees, Indians, and White Sox. Boston stunk, and Guy knew it had nothing to do with their sale of the Babe to the Yanks way back when. It was their stubborn refusal to sign talented Negro players to boost a team's pennant prospects. Here, in 1957, only the Bean Town Sox and the Motor City Tigers fielded all-white squads.

Guy felt a twinge of self-rebuke. He, too, had resisted signing a Negro.

But should he tell Frank he'd likely move up faster in Boston than with the Dodgers because he'd not have to compete with Negroes? After taking a back seat to the talented Campanella all those years, he could speak with bitter authority about that.

Guy flicked his cigarette to the bus floor and snuffed it out with his toe. He was Hacker's coach, not his career counselor. And Frank, being young, would probably reject his advice anyway, thinking that nothing could hold him back, just as he believed at that age.

So, he'd stick with the original plan. Steer Hack to the Dodgers, reap the Reno job as a reward, and maybe, just maybe, lure Lana away from that sonovabitch husband of hers!

• • •

Fred slammed on the brakes, jarring the Chiefs from their sleep.

"What the hell, Fred. You aimin' to kill us?"

"Sorry, Boss. Cattle sleepin' on the road."

Stockman picked his way to the front of the bus. Dark, almost black cows lay like mud buttes on the blacktop, blocking both lanes. With deep ditches on both sides, there was simply no getting around the bovines.

"Honk the horn," Stockman ordered.

Fred scoffed. "Horns don't work for cows. Deer, yes—they're skittish—not cows."

"Honk anyway."

Fred hit the horn in a long blast. The cows turned their heads but didn't move.

"Honk again," Stockman growled.

Fred delivered a second blast, again with no effect. "Guess we gotta herd 'em off."

"In the movies a kid with a stick does that," Joel said with a chuckle.

"Hell, we got sticks," Quarles said. "Everybody grab a bat."

"Ya don't wanna rile 'em," Fred warned. "Some got horns. Anybody got a candy bar? They like sugar." Joel rooted through his duffel and came up with a Hershey Bar.

"Great, Freako. We'll need four herders. Every herder gets a piece."

"I'll do it," Billy volunteered.

"Count me in," Joel said, thinking he'd better stick close to Billy, just in case.

"No pitchers or catchers," Stockman ordered. "Can't have some cow biting off a finger."

"Or a thumb," came a yell from the back of the bus, followed by chortles.

"What about 'Three-finger Brown,'" Q protested. "Rode three digits to the Hall of Fame."

"He had to heal up first . . . " Stockman added " . . . we ain't got time for that."

"You would know, boss."

Joel broke the candy bar into equal pieces, and Billy, Casey, Hacker, and Paskiewicz, followed by the other Chiefs, trooped down the steps for a midnight roundup. Fred stayed behind, waiting for the all-clear, while Quarles warbled, *I'm an old cowhand from the Rio Grande.*

"Here, Bessie, here, Bessie," Hacker cried, extending his long arm under the snout of the nearest bovine—then quickly snatched it away when the cow stuck out a dark, searching tongue, spotlit by the moon and Fred's headlights. "Jesus—it's black! And long."

"You're kidding." Hoades moved to get a closer look while Joel sadly recalled the long gray tongue of the bull buffalo from that magical afternoon with Dinah in Custer State Park.

"Well, I'll be damned—it *is* black," Hoades snorted. "Hey, Meznik—Williams was your bunkmate. Was his thing black and long?"

Maybe it was the scurrilous innuendo. Or, finally he'd had enough of Hoades. With one leap Joel was on him, and the pair fell grappling to the ground.

Still, the only lasting damage came from the hooves of the startled black Angus trampling Hoades's shin—dispatching him to the operating room of St. John's Hospital in Rapid. And then, with nose bandaged and leg cast, onto a bus to Alabama—kicked back on crutches to the Heart of Dixie.

Chapter Eighty-Eight

THE MOMENT CLARENCE WALKED ONTO the field at Sioux Park Stadium, Joel bounded out of the bullpen and clapped him on the back. "You sure are a sight for sore eyes!"

Clarence smiled broadly. "Heard you stampeded the redneck back to 'Bama."

Joel laughed. "Well, the cow deserves most of the credit."

Then, Clarence spotted Billy feeding baseballs to Dick Quarles behind the batting-practice screen. "How's your little shadow? He all right?"

"Has his ups and downs. The girl in Valentine dumped him."

Clarence looked pensive, and for a moment Joel feared his friend might ask about *his* love life, but Clarence merely nodded, his gaze drifting to the Morans' concession stand.

"You hungry, Clare?" Joel asked following his friend's eyes. Clarence grunted, then shifted his attention to the unfamiliar player crouching behind home plate.

"Who's the new backstop—looks real smooth back there."

"Dayton Todd. Played five years in the Cleveland chain—line-drive hitter with some pop."

"First an Indian, now a Chief—guess that's a move up for him."

Joel laughed. It felt great to have his friend back on the team.

Stockman waved for the players to come in. "OK, men, here's the skinny on the Terrys. They're last in the standings, but they got their #2 guy goin' tonight. Not much of a fastball, but he's got a good wet one. So, lay off the pitch 'til you got two strikes. And take a hankie to the plate. Hand it to the catcher with your compliments. Maybe the ump'll get the hint." The Chiefs laughed, and Joel cracked a smile at the flash of team unity. "Schmidy's going for us, Todd's behind the dish, and Williams is in left. You got twenty minutes—get loose."

As the team filed out of the dugout, Kibbee grabbed Joel by the sleeve. Joel stiffened, expecting that Hoades' best buddy might be spoiling to even the score.

"What is it, Clyde?"

"Wanted to express my condolences 'bout what happened today in New York. Hope your people are all right."

Joel frowned, disturbed by his reference to *your people.* "What are you talking about?"

"Nuclear attack. Rooskies hit New York. Front page of the paper."

"You're kidding," Joel said, though his chest tightened at the thought.

Clyde pulled the *Journal* from his pocket, but instead of handing it to Joel, read aloud.

> *In New York City, air raid sirens sounded at 1:45 p.m. People on the streets were directed to air raid shelters. Times Square and other well-known points were cleared in about two minutes.*

Joel's knees buckled, and he stumbled backwards. Clarence grabbed the paper from Kibbee and scanned the headline. "It's a fake, Joel. Was just a drill." He thrust the paper under Joel's nose, so he could read the headline himself. *Make Believe Bombers Strike!*

"*Make believe bombers,* Kibb—you're some clown."

"Clown? Thought that was Williams, back in Baseball's Dark Ages."

Joel clenched his fists and started to rise from the bench, until Clarence placed a restraining hand on his shoulder. "Don't waste your time on this fool."

"Me a fool?" Kibbee swiped the paper from Clarence's hands. "*Your* people don't got 'nuff sense to get out of the way of an A-bomb." Clyde read from the article: *In the Harlem Negro section, there was marked slowness in clearing the streets.*

"Let me see that," Joel grabbed the paper to see who had written this defamatory thing. It was the Associated Press, the national wire service. He grimaced. The slur had been published in every newspaper across America.

"See," Kibbee added, "they dog it just like you, Williams."

Clarence's eyes flashed, but he said nothing. It wasn't the welcome he'd hoped for, but one he'd come to expect. "My people just too smart to fall for a bullshit stunt like that."

Quarles wagged a finger at the Chiefs' erstwhile center fielder. "You're one to be talkin' about dogging it, Kibb—after that swan dive at Lake Kampeska." Quarles shielded his eyes as if peering into the distance. "Is that a limp I see before me?"

"Very funny, Q," Kibbee snarled, hobbling up the dugout steps.

Quarles turned to Stockman at the end of the bench. "Gotta get Clyde back on the field, Chief, and away from the newspaper. Reading just addles his little mind."

Guy nodded, knowing only too well how idleness can turn a sidelined warrior ornery. But would this pass, or had Kibbee taken up the needle from the fallen Alabaman? Now, he'd have to keep an eye on Kibbee, along with Meznik and Williams. Perhaps he'd made a mistake, bringing Williams back. Then he checked himself—blaming the Negro and the Jew when it wasn't their fault and he knew that the problem lay elsewhere.

"And, away from road cows," added Hacker, clapping Joel on the back.

The team laughed, and a warm gust swept across the ballfield into the dugout. And Joel raised his face to the sweet prairie wind and laughed.

Chapter Eighty-Nine

THE STORM WAS COMING—moving through the Hills, turning the sky over the Mellerdrammer an ominous green. The director stepped onto the stage, stopping the show with an urgent announcement. "Foul weather's afoot. Everyone . . . please . . . scurry on home!"

After waiting a precious minute for the Skyliner's retractable hardtop to rise and reposition as a roof, Dinah and Glen sped off in watchful silence, the radio spitting static, the wipers sweeping frantically to keep up with the driving rain.

It began in the valley. Hailstones as big as baseballs. Dinah gripped the wheel as she tore down the mountain, flinching with each strike on the Skyliner. She'd never driven in a storm before—except with Bernie behind the wheel, and then she'd always felt safe.

When the first hailstone struck the windshield, Glen grabbed the dash, straining to see the road through a growing web of cracks. When the second one hit, it shattered. A shard grazed Dinah's thigh and she swerved, nearly losing control. "Oh my God!" she cried, gunning the car toward home. By the time they reached Evergreen Street, the hail had stopped as quickly as it started.

"We made it," she exclaimed, glancing over at Glen. And then, she saw it.

John was the first to hear Dinah scream. Joel, fixing a sandwich in the Rosen kitchen, ran out next. John to the driver's side, Joel to the passenger's seat, where Glen sat slumped against the dashboard, blood streaming down the front of his shirt. John lifted Dinah from her seat and carried her inside. When Joel tipped back Glen's head, he saw the glass in his neck.

Leave it in or pull it out? There was no way to know and no one to ask. Helpless, he cupped his hands around the glass blade and watched as the light went out in Glen's eyes.

. . .

It was the Chiefs' day off, and Billy was pitching a shutout on Canyon Lake playground, bewitching nine hapless batters with his sharp little curve. Then, in the fifth inning, the sky darkened, and a hailstorm ripped through town, sending the players streaking for shelter.

Waiting out the storm, Billy indulged in a favorite fantasy—wiping the sneer off Glen Merritt's face with his new curve and the slider Quarles taught him. But he no longer dreamed of killing him. Ever since he'd been attacked in Yankton and saw Clarence almost get killed, he got queasy thinking about doing something like that to anyone . . . even Glen.

When the storm passed, instead of finishing the game, the boys threw fist-sized ice balls at each other as if it were January in July.

Suddenly famished, Billy jumped on his bike and flew home, splashing through puddles with legs spread wide like wings. Arriving on Evergreen, he was surprised to see his father talking to the same reporter who'd interviewed him for the batboy feature. Was the *Journal* going to profile his dad, too? He wasn't sure how he felt about that—sharing the spotlight with his father whose stinging betrayal at the Y pained him still. "Hi, Mr. Cannon. What's up?"

James placed a hand on Billy's shoulder. "Go to your room, Bill. I'll be there in a minute to speak to you." Billy blanched. Could this be about Andrew Hanging Cloud and the knife? He tried to recall exactly what he'd told the police so he wouldn't get caught in a lie.

But it wasn't about Yankton or Hanging Cloud or his night in the hospital. It was about Glen Merritt, killed an hour before when a hailstone shattered Dinah Rosen's windshield.

Billy could scarcely believe his ears. Just that afternoon he'd been striking out Glen in his mind and now he was dead. "Is Dinah OK?" he asked.

"Yes. She wasn't hurt."

"OK." He picked up a comic book from his bed.

James wondered if Billy was in shock. "Son, don't you understand? Glen was killed."

"Yeah, Dad. I heard you." Billy became aware of his father's eyes boring through him.

"Don't you care? Your friend is dead."

"He wasn't my friend." He said it flatly, then flopped down on his bunk and turned his back to his father. He knew he was supposed to be sad, maybe even cry, but he couldn't be a phony and fake it. His father thought Glen was just a kid who threw snowballs at you, not someone who always tried to cut you down and made you hate yourself as much as you hated him.

James put his hands on his hips. "You'll have to go to the funeral with me and Mom. We must pay our respects."

"Not if the Chiefs are on the road. I'm not missing a game for *him*. I hated his guts."

James yanked Billy from the bed and gave him a hard shake. "What in God's name is wrong with you! A boy is dead—a boy who used to be your best friend."

A sob broke from James's throat. "It could have been you, Billy, it could have been you."

James threw his arms around his son, but Billy stood stiff as a toy soldier, unable to handle the sudden swerve from paternal censure to a father's straight-on love.

• • •

Joel bolted upright in his seat. He'd finally fallen out, but for how long he couldn't tell. It might have been only a minute or two, hardly a reprieve from what haunted him night and day . . . the glass dagger stuck in the neck of the boy, and the look in his eyes the moment he died.

Leave it in or pull it out—a matter of life and death mocking him and his years of study at one of America's great universities. He'd earned top grades in science, but all he could think to do was press his palms around the gleaming blade and squeeze the boy's skin, as if to dam back life with his bare hands.

He looked across the aisle at Billy slumped in his seat, cheek pressed against the window. He was sure the boy was also troubled by the death of a classmate who lived just up the street. Still, he didn't expect Billy to bring it up when the boy hadn't uttered more than a dozen words to him since that terrible night in Yankton.

But today, for the first time in weeks, Billy didn't breeze by him on his way to his new pals Quarles and Kibbee. Instead, he hesitated, his eyes darting to the back of the bus before taking the seat directly opposite Joel, the same spot where his brother once sat. It made Joel wonder if Billy wished, as he did, that they could turn back the clock to that first road trip, when they'd all banded together like hopeful pioneers on a journey of discovery.

"Too bad 'bout the Merritt boy," Fred offered, his eyes fixed straight ahead. That morning, the *Journal* had quoted Joel, speaking unguarded and from the heart: "I didn't know what to do."

When neither Joel nor Billy responded, Fred let it drop. He believed that Joel had a good heart—maybe even a brave one—but like most young men these days was a little soft at the center. A day on Saipan or an hour on Omaha Beach would have fixed that—taught him how life or death was often just a matter of inches and only the good Lord above held the ruler.

Joel reached into his duffel for a letter he'd just received from Rivkah. His hand grazed the strap of the tefillin, the leather boxes containing scripture, which his father had slipped into his bag before putting him on the bus in New York. That morning, he'd donned them for the first time since leaving home, davening in the prescribed rocking motion, facing east in the Rosen basement.

Dinah never came to breakfast. He suspected she was still in her bedroom and that John had been with her all night. He would have given anything to be the one to gather Dinah in his arms, hold her tight, and make love to her, dulling the memory of what happened in the storm. But Dinah wasn't his girl anymore, and now there was even more reason to doubt she ever would be.

Hardly touching his cereal, Joel jumped on his bike and sped for the Stadium. There, he ran laps until his legs throbbed and his mind went numb. On the way home, he spotted Billy peeking out from behind a hedge, watching the parade of people, mostly women with daughters, carrying casseroles up the steps of the Merritts' porch. Joel didn't stop. He wasn't sure why Billy was hiding, but figured he had his reasons, just as he had his for exhausting himself on the ballfield.

• • •

On the bus, Billy felt sick, like he'd been kicked in the gut and socked in the head at the same time.

"Asshole," he swore, his anger welling up. Even in death, Glen managed to make him look bad. This time to his dad, who expected him to do the regular thing and be sad that Glen had died.

But how could he mourn a bully who put him down every chance he got?

Still, he didn't get why he felt so yucky. Fighting back tears, he punched the seat-back in front of him, pummeling the cushion until his knuckles ached. But the knot in his stomach would not ease.

And then it hit him—what he'd lost when Glen died. Not just the chance to show him up by striking him out with his killer curve. It was the chance to prove to him that he was someone that mattered—someone who should never have been dropped as a friend.

Now he'd have to prove that all on his own.

"Hey, Billy Moran," Quarles called from the back of the bus. "Whatcha doin', goin' ten rounds with the upholstery? Give those golden gloves a rest and come play some poker."

Though they'd not exchanged a word, he looked at Joel as if requesting leave to abandon their common pew. Joel nodded his assent. Whatever demons Billy was battling, they seemed knocked out by a couple of sharp left-rights. His own, he knew, would not be so easily vanquished.

Chapter Ninety

JENNIE TOOK A SEAT IN Dr. Latham's waiting room as far from the receptionist as possible. She'd made the appointment but not because she thought Clarence was her baby's father. James had explained that the pregnancy test had been done when she was in the hospital, long before she'd gone to his trailer. The reason she came to the doctor—the reason she had to come—was to find out if what she'd done with Clarence had harmed the baby.

Dr. Latham was shocked when he saw Jennie dressed all in black. For a moment, he thought she'd gone mad with grief, like a character in a Victorian novel perpetually mourning a child. But then he recalled that the Morans lived down the block from the Merritts and he, too, had donned a dark suit for Glen's funeral later that morning. A child conceived and a child gathered in, he mused. The nearest of neighbors, birth and death, practically sharing a backyard fence.

"How are you doing, Jennie?"

"I'm having a baby."

He smiled. "Yes. I gave James the news. How are you feeling? Any more fainting?"

She didn't respond. Her eyes were fixed on a photo on the doctor's desk—of a smiling young woman cradling a newborn swaddled in pink flannel.

"My daughter and granddaughter in Denver," the doctor said proudly, following her gaze.

Jennie's lips trembled as she fought back tears. Dr. Latham came around the desk and stood by her side. "What is it, Jennie?"

Jennie squeezed the chair's arms until her knuckles went white. "I think I hurt the baby."

"Hurt the baby? What do you mean?"

"I had relations."

He nodded, relieved it was just that old wives' tale about intercourse harming the fetus.

He placed a reassuring hand on her shoulder. "Don't fret, Jennie. Women are allowed to have relations when they're pregnant."

Jennie looked down at her lap. "It wasn't James."

Dr. Latham jerked backwards. "What do you mean? Isn't James the baby's father?"

She lifted her head to meet his gaze. "It happened after I left the hospital."

"I see." Dr. Latham walked back to his desk to gather his thoughts. "Is this a man of good character?" he finally asked, wishing he could put it to her directly and ask who it was.

"I'm not sure," Jennie stammered.

Dr. Latham nodded. "We'll take a blood sample just to be sure."

Jennie's eyes grew wide. "Sure about what?"

"Syphilis," Dr. Latham answered, choosing to be blunt—the memory of James Moran's elation at becoming a father prompting his sudden coldness. "Don't have relations with James until I get the results. And this time you can't run out before I examine you. You owe it to your baby."

Her nod was immediate. She needed to know that the baby was all right. She would suffer this exam and all that followed. And pray that God would spare her innocent child.

"And something else," the doctor continued, looking Jennie straight in the eye. "I will support you medically because of what happened last time to your baby. But you need guidance beyond my healing arts. Seek out your pastor. He can provide the spiritual help you require."

Then he took Jennie by the arm and called for the nurse. Returning to his desk, he stared dumbfounded at the blank page in Jennie's chart. How could someone like Jennie Moran—wife, mother, schoolteacher, devout Christian—give in to such a passion?

What else didn't he know about his patients?

What other secrets escaped his eye in his town?

Chapter Ninety-One

A GUNNING MOTORCYCLE BROKE THE peace of an early August afternoon. Rolling his chair to the window, Bernie observed the trespass—a slight young man in leather jacket and boots tracing figure-eights with his Harley through the stanchions of his New York Club sign.

"Damn delinquent," Bernie chortled as the kid drove off. Probably arrived early for the big motorcycle rally up in Sturgis. Then he frowned. Something about the biker reminded him of Glen Merritt, and that disturbed his peace more than any Harley in his lot.

It was Dinah. She hadn't been herself since Glen's death—anxiously biting her nails, picking at her food, crying at the drop of a hat. The morning after the accident she went hysterical when she spotted her car still in the driveway. Later that day he spirited it away to the local garage with instructions to fix it, clean it, and find someone to take it off his hands. Though he doubted anyone would want a car known as the death trap for one of Rapid's most promising young men. Even if he had the car painted another color, Dinah might still recognize it around town.

More concerning was his fear that she'd never drive again. He'd heard of people who couldn't get back on the horse after being thrown. But in a place like Rapid, you had to drive.

Bernie gazed at the photo of his daughter. The Mellerdrammer was dark tonight. This might be a good day to get her back behind the wheel, with him by her side for morale. Just a spin around the block in the Caddy, or up to Rockerville to get her comfortable again with that drive.

Picking up the phone, he dialed the house. Ten rings and no answer. Where could she be, he wondered. Maybe sunning herself in the backyard or wedding shopping with her mom.

He might have convinced himself of that, except for a certain feeling in the pit of his stomach that seldom steered him wrong. Grabbing his car keys, he sped home.

His gut proved right. Parked in the driveway was the Harley he'd seen at the Club, a leather jacket draped across its handlebars. Taking note of the New York license plate, he hurried into the house, calling his daughter's name.

"Out here, Daddy." In the backyard, he found the young man, sharing a beer with Dinah. Clad in tee shirt and jeans with dark, slicked-back hair, he was of medium height and slender build, with a hooked beak and a broad scar across his upper lip.

"Well, well. What have we here?" Bernie asked as casually as he could. He sensed that the biker's presence in the New York Club lot and now in his backyard was no coincidence.

Rising from his chair, the young man started toward him with a swagger so pronounced it must have been boosted from the movies. Looking him over, Bernie saw that his clothes clung too tight to conceal a gun, and with his slight physique and soft face, posed an unlikely threat. Still, there was something about the kid that put him on his guard. Maybe it was his harelip scar, curling like a worm across his lip, making it hard to tell if he was smiling or sneering.

Bernie put out his hand but kept the other cocked at his side. He couldn't recall the last time he'd felt this way in his own home. His tough guy reputation and shadowy past had always been enough to keep trouble at bay.

"Hello, Mr. Rosen. I'm Roger . . . " The young man paused for effect. In his voice, Bernie heard traces of Long Island and a schmear of Philly. " . . . Annenberg—but you can call me Dez."

Bernie blanched. Annenberg. Ranch A. The money. The Mob. The boy's presence in Rapid was no accident.

A self-satisfied smirk crossed the young man's face. "I was telling your daughter that you knew friends of my father's back in New York."

Bernie threw a quick look at Dinah to gauge her mood. But perched on a chaise lounge in bikini top and shorts, she seemed more at ease than any time since Glen Merritt's death.

"Dez's stepmom is Harry Cohn's niece. Harry Cohn's the President of Columbia Pictures," she gushed. "In Hollywood! And Dez's dad publishes *Seventeen* magazine and *TV Guide*. Dez rode all the way out here from New York and is going to California for a screen test."

Roger chuckled, and Bernie tightened his fist. New York, Hollywood, the Annenbergs. An unholy trinity if there ever was one. Motioning for Roger to reclaim his seat, he pulled a chair onto the flagstone path, blocking the boy's sole means of escape. "You here for the motorcycle rally in Sturgis?"

"Nope. My Grandpa Moe had a big spread out here. Meyer Lansky told me about the great parties he threw there." Roger fixed his gaze on Bernie's stony face. "Maybe you made that scene?"

Bernie's gut clenched. So, Lansky was the one who told the kid he lived here. "Can't say I did. When was that?"

"Back in the thirties. Grandpa Moe sold it right after I was born." Roger's voice faltered. "My dad really dug the place. Talked about it all the time."

Bernie shrugged, trying to appear calm. He didn't appreciate cat and mouse games—not in his own backyard. "Never heard of it. Before my time."

"Really? Dad said it was a big deal 'round here. Had a lodge, guest cottages, trout stream, and a huge barn. Called it Ranch A. 'A' for Annenberg."

Bernie could see it as if it were yesterday—Ranch A, on that cold winter night more than a decade ago. Stashing his pickup in a thick stand of pine . . . skirting the trout stream . . . trekking the last mile through hard-packed snow to the grand lodge and an empty stall of the abandoned barn where he found it—the pot of gold that bankrolled his life and livelihood in Rapid.

"Where ya staying, Roger?" he asked, tempering his tone.

"The Alex Johnson, downtown. Cool digs. Western, you know."

"Why can't he stay here?" Dinah asked. "No one's using the basement tonight."

Bernie nodded. Joel was away with the Chiefs, and it might be easier to find out what the kid was up to if he was under the same roof.

"Sure, baby. It'd be an honor to have such a distinguished *landsman* in our basement."

"Landsman? What's that, Daddy?" she asked, throwing him a grateful smile.

Bernie gestured toward the Annenberg scion, inviting him to translate.

"Cool," was all Roger said, smiling at Dinah, making Bernie worry he'd made a mistake inviting a fox to bed down in his hen house.

As soon as Roger rode off to fetch his gear from the hotel, Dinah ambushed her dad. "Dez is taking me to California!"

"Whoa! What about that rock on your finger? Remember John Moran?"

Dinah stuck out her chin. "I owe it to Glen."

Bernie snorted. "What the hell does Glen Merritt have to do with it?"

"He loved me, Daddy. And he believed in me—maybe the only one who did. He said we could make it in Hollywood."

"Make it? Maybe on a casting couch. You know what that means, little girl?"

Dinah sniffed. "I can take care of myself. I've been on couches before."

"I'm not talking about good-looking ballplayers, or the boy next door. I'm talking about balding old men with potbellies and hair growing out of their ears."

"Dez won't let that happen. He's got connections. His uncle's Harry Cohn."

Bernie didn't know about Harry Cohn, but he did know about Mickey Cohen, another Brownsville boy and kingpin of the LA Mob. After his release from Alcatraz, he boasted on TV that gangsters ran all the nightclubs and movie studios in Hollywood. In New York, too. He shuddered, remembering why he'd pulled Lana off that Broadway stage years back.

"LA is full of big-time bloodsuckers, and I bet Harry Cohn's one of the biggest."

"But, he's Dez's uncle," Dinah protested. "And Dez will be there to protect me."

"That punk? He couldn't protect a mosquito."

Dinah bit her lip. Fate had brought her Roger Annenberg—a shining knight on a Harley and she wasn't about to let this lucky break pass her by.

"Don't give me that look, little girl. I'm still your father, and what I say goes. You're not going to Hollywood with Dez!"

Dinah swallowed hard. Right then, she almost told Bernie what she knew and that he had no right to tell her what to do. But she couldn't do it, couldn't tell him all she'd unearthed in Lana's closet. "I could die in a hailstorm, too, before I have the chance to do anything with my life!"

Bernie's resolve wavered. "I'll take you," he blurted. "I'll take you to Hollywood, and we'll call on Dez's Uncle Harry together."

"I don't believe you."

"Have I ever broken a promise to you?"

Dinah blinked to keep her eyes from filling. Bernie might not be her real father, but what he said about promises was true. "When?"

"At the end of summer. I can't go anywhere before the season's over."

She scoffed. The ball team or the Club. Something else always came first. If she stuck with Dez, she could leave now.

Bernie took her hands in his. "It's not that long, DiDi," employing an endearment he hadn't used in years. "Only a couple more weeks."

She pulled her hands away. “What about the Club? You never close the Club.”

“Maybe it’s time I did. We’ll go by way of Yosemite. A family trip, like when we used to go to Rushmore together. Remember, baby?”

Dinah threw her arms around his neck. “I love you, Daddy.”

He planted a kiss on her forehead. “You still gonna marry Johnny boy?”

Her face clouded over. “I don’t know.”

Bernie waved his hand. “You don’t gotta decide now. But I’ve got one condition. Keep off that punk’s bike. His connections aren’t worth a plug nickel if that pretty face of yours hits gravel. Like cheese on a grater. You get the picture?”

Dinah shuddered, and Bernie felt a wave of relief. The pitch to her vanity would keep her local and off the bike. And there was still the chance that John had already knocked her up. Marriage and motherhood would KO any trip to Tinsel Town.

“When Dez gets back, we’ll go to the Club for dinner and see your mama’s new show. Good thing your fiancé’s at work and the junior spy is off with the team.”

“Junior spy? Who’s that?”

“Billy the Kid.”

“Oh, Daddy, you slay me!”

Bernie forced a laugh. He’d never slain anyone, except in the War, but there was something about this kid that made him think he could do it . . . if he had to.

• • •

Bernie stifled a cough from the cloud of hairspray wafting from Lana’s freshly styled bouffant. He’d been awake for hours, puzzling out what the kid in his basement might be after. Their trip to the New York Club had only made him more suspicious. Young Annenberg seemed far too interested in the Club—how long he owned it and how much it cost to build. Was this upstart solving a puzzle, with the missing piece the roll of C notes he’d stolen years back from Grandpa Moe’s barn at Ranch A?

Bernie swung out of bed and headed to the kitchen. At the top of the basement stairs, he listened for signs of stirring from his new houseguest.

This was the first time he’d been visited by anyone from back East. Whatever appeal the West once possessed for Moe Annenberg and his cronies seemed to have died with the man. He liked to think that Rapid was too small fry to be of interest to the Mob, and that suited him fine.

They could keep big towns like Kansas City, Denver, and Minneapolis, but he liked being the arbiter of vice in his own town, a self-appointed gatekeeper barring the insidious reefer and cocaine traffic that had lately become the Syndicate's stock-in-trade.

Bernie poured himself a glass of milk and sat at the table. He wondered if someone had told the kid about the money stashed at Ranch A. Meyer Lansky was the most likely source, though Roger could have picked it up from idle chitchat at a family gathering. He could just imagine the stories a kid might overhear at an Annenberg Thanksgiving or Passover seder. Grimacing, he headed for his desk in the den. What if Dez was just the tip of the spear—sent ahead, like Custer's scouting party, to search for "gold in them thar Hills"? Grabbing his gun from the drawer, he shuddered at the thought of how many hoodlums might follow—fiendish fortune seekers searching for the El Dorado of the Dakotas.

• • •

Bernie didn't take the scenic route to Ranch A. Instead, he chose a shortcut, requiring as little time as possible with Roger. Fidgety from the moment he got into the car, the kid had seemed pleased when he offered to take him there. "Got a supplier up that way," Bernie claimed.

But now, Annenberg was a bundle of nerves, biting the nails of one hand, while clutching the strap of a small canvas bag with the other.

An hour out of Rapid, Bernie spotted what he was after—an unmarked dirt road angling toward a butte north of the highway. He checked his rearview mirror. No cars or pickups or farmhouses in sight. Turning off the blacktop, he sped for the butte, stopping on the far side beneath a ribbony knuckle of rock.

Roger's eyes darted from the butte to the empty prairie beyond. "I don't think this is it."

"It's as far as we're going until you level with me."

"Whadya mean?" Roger asked, avoiding Bernie's gaze.

Bernie scoffed. "What's eatin' you, kid? I know you got more on your mind than a trip down memory lane."

Roger swallowed hard and pulled a dog-eared copy of *National Geographic* from his gym bag. Placing the magazine on the seat between them, he opened it to a color spread entitled *Back to the Historic Black Hills* with a photo of a lone horseman gazing down on a lush, green valley, and on the opposite page, a shot of the interior of a sumptuous hunting lodge.

Roger pointed first to the horseman, then to the same man pictured in the lodge. "That's him. Pete Smith. I'm looking for *him*."

His hand shaking, Roger turned the magazine to Bernie, so he could read the caption:

Ranch A. Home of a Million Rainbow Trout. In the early 1930s a wealthy Philadelphia publisher ordered trout in a Black Hills restaurant and found it so delicious he bought Sand Creek whence his meal came. In time a fabulous million-dollar retreat rose around the trout preserve. The estate is now owned by Peter F. Smith, seen with his horse on the rim of Sand Creek Canyon.

Bernie turned the magazine over to check its publication date. October 1956. Not even a year ago. "So, this Pete Smith bought your grandpa's ranch. So what?"

"Pete Smith stole it. His father was governor of Wyoming when Grandpa Moe was sent to prison. And now, his son lives there like a king."

It was all news to Bernie. No one was at Ranch A that night he'd made off with his grubstake. Since then, he'd not been anywhere near the place.

"Who told you about Governor Smith and his son?"

"My father, but that's *all* he'd tell me." Roger's voice took on a mocking cadence. "*No use crying over spilt milk. Let sleeping dogs lie.*"

"So Governor Smith got the ranch and gave it to his son. What's the big deal?"

Roger began to sputter. "They swindled my family. Ranch A was my grandpa's pride and joy. When he fled Germany, he had nothing but the clothes on his back. Jews weren't allowed to own land there. Here, in America, he worked like a dog. Then this Governor Smith took it away from him. Just like the Nazis. You ought to understand, Mr. Rosen. You're a Jew."

Bernie didn't say a word. He never would have guessed that a magazine could inspire a crusade to avenge family honor and the loss of a beloved western homestead.

Roger mashed Pete Smith's picture with his thumb. "You know what else? Governor Smith had a partner, some fat cat from Ohio named Keener, who put up half the dough to buy Ranch A. And get this—Keener helped build a steel factory in Germany! In 1938! The Herman Goering Steel Works. Steel for guns, tanks, and planes. Concentration camps, too. That sonovabitch helped the Krauts prepare for war, then helped himself to Grandpa's spread."

Bernie was dumbstruck. Lansky hadn't said anything about that when they met up after the War. But now, he savored the knowledge that the booty in the barn ended up in the hands of a Yid like him, not some Nazi sympathizer or crooked politician.

"That's some story, Roger." He lowered his voice to a conspiratorial tone. "But didn't your Grandpa Moe cheat Uncle Sam? Wasn't the ranch sold to pay back taxes?"

"Bet they helped frame him, so they could get their hands on Ranch A."

Bernie couldn't dismiss the possibility that Roger was right. Lots of politicians out here would be tempted, and feel justified, when the landowner was an interloper—an East Coast racketeer and a Jew. "What's your plan, kid? You going out there to buy it back?"

Roger dug into his bag and pulled out a Colt 45. "I'm going to even up the score. Pete Smith and his Guvner Daddy won't know what hit 'em."

"What?" Bernie felt for his own piece, a snub-nosed .38 he'd stashed beneath the driver's seat the night before. "You want to go to jail like your granddad? Your father's got mountains of cash. *TV Guide* and *Seventeen* must bring in millions. He could buy it back for you. Or get you a different spread."

"I doubt it." Roger let the gun drop to his lap. In that moment, he sounded utterly defeated, and Bernie felt a bit sorry for the kid. Maybe he was doing this to impress his rich old man. Or, just to get his attention. As for himself, he never had a father to impress or disappoint. Sometimes he regretted it, but in the end, he was proud to be a self-made man.

Keeping an eye on the gun, Bernie softened his tone. "Did you really think I'd help you kill a governor and his son?"

"Meyer said you hated Nazis. Called you a tough Jew you could count on in a fight."

Bernie snorted, amused by the three-pronged appeal to vanity, reputation, and tribe. Still, he remained unswayed. He'd done some reckless things in life, and some brave things, too, but had learned to pick his battles. He thought about the latest shipment of guns in the basement of the Club. He had bigger fish to fry than helping a rich brat reclaim the family trout stream.

"Thanks for the compliment, kid, but you're fuckin' crazy."

Roger picked up the gun and aimed it at Bernie's chest. "Who you callin' crazy?"

Calmly, Bernie yanked the .45 from the boy's hand. "Anyone who points a gun at me and can't tell the safety is on."

Roger slumped in his seat, his Adam's apple bobbing like a Spaldeen in his neck.

"Listen, Dez. The joyride's over. You're gettin' on your bike and riding outta Rapid, with me on your tail. Do what your father told you—forget about your zayda's ranch. Got it?"

"Please don't call my father or Meyer," Roger wailed. "They don't know I came here."

Bernie nodded. "I don't know your father. And I won't tell Lansky. I turned my back on that life years ago."

Later that night, Bernie handed Dinah a note he'd forged after ushering Roger Annenberg out of town. *Sorry, doll. Had to split. Ciao. Dez.*

"Who cares!" she said as she tossed the piece of paper in the garbage. "We're still looking up his Uncle Harry when we get to Hollywood."

"That's my girl!" Bernie roared, as she flounced down the hallway to her room. Back in fighting form, she'd be driving again soon. Cocking his finger and thumb, he took aim, then blew out the imaginary gun smoke with a self-satisfied puff.

"That there varmint won't be troubling you no more, miss," he whispered.

Then, taking a deep breath, he added, "I hope."

Chapter Ninety-Two

LIMPING BACK TO RAPID WITH their tails between their legs, the Chiefs arrived home from the season's worst road trip. Four games in four towns—with the only sweet spot, a first night win over Watertown, where Joel, given the start, led the Chiefs to a 14-2 trouncing of a close rival.

For Joel, it was a triumph—giving the Club a brief hold on second place, one game behind the Kernels. He was most proud of outdueling Dick Radatz, the Lake Sox ace, who had notched seven straight League victories to that point, including three against the Chiefs.

The road trip had also been a success for him and Billy—a kind of tonic, letting them turn their backs on Rapid and the turmoil unleashed by Glen Merritt's death. For Joel, the diamond had become his refuge, a place where thoughts of the dead youth disappeared. Letting his mind go blank, he could pitch as Stockman had once ordered, with "no thinking tonight."

Clarence was back, too, and the three of them happily shared a room again, watching the superior TV offerings of the East River towns and playing penny-stakes poker, which Billy had to teach Joel. "What ballplayer can't play five-card draw?" he asked with worldly pretense, prompting a chuckle from Clarence and a good-natured yelp from Joel.

Then, back in Rapid, after losing their last three road games, the Chiefs lost again, falling to Huron in the tenth inning. With just ten games left in the season, their record was now 19 wins and 13 losses, and they trailed the first-place Kernels by a seemingly insurmountable three games.

Bernie was worried—afraid that his Chiefs, with four straight losses, had fallen into a losing state of mind. And, while he was proud that his stadium and his team were an overwhelming success, he wanted more than to be a mere contender. He wanted the Basin League Crown!

Late that night, he and Carl pow-wowed at the Club. "You see Kibbee stumbling around out there? If he'd got to that ball in the tenth, we woulda won. But Guy won't cut him."

Bernie scoffed. "Tough shit. *I'm* cuttin' him. We're getting a guy from the Man-Dak League to replace him—Len Hunt, center fielder for the Bismark Barons."

Carl frowned. "Isn't the Man-Dak full of coloreds?"

"So what? Hunt played for the champion Monarchs in the Negro League and four seasons in the Minors. Never hit below .300. Good fielder and base stealer. Great replacement for Kibbee."

"You really think we need another Negro? Look what happened with Williams."

Bernie frowned, wondering if prejudice or prudence fueled Carl's opposition. "We're gettin' him. Airmail special delivery. Base Commander's sending a B-52 to collect him."

"The Air Force will do that? What if the taxpayers get wind of it?" Carl growled.

Bernie chortled. "Ellsworth will bury it. Call it a training flight."

"OK, but shouldn't we get Guy's take on this first?"

Bernie scoffed. He'd never solicit advice from the man who made him a cuckold. "Remember the deal we made with Stockman? He got his pros, but we get to make all the replacements. We'll be doing him a favor cutting his pal Kibbee. He'd never do it himself."

As Bernie figured, Stockman didn't put up a fight about cutting the hobbled center fielder. He was just happy not to be the hatchet man.

And while only a few Rapid Citians observed it thundering north to Bismark, they certainly noticed it when it returned to Ellsworth later that day—a massive B-52 jet bomber, pride of the US Air Force, cruising low, rather too low, casting a giant shadow across the ballfield.

Minutes later, as the Sioux Park stands were filling, a giant military C-34 Choctaw helicopter hovered, then landed in center field and disgorged its passengers—a stocky Negro dressed in a Chiefs uniform, and at his side, his petite wife, Ruth, outfitted demurely in a flowered sundress and white gloves—greeted with a handshake by a beaming Bernie Rosen.

Chapter Ninety-Three

"WHAT THE HELL!" BERNIE THREW the newspaper onto the floor in disgust. "That damn Paddy—accuses me of trying to buy the pennant by poaching Harry Wise from the Terrys."

Joel looked up from his cereal. He'd heard talk about picking up a player for the stretch run, but figured Len Hunt, the new center fielder, was it. "What are you talking about, Bernie?"

"Paddy Olavson's latest editorial, 'Chief Rosen's Big Poach'. He goes after *me*, not Mitchell or Huron. They stalked Wise first, but I'm the only one he names—me, Bernard Yitzkak Rosen."

"Ahh," Joel said, catching Lana's eye, one of a pair rolling toward the kitchen ceiling.

"What?" Bernie said, glaring at Joel. "Think I'm making this up? We're landsmen, kid. Out here us Jews got to stick together." Bernie's laugh was bitter. "Everywhere, really."

Joel stiffened. This was the sort of thing his father often said, which he halfway believed, but coming from Bernie, it felt sinister—corrupt—like Mob talk.

"What's with you, kid? Everything I say, you stick between your teeth, like it's fake." He mimed biting down on a doubloon. "I don't know why. I've always been straight with you."

"Straight *at* me," Joel was tempted to retort. The memory of being pinned against the stadium wall by Bernie's Cadillac was something he'd never forget. And maybe never forgive.

Bernie paced the floor. "You should only know what the locals think of our tribe. Just yesterday, I stopped at a place I heard had great schnitzel—*Bavarian Inn*, down by Custer—and on the lobby wall there's this huge map." He spread his arms wide. "'Deutschland, 1938,' in big red letters across the top. Nineteen thirty-eight—same year as Kristallnacht—like they're hoping Adolf will rise from the dead and walk the land again."

Joel shuddered, and Bernie fixed him with a penetrating stare.

"What you doin' tonight? I've got something I wanna show you that you won't see anywhere else in the whole U.S. of A. And it's just fifty miles from here."

Bernie's tone put him on edge, but Joel had no plans—no girlfriend and no game—and Bernie knew it. "I'm up for anything, Bern—whadja have in mind?"

"How about some good old-time religion—Nuremberg style?"

Joel's throat went dry. "You takin' me to a KKK meeting?"

"Somethin' like that." Bernie frowned. "But first I'm gonna make you earn your keep. Gotta shipment of Seagram's coming in this afternoon and Buck's out getting a couple teeth pulled."

Joel nodded. "Fine with me—a little heavy lifting might help my fastball."

...

Depositing the last of a dozen cases of whiskey on a long banquet table, Joel listened for Bernie's footsteps on the stairs. It was his first time in the murky depths of the Club's cellar and his first chance to check out Billy's story of a secret munitions cache. Crouching, he parted the pleated skirt hanging from a long tabletop, then swung his arms back and forth into the void.

Feeling nothing, he rose to survey the vast space. Nothing suspicious and no wooden crates—only surplus chairs and kitchenware. Then he spotted a large, chalked rectangle on the far wall with an "X" at its center. Joel smiled—Billy's practice strike zone. No sign of traitorous gun-running—only powdery proof of a very human Bernie Rosen, a hard case with a soft lining.

It was then that his foot found what his eyes could not—his shoe striking an object, hard but light, sending it skimming across the floor like a hockey puck. He chased after it, then was sorry he did—for there on the concrete floor lay a splintered slat of wood stenciled with "US Army"—just the kind of wood used in heavy packing crates. Joel stared at the fragment, then flung it under the banquet table. He had hoped Billy was wrong—that the guns were a figment of a young boy's overactive imagination, but this wood scrap was too real to discount.

Heart racing, he steeled himself for the trip to God knows where with Bernie.

...

The drive to Spearfish on a winding canyon road cut through some of the most breathtaking scenery Joel had ever seen—towering ramparts of red, white, and black sandstone above a rushing mountain stream, which he would have loved to dip his toes in. But he didn't dare ask.

Bernie's face was like the rock wall itself—eyes slit narrow and his mouth a tight fissure offering no commentary on the landscape and hardly a word since leaving the Club.

After about an hour Bernie steered the Caddy into a huge parking lot, already three-quarters full. There they joined a throng of families and couples—a procession of pilgrims, it seemed to Joel, along with nuns in habits, wending their way to the entrance. Above it hung a huge sign . . .

BLACK HILLS PASSION PLAY.

"What have you brought me to, Bernie?" Joel whispered.

"You was warned." Bernie plunked down three dollars for two seats. "My treat."

It was a packed house, but they found seats near the rear of the grandstand. Below them stretched a stage several hundred feet long, with the gates of Jerusalem at one end and a hill with two raised crosses at the other. Six buildings marked the set as an ancient Biblical street-scape, with two of the buildings featuring prominent, six-pointed Stars of David . . . Jewish stars. The larger one, Joel assumed, was the temple where Jesus expelled the money changers.

"Three shows a week: Tuesday, Thursday, Sunday. Six thousand seats and they fill 'em every night," Bernie said. "The guy who plays Jesus came here from Germany with his troupe in the early '30s. Brought more than a little of his homeland's love of Jews with him."

When darkness fell, the crowd hushed, and a spotlight found a solitary figure robed in white. Radiant in the light, the Christ figure raised his arms and began his prologue.

"Oh, ye children of God, open your hearts and receive with childlike confidence His great message."

For two hours, they watched the enactment of Jesus's last days on earth—his entrance through the gates of Jerusalem, the celebration of the Passover seder that was the Last Supper, and his crucifixion on Calvary, which the Christus climbed, stumbling while dragging his own cross, amid orchestrated booms of thunder and flashes of lightning.

It was a moving performance, but what struck Joel the most was the unrelenting portrayal of Jews as monstrous betrayers of the Savior, repeatedly pressuring Pontius Pilot to kill him—with the Temple elders forcing his hand, while the Jewish mob screamed for blood.

"Crucify him! Crucify him!" The cries of the Jews rang in Joel's ears as the spotlight on Jesus's cross cast an eerie shadow across the night clouds.

Joel broke into a cold sweat. Looking around him at the families—parents and children, many seemingly enthralled by the libel—he felt privy to the Christian world's view of his people, and it chilled him to the bone. *Crucify him, crucify him.*

On the drive back to Rapid, an hour passed before Bernie broke the silence.

"Now you've seen it—normal, decent people bringing their children to this spectacle—learning to blame us for all the world's troubles. It can happen again. It can happen *here.* Our neighbors, even some of our friends—turning a blind eye to the smell of burning flesh, laughing at the skin lampshades." He squeezed the steering wheel tight. "What I saw in the camps at the end of the War I'll never forget as long as I live."

Joel couldn't stop the question. "Is that why you had guns in the Club basement?"

Bernie arched an eyebrow. He wondered how he knew about the guns. The latest cache had been shipped to their destination, and he didn't think Joel had worked in the basement before today. He'd have to find out if anyone else knew and locate another way station for the next batch. Maybe buy a cave or an abandoned gold mine in the Hills and store them there. But no rush. He was in this for the long haul. At least now he could truly be straight with Joel.

"They're for Israel."

• • •

That night, in his office, over a bottle of Jim Beam, Bernie shared his story.

"I flew some congressmen to Buchenwald in April of '45. You know what was engraved on the entrance to the camp? *Jedem Das Seine.* 'To each what he deserves'. What did we Jews do to deserve that kind of hell? Not that the Nazis invented anti-Semitism. They just took it to the end of the line. The rail line." His laugh was bitter. "But what you saw tonight was the root of it—a play they've been putting on in Europe since the Dark Ages. Top of the 'Jew Hate Parade' for centuries."

He downed his bourbon and poured himself another. "And not just the Krauts. Some of the places they invaded—Poland, Romania, Ukraine—fell over themselves helping the SS round up their Jews. Afterwards, too. In '46—just a year after the Nazis' surrender—over forty Jews were killed in a pogrom in Poland. And now we got the Arabs. Must be a hundred Moslems for every Jew left in the world. We don't stand a chance."

Silent, Joel contemplated the frightening odds for his faith. "Then why don't you live in Israel?"

Bernie rolled his eyes. "Have you met my wife . . . and daughter?"

Joel snorted. He most certainly had.

"Seriously, kid. I'm an American. I love my country. I would have given my life for America in the War. But even if you love America—and I *love* America—you never know when what you love is gonna turn on you."

Joel regarded his host and benefactor, a tough Jew walking the tightrope between country and tribe. "So, why not start a congregation? There must be other Jews in Rapid."

"Only a handful. And Lana and Dinah aren't Jewish, you know. Just me."

Joel didn't know, but he probably should have guessed it. Instead, he let himself believe that all three Rosens were Jewish—of the lapsed, bacon-eating variety, like his friend Morrie back in New York—and most Jews, he supposed, in an isolated place like South Dakota. Now he wondered if he would have fallen so hard for Dinah if he'd known. Or was that just something he'd tell himself to soothe his bruised ego—and maybe, also, his heart?

"And it's not about praying," Bernie continued. "It's about doing. America will always survive. Most other countries, too. Hell, Japan bounced back after two atomic bombs. But Israel? It wouldn't take much to wipe her off the map forever." He snapped his fingers, "Like that."

Joel nodded. All summer long, he'd put aside the yarmulke, tefillin, and Jewish dietary law—betraying his faith, as his father would see it, for a dream, an American dream. But, the survival of a people, *his* people, well, it didn't get any more basic than that.

He recalled the words of Hillel, the ancient Hebrew sage: *If I am not for myself, who will be for me? But if I am only for myself, who am I?*

Bernie had found his answer to this age-old quandary. Love America with a backup. It might not be how he would answer Hillel's questions, but for the first time, Joel felt a true bond with Bernie, and profound relief that the guns were for a cause he could support.

"But out here, it's better to keep a low profile," Bernie concluded.

Joel laughed. "Some low profile you've got, Bern."

Bernie poured each of them another finger of bourbon. "Gotta ask you something, Joel. You tell anyone else about the guns?"

Joel hesitated but knew from experience that hiding anything from Bernie was futile. "No, but Billy's the one who found them."

"Musta been when I taught him the curve. What did he think they were for?"

"Fighting Commies—or aiding them."

Bernie's face fell. "Why would Billy ever think I'd help the Russians?"

"Well, Bern, the night I told you about Guy, Billy saw you and Lana through the kitchen window. Thought you were spanking her on the table. It really upset him." And, while Billy said he hated Bernie, Joel didn't repeat that, knowing it was just something a kid might say in anger.

Bernie sighed. "Poor kid—has no idea what's in store for him . . . " Catching Joel's look of alarm, he quickly added, " . . . with women, I mean."

Joel smiled weakly. "He already got his heart broken by a cute girl in Valentine who works the concession stand there."

Bernie hooted. "No kidding. Heart got broke in Valentine."

The men shared a kindhearted laugh, and Joel had the odd feeling that he and Bernie were talking about their own son, one they were raising together. "What you gonna say to Billy?"

"Nothing. He's just a kid. And the guns are long gone. This ain't Nazi Germany, or some Commie nightmare—with kids ratting on their parents. Even if he goes to the police, I ain't worried. They'll think he's one of those crazies who report flying saucers."

"Better clean the basement, Bern. I found a piece of a wooden crate with the words 'US Army' stenciled on it. Tossed it under that long table."

"What? Lookin' for proof?" Bernie laughed. "Guess it's a good thing we took that little field trip tonight." Sweetly drunk, he gazed tenderly at Joel. "So, what you gonna do after the playoffs? Head home to med school and that Brooklyn girl who wrote you?"

"I don't know. I'm still hoping to get a call from the Dodgers."

Bernie nodded. "Could happen."

Joel shrugged. "You might not appreciate this, Bern, but I'm itching to see California and everything between here and there. If I go back East now, I might never get a chance."

"Christ, you'd think California's the fuckin' Promised Land! You know they've got earthquakes—big ones, and wildfires."

"And perpetual sunshine and movie stars and the tallest trees and the wildest surf."

"*Pfff!* We got big trees and plenty of sunshine here, too. Our motto is the Sunshine State. It's printed on our flag. And people are people. They all squat to shit and take off their pants one leg at a time." Bernie leered. "Their panties, too, unless she don't wear none."

Joel laughed. "You ever been?"

"No, but if the Dodgers make their move, maybe I'll break down and take the girls."

"Just don't let them out of your sight."

Bernie chortled. "You really think you had to tell me that?"

Chapter Ninety-Four

THE CEMETERY AT WHITE OWL was better tended than Jennie expected—weeds pulled, grass mowed, graves and headstones cleared of debris and bird droppings. She'd not been there since before baby Lily was buried. There'd been no funeral and she'd never seen the headstone James had chosen. She wasn't even sure that he'd bought one.

Standing outside the wooden gate, Jennie peered across the rows of graves to the corner plot. Her mother had buried Florence here, believing it the most heavenly spot around. Set on high ground and surrounded by a boundless prairie, yet far enough from home that between visits she could forget the awful violence that had shattered their lives.

Turning her back, Jennie braced herself against a wind that set her dress slapping against her bare legs. In the distance, a young woman galloped across the low hills and Jennie recalled a long-forgotten poem from her youth—a prize-winner at school penned just before her sister was killed.

ON HORSEBACK

We claim the wind,
the sun,
the storm,
and all that lays
across the range
of days.
Beneath our hooves
it matters not
what takes and breaks
our spirit soars
above the fields and farms
to ride
on roads of mist
and dreams untamed,
again.

"Can I help you?" A gruff male voice jolted Jennie, and she let out a cry of alarm. She'd not heard the pickup truck or the footsteps of the elderly couple—the man, tall and scarecrow thin in farmer's overalls, and the woman, short and portly in a faded gingham smock and straw hat. It had been years since she'd seen the Sheriff of Meade County and his wife, Ruth, but there was no mistaking them. "Jennie Nilsen—sorry," was all the old man could say.

"Moran," corrected the round-faced woman. "How are you, dear?"

Sheriff Markinson shuffled his feet and peered into the distance. Now that he knew who the visitor was, he was ready to leave. Jennie conjured up darker days—the death of her sister Florence—ruled a suicide because of the shame of her out-of-wedlock pregnancy—and his possible mishandling of the only capital crime in his twenty-nine years as County Sheriff.

"I didn't hear . . . " Jennie placed a hand on a fence post to steady herself.

"It's that darn wind," the old woman commiserated. She pointed toward the rider on the horizon. "Our granddaughter saw your car. Don't get many visitors here, least not in the middle of the week." She smoothed her dress with a chapped pink hand. "Roy retired a couple years back and we bought the Clausen place. Being caretaker at White Owl went with the property. Looks a whole lot better than it used to, don't you think?"

The old man cleared his throat. "Guess we should leave Jennie to her people. Gates are open, stay as long as you wish."

Ruth put a hand on Jennie's arm. "Never saw you after you lost your baby. Wanted to tell you how much I liked her headstone. Such a lovely way to mark the passing of an innocent."

Jennie whirled around, her eyes wide. What had James done? She could just make out the simple headstones of her sister and father, but they blocked the view of Lily's grave.

"We'll be going now." Roy took his wife by the arm and led her back to the truck.

Jennie unlatched the gate and started down the path that split the small cemetery in two. The first stones she passed were grainy, their faded inscriptions like whispers from another time. Her family's plot lay beyond and, unlike the others, held just three graves—her sister, her father, and Lily.

It was a lamb.

James had picked a headstone with a solitary lamb curled peaceably on top. And on the side of the stone facing the grave were the words . . .

"Called by one who loves you dearly, Lord, we offer our littlest lamb."

It was an inscription she would not have chosen, nor the lamb. She spun around to confirm what she already knew. Other babies and children were buried here, but Lily's was the only grave so adorned. What had possessed James to make this grand gesture, she wondered—a showy tribute from someone who never seemed to give a thought to their lost child?

And yet, standing by Lily's headstone, she couldn't help reaching out to pet the lamb's rough-notched body and shiny, rounded head, worn smooth by the touch of strangers—other mothers, other children—and maybe by James, too.

Looking up, she saw the young woman on horseback wave to her before riding back across the fields to her grandparents' place.

Falling to her knees, Jennie wept as she never had, for Florence and for Lily and for herself, too.

Chapter Ninety-Five

THIS WAS THE STRETCH RUN. With just six games remaining, Rapid was only one game behind the Mitchel Kernels.

Neither club could afford to lose even a single contest.

Every fan in Rapid knew it, and the crowds and excitement grew ever greater, with the question on every fan's lips—could the Chiefs keep their winning streak going to the very end? Could they run the table?

Back home in Sioux Park, Joel went the distance against the Hearts, scattering five hits and, remarkably, issuing a season-low two walks before a boisterous crowd. Len Hunt, Kibbee's Negro replacement in center field and now the Chiefs' leadoff man, garnered three hits and stole two bases, and made a sparkling, rally-ending catch in center field.

At game's end, Billy whooped loudly as he retrieved the last of the bats. Until he saw something that stopped him cold—Ginny of Valentine, standing at the fence by the Chiefs' dugout.

"Yoohoo! Chief Billy." Dumbstruck, he stood frozen on the chalk line.

"What in hell is *she* doing here?" he thought, then quickly remembered—her boyfriend, the Hearts' second baseman. "Come on over, Billy. I want you to meet someone."

Billy threw a beseeching look toward the Chiefs' dugout, hoping that Joel or Clarence might reel him in, and out of her orbit. But the ballplayers, reliving their triumph, were oblivious to his torment. "Uh, sorry. Got work to do . . . the bats."

Ginny laughed. "I saw! Come on, Bill. Just a minute. You won't be sorry."

Dragging the bat behind him, Billy trudged to the fence where he angled himself so as not to face Ginny head-on. "This is my friend Maryanne. Her folks owned the farm where you broke the egg. She's the one who moved to Rapid."

Billy winced at the memory of the egg and their kiss at the pump, his first and still his only one. Squeezing down hard on the knob of the bat, he welcomed the sting of a rough patch of ash—an ache he could stop at will just by letting go.

"Hi," the girl said shyly. Happy not to look at Ginny, Billy turned to her. Cute in a Shirley Temple way, with curly brown hair, and a pert, upturned nose, she looked much younger than Ginny.

"Maryanne's going to West Junior High this fall. Isn't that where you go, Billy?"

Before he could answer, a lanky ballplayer in a Hearts jersey jogged over and stood next to Billy. Extending a long arm over the fence, he encircled Ginny's waist. "Hey, Gin. Are these the little friends you were telling me about?"

Little! Billy thought, fuming. Then he caught sight of Maryanne, flushed red and similarly peeved by the put-down.

Ginny laughed nervously. "Parnell!" she admonished.

"Yep, that's my name, don't wear it out," issued more like a warning than a joke.

Then Joel appeared at the top of the dugout steps. "Thought I heard a familiar voice," he said, smiling briefly at Ginny before extending a hand to Parnell, forcing him to release the girl's waist. "Some shot you hit back through the box. Nearly took my head off!"

Billy kicked a clump of grass with his cleat. He couldn't believe Joel was praising this asshole, not flattening him.

"Just a loud out." Parnell snorted, shaking Joel's hand.

"Well, that's what shortstops are for. Right?" Joel pivoted to smile at Maryanne.

"So, who's your friend, Bill?"

"Her name's Maryanne. She's starting my school this year."

"Have Bill show you around Rapid, Maryanne," Joel prodded. "He's a great tour guide."

Billy threw Joel a quizzical look, which Joel answered with a tilt of his head and a smile. Not exactly Morse code, but Billy got the message. "Ya got a bike?"

"I sure do!" Maryanne beamed at him in a way that made the corners of his mouth turn up in a goofy grin. All at once, new possibilities dawned. The girl was cute, but not someone a college boy would try to steal. He could see clear to the new school year with a real live girlfriend, one who might look at him in that special way for more than just one afternoon.

Ginny watched the newly forming couple with unexpected interest. Billy was a sweet boy, much sweeter than Parnell, but it all made good sense with both living in Rapid. And how could she be selfish when she already had a boyfriend—a college man, who played baseball and football and owned his own car? Still, she couldn't help feeling a wisp of regret at what she was giving up.

"Wrap it up, Parnell, or you'll be thumbin' it back to the motel." From across the infield, the Valentine manager called for his last errant Heart.

"OK, chief." Parnell jerked his hand in the coach's direction, then planted a long, branding kiss on his young girlfriend's lips. Billy and Joel looked away, but Maryanne took it all in, as if picking up pointers from a Hollywood love-scene. "Be good, babe," Parnell warned, throwing a wary look at Joel as he jogged across the infield to join his teammates. "See ya tomorrow."

Maryanne glanced at her wristwatch and frowned. "Was that a quick game? My Dad's not coming for half an hour."

Billy looked puzzled and Joel smiled, doubting that the boy ever gave a thought to the matter of time in baseball, a sport that turns a blind eye to the clock. Joel imagined that every hour on the ballfield flew by for Billy—as it had for him, too, at that age.

Just then, Billy's stomach growled aloud, and the girls giggled as his face turned beet red. "Guess I'm not the only one who's starved." Joel chuckled, covering for the boy. "How 'bout you girls. You hungry? Bill can take you for hot dogs and Cokes."

Joel nudged him with his elbow and Billy's face brightened. "You bet I can!"

"Oh! That's right. I almost forgot. Your folks run the concession stand." Ginny winked at him as if they shared a special secret, but Billy, newly wise to the flirt, directed his response to Maryanne alone. "You should see all the candy bars in our freezer at home."

"I'd like that!" Maryanne said.

"Bill, why don't you bring the girls up to the Stand while I pack up the bats." Taking the Louisville Slugger from Billy's hand, Joel descended the steps to the dugout, now empty except for Clarence, who offered his own bat with a twinkle in his eye.

"So now *you're* the sportin' man, dishing out love advice?"

Joel tipped his cap in Clarence's direction. "Learned from a master."

Clarence roared. "Then how come he's sportin' two girls and you and me got none?"

"Pupil outshines teacher. Happens all the time."

"You did a good thing, Freako. Makes me miss my son, though."

Joel placed a hand on Clarence's shoulder. He'd finally leveled with him about Cherry Mae and the children moving back to Indiana. Said they couldn't live so far from kin anymore, and that he'd put in for a transfer to join them. "You'll see him soon. Right after we win the pennant."

Clarence shrugged. "Still gotta hear from Uncle Sam 'bout that."

"Maybe you could ask Bernie to put in a good word with the Base Commander."

"You kidding? Bet he used up all his chits gettin' Hunt flown in from the Man-Dak."

Joel laughed. "Talk about your grand entrance—a B-52 *and* a helicopter."

"Knew he was coming. Did the final check on the bomber that morning."

Clarence's voice was oddly flat, and Joel remembered Bernie saying that, back in '50, Hunt, then a Kansas City Monarch, had been signed by Organized Baseball and played in the Minors. He figured that might be a sore point with Clarence. All his years in the Negro Leagues and never getting signed. And while Clarence and Hunt ended up in the same place, the semi-pro Basin League, Hunt at least had his shot at the big time. Still, Joel wondered how Clarence felt about having a fellow Negro on the team, though he wasn't sure how to pose the question without causing offense.

"How is it now . . . I mean . . . how do you like . . . having another—?"

Clarence cut Joel short with a hoot and a clap on the back. "You're too much, Meznik. One more brother don't make this team the Clowns. And Hunt's hitched to a pretty, little wife. He ain't lookin' to buddy up with big old Clarence Williams."

Clarence's tone took a serious turn. "But bootin' those two rednecks, Hoades and Kibbee? Best news ever for this here Nig . . . brother."

Chapter Ninety-Six

HE WAS NOT THE KIND of customer Bernie was likely to miss. Ruggedly handsome and about six-foot-seven, the stranger was dressed in a bolo tie, ten-gallon hat, and a white western shirt—a patrician cowboy who towered over his companions.

Standing at the bar, Bernie and Carl were discussing Rapid's playoff prospects. With only three games left in the regular season, it was certain that the Chiefs would qualify for the four-team playoff. But which team, Chiefs or Kernels, would cop the Basin League pennant?

A week earlier, Rapid trailed the Kernels by three full games and led Watertown and Huron by only one game. Then, the Chiefs took off like a rocket, seeming to forget how to lose—leaving everyone in the dust except the Kernels, the team they'd battled neck and neck all season.

Bernie credited the Chiefs' long winning streak to strong late season defense and pitching. The team's hitting, except for Hacker, had tapered off in the stretch run, but the fielding and pitching had tightened up, with Joel, to his delight, applying his share of the torque.

Now, the two hot clubs were tied. If they ended the regular season with identical records, some means would have to be found for determining the winner. And, not just for awarding the pennant, but also for seeding the four-team playoff. The Chiefs had the better head-to-head versus the Kernels—the usual way the victor was decided—but Bernie had his suspicions. "The fix is in. No way they'll let the new kid on the block—the new, *rich* kid—have the advantage. Mark my words, they'll come up with some scheme to put the Kernels on top in the end."

Suddenly he spotted the tall stranger across the room placing a hand on Dinah's bare shoulder. Filling in for the cigarette girl, she seemed to welcome the contact, rewarding it with a warm smile. Bernie watched the man chat her up, eliciting laughs and lingering longer than required to purchase a pack of smokes.

"Damnit," Bernie cursed, arriving a moment too late to overtake him. "That guy was awfully chummy," he growled, grabbing a pack of Camels from Dinah's tray.

"The tall guy? He was just being nice, Daddy."

"What were you two jawing about?"

"I dunno. He made some joke about smoking."

"What was it? I love a good joke."

Dinah shrugged. "I don't remember."

"Really? You laughed plenty hard."

"OK. He said he was Smokey the Bear 'cause he's a 'bear' when he runs out of smokes."

Bernie snorted. "Some comic. A regular Uncle Miltie."

"You're the one who told me to laugh at the customers' jokes," Dinah countered.

"Did he tell you his name?"

"No, but he said I reminded him of his daughter."

Bernie rolled his eyes. Some line. "He was here a long time. What else you talk about?"

"He asked me how old I was."

"Really? Well, at least now he knows you're underage."

"It wasn't like that. I felt sorry for him. He seemed sad."

"Sad you're underage."

Dinah's eyes flashed. "We were just chatting. Why are you so suspicious?"

Bernie tore a cigarette from the pack and squeezed it between his fingers. "I don't think I'm going to have you fill in anymore. You flirt too much."

Dinah gnawed at her lip. Was this a preview of what he'd do in Hollywood—pull her off the stage to end an audition or screen test and ruin her chances? Maybe it would be smarter to make John take her. She'd already picked out a wedding dress and she and her mom were soon going downtown to choose the invitations. "I wasn't flirting. And he was a perfect gentleman."

Bernie scoffed. "There's no such animal, cupcake. There are only men."

"Daughters," Bernie grumbled, as he rejoined Carl at the bar and motioned for a refill.

Carl chuckled in sympathy. He had two sons and only one daughter, but the girl gave him ten times as many sleepless nights as the boys.

"Did you see that guy making moves on my Dinah? Told her she reminded him of his daughter. The nerve of him. Old enough to be her father."

Carl's face turned grim. "Don't you know who that is, Bern?"

"Never seen him before in my life."

"Thought you knew everyone around here," Carl teased with more than a hint of sarcasm.

"Cut the crap, Carl, spill it."

"That's Pete Smith. His father used to be Governor of Wyoming. Owns a big spread up near Beulah called Ranch A."

Slipping through his fingers, Bernie's drink snaked down his pant-leg like a trout stream.

"Jesus!" Carl handed Bernie his pocket hankie, then recounted what he knew about Smith. "I supply a tavern up that way and the bartender told me what happened to Smith's daughter. A real tragedy. 'Bout five years back she went missing from a summer camp in Connecticut. Only ten years old. Never found. Think some pervert got her."

Bernie shuddered. Ten years old in 1952. She'd be fifteen now. Almost Dinah's age. "What the hell was she doing at a camp in Connecticut?"

Carl shrugged. "I think her mother was from there. She and Smith were divorced. His father—the ex-governor—offered a $3,000 reward. Posted missing person circulars all across the country, but no luck. Terrible thing."

Bernie's blood ran cold. Kidnapping, abduction, murder . . . Murder, Inc.

Let sleeping dogs lie, Walter Annenberg told his son, Roger. Had the Mob already avenged the loss of Ranch A, in the most despicable way imaginable—by killing an innocent child, a little girl like his Dinah?

Bernie downed the drink Joe set before him and signaled for another. And what about Roger Annenberg—out West somewhere? Could he be plotting his own payback? He imagined the young punk stewing on the thousand-mile ride to Hollywood, and coming up with some tale, maybe citing the motorcycle rally to explain his detour to Rapid, then grousing about the shabby treatment he received at the hands of the owner of the New York Club, the 'tough Jew' Meyer Lansky had once showered with praise . . . exaggerating the opulence of his home and the Club, making Lansky wonder how a broke GI could swing such a venture straight out of the service.

"Ran me out of town—like he had something to hide . . ."

Or Roger might spark interest in the place. Put Rapid on the map—the Mob's map—virgin territory, ripe for ravishing. With two quick swallows, Bernie killed the third highball.

"Should have snuffed the kid when I had the chance," he thought. Left his body behind the butte for the coyotes to finish off. No one knew he'd come here, but now he might be telling his tale to people who'd take up his cause and come lookin' for him, or Dinah, to settle the score.

Bernie looked across the room to the coat check where Dinah stood replenishing the cigarette tray. Watching her sort the packs, his eyes brimmed with tears. He'd held those hands when he walked her to school and taught her to roller-skate. Warmed them with his own after building a snowman together in the Club's parking lot.

Dinah dropped a handful of matchbooks on her tray. She was ready to work the tables, including the one where Pete Smith sat drinking with his pals. Bernie clutched his bolo tie, suddenly tight around his neck. What had he done, not killing his past when he had the chance?

"Excuse me, Carl." He strode across the room to the coat check and placed a restraining arm across Dinah's tray. "Sorry, Didi, no more smokes. I'm taking you home."

"What?" she sputtered. "Why?"

"This is no place for a girl who's about to be married."

Arms akimbo, she dug her fists into her hips. "I'm not leaving."

"Oh yes you are. I'm still your father and you have to do what I say."

Dinah squared her shoulders. She remembered it like it was yesterday. She and her mother—pulled out of that theater in Times Square, helpless as rag dolls in his unrelenting grip. Only one thing could stop him from riding roughshod over her dreams.

"My father? He was some cowboy Mom screwed before tricking you into marrying her."

Bernie recoiled. Staggering backwards, he pulled the cigarette tray with him, sending it crashing to the floor. The bar became silent, as all heads turned toward the clatter. "Whoever told you that is a goddamn liar," Bernie hissed, his heart breaking into a million pieces.

• • •

Darting from the Club in four-inch heels, Dinah tottered along the gravel shoulder, weeping so loudly she didn't hear the catcalls from passing cars and pickups. Before long, she began to hobble, her sobs replaced by winces and groans. Removing her shoe, she ran her finger across an angry abrasion. If only she could call John and have him pick her up, but she'd run from the Club without her purse, or a nickel for a call.

She didn't notice the T-Bird until it pulled up alongside her.

"Get in," her mother commanded, leaning across the seat to open the door. Lana was still in costume, her face made up for the stage, and Dinah realized she'd walked out on a performance, something she didn't think her mother had ever done before.

Dinah got in without a word. Slumping in her seat, she picked at her nail polish, a habit which usually elicited a swat from her mother but tonight was ignored.

Pulling into the lot of a supermarket, Lana parked beneath a single streetlamp and lit a cigarette. Then she pulled a hankie from her purse. "Here, take this. You look like hell."

Dinah blew her nose, wondering who'd speak first.

"So, who've you been talking to from my deep, dark past?" Lana finally asked.

"No one."

Lana shrugged. "Don't matter. It ain't true."

"Ha! He was tall and blond, and you met him at a rodeo, and he had one of these." Dinah made a stabbing motion at her own distinctive chin dimple. "Just like me."

Lana exhaled a long line of smoke. "Ya got me there, but I never tricked your Dad into marrying me. He knew I was pregnant, and it weren't his, but he wanted to marry me anyway."

"Who's my real father?"

"Don't matter. He's dead and buried, somewhere between here and Montana."

Dinah turned pale. "What?"

"Six feet under." Lana paused, but decided to say it, "Good riddance to bad rubbish."

"You didn't love him? You went to bed with him, didn't you?"

"Do you love John Moran?"

Dinah looked away. "I guess. I don't know."

"Well, I guess *I* didn't know, either, but I married him."

Dinah's jaw dropped. "You were married before Bernie?"

"For three whole months. Got out of it the easy way when he died joyriding with his girlfriend." Lana snorted. "One of many."

"I don't believe you."

"Why? 'Cause I'm so special no one would ever step out on me?" Lana shimmied her shoulders in a vampy way. "Men are dogs, always sniffing 'round fresh butt. But they can be sweet like puppy dogs, too, if you know how to train 'em—like Bernie, most of the time. You of all people should know that, Dinah. You got the Big Dog trained better than I do."

Dinah shrugged. "He feels more like a guard dog to me."

"Guess he thinks you're worth it." Then she cackled. "'Course, dogs guard junkyards, too."

Dinah fumed. She couldn't believe her mother was having so much fun with this. "Why didn't you tell me about him?"

"Guess I never thought you'd find out—not like he was gonna start comin' around."

Then she hooted. "Now I get it. You found the scrapbook in my closet. That's how you know about the dimple in his chin. Thought things looked messed up in there."

Dinah's face turned solemn. "Bernie's never gonna forgive me."

"Men are prideful, but at least you didn't shout it so loud everyone could hear—just the drunks at the bar, and they don't remember much."

"I hope you're right."

"Bet you never thought I could teach you anything," Lana added smugly. "Listen. Bernie's your father. The only one you ever had. And a whole lot better than the sonovabitch who spawned you." She flicked her ash out the window. "If you apologize, he'll forgive you. Just don't start calling him 'Bernie' instead of Daddy. That he won't forgive."

Dinah pouted, recalling what had triggered her outburst. "But he's never gonna let go!"

"And you can thank the good Lord for that. You should know how rare it is to have someone love you that much."

"Doesn't feel like love."

"Yea, well, love can be funny that way."

"Do you love Dad?"

"Yes."

It was the shortest answer Lana gave that night, but Dinah could tell from the set of her jaw that was all she was going to say on the subject. For the first time, she noticed a fine web of wrinkles at the corners of her mother's eyes. "He said he'd take me to Hollywood."

"Who? John Moran?"

"No! Daddy."

"Really? Well, maybe he will, someday."

"He said after the baseball season's over."

"No kidding?" For a moment, Lana considered breaking the string of Bernie's lies. She doubted he had any intention of taking Dinah there. And, deep down, she wasn't sure she wanted Dinah to get the shot she never had, the same shot Bernie had promised her, too, sixteen years ago.

"Better have John Moran take you if you want to do more than meet Mickey Mouse."

"I don't think John wants to go back there."

"You're smarter than I thought."

"I almost ran off with Dez," Dinah bragged.

"I take it back, 'bout being smart. That boy was trouble." Lana laughed. "And not the fun kind. Plus, he'd never protect you. At least Moran would do that."

Dinah folded her arms across her chest. "I don't need protection."

"Really? I wonder how crippled you'd be if I hadn't come along. Have Moran take you. He's a bigger puppy dog than your Dad." Lana's tone turned serious. "You been using rubbers?"

"We only . . ."

"Tomorrow we're gonna see this doctor I know. If there's a problem, he'll take care of it. The earlier, the better."

"You don't think . . . ?"

"Whadja think—you were made on my wedding night? Back of a pickup, like a lot of brats 'round here."

"Thanks a lot, *Mom*." Dinah scoffed, then recalled her own reckless moments with John—twice in her bedroom and twice in his car.

"Well, you're lucky it's 1957, and you won't have to go to some back room in Deadwood to take care of it. But don't go telling your dad or John. They could have different ideas about a baby. Women's business is women's business. The less men meddle in it, the better."

Dinah nodded. "Can I ask you a question, Mom?"

"Shoot."

"Why didn't you do that to me?"

Lana snuffed out her cigarette to buy a little time. It was Bernie who'd talked her out of the abortion. If she hadn't met him, she would have done away with Dinah for sure.

"Guess I wanted you," she said, proffering the lie, though she wasn't exactly sure why. Maybe she was enjoying their first mother-daughter talk more than she'd imagined.

Dinah beamed. It was what she'd been waiting all her life to hear. Hungry for more, she pressed on. "And you didn't want another child with Bernie?"

"Couldn't. You came out upside down. Must've been grabbing at anything you could to stay put. Took too much of me with you on your way out."

Dinah gasped, and Lana patted her daughter's knee.

"Worked out for the best. Not exactly 'Mother of the Year' now, am I?"

Chapter Ninety-Seven

THE DOCTOR NEVER TOLD DINAH she was pregnant. Just that he needed to remove "a little growth" and that she couldn't have relations for a month. Before the appointment, Lana made Dinah remove her engagement ring. "And don't go talkin' 'bout your fiancé. You're just another teenage girl who got careless. He sees 'em all the time." Dinah wondered how her mother knew about that. She didn't think she had any girlfriends, and certainly none with teenage daughters. Maybe it was something she'd overheard at the beauty parlor. Maybe one of the hairdressers had a careless daughter, too.

Later, after sleeping off the anesthetic, Dinah told John what the doctor said about cooling it for a month. Alarmed, John asked, "Are you OK, sweetheart? I didn't hurt you, did I?"

"No," she answered, "it was just a little growth that had to be removed." But she couldn't meet his gaze. And there was something about the words "little growth" that left him unsettled.

They'd done it just four times. The first magical time upon his return from California. The second and third, in the back seat of the Belvedere, reckless but half hoping to get her pregnant. And the last when he'd comforted her after Glen's death. Never had he felt so close to her as that fourth time, when her need was so desperate but had nothing to do with desire for him.

That night he barely slept, thinking about Dinah's visit to Dr. Mulson. The next day, he walked by the doctor's clinic on Kansas City Street. At the library across the way, a young mother shepherded two little girls up the stone steps, the same steps that he and Billy had climbed every Saturday morning with their mother when they were small.

John squeezed his eyes tight, like a child making a birthday wish. Try as he might, he couldn't imagine Dinah in either Jennie's or this tender mother's place. Nor could he muster any paternal feeling himself. He didn't want to be a father at age nineteen. This baby, this "little growth," was just something that might have clipped Dinah's wings. But it wasn't the future she'd dreamed of. A sob caught in his throat. What had once been a fairy tale come true was now a twisted tale of lies and deceits.

Just then, a pale young woman emerged from the doctor's office clutching a pocketbook to her chest. John watched her cover her ringless left hand as she walked to the curb. A moment later, a blue Chrysler with Wyoming plates drove up and a grim-faced older man reached across to open the passenger-side door. Without a word, she bowed her head as they sped off.

Sinking to the curb, he thought of how he could never tell Bernie or anyone about this. But he couldn't keep lying to himself either, pretending that Dinah loved him for himself alone and not as her ticket to Hollywood. And yet, if they broke up now, how could he stand seeing her with other men? He'd have to leave town. Give up on her and the chance to get in on the ground floor of Rapid's new TV station.

John held his head in his hands. On his desk at home lay a bill marked "For Immediate Attention—$225 Past Due." Yale college costs not covered by his scholarship. The car, the ring, taxes, and his investment with Bernie had wiped him out. And he couldn't get his money back from Bernie, who'd been counting on him for the new TV station and would be furious he'd ditched his daughter, practically at the altar.

Maybe his dad would give him a loan. Just the other night he bragged that his original profit projections for the Stand were working out, thanks to the extra playoff games.

John drew a deep breath. Resolving his finances was child's play next to untangling his heartstrings. He'd have to tell Dinah that the wedding was off, but for that, he'd wait until after the Championship in Mitchell. And, he thought with a snort, after Joel left town.

• • •

"What? You've decided to go to Yale? What about your job at KOTA and the place in Robbinsdale?" James asked, stunned by the U-turn in John's plans.

John frowned. Clearly Billy had snitched to their dad about Robbinsdale. "I already gave up the house. Put my money into something with Bernie, but I'm not at liberty to talk about it."

"So, you're going to take your bride to Yale. They'll let you do that?"

"You don't understand, Dad, I'm breaking my engagement with Dinah."

"You are? Did you tell Bernie? He's planning some big shindig at the Club."

"I'll tell him after the Championship game."

"Why wait?"

"Dad, stop with the twenty questions. I've got my reasons and I have to keep it secret. But I need to borrow two hundred and twenty-five dollars to pay Yale."

James was shocked by the sudden turn of events. Why was John breaking up with Dinah? Couldn't he keep working at KOTA and attend the School of Mines? And why so desperate for money? Had Bernie swindled him? He wanted answers, but was told, "No more questions."

"Listen, John, I wasn't going to tell you yet, but your mom is pregnant."

John started to laugh, a laugh that fed on itself until it doubled him over.

James's face reddened. "What's so funny? You think we're dried-up old prunes?"

"No, Dad. I'm sorry, I can't explain." John stopped for a moment to catch his breath. "A baby. Wow! Is that why Mom's been acting strange all summer?"

"I think so." James's face darkened. "I hope so. But don't tell your mom I told you. Or Billy."

"So, where's the baby gonna sleep? Not with Billy, I hope." John remembered how his father, stumping for the Baseball Bond, had embarrassed Billy at the Y. "He's thirteen and deserves some privacy, you know."

James grimaced. He hated to be reminded of how he'd hurt Billy's feelings that night. "That's why I can't lend you money. We need to add a room, and your mom has to stop working."

"Don't worry, Dad. I'll figure this out myself."

"I'm sorry, Son."

"Don't apologize. You're going to be a father again. I think that's terrific."

"Thanks, John. And don't tell Mom I didn't give you the money. She'd be livid."

John nodded, then grabbed two beers from the refrigerator and handed one to his father. They both harbored secrets but his, about Dinah and the baby, he would never reveal.

Were all families like this, he wondered—living with secrets and lies? It made him doubt he could ever have faith in family life again.

Chapter Ninety-Eight

BILLY WOKE UP HAPPY. He couldn't believe how well things were working out this summer. The Chiefs were in the Championship, and he had a girlfriend, too—a cute girl who laughed at his jokes, cracked a couple good ones herself, and didn't seem to mind when he talked about baseball. She even beat him in a footrace which he didn't let her win! Hand in hand, they'd walk to the Stand to share a treat and a chocolaty kiss after every home game. Just a quick, shy kiss behind the Stand, it fueled his dreams of one day 'circling the bases' with her—something Kibbee once said on the bus, whose meaning Joel stubbornly refused to explain.

Suddenly he heard unfamiliar voices outside. Darting to the window, he was met with the oddest of sights—Dinah and Lana, in gauzy robes, talking to an old man in a baggy dark suit and hat, and a young woman in a plain white blouse and long gray skirt. Curious, he rushed outside to get a closer look. The strangers had crooked noses—though the woman's was smaller—and both had darkish skin, like Joel and Bernie. And the woman had curly black hair like Joel, too.

"Are you Joel's father?" Dinah asked as she eased down her sunglasses.

"No. I am Seymour Slotnick, and this is my daughter, Rivkah. We are friends of Joel's from New York." The man spoke with an accent that reminded Billy of the Nazis he'd seen in war movies.

The young woman locked eyes with Dinah, before letting her gaze drift down to the engagement ring sparkling on Dinah's left hand. "I'm Joel's intended," she declared as the man threw her a disapproving look.

"His intended what?" Dinah asked, and Billy wondered, too, what that meant.

Lana stifled a snort, then smiled. "Joel's not here right now. Let's go inside and have some refreshments. You must be burning up in those heavy clothes."

Waiting until everyone stepped inside, Billy darted across the driveway to an open window shielded by a bush. Crouching below the sill, he listened for the conversation to resume.

"Lemonade, Seymour, or can I offer you something more bracing?"

"Thank you, no, this is good," which sounded to Billy like "goot."

Lana walked to the wet bar and poured some gin into her lemonade. "I'm taking the Tom Collins shortcut. So, Seymour, you two came all this way just to see Joel?"

"Sadly, no. We had a funeral to attend in St. Paul, and St. Paul was not so far away."

"Not so far? St. Paul's all the way in Minnesota," Dinah countered.

"But the bus ride was pleasant, a wondrous country, so different from New York."

"Close relative?" Lana asked with a twinkling eye, figuring the funeral was just an excuse to check on Rivkah's wandering *intended* and make sure he'd be returning home to Brooklyn.

"Yes, my cousin, Herschel. We grew up together in Germany, before the War."

"Oh," Lana said, no longer delighting in her banter. Crossing the room, she switched on the window fan, letting the breeze rustle her thin robe. "Feel free to take off your jacket and hat, Seymour. We're not formal here."

Keeping his hat on, he removed his suitcoat, revealing a short-sleeved shirt with stained armpits. But what caught Lana and Dinah's eye was the small blue number inked on his forearm.

"What kind of tattoo is that? Were you in the Navy or something?" Dinah blurted.

"Something," Seymour repeated flatly, as Rivkah's eyes widened. "I thought Joel said this was a Jewish home," she said in a frosty voice.

Lana bristled. "My husband is Jewish. He's never tried to hide that from anyone."

Just then the door swung open, and Bernie burst in, his shirt splattered in a ruddy grease. "Damn burger bled all over me." He grabbed Lana's waist. "Help me outta this, doll."

Lana pointed to the couch. "We got company, Bern. Friends of Joel's from New York."

Bernie released Lana and took a quick look at the visitors.

"They're Jews," Dinah added with a smirk.

Bernie flinched before throwing her a warning look. Though she'd apologized for her outburst at the Club and swore it didn't matter that he wasn't her real father, he had to wonder if she would have made that crack if they were bonded by blood.

"Uh, welcome. Didn't see a car. I'm Bernie Rosen. And you are . . . ?"

"Seymour Slotnick and this is my daughter, Rivkah. We took a cab from the bus depot."

"She's Joel's *intended*," Dinah said in a mocking tone, and Lana realized her savvy daughter knew exactly what the phrase meant all along.

"We are just family friends," Seymour asserted.

"Well, any friend of Joel's is a friend of ours. He's a fine young man," Bernie offered, as he shook Seymour's hand. Spotting the mark of Auschwitz, Bernie swallowed hard. "Are you here for tomorrow night's game? Joel's slated to start." Noting a look of confusion, he added, "Scheduled to pitch. You know, baseball?"

"No, our bus leaves tonight. We must return to New York before Shabbos."

Bernie was relieved. It occurred to him that having Rivkah and her father at the game might hurt Joel's performance. "Joel's running errands for me, moving merchandise between my two businesses, the New York Club and the Coney Island Club."

Seymour smiled, "We would be honored to see what New York and Coney Island are like out here in the Wild West," which he pronounced, "Vild Vest."

Dinah snorted, imagining these priggish Jewish pilgrims at the Coney Island Club.

Bernie glared at Dinah. "Sure, we'll go to the Club, but the food's not kosher."

"Thank you, we are good for food. We are ready to go with you now."

"I'm coming, too!" Dinah popped out of her chair and started for her bedroom to change.

"No dice, Dinah. Your mother's taking you to the Mellerdrammer." And then, with intended emphasis, added, "Unless your *fiancé*, John, is driving you today."

Rivkah's eyes brightened as Dinah glowered.

"Don't give me that look, little girl," Bernie scolded. "Seymour and his daughter didn't come all this way to see *you*."

...

Breathless, Billy caught up with Joel in the parking lot of the New York Club. "Joel, your friends from New York are at Bernie's house!" he shouted, hopping off his bike.

"What? Who?"

"Some old German guy and his daughter."

Joel couldn't believe his ears. Could Rivkah and her father possibly be in Rapid City? He'd just got a letter from his folks and they hadn't said anything about the Slotnicks coming.

"Germans? You mean Rivkah and Seymour?"

"That's their names. She said she's your 'intended'."

Joel was dumbfounded but also pleased. Rivkah had been true and had waited for him—unlike Dinah and also, admittedly, himself. "She said that to *you*?"

"No. To Dinah, but what's it mean . . . *intended*?"

"Well, she was my steady girlfriend back in New York, and I guess she still is."

Billy's eyes widened. Did that mean Joel had another girlfriend at the same time he was dating Dinah? Had either of them known about the other one? "Someone died in St. Paul, so they came by bus to see you. They're leaving tonight," he added with an urgent tone.

Joel needed a moment to take it all in. The last people he expected to see in Rapid were Rivkah and her father. "How come you know all this, Billy?"

Billy beamed, proud of his spycraft. Letting his tongue hang slack and bugging out his eyes, he mimed a noose tightening around his neck. "Pull out my fingernails, I'll never tell."

Joel frowned, less charmed by the boy's antics than usual. "Never mind," he said as he grappled with what he might say to Rivkah, after all he'd seen and done that summer.

Bernie's Caddy intercepted them in the Club's lot. Motioning to Billy, he barked, "Pick up Joel's gear and bring it to practice—and put on some shoes while you're at it."

. . .

Rivkah and Joel hugged briefly outside before Bernie ushered them into the Club. Hearing Brooklyn in her voice and gazing into her dark Semitic face, Joel felt as if he'd been roused from a fantastical dream, unsure of where he was or how he'd gotten there. He wished he could kiss her and orient himself by taste and smell but wouldn't do that in front of her father. And he didn't want to give her a false notion of his feelings, when he wasn't himself sure what they were.

Bernie directed them to a corner table, then took Seymour on a tour of the Club. For the first time since crossing the Hudson, Joel kept his head covered indoors, employing his Chiefs cap as a stand-in yarmulke.

Rivkah spoke first, breaking the silence by explaining how her cousin's funeral brought them West. Then, she surprised him with a question he didn't expect would be her first after their summer apart. "Tell me about the baseball. Was it all that you dreamed—your baseball summer?"

Joel paused, overwhelmed by all the stories he wanted to tell—of Clarence and Billy and Hanging Cloud and Hoades, and Bernie and Lana and Stockman . . . and the Passion Play. Other stories, too. Ones he could never tell. "No, but being here was a revelation in so many ways."

"Did you get signed?"

Joel cocked his head. He didn't think she knew about that, much less the baseball term for it. "I was seen by a Dodger Scout but haven't heard from him yet. I pitched well and the team's in the Championship, so I may still get an offer."

"Would that make you happy? Have you been happy this summer?" Her eyes were soft with concern. "I got the postcard of that cathedral and had to wonder."

"Happy? Sometimes. It was different than anything I'd ever done. I met a lot of new people and saw places I could never have imagined, but there were other things, too."

And then, he told her what he most wanted her to know. "A boy died in my arms."

"Oh, no!" Rivkah reached across the table and covered Joel's hand with hers. "Tell me."

"There was a storm. Hail as big as baseballs. One shattered the windshield of the car he was riding in, and a piece of glass cut his jugular. I didn't know what to do. Pull out the glass or leave it in? He was just fourteen. By the time the ambulance came, he was dead. I asked one of the doctors what I could have done. He said 'nothing,' but maybe he was just being kind because the boy was already dead. Maybe if I'd been . . ." Joel bit his lip and his voice trailed off.

Rivkah shook her head. "No, Joel. I'm sure the doctor told you the truth."

He shrugged and looked down at his hands.

"What will you do now?" she asked after giving him a moment to gather himself.

"It made me think it was a sign from God that I must go to medical school. Then I pitched the next day and it was the only time I stopped seeing the dead boy's face." He did a seesaw motion with his hands, as if weighing baseball and medicine on a balance scale. "And then, there's America. There's so much country out there I want to see."

Rivkah's eyes lit up. "Oh, yes—on the bus coming across, it took my breath away. It was like a canvas unfurling outside my window. I wanted to see it all."

The fervor in her voice emboldened him. "Me, too. Yellowstone, the Rockies. California."

"Alone?"

Joel guessed that she was probing. She likely met Dinah earlier at the Rosens'. "With a team, I hope."

"Yes. We've been hearing rumors about the Dodgers moving out West, but there are medical schools in California, too."

"Of course, but I couldn't do both—go to medical school *and* play baseball." And still be an observant Jew, he added to himself, though he wouldn't suffer that reckoning until he had to.

"It's been done. Not that long ago."

He was incredulous. "Really? Who?"

"Bobby Brown. He played for the Yankees when they beat the Dodgers in the World Series. He went to medical school at the same time."

Joel's mouth dropped. He was thirteen in 1949 and had listened to that World Series on the radio, but never heard anyone mention that Brown, the Yankees' third baseman, was in medical school. Or, if they had, it hadn't meant anything to him at the time. "You're kidding."

"No. I'm sure of it." She said it with such certainty that he was convinced it was true. Still, he was shocked that she knew anything about the '49 Yankees—even Joe DiMaggio or Yogi Berra—much less Bobby Brown. "How do you know this, Rivkah?"

She fixed him with a cool stare. "Someone told me." And then with a boldness that caught Joel completely by surprise, she added, "I had a summer, too."

And he knew that 'someone' was a man, but that he wasn't going to ask about him. Just as she wouldn't ask about the women he'd known that summer.

"A Yankee fan! Who woulda thunk it?"

Leaning across the table, he kissed her open-mouthed—a promise that in a week, or maybe two, he'd be heading back to Brooklyn to see this through.

Chapter Ninety-Nine

GUY STOCKMAN ROARED INTO SIOUX PARK, the sun blazing off his fiery red Pontiac. He'd done it! Won the Basin League Pennant! Well . . . tied for it with the Kernels, but who would quibble with that? Now they were ready to take them on for the League Championship. Grind them up and spit them out like chaw. And his red-winged chariot, once imperiled, was his. Lock, stock, and barrel.

Guy snorted. The season had been a roller coaster. Early on, the bats belted out hits, but the pitching, fielding, and baserunning lagged behind. Then, in mid-season, the bats cooled, while the pitching and defense gelled, and the baserunning turned smart. Finally, in the stretch run, everything clicked, and they went on a ten-game winning streak to close out the regular season and prime them for the playoffs.

Grinning, Guy hustled past Bernie's parked Caddy and gave it a knock. He hated to admit it, but the man deserved credit for signing catcher Dayton Todd and bringing in outfielder Len Hunt. The ex-Negro Leaguer regularly delivered—a clutch hit, a run-saving catch, a critical stolen base—the full repertoire of the player he was touted to be. Hunt was the lightning and Hacker the thunder in a one-two punch dubbed "Thunder and Lightning" by the *Journal*'s Paddy Olavson.

And without Hoades or Kibbee around to strike the match, he never had a fire to douse.

• • •

Surveying the crowd, Bernie saw that it was the largest draw of the season, with fans sitting cross-legged in the aisles and standing shoulder-to-shoulder along the crest of the little hill that extended down the foul lines. It seemed as if the whole town had shown up for this, the Chiefs' last home game, the first matchup in their best-of-three championship series against the Kernels.

But how could it not be so, he bragged to himself. As the season went on, every home game, or every important one, saw a larger audience than the last. In fact, every place they'd played reported record crowds when the Chiefs came to town because Rapid was the League's only real city—its "Big Apple"—and the Chiefs, its Yankees. And it was the only team with a Negro—now two—and a Jew, and for a brief moment, an Indian. And, most important of all—slugger Frank Hacker, the Chiefs' own Babe Ruth, one of his collegians, not one of Stockman's vaunted pros.

Bernie puffed with pride. Tonight, his Jewish southpaw, Joel Meznik, would get this important start, and solely on his own merits. He couldn't be prouder if Joel were his own son.

...

It was eight o'clock on a hot August night, and the light had already begun to wane. Joel recalled his pitching debut in Huron, and how bright the sky had been at that hour in June. But now his summer was drawing to a close, and he'd be leaving behind all those who'd been part of his new world—Clarence, Billy, Bernie, Stockman, and Quarles—all present tonight. And Dinah, Martha, and Lana, who were not. When he took the mound, he knew it was the last game he'd pitch for the Chiefs, and maybe the last he'd pitch for any team that mattered.

Joel glanced at the on-deck circle where Mitchell's leadoff man sliced the air with restless anticipation. The Kernels were hot. Like the Chiefs, they'd ended their regular season on a high note, hammering the Lake Sox 19-10.

To Joel, that score sounded ominously like the Kernels' early season 20-10 battering of the Chiefs when ten home runs flew out of Sioux Park, seven slugged by the Kernels. It was the game that inspired Paddy Olavson's column mocking Bernie's free steak offer and his undersized stadium, calling Sioux Park a Little League field. A shiver shot down Joel's spine. Tonight, he'd be facing those selfsame sluggers, and defending those selfsame Little League fences.

Still, despite his concerns, he was proud to get the start. He'd earned it—tossing a shutout in his last outing, then working effectively in late inning relief, both commendable performances, and both after the death of the Merritt boy. Somehow, the tragedy had changed him, triggering a sort of hypnosis that settled him into a curious calm as soon as he ascended the mound.

And yet, the challenge Rivkah raised sent him reeling. Was it really possible to pursue both medical school and professional baseball? Could he do what the Yanks' Bobby Brown had done?

Joel felt the energy shoot off him like sparks from a campfire. Closing his eyes, he turned his back to the batter's box and recalled that time at Sylvan Lake when Dinah gathered herself on the rock before knocking his socks off with the song from *Damn Yankees.*

Yes, this was his Sioux Park swan song, and it was up to him to make it a showstopper.

• • •

Entering the ballpark, John was struck by a deep sadness. For months, he'd looked forward to Rapid getting a team but had seen only a handful of games. Some were missed when he was in Hollywood. Others he skipped to avoid Dinah and Joel. Now, he was loath to run into Bernie because of his impending breakup with Dinah and his decision to go to Yale. The simple pleasures of baseball had again become sorely entangled—hopelessly snarled like a kite in a tree.

John looked up at the press box. That could be the place to hide out. The men might ride him about his last stint in the crow's nest, when Dinah cursed him over the airwaves, but they wouldn't question his right to be there. What did it matter if he pretended to be on assignment. It was just one more lie in a season of hits, runs, and far too many errors to count.

John mounted the stairs and stood for a moment at the mouth of the press box.

"Johnny Boy!" Paddy, holding the score book, greeted his former protégé with a smile and an outstretched hand. "Lookin' for your old job back?"

John eked out a smile. Clearly, Paddy was tonight's Official Scorer. "Wouldn't deny you the pleasure, Paddy. Just figured this was the best seat in the house."

Ex-Mayor Baker clapped John on the shoulder. "Glad to have you, son, but lock that door behind you. No girls in the treehouse. 'Specially loud ones."

KOTA radio's Verne Sheppard chortled. "Oh! that's right. Heard you're engaged to the young woman now."

John's throat tightened. He'd anticipated a tease, but this was more pointed than he expected.

John forced a smile. "Don't worry, she's the damsel in distress in Rockerville tonight."

"Hope you slipped the archvillain a couple bucks to keep her tied to the railroad tracks."

"Give the kid a break, Paddy," Baker said. "Who among us hasn't had trouble taming the so-called weaker sex?"

"Ah-men to that!" *Journal* Sports Editor, Bob Romaker, chimed in, as he slid down the bench to make room for John. "Have a seat. You can help me with tomorrow's column."

...

Taking the mound in the top of the first, Joel wondered if he was up to the challenge of the playoffs. Warming up in the bullpen, he kept bouncing his big curve, and while an adrenaline rush boosted his fastball, it was high and wild, missing its spots. Only his slider behaved. Still, over the course of a game, he knew it could all change, and he might regain command of his full repertoire.

Greeted by warm applause from the big Sioux Park crowd, Joel proceeded to plunk the Kernels' leadoff batter and walk the two men that followed, loading the bases with no outs. He began to sweat. Joe Lutz, the Kernels' manager and cleanup hitter, was up next. A former Major Leaguer who'd led the Basin League in home runs the summer before, the lefty Lutz was known as a dead fastball hitter.

Joel took a deep breath and broke off a slider. The ball was aimed at Lutz's hip but broke over the inside corner of the plate for a called strike. His confidence growing, he followed with another slider, this one low on the outside corner, looking like a fastball but breaking outside the strike zone. Lutz lunged for it and missed. "Strike two!"

More confident still, Joel shook off his catcher's call for a curve. He knew what he needed here. A fastball, but not the one Lutz was hoping for. Chin music, high and tight, it backed the burly slugger off the plate and dimmed his memory of his foolish lunge the pitch before. Ball one.

Then, the coup de grâce, another slider, this one lower than the first. Looking like a fastball and a strike until the last instant, it broke wide of the plate and again Lutz lunged and whiffed. "Strike three!"

Joel bulled his chest. Out number one. Another strikeout and a fly-out ended the threat. No hits, no runs, no errors—a snuffed-out Kernels' assault. Everything he ever wished for as a pitcher—tactics, finesse, command. He could now say he had it all.

"Loved the chin music, Joely. The mighty Maglie would be proud." Quarles, always the proud teacher, clapped Joel on the shoulder as they jogged back to the dugout.

In the bottom of the first, Len Hunt got things started for the Chiefs with a grounder that struck a rut in the infield and ricocheted through the shortstop's legs like a croquet ball through the wickets. Then, a skittish O'Toole walked Dayton Todd, and Quarles hit a long fly to right scoring Hunt and Todd. The right fielder appeared to have a bead on the ball, but a gusty wind stopped it cold, and the ball struck the fielder's elbow and dropped to the ground.

"Hit or error?" Mayor Baker asked—as Paddy held off on his call.

"Hit," Paddy declared.

John agreed. Can't call an error when Mother Nature is at fault.

Visibly shaken, O'Toole failed to flag down Hacker's grounder through the box, which sent Quarles to third. Then Q stole home without a throw. A wild pitch was followed by a passed ball, a flare to right that dropped, and a soft liner to first that was muffed—this, by the peerless first baseman, Lutz, who appeared to lose the ball in the glare of the setting sun. At the end of the first inning, the Chiefs had a commanding lead—6-zip.

In the press box, John was dumbfounded. It was as if someone were sticking pins into a Kernels voodoo doll. Every break had gone the Chiefs' way—errors by four different Mitchell players, an uncontested steal of home, and both a wild pitch and a passed ball. Clearly, O'Toole and his Kernels were spooked, with Mother Nature appearing to side with the Chiefs.

"Is this how it is with baseball?" John wondered. Less predictable than other sports because in baseball, the capricious "Mother" gets to play with all four elements: earth, wind, water, fire—a rutted field, a rain-slicked ball, a blinding light, or a 'Sioux Park Special'—a wind-carried baseball sailing out of the high-altitude stadium. Or, a storm of cottonwood fluff, John thought with a wistful smile, recalling that hopeful first road trip to Pierre.

In the second inning, the Kernels got back a run when Joel again walked the first two Mitchell batters and gave up a long double to left center. If the ball had not bounced over the fence, the blow would have scored both baserunners. Then Joel rallied to retire the next three Mitchell batsmen and walked from the mound with a 6-1 lead.

John shook his head. Clearly, Joel had benefited from good luck in the inning. All three outs had come on hard hit balls—two scorching grounders right at third baseman Paskiewicz and a 'frozen rope' to Clarence in left. Good fortune, but could it last?

In the bottom of the second, Rapid continued its assault on Kernels pitching, plating three more runs. O'Toole was gone now, relieved by a journeyman minor leaguer who gave up a walk to Hunt, a double to Todd, and as the big crowd buzzed, a blast over the scoreboard by Clarence.

John figured that with an early 9-1 lead, Joel could surely relax, but it wasn't until the fifth inning that he hit his stride, needing just ten pitches to strike out the side.

Then in the sixth, it all fell apart. A walk, a 'seeing eye grounder', and a high-bounding 'Baltimore Chop,' loaded the bases. The next batter was Doc Dougherty, another ex-major leaguer. After two quick strikes on high inside fastballs, Dougherty lifted a short fly down the line in right. With two outs, the Mitchell baserunners were off and running.

If the ball dropped, it would produce at least two runs, but three Chiefs were after it—Hacker charging in from right field, Quarles retreating from first base, and Lee Casey, scurrying into the outfield from second.

The ball landed in fair territory, a base hit. As Hacker lunged forward to make the catch, his shoulder delivered a knockout punch to Quarles' chin. Stumbling over the flattened Quarles, a remorseful Hacker lumbered after the errant ball but he was too late. All three Mitchell baserunners and the batter had circled the bases, cutting the Chiefs' lead to 9-5, and bringing Stockman out of the dugout, calling for the ball.

Romaker shook his head. "I'd have left Meznik in. That dunker shoulda been caught."

Paddy agreed. "Early on, New Yawk pitched like crap but had eight good gloves backin' him. Now, he's pitching OK, but Lady Luck turned agin' 'im."

John nodded. He'd seen it in games he'd scored with his father—a pitcher throwing well, but relieved because the manager thought Lady Luck switched sides and would return only after he changed hurlers.

"Mother Nature had a hand in it, too," John added, recalling how the wind had carried the ball. "She whisked it away with her broom."

Paddy hooted. "Mother Nature and Lady Luck—two fickle bitches if there ever was one!"

Musing on Paddy's quip, John was spurred to tally how he himself had scored with that mercurial duo—Polio, Dinah, Joel, Groucho. Bad luck, good luck, flipping back and forth. But, to be honest, Dinah counted as both.

Raising his eyes, John looked at the scoreboard—far from a perfect performance, but not bad either. Probably good enough for Joel to get the win.

Spotting the lights of a plane jetting east across the prairie, John hoped that, someday, he might say the same for himself.

• • •

Joel surrendered the ball to Stockman's outstretched hand.

"That's it, young man," Stockman said, "Dalluge will take it from here."

Walking from the mound, Joel saw Billy waiting on the dugout steps, a Hershey bar in one hand, a warm-up jacket in the other. Then, he spotted Red, the Dodger scout, sitting on the aisle. Had he just shown up? Joel couldn't believe he'd missed him.

Joel glanced at the scoreboard, though he already knew his line score. Pretty good, he thought, given the prairie wind. But was it good enough for the Dodgers? Only time would tell.

Turning to the crowd, Joel tipped his hat to the warm applause, capping his season as a pitcher in Rapid City—and maybe anywhere else, too.

Chapter One Hundred

JENNIE STOOD AT THE GARBAGE PAIL, scraping dried egg yolk from John's plate. She'd risen early to fix breakfast for the menfolk before their trip to Mitchell for the second, and possibly deciding, game of the best-of-three Championship Series. Billy would be on the bus with the team, and James and John in the Chevy, because John's Belvedere was in the shop. "Transmission trouble," he offered with a shrug.

She'd nodded, though she didn't think a transmission should be a problem in such a new car. Still, she didn't want to criticize her son, though it was hard not speaking her mind, especially to John. But this was the summer she'd learned to conceal, and she resolved to put this newfound skill to good use, mending the frayed fabric of the family . . . for the sake of the baby if nothing else.

Jennie grabbed the edge of the sink as a wave of nausea hit her. Just yesterday, Dr. Latham told her that all was well with the pregnancy, including her syphilis test.

She was not there last night to see Clarence play his final home game, and later, she feigned morning sickness to escape Billy's spirited play-by-play account. James's edict barring her from the Stand proved a godsend in her vow to banish Clarence from her thoughts. She couldn't wait for all talk of the Chiefs—and of Clarence—to pass from the house like a summer fever. That, she believed, would do more for her peace of mind than any spiritual guidance she might seek.

And last night in bed, she and James had relations for the first time in months. Touching his shoulder as he lay down beside her, she simply nodded when he turned to her—and that was that.

Through the kitchen window she watched as James and John drove off, followed by Billy, Bernie, and Joel headed for the team bus in Bernie's Cadillac. Each carried a small suitcase for their overnight in Mitchell.

Leaning against the sink, she drew a glass of water and waited for the queasiness to subside. From the street she heard the familiar clank of the mailbox. "Postman's early," she thought, glancing at the clock. Out the kitchen window, she spotted mechanics from the local service station dropping off a mint-green convertible, and a minute later, Lana and Dinah loading suitcases into its trunk. They must be going to

Mitchell for the game, she thought, though John hadn't mentioned that Dinah was making the trip.

That didn't surprise her as she and John had barely spoken all summer. But this morning, he'd kissed her cheek while swiping a piece of bacon from the frypan. For a moment, as her eyes filled, she imagined she'd been carried back to a breakfast months earlier—before Dinah, Clarence Williams, and the Chiefs had roiled all their lives.

Now, she resolved to hold her tongue when it came to Dinah, who'd soon be joining the family and likely bear her a grandchild not long after her own baby was born. John's kiss that morning was a sign he was willing to let bygones be bygones. It was up to her to meet him halfway.

"Get the hairdryer!" Lana yelled from the Rosen driveway as Dinah dropped two more suitcases by the side of the car.

"Four suitcases and a hairdryer for a short trip to Mitchell." Jennie smacked her lips with a disdain she couldn't suppress. Such pampered princesses, who couldn't go a day without indulging their vanity. As she watched the Rosen women drive off—the sun glinting off the hairdryer's silver dome—she thought, "Maybe they'll crash," then waited for the stab of remorse that never came. Grabbing her grocery list, she wrote down the words that did.

CRASH VISION

Some will look, and some will look away
I can't help myself
And I can't make it so . . .
So, I drive on.
Past shacks and soddies that stood and sheltered
now bend and kneel.
There will be no mercy
in a land that swallows its seed
and spits back dust.

She tucked the paper into her apron pocket and headed down the driveway to check the mail. If the baby was a girl, she'd name her Flory Clare—Flory for her sister and Clare for the man who brought her back to verse. If a boy, she'd name him James.

There was just one letter in the box—pale pink, with no stamp, addressed to *John* in a florid hand. Most strange was the impress of a circle joined to a small, sharp-edged stone.

Holding the envelope up to the sun, Jennie gasped.

To her surprise, her first thought was of John and how hurt he would be.

Then the laughter struck, clear as a church bell, bounding up the street like a skip-roping child.

Chapter One Hundred One

BERNIE WAS RIGHT. THE LEAGUE had found a way to screw 'the new, rich kid on the block'—awarding the Kernels the number one seed because they'd led the most days in League standings. Officially, the Chiefs and the Kernels shared the Pennant, but in the Championship series, the Kernels would enjoy home field advantage, hosting game 2 and, if needed, game 3 in Mitchell.

When Bernie learned that half his Chiefs would leave for home straight from Mitchell, he ditched the idea of returning to Rapid for a victory party and reserved the Mitchell Country Club—just in case. He also sprang for a bus to ferry the team's most ardent fans, including the few players' wives and any collegians' summer flings, so there'd be women there to make it a true gala.

But not Dinah or Lana, because both the Club and the Mellerdrammer would be open for business on this, one of the busiest summer weekends of the Black Hills tourist season. At least, Bernie would be spared seeing his wife and Guy Stockman together, something he'd managed to avoid all season. And Buck was stationed back in Rapid to keep an eye on the girls.

...

It was a hot August night on the Dakota prairie and Kernels Park was packed with its largest crowd of the season. Most were from Mitchell and the surrounding countryside, but there were also delegations of fans from the nearer Basin League towns, eager to check out the latest Corn Palace tableaux, and watch the big game on the converted cornfield. And, of course, busloads of fans had crossed the State from Rapid, as well as many by car. And Governor Foss and Congressman McGovern were there. And Red, the Dodger Scout, too.

Surprising himself, Guy felt calm. Of course, he wanted his Chiefs to win that night. But even if Wiegand, the old pro, failed them—they'd have another shot at the championship the following evening with their ace collegian, George Schmid, rested and ready.

Still, one thing troubled him—Red, the Dodger Scout. Last night, he'd rushed out as soon as the game ended. Was he ducking him? He said before that the Dodgers' Reno job was opening up. It was just what Guy wanted, and he'd told Red that, straight out. Had he been too pushy? Did the job go to someone else? Would winning the title mean nothing in the end, just another way station on the road to nowhere?

• • •

Even an old pro can play a bad card, and Dick Wiegand's hanging deuce to the Kernels' Gene Duffy with the bases loaded in the fourth was fired back like a canon shot in a cornfield—carrying to the far reaches of the ballpark, while the three Kernel baserunners, flushed like pheasants from their stations, circled the sacks in a wild, mad flight toward home.

As Len Hunt chased after Duffy's long drive, Dayton Todd, the Chiefs' catcher, waited at home plate, counting Kernels as they crossed. One, two, three. The score even now as Duffy, the tie-breaker, flew toward home, where Todd, standing his ground, reached out for the baseball.

The sound of the collision hit Stockman's ear like a thunderclap. From his low dugout perch, he saw Todd crumple into the dirt, moaning and writhing, his left ankle bent under him in an impossible angle, with the baseball, the instigator of it all, resting innocently on home plate.

Watching from his position in left field, Clarence Williams winced and shut his eyes. Even from that distance, the sound made him sick inside. He'd suffered some bad crashes himself over the years, though he'd never been felled just that way. But then, he was a much bigger man than Todd and supposed that had protected him. He just hoped this wasn't as bad as it looked—though bad enough for him to offer up a prayer for the young man.

Then, it came to him—no one could carry on after that smash-up. He would have to step in as catcher.

Or Stockman might. He'd recently put himself back on the roster, but hadn't done much of anything except throw batting practice a few times.

Clarence looked in at Stockman, but the man wasn't looking back at him. Gazing up at the sky, Guy seemed to be waiting for heaven or another Choctaw helicopter to deliver him a replacement ballplayer. Clarence snorted. Was he thinking of handling the position himself? Bigot or want-to-be hero, the man was no manager.

"It ought to be me," Clarence declared to himself. Though his ribs still ached from the attack in Yankton, his hands were good and his throwing arm as strong as ever. And, unlike Stockman, he knew he could hit. Clarence spat in disgust. At times like this, you saw the true measure of a man. And, from where he stood, Guy Stockman looked pretty damn small.

Guy watched as Todd was carried off the field. Dusting off home plate, the umpire threw him an impatient scowl. He had to make a choice and he had to make it fast.

Just that morning, he'd considered letting Williams catch and putting Todd in left field. The two men were roughly equal as backstops, but Todd's greater speed would allow him to cover more ground in Mitchell's big outfield.

But he just couldn't do it—couldn't shake the memory of his own years in the Minors, dreaming of someday taking over from Campanella, the Dodgers' veteran Negro catcher. He figured that Todd had suffered like him, toiling for years in the Cleveland chain, blocked by their all-star catcher, Jim Hegan, without ever getting a shot at the Big Leagues. And so, he decided. Todd would catch. Williams would stay in left field.

But now, in the fourth inning, with Todd gone and five full innings ahead, he had another decision to make—himself or Williams behind the dish. His broken thumb was mostly healed, and he believed that he called a better game. And this might be his last chance to lead his team on the field—his best chance to bring home the Basin League Crown.

Then his doubts crept in. What if his thumb couldn't handle the pounding of a hard fastball for five innings, or his rickety knee not hold up? And he'd only taken batting practice once since returning to the roster. What if he struck out in a big spot—embarrassed himself in the clutch?

Embarrassment—the fear of every ballplayer on the downslope of his career.

No. He had nothing more to prove as a player. His future in baseball was as a manager. Williams would catch, and if *he* fucked up, the loss would be on *him*.

Guy turned and raised his arm to wave Clarence in from left field.

• • •

Sitting in the dugout, Joel watched Clarence jog in and don his gear. He looked calm and collected—not shaken by what had just happened to Todd. Knowing the man, he wasn't too surprised, but shouldn't he at least feel rusty? He hadn't caught much that season before his ribs were broken, and only a bullpen or two since returning to the team. But a bullpen session wasn't a game. And he couldn't help thinking about that brutal collision that just happened and could happen again. Joel shuddered—the collision playing again in his head in slow motion, like his recurring nightmare of Glen Merritt dying in his arms in the Rosen driveway.

Clarence plopped down next to Joel and clapped on his shin guards. Bending forward as if to tie his own shoe, Joel whispered in Clarence's ear. "Hey, buddy. Be careful out there."

Clarence laughed and slapped Joel's thigh. "Yes, Momma," then hustled onto the field.

Clarence was not careful. Despite his bruised ribs, he played without restraint, blocking pitches in the dirt with his big body and tumbling into the Kernels' dugout after snagging a foul pop. And always he was the field general—barking out orders, calling a smart game, arranging the defense. It was an outstanding performance, the best of his Basin League season.

Then, in the bottom of the ninth, with one out, the score tied, and a runner on third, the Kernels attempted a suicide squeeze. If the play worked, the Kernels would win.

Joel saw it coming, though all he could think of was another terrible crash at home plate—this time, with his friend Clarence suffering the blow.

Paskiewicz, the third baseman, saw it, too, charging down the line to field the bunt, shouting, "He's going!"

Wiegand heard the third baseman's shout as the Kernels' batter squared around to bunt. Finishing his wind-up, he threw a fastball straight at the batter's head. The batter ducked and Clarence, rising from his crouch, calmly plucked the baseball from the air and tagged the startled baserunner before he could touch home plate with the winning run.

It was a spectacular play, Joel thought, in a low-key, Clarence Williams sort of way. So smooth and solid were the three old pros—Paskiewicz, Wiegand, and Clarence—that they'd made it look easy, as if they'd practiced the play a hundred times . . . knowing that the batter would duck to save his skull and not lay down that precious game-winning bunt.

Then in the top of the tenth, with the game still tied, and Chiefs on second and third, Clarence fought off a tough pitch and fisted a grounder to the right side—exchanging an out for a run and giving the Chiefs a 7-6 lead. In the bottom of the inning, Q came on in relief and closed out the win.

Later, thinking about the game, it seemed to Joel that the veterans had simply shown the college boys how the game was meant to be played. But now he stormed the field—with Billy, Stockman, Clarence, and the others, whooping and hollering—pros and collegians alike—the unified tribe they'd finally become.

Chapter One Hundred Two

IT WAS NOT THE CELEBRATION Bernie had hoped for—three hundred miles across the state in the corn-fed belly of the beast. And, to his surprise, the Mitchell Country Club was drab, decorated in beige and brown as if all the color in the town had been harvested for the Corn Palace.

But his Chiefs, flushed with victory, seemed not to notice.

Standing at the bar with Carl and James, Bernie surveyed the handsome young ballplayers. Many of them—for reasons of race, class, or creed—had never set foot in a country club, but tonight, they all were there as a team—a championship team—and he was proud and a bit tickled that a Jew and a Kraut—he and Mueller—had made it all possible.

"We done good, Carl," he said, raising his glass for a self-congratulatory clink.

"And you too, James," he added as an afterthought. "Had the Stand humming like the Ford assembly line. Except that time your wife passed out, and when the girl was left alone to man it." He shook his head as if those episodes had spoiled a no-hitter. "Where's Jennie been keeping herself lately? And the girl you had popping corn? What happened to her?"

James blanched at the reference to Martha. He'd managed not to think of her in weeks. Taking a swig of beer, James racked his brain for an explanation his canny neighbor might swallow. "Girl broke her arm and Jennie just tired of it—never liked baseball much, anyway."

Bernie smirked. "Oh, I don't know, James. She seemed pretty interested, at times."

James chose to ignore Bernie's cryptic comment, which like most of his observations about Jennie came across as barbed riddles. He had something he wanted to pitch to his neighbor —something he hoped would help him stay close to Billy. And he needed to do it before Bernie learned that John was breaking his engagement to Dinah.

"Sure, Jenn had some interest. But not like us men."

Then, he told Bernie about a customer who started the Little League in Wyoming. "Hard to believe Wyoming got Little League before South Dakota. Riverton, Cody, Douglas, Glenrock—all have teams. We should start Little League here. Kids like Billy would love it."

"You angling to get the kiddie concession, James?" Bernie joshed, with a wink at Carl.

James bristled. That wasn't his intention at all. He just wanted Billy to play baseball on a proper field, with uniforms, equipment, and umpires—not the helter-skelter sandlot ball of Rapid's playground league. He'd get back into coaching and manage Billy's team. But it would take money, and for that he needed Bernie's help. "Nah—I'll stick with Sioux Park, but kids in Rapid have been inspired. They want to be like the Chiefs."

"First in the Basin League! First in the Little League!" Bernie bellowed. "Can't argue with that." He pumped his neighbor's hand. "Count me in. Billy will get his team. And I'll coach it!"

• • •

For Joel, the celebration was bittersweet, for he'd soon be leaving Rapid and might never see any of these people again. With sentimentality heightened by drink, he made the rounds of the ballroom, resolved to thank everyone who'd helped him that summer, including Stockman for giving him the start in front of the Dodger Scout, Quarles for his pitching advice and wise counsel, and Fred for his amusing yarns and the driving lesson in the hearse. That was a story he'd relate back in New York—one he could tell without censoring.

"Couldn't have asked for a better tour guide, Fred."

"You was a good listener. Asked smart questions, too." Fred's face darkened. "Most times."

Joel figured he meant his clumsy probing of Bernie's politics. Still, he had one more question to ask. "I was wondering about Andrew Hanging Cloud. Did his child recover?"

For a moment Fred looked confused, as if he'd forgotten that Joel hadn't been clued in on the real story. "Oh, yeah. Kid's OK."

"With that wicked curve, I was sure he'd be back for the pennant drive."

Fred shrugged. "Heard he headed up Canada way."

"Pitching in the Man-Dak League?" Joel asked, hoping it was so.

"Could be. Better place for 'im," Fred said without conviction, then headed for the bar.

Finding himself marooned, Joel spotted John slumped at a table strewn with beer bottles. When they'd first met, he thought they'd be friends, but the younger man seemed to have a chip on his shoulder from the start. And when Dinah entered the picture, that chip became a boulder.

Joel took a seat next to his erstwhile romantic rival. "Never congratulated you on your engagement, John. Don't have to tell ya, you hooked a great gal."

"Thanks. You headin' back to New York now?" John's words were slurred, but Joel could swear he heard him mutter, "I hope," under his breath.

Joel's eyes twinkled as mischief beckoned. And for once, he answered its call. "May go out West first. Get on a quiz show—win me some wheels and drive back to Brooklyn in style."

John sidestepped Joel's obvious gibe. "Aren't you leaving from here?"

"Nope. Gotta get back to Rapid—something there I need to take care of."

John got up from the table. He'd had enough of Joel, and, with the New Yorker returning to Rapid, he'd have to wait a little longer to break the news about Yale to Dinah—and to Bernie, too.

Sorry that he'd razzed the younger man, Joel searched for Clarence but instead caught sight of Billy sneaking a swallow from a beer bottle left on one of the tables. With a furtive glance, the boy moved on to an abandoned highball. Joel was about to stop him when he remembered that Billy's father was there, and his own guardianship had come to an end.

But, as his final duty, he sought out James to suggest he keep an eye on his scavenging son.

Standing at the bar, James downed his bourbon in one swallow. His Little League pitch had spun out of control, with Bernie again staking his claim to Billy. And then the man brought up Martha. James's frown deepened as he spotted Joel heading his way. He braced for a second hit.

"Mr. Moran—nice to see you again. Seen Billy around?" Joel turned his head from side to side, hoping James would follow his lead and see what the boy was up to.

"No. Sorry." James angled his body away from Joel and signaled for the bartender.

Surprised by his rudeness, Joel recalled the day he went to the Morans' to ask for Martha's phone number. "I was just wondering . . . if you'd heard from Martha since her accident."

Gripping the edge of the bar, James turned to Joel—a cold, hard smile on his face. "No, I haven't. Have you?"

"I called once, but her father wasn't very . . . friendly."

James grunted. "Fathers can be funny that way about their daughters."

Joel nodded. "I'm sure you're right. Guess you'll see her soon. Please say goodbye for me."

"What?" James asked, his heart skipping a beat.

"When school starts. Isn't she one of your students?"

"Yes. Excuse me. Bartender!"

James moved to the end of the bar, leaving Joel to wonder what it was with Mr. Moran. Was he like this with everyone or just him? And Mrs. Moran had been cold from the word 'go'. Maybe Bernie was right—that this place had a kind of endemic anti-Semitism. Though Billy seemed to have dodged it. When the boy turned frosty, it was purely personal.

Stranded again, Joel surveyed the crowd. He'd sought out Fred, Quarles, John, and James. Only his chat with Quarles had gone well. Finishing his beer, he waved to Clarence across the room. He'd caught a great game. He was happy for him. Too bad he hadn't been behind the plate last night when the Dodger Scout witnessed his subpar performance. It might have made a difference.

Clarence bounded over and clapped Joel on the back. "Got my transfer." A big grin spread across his face as he jerked his thumb in the direction of the base commander. "And a new car, too! A real bargain."

"The base commander sold you a car?"

"Nope—Billy's brother. Heard me talkin' about needin' to haul the trailer back to Indiana, so he sold me the car he won in California."

Joel's mouth dropped. "John Moran sold you the Belvedere?" He couldn't imagine John and Dinah managing with just one car in Rapid, though that might keep her from skipping town.

"Now I can haul my Dakota soddie back home in style," Clarence exulted.

"You think your wife's gonna be happy 'bout that?"

"Don't matter. No way we're livin' in her Daddy's house! And, if I get itchy, we can hit the road with the trailer."

Joel hooted. "You get itchy, come visit me in Brooklyn."

Clarence smiled. "You know, I might just do that."

• • •

Grabbing a beer, James walked out of the Country Club to the Chevy. He hadn't been to eastern South Dakota in years and was struck by the steamy air—so different from Rapid where the cool, dry nights made you forget the searing heat of the day.

Slipping into the Chev's moist womb, he flipped on the radio as a silly ditty came on, a satirical verse that seemed to mock his inner turmoil.

Trans-fusion, trans-fusion. I'm just a solid mess of con-tusions
Never never never gonna speed again. Slip the blood to me Bud.

All season long, like a kid drunk on summer, he'd scarcely given a thought to the approaching school year. But in little more than a week, the Basin League and the concession stand would be packed away—mothballed like Jennie's winter woolens—replaced by lesson plans, attendance sheets, and Martha. Every day, Martha. Passing her in the hallways, seeing her at assemblies and in the cafeteria. Maybe in his own classroom, too, a daily prick of conscience, a cruel reminder of her sorrow and his headlong stumble into sin.

James laid his head on the steering wheel and sobbed. So, this was how it was going to be from now on. And there was absolutely nothing he could do about it.

• • •

Bernie approached Stockman with his hand palm up. "Keys, please. To the Pontiac." He snapped his fingers impatiently.

"What?" Stockman protested. We just won the Championship!"

Bernie shrugged. "The bet was for the pennant. Which you did not win."

"Are you kidding? We tied Mitchell for the top spot."

"Gotta read the fine print, my friend. A tie is not a win."

Stockman balled his fist and Bernie did likewise, thinking he'd like nothing better than to beat the crap out of the man who'd cuckolded him. The broken thumb hadn't evened the score. Meted out—as it had to be—by Buck, it robbed him of the satisfaction of flesh pounding flesh. But a fight now would spur questions from Carl and the Morans—questions he wasn't prepared to answer. And the story would surely get back to Rapid and to Paddy Olavson, who'd have a field day with it in the *Journal*. No. He'd kept his cool all summer. He'd have to do it one more night.

Bernie smiled through gritted teeth. "Just pulling your leg, Stockman. You get to drive home, wherever home is for washed-up ballplayers.

But I docked your last paycheck. You only get half for a tie. Thanks for helping pay for the party." Bernie turned on his heel and walked off.

"Cheap kike," Guy thought, then cursed himself for not telling Bernie how he got the good word from the Dodger Scout after the game. A bit of a surprise that all this time Red had been scouting him, too.

So, tomorrow he'd be on his way home to Johnstown, PA, and come spring, to the Dodger Camp at Vero Beach, Florida. Then on to Reno, 'Biggest Little City in the World' and home of the Dodgers' Class 'C' affiliate in the California League. And, while Nevada wasn't the Golden State, it was right next door, and with Reno's swanky nightclubs and speedy divorces—close enough to lure Bernie's Lady Lana away. Even if it took extra innings to do it!

...

The celebration broke up at one, but players with girlfriends or wives—and Guy with a willing waitress—left early to top off the festivities in their motel rooms. Fred stayed to ferry Joel and Clarence and the other chaste ballplayers—and a green-faced Billy—to their lodgings.

Bernie paid the bill, then drove alone to the motel where the night clerk handed him a note marked "URGENT!" along with a chilling message in capital letters. "CALL THE CLUB!"

Panicked, Bernie ran to the pay phone and dialed collect. Buck picked up on the first ring.

"Lana never showed, and the Mellerdrammer called lookin' for Dinah. Your house is locked up, but the T-Bird's still in the driveway."

Bernie broke into a sweat. "Why the hell didn't you keep an eye on them?"

"I drove by at noon. T-Bird was there. Figured they was home."

Bernie could hear the bristle in Buck's voice, but he didn't care. "Stay by the phone—I'll call you back in five." He snapped his fingers at the desk clerk. "What room are the Morans in?"

Racing down the concrete path, Bernie pounded on the door until John answered, a toothbrush jutting from the corner of his mouth.

"Lana didn't show for work—neither did Dinah. Did she say anything to you?"

John chewed on, ruminating on the news. Infuriated, Bernie had to squelch the urge to shake him. "Spill it, Moran. What do you know?"

John spat a clot of toothpaste onto the grass. "Nothing for sure, but I never figured it'd be Lana who'd take her."

"Take her where?"

"To Hollywood—where else?"

Racing back to the pay phone, Bernie called Buck. "House key's under the girlie calendar. Look for a note on the kitchen table by the napkin holder. Then call me back."

The note was exactly where he said it would be.

Dear Bern,

Getting a head start on that trip you promised Dinah. Will call once we get settled. Say goodbye to Joel for us and tell John that Dinah's sorry. The ring's in his mailbox.

Love, Lana

P.S., I took your gun.

Bernie slammed the side of the phone box so hard that Buck heard it clear across the state.

"You OK, boss? You want me to go after 'em?"

Bernie started to laugh, a laugh so thunderous the desk clerk came over to shush him.

"Hey, buddy, keep it down."

"She took the gun," Bernie cried, teetering between panic and pride. "She took the goddamn gun!"

Chapter One Hundred Three

SHORTLY AFTER DAYBREAK, BERNIE DROPPED Joel at the bus depot but didn't wait to see him off. "Gotta close up the Club. Hell, Lana did me a favor. Can't wait to dump that money-sucker."

At breakfast, he'd been blunt, explaining the women's absence to Joel. "Made a break for Hollywood when we were in Mitchell. Flew the coop in Dinah's Skyliner."

"So, she's not marrying John Moran after all."

"Nope. He's headed to Yale."

Joel didn't ask Bernie if he was going after the runaways but seeing how drained the man looked—as if he'd aged five years in two days—said the only encouraging thing he could think of.

"They'll be back, Bern."

Bernie grunted. "Yeah, I ain't worried." He'd decided that if the girls tracked down Dez Annenberg at Columbia Pictures—which might take just a bit of sweet talk at the studio gate—they'd be safer without him there to rile the punk kid.

If it worked out, they'd call home. If not, they'd come home. He took comfort in knowing that Lana was a crack shot. And maybe a better mother than he'd given her credit for.

• • •

Billy rode his bike to the bus station to wait with Joel until he boarded. The boy was out of sorts, and Joel figured it wasn't just from the hours he'd spent vomiting in the motel bathroom—ministered to for the very last time by him and Clarence.

Billy thrust his hand into the chute of the bus depot's gum dispenser, hoping to find something left behind. "Damnit," he swore, giving the machine a hard swipe.

Without a word, Joel fished a penny from his pocket and slipped it into the coin slot. Billy reached in to catch the gum, stared at it for a second, then broke it in two, offering half to Joel.

"No, Bill. You take it."

Joel understood that the end of a season—even a victorious one—was always sad, and for a kid seeing his team disband and scatter to the four corners of the globe, it had to be especially rough. He imagined that his own leave-taking might be the hardest part for Billy.

"Come see me in New York if you visit your brother at Yale. It's not that far. We could go to a Dodgers game. Maybe when your Braves and Eddie Mathews are in town."

Billy kicked a crumpled cigarette pack across the floor. "Fat chance of that." Last night, his folks explained about the baby, and how they'd all have to tighten their belts. He figured there'd not be any money for trips. And, with John leaving town and no Robbinsdale house, there'd be no TV either—no *Dragnet* or the World Series, which the Braves might be in this year.

Seeing the boy's upset, Joel went on. "Then study hard the next few years and come East for college like your brother. Maybe Columbia. I'd write you a recommendation."

Billy made a face. "I'm not an egghead like him."

"So, study with Maryanne. She's smart *and* pretty. A study buddy like her can make homework fun."

Billy's face brightened. "Now you're talkin'."

Joel laughed and put out his hand. "You're some pistol, kid. One in a million."

Giving Joel's hand a hard shake, Billy turned to the schedule board to hide his tears. "Which bus you taking?"

"Whichever leaves first."

"You kidding me?"

Joel chuckled. "Yeah. But there's this movie—*Best Years of Our Lives.* Toward the end, the hero's itchin' to get outta town. So, he goes to the airfield and the dispatcher asks if he wants the plane heading east or the one heading west. And the hero says, 'Whichever leaves first'." A wistful look crossed Joel's face. "Always wanted to say that."

Billy twirled his index finger by his temple. "You gone loco."

Joel smiled as he gazed at the hills to the West, their soft summits bathed in the rising light. East or West? Could these be the best years of his life? Only time would tell.

• • •

On the road to Yellowstone, the bus made a rest stop in the little Wyoming town of Riverton. Joel bought a Coke and walked behind the filling station to stretch his legs. Before him lay a ballfield, less than half the size of a standard field, but well-tended, with freshly painted bleachers, concession stand, and ads from local merchants neatly spaced across the outfield fence.

"Baseball tucked into every corner of America." Joel repeated the Columbia professor's words from what seemed a lifetime ago. Smiling, he surveyed this gem of a field, its every facet sharp and clean and polished.

And yet, beyond the center field fence was a low scoreboard tilted askew, as if it were an afterthought, like a label carelessly sewn into a suit. To his surprise, he was reminded of what his father once told him in the back of his tailor shop, imparting a commonplace of the trade.

"A shmata," Mordecai said, pointing to misaligned pinstripes on the shoulder of an otherwise fine-looking jacket. "Nisht gut," he added, with a stern shake of his head.

A rag. No good. At the time, Joel thought it a reasonable appraisal. Now he wasn't so sure. Imperfections—flaws—didn't render a thing worthless. If he'd learned anything from baseball, it was that perfection was beyond rare. Don Larsen was the only pitcher ever to throw a perfect game in the World Series. You could sell your soul to the devil and still not bat a thousand.

The same could be said of the people he'd met. Quarles took delight in mean jokes but was a generous teacher. Bernie Rosen could be both brutal and uncommonly brave. Lana, an unabashed adulteress, did right in the end by her daughter, letting her test her mettle in Hollywood. As for himself, he'd stood up for a teammate one day and was ready to sabotage him the next.

Saint and sinner, a bit of both in everyone. Well, maybe not everyone, Joel thought with a snort. He'd found nothing saintly about Hoades and little to recommend Kibbee. Though perhaps, as his Columbia buddy Morrie once joked about Hitler—they loved their mothers and their dogs.

And there was no denying it—they were damn good ballplayers.

Down on the field, an old man in farmer's overalls poured lime into the bay of a wood-handled spreader. Crossing the infield, Joel watched him line the batter's box, the chalky confines of the game's central conflict—hurler vs. hitter, a noble duel that Joel wasn't sure he'd ever be part of again. "Nice field you got here. Is it a school field?"

The man slowly straightened, taking a moment to size up the stranger and decide if he was worth the breath and bother. Noting Joel's baseball cap, he responded.

"Nope. Little League. Won the State Championship. Beat Glenrock, then Cody." He said it matter-of-fact, without boast or brag, like delivering the farm report.

"Wow. That's terrific. Were you the coach?"

The old man's mouth twitched, signaling amusement or annoyance.

"My grandson were the pitcher." This time he couldn't strip the pride from his voice.

Joel, both a pitcher and a slugger at that age, pointed to the crooked scoreboard along the fence. "His work, too?"

"Yep. Home run. Hate to fix it. Were the game winner."

The flaw in the diamond. The thing that made it special.

Joel smiled. "Yeah. I'd leave it. It's perfect just the way it is."

THE END

ACKNOWLEDGMENTS

To Jay for his stories; Emily for her many edits, support and advice; Jack, Elizabeth, Ruthie, Jesse, Jane Bal, Jean and Diane for their reads and suggestions; the Rapid City Public Library and South Dakota State Prison for their help with source material; Jake, Lou and Eileen for legal advice; Jane R and Lee for their referrals; Julia for her help with the cover; Eric of RC for his guidance; Claudia for her initial enthusiasm—even though it didn't work out—and Dean Burrell, our book producer, for his patience in shepherding our piece. And to all our friends and family: Abby, Anda, Jane Bud, Bill, Fitz, Pam, Allie, Elaine, Maureen, José, and Eugene for listening to us obsess about our "Dream" for well over a decade. Thank you all.

ABOUT THE AUTHORS

When a girl from South Chicago meets a boy from South Dakota, the result is *Rapid Dreams.*

Debbie Kling and Jim Quinn, both volunteers with the West Side Little League, met on the ballfields of New York's Riverside Park. Years later, on the first of many trips to Jim's home state, he showed Debbie the ballpark in Rapid City where his parents ran the concession stand and he served as batboy for the Chiefs, a team in the semi-professional Basin League.

There, in that very ballpark, constructed in 1957, they envisioned *Rapid Dreams.*

With extensive research of midcentury Middle America and trips to the small towns and cities of the Basin League, *Rapid Dreams* required more than a decade to write. During that period, Jim and Debbie also coached girls' softball teams and Debbie became President of the West Side Little League. And she appeared in the movie *What Happens in Vegas* along with players from their teams.

Debbie and Jim live on the Upper West Side of Manhattan where Debbie continues to serve as League President. They are currently working on a novel based on their experiences in the Little League.

Printed in the USA
CPSIA information can be obtained
at www.ICGtesting.com
CBHW020902250824
13581CB00053B/686

9 798989 926305